a novel

Andy Warhol®

Published by Virgin Books 2009

2 4 6 8 10 9 7 5 3 1

First published in Great Britain in 2005 by
Virgin Books
Random House, 20 Vauxhall Bridge Road
London SW1V 2SA

www.virginbooks.com
www.rbooks.co.uk

Addresses for companies within The Random House Group Limited
can be found at: www.randomhouse.co.uk/offices.htm

The Random House Group Limited Reg. No. 954009

A CIP catalogue record for this book is available from the
British Library

ISBN 9780753519301

The Random House Group Limited supports The Forest Stewardship Council
[FSC], the leading international forest certification organisation. All our titles that
are printed on Greenpeace approved FSC certified paper carry the FSC logo.
Our paper procurement policy can be found at www.rbooks.co.uk/environment

Printed and bound in Great Britain by CPI Bookmarque Ltd, Croydon CR0 4TD

Rattle, gurgle, clink, tinkle.
Click, pause, click, ring.
Dial, dial.

ONDINE—You said (*dial*) that, that, if, if you pick, pick UP the Mayor's voice on the other end (*dial, pause, dial-dial-dial*), the Mayor's sister would know us, be (*busy-busy-busy*).   DRELLA—We should start for the park, right?   Okay.   Hmm.   *Coin drops. Money jingles as coins return. Car noises in background.*   You're a clunk. Are there any way stations on the way that we have to (*honk, honk*) like uh, I, wha—(*noise*). If we go through, through the park, is there ANY place we can keep calling your uh, I mean right through the, uh, phone call. Is there any place where we can keep call him if we—   Answering service . . . Are you (*cars honking, blasting*).   Are there difFERent places—are there different places where we can call your ans—oh.   Want some cake?   Nah.   A little juice, anything?   I know where we can get some.   *hurriedly*—oh yes, let's get some.   Fantastic, baby. Yeah. Good. Oh you can't pretend that you're not here.   Oh, okay, all right.   You're uh, I mean—   Aw right.   You're uh, you're uh, here, yeah.   Okay.   You're here. Okay.   You definitely are here. Uh (*noise*). Hey, what time is it? Do you know it's exACTly—it's two o'clock?   Uh, Gerry made me, uh, I had to wait for him.   It's all right. D'ya know what happened? I fell asleep on the bus.   *surprised*—You did?   And, uh, yeah, but I got off, uh, I got off, in time and, eh, I realized that the bus ride was so long it's ridiculous. It's, its—the Fifth Avenue bus takes forever. Let's see . . . The bus was, was, was—   We had a fairly good time last night, but not too special.

Um.   Nothing, really (*sigh*), just put a coupla sheets on and went into somebody's house (*giggle*) and scared them, ha huh HUHha. It was all. I felt like a ghost. Yeah, uh, some of stolen Rotten Rita's causes. And, um, some of my throat is gone.   Really?   Yeah.   Aw, what is it from? Blowing?   No, I didn't do a thing last night. Just, general, you know, just staying up and all that, just talking. This number in front of us is too gorgeous.   Do you need some Obertrols? . . . Need some Obertrols?   Do you have any?   Blue ones.   Oh, they're five milligrams. Yeah.   That's good. Ten milligrams. No, they're—are are the—are they ten or five?   Ten.   Ten? Oh well, then I need—   I'll try to get some orange ones, yeah?   Oh the orange ones are divine.   How many do you want of the blue ones?   Ah, let's see, twenty milligrams of forty . . .   Ten.   Sixy, ah, ah ten.   One*two*three*four*five*six!   *Kid yelling:* Ay, ay!   That's too many to take. Whish! (*Giggle.*) Sixty milligrams.   *Kid:* Waah, yaie.   Let's see, a setup would be, oh, you can't blame the front of his outfit. It's all bare skin.   *Kid:* YAAEI.

Oh, that's horrid.   It's very stupid.   Bluh, he has a horrid face. Really?   Yuh, he looks like a, y'know, but what a body.   Really? Ah!   Oh, I was wondering what you would like to do too, besides that, cause I mean if we're going to spend this whole day and we should really—   Oh, did you enjoy the con? What did you and Rita speak about last night first of all and isn't she marvelous?   Yeah.   Isn't she tru-truly marvelous? She's the meanest girl in the world but she's so fun.

Really?   Yeah, she has a, y'know, like, like a, like a, like all mean girls she's been—she been roughly treated.   Oh, the bakery's open. It's the best bakery in town.   What's the name of it?   Greenberg's. Greenberg's, ooh that's a Jewish bakery.   *Laughter.*   Yah.   *Laughter*   I thought it was a ChinESE bakery! I sat down next to an old woman in the park and she got very indignant.   Really?   Because I sat there.   Why?   Well, it was her bench obviously.   Oh. She must have had it since, since sh-she was a child.   Really?   Sh-she was—people are not going to believe this.   Probably thinks you're a star.   Eh, well I am. I, I just like to accept that I really—   Wha? didn't stay up last night.   *Washed-out noises.*   It's a pity. Huh? (*Pause*). Dum-tum. I hate all that. I hate all that business of having to train them—   Train people?   *Laughter.*   Yeah. When they're that young.   Oh!   Oh, how horrid.   Horrible.   *High-pitched honk.*   Oh, what'll we do?   Well . . .   We'll (*honk*). Should we try another bakery?   Yeah.   Do you know of another one around here? I's-I's-I was comPLETEly for this neighborhood. Completely new for this neighborhood. Feature uptown all right but it's this is uptown. Uptown on the East Side. This part of town is uh, I like that sh—I like that shirt. It's very nice. Uptown, uptown on the West Side, it's very hard to get to. I wanted to—   What? It's, it's a very—uptown on the East Side, ah, it's very rare. You don't take—ge-get to it very easily. Maybe we should have a cup of coffee at some, some—a cup of coffee like Thelma Ritter.   All right, we'll do that. Let's get some cake and then we'll have coffee.   A glass of beer or something.   Okay.   A glass of beer (*laughs*).   Ah, who, let's see, you left last night at what time?   Aah, four o'clock.   I'm trying to find out what I did last night. I don't remember. I remember we—   You went to the uh, the uh, the the whore house. The whore house. But everyone is always going there anymore and they don't have any electricity.   Oh really?   And they have electricity from the outside piped in and there's always trouble and someone always loses something. I've been robbed twice down there.   You were? Oh yes, of all my amphetamine and then this time I lost it.   Oh ah. Awfully sweet.   Huh?   I guess this is a Jewish delicatessen. Open Sundays but I guess they're closed every other day. (*Laughter.*) Here we are now in the famous bakery which is very Jewish.   *In background:* Yeah, okay.   Anything a—   Won't you, I don't know what to order here cause—an ice cream tray.   Oh well.   All those things look very good. Maybe (*sigh*), I don't know. I looked. Where are they?   I don't see anything there. Looks like a cake, do you?   No, do you want any cake or should we go somewhere else? Want cookies or cake?   I think we better go elsewhere.   Okay.   There's some cake there.   It's a day off. They are closed on, on every other day. They're only open on Sundays. What, that's too much. That's so precious, that store—it was like going into a who knows? Who knows anymore, Drella? You have to let me help you carry something.   Yeah wait, just hold uh, just hold the cap and microphone too.   Good, okay.   While I put—   Okay, go right ahead. We're now on Eighty-fifth Street and Madison Avenue and we're very upset.   You're very upset?   We are. Drella and myself are very upset. Mangos and Rosemary Clooney right next to it.   Do you want to go to Stark's?   Huh?   Do you want to go to Stark's?   Stark's, Stark's has appeared. What is Stark's? Oh, that's, I, I know what that is. It's like a, a, what is it called? It's like a—   It's like Childs.   Or Longchamps, yeah, doesn't matter but it sounds fine with me. Moby Dick sounds (*laughter*). That's very good too. People aren't equipped for my filth. I realize that.   What?   People are not equipped for my filth. I don't know why, it's amazing. I, da, I, I cut through everything, like I lose lo-lots of friends and everything.   Really?   And all the tricks, you know, I mean first of all I can't be deceptive. If there's any kind of subterfuge I have to use, it has to be very obvious nad very funny. You know, I mean it's gotta be a ss, uh, it's gotta be—amuse me at least and uh, so now that we're interviewing you, you have to like living up here for a time?   Oh it's terrific.   Oh isn't this a riot.   Especially way down there, it's really wierd.   Oh there must be some restAUrant. Maxine's is out of the question cause the dress is out.   I, I thought we were at Seventy-ninth, that's higher than Seventy-seventh.   Eh?   That's all right. You wanna walk down?   I don't care, certainly—what was I going to say? Oh yeah. Hey listen. Why don't we take ourselves to the baths or something. It might be definitely—   Are you serious?   We would be such a hit at the baths.   Really?   Do you think?   All the women, AöWö's.   There would at least be a few, a few others blowing around there with just—   What do the others know? Like sport cars. Y'know. We didn't have to know or b-be— Florence Lustig? Oh no—I thought it was this famous Florence Lustig. The other one's the quie—everything looks good today, doesn't it?   Yah.   It's just one of those days. (*Laughter.*) I don't know why but—   Yes, why is it that—   It's just one of those days, it's just a fabulous day that everyone looks so happy, and everyone is good. On a day like this everyone is divine. The Duchess's in the hospital.

Oh, we have quite a good visit.   Poor darling, we used to go to the uh, uh—Rotten Rita will, will wing for—for the first time she will be recorded.   Oh really?   And she will, yes she'll even acCOMpany herself on the piano, and then we'll all go and have a magnificent brunch.

Uh, uh—   At the Ethel Roosevelt Hospital—   Oh.   where the Duchess has managed to take—she's got the blood-pressure machine.   Oh really?   She has.   *Laughter.*   Where'd she ever get the blood-pressure machine?   Wow! She's afraid of having her blood pressure taken because she knows it's zero.   Oh really?   What a weird little wagon.   Yah.   Ow, ow. My gook was pinching my arm. Do you want to hold any of them? Oh dRILLy dum dum—It's awful working for Taxine.   Why?   You can't, you can't support yourself.   Oh. (*Ondine laughs.*)   Well, she went out today, uh, as soon as she gets, uh, really, uh, as soon as she gets— I wonder, I wonder if she's still— I wonder if she's still going to uh—   No, she's out on two or three—two big nights, night, night club acts.   Well, well y'know, we advised her about that.

Oh you did?   At least I tried to and I told, you know, we told her that anything prepared would be out of the question.   Anything what?

Prepared. Anything prepared would be out of the question and her sponsor may, may, will, would do this thing that would save her, and if she, if she got insulted, if he, if he acted like he was insulting her in, in any way, well she would merely say, "Excuse me, I won't answer that," and just go, go off the television set.   Wha, what o you gonna think of Taxine?   I very, really, I think an awful lot of her.   Oh really?

Yah.   Tell me about her.   I do. I think she's uh, well, you, y'know (pause) uh, what can I tell you a, about her. Every—everybody, I found out last night, what uh, what I suspected was happening, was happening.   What?   That people are believing uh, that we're having sex and uh, and uh, everything.   Oh.   Which is not so.   Who, who, who, uh—   Oh, oh you know, everybody does.   Who?   Oh, oh all the . . . what does misanthrope mean? It sorta means a powerful person right?   Yeah.   Well, these are not the powerful ones, these are the pilot fish, what, whatever-ever that stuff's supposed to mean. The ones that spread rumors, y'know. And they said, and they said you and Taxine, you're really, someone said, said last night, you're really fucking her up, aren't you? I said, well, what do you mean? What drugs do you put in her morning coffee and, and how stoned do you get her?   Who said that?   I said oh, uh, no names, I said oh I said, "Oh don't be ridiculous." I asked Taxi if she wants a drug and if she wants a drug she takes it I said, I mean it is completely aboveboard. I said that the fact of the matter is that very rarely she says she wants anything, and we both agree that that's the best ticket for her. And she, and she's marvelous like that but she does have a problem with, uh, slipping barbiturates— Oh really?   with her sleeping pills, yes. She takes too too many of them in the nighttime and uh, she should cut down. Besides, I'm beginning to talk like her, my voice sounds like uh, I can't bear it, I don't know what to do—   DoDo Mae Doom is such an excellent girl.   What do you, what do you think of Rink Crawl?   A lot. I think Rink is marvelous. I wish he'd stop doing things with his hair—   Oh—And leave it one way or uh t'other cause it's quite jolting to see him there with—Rotten didn't know it was the same person—   Oh really? Because I—   —he said I never met him—I said Rotten Rita doesn't—I said I never met him—I said that's the boy you saw last night you know, I'm vaguely interested in him, Ondine, and I said oh—he said he doesn't look like the same person —well he is. Finally I left them all and uh we—after the whore house— we just left them there.   Oh really?   We had to go off on our own because it was—OH—   Ah who's that?   O look at the French Coffee Shoppe—we had to go off on our own because, oh Gerry, Stu Denta, my- self, uh Gene, gene Rawson, uh, that was his last name and what was— who was the other person? I forget—it was an extra and I don't remember —who was the mysterious missing woman? (*Laughter*).   I don't know.

Of course your presence will solve it in time.   Oh really? Gerry would roll around and say Drella (*laughter*). Oh Gerry was so funny the other morning.   Oh really? Why?   Oh I know who was there— Debbie—   Oh really, Debbie Lee?   No, no, no, oh Debbie Lee, oh you take your life in your hands when you go anywhere with her (*honk*). Oh stop it now, uh, somebody else was there but I don't remember who —that looked like Chanle.   Yeah, oh really?   I wha—I finally got so annoyed at Roger—   Oh really?   When we both a, a, you sound like Greta Garbo!   Oh really? (*Laughter*)   I find that so annoyed that Roger that day I started to eat yogurt—   Ya!   —a strawberry yogurt, and he said "Oh dear," he said, "I thought that's the least." I said, "Do you hate me?" God, he slept over last night and another word like that and I'm gonna throw it in your face. I said, "How dare you." You know he's got three cans of uh of of yogurt there and he's afraid somebody's going to eat it. I was really furious. He shouldn't act like a little mother. He's not, you know? I wonder when he's gonna stoy or who's gonna stop him. Oh, I almost did the other day with—   Oh really?   —with the

cleaning woman who loved me.   Oh?   He looked like such a fool.
What happened?   Well, I, I just chewed the bubble gum and I
(laughter), well he and DoDo Mae, you know, came over to help Ttxi
with the, the letter and she was try—oh—what an enormous flower
(laughter), and she was, they're what? They're not, they're not . . . big
ribbon but they're not too big at all—you know a lot of people. It feels
so wonderful to walk down the street and have people meet you. Is that
an old friend?   No, he's from a gallery.   Yeah, thought so. Gallery
people are, are all right. (Noise.) Do you want to sit at the counter over
here, or what? Who's that? (Noise.) Who's that? That's Wee Carter-
Pell.   That's uh, Wee Carter-Pell? (Laughter.   What a marvelous,
eh—   Wee Carter-Pell.   He doesn't know who you are. Yes, shall
w go inside?   Isn't that awful?   It's just just that he can't even, never
learn that 90 per cent . . . Laughter.   I can't believe it.   Neither me.
He's snobbish   Isn't that AWful? He's with Rauschenberg.   Isn't
that awful? We're being snubbed.   It's Rauschenberg.   Who?   I
mean, are they from here or are they on this side?   I always say who
cares.   Uh, Wee.   He, he, he won't say hello. When they're like that
they're just like that.   What can you . . . It's horrible isn't it? I wonder
when they'll crawl out? I said I wonder when they'll crawl out. I wonder
when . . .

He saw me.
Why didn't he stop you?
I don't know.
Think it could be a private booth?
I think so.
(D) I'll fix it for you.
(O) Please do.
(D) I think it wasn't even him.
(O) Oh. that's what I said. I didn't
even know who he, he, he is. Ah,
let's see, do you want some-some-
thing to eat, Drella?
Oh, can I have some fresh orange
juice. Yeah, a large one, that's all.
I think I'll have a, a grapefruit
juice. Do you have a grape- grape-
fruit juice? Freshly squeezed
grapefruit juice? Yeah, is uh, no,
I don't think there's any more
fresh grapefruits. They're out of
season, uh, and a cup of light
coffee and uh some kind of a bun.
Aren's you going to have—light

coffee—aren't you going to have
some eggs or hamburger"
No.
They make terrific hamburgers.
No, I'm not hungry. Well I'm
not that hungry. I couldn't eat
after that frunch. I'm not hungry.
Just slap me in the face. I wonder why h did that? You know I
hate when tha-tha-that happens.
Which one was taken? Oh, that's
who, uh, what kind of buns do
you have? I mean, what kind of
rolls. What kind of uh—Dan-
ishes—you have. What kind of
cake do you have? Pasteries?
What's a schnecket?
(D) I don't know.
(O) What is a sch—oh I'll have a
schnecket. I couldn't resist. No,
a schnecket is enough for me.
Wanna schnecket? Where is, I
don't . . . understand.

(D) Wha?

(O) I don't understand why people do that.

(D) Ah.

(O) It doesn't—

(D) Maybe it isn't him.

(O) Which one was him? Was it the one—?

(D) The one in the suit.

(O) In the suit. I don't even know who he is.

(D) Huh?

(O) Is he one of theee Carter-Pells —is he one of the Carter-Pells, Drella?

No, I can't seem to be abl to tell.

Who is he?

Johnny Fatts' lover.

Who's Johnny Fatts?

He's Bill's, et, the . . . secret . . . building.

Oh, how wonderful! Oh, that's a lovely building. Bedroom Billy.

Six or eleven. Do you want to take 'em right now? Oh, you mean your orange juice?

Stick 'em in the grapefruit juice.

(D) I've just four left.

(O) Let me take those little orange ones.

Don't you want just four or you want five? They're actually ten.

Five'll be . . . the MINute we get to Rita's they can be replenished. She has, she has this little tiny marble picture.

Take ten.

This little tiny marble—

What?

This little tiny marble—

(D) Ten.

(O) The ones that were, at the time to which . . . the ones that tasted, oh, horrible.

(D) Here's your fun. Oh. (*Noise*)

(O) Ah (*swallowing*) that was five

Obertrols. That's a hundred milligrams, like pure gaiety. No, it's not hundred milligrams.

(D) No, it's not, it's fifty.

(O) It's only fifty. Aah! Cause I go under like a wonderful third time. You have to swallow some, if they melt in your mouth, ro you'll go crazy. Here, have some of my carbolic acid.

(D) That's all right.

(O) You believe grapefruit is so wretched. That all you're goin' to have?

I just don't know. I'm having uh, orange juice.

Orange juice, yeah, but I mean is that all you're going to have?

(D) Yeah.

(O) I don't look very good today. I was a little under it.

(D) Huh?

(O) I was a little under it last night.

(D) Really?

(O) Yeah.

Why?

Oh, I don't know, I was sieged.

(D) Why were you sieged?

(O) I get very upset you know with with, with sex-sexual scenes, uh . . .

(D) Oh, really? Why?

(O) I, I can't pre-pretend, you know, or, or like, uh like, like, you know, pretend like I'm someone else and all of a sudden sneak out on the balcony with someone. I can't do that.

(D) Yeah.

(O) Cause I don't think it's worth it, first of all.

What does that have to do with yesterday?

Well, that was all, that, you know, there's so many thing involved.

Oh, that must be our schnecket.

(D) Yeah.

(O) It's from Australia.

(D) Hmm? Is it?

(O) My schencken looks like it's from Australia. That woman came from . . . Anyway, ah, I, I don't think it's worth it first of all.

(D) What?

(O) To pretend ce-certain uh, sexual scenes and then to do other other than I am what I am.

(D) Why were you?

(O) I wasn't do—I couldn't, I mean if I could've I would've uh, been able to score but I didn't so I wasn't able to uh, you know, meet the requirements which is to pretend you're something else and then uh, go off with the spoils. No, I can't do that. I have to go in and scream and holler at Rita and blame myself and then you know I really feel tha—oh goodness, uh, uh take milk uh, and then uh, you know, I always feel that if someone is courageous enough to come throught it and still register and then just more than that, that's pretty good. Of curse some people are dazzled by my madness. Who's that? Looks like an ORFA-SIR of the law.

(D) What?

(O) An officer of the law.

(D) What?

(O) It's an officer of the law.

(D) Oh.

(O) Want some sugar in your orange juice?

Yeah. No, you did put some sugar in my orange juic.

So yoeu, you wouldn't mind going to the hospital to see the Duchess?

(D) No, no.

(O) She has 3,000 livers.

(D) Oh really?

(O) Yeah, she's, she's got that an a stethescope and oh she's got the dotcor's coat and she said an oldl woman's taking up ward patients. Wonder if we should go over this afternoon, which I think is a step ahead for her. Won't you have some schencken? Drella, what's going to happen to me when I start . . .

(D) What? What?

(O) Oh, this custard is delicious; I wanna go to the bahroom after this.

(D) Oh, you do, oh you can't go.

(O) Shall I take that with. me?

(D) Yeah.

(O) Have they left yet? Have they left yet?

(D) What?

(O) Have they gone yet? . . . They don't dare, do they? They don't dare. What's tha? Oh that's the art gallery. Oh the coffee's too hot. Umm, that schenken's delicious. I figured that you wouldn't be up by eleven, that's why I didn't call.

No, I uh, took all these ObErtrols yesterday, and I was up all night.

What'd you do?

(D) Huh?

(O) What'd you do?

(D) Just read magazines.

(O) Oh, and you can't get a . . . How can you, I can't get interested enough to read them.

(D) Really?

(O) Positively anything, I get, I'm starting—

That's why I read the same one over and over again.

I'm starting, I'm starting to find an interest in some, some things and it's good, but I can't, I can't get enough interest in anything to really read it.

(D) Oh really?

(O) Yeah, it just doesn't, I don't have it. Um. I like that one. I mean, I mean, I don't mind reading documentaries or Schwann catalogs or lists of one sort or another. I don't mind that. I really don't mind reading biographies if they're, you know, fairly well written, but I can't take reading novels or anything like that when they're . . . I just can't do it. Anyways, isn't that, isn't that heartbreaking news? I was shocked when I found out that I wasn't reading novels.

(D) Really?

(O) Oh, novels, what novels, Ill read any novels.

(D) Oh.

(O) I used to read romance, every romance.

(D) Oh really?

(O) Oh, no, no more.

(D) Want some water?

(O) No, this schnecken is very, I don't know what to say that's not an critic for some reason. No, y'know, what is it that's bother ing you?

(D) Oh, the newspaper.

(O) No, really. Have you thought about what you'd like to do after this?

(D) Uh.

(O) I mean besides . . . I mean after Rita and the hospital.

Uh, I would like to meet her. Call me at Taxines.

Yeah, good, she's going to uh—

She's gone already, too, big appoint-

ment.

Yeah, she's with Les Crane and let's see who else?

(D) The other one is Night Time.

(O) Oh, Merv Griffin or someone. Les Crane can sometimes be very evil.

(D) Oh, uh, he's . . .

(O) Well, she's going to hem them into that world too. I mean, she, she believes in what she's doing, what she does, then, she doesn't like to go anywhere, like a, because it's just not—this schnecken took the rest of my voice away, uh, ih . . . it's completely gone. When will it return? Next Tuesday. Um.

(D) Hmm?

(O) I'm scared. I believe you (or I feel easier) because everything I eat I lose weight. Have you spoken to our technician yet?

(D) What?

(O) Our lab technician, have you spoken to him?

(D) No, I didn't speak to him . . .

(O) I like him . . . but the reaction that he had getting off the train was fabulous.

(D) Oh really?

(O) Ah, I said, "What happening" What's he doing? I didn't know WHAT I was doing, I was going, was going to buy a record, I think. Yes, I left the record at the factory.

(D) Oh, which one?

(O) The Callas record.

(D) Oh really?

(O) Yes, because it was, it's a bit safer there, rather than be en route with me. I lost so many things last night.

(D) Oh really?

(O) Like my marbles.

Where'd you leave them?

Along the rough.

(D) Really?

(O) I kept hearing them drop out and I got scared. One by one. CLUNK.

Would you like a cigarette?

(D) No.

(O) Those five Obertrols are go—

(D) What?

(O) Those five . . . I thought that fifty milligrams of Obertrols is gonna be . . .

Which ob—what all . . . when?

A few minutes, in a few minutes I should go up to the factory.

(D) Oh really?

(O) I have to (clearing his throat), I have to get to a phone call.

All right, wh-when, when are we leaving?

As soon as—right after you're finished. I'm not even gonna go to the rest room. Hot as a witch's tit.

(D) Hmm?

(O) It's hot as a witch's, whatever that it.

(D) What is hot?

(O) Coffee. No, it wasn't even hot. I just wanted to make that slippery noise. I like that . . . that boy's nice.

(D) Hmm?

(O) That boy's nice. Have you ever been to St. Mark's Baths or the (Everhart's?)

Uh no. Tell me, tell me about it.

Well for twelve hours, for $2.50 on a wekend, you know, twelve hours of facilities, which means you can use the dormitories, you can use the swimming pool, the uh, roof, which has the sunbathing and um, the masseurs, and uh, three floors y'know

of complete utter gaiety, and a cafeteria that serves Manning's coffee. It doesn't really serve Manning's coffee; it just has Manning's coffee cups and it says Manning's coffee on the side of it. You were up all night?

(D) Yeah.

(O) You didn't sleep at all?

(D) No.

(O) No-no rest? Are you a little bit peaked?

(D) No.

(O) Don't you feel marvelous?

(D) Yeah.

(O) Aren't Obertrols he-heaven? Did you do that on dexadrine?

(D) No, no, I . . .

(O) Then you'll drop dead.

(D) Yeah.

(O) Really! They'll take care of your heart. Almost strength like this.

(D) Really?

(O) You know, you can't use dexadrine because it's not good for you. Obertrols, I know, would take it off the market. I gotta do . . . oh no. Can I have—lock this up and when you want to unleash just tell me, I'll take, take it odff cause it ruins the . . . I'm gonna finish my carbolic acid and then we'll be going.

Do you want to meet Rauschenberg?

No.

(D) No?

(O) Who is he?

Uh, the number one artist.

Is he really?

(D) I think so.

(O) I don't believe it. I think you are. Oh, come on, Drella, he doesn't make movies . . . . he doesn't make movies.

(D) He's trying to.
(O) *with sarcasm*—He's trying to.
   Have I ever seen any of his work?
(D) You might have.
(O) What's, *what's* his most fa-
mous thing?
(D) Uh, he's just very famous.
(O) Does Norman have any of his
   work?

1 / 2

Oh there's this nice breaking crockery.   You mean, how do you
mean . . . board Hopplehaney . . . What do you mean, Denny can't
afford it?   Uh, it's $40,000 a painting now.   Well, that pretty good,
isn't it? It's an awfully high price.   Describe himself.   Divine, yeh,
high. Yeah, but what does he do? How does he paint? Is he a pop, is he
considered pop artist?   **He is the father of art.**   *With surprise*—
What?   Well, he can't be like Jack Daniels.   He came before Soup?
I don't believe it, I don't believe it.   Well, in a different way. He's half
expressionism, half . . .   Oh, oh, I don't oh, oh, oh . . . I'm right, well
then . . . and like *Bob Dylan* either. Of course you realize that, hat Taxine
is so odd.   That you, you know . . .   Yeah, I was wondering, I was
a pop tart.   Yeah (*laughter*), uh year.   There's a new cereal called
pop tart.   Oh really?   Yeah.   Pop tart?   Yeah. In this little
squares of . . . would you like a cigarette?   No.   But you know
what's . . . I'm not really pop. Yes I, I am pop in many ways but I'm you
know I'm not really though. I'm sort of a little bit 1930 bohemian.
Really? Oh, no.   Oh yeah. There's a little oh yeah there's a little of the
natural Bodheim in m, and I can't help it. It's, I know it's tacky but . . .
   Really?   Oh, of course. I'm truly tacky, didn't you know? I don't
care if he's the number one artist or the number ten artist (BURP) You
know my opinion with honesty. I haven't seen any . . . I don't know, but
I know Jack's an unpleasant soul.   Oh yeah?   Shall we go?   Uh,
yeah, we'll make phone calls.   All right.   Oh.   Check the daily
. . .   Huh?   Check the daily . . . does it look like the uh, bus is
here?   Huh?   Do you want to take the—   No, no I'll do it—
let's get some change.   the five over.   I'll put this back here on the
   table and then I'll make my phone call.   I can I can I can.   Do
you want to hold it?   Sure.   There's nothing to hold onto.   I
have one.   Oh.   Can I call any place for, for you?   Ah, no.
Huh, huh, ho (*coin drops, dialing, phone ringing*). Hello? Hello Arlene?
Is, is, is Roten awake? This is Bob. Yeah. Bob Oliva, y'know, Ondine.

Okay, okay, bye-bye. Are you going to Rotten Rita's house? The Mayor of our fair city.   Uh.   He said to come right over. He said to come right over. So let's go. What is your opinion of Star?   She's very . . . austere.   Austere?   I have to make a phone call.   Oh, oh make it from Rita's.   Oh no, oh no, I have to make it from . . .   I'll wager . . .   You can talk to Wee.   No, I'd rather go outside . . . Oh here I am going outside. And now I am outside. (*Traffic noises.*) Someone just said it's tragique, the sky. (*More traffic noise.*)   Eh, oh two-thirty-one Forty-seventh.   Between Second and Third. Uh, between Second and Third. Uh, did you just fix something up?   Oh, no, yeah, they're coming at three with uh, and it's after three. Oh, it's I don't know what happened.   What happened?   Well, uh, he just called and left this message, and uh, it's nobody's, nobody's at the studio, and I—   Nobody's there at all?   No.   (O) Oh listen, driver, would you please get there as soon as possible? Oh I mean I hate to sound like an old movie, but step on it. (*Laughter.*) It's imperative. It is really important.   DRIVER—Yes, well, the lights let you get there.   (O) Yeah, please, because, uh, UH MY GRANDMOTHER'S BEING DELIVERED and uh, if I don't go to get her . . . she, oh who, so which one was us . . . Rauschenberg.   He wa he wa he wa he was the one behind the pole, right?   Yah. He's very famous, he's very, he won in the centennial last year, very, he's with some gallery, he's with The Cattleman. If it wasn't for him I wouldn't be able to do the kind of work I do.   Well, I'm sure that you're grateful and all that, and I . . .

Oh no, well it's not the same kind of thing.   And, and I like him, but I don't know any of his work so I can't say. He looks a little arch. He's uh Star Philixer's boy friend.   Who the hell is that?   Star Philixer. Star is with the Judson music series.   I don't know Star.   You know Star, don't you? You remember Star with Merce Cunningham and then—   Oh, I never go to any of those things. I couldn't possibly. Oh really? I thought you did.   No.   I see you around.   No, but not there.   Oh.   When, whenever you see me around it's with you.   Oh.   I don't bother with anyone else.   Oh really?   I couldn't . . .   I used to be there so . . .   Yeah, but I can't afford to bother with anyone else. It rEAlly comes to that. I don't know, y'know, Merce Cunningham I've never seen, and I've nver seen Ian Coop, I've never seen patrick deal.

Oh really?

I, I, I don't know any of these people; I met them only at sort of a uh, associatively and friends of Binghamton Birdie, who was, when I was with Binghamton Birdie.

What were you with Binghamton Birdie?

(O) I was Mrs. Birdi.

(D) You were Mrs. Birdie?

I WAS THE SECOND MRS. BIRDIE?

Awful. Who was the first Mrs. Birdie?

Yetta Blini.

> Oh really? You're kidding?

Yes and the other day she was at the Factory.

> Oh.

Oh with . . .

> Really, yeah.

Step Stubble. My dear, I have never seen anybody run in my life.

> Oh really?

She ran down the stairs and I didn't know it was her.

> Oh.

Step came over to the window and said, "That's Yetta Blini." I said I, Yetta, I didn't, and the minute I recognized her, uh, put the bead up on her—

> Yeah.

She took off down the stair and I said "Yetta" and she went "Oh Jesus" and she ran all down the . . . she didn't say hello, good-bye, she just said "Oh Jesus" and ran down the stairs. Now I didn't know what caused that, but he said she wouldn't return. We didn't think that she would but we don't want him to return. So we put Ellen by the door. Elaine and every time he said his nam she'd say again, "Who is it?" And he would say, "Step Stubble." "Who is it? Louder please." This went on for fifteen minutes.

Wh-what do you mean?

We kept saying to her do not open the door; just ask, "Who is it?"

Oh, oh.

"Who is it?" And then just opened the door and handed him his jackt and that, y'know, that would be the end of that. (*Laughter*.) But she couldn't, she couldn't, she couldn't do it. She just couldn't do it.

> Oh really?

So, by the time he came inside he was uh, he's thoroughly conquered. Rita's showering and getting ready.

> Oh really?

(O) Rita's uh, Rita's sister is uh, over there.

(D) Oh perfect.

And Rita's sister is a beautiful girl. She's us, Rita's uh, Rita's mother bought, bought, bought a horse.

Oh.

And she keeps it in a chicken coop. Isn't that fabulous? Doesn't everyone's mother want a horse? My mother does. I know that an you, you, you've got a horse in your apartment . . .

Three.

(O) Your apartment, your apartment . . .

Three.

Uh?

Three.

(O) Three horses?

(D) Yeah.

I just saw one, well, oh, but Carmen Miranda's shoe. Oh Drella, what an aura about it, it just, the minute I saw it, it looked like something so precious, it has that feeling about it. Oh the Delmonico Hotel, they have the nice PLEASE DO NOT DISTURB sign.

Really?

(O) I'm, I was, I hope I wasn't rude.

(D) Oh no, no, no.

Because I didn't mean to be. I just didn't want to sit at the table with them or talk with them, because I never know what to sayto them, y'know, because they say things like . . . I said that the atmophere in her is ah—You knwo Wee Carter-Pell- You never met Wee Wee Cater-Pell. He's been always here when you're here. Well, I don't know him. I thought, I thought he was, who was the other one? Uh, Uh, he just, his wife just lost a baby. He just works as a, y'know—Oh, he's just a heterosexual, that's all.

Yeah.

How boring.

Laughter.

Very cute, very cute.

I know but, he's probably, y'know, off boys or something. He's not the least bit, uh—

Yhy is it that they just eh, the really top people are, are homosexual. It's insance, Drella, do you realize that that there's just no one else is . . .

Why is that?

(O) I don't know, they must've, they must be really . . .

(D) Or Jewish.

Well, they're so far—   Devote your maiden   Oh, well, look at Rauschenberg, it's inSAne.   He's not Jewish   He's not? Well he should be. *Laughter.*   With a name like that he shoul definitely be Jewish. Is he—   It's funny, he uh—   Is he, is he a German?   I don't, I don't know really.   Oh he could be Swedish.   But it's very funny, the people of the uh Church always, always look, the Catholic Church, al-

ways look Jewish. I never understand that.   They always look Jewish.
    Yeah.   Well, well, you know. The Mediterraneans, they're all the
same and they're all, like Italians, Armenians, Greek,s uh, Jews, uh, they're
all traders, t-r-a-d-e-r-s. By just, by, by uh merchant, just, just by uh, just by
the fact that their long history of being so, and they all have those charac-
teristics, like they're swarthy, short . . .   Gee, they're really sexy sometimes, yeah, the Jews are, can be terribly sexy . . .   Are they?   Yeah.
    But that's a combination of uh, asthetic beauty and sex, it's uh, it's
unbelievable, eh.   Sergio I thought was a Sephardic Jew when I first
saw him . . .   What, what . . . No, he was just a Chilean to who you
lend a couple of million . . . a Chilean Jew *Laughter.* Eh, Sephardic
Jew. I understand that most of the people who inhabit, who live in Chile
are the Basque country, originally they come from the Pyrenees. (*Singing:*)Oh, New York is a helluva town, the Bronx is the battery's down.
Ah, oh I, is he playing a musical instrument? Is he, it's no time for a concert, driver, we are, we are in a hurry. My grandmother's being delivered;
my grandmother was delivered on Thursday by my sister Joa . . .   (D)
Oh reallq?   (O) Yd, y'know they keep shipping her back and forth
from my mother to my sister and it's, they're they're, I get it, it looks
rather slumpy and sexy. Oh when am I going to be sated? Ahh, not mated,
sated.   (D) Oh when am I going to find someone who will like A.W.
    (O) Everybody does—they just, first of all there are the . . . oh,
Drella, the categories are insane.   (D) What are they?   (O) There,
there, there are the people who admire, but can't let themselves go because . . . they would blow their whole sexual scene.   Yeah.
(O) Oh, let's see, so that was one group out. The second ones are ones
that are competing, because they have, are like, well let's give un an e.g.
I suppose, eh, Roger Trudo Trudow, who even named himself A.W. and
is not . . . you can't name yourself a witch if you're not a witch. What're
you going to—who who whoo is he kidding, y'know. He's, he he gave
himself the name of Heckedy, that's eh, that's eh (*laughter*). Doesn't he
know that Heckedy is the goddess that I pay homage to every night?
When I point towards uh, my homeland, the golden fleece and bow,
y'know he doesn't know, know that.   (D) That's, that's terrific—
(O) Eh, that's eh, two groups and then, then there are the young things
and the young things, and the youg things y'know, the young things are
always in, the young, there are a few young things yet they're very intelligent, will be attracted and will do everything in their power to stay with
the A.W.'s but there are very few that are that courageous, that group,
winding up sometimes in a mental home.   (D) What about mislead-
ing all these A.W. girls, I mean uh . . .   (O) Uh, uh, what do you
mean, sixteen-year-old girls?   (D) Sixteen-year-old girls? Well, that's

because they're all throwing themselves at my feet. (O) They're all, they're all giving you their virginity.   (D) How do you get the sixteen-year-old boys?   (O) I don't know, darling, but . . .   (D) I mean y'know but where . . .   (O) Well listen, we'll find a way.   (D) all right.   (O) Drella, if there's ever been a way, we'll find it. Because they can have the sixteen-year-old girls   (D) Yeah, well, we have to, you have to make a lot of studio apologies up there. You have to invite all these things down.   I will, I will.   You have to uh . . .   I'll put, I'll put and I'll also, I, I, I'll also enforce it.   Yeah, well, we'll well, a little further down. A little further down by the green door, right behind the garage Right in front of the . . .   Oh, oh, there's nobody here.   (O) Right, there's nobody here? Oh God, I hope it doesn't come . . .   (D) And I hope . . .   (O) Shall I take this all out of your hand? And, and rush, rush upstairs?   Uh, yeah, would you help me? Uh . . .   Fine. We're gonna run upstairs and see if anything has been delivered, just I'll look in the mailroom. Uh, there's nothing here. Not a thing. Yes, here's some mail   They're not in the mailroom, they must've, I don't know, here's some mail.   Oh well, over here, Oh I guess nobody was by.   Do you think he came by already?   Oh he can't because it's our big new television set.   Oh, oh, he, I don't think he was here.   Oh, oh, oh.   Well, wouldn't he leave a note if he came?   No, no it's just not there—no.   Is there some place we can call and find out if he did come by?   Uh, yeah, yeah, but we'll just have to wait.   Oh yeah.   Stephen?   Stephen who?   Have you been here long? How long?   Was it open Has it been open upstairs or what and who was here?   Oh, oh.   And no one's here? The door is locked.   Well, that's all right.   Oh well, then he sort of guarded it.

They'll probably, probably yeah . . .   Yeah good. That's heaven. Oh, oh.   Oh we really made it. I'm very very, very glad, I bu—I won't jump the gun though. No, no, I don't want any music; I want my glorious Welch Aid. Uh, I, there are many things to do. Oh, ho, it looks so good. That's, that's Rita's.   Oh, oh.   Isn't she fab-fab. That part of her material and she said, she said "Ondine," she said, "when it, when it drives take it down and do what you want with it." But isn't it lovely?

Oh very.   She puts it up. And Gerard got, got demented because she used the spray.   Oh really?   Yeah, well you know he can't tell, you know, she seems very mean but she's really a darling. Here we are at the Factory and there's nobody here and there's no camera.   Uh Stephen, I would like you to tell them of your problem.

STEVE—Who was there was . . .
Posterity.

No, this is just all right. I think you should tell them. Give them your bit on uh . . . why don't you give me your problem? Why don't you become a homo-sex-sexual?

(S) Oh, I don't know.

(O) Well, because pretty soon if you're not a homosexual you uh, you won't be allowed up here. That's because you won't be one of the group. (*Laughter.*) I did on Sunday for a while; Billy and I did.

Oh, uh.

Okay. Uh, HOW TO BECOME A PROFESSIONAL HOMOSEXUAL or how to be a good fag. It's hard. xxxxx It's gonna be hard work because you—you're obviously off to a late start. I think I have a dime, Drella.

What's the . . . us I'll tell you all about it.

Well, come over here. What the hell is this? Would you hold it? No this. (Drella talking in background.)

Okay.

D in background—Oh okay.

xxxxxxxxxxxxxxx Whose are these?

(S) I don't know.

It's perfection.

Maybe it's Rink's.

Have you ever seen anything more perfect? What kind of a pillow is this? Shall we smoke.

Is this plugged in?

Uh no, but maybe we can.

I guess it's plugged in. It's working. We just saw Wee Carter-Pell and Bedroom Billy and somebody else in uh Stark's and uh . . .

You're going to give me your lesson now?

Tell me what you want to know.

Oh well . . .

What's troubling you?

All right.

(O) The oracle is open.

The oracle is open?

The oracle is open. What do you wish to ask the oracle?

Oh, I don't know.

Hey, I'm going to see the Beatles.

When? When?

This Wednesday.

Fabulous.

Oh fantastic.

There's a fashion show at One Fifth Avenue. A friend of mine uh, a friend of mine has reserved three tickets for me. It's it's kind of a weird fashion show, um, and . . .

Stephen, you're supposed to follow him around. Would you do that or . . .

Come on, I'm going into the bathroom. No, come one, get up, get up. I'm gonna go into the bathroom. I just wanted to talk to you.

What's this other wire for?

I don't know; it has no imporTANCE. Tell me what your problem is, Stephen. That's per-fection. That's perfection. It's a weird, strange, difficult, but it is absolutely—

Is anyone's name in it?

gorGEous. No one's name is in it of course. How should, whoever, anyone have a name in it? I suspect it's really being the cleaning woman's. It is, isn't it? Don't try to hypnotize me with that thing now. What do you want to learn? The oracle is open. It will be closed shortly; it's Saturday.

(S) What are your hours?

(O) The oracle, it has twenty minutes on Saturdays and then she goes into deep meditation.

(S) But it's Friday.

(O) Well, then we, we'll pretend it's Saturday, okay? What do you want to ask the oracle?

(S) I don't want to ask the oracle anything.

(O) Then get out of Adelphi. You have no right to come, to come up here; you people who can come up here and waste the oracle's time, do you realize how busy she is? The all-seeing . . .

(S) I was up here before you were.

(O) Yes, I know, but there was no one in here.

Well, that's true.

Who's jacket is this?

Looks too small on you.

It is not . . . it's . . . . that's how much you knew you know know about perfect fit. It's a perfect fit. Look at it, it's a perfect fit.

It's too tight.

It is not too tight.

It is too.

Stephen, you have no eye.

I have no eye.

You haven't and your own. That's too tight I suppose? Don't you under-stand how fabric is cut? That's too tight, isn't it, huh?

It is.

Don't be an ass. It's perfectly divine. Whose is this?

It's Rink's.

It's magnificent. It's just magnificent.

I told him that you'd probably take it.

Well, I've never seen anything that made me look more like Rosalind
Russell.

It's beautiful; keep it.

He said it's too tight.

No, no . . . that's just perfect.

This is exactly perfect.

Yeah, it's perfect.

Yeah, I mean I look—don't switch it back and forth, the microphone
has been taught, been trained to pick up, up. Well, listen, Drella, so
then whe (*Drella says something*). Oh all right, so shall I call Rita?

Uh, yes. Oh uh, please. There's something you can do.

Oh come with me to the phone. Oh can you give me a dime? Do you
have any money on you?

Yes oh . . .

So you like that?

Huh, oh I love that coat.

Isn't it, isn't it stunning? I mean is it, aren't they, are we (*phone rings*).
Answer it.

Aren't they heavy? Hello, who's calling? (*Voice on phone: Did you
get the tape in?*) The video tape machine? Did, did you get the video
tape machine yet, Drella

No, were awaiting it. who is it?

We're awaiting it. It's Paul.

(D) Paul who?

Uh, Paul who? Paul.

Oh, no, no, it's coming.

It's coming, it's coming. Yes I suppose. Yes, Drella's going to wait
for it to come in and then the Factory will be closed because Drella's
going away after, after that. Yes, who is, do you know me? Where? Oh
Paul, oh you mean Juan's friend. How's Juan? Has he ever recovered?

PAUL on phone—Yeah, yeah, he'll come up and see the video tape machine ift it's there.

Oh, no, no, no, no, no, no, I don't want to frighten anybody.
There's no reason. Did he ever say what was the matter?

Ho, he just sorta gets that way. I don't know, I think.

Oh because I mean we we stomped and screamed and said good-bye.
It was nice meeting you . . . never answered . . . I thought he might
have been terrified.

(P) Yeah.

(O) I mean I would beterrified. Well, good-bye Paul.

(P) Well listen, I'll get Ed up there if your're gonna wait for him. Paul said he, he's heading up here because he can't wait to see it Drella. Drella said, "Oh great." (*Laughter from phone.*) No, he's, he's reading his correspondance.

(P) All right then, thank you. Adio.

(O) *coughs*—Ahdeeoo. What, wha, what.

(P) Ondine, I'll see you later.

(O) N-no, you, n-no, you just said something. What'd you say?

(P) I said uh, "Thank you very much."

(O) Oh, it's my pleasure Paul. If I can ever do anything for you again let me know. Ahdeeoo. (*Hangs up.*) Mississippi that call came from. Now, you wanted to know something? The oracle is just about to close, it's twenty minutes later.

Close your oracle, close the oracle.

Close my oracle? Close your orafile. You shouldn't

Close the oracle.

Have you leaned a great lesson from to-day's session?

I've learned nothing.

Ah, but then you've learned it all.

I've learned it all.

You know the way—I yeah, but he says he doesn't want . . .

You can't mean that.

Oh Drella, it's—

It's not bad at all, I, Drella, listen Stephen / / / / / why don't you, why don't you do something about it? Show it a little bit. And get those fucking girls form around your knees. The streets are just full of el-ligible men. Don't you want to become a woman?

No.

(O) The streets are just full of eligible men. Don't you want to become a woman?

No.

No? !

Not really.

Well then you(ll never know what it is to be all woman will you?

S—You mean A.W.?

You mean you're going to spend all of your life a . . . board? Hover-ing between womanhood and manhood? No, be all woman and there-fore all man. Just to have, to have, to first of all, well the first thing you have to do is to eat an asshole. I'll tell you.

S—Really?

You have to learn that first of all and you have to go down with an asshole face and say, "Oh, you've been ea—" You mustn't point at the first one you see. I'm calling the Mayor. There's a big red thing and you, you pucker like this, Drella goes over there's the guilty wear it.

(S) Oh really?

They wear it.

Laughter.

(S) Oh really, is there somebody who's hard-assed too? I mean, one with a real, people with uh very tiny hard lips, are, are they the ones?

I remember, you can(t tell, tell by—

(S) You can't really tell?

If, if there are pieces of filth— it's just a certain guilty look that they wear which you know.

(S) Really? Can you point one out when we're in the street?

Yes, absolutely. Oh I don't know if we'll see any on the street because that's uh, y8know . . .

(S) Where can you tell?

Uh, when they're just finished. When they're just finished. I say that's why the baths are such a xxxxxxx marvelous place cause you can spot them right off.

(S) Oh really?

Yeah. (*Dials phone.*)

Oh.

I go through cycles y'know, in the baths, either nothing happens and hen all of a sudden—oh she's busy.

Would you like to BE RIMMED?

Oh, I, I don't mind it, y'know, it's as nice as anything else, but certain days I guess my asshole must have a special flavor.

(S) Why?

Because after . . . that's all anybody does, and I walk out and they don't do anything selse and I walk outside making suction noises, and say, "Oh, Jesus, my God," and the back again it starts, five, six times y'know, and I just can't, if somebody says to you, "Oh please sit on my face," what, what can you do? You've got to uh, acquiesce—is thaat the right, yes, you've got to it, I mean you must be friendly, at least. If somebody says sit on your face, on their face, I would do it. I mean I'm not a snop, I never have been—

S—And you never will be.

and I would do it anywhere, no matter where it is. I'd even do it in my parents' home. Where I have done it, by the way.

Well, I like the experience you had once when a kid almost came at the end, you came in and the guy ate it out afterwards.

Oh that was fabulous. Oh well, I had the baked bean one was even better.

Who was the baked bean one?

This was, this was a real weirdo. He asked me to please squat over his mouth and sit in it, and I said, "Oh—".

Oh really?

"but I don't have to go to the bathroom." He said, "Please try it." I said, "Well, I'll try, but I'll feel silly." And I couldn't do it. I could not do it. I said to him, "I know what we'll do, let's get a can of baked beans, open it up, you take the pork out and you put them up one by one, would you try, and then I8ll squat over you, and I will shit them out." And I did. And he was in seventh heaven.

Where was this?

It was hysterical. Right down in the middle of his living room floor in Brooklyn.

How long did it take?

Uh, about twenty minutes, the whole process getting warm and everything, and then he said, "Did you," eh, I said, "Did you get anything else?" I said, "No, I told you I didn't have to go." I know when I don't have to do things. Y'know, but they think that you're just being modest.

Put the whole can of beans up your ass?

No, just two uh, two or three mouthfuls.

Oh really?

No, about twenty-five, thirty beans.

Oh really? Wow. That's fantastic.

It was a can. Oh it was really funny. I had string beans once there and mayonnaise and then . . . I . . .

Where was that?

Somewhere on Fire Island, and I said, "Please . . ."

He loves bananas, oh, I think it's what you really have done.

But that's—no, that was a once-in-a-lifetime thing, that slippery banana was a once-in-a-lifetime—

Oh really, oh but that, that, that's the thing you should recall, I mean you . . .

There was this one guy the other night who I met in the dance who told me he was a real— I was sitting in somebody's room with, with two people and I looked outside and I said to the boy, I said, "Come, come in here and he ju—without enormous hes-hesitation he walked right in, and you know, I showed him what had to be done and he went right down and then he tol—then he told me about this man—

Who is it?

Who, who is it?

Oh this is it.

This is twenty-three, open up.

Oh are you delivering something?   MAN—Yes.   Oh well, there's an elevator—wait a minute. The elevator's—wait, you can go down by elevator. Are you delivering a camera?   MAN—Yeah, a camera.   Oh terrific   MAN—Seven, Seventh car.   Wha?   MAN—Seventh car. Yeah, yeah okay, okay. Why don't you take the elevator down?   MAN— Yeah, all right, okay.   Yeah, I'll call him for you.   It's here, it's called—   Oh here it is, oh no, it's arriving now.   Okay, it's uh, the bottom on this side, so uh, push one . . .   Yeah, one.   MAN—Would you all give me a hand truck?   Oh yes, give him a hand.   Yeah, uh, do we? Oh no, we don't, uh, okay, all right.   That's—   This thing? (*Clatter of objects.*) Is this all right? Okay. This all we have? How exciting, my new camera. (*More clatter.*)   MAN—Did you say push this?

Now push one, push one and then the one, it's right where, it's right on this side, where it says four uh, 4W, no, on this side, yeah, because you'll get it on the other side if you go on . . .   MAN—Just when . . .

When you're coming back up . . .   And make sure that this door's closed like this, so that it, it rides.   MAN—Okay.   Okay?   MAN— Al lright.   Oh uh, oh uh.   So he said to me . . .   Okay, wait a minute, uh . . .   Oh.   Oh.   He said to me . . .   No, no. Okay. (*Phone rings.*) Answer the phone.   Hello, no Gerry's not here. Who's calling?

2/   1

Oh, so, wherever I was in these stories we called him in and showed him what was what and after it was over he told us about helping a man fuck himself.

Oh.

He said his dick was bent the right way, and he could help him, and so I immediately got excited knowing that mine was bent the right way . . .

Yeah.

And he said, I told him to uh, uh get the . . . with the help, with the aid of someone else you

can fuck yourself.

Oh really?

Yes.

How?

Well, because you see, when I get a hard-on my, it comes like this.

Yeah, yeah.

Y'know, and that, that reaches and and you can fuck yourself.

Really?

With somebody else's help.

Oh really?

Wouldn't that be heaven?

You'd like it?

I don't know. I didn't do it yet . . . that's still good.

Oh, oh.

It's gonna be a new one for Ondine!

Can you have balls too at the same time?

Uh, no. I don't know how far you can go, go, you know, into your own ass but uh, but uh, will luck, will have luck, will have it, I'll get my diet pilll. The girl did call . . . Josephine? That's for Gerard?

I think maybe it was for me.

Dear Gerard, no, no—is Josephine Levine? You don't want her.

She's probably onto . . .

Oh she, she's fit, well, she, she's not giving her cherry to you too, I hope.

Huh?

If she does, don't accept it because she doesn't have it left.

She said she'd be here. How do you know?

She hasn't got, she hasn't even got a pit left, or a stem. The girl didn't call Josephine Levine, Gerry.

Oh, that's who, why don't you like Josephine? She's a good, you'd make out well with Josephine. Tell her about Josephine.

You you like uh, Diana uh, Cunter, right?

Do you like to uh . . . yes.

(S) Yes.

You're in, are you in love with Diana Cunter?

Oh he's in love with uh, Sandy, any, any girl . . .

Sandy and you would look good with one another.. They would, you, we would both be very uh—Handsome couple.

(S) That's a lot of truth.

Lanky & ill-looking. (*Laugh . . ter.*)

It would be very very—no, no, very very beau— Ithink you should, you you you you should learn how to handle a prick first, though, it's most important, as having a woman it—

Does he, is he going to give us a big car?

I don't think he's badly sized at all.

He can only tell us.

He could show us. When that little man goes you can show us, for . . . sake and then we'll all judge.

He's getting nervous, he's getting all—

Well, of course.

(S) Well, yes, I am.

He thinks his analyst is here so that's the reason he's scared.

Everybody does. Your analyst is away.

(S) Yes.

Well, when he comes back poison him.

(*Laughter.*) Did Jeffry call?

(S) No.

No?

How big is it? Did you ever measure it?

(S) No.

I mean as a child, you must have. You mean you you kids didn't play the games . . . how big is it?

(S) Where?

Yeah, listen, will you, will you submit to this test?

Average size.

(S) Oh sort of small, smaller, about like this.

Six inches?

(S) I've never measured it.

Well, can we measure it?

(S) No. You can't.

Well, this is only a clinical study for heaven's sake. What do you think this is? What do you, what do you think I'm going to s-swoop down on it? Don't be silly. I mean you've gotta learn if if it doesn't reach a certain size you, we we just have the proper exercises, that's all.

(S) Well, what are the proper exercises, that's all.

You tie . . . they're Arabian, by the way. They're heaven.

(S) Oh yeah, well, tell me what you do?

You tie a rope around, a rope?

Yeah.

ROPE. That's how Marie Mc-Donald would say it with an R.

Yeah.

A rope—

Yeah.

AROUND THE HEAD OF YOUR PENIS.

Yeah.

And you sit like this at the edge of a stool. Uh, a boxer. And that's wha—that's what we did. And you move it like this, forward and then back—

Yeah.

Forward and then back. This process goes on for six months.

Yeah.

At which point uh, you have stretched it out. You have pulled your prick out a a bit. Cause you can't expect to have steel, it'll be a little like uh, an uh, asparagus tip, but maybe two, up to two inches.

Really?

Which is heaven, isn't it?

You're kidding?

No I'm not.

Well, why don't you do it to yours

os you, you can . . .

Oh, because I think mine is so uh, all right, you know, I mean, I don't—besides, if it's, if it, if mine did ge ttwo inches longer it, I might be fucking myself every minute of the day . . .

Ondine, that's . . .

It would be ridiculous. It's heaven, it's so ancient, it's whorey.

Yeah, it's been around.

It's been around, yeah. That's what Rotten said when he saw my face. "Ah, that face has been around," he said. After eight years; I hadn't seen him for eight years.

Oh.

Because I met him at the park, at Reese Park, and I was on the swings singing "Struda la bamba" and he came up and said, "AH ZOO CHAIN AH," and we became friends and then we both decided that Rita Stevens would make a very good Ah Zoo Chain Ah.

Who's Rita Stevens?

Rose Stevens.

Oh, Rise.

Yeah, yeah, and then uh, we didn't see, see each other for eight years.

Oh. Rise? No, you mean the Mayor.

I mean, yeah. Rotten Rita and myself. And then all of a sudden . . . Do you know what Taxine's name is?

What?

Rocket Rita-Taxi.

Rocket Rita?

Laughter.

No, Rocket Taxi.

Rocket Taxi. Oh, ejected. Taxi, no, you have to do something with the "T."

Rocket Taxi.

Rocket Taxi pretty good.

I, I thought it was Rotten Taxi . . .

I was so happy . . .

·*Laughter.*

Rotten Taxi something with a *T.* I can't think of a, can you think of a *T?*

Taxi, Taxi, Tavxine, taxi, taxine, Taxina . . .

Uterus, I guess—no, that's just plain U.

What?

How do you spell "uterus"? U-t-e-r-u-s or e-u-t—?

Urasion, Urasion Taxi.

No, I like Rocket Taxi.

I think that's very smart too.

It goes with . . .

With Rotten Rita. Rocket Taxine and Rotten Rita and the Duchess. O Jesus.

Isn't she incredible?

Yeah, I think she's fantastic.

She does things like . . .

If we didn't have Taxine around, she would, if we didn't have Taxine around she'd really uh . . .

Uh, she's in the hospital now.

Yeah, the poor—

(O) darling.

(D) girl.

We would really make her a star if she'd come . . . a recording actress.

Well she wha—listen, once, she can certainly uh, uh, uh, work her way up.

Yeah.

And uh she, I mean uh, once we uh, we uh, once we top control of the first pa-papers we can do anything. Her, her parents have control of the KELLOGE

PAPERS which—

Oh, I know they do.

means nothing can stop us. We can start another Spanish American War. UGH!

We could, we could be the new uh, you could be, you could be the new . . .

I could be the new *Dorothy Killgalan.*

No, no, not the *Dorothy Killgalan,* the uh, NEW uh . . .

Marianne Davies.

Marianne Davies.

Yeah, but . . .

Wow, why don't you, why don't you marry her . . . why don't you make her give up her husband and you marry her?

The Duchess?

Yeah.

I wouldn't want to fuck her all the time.

Well uh, she doesn't want to be fucked; she's a lesbian.

She went down, oh no, she likes to suck and she went down on me—

Oh.

once in the bathroom . . .

Oh really?

And in the kitchen, yeah, she ju— y'know, and she likes things in her mouth and I don't, I mean I want to, I like to, when I'm blown, like to be really calm about it. What's wrong with the girl's mouth in the boy's mouth; is there a difference?

Yes.

What?

Uh, but the Duchess doesn't suffer from this.

Yeah.

Yeah.

Most girls think that, that, that, that they don't have to, that, that they have a conscience . . .

Yeah.

And that they don't have to do anything.

Oh.

Y'know, so it's like doing you a favor that they blow you.

Oh really?

Which means—

Oh, I didn't know that.

you have to be really raunchy and piss on them or something . . . but uh, uh, uh, boys are usually better, you know, you just know them, and boys have better assholes I mean, and assholes is definitely more . . .

GIRL—what's wrong with girl's assholes?

No, but, no, they, they, it's what's wrong with girls' asses. They're flabby and uh, you want muscles and cheeks and places for your hands to fit and someone to be able to move like a, and girls really don't uh, you know, they feel that the world owes them a child or something just because they can . . . they have a clam, who cares?

The Duchess. The Duchess always got me. She, she has a pretty face, I, I think she's pretty. She's a lovely fiirl.

Uh, ah, uh, her ass. . . .

She's been a drug fiend since she was twelve years old.

Oh really? Oh.

Twelve years old and the child has been drugged . . . I mean I think that's funny.

Well, Taxine's been drugged, hasn't she? And she's pretty young too.

Well, Taxine has, Taxine has told me bits and pieces of her story and uh, her parents are just, just

deadly. I don't know how anybody grows like that, you know, I just, I just . . . Taxi was I guess, I guess uh, uh, because all the kids were very big and uh, Taxine was out a little uh . . .

Small.

Leftover frail.

She's uh, she's a heavy girl, except she gets too frantic . . .

Oh.

And she indulges herself . . .

Oh.

In the franticism.

Uh, oh Taxi wants to see you, so I mean why, you should, you know, like you should make arrangements so you can go up like towards the week or something like that.

Well, I couldn't mind going up but uh . . .

Yeah, well I'll fix it up.

But you, you don't know what it is, Drella. It's the uh, first of all . . .

No, she's very nervous about her uh, appointments and she just has to . . .

Her disappointments?

Her appointments.

Oh uh, I think her disappointments is true too.

And, and it would've, it would've been disappointing.

I think, I think if she, if she disappointed one one would, well, just of all she's trying, she wants . . .

She adores you, I mean.

I know but, well, because, because, well . . .

I've seen parts about you that I know everybody loves.

But Drella, she wants to believe very desperately in what she's doing.

Yeah.

And perhaps she doesn't quite believe it as much as she says.

Oh.

Well, she makes it frantically, but once she would, does, she, she'll just rest assured.

Yeah.

Y'know, because she is that good.

She is that good.

She's gorgeous on screen, she's really beautiful. She looks beautiful, she act beautiful, and what she considers a nervous, huh, huh, huh, is heaven. She's—

It's really uh, yeah.

the sexiest sound I've heard.

Yeah.

And every little frantic movement of hers is beautiful; it's not because I just dig her.

No, no.

Because I don't, I, I understand women. Imagine, understanding women. Well, that's what comes if you're ALL WOMAN.

Isn't it funny, I don't. People like that are usually nymphomaniacs or, just the other or opposite. She doesn't go either.

Well, she wants to, she wants to uh, have a family and—

Yeah.

children.

But I mean, but she's uh, very careful now not to get involved because she's not ready, and if . . .

She's, he's, she's lies, oh she's lies, oh God.

That's great. I, I mean that's so funny, I mean if she were just eh, just eh, if she were a nymphomaniac say, if she were, now there's nymph—now the point of nymphomania raised, raised to-

towards height and bright to its extremes is Gloria Savage.

But she's not—is she a nymphomaniac? Is she like Donn?

Indulgent.

Really?

She indulges her own passions besides the point she must, that she hates herself viciously for it . . .

Oh really? Oh.

And, and no one else would torture herself and her children and he rhusband in such a manner. There's no point to it. Why, why, why torture your, your family. I figured that out a long time ago when my mother said—"Please ago when my mother said— "Please don't come home for Christmas," she said.

(D) Oh really.

"You're so awful." I, I laughed. I said, "What a beautiful saying." . . . my place for Christmas, because I don't . . . No, no, no, no. . . . neither do I and she knows I don't and I tell her Mother's Day should, all mothers should be burned and everything, and she says . . .

Oh really?

She always drags it up to my face, my mother is great, my mother is the absolute. Her entire family hates her . . .

Oh really?

Because she's so great that she's just hated by everyone.

Oh.

Oh, I'm a product of her, there's no question about it, and my father is the product of an old maid.

Well.

My grandmother was resigned to

being an old maid when she was a young girl because her two younger sisters were, were, were ma—

How could your grandmother be an old maid?

But her two younger sisters were married before her, and like she figured she'd be an old maid.

Yeah.

And she didn't think that her parents would contract a marriage with someone in Italy.

Oh.

Besides, my grandmother had a squashed nose.

Oh really?

She looked like the banana woman. I've never seen anything like it.

Oh really?

But she married this man, sight unseen, from Italy.

Oh really? He didn't . . . upset, disappointed?

o, not, y'know, he didn't expect anything much uh . . .

Is your grandmother still around?

My grandmother's still around. She's taken to wearing my grandfather's pants and everything.

Oh really?

Fainting in the hallway. She's the one who's, who tried to kill herself with a plastic bag, first of all.

sadly Oh, aaaw.

laughing With a plastic bag.

Aaaw, your, your grandfather leave her?

No, my grandfather died uh bu— of uh, I think in a texacholosomy bag. I'm not sure, I didn't see them in the—the lady asked them. My aunt moved them out to Queens and put them in the cellar (*phone rings*) and I wouldn't be bothered.

RING RING RING RING

Oh really? Oh.

My aunt was such a mOTHerfucker. Hello? No, this is Bob. Who's calling? Who is this? Yeah. Who is this? Who is this? I can, I recognize the voice. Oh yes, I can recog— Bobby. Biscuit. Yah, you told. Well, I told then. Well, I told. Tha-that big mouth. I can have, I have just a . . . I'm waiting for the delivery of my grandmother and then I'm . . . everything will be all right. Yeah, my grandmother is being delivered parcel post. No, my real grandmother and Nikita Khrushchev. She's being delivered parcel post. What are you doing?

BOBBY *on phone*—Uh, I'm watching my . . .

THE DUCHESS IS IN THE HOSPITAL.

THE DUCHESS. IN THE HOSPITAL?

They went, she went to the dentist yesterday and the dentist wouldn't let her out; he sent her right to the hospital. Isn't that fabulous? For being bruised and demented. I wonder who's gotten her bag? So far do you know what she's gotten from the hospital? The blood-pressure machine, three, three thousand libreums, she, and I don't know what else she's racked up. I think she has a nurse in her closet. I'm not sure but she can't go to bed alone. I know that. They took her away but she's having a nice t— y'know she's resting and we're gonna take her on an LSD trip this afternoon. We're gonna go up to the hospital and put her on LSD. And we have a, we have a doctor's coat for her. A and Rotten Rita the Mayor. Billy's uh, would Billy be at Norm Bil-Bil-Billardball's?

Yeah, Billy would be at Norman Billardball's.

I don't know, I don't know if he, uh, uh . . . I think he may be asleep there.

Yeah, Bobby, uh, yeah, this is, this is, this is a very weird day; this is a day of uh, twenty-four hours with Ondine and it's uh, on tape and so are you right now, and uh, I mean like uh, I can't uh, I had certain things planned like a visit to Gracie Mansion, and to uh, unwrap my grandmother and a few other things, but y'know, I'd, I'd . . .

(B) Ah, ha!

(O) And I'm not sure; but we're waiting for the deli, the delivery of a, of a television studio now, really. CBS is coming over here, yeah. The Pa—the Patty Duke Show is being filmed.

Great, great.

Ducky.

(B) Yeah.

(O) Let me get off the phone.

Okay sweetie, and uh, when will you be around?

Uh, probably Monday cause I, yeah. Okay?

(B) Oh, that's a long ways off.

(O) Oh no, that's right. I keep thinking that today is Sunday. Uh, preferably Saturday evening then. That's tomorrow night, right?

At the Factory.

Yeah. Okay, Bobby, gi-give my love to y-your, to your darling wife.

Okay.

And I will see you uh, I'll see you soon.

Okay, uh . . .

And to you. Bil-Bil-Billardball's number?

(B) Right.

(O) Bye-bye. Oh, here we are. He's, he looked like a particularly uh, he looked like a particularly insipid uh, service girl.

Why can't we go now?

She a WAC? Oh, she's crazy. Hey, mad woman.

Why doesn't he just park up here?

Look at her; she's gonna have a little bit of difficulty.

Look at that camera. Oh, we've got to keep that.

You've got to keep that under wraps.

Oh.

My dear, under wraps.

Are you renting it, or are you buying it?

No, they're giving it to me for a month.

Oh how fabulous.

Who?

Who?

Norelco.

Norelco.

That's who it is, yeah.

My God!

It's a fantastic thing, it uh, you can put it down in the window and it takes pictures. You can r-race it off . . .

Oh Drella, oh Drella, oh.

You're going to be a big star, you're starring with . . . might be in space.

Drella DrELla DrellA.

In space . . . *Laughter.* He's all woman in the ass.

Oh but darling . . . wanted . . . *Laughter.*

Uh, oh, so that proposition is still

around, is it? So you know, but I don't think that that should be a film.

Why?

I think that that should be, if *Alice in Wonderland* is done, it should be done day by day and uh, people should pay to see it and it should be a running kind of a . . .

Project

Like, like here, no, no, I mean just certain hours of the day . . .

Oh, you're, you're right.

And make them, make them pay for it.

What for, to come in an dbe in it?

To come in to see it.

To be in it.

To do whatever happens here; they'll be in wonderland. They are right now but they don't know it.

Oh.

And someday soon you can, y'know, film it if you want to and if you don't want to (fluff down)? and all that.

Oh marvelous, Ondine.

But they should pay. I mean why should we all the . . .

To be in? To be in? Okay.

Yes, why should . . .

Ondine, you're our business manager. I just . . .

Oh, of course. I thank God you're out, darling, because I'm out too.

Okay.

All right. This is Ondine business, seeing I gotta get my dress on.

You know what you have to find for us?

What?

A little girl who's sensible, who doesn't know anything, to answer the phone.

Just to answer the phone.

No money.

No money, just to answer the phone. Okay.

Just to be around.

I'm thinking.

Okay. Do you know anybody?

I'm thinking . . . my cousin Angelo.

Laughter.

(S) He's beautiful, seventeen, and rich also.

Yeah, rich.

Oh rich. I know no, I know very few rish people because uh, the Duchess knows a few . . .

Well, we could even ask her.

As a matter of fact I know a few through the Duchess.

Oh, maybe we'll use the Duchess.

The Duchess is in . . . oh, she would, my dear, oh you'll never get through. "Hello, this is the Duchess. Do you want to poke?"

Poke.

She needs an injection and I poke fast and when I come in for an injection she gives you vitamin B12 and dehydrating and aren't these obies divine?

Yeah.

Oh now.

I'm just on two and I feel fine.

They're uh, beautiful pills, y'know.

You're for, you're for five.

Fifteen milligrams.

Oh, oh.

That's a combination of my overindulgence, your caution, and a final compromise which is so beautiful, and five is such an umph, umPHINately inscrutable number.

Yeah, yeah.

I feel like it too.

With your society teeth.

What do you mean? Duncan Mc-

Donald?

Yeah uh.

Kaye Ballard had an interview with her on the air and all Kaye Ballard kept saying was, is, "Duncan, that's such a wonderful name, I think, for a woman." Duncan. Duncan McDonald, the woman who announces for W— she has an interview show on at 2:30 on WQ-WQXR and she, and her sponsor is Beshard Rug Company nad Lord & Taylor.

Oh Really?

And all Kaye Ballard gept, kept saying was, "Duncan is such a fabulous name, isn't that the cuningest name you ever heard?" She was great.

Do you wanna, do you wanna meet . . . uh, do you know her?

Duncan Mc—

Kaye.

I love Kaye Ballard.

Would you really, oh.

Ooh, she's uh, I think she's h, one. I think she's one of . . .

I know her very well, I know.

I thing Bea Trice and Fay Lard . . .

You can really get involved with her.

Yeah, no, but, well, but she, but she got in trouble for being that.

Oh really?

And she went through a very great men-mental strain and she's uh, sort of—

Oh really?

changed.

Who told you that?

She sorta told it herself on television. I, I, I remember she used to go over with Yunna Hooah.

Lovers?

Yes. Yunna Hooah. . . .

Yunnah Hooah . . .

Yes.

Fantastic.

And I used to go with Yunna Been.

You did?

No, no, no, I mean Yunna was.

Did she really only weigh . . . ninety-eight pounds?

She was twelve younds and that was padding that way . . . ninety-eight pounds (laughter). What did she die of again, acute leukemia?

No, earache.

Oh. (Laughter.) Linda Darnel is the second woman to go up in a blaze.

Oh, I know.

Madame Of-Ofsky of-the-sky was the first—that picture with Ronny Navel in Dragnet and his brother's leg in drag, it left me cold.

Oh, you mean with Jack Strap.

I don't understand transvestitism.

Yeah, I don't . . .

Yeah, I never have; if you're all woman there's no need to be a transvestite.

Uheauh.

How are we going to write "Oouh"?

It's hard but we'll find a way. Uheauh. We have to get, there's . . . my throat.

That, that—

Really?

was born eight years ago in Riis Park.

Really?

When Madame Rouche said that these are the pants that Bill . . .

You were actually thinner last year.

Yeah, I know but, I, I'm getting that pleasant . . .

But I, why, why is it that you can eat and Billy doesn't eat? Is there a reason for that or . . .

The glandular I guess or, I don't know.

Oh really, is it? But you eat more, don't you?

Well, I make sure to eat bec-because I like food.

Yeah.

I love the taste of food.

But I thought all this stuff is supposed to make you hungry.

Well, it's supposed not to.

But if, you mean if you don't want to eat you don't have to?

The minute I take amphetamine I go to sleep and get hungry.

Oh.

Which is the opposite of what it's supposed to do.

Oh really?

Which is great.

Oh.

Darling, darling, join in.

Oh really? Oh I—

It really does, and aft-after after you've taken amphetamine for a while it does this in everyone. It makes me so hungry.

Well, did you ever see him eat?

Jimmy?

But Ji— how could Jimmy possibly be hungry?

Oh uh, is Jimmy and Billy uh, still uh . . .

No. I doubt it.

Well, wha— have they broke up again?

Well, they, I think this time it's for keeps.

What happened? Well what happened?

I don't know; maybe they got wise. I don't understand.

Oh.

Billy told me one thing that was very revealing. He said he couldn't stand Jimmy doing crossword puzzles . . . which is beautiful, isn't it? I saw him one night here doing a crossword puzzle for 3½ hours.

Oh really? (*Ondine breathes in deeply.*) What do you . . . who taught him a crossword puzzle?

I used to do them all the time.

Hey!

Which is really too much for anybody to endure.

Fantastic.

Poor Billy, he . . .

He was thinking about you then.

He, he was imitating me, he never thought about a-any-anything in his life.

Really?

We, we—

Was he, was he . . . he's not an A.W., is he? Is he?

No, he's—

He's all man?

He pretends to be. No, he's not all man or all woman; he's uh, uh, uh . . . he's, he's, I don't Know. He's, he went to Zorba Pachukas' psychiatrist and Peter Hopper's, and they all went to the . . . he's very sick now. Jimmy is very sick.

Can you see . . . wha-what happened to the . . .

He's the last of the old S-an-M's.

Oh he was?

Yes.

Was he?

Uh, he used to, y'know, he'd be-LIEVE and all that uh, Arcade shit.

You mean, beaten? He's beaten you or you've beaten him?

No, y'know, he just does all that regular nonsense and he didn't do it for fun; he did it becau— see, Jimmy has a lot at stake.

Yeah.

H-His mind for one thing.

Is he intelligent? Oh he must be.

He has intelligence about him but he refuses to make—

Oh really?

it function.

Oh.

Because he's, he, he's just a (sniffs) well, he comes from that kind of family, my dear.

What? What kind?

Well, his mother, he, I, I overheard his mother on the phone one night say . . . he said, she said, "Jimmy, what are you eating?" And he said, "Pasta, a plate of pasta." She said, "How vulgar." That's the kind of family . . .

His mother?

And she also wears white gloves, she also wears little gloves. She also does not eat rye bread in public. Rye bread in public? Because I don't understand that but his—

Oh he is?

mother is out of her mind. Jimmy?

Yuo met her?

Oh, I would never . . .

Oh.

Thank God I didn't meet her. Ah we's I we's I to be tortured and tormented with guilt living in Flatbush, at the same time this unbearable . . .

Does he, does he ever call you?

I love Elsie. I love Elsie. No, he's just deadly afraid of me.

Oh really? Why?

I, he owes me $75.

Oh.

And everytime he sees me he crawls up inside himself and dies.

Oh.

He burned me for $75. I-I-I-I could little afford it.

Do you think you'll ever go back to him?

No! Go back to what? A house, full, full of dog shit?

Whose dog?

His dog. Sigfried.

When did he get Sigfried?

Oh, he had Sigfried a long time ago and then S. WEISS lost him.

And you found him again? Where?

No, no no no. We ddin't find him; we've been feeding it to-to Jimmy every morning. He eats that f-f-from . . .

Who?

Sigfried he has um, chopped up uh, Doberman pinscher.

Really?

It's divine.

Is it really?

We told him the other day—oh we also told him that Taxine was a murderer and we gave him a list. Rotten Rita gave him one list with my name on the top of it and I gave him my list . . .

The murdered? The murdered?

No, the ones to be murdered.

Oh, oh.

So, I'm on the top of Rotten Rita's list and she's on the top o my list.

Oh.

He's completely out of his mind. But he's got the perfect face for a murderer.

Oh really? Of . . .

Yeah, well anyway I feel so excited that I'm go—I think that this should be shut off for just a

Oh, oh, no. Why?

second or two.

Well, cause I just feel like doing something, like putting that dress on.

Oh well, oh that's all right.

I wanna wear it.

You can put it on.

Can I put the dress on?

Oh uh y'know, I mean this is all you. I'm just following you around. You know this is twenty-four hours of you, or twelve hours I think.

Twelve hours. Oh like the baths like the (*laughter*) like . . .

Oh that is beautiful.

I have other pieces of material I can fit my statue.

Really?

Yeah.

Where'd you find it?

Rotten Rita is y'know, works for a . . .

Rotten Rita gave me a lot of information yesterday, I was very surprised.

Rotten Rita is that bad . . .

Come here, you see I'm doing wallpaper and Rotten Rita's . . .

She . . . so much like . . . do you . . . if that Vivian Shrieker was able to listen to her.

Yeah.

And he wasn't, cause he was so busy with prejudices and so busy being a queen and the Duchess wanted to be one of my lovers at one time.

This, this, well, he says he knows so much about music that blah, blah, and he's really just a fag. Well, I, he had listened to Rotten Rita and he he h-hadn't minded her manner . . .

Yeah.

He would have heard that uh . . . she told him in three sentences what to do with his apartment and to make it look presentable.

Yeah.

Cause it looks like the back of a Viennese warehouse that's just been . . . that only the valley has just vacated. She, he's told her the fabrics to use, the way to use them.

He doesn't have . . .

What to do.

He really doesn't.

But he told her how to do it.

Oh.

Everything, and she just refuses, she said, "Oh please, don't talk while the record's on." He said what?

Oh, but the music there is gorgeous.

It's not even played right.

Oh really?

He had the Callas album there and it sounded, and it sounded atrocious.

Oh really?

The volume was all fucked up and everything.

Oh.

And we heard it the other night and we just went—

Really?

berserk . . .

Oh.

It was so beautiful.

I thought it, I thought it was just, I thought it sounded fantastic.

He plays certain tapes well.

Did you go downstairs too?

No.

Oh, you should go downstairs.

Well, you see Walter was there y'know, and Walter is, Walter is too uh . . .

Oh.

Oh well, this is gonna be a new one.

Well uh, we have to stay maybe, cause they're gonna send a man over.

OH I HAVE TO CALL RITA
NOW.
I forgot to call Rita . . .
Yeah . . . well he . . . we'll get,
    we'll pick them up and uh . . .
She was over there on the side of
    the street getting the thing; I
    couldn't believe it.
Yeah, I know. She sort of parked
    her car right in front of the place
    (*dialing phone*). Drella, who's
    going to assemble it for you?
I don't know; maybe they'll come
    Monday, or . . .
They should be, oh it ha—it ha—
    it has to be done by a technician.
It's like uh, it's like space. It's uh
    . . .

Do you want me to—Hello, Rotten. It's me. I'm at the Factory. I know
but I couldn't help it. Rrella ran out of the restaurant and told me that
they were delivering a camera that no one was here to receive and he had
to go and the camera has sevnten parts to it and it's enormous and it's
just been delivered and I've ben calling you since I arrived here and you've
been busy . . .   Why is he so busy? He's always on the phone.   He,
he's got to be, he can't help it, everybody calls him, well, everybody calls
him.   Really?   Yeah.   We'll be there, we'll call Billy and, as soon
as Billy gets here we'll leave (*person on phone talkingℴ* (o) hah hah (and
she said that she's not coming up here) aw too bad for her. Well, tell her
why she had friends like Dennis Seco . . . Rita, you can't believe the size
of this camera. It is enormous. I'm sorry baby, listen, I'm sorry but I, I
have been calling you since I've arrived and you've been busy; this is the
first time you haven't been and there was nobody at the Factory and there
should have been someone here to receive the uh, the camera. This is, it's
really, and uh, oh it's such a camera. Billy's not here and who knows where
he is . . .   Oh, but he said, he said.   Is he at Norman Billardball's?
    Norman's, and he said that, he said he'd be here soon.   Billy said
he'd be here soon.   Yeah, I'll call him to come here soon. (You said
that you'd be in touch with him.) I-I didn't call him this morning. I-I
didn't call him this morning.   What's your apart—can I . . .   What's
your apart—   Listen, Rotten . . .   Which one . . .   Is Arlene all
right?   Which one, sometimes. (Keep the heavy one.)   Yes Dr-
Drella wants to to go and so do I.   Yeah, I wanna see the Duchess.
We had to wait for the machine. It's just been delivered. It just got here.

The man is taking his ? from his car outside and bringing it . . . well, don't be teed-off with me because I, it's not my fault, my fault.   (D) It's my fault.   (O) It's not your fault either, Drella, why wasn't there, be someone here to receive it?   Well, uh, okay. Tell him to wait for us, because I uhm, want to get a riiii . . . . uh.   (O) Yeah, I'd like to go there too. Shall we meet you there or what, baby? . . . Well, we have to wait until the man delivers the thing—he's got to bring it up to the elevator and put it here and then uh . . .when will Billy, and whenever Billy arrives we'll, we'll leave the minute that he comes here.Wehaveto. Ohm, thanks very much.   Billy's at Norman's.   I'll call him right now.   Well, I'm gonna call him right now and then I'll call you right back, immediately, and tell tell you uh, yeah, I have to get off the thing because the man has to use the phone—ah I'll call you right back. Bye. (*Hangs up.*) I'm glad to hear he's a nervous wreck.

What a refreshing difference. Because he's been, because his sister fainted at work and had to be brought there and he's bringing her to the hospital; he's bringing her to the hospital when he goes to see the Duchess. She fainted at work; she just kept that . . .

Why?

Her boss drove her there, drove her to, to, to . . .

And she's still . . .

No, at his house. She's lying down.

Why, why, why did she faint?

I don't know; I think she must be Le-Leanora in *Trovatore*.

How old is she? Younger than Rita?

She must be twenty, yeah. She's a little younger than Rotten.

When's he taking her to the hospital? Is he gonna put her in?

No, he's bringing her to the hospital when he goes to see the Duchess.

Why?

Y'know, I don't know but Rotten Rita always has a plan.

She'll probably crawl in bed.

She might, and w-we oh, and then we, that's how we can get the

Duchess out. The Duchess.

Oh.

We can pretend that she's the Duchess.

Oh.

Leave her in bed and take the Duchess.

What is wrong with the Duchess?

I, I don't know. I think her brain.

Oh really?

I'm not sure. I don't think she should have done all the things she's been doing, she doesn't eat, she just drinks vodka and she . . .

She doesn't eat?

Doesn't eat? I know but she doesn't eat.

But she's so fat.

I know she doesn't eat. Do you know she went out shopping to get something to eat and she wound up with two cans of as-

Oh really?
paragus?
That was all. The rest was . . .
But she's a secret eater.
She never ate. She's a secret blow down.
No, she eats.
She doesn't eat a thing. Drella, it is liquor that has made her like this.
Really?
It's, she used to drink three quarts a day of vodka.
Oh she, nobody can drink three quarts. Somebody's at the door.
She, she . . .
Who is it?
Lucky—It's you.
Oh, oh, oh.
(L) Ah, what you should get is a blimp. B-l-i-m-p.
Okay.
(L) A blimp, blimp.
What're you talking about?
(L) For the Hassels.
What Hassels?
(L) The sound Hassels. All right.
I don't know what you're talking about.
Oh, no, you go down the elevator because you have the thing on it.
(L) Yeah, I have. Oh wha—here, here. Oh it's there; we left it up, you don't wanna walk.
I'll have the drug for you.
(L) Yes, oh all right.
Thanks very much . . .
(L) Yeah, you're welcome.
Is that yours?
(L) No, that belongs to me.
No, that's his.
Oh all right, good night.
(L) Oh, good night.
Blimp, a blimp, it wasn't . . .
Maybe you should blow him for uh, for tape.

What for—who, Lucky?
Lucky.
Ohm, I've never blown Lucky.
Maybe Lucky can blow you for tape?
Lucky and I wouldn't do that.
Oh.
Is tha—it would be so imp— y'know, our affair would have to be very 1930's.
Really?
Very personal—very 1930's are personal.
Oh really?
For heaven's sake, you can take your thing out and . . .
(you should maybe we should)
How big it was . . . see if you can. (Laughter.) Wait, I've gotta mark this A.W.
Oh my, A . . .
Yes.
Oh my crud, A.W. stands for Andy Warhol too.
Didn't you know that?
No, I just got— (Laughter). It also means "all woman."
And "all witch."
(what is all this here)
That is . . .
The new camera.
The new camera for our television serial.
Voice—New camera?
It's called TV.
    Laughter. I love you
(I do on the definitely so)
Oh Mrs. Lockwaldatross, I'm taking my dress off. I just can't stand around in my . . . I just can't stand around in my . . .
Your dress on—oh this dress . . .
My whole dress, my whole outfit.
Yeah, ohm, here's a dime.
Oh well, call Billy now.
Ohm, okay. Lucky, what happened

to your eye? RH 7-9718, right?
He was fighting because of the—oh
can you hold one. Oh, go ahead—
R, H, 7 . . .
Twenty-four hours of Ondine.
(24 hours of Ondine)/?
You should try that anymore hours
are decreed, right?
Right, just hold . . .
Damnit, look, it's the baths. We

started off the morning by meeting at at the park, then in in to
to Stark's for a severe atmosphere
and I had schnecken for the first
time, which cleared up my voice
entirely.
Oh, did it?
Yeah, oh I uh . . .
I thought it was the five obertrols.
No, the five obertrols didn't work.

2 /   2

This way, pack up your packs, and
if *he qua ponta la gusta*, that's
all okay, bye-bye.
Was he there? Was Rotten there?
Nobody there. Now I gotta call
Miss Rat Rotten Rita our dear
beloved Mayor, and then we have
to go to the Duch—we have to
go to the Duchess's. Listen, we
have to start instituting rules,
rules here. Nothing but the—
Studio policies.
Nothing but the best-looking
(*laughter*) women are allowed in
here.
(L) A.W.'s.
And without cunts. Uh, let me see,
what's, uh what's uh Rotten
Rita's, what's our Mayor's number—oh, EN 4 . . .
Studio policy.
Englebarg. Each person—oh and
three's going to be a—
(L) Policy?
Yeah, that's the policy.

And we've got to find a moron girl
for the phone. Do you know any
mo—Lucky, Queens is full of
these little girls, like . . . just pick
out one, drag her here and . . .
she's at the phone.
(L) Oh, you mean the switch-
board.
We need a non-paying moron like
like Ruthie on the Uncle Miltie
show. "Hello, Ruthie." Hello, I
just called Billy; he's not there,
he's on-on-on his way. He said
Billy's there and he's sleeping;
he's been calling there for two
hours.
He is not.
He's not. Drella said no.
Cause I talked to him and he, he
slept last night.
He spoke to him and he said he's,
he's on his way down.
I tried yesterday.
When did you speak to him?
Uh, uh, two o'clock.

He spoke to him at two o'clock.
He promised me.
Pause.
I'm sure he's not there. I'm sure
he's not there cause I know when
Drella tells him to please please
be here for a delivery or some-
thing. He w-wouldn't be st—he
wouldn't be stupid enough not to
If he does, my dear, it's not
gonna be for long, cause . . .
Here Gerry's coming.
Cause cause Gerry's on his way
downtown, which means we
should leave here in about fifteen
minutes.
Yeah.
Yeah—no, wh—
Tell him to call us at the—
No, where shall we go?
When he's leaving tell him to call
us.
(O) Yeah. Well, Rotten, listen . . .
no, let her do it herself. Well,
why don't you call up the New
Yorker and say things to her?
(RR) Wha?
(O) Call, call up the N-New Yorker and say things to her. Good.
Well, well then, now . . . now I'll
call up the New Yorker and de-
stroy her. You, y'know Sunshine's
bten a friend of mine for years
and she has some nerve, boy. But
she was pretty insulting to me
last night too. I'm afraid she just
deserves a a little bit of a rough
time.
(L) Eliminate the sound Hassels,
the blimp.
Huh?
(L) It's something, uh . . .
(O) Rita, if you leave for the
Ethel Rossevelt Hospital before
we uh, leave here, would you uh,
call here? Please, and you tell us

exactly—I know, I know that it's
building G, floor 9, I have the
adress.
Building G, floor 9.
Would you . . . Rotten Rita gave
me the address.
Darling, I'm sorry, I didn't, I told
you, I explained it once before.
G-905
That it wasn't, it's not due to any-
anything from—yes I know, and
I had to wait for Drella.
Obertrols.
And I told you, my dear, I told you
when I got off the phone, you go
back to sleep and I'll call you
when I meet Drella. Try and get
some rest. I don't know if that's
being horrible but it sh-should
. . .
Huh?
Uppies, ves hippo.
Well, I didn't expect you to really.
No?
But I got, but the Fifth Avenue
bus took me about one and a
half hours to get across to where
I was going. I fianlly got there
and Drella arrives and we went
off to, we wen, we went off to
call you. The line was busy.
(Pause.) We went up to call you
and your sister gave us the message, which was "Come over,"
she said, and we were and then
an dthen Drella came out and
said that they're delivering a
camera which is essential that he
get there. It's about seventeen,
how much money is this? It, it,
it's-it's-it's . . .
$15,000.
It's fifteen thousand worth, worth
of equipment. It's an enormous
camera; it's like a TV camera.
It's fabulous, Rita, really, hon-

estly, and no one was here to receive it.

No, no, they're just uh, it's not mine.

I . . .

(L) Did they rent it to you or . . .

$ $ $ $ $ $ $ $ $ $

You know personally that I would never do anything like that to you.

(L) What are you going to cut— a closed circuit job?

I know. Oh, I won't go without you. I won't go out, I won't go there without you, my dear. (*Pause*) I don't blame you. I don't blame you. Good-bye, my love. He's—no, he's furious, he's so disgusted with people he knows and disgusted with the telephone and—good, we don't have to go.

Oh, we *have* to go.

No, Rotten Rita's gone out for a walk and then . . .

Oh is . . . nothing.

The Mayor needs a . . .

Oh.

The Mayor needs a stroll.

But, but what happeend to uh, aren't we going to see the Duchess?

We, we, she calls every fifteen minutes and says, "Honey, baby, I love you." She's nine hundred pounds of woman, and . . . she, $ $ $ $ $ $ $ $ $ $ oh, she sleeps on the edge of a coutch t-to be cute. (*Phone rings.*)

RING RING RING RING

Huh, hello who's calling Margaret? No, he's not here but can I leave a message. Margaret who?

Uh, do I know where he is? Yes, he's somewhere on Eighth Street

Mar-Margaret who? Would you spell that please? B-o-y-c-e hyphen C-a-m-. And uh, what message do you want to use? (*Giggles.*) Pierro's movie is being shown where?

Oh, we're showing some movies tonight, oh yes.

Where? Cinematheque. Okay, darling. Thank you very much. Bye-bye.

We're showing uh . . . or we could show your *Blow Job* or something.

No, but I don't want to see either.

Laughter Oh, y'know you have to go everywhere we go.

I know I have to go everywhere . . . no, no, you have to go everywhere I go. Hah, hah, hah, ah hah, hah, hah. She said, "This is Margaret Boyce-Cam." She said, "I'd love to speak to Gerard, is he there?" Oh, the best one was a woman who got on the phone and walked up and said, "Hello, this is Marjorie." I said, "Marjorie?" She said, "Yes," she said, "What are you listening to?" I said, "*The Marriage of Figaro.*" She went woo—she was, that was really good.

(L) I'll get . . .

Uh, just anybody wanted to bring the films.

Stephen, why don't you bring some of the pictures that we can see?

He's just uh, you should bring up the . . .

You shouldn't be like that, that's terrible, I mean, really. First of all, I allow you to take pictures of myself, and I really am a property. You should at least let me see my own picture.

(S) I don't have them.

Well, get them.

(S) I can't get them.

Well, try. Don't come back if you can't get them.

(L) Do you have any candy on you?

No, I have some amphetamine if you'd like it.

(L) What time are you going?

Well, I know it it's . . .

Everything's signed now, A.W. There we are already signed. I've got to put my new dress on and I'll be all right.

Oh which, oh terrific. Do you have uh . . .

Do you like it? It's a steal Chapman, they they designed it for uh, uh, what's her name, Jane Froman, but she's, she's been crippled.

Is she still crippled?

I think. She's so sweet. Sure she is, she used to dance like . . .

You know that's great with the uh . . .

Isn't Rita wonderful? I hope she walks down here, our Mayor.

You think she will?

I hope so. I hope she's not hurt. But Rita jumps to conclusions, you, my dear, what can you do? The Mayor is sick. The Mayor needs a doctor. And the doctor's in the hospital. She, she's in love with Rotten and I, and they write notes every night.

Oh really?

"Dear Rotten" or "Dear Rita, I love you," signed "The Duchess." Oh please, The Duchess's people own the uh, or manage the *Kelloge* uh, all the *Kelloge* papers.

When'd you find that out? I knew that years ago.

Isn't that too much? Can you imagine us with *The General Mills* behind us, it would be heaven. I'd have Dorothy Kilgallen immediately flailed . . . in public. All right, girls, take her skin off.

Show uh, what's her name, the uh . . . oh he's not here.

Stephen doesn't care about my dick if you uh . . . or do you? I mean uh, I uh don't want to answer for you, Stephen, if you'd like to, if you'd like to see it and hold it, and know it as your own, you can, I'll be very gentle. And you'll learn from the oldest—I'm a nine-thousand-year-old   whoosh, it's a—ow! a cramp. You know what I need, Drella? I have a mole on my leg.

Oh really?

Uh, uh whatever this is. That, that-that's a beauty mark.

What's beauty mark?

Could someone do something in there?

Yeah, I could do something right now.

Oh, would you? You're the only one with courage, I swear to Christ. Everyone says, "Oh, now you need an engra—" Thank you. He's covered it! Very smart, my dear. I wanted a picture of Margaret Dumont. It's heaven. Look at my back from-from-from the injections. Are there any, any—

Yeah, big marks.

Oh, oh can I use that?

Where'd you get that from?

The Duchess. You want a little poke, you . . .

I, I have to get a better colored—your-ass-color skin. Y'know, these come in different colors.

Wha-what, what is my ass color?

(L) Hoory pink.

Oh.

(L) H-o-o-r-y.

Oh all these things, I oh—wow, can you make your ass hard? Oh, Ondine makes his ass hard, oh, wow.

Ondine makes his ass hard, I used to have an ass like an overnight bag.

Really?!

I used to . . .

And how, what happened to it?

Yoga.

Really?! Yoga or yogurt?

I—Yoga, for two years I learned how to be all woman.

Oh really? But you have an all-man's ass.

I know, but that's how you, that's the only way you can.

And your cock is so big. Huh, oh, uh.

Isn't it warm at all today?

No, I, I think it stands over here.

I'll bet that Rita's right though, that uh . . .

What?

That Billy's not coming.

Oh really? No, I don't think so.

I hope it's not the police.

Why?

I mean what, what would I, how, how would I explain this to the police? I'd say they're just spraying me. And you'd grab a can of spray and . . .

You're getting up out of the shower.

Did you hear when I helped Billy paint the kitchen in Norman's house and I painted myself white from head to toe?

Really?

And he wouldn't let me get back in

the room, to paint. He thought I was going to paint him next. But I looked so phenomenal.

Really?

All white. It was that water-base paint y'know, it comes right out. Oh, I'm so sick of On—

Really?

No, not really. I'd never be. How could I be, I owe it to myself and the world. What could I do, why shouldn't I deny them the right, the pleasure of seeing me in . . .

Who, who should we have play in the movie?

What movie?

Well, should we call the movie *Ondine* or

What movie? Is there gonna be a movie of Ondine? Oh no, please no.

Bob, it should be *Bob*.

No, no, no—no, that's even worse! No, don't make any movie about me please. Just let me be in movies.

Okay.

Or businessmen, because once there's, once there's a movie about about me, my my . . . I don't want a biography now.

Really?

I don't need it.

Well, every day's a new day.

(O) Every day is . . . it's time for another sch-scheneck, schnecken. Schnecken. No, I'll go and get some at the store at the uh, what you call it. Stephen, would you go to the store for-for-for us please? Schnecken.

(S) What's it called?

(O) Any kind of a roll that has an almond paste in it or a, or a, huh? There's uh, aw, Stephen, there's a, there's a Bickford's, you can get . . .

There's a bakery right down there.

Yeah, just down the street a bit. Please, hum? You'd do us an immense favor. You would.

Oh . . . well, why don't you uh, photograph Ondine while I'm calling?

No, he's not gonna get another photograph of me if—

Why?

Because I can't see them.

Just like this.

I wanna see, before you take another picture, Stephen—

Oh, let him take some pictures, please, just . . .

But he won't show them.

Yes, he will. You just haven't been here when he brought them.

Go ahead, take them. They're for a book all right.

Well uh, all right.

That's why he's definitely . . .

You have to turn on the light yourself.

I don't want them, Drella, I don't want—he's a nasty boy.

No, he isn't.

Yes, he is, he's nasty.

No, he isn't.

He's, has some . . .

We're trying to teach him not to be nasty.

Well, it's too late.

Really, can you tell, you can really tell, I'm—

Well, he won't go to the store; he's lazy and he won't suck a dick or anything like that.

What is he good for?

I don't know; he's gotta prove himself—who knows? Bring those pictures in. Please, Stephen, I have a right to see my own pictures.

(S) Okay, I'll, on Monday and I'll try to get them.

What kind of an effort did you have to make in the first place? None, but just talk totem, which you didn't do. I know the whole story because I'm, I'm never guilty of it but everybody else is.

What?

Of going out of your way.

Yeah, I know, Stephen doesn't go out of his way.

No one else does; you do, I do, Lucky L does. Unfortunately Lucky goes out of his way more than I do. But uh, you, you should go to the store, Stephen, immediately and—(phone rings). Hello, hello, who's this? Jonas calling. Neither Gerry nor Drella are here.

(D) Oh, I'm here.

(O) Oh no, Drella is here, that's right. Uh, he's holding the microphone; here he is.

(D) Hello, oh hi, Jonas.

(L) So what's this world of uh,

Nothing, no, no . . . please go to the store, Stephen, please. (Noise) They have—oh (whispering) get the day-old pictures you, uh . . . don't speak . . .

Okay, all right.

Don't speak to me, don't speak to me. Demand them, say, "I want my pictures."

(S) You want some proof sheets?

Oh, anything, anything.

(S) Oh, I'll show you the proof sheets, um.

(L) Are you coming in Monday afternoon?

(S) Gee, I don't know, but, but, but why don't . . .

(L) The G.B.S. thing now.

(S) What, what, what are you

getting?

I don't know. I might've known but I'm not sure.

Saturday and Sunday, the last week in August . . .

If, if like I'm dead, bring them please, please.

Has Gerry been down yet or . . . oh.

Isn't his voice shaking? No . . . Lucky L.

Okay, okay all right, yeah /// I'll try to be. We're showing some movies, uh . . .

What did, what did he, his voice sounds so shaky . . . who . . .

He always talks that way.

(O) Is he, is he, is he very old? Or is he just frightened to death? I never, we walked in-into the the Cinematheque and he was, he was sitting in a chair like this and he went, and the coffee container went all over him and all over the floor and Taxi and I just went, y'know, we were already stoned from, we halluc—we hallucinated road blocks and cops and everything we smoked so much pot and uh, uh, Stephen, please go to the store, darling. I don't—for some reason. Drella, could we shut it off for just a moment or two, I wanna go to the shithouse?

(D) Oh, that's all right, I, that's all right.

(O) Oh, no, don't be silly, no, I'll take it with me. Okay, I will. I'll just make or-or-ord-ordinar. That shithouse doesn't work very often, does it?

(D) It doesn't, no, no.

(O) No, oh I wish I did, I'm so upset. No, I don't have any pot, I don't have anything except a photographer.

(D) Photograph Ondine shitting on the toilet with me holding the microphone.

Laughter.

(O) No, don't.

(D) Oh, please.

(O) No, oh Della, please, I, I, my . . .

(D) Oh Ondine, I . . .

(O) It's uh, my turds is a personal . . .

(D) They're not. They can't help it.

(O) Do you know when you had that big party here?

(D) Uuh.

When was it that I threatened to throw cigarettes in your camera like that? Oh the night that you showed the films.

(D) Yeah.

(O) Now I'm gonna close the door.

(D) No, uh, no, Ondine.

(O) Oh please, Drella I want to be—

(D) Just once.

(O) behind it myself.

(D) One picture and you can close the door. Okay? So just sit on the john and I'll, oh just, just one picture.

(O) I can't take a picture like this. No, no, oh I . . .

(O) I can't sit on that john. Oh there's something in it. I think it's speaking. Can you hear it? There's a message. It's just saying shsss and . . .

Oh no, listen do, do this.

(O) No, I don't wanna sit. I'm so sick of my dick being shown and everybody talking about it.

Oh, I don't want yo to, oh I don't want you to show your dick. Just sit on the toilet, it won't be shown.

(O) Must I have the light on?

(S) Yeah, just for a minute, just for one picture.

(D) And then you'll go downstairs?

(S) Yeah.

(O) Merry Christmas everybody. Er, one, one, enough, enough, enough, Stephen, enough, Stephen.

We're not done yet.

They're no good.

Now go downstairs, like you promised.

(S) Okay.

Buy a good, buy a good cake.

Ohm, I don't know what you want. Just uhm, oh uh, like a Danish pastry.

Let's see if you have anything in here that we can drink.

There's some uh, uh pop.

Oh wow!

It's just for you.

Um, I'm, no thank you. I'm, would you answer that, Steve, please? Would you like some soda? Lucky, some soda?

(L) Yeah, that's nice.

Oh certainly.

Who is it? What?

Drella, it's . . .

What?

Ed Sommers

Who?

Ed sommers. Ed Sommers from the . . .

Ed something or other for Drella —Saunders?

(S) Sayer or something.

Oh, d oyou want to hold this for— oh.

I, I, I can hold it.

(L) Ondine, now I'll do the interview.

Let's have it again.

Lucky, what happeend with uh . . .

He had a delightful . . .

What happened to you, what happened to you?

The light bulb is going on.

(L) Going on, it's reality, at all times, why that's uh, c'mon, here we go.

What's you drinking it out of a saucer for?

(L) Well, a bissel.

A bissel, huh. Hello, I'm a bissel virgin.

(L) Hello, I'm a bissel virgin. Hah hah hah . . . a little zonga, he's putting some zonga in . . .

You can't

No, I'm extracting it and stow away from the, with that . . .

You'll have to excuse me for being so dominant; it's just that I'm aggressive.

Not just any—I ever saw (*Laughter.*)

I think that you may be the only one to rise above the, your circumstances. You may find that you're, you're having an awful lot against you, Lucky L.

Yeah, well I . . .

Pe-people who are destructive, ah . . .

(L) Yeah, raspberry flavered yogurt.

Sh.

Oh how elegant.

And me, with, didn't eat . . .

You think, you think we'll let the bourgeosie (*strangulation*)

No, the bour—

It just stays with you

I love to, I lost that . . .

They'd love to go; they don't want to be around anymore—look at the (*pause*). You're not going to believe that you shit down that you're going to hear that marble cake burst and my head's gonna choke it's so expert and so bearable she's really incredible it's so —oh yes, I'm sorry, pardon me, I didn't know, you're gotta get off the pot. You really must be-c-because y'know, you you have some talent and eh, second of all . . .

Stop being agreeable to me, please, I don't feel that well.

N-no, you, Ste-steve, I haven't know you when you, when you have felt well. You should jug off more or get youself a partner, put that dick in a hole, darling. Put it in Oilbert first.

The furniture in the raw? The furniture where?

GIRL In the raw.

(L) Furniture in the raw.

Oh, it gets polished, doesn't it? (*Laughter.*)

MARILYNE—It's in here somewhere, in this building.

Aw, I have no idea. This is the fourth floor, 4W?

Yes.

This is the Patty Duke Show?

Yeah.

Do you know any of these?

Yes.

Yes.

Oh, all right.

Do you want . . . or what?

There's furniture in the raw.

CAPPY—Yeah, there's furniture in there too, but we were looking for . . .

I don't know if they're open.

Furniture in the raw, Tempo, right?

It's empty, it's empty.

Tempo Furniture Company.

I guess they're not . . .

I have an idea. Go down to the garage and have them, have, take you up.

Oh the'yre for Gerard.

Oh. Oh you're, well, he's not here, tsk tsk.

(L) Gerard is furniture in the raw (*laughter*). He is . . .

Drella, want some raspberry yogurt?

(S) Oh, there might be your Factory receptionists. Hey uh, hey uh . . .

Oh yes, would any of you like to, later, yes, yes, yes, yes, all right subject

But you're all 17.

You have to come in.

ROSALIE—18 . . .

Oh good, 18.

(L) Working papers.

Different shifts.

(M) That's all right.
Noise.

(L) Eight hours at a time, 24 hours a day, 8 shifts, 8 hrs. Wednesday.

Fantastic.

You still have this thing they just . . .

Okay, uh, uh, fill out your applications, telephone numbers and uh, and uh . . .

I'm gonna start, okay?

We want somebody there Monday.

First things first.

First things first.

That girl's first.

Your name?

CAPPY—Cappy Tano.

(O) Cappy what?

(C) Tano.

(O) You, that sounds—oh you're Italian.

(C) Well, I'm American, but . . .

(O) You're Italian American.

T-a-n-o? Tano, that's not an
Italian name.

(C) Yes, it is.

(O) Oh, Cappy. C-a . . . that's not
Italian. KahtahREENah. Uh
please, I mean, where you live,
your telephone number . . .

(C) Ruentin Road.

(O) The Bronx?

(C) No

(O) Brooklyn. (*Laughter.*) It's
Brooklyn, Brooklyn.

Tee-hee

(C) That's cute.

Well, go ahead.

(L) Start in, here we go, 1, 2, 3 . . .

Ruentin Road, go ahead, oh yes.
You have to say "Factory."

(C) "Billy."

Oh, I'll speak to him. Oh hi, Billy,
we're just . . .

Ruentin Road?

(C) R-u-e-n-, Ruentin.

R-u-e-n . . .

(C) ti-n.
Yeah, oh it's it's just . . .

Hmmmm, I know that.
Yeah.

And telephone number?

(C) NI 5 . . .
The whole, the whole bit, yeah, it's not, it's
not that, it's Nor-Norelco.

(C) 4914.

Okay, and now do you do anything
during the day? You work where?
Uh what are your hours?

It's very lax.

Oh, on Fortieth, oh good, Forty-
fourth and what?

(C) It's, it's nineteen West Forty-
fourth.

ineteen West, right off Fifth.

(C) Hmm hmm.

Nineteen West, okay, and uh let's
see, would you be able to be
down here about eleven in the
afternoon say, and then stay till

about uh, it, it, it would vary,
three some days, four maybe, two
maybe, even 1 if there aren't . . .
this is verry important job.

(C) If I can, if I can stay in the
city—no, if I can stay in the
city . . .

Does Brooklyn call you?
Oh that'd be great.

Does Brookl—oh, I mean, if you
can't stay in the city, where are
you going?

(C) You, I mean if I can stay at
someone's house. Oh, I don't live
anywhere.

(C(No, I have friends.

Don't live any, don't ev—don't
even live with friends; they get
boring after a while.

All right, when-when-when-when
you, you'll let us know?

(C) When should I let you know?

You don't realize how important
this position is.

If you have, have to realize how
important this whole thing is, uh,
we're on. All right, don't call us
we'll (*laughter*). Tano, what
kind of Italian name is that?

(C) What kind?

Yes, Varasic, Piedmontant . . .

(C) Oh, Sicilian.

Is it really?

(C) Well, that's what my father
is . . .

And your mother is Italian?

(O) Uh, her parents, she was born
here.

Yeah. My grandparents were born
here too, but their last name is
Ovatado . . . You're next; dear.

(R) Rosalie Goldberg. Rosalie,
R-o . . .

(O) Now your last name, please.

(R) G-o-l-d-b-e-r-g.

(O) And Rosalie first, first name,

right? Oh, what's her age?
(R) Eighteen.
(O) Ddo you know her birthday?
(R) May 6.
(O) May 6. No, May is 5 .
(R) May 56. Capp!
(O) May 6? What year? Nineteen, okay now, excuse me, Rosalie, address . . .
(R) Forty-nin-e eighty-two . . .
(O) Hyphen?
(R) No. Avenue V.
(O) V?
(R) Yes.
(O) Brooklyn. That's my old stopping grounds.
(R) It's terrible.
(O) Your uh telephone number?
(R) Dewey, DE 8–8953.
(O) Uh, now, uh how bout you, do you work in the city or or . . .
(R) No, Brooklyn, occasionally.
(O) Occasionally? Uh, you're, you're, would you be over here, would you be able to be here uh uh uh almost everyday maybe except Saturday and Sunday?
(R) Well, I have to see. I've got, I gave, a certain job and I don't know definitely how long it will take.
(O) Okay, and and your birthday, please?
(R) June 22.
(O) 6/22. You're on the cusp. Forty-seven? Number three, may I have . . . number three step forward here . . . oh, you're not applying. All right, okay, now we'll let your girls know uh, let's see how—you haven't gone out yet?
(S) No.
(O) Please do.
(S) I feel better now.
(O) I don't really care, I don't really care if you choked to death.
(S) I know you wouldn't.
(O) But that's for Drella, not me. I have my raspberry yogurt. Oh just, you mean you're not going to . . .
(O) No, I'm gonna go talk to the girls. Oh I'm sorry, Lucky, I keep forgetting. Would you hold this for me? No, I'm gonna go talk to the girls—oh, I'm sorry, I keep forgetting—would you hold this, no, just this, watch it, the—in between—I can just now uh, Robert Oliva, Bob Oliva, Bob Oliva, they call me Ondine. I don't know why, well what do you mean, why are there names like that? (*Pause.*) That's good, I'll (*shakes it*) with it, that's funny.
Who is?
(O) The liquid with it disappeared; you you can't see how much is in it. What's with this furniture in the raw? Yeah, you-you want, you want to buy some right? You-you-you're furnishing an apartment and you look but they're, they're living in uh, Sherwood Forest. Why don't you just get some orange crates?
(C) What?
(M) Orange crates?
Just, just get some orange crates, they're a lot more gilt in your outfit.
(L) I have some uh, milk carton milk crates.
Do you have, they're fabulous.
(R) I love it.
You, you can make units and things, they're insane I know, I tried.
(R) I only have one.

Just one?
(R) Yah.
Go, go around—where do you uh,
  I don't know Brookl—what
  Brooklyn is like.
(R) there are a lot of them.
Bu-but the Lowes East Side has
  loads of milk con—
(R) Yeah, but . . .
The uh, steel uh . . .
(O) They have steel on the out-
  side. No, even . . . but I mean
  just the separators.
(R) Oh, I know what you're—
Oh, I know what you're—
Oh, they're marvelous too; you
  can, you can use them for any-
  thing. You can pile . . .
Oh yeah that's good and you have
  them one right next to the other,
  and you have just shelf space, it's
  fabulous, but if they catch you
  stealing then it's death.
(R) Oh just take one at a time.
And you have to sneak out on your
  toes.
(R) I did, we did it in broad day-
  light.
Just take it right out of there but

you can take three or four too;
  say you're a delivery boy or
  something, they'll never know,
  they never check. Did I lay a
  drink down somewhere? Yeah,
  over here, okay.
(C) But by the way, what does
  this entail?
What?
(C) The recep—
Just answering the phone.
(C) Answering the phone? That's
  wonderful because I do that all
  day.
(O) And enjoying the uh, the rest
  of th things that are so, the
  notorieties.
Um.
(O) The degradation, dishonor and
  renewal. And why don't you
  wanna apply for a job, dear? Oh
  I know, you disapprove of something, but I wonder what?
Oh, I just don't want to come here
  every day.
Well, then don't, I don't blame
  her and I don't think either one
  of you will want to come here
  every day either. I'm serious.

3 /   1

It probably did, so far okay. I would especially like to hear the one
at Stark's—this atmosphere is very stark. They have to be labeled right?
The yogurt's good, wow.   Oh I know.   Which one is which?
I'll mark them for you.   (D) Oh I have them marked.   (O) All
right. Does anybody want some yogurt? Uh it's very very good.
Did anybody see a glass with uh grapefruit soda in it?   What?
(O) I put a glass down with . . . in it.   There's soda there.   Well,
I'll see if there's anything on the floor. What's the matter?   I can't,
I'm mixed up.   Oh well let me help you.   No, no, oh get—   Oh

what's wrong? What's the matter? Oh you're mixed up. I don't believe that, trying a new form. Uh where's Bill going? They're leaving.

Well, you're all gonna take time for answering the phone. Aren't you . . . Yeah. If you'd like to, why not— Well is there, have you hired one of them? o, I told them we'd let them know and we could, because they're not made up, their minds aren't made up yet.

Oh, are you free for the whole summer? You have a job? (O) They're very particular at their jobs, they're all nice girls. The blonde is marvelous; she said, "I just don't want to come here everyday." Isn't that wonderful. No, no one does. I think it's marvelous. You can take the fire escape down; it's very quick and it's charming. No uh, well I mean are you gonna do it or not or, or you will? Okay, well why don't you both.

(O) Why don't one of you stick around if you get a chance, and then you could just answer the phone and see if you're, you'll, you'll like it; if you don't like it, then don't uh. You can learn to say that to certain people Drella is out of town. Yes, there's a certain, yes there is the one trick you must learn and that is signaling the person because we're always saying . . . You have to say when you answer the phone . . . "Bozo's on the phone" and then say no, no . . . Uh "Yes, it's Mr. So & So" or it's Step Subell, don't let him hear you. And then they go . . . Or they'll say "Is Drella here" and you say "Who's calling?" without saying he's here. She does that, she's not uh, oh, all right, you're hired. Do you want to start now? When do you want to start? You could start Monday. Is today Friday or Saturday? . . . need about half an hour to test your voice. I'll be down at the phone booth and start calling.

Oh don't you feel too badly now, do you Stephen? No, I know Stephen, if, if you were, if you had robbed the cookies they might have stayed. Mmm, isn't he lovely? Yeah. No more pictures with me dear. No, don't oh, you're, you're a tantalizer aren't you? My father said . . . one day. I don't believe it. I will. Awright Cappy, why don't you put your bag down. She has, she has to go. Take your snood off and relax. Well put your stuff down anyway. Relax, chin, do something and re—y'know just enjoy yourself; put on uh, no I won't go into that, put on uh. Well, what time can you come on Monday?

Adress. I said around you or so would be . . . Oh what time's that uh. There should be someone here before then, but that's all right, it's the summer. Well CBS is coming at 2:30. It would be nice if you were here. On monday? Yeah can you come here? Well, I mean I don't know. Well why don't you come around 2:30. (C) Cause I think . . . (O) There's no pay. She she know's that, she knows I'm gonna gro wthis yogurt on somebody's had, motorcyclists head. All right. (C) Huh will Gerad be here tomorrow? Yeah he'll be here

today.   He'll be here; he should be here now.   Did you do any more
articles about him or oh . . .   What paper do you wirte for?   The
French American Student. Laughter.   Oh Rita looked in here and said,
"Wagner" (*laughter*); she meant "Vagner."   Did you get a job in a,
in a art at all?   Well the thing . . .   Yeah well I told you I'm
stumped.   Are you?   I tell you I'm so tired it's enough for me to
say I'm so tired. I for one am exhausted.   Well I'm so tired I'm going
right to my hotel room and get some sleep. Ah that's what you told me
you were tired and I thought that you were tired. You said that you needed
sleep. Now I'm doinge funny face, now this is funny to . . . I wouldn't live
anywhere, hotel or, I wouldn't live anywhere.   Except the baths.
The baths. I don't live that—I merely go to the, to uh, relieve myself of
the hot tensions of the city, and uh catch up on a night's uh, you know.
My plumbing has to be done. It's an essential, darling, I mean I can't
stand a rusty pipe. I never could and I never will.   Wagner, Wagner???
Why do I get letters like this all over, Mark, LT17548, who is that?
Oh it was a message for you.   Obviously.   He called 15 times.
LT is lettuce and tomato, who is Mark?   He called 15 times   Do
you know that number?   British, he said, "Is there Ondine there?"
    Mark—he said "You sound like Ondine, Ondine," he said He's from
Brooklyn, he's not conditioned. I said "Ondine is English, he's just faking
it." (*inverted sigh.*) And and this one was was English I think I think
I'll call it now. Has anybody got a dime? I'm out kids.   I've a dime.
I'm really busted. Do you, do you know that I'm out; I'm just broke.
You're my ward for today.   Why am I broke?   STEVE—Do you
still want me go down, go down and get . . .   Oh uh, go get something;
get the girls something.   Yes, get the girls something, something that
they would like.   Where is the uh . . .   I wonder who I know this
Mark.   Aw, or who is he.   Well you don't know.   Où est Mark?
    Hey, well what was he . . .   I was dazzeld, I was English and
faking it, that beaut—   (S) It's just a little thing.   No, no please get
something . . . Ondine . . . to do it.   Well I have the yogurt; that's fine.
    Not donuts . . . that's . . .   Oh I don't want any donuts.   No
uh, rolls y'know, like Danish rolls.   I, I'm fine with the yogurt, baby.
I really am fine.   Oh, are you leaving?   Don't go down at all.
(S) I'm glad you said that.   You lost, you just lost it. He's not answering.   You know I didn't, I don't know what I did with the number. I
just had it.   There it is. On the cardboard   Oh thank you.
What? Lettuce and tomato.   (S) LT 1   Oh, thank you, would you
dial it please? LT, LT 1,   (S) 7, 5 . . .   7, 5, I don't know who this
is even. Burp. 8, 0, pardon, America. Hello, Molluck. This is de fat woman.
    Is he on yet?   What? No, there's, I don't hear a thing. Hello

darling, this is for a moist? Oh. What's that third word?   For a moment.   Oh, I thought it said for a moist.   Yeah, look at this. And it does not answer.   Oh, you lost your dime.

(O) Shit, pardon me girls. You girls don't mind when people say things like that. D-do you? Your y-y-you have nothing to do with the Victorian Era, right? Shit's a perfectly acceptable function, I realize. Isn't it?

(S) My father walks by . . .

(O) Shit on Shineola?
Laughter.

(S) My father goes by Keane's Gallery on Madison Avenue . . . Oh, Mark, Mark, where are you?

(S) . . . he said, "Oh shit."

(O) Everybody says, "Oh shit." I used to go out with a girl who used to say, "Oh shit." You used to go with the same girl.

(S) Who.

(O) Emily Arnold. Thomas Mitchell of her set. She's (*laughter*) she looks like Thomas Mitchell. She was once the most beautiful girl, just gorgeous, and now she looks like Thomas Mitchell, the father in "Gone With the Wind." She looks just like him. *pause.* Oh, Drella, Drella. Isabel. It reminds me which one.

(D) Which one?

(O) Please, basta, with the tape Drella, for a little while. Shut it off, let's relax 'cause we'll go crazy. We owe ourselves a well earned rest for a minute. I'm done. Oh objection from. Oh Drella, please we need a rest. Bidawee Home is perfect for us. Stephen get out. Stephen come on; do something constructive like take off your jacket and put the camera down and get to work.

(D) Photograph Ondine.

(S) Let me photograph you.

(O) Oh, do you want to photograph me?

S—The pictures become mine.

(O) Oh no they don't. Oh no they don't. I treat your pictures the same way you treated mine, with inconsideration and bad taste.

Where is Gerard?

Where is Gerar . . .

S—Oh, you can ask you know. That I've brought them up here up many times. You can ask Andy. You just weren't there when I . . .

(O) Well, why don't you leave them there with someone, certainly you trust people here.

S—Not really.

(O) Well then why (*inverted sigh*). What a terrible thing to say with a slap in the face.

S—My agent . . .

(O) Oh, what a nerve. Stop it, you've said enough. No more. You're getting yourself in deeper and deeper earth quicksand.

S—I told you I'd bring the proofs. You said . . .

(O) — I don't believe you, you know. (*Phone rings.*) Hello, factory. This is here Robert Olivo. Hello darling. Who is this? Lucky who? L? Oh you, you're not Mark are you? Oh well, someone named Mark kept calling. I thought it might be you. No, would you tell me uh what

when the show is for? What.
Money? Oh you have money.
But tell me about the shoe cause
I, I wanna tell Drella who's
right here.

(D) What show?

(O) He's gonna tell me now.
What money? o, he can't because I've got the other kind. I
have the other kind. Should I
put it on? Wait. (Pause.) When
have, when when have you made
the invitation for?

(D) Oh, this is the fashion show.

(O) The 24th. Tuesday, the 24th
for how many? Yeah. Drella and
myself. Okay. Good. That's all.
Yeah? He wants to come see
both of us at once he says.

Who's that?

Lucky L.

Who's Lucky L?

Oh, he's an old friend of mine and
McDuff's and he's a very . . .
He's uh rather handsome young
salesman.

Oh. What is he going to sell.

What do you want to see us about?

Oh well well Gerard's down there.
Come on out.

Please go on—please go out and . . .

Tell him to come up.

Yeah, tell him to hurry up.

Come on over, oh Ronal Fels-
No, right, yeah yeah of course.
O.K. fine.

(O) You were here once, you were
here once in your car 231 East
47th between 2nd and 3rd. 4W
. . . East 47th. Apartment—none.
Floor 4W, okay? Bye Bye.
Doesn't even know that you're
here.

(D) I know and . . .

(O) Now he says he's got money
and he also has tickets for for a

fashion show at at One, One
fifth avenue. Some kind of a
weird fashion show. For uh uh
you and I.

(D) Oh when?

(O) I don't know. He works in the
garment ind-industry and this is
a big surprise for him.

Did you meet Diana?

I know Diana. Sure.

Oh, oh, all right. Well uh, uh, I
can't, because uh uh . . .

No this is my day, what do you
mea,n this is well this is . . .

12 hours . . . 12 hours.

And I refuse to let the tape go . . .
ahdjf . . . you told me. C'mon
Drella let's go somewhere.

DIANA—Drella this is Barbara.

(D) Hi.

(Di) And cousin Gilly.

(D) Oh hi.

Cousin Gilly?

(Di) This is Ondine.

S—Hello cousin Gilly.

And this is my . . .whose motorcycle is that? I'm sorry Drella
I can't move too quickly.

GIRL—I brought that for Gerard
to play with.

Oh.

Well, here we are.

GIRL—Do you have any money?

Huh? You'll all have to go now.
Come on, quickly, get out
quickly, all of you.

Wait for Gerard for . . . here he
comes.

Thank you. Wait, what is it?

It's a screen.

Uh, ooh. You'll all have to go,
come on.

GIRL—We're going in a few seconds.

These huh? Come on; we need
peace and rest here. This is uh,

this is, we we're working, good-bye.

Where are you going?

To Ithaca.

Oh.

Adio children. Stephen can you put this outside?

GERARD—If the screens get any Bgiger, if they get like that, I can't take them.

Oh, I didn't know they were going to get that big. I thought, we could have called uh, I didn't know we were take a risk.

G—You'll have to check on the silk screen.

Oh really? Oh, uh. Oh I oh if you don't talk it's all right; don't talk, just hold it around. Yeah.

Oh.

Hold it around.

I hope you didn't mind me getting rid of those people because . . .

No, no no.

I can't stand all that, I mean I don't want . . . Do you want all those virgins?

No.

Do you? (*Laughter.*) I didn't think so.

Do you think it's here yet?

G—Uh, no I had to bring . . .

Ronal Rels coming too Lucky.

L—What?

Ronal Fels.

L—What? Here today?

With Lucky L. They both should be up in a couple of minutes.

 Voices in background.

This is exactly what THE DUCH-ESS looks like. I swear to you, Lucky, she looks like that and she's now in the hospital and is going to . . . He's on 8th Street.

Diane, don-don't bring tho-those girls up.

DIANA—I'm sorry. It's just . . .

I know, y'know it's, but it's like being in a cage. It's like being in a cake. Yo, you . . .

Di—She's just . . . she's just crazy over . . .

Well, who cares?

Di—All right, I . . .

You're fine you know.

Di—I'm not allowed here.

Yes, yes you are

Di—No, I'm not.

Just don't bring those tacky crea-tures up.

Di—I'm not allowed here even now.

Oh well then goo-goodbye.

Di—Goodbye.

If you want to be sick about it.

Di—No, I'm . . .

(O) Get out of here, we're busy, busy, just, but just don't bring those creatures around because they make us feel like, like, like zoo animals. Which way is this suppos-supposed to be turning? There, that's the right way.

 Music—opera starts playing.

(O) Aah! Diana says she's not al-lowed up here and I said and you would be if you wouldn't bring all those fucky girls with you I said because we uh, we don't, we don't like feeling like freaks. I mean it makes us fell like zoo, uh, cage, uh, animals in a cage. Y'know, she said "I'm going out immediately, goodbye." I said "Goodbye." Who cares about Ithaca, New York? I don't. Hello darling, how are you? Are you Irish? Yes you are oh, I love the Irish.

xxxxxxxxxxxxx

I had a fight.

With who?

A guy.

(O) Hm, always disappointing; you might lose. Ger, when did you break up last night?

(G) I woke up this morning.

(O) Yeah, when?

(G) One o'clock.

(O) Oh wha, what was Stu?

(G) STU said that he uh had you turned on so much, the talking. Is that true?

(O) I tried to kill myself.

(G) STU said he saw a vision.

(O) Yeah.

What happened last night?

We went berserk.

Really ? xxxxxxxxxxxx

But no sex or anything.

He's sleeping now.

He should sleep, he needs rest. What are these?

It's from Blow Joe's.

Hello Paul.

PAUL—Hello. How are you?

Fine, how are you? Are you excited about the new camera?

P—Yeah, I wanna see it.

You got, you gotta, you got, sit down here on the xx couch and tell me about it please.

(P) The tape recorder, right? You set a aim at, this microphone at people. You aim the, the lens at the people.

Oh.

P—And the microphone.

Oh.

P—And the picture goes onto the tape and then you push the tape. . . . .

Oh, do you hear this Lucky? Do you hear how this thing works?

And you push the tape just like you play back your tape recorder and the tape plays back through a television set.

Oh man, and you get a picture too.

(P) Yes, immediately.

Oh wow.

(P) So the sound . . .

This, it's in films?

(P) Right. The sound . . . adequate or the lighting is not good . . .

You could fix it immediately.

(P) You stop it, you look at it and you say "Okay, let's do it again." or "Let's continue with this light."

Is this a new product?

(P) Yeah. You remember Hamlet in Richard Burton electronovision.

No, I never. I don't know anything about it.

(P) They had Richard Burton in "Hamlet" in the movie theaters.

Oh, og yeah, yeah.

(P) Electronovision, this is electronovision. You see they make it very cheaply but then they transfer the tape to movie film.

You got . . .

(P) To movie theaters.

Can they do it without the person knowing it?

(P) Yeah.

And being filmed.

(P) Well, they hide the camera, yeah. They put the camera back there and brought people up here.

What about behind the mirror?

(P) Yeah, you could. Well the sound, you have to have the microphone somewhere where you can pick up the sound. What about the sound here? . . . have difficulties, you find out what . . . really correct a lot of problems but with a machine like this you might have a tendency to become kind of a perfectionist.

How true, auhoueih (*Ondine sound.*) . . . .

(P) What . . .

(?) A perfectionist about the whole thing.

(P) You're gonna sing?

(O) Yeah, but I'm not, I'm gonna go walking around and see my-sefl. I wanna get loose.

(P) All right.

(O) If I don't get loose I can't sing a damn thing.

(P) Can I, how do you play this back?

(O) I don't know anything . . . I don't understand.

(?) You clip it on and just walk around if you don't feel like say-ing it, don't say it.

(O) Do you know how far we're getting? I, I really (*starts singing*) oh, the one, the only the true, the ever popular Maria Callas. Not quite altona the last, the last aria in (Che . . . ?) is Cinderella. This is how the opera ends with this aria (*singing again*).

(P) Is that a happy song?

(O) She says, I no, I no longer y'know have to sit by the fire; I no longer have to go she says, brothers it's, it's a Rossini. It's so gorgeous but she's the only one who ever does Italian like this. They all go la la la la la and they make the most boring kind of music. She's so, this record really, I just when I heard it I shit right down my leg. . . . She's better than . . . that's what's so sick about it. She's better than wih nothing, oh . . . she's sick. No put that veil over that singer. . . . She's out of her thing. You know you did just what.

(P) How old is she now?

(O) Forty-two. You did just what an English critic wrote. He said, "After I heard her to the Falk to . . . I just jumped up for joy." You just did it. (*Sings along.*) Listen to what they do at the end of this arrangement you'll . . .

(P) She sounds like Mother Bell.

(O) She's, have God bless her for singing that way. Lisa is the big-gest big who ever lived. She wanted her mother to be an, she wanted her daughter to be another Diana Durbich. (*Opera finale.*) You know that, you know that singing, I mean that time . . . (*finale*) divine, that that that's considered the great-est thing am, amphetamine hy-drochloride.. Considered the greatest thing in the world with the world's most powerful organ, be it Wurlitzer or whatever it is.

(P) What do you do with that?

(O) You put it up your nose, you can shoot it, you can swallow it, but they, Bergin . . . sing nor-mal? She said, "No, I'd wait for 5 years before I sing normal."

Bergin Yulfors said that?

(O) She's saving her voice . . .

You know how old Be . . . is? How old?

About 36

Isn't it awful?

Certainly, she . . .

Siegfried Nielson, You wanna know how old she is?

She's in her 40's?

She's 53 now.

Bull shit.

She is, I saw it in the *Times* last week, she's 52.

(O) Oh, that, they misprinted it. No she couldn't possibly be be-

cause she, no she couldn't be 52,
I know why she couldn't be.

(P) I don't think she could be
either, but I did see it.

(O) It must've been am, a missss-
print because xxxxxxxxxxx she's
just too uh, but no, anyway, she
won't sing normal because you
feel there's too much wear and
tear on the voice.

(P) I think that stolen opera is
uh . . .

(O) It's not for . . .

(P) Chewing gum.

(O) But she's not, she's not even
a turned out, they only turn
down Caillas.

(P) She sings so . . .

(O) She sings it as it was written,
which Nielson doesn't—Nielson,
Nielson has the trouble to save
her voice and . . . the energy . . .
y'know and it's just when you
get "throngera (singing along in
Italian—check the record or
Ondine) aschulta" where there's
no   pause—"familia,   sculta"
(singing again) she can't take,
you can't take a rest there where
there's no rest, what is she singing? Who wrote it?

(P) She goes to . . . at . . .

(O) Who cares? I, you, can make
a Wurlitzer organ go that right.
You won't, I want feeling. I
want I want a pair of tits and a
cunt and an ass hole and . . .
she won't stop his view.

(P) Oh yeah?

(O) And Eugando Fernandi has
the prints, it's like his own recording he's had, he's he's so
beautiful it's like a freak. It's like
it's something like a catch of
Gizelle or something it's so
beautiful . . .(opera) . . . Callas

is the only one . . . Callas is the
only one who really, imagine(?)
singing it like this.

(P) She, she's (?) she she's . . .

(O) A dog, a dog—an Australian
dog. o, she's even worse, she's an
Australian dog that she, who—

(L) She has elephant tights.

(O) She has the trouble to to have
a fairy for a husband, who thinks
he's velly (laughter).

Ooh, I don't want this, what am I
going to eat it for? I'm gonna
put it in my ear . . .

(L) I think Drella's have a microphone fit.

(O) I think he's having a good
time. Certainly, I am, Drella.
Did you warm these buns up, er
Steve?   They're   very   good.
Where'd you warm them, they're
heaven. Oh it's it's like an arti-
choke heart. Here darling, the
microphone   wants   something.
Drella the moment I, I have to
have rest, I feel like . . .

(D) But Ondine,

(O) But I . . .

(D) You, you just pretend I'm not
here.

(O) But how can I do that?

(D) Just, just . . .

(O) Do you have any sort . . .
oh, all right, I won't talk. Mum
is the word. Stephen say something about your dick. We wanna
know the size of it.

You look so clean, wow,

What can I tell you about (?) except that she's topless.

Wow. and a new tie and a shirt.

You looked good the last time I
saw you too.

There's something else there.

Sutherland in his topless and no
imagination and she's ugly, ugly,

she's a cow, a cow. An enormous cow who is green velvet green satin with purple satin shoes and red hair. She's so phony.

(P) But they don't sing the same parts, do they, except now they do.

(O) They couldn't sing the same parts, Callas has no rivals. God, are you serious? Can you imagine (?) singing Medea? Now just be a little serious. Can you imagine (?) singing Luchea? No.

(P) (?) sings those Handel rhythms.

(O) Badly. She even sings her own language badly. It's whoop whoop whoop. She can't even sing her own language well, the fooNl.

(P) The terlit door?

The uh, ice-box uh . . .

(O) Well is the shithouse door open cause the horses escape are through, the horse is waiting for me—cause it's what's Grahilda's horse's name, Verona? Look, I don't want to say this because I've been saying it for the past 12 years. Duh, I saw her, she's ju, I saw her last year, this year's Tosca, and I have never seen anything like it. The way she raised Puchini's music in my mind she made it something ethereal, and it was only her. Where . . .

(P) I . . . at the Metropolitan?

She was shocking.

Who?

You know she didn't sing like Maria Urista with one tit out and all and like this one used to sing it on the back balanced or melon objects. She used to bat here eyelashes.

Do you know a lot about music?

(P) What?

Do you know a lot about music? You seem so delightful.

(P) Music, yeah.

You seem to have a Nordic taste about things though. You must understan the Mediterranean folk heh heh.

Where has Paul Paul been all my life?

I don't know. Where have you been all my life? 49. I really would be uh the divine wife. I would churn butter and everything, and oh I'd be so devoted. You can have me for a drink. You can have me—what's that? What do you want me to do? Do a Madame Butterfly or something. laughter

You'd be having Paul cutting up your uh . . .

(O) My dear, I am so faithful when I wanna be—certainly! I went out with a friend of his who was —who went to school with him, yeah, I know, very faithful, I drove him crazy but I was faithful—in fact he went into a madhouse.

(P) He became a talking abstract expressionist.

Can you imagine someone becoming a talking abstract expressionist just just used to go like that.

(P) Stop talking about my . . .

Paul is very cute.

Paul is beautiful but I, you know I don't even dare to hope about things like that. Ha ha ha, oh what can I do with . . .

This is mine, Lucky L.

Is there any hope for me, Ondine?

Not mine—is there still hope for you what? A woman in her prime like you. And Mildred's just starting all over the country—a chain of restaurants, Mildred! laughter

What does that have to do with me?

Mildred Pierce! Aren't you Rita's mother? I thought you were Rita's . . . That's Rita Pierece, I swear to God Rita!

—Or Vita herring.

Vita herring? (*Laughter.*) It's Rita Pierce though isn't it? Stephen, why don't you sit down, darling? Rita Pierce—in black.

L—. . . Vita herring . . . think so . . . every other . . .

It was her only good movie. Oh, goodnight.

(S) Oh, oh are you going to the films?

Maybe 8:00, I'm not sure.

(O) Hideous women. Why do they look like that? You like girls don, don't you? . . . Boring. Oh thanks. Blah, blah, blah, I asked him if he was completely hetero-heterosexual.

Oh, what did he say?

He said he doesn't speak about those things. Isn't he smart? Now that's a gentleman.

Mm.

You would be a credit to my name.

Pos-possibly I have the same problem as Ondine.

Wha-what's that? Shineass?

No, (you don't have any come on.

What? And what's this hangup?

Do you have any sexual problems?

Of course not.

Tight ass.

Tight ass?

Darling, there's always the Mar fac job

What?

Do you know the only way to loosen up that ass hole is to put it over someone's face and it gits you just, it loosens right up you say "Okay dear, here it comes." Ploymouth Rock.

No I didn't mean it that way.

Oh you mean you you have tight ass problem with other, with other people.

What?

You have tight ass problem with other people. Well how did you mean it? Please uh Drella,

I'm bewildered uh

(L) You you got, I heard about the, the wild experience you had in the baths.

When? about the person who told me about . . .

(L) No the oral thing with the person, uh, the testicles . . .

What?

(L) In the mouth, I've, whole testicles and penis I can't believe it.

Isn't it astounding? But when she did it I was so amazed.

It's turning red?

Listen, you have genitals, right? We all do and uh the care and tending of them, the care and tending of them is very important.

What?

Of genitals, y'know.

Balls are really . . .

I had them out when I was young.

Oh, did you have them removed? I was going to have mine, mine removed but the doctor said that I, that I really, really didn't have an acute . . .

Are you asexual?

Huh? What does that mean? No sex at all?

Yeah.

No, I like men.
(P) Listen, you know what I thought?
(L) Are you asexual?
Uh, no.
No, no he's not. He's A.W., not asexual. A.W. is . . .
What?
(P) You know what I saw in the paper yesterday? The president of Macy's. They said the president of Macy's, I guess. His name was Richard Yunich.

Hu hah!
(P) N-y-u-n-i-c-h, Y-u-n-i-c-h, Yu-nich.
How would you like? Oh no I can't do that with you, I'm sorry.
You have to be yunich.
Yeah, I know, it's good to be yu-nich but you have to be in that nice sand.
Yeah.
They put you in sand, the right kind of sand it's okay.
(L) What do you mean?

3 / 2

Lucretia Borgia. Right, do you understand, well Samurami, it's an aria about a queen who makes love to her son. It's incestral, the whole thing is. I don't know who wrote the original. I think uh Cole Porter. Then Luretia Borgia's singing to her son too. She sees him sleeping under a tree and she says, "Oh what a lovely penis." What's that? Oh ROT-TEN's. It's rats rent.   Oh.   (O) Gee, I wonder if one of us should pay it. (*Laughter.*) Right. Right? Oh it's this music is gorgeous.   Well, I'm straightening up, huh?   Oh well—A.W. I would've I would have cut your hair. Oh I wish someone . . . PAUL, I've got a student special head. I can't answer the phone anymore. You're too . . . gentle-man's . . .   No, I, I'm only kidding around . . .   LUCKY—I got like . . .   (O) I want you to hear this, this is Rossini, I think this is the best thing Rossini wrote, it's just as a . . .   Who is that, Gerry?
(O) Aria, it just has uh, it's so beautiful, what can I say? The other one on the other side is my favorite.   PAUL—You have a lot of favorites.
    (O) Oh, you can't have one favorite.   (P) No.   (O) No. I don't really care for what's his name? Gomez's "Las Cavo." I don't really care for that opera, but uh . . .   Uh, he's down at an appointment.
    I think it was called . . .   L—Y'know the Hunchback of Notre Dame?   Yeah, oh, the . . . Le Gent . . . de Notre Dame.   (L) Oh which one, who wrote it uh . . .   Uh, tell her to call back in a little while because uh . . .   Montrimessi?   They're on the uh, they're on the television program.   What the hell . . . the, the, the Hunchback

of Not—   (L) I think it's "Rigoletto."   No, but uh, yeah, no it's the, the Juggler of Notre Dame.   (L) Thomas.   No Ambroise . . . the one who wrote "Hamlet"?   Yeah.   (O) Yeah, he might have wrote written in . . . It appeared in 19—in the 1920's in Chicago. Mary Brighton sang it. Yeah that, that's le, le gens . . . no, I, I don't know who sang it. Who . . .   (L) Part of it.   (O) I must put this a little louder; it does us all an injustice. Just a little louder, just a little cause we can be heard. (*Opera becomes very loud.*) I'll just lay on the floor and you could put it on.   (P) Do you know the movie "Ikearu Persowa"?   Japanese movie?   No.   (P) Do you know what, in that movie he used for his music he used the uh Johnny Sh . . . music   Johnny . . . (?) that's beautiful!   (P) And he, they sang the song and they made a Japanese version of it. They used it as an . . .

(O) Well Puccini you know is a very underrated composer He didn't write just pretty tunes. He wrote really great operas.   (P) Pretty tunes are the hardest things to wrie.   (O) No, no, no, no, no but I, not, not necessarily; I mean . . .   (P) Some people can't do it.

(O) Some people are prolific though, look at Mozart. Look at Mozart, he could write a pretty tune at the snatch of a hat or Tchaikovsky, so that doesn't prove anything. Tchaikovsky wrote some of the most beautiful melodies I've ever heard.

(P) But, but wait uh, Beethoven is very poor on tunes, a lot of composers are poor on tunes.

But Beethoven was, wasn't poor on imagination.

(P) No.

(O) No but but the thing is like, like Puccini didn't make . . .

(P) You don't like Beethoven's opera, do you?

(O) I love it. McDaniel is great; it's so impossible it's unbelievable, it's the, it's the most impossible opera ever written.

I think "Norma"   is my favorite opera.

(O) Yeah, "orma" is the miracle, yeah it's anybody can live through it oh it's, if you're really there forget it. No, but anybody uh, I don't know about my . . . after seeing her do "Tosca," It's, I can't get over it. I understand why the Tosca jumped Russians, driven to it, and I can't believe the values that the woman has in question that she can raise that crummy Met thing up to wha, what it was. I don't think there's, there's no experience like her.

(P) Did the critics uh think . . .

(O) A little more. Al-Alan Rich was the o-only one who really really knew what he was writing about; the rest, Harold Square, says he's a cross between Sarah Bernhardt and Brabra Striesand. Wouldn't you like to cut his balls off. That stupid cocksucker, he should be murdered. At his desk he should be murdered. He's also responsible for . . . Bel Canta was brought to America by Franco Corelli, Leontyne Price, and Joan Sutherland. Isn't that a statement? This Mr. Square is a very, and he's a very oh and then the new the new Carmen. Irving Callen said he never heard anything as gorgeous as Leontine Price. She doesn't even know how to sing one rhythym right, i'ts impossible. She's the best Carmen that there . . . . oh, everone's eating . . .

(P) Carmen, Carmen.

(O) As Carmen, oh wasn't that an atrocity, Carmen ,except for one line when she picks her leg up and says "What's mine is youds, John," and then goes right on down the line. That's the only good line in the entire movie. But there, you walk just like my ma and talk just like my, in fact I think you are my mother (*laughter*). And Joe, you are ju-just my Joe and dat's love, dat's love and der's a cafe on da cor-ner. Oscar Hammerstein the sec-ond. Why do they do that to Bizet? I mean, honest to God, he didn't deserve that. Did you ever see "My Darling Aïda"? (*Laughter.*)

(P) No.

(O) Dorothy Sarnoff and Elaine Malbert and my darlin' Aïda take place in the Civil War. Bang. You, I don't know who did it but I just, I just shook. Then there was a popular song made out of the last duet in Aïda, "The mak is off so sonw I see you're not the girl."

(P) There's a popular song made out of Musetta's Waltz.

(O) Oh yeah with Della Reese (*laughter*). Miss Chin actress. (*Phone rings.*) Who's calling? Lucky, it's for Gerry. He's right

over there; he, he's he'll, he's coming now. Here he comes. I can't stand it, I'm fainting.

(L) Thank you Ondine.

(O) You're welcome darling. Oh, oh, oh please, eats your heart right out. The spoon, something, the silver spoon bent right in my mouth. (*Music.*) What were we talking about? Oh. We were talk-ing about something . . .

(P) Do you know anything about modern operas?

Modern operas?

(P) There's a lot of it . . . I'm serious. They're not know here though.

(O) He wrote some good (*cough*) pardon me, some very, very charming very good music. Never played well. I like Tchaikovsky's operas especially.

(P) Yeah, I like him.

(O) I don't know, what were some of the names of Rachmainov's operas. Fabulous, I, I know that one of Yailing's is so great.

(P) He had a silver Russian Phil-harmonic . . . fantastic and then I, I heard the recording of it. (*Music overpowering.*)

You wouldn't mind if I uh, no whatever happened to . . .

Don't beat him up here.

No but uh . . .

(O) Don't make my dress wet. (*Music.*) Well, you're not go-ing to write about it. You're not gonna write about it, I know you are.

Paul says something.

Well what . . .

(O) No, no, I like . . . it's so wicked day y'know it's so reg . . .

Yeah it's got an aria. Bela Lugosi.

(P) No that one, I mean the

one . . .

Oh.

(P) the one that's called "there is the garden."

(O) o, I, I don't even really know it . . . very very well.

(P) Then then there's . . .

(O) Leonard Bernstein I stay away from as much as I can. I mean I like Candice greatly and I thought that I thought that s . . . was very nice but I don't really think he's anything special as a composer.

(P) Do you think that he's stealing . . . opera standard in the Ondine sings along with record. aria?

(P) That's a Mozart melod—eh, Mendelsson.

(O) Straight from heaven. Please, he's insane; he does everything, he steals everything. But I uh, look he's too busy right, he's designing journal and and playing in it, and then uh, expect to write opera too.

(P) He's been writing opera.

(O) Married to a telephant, television actress who up ta, she's all of 12 parents (laughter). Mrs. Montelegro (laughter), with a name like that should she be a cemetery? Honestly, I can't believ that Felicia Montelegro Miss Kraf television cameras. This is Lucretia Borgia. Now Lucretia Borgia is a fabulous opera. They cuoldn't even call it by its name in Italy; they used to have to call it "La ra, La vinagartta."

(P) Oh.

(O) Which means something like "The Revenge" or something like that. I hate when I have Grapes of Wrath feet. With sandals you have to wear, have nice clean feet or else you feel disgusting.

(P) Tan too.

Taking it all day too.

(P) Tan, sun tan.

(O) Y'know I haven't even seen the ocean yet, Lucky?

(P) Is it . . . ?

(O) No, I love the ocean. Do you hear how her, her, the voice is different in this . . . from the uh last song? She just, every color is different. I can't—what do you think I have this in my hand for? You can, you can . . .

(P) I like to hear you tallk.

(O) And you can keep the microphone here and get other sounds.

(P) Bob, Bob.

(O) If you are to what? . . . this, no, no I want Paul to shut me up.

(P) . . . go on. I might as well talk.

(O) Well, I'll talk but I, I . . . afterwards . . .

(P) I want Drella to unpack his machine.

(O) He won't.

(P) Oh.

(O) The other men are going to do it. The r . . . . . that came and I don't blame him.

(P) Yeah.

Y'know because they might just . . .

(P) No, I don't . . .

(O) What kind of name is Paul from? Is it Irish? Oh I couldn't tell.

(P) A lot of people can't but it's a very ordinary Irish name.

He's very sensitive.

Paul? He's very, very good too.

I don't usually follow . . .

What?

The rest.

It hurts too.

The rest. It's all on this side.

No, no, I mean I do well, but that's right we, we all do but many people think we don't. Most people confuse me with being a vulgar pig.

(L) Cause that's because they're tripping over their own noses. Which I amn't.

(L) Well that's . . . (*Music gets louder.*)

Lucky, there are a few vulgar pigs left in the world.

(L) Vulgar. That word vulgar's all . . . anyway. It is.

Vulgar can only exist when the other exists with it. Right?

(L) Right but . . .

(O) But Paul has one thing in particular that I like. And we'll leave it at that (*laughter*).

(L) He's, he's very select too.

(O) He's yeah, he's a very, he's a gentleman too. Let's not go on about it. I'm (*pause, talking not understandable*) married. Isn't it . . . stop him, I wish that she had been drinking from cause she's only been there twice uh, by Dame Clara—but that really is a name and uh, could you imagine her husband's name is something like Harry Horn or something like. So Harry Horn and and Ernestine . . . going to uh . . . I think she's . . . designed pianos or they design pianos I can't . . . this music is so gorgeous. Goodness, everything is so beautiful.

(P) Do you know the movie about Don . . .

(O) Oh, isn't that horrible? The . . .

(P) No . . . I'm thinking about, I'm thinking about the Italian movie with . . . the other one.

(O) I don't know. I saw the Rossini, I saw the, it's the funniest thing I have ever seen, the two of them. Oh that's even funnier, I saw that too, I roared. The Italians can mN-make movies like that; they, they just fu-fuck right up. Where can I hook this onto my hair. I think if I wear it like this I should get a . . .

(P) . . . is really big enough on that.

Sure it is, every oh, I've heard it.

(P) Oh.

(O) How could I do it. I don't mean to speak to Borgia through the Lucretia Borgia thing uh, this, do you know that there was Lucretia Borgia she had just given of the American opera society and they had a new soprano they called Monsorette Caballé, Monsorette Cabari, and all these fags are running around saying "The new . . . she's a combination of De Los Angeles and Crespin. And all she ever says is "Ohh," she's . . . (*very shrill music*). Hi darling, can I take a rest? He's a slave driver y'know—Simon La Warhol.

Eight more hours.

(O) Eight more hours?!! Ballet Russe are you ready? I'm gonna do my imitation of Nina Novack in "Scheherezade." Did you ever see the Ballet Russe of Monte Carlo? Her Scheherazade was so wretched. Nina Novack is the worst dancer . . . that ever.

(L) Do you wanna do our tape now, I mean do the tape. Do you really wanna do it? Where? Where?

(L) Roll out the tape and we'll just wait.

Where will we go?

(L) Right here.

What're you doing?

What do you want to do?

(L) We wanna do a whole tape.

(O) Lucky, you're suggesting something, yes it is if, if, if we, we, but we all have to be pushed, uh well, darling, all you have to do is put me on those bars and I'm ready—an orgy. How can we have an orgy?

No just stand.

I will. That's not so.

(L) Six hours.

(O) It's not fair to the rest of the people, six hours of madness and then a lifetime of regret. o I don't want Paul to rise, please I want, I want Paul to shut me up if he can

(P) What does that mean?

What does that mean? Caught.

. . . Ondine.

(O) Oh Drella, don't tell that story cause I'm . . . You have, you've got a walking heart on today huh. You do. That's a little amphetamine and bang. I love. They used to tell me, they used to tell me amphetamine didn't do anything for you, they thought oh it's a wonderful drug, you don't, you don't get sexy. That's until you don't know about it and then you walk, and then it becomes a, you come and put the heart on. Paul Paul, are you from Brooklyn?

(P) Where, Yonkers.

(L) Yonkers?

Yonkers?

Yonkers. (*Loud music.*) Yeah. Ruth uh, Ruth Noonan not Ruth. Ruth, Ruth Drake, Ruth, Ruth Drake That's it. She played in the "Watchmaker." She was the . . .

(L) No that's Ruth Borden.

That's the one I mean. She's that that that's that took place in that that that took place in Yonkers.

(L) Yeah.

I even liked Shirley Booth when I was . . .

. . . Lucky and I pick out a story.

Am I . . . one of Paul's stars?

(L) I think you should use your new video tape for a big long interview with Ondine.

Well, I'd love an interview with Odine.

(P) It's very easy just . . . close up maybe not even . . .

Oh, the men are coming at 9:00 in the morning. . . .

Ondine sings.

(O) You can feed me anything Paul, only don't get nasty. (*Laughter.*)

(P) Oh but it's . . .

We have to . . .

(P) When, who's gonna come too Monday?

Oh, no, CBS.

(P) Oh CBS.

(O) The Patty Duke Show and I don't want to be a Patty Duke substitute.

We-we're going to be uh, Ondine's just become business manager. He's gonna . . .

Oh really, I could run this, I could I'll make this thing.

What do you want to be in? The video tape?

(P) Yeah, I'll be interviewing.

Yeah, we'll call you Linkletter or something or other.

Interview you.

You're, you're Linkletter Paul.

If you want to be part of the studio you can be something.

Just be around Paul. That's all, just hang around the back—just, just, just, just, just.

Just tell Taxi that exerything is all right.

Just put a tea bag in my coffee every once in a while.

Yeah that's what.

Yeah but for three weeks.

Yeah, everything's right.

Ah, in God's lil heaven.

(P) How good how how long . . .

Yeah, that's right.

I'm putting a fog in the mike.

I never thought you smoked.

Sure I smoke everything.

Oh.

From pipes t-to to cigarettes to uh, butts. . .

What are the best?

Best? Smoke? White Owls (*laugh*) What else could I say? o, the best smoke in the world is uh, I don't know, I haven't thought about it much. I guess snuff is pretty good. Aarrrh.

(P) Huh, huh. What are some other titles available, set up?

The Children's Hour.

Well you're so new so uh . . .

What do you mean? Did you arrive with them? Did they come with you?

Yeah.

Are you serious? Oh, that's all right. That's all right. This is Lucky L. This is Drella Drella. Ronal? That's Ronal Blinny Felso and he's he's he's looking at those tubes. (*Opera.*) This is, did you ever meet Dr-Drella? He was up here once, I think you had just,

you went to the World's Fair the day he came it was. This is Paul Paul. Lucky, you know Gerard

(P) What's he reading in the Woman's Wear?

. . . reads Woman's Wear?

No I don't read Woman's Wear but uh . . .

(P) You want to know what's going on . . . (*music*)

Ondine, do you want to go to the movies tonight or . . .

Factory's closed, that's all right.

Well uh, uh you uh (*kid's voice in background*) (*opera*). I'm gonna have to say something in a minute you know.

(P) That's good, have you seen any good movies, have you seen "The Sandpiper" yet?

I won't see Elizabeth Taylor movies. Oh, what do I look like Otto Preminger? What, what what're what's leading through through this thing?

Are you gonna pose for a portrait Drella?

Oh, I don't know yet.

No, no you can't. You're working with me today.

Okay uh, n-no uh, are you going to the movies because I have to decide . . . Now.

No but huh . . .

Can he put your name. Oh what's this?

Where?

Can he put your name on million's of people's backs. Quiet! And and don't move that thing, I'm listening to the record.

Shirts, no just Drella huh.

Lucky L—More than Drella.

A.W.

Look, look at this last line (*opera*

opera). I think we should just leave it on the picture. Well I got that right in time. Look at the last line there . . . (opera) . . . I figured one of the children delivered this.

We wanna make a shirt and sell millions and millions of shirts.

Oh. an Andy Warhol shirt.

Yeah. What what kind.

Sort of pop art.

Like a good-guy shirt?

No a bad-guy shirt.

Well he'd have to bad guy shirt!

You mean the Beatles right?

Huh? No.

You mean the Beatles, right?

(P) Beethoven, Bach.

. . . and brown hair.

Oh, I really can't take this.

Oh, no.

Beautiful prints.

P N-not a, not a not a uh wha uh sweatshirt, uhh shirt.

No.

I'm gonna have to put . . .

(P) An actual shirt with a collar?

Oh.

That's the only way to do it.

Oh.

Hi, us Blinny, this is Drella.

BLINNY—Hi Drella.

D Hello.

B Uh, I haven't seen you in a long time.

How are you?

B How you doin'? Where you been hidin'?

Uh, in front of the movie cameras.

B In front of a movie camera?

Wh-where have I been hiding? I've been buried in Queens. I've got, I've, I have to put some . . . Isn't that disgusting? I mean, that's really offensive.

Hmm?

She's really offensive. Come in the back with me and I'll get everything.

Yes, we're going into the back room.

Speak.

(B) Oh, for heaven sakes.

Speak and we'll listen.

I wanna make the shirt, *Life*, *Playboy*, sell it coast to coast.

Uh, what kind of shirt?

Night shirt.

Oh.

Print on it.

Yeah, you mean just print would be the most important thing or it should be a design?

It should be a design.

Oh, what should it be, Ondine?

I don't know, I I I I'm trying to think and I can't, think of . . . think it should be something uh, we'll work it out.

I like Heinz Ketchup.

Oh yeah.

Spilled over on the shirt.

That's a terrific idea.

Bob, I have to find something that's gonna get rid of her. Coulld I say something, is there such a thing?

Of course. It's just a journal of Ondine's life.

Oh, it's just my life that's all *laugh* . I'd like some lemon water. There's all kinds of things back there; just help yourself. Go in the ice box.

I don't think there's any there.

There should be some.

I mean something like we had, had to, that woman . . .

Oh you want the other kind, yesterday kind.

Yeah.

Oh, you want some amphetamine.

Yeah.

Sure darling, I'll put some in your drink or up your nose or wherever else you want it.

I'll do it myself.

No, let me administer the drug please. I'm the doctor here.

He's the doctor.

Look at Billy ame, look at Billy Name's photographs, they're so fabulously imaginative. They're incrdeible. Look now isn't that gorgeous? Loger(?) caught on the mike. God! No, he's really fabulous. This one, this one's a little bit cute but . . .

What about the shirt?

Look at Paluta.

Well uh, we'll have to think about it.

A group of lions.

Okay.

I'm gonna put the, s-stop stepping on my tape.

I don't think the tape uh, works.

Sure it does.

Does it?

Yeah.

Oh come on, let's follow (*pause*). Will you hold this just for a minute Ondine while I get another tape?

This is, this is almost done.

Hold it.   (P) How much power does it take to get . . .   I must administer it in my arm.   Okay darling, I'm just gonna put this tape in.   I'm getting you uh, a present.   You, you've always been sweet.   But this one's tremendous.   What is it, I hope it's something I like.   It's a turtle shell.   A turtle shell! (P) Can you scrape together 7000 dollars?   You like the electron, you like the quipment in here Ronal?   (B) It's supposed to be over Palisades this weekend.   (P) ot like this.   Isn't that beautiful?   (B) Isn' tit? No, it's, I'm fixing the whole thing up.   I, I thought it was broken. You sure it's not broken?   No, no, yeah, he he's been playing with it.   Oh he has. Oh he isn't the only one that's been playing with it. It's a wonder it's not not ste-stereo oh oh.   No this his his fix it, in fact he he recorded the Luchea.   Oh terrific.   Wait a minute— there there was . . .   I'm not sure.   No, no, neither am I. Lets take it off.   Take it off through here.   Well will it, him, it if it uh . . .

Yeah—it might fuck it up.   Well uh he he can play one track tape—   Well this is four track—that's what I mean.   Uh . . . well no, this can't play . . .   It's spaghetti.   No it's . . .   Yeah, but I don't think that this will work. I'll I'll get some some some Nom-meal, I'll I'll think of something . . . and theNn we can and then we can— we'll havt to stop recording for a little while and we'll have to stop recording for a little while until she goes—but it'll be very loud and we'll run around.   Where are the shirts.   Hmmmmm, I have no idea. Beautiful—   What?   The next, in the next, I whu—you shouldn't have put the tape because we—this is this is this is called called getting rid of of this is getting rid of Gloria Savage time.   Oh.   And and I I

gotta put it loud cause then she'll go (*long pause*) you're gonna tell us about the thing now? About One Fifth Avenue—please.   Oh that's going to be fun.   Because . . .   I don't know.   Hmmmmm.
          I haven't been there.   Oh.   Do you, what kind of a fashion show is it please please.   Oh who knows who knows, I haven't been there.   Well what what is it called?   When is it?   It's called, Oh Aug, August 24th.   August 24th?   Oh it's gon-na be hot isn't it?   No well well we won't be around.   Do do you wanna hear Norma?

Norma?

Medea.

          It's only for 2 days y'know. I asked for reservations that, for all the days.

Oh terrific. Why is it so special?

I mean well is ther esomething happening or something?

          I don't know, I've never been there.

Oh.

Where the hell does he have Norma?

(P) Can you people get out of the light for one second?

(O) Norma is not here honey. I know. Palacchi it says here. (*Long pause.*) So where is the Norma? That Norma is missing. Do you think she's out for a coffee break? She has no right leaving without letting us know. Drella, Norma's not gonna work now, what what else can we put on: Rigoletto, is that here? . . . Oh that? Delmonico's, I don't wanna hear that . . . is too gay. I gotta choose well.

          Olivo.

          What?

          That turtle, is . . .

          Why are you giving me a turtle?

          It's a, it's a, it's a snuff box. gold snuff box.

          Oh how beautiful.

With a leather tortoise shell.
Sorta of a on top . . .
Oh that's fabulous Lucky
thank you. . . . It's great, oh that's
fantastic. When am I gonna
have it?
Whenever they come.
Are you serious? That's gonna
be gorgeous.
I know.
Thank you dear.
You're welcome. It has it has,
listen to this . . .
That's very nice of you, I think
you're a beautiful boy.
Listen to this. It has 2, it's
this big only, an inch and a half
by an inch. And it has 2 compartments.
2 compartments?
Yeah and inside is white leather.   Oh.   This should do, this
should do it right? Hi Ronal.   Gee I haven't seen you around in a long
time.   Maybe it's because I haven't been around in a long . . . I'm
looking for a special record I think has just walked out. Uh who's that?
Oh Lucky.   Lucky who likes to drive.   Oh I don't know,
correct . . .   Who which one, what's his name?   Oh, it's very
easy. He always remains that way.   What's his name.   . . . . .
bother with . . .   Jimmy.   You know it's just that some people
ug . . . Is that a tape recorder? Get to be very obnoxious I, I, sort of I,
I . . . *2 conversations at once.*   Say um . . . F.B.I.   Oh really? Oh
he designed paper covers? Who?   Madame Butterfly—I made just one
for the uh Gemini space capsule.   Oh.   Wasn't that a thrilling
event?   We just got a video uh movie video tap . . .   Oh oh video
tape—huh . . .   Oh wow, where is it? Gee and . . .   Records, both I
started it, Drella, all the Carlsons have gone. The   Norma's not here,
the Butterfly's, nothing's here.   Oh.   Where are they? This is very
strange. I don't understand y'know that really is weird. Maybe I'm having
hallucinations and I don't see it, but I just don't see them anywhere, can
you imagine Drella that they're all, is he taking a walk to Norman?
Kids in background.   How long do you get one tape?   "La Bo-
heme," I guess.   Half an hour.   Nope.   About ½ an hour one
side and ½ an hour the other side.   No, we won't play . . . at all, we'll
play this, we'll play the firstact of Verdi's "Traviata' by Toscanini. That
would rush anybody anywhere.   Okay.

I'm going out to the . . . we are now, oh look . . .   Oh uh, what happened?   Oh it's just ruined just signaled. I don't bel—   . . . Ondine. Oh here, I have it.   No, I mean I just have, it's not armed.   *Ondine sings—Phaedra jalous.   Kids in background.*   Oh stop that noise. Basta with the noise. (*Ondine mutters.*) Stop the eternal racket, my ears are killing me. (*Pause.*) Maybe we're doing the right thing without doing anything. Do you think I should try a tape?   Uh maybe you should wait til Billy comes.   This is always there.   W-wait . . . (*pause*). Turn it louder.

(O) We must get rid of that woman and her children. Eh, is this all right though?

Yeah. (*Pause.*)

(O) Isn't that a beautiful picture?

Hm.

(O) Beautiful pictue. (*Paunse. Noise and kids. Music starts.*) This is, this is a huh? This is the record that will get rid of Gloria Savage, I hope. For her sake. (*Music. Ondine sings along.*) Oh this is so beautiful. It's uh the f, the last night of . . . . . (?) This is uh, you you you can put this tape down. (*Music.*) She, sh-she . . . Do you think maybe we should take the tape off and put in another tube? Please, really because this is going to be so light it's gonna be impossible to hear. (*Music—singing along.*) I'm singing. No, I don't want to. Let's please, push that . . . (*music is loud*).

I don't know.

Ondine sings along.

(O) That's, that's the way you always react to the, to the line and I, I don't know why. (*Laughter—loud opera.*) All right Maria, do your work. Aw, she fell. Please, please please (*loud music*) in minutes that'll be the end of this. From here to there and then about that much on side . . . and that's all.

That's all right. We'll have to . . .

(O) . . . record anything (*sings along*). Liberace and Elvis Prezel. Lucky (*loud music*) it does, it ain't though. I guess the queen and the dowager queen. But it's Tito Ciari that stuff, it it, the Telstar.

Yeah.

(O) (*Ondine blows into microphone.*) That was just a sigh. Uh, Lucky L. He's the one that got us the tickets to go to the uh, fashion show.

What? You know he gave us a bargain. Don't you know wierdo, even . . . who was it that asked me that about you? They said, "Is he Rink, is he weird?" (*Music.*) Hey Lucky, you Czechoslovakian? Are you Czechoslovakian? (*Music.*) Are you Czechoslovakian? See I told you, they're all weird, everyone of them and they're strange names and everything. (*Music.*) . . . the cartoon from *Esquire* magazine. (*Music.*) Oh you know it wasn't like the cartoon from *Esquire* magazine that you should have announced that it's closed when when when it's closed, it's closed, right? (*Music.*) Leave after this act? We, y'know we we we wrapped them a lot, we want to wrap them all . . . the fall. Who's? Who, Steve's? Steve, Steve . . . your change, your change.

(S) What?

(O) Steve will give you his change? (*Opera.*) That's . . . be a cow painting. You want to give me a cow painting?

What?

(O) I've never hit a pregnant woman but I would. I can't stand her. Oh how I, funny but I, I'm going to this other side, I'm going to this side of the road. Oh oh, Paul's going to fall dff the fire escape, I know it. Gerry, Ger, please get him off the fire escape; he might get hurt.

Get him off.

(O) Because I don't think it's . . . where did I put it? (*Music.*) Close the door Gerry too please. Look, if he fell I would die. God. (*Piercing music and Ondine sings along.*) Help. (*More piercing music.*) I think this . . . . . (?) has anything. Here he is. Lucky, you look cleaner.

Is is that a Little Lulu in your bag? Ooh, what a knife. My God, you can certainly stab Edward Arnold.

(LL) Can't I do it?

(O) No, because it's a very tricky situation.

(LL) Put it out.

You mean his nose.

No.

No, I mean he wa he wa he was, he has to swallow it.

Swallow it?

(O) Lucky I tell you what, get yourself a glass of soda, like there's one in the, in the, in the refrigerator.

He'll need it Ondine.

Oh, Bonjourno! Oh.

Oh the movie's here, the camera. No, how was your, our day? Hey, how was, I'm following Ondine, today, Taxi. (*Ondine sings.*) Taxi I'm following Ondine today. What happened?

TAXINE—I don't know. (*Lots of different voices.*)

No No No

(T) We're all . . . whose are these, Drella? They have, htey'll take it was devastated.

Oh hahaha.

I wanna, I wanna get them down.

I wanna get them out and it's the the minute that they get out we'll we'll be fine . . . duh . . .

We'll do it in the car later.

Ondine has to come with us all evening.

Yeah.

(T) Tapes?

RINK—No, I mean we can't really talk about the interview.

(T) Okay. (Music.) Where is Steve today?

(O) Oh, well ohm as long as you're here. I'll play you the Callas al-album okay?

(T) I might go right out of my mind.

(O) So beautiful that it will calm you. Yeah she . . .

(T) And I got because of my cold I got my money. (High soprano.) I, you know what? I have $35.00 to live on the next month.

Do you want more?

Oh.

(L) Yeah, I'll take some . . .

(T) I spent a thousand dollars . . .

I don't have that much. I'll give you more when I when I get some.

(T) Send me enough to cover the fact that I . . . Do you know what happened to me today?

What?

(T) People came to the door saying they had checks from like two weeks ago that were bouncing and that I've written three checks since then ohhhhhhhhhh! And so I, I called mummy and I said "You, I'm doing this because uh I'm trying to say what I really think and believe and and you've twisted me basically ever since I was born and I've made mistakes but I've you know I've done it in in a way that was genuinely Micky(?) and I fe—and I'm doing it now in in a much more wide open space and I and the reason for the publicity is to avoid being squashed out by people that use you like dirt. I don't know where I put it.

That one's dirty.

(T) What?

It's sort of dirty, it's broken.

Oh oh.

Here it is.

KID—I want some soder.

I'll get you . . . some I'll . . .

KID—I want some soder. I WANT SOME SODER.

What kind do you want? Half grapefruit. We have lemon or lemon twist.

Did you put anything in his water? Put some in his water.

(LL) Did.

You did?

    turn on the light.

Did you make an appointment?

    This way.

We don't have Coca Cola honey.

    Does it really go away in water?

Yeah it vanishes. Throw it in there; it just disappears or something—

    You mean it's it's in there and I can't see it?

Lucky I said. I didn't know you would crawl up under my armpit like
    mat what a . . .

I said would you excuse me . . .

You? I don't have to excuse you for anything.

Oh you're talking about Lucky?

Yeah. No Lucky was crawling up under, under my armpit and you said
    "You going gay?" You've been crawling up under my arm. My glasses
    and (pause).

    Be prepared! that's the Boy Scouts' marching song. Be prepared
    (Opera). But I have one doubt in my mind and—Drella—when can we
    relax?

Who went with Taxi and Rink?

No, but I mean when can we start recording for for a second?

Oh we're going . . .

Where are you going?—oh—Debbie's house?

Uh . . .

Because because Gerard you better help us, Gerard you better help us.

Are we working here?

You've got you've got you've got to help us. Gerard—please Gerard you
    must help us.

Is that for me?

    Darl-Darling we and we also want to get rid of Gloria—please you've
    got to help us get rid of Gloria. Bravo . . . what?

    Do you have any cough medicine?

Cough medicine.

Gerhimmmm!!! Cough medicine . . . no I have Rhim cough medicine.

They really do have good cough medicine, it's cocaine, yes . . .

Oh it's . . .

What?

Gerry. (Ondine singing along.)

. . . they come in grams—cocaine . . .

(singing) minds . . . minds . . . yeah. . . .

Gerry why start home for an hour . . .

(Ondine moans to music.) This is Cinderella, can you believe it? She's out of the cinders.

What a gorgeous record ohhh yes, yes . . .

Do you want to see my shirts?

I like to feel, I like to see art Drella stop that. What are you feeling in your balls for in your shirt—that's a nasty habit. Lucky, that you Irish people have of feeling your thing—it's terrible.

But . . .

I'm sorry you checked sir, all the . . .

This guy's a Russian.

Well we'll we'll I'm I'm I'm Alaskan, I am, and then she's a Hawaiian.

Cherokee.

I'm an Indian.

I'm really cherokee.

Cherokee.

Yeah. Warhol . . .

Toot toot toot toot! I hope so he's giving us nice presents.

Huh? Oh yes? (Opera.)

Ask your mommy first.

Do you want to go out and show some of my films?

No.

How come you're recording his voice?

Cause cause it's it's you heard what I say darling.

(D) Not really, that's how he says it. I'm doing a a 12 hour uhhhh a 12 hour novel.

(O) On me and my time.

What's interesting about Ondine?

Ondine?

(O) More than you'll ever see sir.

(LL) You know something? I don't understand, I've been to more places than him, did more things than he ever did . . .

You just haven't got a facility darling (sings). Look at, look at yourself. Have you got a big heart? Besides you're gonna have to leave in a couple . . . an hour. (Sings.)

Will you gentle things join me please?

Oh I want to go . . . no, no I, I, don't want to go in there.

. . . follow me.

I haven't don't even go to this Lucky it's . . .

Hey close the door. Let's make that shirt.

You still gonna make a shirt in here? Let's make that shirt? What a kooky thing to say to anybody.

    Trillions of them, billions of them.

What's gonna be our cut?

    Tell me . . .

Oh I don't know. 75%, what? Oh?

Okay.

What should er take? I don't know. It's up to Drella.

    What'd you think?

I'll have to think about it.

    How long does it take you to think?

Well, he doesn't think if he can help it and he's wise uh who thinks?

What company is this?

    My company.

Oh it's called your company. Oh is it?

    Yeah.

Really?

    Yeah.

Well I've never bought your shirts.

    I didn't even have a company till the other day.

You gotta bring us the things first and the papers. Show us what you want to show us.

The papers, signed by the, your honor, Rotten Rita. If the Mayor signs it we'll pu it into law.

Is he a friend of Rotten Rita's?

Huh?

A friend of Rotten Rita's?

    No, he's a friend of Rotten Rita's.

He doesn't know who Rotten Rita is.

Oh.

  Ondine sings.

That's your coarseness price.

    For what?

For the cameras.

For the cameras.

    For the cameras? What cameras?

There will be, there will be, there will be picturing our love making. That's the price he wants.

    The price for what?

The shirts.

    For shirts. Mm hm. You're gonna have exclusive rights.

Why?
>Uh huh, because you otld me to go to bed with her. I can't go to bed with anyone. You've been telling me to anyway.

(O) Why not? You could go to bed with anyone. Did you ever go to bed with a bear? I've been to bed with bears, skeletons, and (*inverted sigh*) someone stabbed her. Billy Name. (*Laughter.*) It's so funny.

I know another Lucky L.

Fifteen minutes, then clear out. (*Pause.*) Is that the only way to do it? Must I be rude?   I hate being rude. Oh that's lovely. Wait, I'll put put my mask on and we can play "What's My Line?" This is where I made my first film. Oh do you remember this, Ralph Edwards, uh this is your life, Ondine.

Shall we show it down or should we send it?

No, no please. Let's not. Fanny Hill Johnson is in . . . duh, and I¹ would hate to walk out in the audience after they saw that Seven-Up bottle. I'd have o . . . . . (?) my leg's in that picture, flapping around.
>You would be nice on a shirt, on a shirt.

I'd look, I'd be nice on anything.
>On a shirt.

On a skirt?

Oh a shirt.

(O) Here's my shirt. I want this emblazoned on every headline all over America—whoosh. Well you can get that on it, you have my name too. You know I have a thing, a scarf that fits at the bikini. But, but, it, it's this tree is right there, a clump, a bush in a long tree and it looks like a prick, and it's so gabulous, as a matter of fact . . .
>I went fishing the other day.

And you can go fishing now if you can't . . .
>And do you know what you know what the guy gave me instead of putting my fishing pole on . . .

What?
>A sycamore tree and a sycamore tree had a V y'know like this and on each side was a . . . whatleroytheosycampreinalachiside—
>It's brown . . . long (*opera*).

He's getting nervous.

You you just here here's a color rag. That's, open it up and hand it in to Gloria. Y'know. It's just (*laughter*) music what's the matter with her. . . . Is she stupid? Or is she . . . Do you know Gloria?
>No.

You're lucky darling.
>How come she's stupid?

I don't know.

She paints nice pictures.
That's nice?
Not bad.
He paints nicer ones.
That cow is very nice.
Isn't that cow fabulous oh it's really beautiful oh you can do so many things . . .

What'll I do with the cow? I'd love to ride it, I tried to ride it.

You'd like to ride it like a bull would. But you'd probably try to fuck it I mean he he wants to the little bitty small girls in protest and he tied he rup and put her in the bathtub and pissed on her and then the water run . . .
Oh really?
For 2 hours she was in the bathtub. She called him up the next day and said thank you very much, it was the most glorious experience of my life.

You don't you don't go near them—they don't go after you . . .
Mean it too.

They got bulls too.
There's uh that oh wha? Bulls are all right, I've never minded bulls I tell you I can get along with them.

Yeah I . . .
You have a lighter?

Yeah.
You want to give it to me? I'd love . . .

No.
I love presents, is that a lighter?

No the lighter is outside.
Was was was that is that my pay check? For heaven's sake, it's late in coming, ohhh do you know what you can do my dear?
What? What?
Okay I have done, what we all have done—magic marker shirts.

I know I wanna get them.
They're indelible and you know how and they don't come off but they when you wash them they . . .

Mr. Clean's grandfather's sending me Bra—beads from Brazil.
Well, if you take me with you

To Brazil?
And Drella (*inverted sigh*).

Brazil.
During the, yes during the during during Mardi Gras time we wo, we would be . . .

I don't think I'm going.

(O) Well take us with him. Tell Mr. Clean that and Mr. Clean's grand-
father tha-that Drella and Ondine belong there. Well, we could oh
Drella wouldn't . . . wouldn't it be fanta la gusta?
        Think it would be great.
I'm certain it would be great, don't be silly.
This is certainly monotony we did here. We're doing a movie over again.
Which one is that?
Well I'm anxious oh I'm using uh uh uh Gregory Baltcock is uh . . .
He was in Horse.
I don't know what should I do?
Uuh Tarsha's boyfriend.
OH I don't know well they they must be all right.
Well, we want some body to draw them for a certain. . . . Do you know
    anybody? It's very cute.
Me of course.
Really? Don't think I would do it.
But well uh uh uh . . .
Cause I have yeah oh no no I no it's it's it's not that I gotta find out what
    type he he is.
Well, it's just I'm gonna do the face of him . . .
No no but well I I if I get credit, I'll do it starring . . .
What?
        Townshend.
If I get credit I'll do it.
Oh yes.
It's bread we need, money.   Oh course.   Drella contrary
to what we need is not, oh millionaire.   Neither is Ondine the French
maid. We need bread. And lucky you always have enough money oh you
to take care of yourself and a few friends in style. I've never seen you at a
loss   Well I certainly would love to go to Rio de Janeiro
Well I certainly would too.   So let's make the fuckin trip get the
money.   Do you have to do that?   You know what I'd like to
do with the sh . . . with the fucking money?   There should be no condition.   Do you know of course not there isn't any   At least
get my tickets to Rio because we . . .   Listen to this I wanna buy
a fuckin island.   I feel if I can find the tin foil that would be the last
. . . (music). Who wrote that?   Olivo—can't I take some
amphetamine to New Jersey or . . .   I don't have enough Lucky.
        Where can I go get some? I don't live in New Jersey. Huh—   Do
you live in Trenton? I don't live there.   I'll try and get you 10 if I can.
        I have to get to New Jersey with Beach Haven.   If I can't
get you . . .   I want something . . . else   I can't Lucky. If my stuff

hasn't been stolen it would go without question that you would have whatever you wanted but this stuff was stolen from, from from me until we Americans could do something about that then ug . . . will have to go without there is because I told them I go toff the bus and the guy says says to me . . .   I fell right into the trap. A-Head I said "Oh." He said "Y'know baby" he said "I was just burned for 30 dollars" and he said "I don't have any bread or any amphetamine." I said, "Come with me, and I'll take you and get you shot up, and then I'll give you some." I pulled some out of my bag, and I got him shot up and gave him 2, I gave him enough to sell a a dime bag and some for himself (*opera and laughter*) he's so he returned a half hour later with a friend and robbed my bag while I'm asleep. But he, that's that that's—*Opera*.   Whatever it is. Oh I don't want him to die I think, I think his skin will kill him . . .

I don't like him touching that radio.   Kill him?   Oh I think his skin will kill him.   No but you're touching that raido. With uranium.   Oh with oh with the I thought you said radio.

No, uranium, oh you can put it in his radio.   you can put it in his pablum too, give it to his mother H.O. Farina that is.   WILhemina, y'know (*opera*).   You can make you could have a safe and put your amphetamine in it and have no problems.   I don't want an amphet- amine that I have to hide, or hoarde and guard and all that. Right.`   Bernado do do know   Just bought Drella. There's a fishing pond . . . in in the . . . I just got one wait oh this fish is fileted well, well, serve it to Gloria for breakfast.   Darling I . . .   Who's Gloria? The lady with the pictures? . . . Oh yeah.   Yeah she's uh us she's . . .

Why don't you go over there and kill her. I can't get shit out of her.   The top model for Vogue Magazine—1950.   The minute I met her I beat her up.   She's an actress now.   An actress? Yeah she's an actress, she's a dying fool.   she cuts her chil- drne's hair kind of funny.   She's got a mean figure too, she looks like a pygmy. She looks like an *Esquire* cartoon.   It's another success, yeah an another, that's uh Gerry, that's wet y'know.   Oh it is?   Here look.   Oh.   Oh. A message wait a second.   Quite a bit of . . .   There's a Negro where. Oh I I picked up an . . . okay boys whip im out I was picked up in a car by this colored man and I said "It's funny" I said "but, you colored people" he said "Ah prefer being called a black man" (*laughter*). Well I said why he was attractive to me (*inverted sigh*) . . .   I was walking down 2nd Avenue . . .   and Lexington

I took a little card that had a picture of a little colered boy and somebody said to me, "What's that?" And I said, "It's a nigger."   It's a nigger   And a guy or nigger walked by and gave me a dirty look you know, a really filthy and mean one, real quick.   I hope you said, I

hope you said . . .   "Excuse me."   Cool it. (*Laughter*)
        I said "Excuse me."   I wanna design, some design something . . .
        With the . . .   Some . . .   (*Opera*).   He said he
didn't want to go.   Didn't what? (*Opera*.)   He didn't look like a
pretty to me.   I want that shirt I want to make that shirt I need
help.   What do you want me to do bring my sewing machine? Slide
for 64 thousand dollars. Isn't that nice. Slide for 64 thousand. He let me
slip by and get in, put it in *Life* magazine, O God.   She's so old.
        I gotta put it back.   What a wierd character this is here, I don't
know how she called up her gazebo—very frightening in here. OH it's so
hot please take out your dicks please, or get out yes what did he do with
her $10? That's good enough.   Maybe we'll think abou it.   Huh?
        You have to pay the bills from Ondine, then we'll think about it.
        Then we'll have to all pay the price, I want the deed to your mother's
tomb, you fools.   My mother's tomb?   The deed to it is all I
want nothing else.   Somehing's too precious.   They're very
fashionable, they're wool   I have plenty of wool.   Ah yes you
you would gather alot I . . .   I have lots of wool.   I got it
again.   So much wool.   Oh.   I have mor than wool I have
cotton balls.   I have cotton too.   Oh.   Have you
seen his dick at all?   Oh I never saw his dick. He's been a friend of
mine for for years and we never run around in bed though he tease the
shit out a me in a car. And he leaves me waiting for 7 or 8 hours and I'm
frantic. Lucky was being arrested . . . since then . . . Do you really like it,
should I should I go out and introduce it to America?   All right America
the new wool Bracelet and it's also quick for a convenient family jokes.
        I get a black one.   It is oh marvelous for at the baths ohhhh
where did it go. (*Opera*.) Isn't that beautiful? (*Opera*.) It's convenient
to get out of here.   It is pretty nice.   It's a beautiful picture. It's a
beautiful . . .

4 /   2

Yeah Drella's Drella's here, but he, but but but he's he's in the bathroom
what? He's trying to kill some of it, he's strangling some of the toilet.
(Pause.) Oh uh well, I don't know y'know uh I don't know what I'm
doing really because   tell him we don't know what we'll be doing
we don't know y'know it's just we're we're just cut, we're cutting alot of

we're we're just trying to have a lot of fun in New York City, that's all. Here here he is. Oh he's not here at all. Here, here I am. Hi. Darling, Drella's not on the phone even, he's in he's in he's in the bathroom. Darling. Hello. Why not? (*Pause.*) He's not . . . Rink? Paul, you didn't ask for . . . Does anyone want to speak to Steve? Drella's Drella's not not not available he's really in the bathroom. What you heard, I think, was Gerard Malanga speaking to him to him. Do you want to speak to Gerry?

No.   I I don't know. Probably Apause   I don't know unless he's got a special tunnel in the bathroom that get's him out of there which I don't know I don't think, where you going? I'll take care of the broom, Gerry, you're you're . . .   Don't rise uh Steve. . . . I'll see you . . . Why not say it's for Gerry?   Huh? look now. I don't . . .   Huh? Look now I don't see the point in it cause we're all gonna leave in a half in in about 10 minutes, right?   Yeah.   We—listen be prepared to leave in 10 minutes every— body. I gotta sneak up come come come. Turn out the light.   Hey it it unplugged.   Oh no it didn't, this one n-n-n-no just this one it it it's recording.   Oh oh Olivo. (TAXI) Call . . . a half an hour.   Will you wait one second please. It's all my fault.   No it isn't.   All right but I wanna get rid of it.   Don't pull the noose. What a horrible choker. I don't want that. Look, it has it has a clip, Lucky (pause). I don't know, I think so. Go ahead.   OH I wanna make that shirt.   All right we'll get the material—make the trans—get the material and bring it in and we'll we'll we'll well first, I'm gonna have to sweep up here, excuse me, you're gonna have to excuse me.   Express yourself, he get's involved we'll be uh . . .   And we're gonna have to leave in half an 'hour, in ten minutes as a matter of fact, so you might as well put that away. Don't let that thing go below.   Hmmmmmm?   Isn't Bob . . . (*laughter*). But no, I'll think about it. (*Pause.*) Oh he's sweeping it the other way. (*Long pause.*) Hey Lucky would you help me fol—oh no you're busy engaged in conversation.   I finished my conversation.   N-no you, I meant him .   Oh.   Oh would you help would you like to sweep? I would appreciate it greatly. I'm very tired. Thank you I I'm I'm gonna hang fo a second (*long pause*). I'm hanging here now (*long pause and banging*). Wasn't that record beautiful Taxi? Really heaven?   (*Pause.*) Help!   fall on your head   Oh no not I did that once in Brooklyn and I'm not gonna (*pause*). Oh what a relief to hang here. Well, 33 in what booklet. Sweep. Don't sweep like that you may knock me over (KID) I wanna see him do it again.   You wanna see me do it again? Okay! I will.   Where are you?   I'm hanging up here. That's all right I'm all hooked up. They hear me. . . . He wants to see me do it again. It's a request, okay. Do you want to see me do my special number

. . . or?   (KID) Hey look.   Yeah this is just for you (pause). A right?
Can I get down? (Pause.) Whew. (Pause.) Here no well no I uh . . .
    Take my dress quickly (banging and pause).   Oh I like the idea
of ketchup.   Yeah.   ketchup bottle   (O) Oh Drella
Drella this is . . .   (D) What?   (O) this is the n-n-no no it's . . .
and I don't mind it at all. It's just tha uh I've told people that we're
leaving and uh they don't seem to want to move. . . . We have to get
people out. Business—another tit, that's all that's how you talk business
anyway. That's it now and contact with Mars.   He looks like Phlegn
doesn't he?   Phlegn who? I don't know, I tell you I never knew
Phlegn Phleymer, I just met him that one night at the Dom. .   You
didn't meet him at the Dom? He wasn' there.   Yes he was, I was at
Brooklyn Hall too, I think it's . . .   only real way with all the big tables
. . . What do you mean . . .   yeah oh the Jill Johnston Show too.
No joke . . . people   He doesn't want a good shirt.   Man it's
some really something oog I wan-want it fuckin to fuckin to blast off once
after I bust it off then here's tgonna be fuckin . . . one housand other
guys blasting off when I blast it off.   But wh-what what would be so
different about your shirt?   What because nobody has it.   It
wouldn't be a novelty.   what   the shirt   oh wh-what kind
    It's a night gown sort ofthing.   Oh.   It's tee shirt like
this here it comes all the way down.   Drella, Taxine's calling.   It's a
tee shirt.   That's a nice idea.   It's sort of this . . . it comes all
the way down to the knees. Boys and girls wear them they wear them to
the beaches and a lot of places . . .   Oh can I get a wrink of wa—
Oh I know where where they . . .   Do you think it'll make a big hole
in . . .   no, I'm gonna . . . I'll do it my . . .   the shirt's   well I yeah
well yeah   It's gonna be the roast . . .   Uh well uh let me uh think
of uh if I can give you an idea or something   yeah the way to the fire
escape. (Pause.) Rink, maybe you'll help me.   (RINK) Arrival at the
beach.   We have to be, let's start getting people out of here.   (R)
Okay in a minute I, I'm allready. Oh. (Pause.) (Door opens.)   All
right police it's fine. (Pause, phone rings.) Hellp. Who's calling, Bill
Bomber? Would you hold on please, I'll see. (Pause.) Is Drella here? Is
Drella there?   (TAXI) He uh left already.   No I'm not here.
(T) Ondine.   (O) Isn't that album divine? Do you want to speak to
Bill Bomber?   (T) Who?   (O) Do you know Bill Bomber?
(T) Who's Bill Bomber?   I'm on the phone.   (T) Oh really? Is he
somebody Drella met?   I don't know.   (T) Hallo hallo hallo.
Hello? How are you? this is Drella.   (T) This is Drella.   Hello,
Drella.   (T) You must be joking you must be . . .   joking darling
    Who is it?   Drella who. We never heard of him.   Hel—lo. It's

Drella Who here. (*Laughter.*)   He must be getting   where is
Drella   He's not here.   Drella (*loudly*).   Drella what . . .
You've got the wrong name.   He isn't here.   There's no one by that
name here.   Is it the wrong number?   You got the wrong number, I
never heard of him.   Drella it's the wrong number Drella. There's no
Drella here. There's no Drella here. Keep saying it.   You must have the
wrong number. It's Amos . . . Who is calling?   Bill Bomber.   Fabulous he hung up.   He hung up, oh you scared the shit out of him, no
wonder you   *Drella in background*—Who?   I don't want to speak
to someone else because I said you were Amos, and I . . .   She
screamed she screamed.   You wante dto speak to him.   I didn't
want want to speak to him. No.   You didn't have to carry on.   Oh
well, we were just   She she shouldn't have said, Andy Warhol.   I
. . .   Amos Warhol.   Oh.   And you indicated that if . . .   Oh
it's uh oh uh it'll be all right.   I can't clap my hands to that or I
(*claps his hands*).   What do you . . . it doesn't matter.   Well, I
mean I . . .   you . . .   Children we'll have to get out. . . .   Because
I . . .   we haven't . . .   Oh shit. We must there's something you
should have told . . .   No! H esaid "no" he didn't want to talk to him.
    . . . epidemic yet   Oh well then I don't . . .   This this this he's
just having hysterics. It's his susual fit. He has an artfernoon fit. We're
leaving (*screams it*).   Uh well . . .   Good bye . . .   You're coming
with us . . . ah shit . . .   Gerad—   Oh I uh bye.   (*Ondine sings.*)
Isn't that aria gorgeous? Isn't that album phenomenal, it's so beautiful.
    In Europe it's so directed.   I know it's going to ruin me.   Oh.
My darling but I have a far—excuse me I didn't expect to see just
. . .   Jersey tomorrowand you can take pictures in a car with Gerry.
    Where?   New Jersey   What part of New eJrsey?   Forget it
New Jersey.   What partof New Jersey?   Just to get to New Jersey
is another matter. Otherwise I'll buy you a shirt.   Wait what part of
New Jersey would you like to go to darling . . .   Uh.   Where is it
because uh . . .   Well I have the uh . . .   I wish . . . car . . .
oh . . .   What more can I do?   You better do it.   I've done all
that is possible. *Pause.*

    Yeah you could give me some amphetamine.

    I don't have enough darling.

    Do you have any grass?

No but here's a 2 in all.

    But what you give that day?

Amphetamine.

    Oh, those little yellow things.

Shhhh . . . swallow this. You've cut yourself again, didn't you?

Yeah, I'm not shaving for the next few days.

Oh must we hang around and talk and we have to go . . .

Can I ask you a question?

No, what?

What you gave me theo ther day the yellow . . .

Shhhh.

You shouldn't have gave it to me?

Shhh . . . ake your pen out of here and play calmly, it's an opportunity it it's a raving mind.

What what what's what you gave me the other day?

It's called an ambersol(?), darling.

What?

That's why we have to be nice and quiet about it.

Why?

Because they weren't mine.

Who who's were they?

Taxi's the last time.   Oh excuse me darling.   Whoever drinks top job is gonna have a good time. *Laughter.*   Olivo.   What's, uh not my name, my name is Cotildia.   Cotildia   What is this? Whose shirt is this? Whose white shirt is this? Gerard, is he wearing a white shirt?   When can I talk to you about the shirt Bob? When y'know whenever you contact me . . . I'll be around tomorrow, today, all over, I'll be around tomorrow, today all over I'll be around . . . I'm always around.   Where shall I come up for you? I won't be around.

Just call me, that's all darling. You won't be around uh well I'm going to New Jersey tomorrow myself   You want to go down to Beach Haven?   I wanna go to the beach I haven't seen the ocean, and I'm *******???   Fuck you!

Do do you know how terrible it was was that I didn't couldn't give give you more?

Do you know how long I stayed on that stuff?

How long?

For a day and a half.

The stuff that I gave you?

Yeah isn't that sweet?

That's good stuff, though—no it's fabulous stuff. Doesn't even get you sick—beautifu, beautiful stuff.

Yeah, but wow—for a fuckin day and a half.

Yeah—it's that good.

Where's my cup?

It runneth over. Have a clean one

You gonna runneth it over? *Laughter.*

I'm gonna runneth you.
  Alright—when do you want to see my shirt?
When y-you have it—as soon as have it.
  I'll have it Monday.
  Alright then, show it to me.
When are you going—I don't want to do it by myself. Yeah?   Okay.
How do I shut this one off?   I don't know. (*Pause.*)   Time to go
 humming . Oh, oh you mean you mean oh—okay good—then I just have
to get dressed right?   Yeah yeah—but leave that on and oh—what are
we going to do about Rotten Rita?   Oh well, oh well oh, oh.   Sh-
should I call her now?   What's the matter?   Oh oh the openings.
I dunno.   Those are undone.   Yeah, Rotten Rita did it.   I'm
coming, I'm coming—hey Lucky are you a d . . . . . are you a . . . . ?
    He isn't.   Isn't what?   Receptive.   To what?   Ideas.
Oh don't be silly—you're not receptive to ideas.   That's true.   We
all have our failings darling, don't don't—don't cross my . . . ah ah—do
you see this? A human bite.   Lemme see—some prick tried to get
through my whole finger. It wasn't! It was two weeks ago—but now it's
gone. What am I going to tell the Mayor?   Why don't you you come
around more often?   Where, where, where, where? Where can I come
around?   Lucky's basement.   Don't be silly.   Smoke pot in his
basement.   Ball Lucky in his basement, Lucky's oher . . . . whada
ya mean blow pot in his basement?/What's this?   I'm goin to speak to
the mayor now   may I see something?   hol-hold it . . . .
But may I see it? It has gold pages that I like, gee . . . she's not there,
Rotten Rita's out! Ro—I bet Rotten Rita's behind the rock in he park.
    Rotten Rita's maybe getting rocked.   She she's gave me rocks
grrrr lucky I think . . .   so come over for dinner whenever you get
hungry   where?   my house   in Queens?   yeah   oh, and then
my I can't Lucky I can't I, I the family scene now would be just redic-
ulous I'd rather blow my brains out—as I well do now—Bleck **yahhhhhhh**
get out!   I'm going this guy gave me amphetimine it kept me up all
nite   UMMMMM I love amphetimine I love amphetimine I love
a mphetimine   yeah that s you r life   what life?   amphetimine
    amphetimines not my life—my religion—my life is so much my dick
is my life my balls are my husband and myass is my mother in law Now
you have the whole family tree my tits are 2 children— . . . . the hairy
outter arms—now just you r eyes—forget it . . . you don't even see
correctly.   Color hairs? Do you color your hair in different   never
    do you kno—thats the same reason I recognize you—as you are—
your voice.   Oh but, and that's changed completely.   No—your
voice.   My voice has changed completely—honestly I have a terr . .,

my voice has changed completely and I know what I'm talking about. What, how you say it and how you phrase it and how you word.   You mean me that's another story. I happen to be an individual; that's all its easily recognizable.   Yes, it's easily recognizable.   Isn't it true? It's true, well because I'm drunk, no I'm not drunk, I'm really . .   No, no, n othat's Ondine.   There's a lot more to me than meets the filthy eye.

(RONAL) Yeah, you certainly would say that "There's a lot more to one that meets the filthy eye."   (O) You don't have to say everything please Ronal. You're trying to make a mockery out of me in my own. (R) No, I'm not, I' mnot.   (O) I know you're not.   (R) You know, you're typically Ondine. You're, you're not . . .   (O) Oh are you seri- ous? I hate to be t-typical.   (R) Typically Ondine.   (O) You, you know, know what you can do to those people across the street at the Y? Oh yes, you can see a whole—have you ever sat at dinner and seen a whole group of yourselves eating oh ho ho that's fun . . . twelve people eating you. Good night boys, sleep tight. No I'm talking to the railroad boy.

(LL) A, a burp. Looks like syphillis.   Katunga.   Oh, I haven't been in the river to insure candidates. We've got to do sound.   (PAUL) Music huh.   You're coming with us?   Where are you going?   Uh uh Irving's   Aaaaaagh!   We have to.   I say if Judy Garland's there . . .   No, no.   eating spaghetti and sniveling, I'll faint. Oh no please Drella I don't want to see.   See you kids. (Pause.)   Here's a match, AHZUCHAINA. I heard your voice reputing Taxine. Oh ho ho that's what I think of you in wood, hey Rink, Rink psst, La Gurda; This is your right?   (RINK) Yeah.   May I borrow it for this evening? To wear it?   Sure.   You're a doll; this is divine   Really. I bought it from a hustler.   What is it? Ohhhhhh! Well it's a hustler-type piece. It's soo Bette Davis and beyond the forest. No, you're not allowed to make a call. Tell me what this looks like tho . . . it looks good with a palid shirt and then this, like this.   It feels funny sometimes when you wear it like this, it it feels, gets tight on the shoulders.   Ridiculous, like Gerella Massina. (Pause.) That's a tortle -g-g-giggle and laugh and don't care look.   Ask him if he can.   We're at rests. What's the giggle question, what is the giggle question. I never . . .   The kind of question wh, you asked me before.   Oh, that one, oh that makes everybody giggle; isn't it funny? You should make them flex.Boing!   Does this look horrid?   No.   I think it looks rather uh, a new gamée. I think, I just . . .   Huh?   Oh I gotta wash my feet; I hate dirty feet with sandals. Hummmmmmm. (60-second pause and the sound of washing feet.) Is everybody ready?   I think so.   Oh come. Yeah cut out lwts just—oh oh trouble trouble ahead oh 9oh drugs.   who's that?   I won't it's hard it's I won't lose it I promise, Not like I lose the amphetamine an

anyway. I'm so sick of lasing that fucking drug (pause) who? It's fucky
Nancy (pause) oh oh where is it (long pause) (noise of children)
what're you doing?   all right darling I'm terribly sorry I just put it off
aminute ago.   I mean uh   I just put itoff one minute ago. It's right
here.   where are you gonna be later? Do you know or   well yeah and
then I'll uh   which oneyou want?   Do you know where you're going
to be tonight cause I might g to New Jersey and uh   what part of New
Jersey?   uh   well, uh early I don't know y'know I mean uh it's up
to there people (pause) do you feel all right Ondine   then huh
are you all right   No I'm going to put it in the sink.   GERARD
Should I come up in the morning, then?   Well I'm not sure wh what
time we we're going   I'll put it in apie e of tin foil the uh now
shall I get you a piece of tin foil the uh now   shall I get you a peice
o rreaach over here   I think just   Why don't you leave word with
your answering service?   okay oh why don't you tell meor lea ve word
where you're gonna be   okay   you're going to be at 70'd right
yeah, I'll probably be   that machine doesn't have a number—can you
belive? d do you know how long that took?   Diane was up here.
yeah   D ebby too?   I don't think so   what do you think of
Lucky L?   Oh we'll see, I'll Lucky, as soon as Ondine's down I'll be
right down. Bye Gloria.   As soon as Ondine's puts it in we'll come
right down.   Baby, what do yo uthink of Lucky L?   Are you going
downtown?   No, up to uh Irving's   Once in a while, you know he
has magnificent ideas and they really pay that's Lucky Lucky.   Lucky
who?   Lucky L.   Oh.   But but he he sounds a little right now.
    Yeah he's a fairy isn't he?   No he's not.   Really?   Isn't that
isn't that amazing?   That's weird, oh he's so   he's dying to be a
fairy but   yeah   but but he never will   really oh because Irish
are very strange . . .   Never will he's brother is a boxer and uhm I understand should be even more of a fairy than he should but do you know
    what it took to get fuckin Gloria out of here?   huh   Isn't it
annoying? But do you see how long she waited well, she really gets a
pest. She really is a pest Drella, Levine called did you get the message
already?   Are you gonnabe in the movie with Josephine or   No no
she called about gettinga girl for a movie   Oh oh y ou gave her athe
girl?   I didn't   Oh   I forgot   went out of it too   Went out
ofwhat?   when he said "All rightwe'll callyou at the place and make
6,9 hours each" wasn't that funny? Paul Paul isawfully nice.   yeah
uh uh   It's like baking a cake   I's so delicious oh Drella (pause)
I'm already to go (pause) oh I wouldn't ve minded, oh wait cigarets I
have them all over, I wouldn't mind staying here her name wasn't here
you're leaving here?   Hey Gerry—   what?   goodnight   good

night   Good night Do we lock this up?   oh shall I close it?
okay   oh, so calle me later and leave a message where you're gonna be.
    Lucky L had it, I don't know where it couldhave   Okay Gerry.
oh yeah   well you just look at the ball that I makethe amphetamine is
    Gerry   Is the el up   yeah oh it's beautijul ball with the amphit-
iminethat I made   oh really oh   look at it it's hysterical   huh
look at thething   it's so big   It's just a little bit in it. Okay darling.
    oh really   She knocks me out I can' tstand her. (*Elevator door
opens.*)
These people really look exhausted.

5 /   1

. . . and who was that man that she dragged in?

I don't know.

He wasn't bad, but uh he kept looking at me like this. He opened his eyes and opened his mouth and looke dat me. Hey you gotta tell us about the things that happened, honey Taxine, you've got to tell us about the interview please.

We've got a place—

No oh . . .

We're gonna go to Lexington.

Let's get a cab. Taxee!!!! Taxee my brace. (*Cars zoom by.*) I'll sit up front with him.

I know I'm just I'm (*traffic noise*) no uh listen . . .

RINK—5th and 1st Ave please.

DRIVER—Where?

(R) 59th and First.

59th and First yuh oh there's no more cigarettes in here.

That's we . . .

(R) Yeah.

So tell us about the interview.

Well just tell us a little bit.

Just tell us which one did you do first? Les Crane or what

(R) We went to a place on Madison Ave., a building, an eleven floor building which was the office for Nite Life.

Nite life is the *Merv Griffin* show.

(R) Nono Nite Life is *Les Crane*.

Oh.

Oh.

(R) And that's like a it's like they set up i there 3 nights ago and they got gas.

Yeah.

(R) And it's this really ratty place, y'know it's like and

(T) And we told them even y'know like, we wouldn't be there til half an hour later.

(R) We came there a half an hour late, but we called to ask if we could and they said yes but when we got, it was like a Grand Central Station because you had to walk into the office, it was very difficult to keep up a conversation when . . .

Was was there an audience.

(R) No it's just that there was a girl who was sort of in charge of the thing fairly nice, someone fairly bright and fairly sensitive also had her own sick ideas and things.

(T) She also wasn't pretty, wasn't young and . . .

She was wasn't . . .

(T) Had a few hangups.

(R) She she was 28.

(T) Yeah.

Had a few hangups!

Oh and she had th—

(T) She I mean . . .

Oh.

She looked as though she were having a rough time. Look at her, like she looked as if she were, she might not have been but she did look it.

Do you remember that reporter from the *N. Y. Times?*

(T) I mean her hair was scraggly and her expression was somewhat . . .

With that sweet expression on her face.

Did she like you?

(T) Well she was very interested in the process.

Yeah.

(R) She was she was . . .

(T) And Rink told her all about the movie thing and I sort of did a thing about how that was the point and . . .

(R) This . . . very interested in what's happening the Men . . .

(T) We don't really know.

(R) They don't they don't know what they're interested in, so now . . .

(T) But neither do we know how to communicate with them.

Did Les Crane uh interview?

(R) Les Crane didn't.

DRIVER The east side of Lex Ave? Right.

He wasn't there but nobody was sitting in his seat.

Right right right no that's right this is the . . .

(R) And uh there was a man who was there when we arrived who—

(T) He was very awful and like and he had his feet up . . .

(R) Fat Drella y'know and he had his feet up . . .

One second one second that's uh . . .

(R) Very rude.

That *Les Crane's* better better snap it up.

⎧(R) Without knowing it.⎫
⎩Y'know what I mean?   ⎭

Cause he he is is

(R) Yeah.

About the *Merv Griffin* show that that may be too much of a family type thing.

(R) Yeah.

(T) Well, they they were, they the man who interviewed us, wa like I told them, well first of all after we got into the first interview . . .

Can I have a match please?

(T) I don't know how to I don't know whether—

It it's all right just

(R) So first we weer basically left alone with a girl after about 10 minutes, so the man . . .

This is sick.

(R) talked about Taxi's—

(T) Except the man was as though he never even listened to what we were saying.

(R) No he was just sizing you up.

(T) And also he kept asking . . .

No, I know the man, and was he, I know the man from the *Les Crane* show . . . no uh a young guy named uh Smith.

(R) There was another there's a young guy in the room . . .

Smith.

(R) He's so . . .

Oh an Italian guy.

(R) Oh yeah he was he was owner wasn't his name Louis?

Yeah.

(T) They're they're the ones that told us that they didn't take Drella.

Yeah that's the one.

(R) He was the coy one.

Drella what?

(T) They said they didn't take Drella's movies.

(R) He's saw, he didn't like Harlot but . . .

Oh I know that—

(T) And then I was aying that what I was doing is very boring he . . .

(R) Liked you.

(T) But but but my point of view what happeend is first of all it was very y'know it very officially saying the process. And then I said . . .

DRIVER Would you keep a quarter out of here.

(R) Getting exhausted.

(T) No I guess I better . . . okay.

(R) see, it'd be silly . . . (noise).

Oh I have it.

Blahhhhhhgh (honk honk honk HONK!*†!!).

Is that enough? Do you think he's beeping for us?

I don't know. I hope not

Oh . . . it's Alexander.

(R) That's mine.

I got a feeling of the same streetness. OH I would spend the night there, in 400.

You did with who?

With somebldy else, a Greek.

The place is so dirty.

(O) Look at my feet (Drella laughs.) I couldn't get out because Gloria was in the bath was was 4 in the sink all the time. Oh I was the only, I've gotta take . . . I feel filthy.

Huh?

that . . . who was scratching his head.

Yes this is the same place.

Is it? You said you've never been on the east side.

upper in the 89's

Irving du Ball.

We're the Irving da Ball fan club. The Irving du Bull Fan club.

(T) This is the first no but the other was the process it wasn't the people it was the process.

(R) Merv Griffin is

(T) And what's we're . . . he doesn't mean that.

(R) He couldn't find way to

(T) It was all one interview but we were just 2 people—yeah and there was nothing but process.

(R) This gurgly old man pity and he was in that y'know

(T) Well I don't know what to say

(R) And he was in, uy'know uh

(T) I sat down and

(R) In Sardi's and grabbed drinks and he said he said a lot of things that weren't funny and sort of overly . . .

Ohhhhhh.

(T) Well he's a goose, I mean but so what can you say?

Well that's the kind of thing that he's . . .

(T) So, I just just told him but I also was reacting to the other interview which seemed to me too processed.

Yeah.

(T) But Rink explained the whole process was correct but but I really didn't say anything about why I thought eithter of us knew what we mean.

(R) But that's after the part where she said she was she was

Oh quit it.

(R) It was an adolescent who was interested in playing games but that wasn't it at all you two are

(T) No but she said that one instant like, what you said also I might have said.

(R) But three three quarters of the interview

(O) I hope you're going to explain t-to us what what went t-t-t-ook place because it it's it's not happening you two are so far into it now, that we have to that we have to wait until we see it.

(T) They're all a bunch of maniacs.

Oh no it's not so it's just summer.

(R) Very tired and it was

How can you say that uh we're gonna visit our hero Irv duBaller Our hero—

(T) Who said that?

(O) Irving du Ball we're going to the uh our fan club, yeah we're the Irving du Ball fan club aren't we?

Yeah oh oh oh oh.

How awjul oh the person . . .

Who can?

(O) I can't bear being this dirty, but Gloria wouldn't get out of the seat.

(T) Do you want a . . .

(O) So don't don't try to explain to her what happeend, because you two ate totally . . . y'know.

(T) Yeah, I know.

(O) And it it's so confusing it's obviously that you two are enjoying it y'know.

(T) No no it's the worst part of it was we were all playing ourselves.

But I wish we were there we were there.

(T) And they're not quite the same.

Oh, I like what they did to your hair. I like what they did to your hair.

(T) Oh a witch—they did it.

I like that. It should be a little more silver but I like it.

It's golden it's I'll have to put it back again there you are . . .

Oh yeah.

(T) Yeah. How are you?

There you are the hotel boy delivering groceries there you are.

Is that he's not the delivery boy he's the Schrafft's boy. Is isn't he?

That was fast . . . she'll be a little bit older that way.

The Duchess, there you are she said.

That's weird wow nice.

May maybe he hates us. Maybe Judy's there and she wants to sing of well wait'll he sees filthy Ondine.

While you were recognized she doesn't know who Drella was.

Oh really? she told me that . . .

I'm, I have a terrible cold.

(T) I did that's it.

You're weak, you were about to die so I'm taking a bath so just wait . . .

(T) It's you're . . .

I'm Dimita we're all together.

I am D-Dimita Dunn.

You're Dimita Jones?

I'm Dimita Jones.

Hello.

Oh aren't we special? After you.

IRVING—After you Ondine, if you don't shut that fucking machine.

Oh, but you can't he can't. It's . . .

It's uh I'm following Ondine.

He can't leave me alone.

(I) I've never seen such . . .

Look at the dirt.

(T) Throbs and throbs (C) no but

(O) Irving, may I use your bathroom?

(T) Can can I save this?

(I) Yes, I think you should. . . . While we're here . . .

Look at this, of course you could come with us.

(I) Are you serious?

(O) I—Gloria Savage was in the sink with her children for 2 hours.

Should we use the private or the uh?

The private, would they all know how to climb to to come in. (Rock and Roll.)

Oh lovely oh oh oh food excuse me.

I'm following Ondine all day today soanyhow.

And I want to be saved.

(I) I don't want them in my room.

He said show.

(I) It's a private room.

It's it's a bathroom—oh I don't know this.

He's afraid they're scared they're afraid of us—they're

(I) No no no no no no.

If you want to know I have an orange and purple . . .

. . . put this record on if you like it . . .

. . . heaven . . .

How long?

Oh what a snubbing turn to the public bath.

Why am I carrying 2 dimes in my pocket?

You're like that. Who's that boy?

Why can't you go and make it with him?

I don't know, I guess he wants to keep us away from you or something. I don't understand all this who are you anyway?

He's Peter NOTHING.

Peter how do you do? I'm y'know, Peter Nothing, how do you do? I'm y'know, I feel like a slut being thrown into the public bathroom. Huh? It's all right.

We can do all kinds of wonderful things without—

Really?

I have materials now we can . . .

Really?

(D) You're gonna take a bath?

(O) I have to Drella, I feel like the original piece of filth. (Pause.)

What?

I suppose we ought to leave the door open. (Drella speaks.)

It's all right Taxine's O.K. she's different she's the new kind of girl (heavy breathing).

Really? Oh my camera I goofed.

Nobody can who has truly blushes, you'll never know that, you'll be tormented with it

You're wearing Rink's coat.

Yeah I asked him—

Do you know that?

(O) Now what else do I need?—Sedatea—what is this? This is called Rinse all oh what woulld this be us it smells like wine.

It is wine—ugh. Take a bath.

(O) Here dear, all right I'll jump into the tub—I have to have all kinds of medications you know—

Dorothy Gray—Hole cream . . . it's ass hole cream (*laughter*) wha— it was a very nice day today Drella wasn't it—how do you like that? we didn't get along with Dick after—uhh EXPOSED —do you believe it? A terd in our midst.

Really?

(O) That was a terd, why must I be faced with these vicious . . . it was a full-fledged terd—I saw it. I swear to you Drella—I don't lie.

Why don't you take a shower?

(O) Oh because they're so Janet Leigh you know I'm always afraid of being stabbed I really am—in fact it scares the shit out of me— I wonder if I can use the razor too—oh no, very smart Irving, look at this do you want to see something funny? What what what do you want me to do? Take a bath in a coal shute? Little rusty ain't it—I I I wouldn't even wash my mother's feet in that I'm going to let it out—I

don't expect anybody to understand—thank god I have something substantial to hold on to (*laugh*).

Take a shower.

(O) What a strange bar of soap— I'm terrified in in this rusty sloth. I think Arlene Judge was here yesterday.

Oh I'm starved.

(O) Yeah oh I love fogs or fens oh wens oh wen; what's the difference between a wen and a wart?

I don't know.

(O) A wen is some some something————that was brushstroke—this should be a mirror —I hate to be like that—I hate to say things that upset people.

What?

(O) Oh don't mind m—I'm mumbling to myself these these are my pre-bath prayers then I have after-bath prayers which I include Sataris Bete—oh—

Talk louder.

(O) Okay Darling! we don't need them—now I am taking a bath this is an ONdine this is water—that is a sound of water (*sound of water*) that . . . it's the sound of music, can you imagine it? Drella—I'm getting to that filthy pun stage where where I throw out every line that's in my reservoir and I get embarrassed by it. . . . I must sail ch—for this razor—oh my hand was inside I need a new one and that one's old whose shave is that? guy kippy? He shaves his feet with it. Now rrrrrejecet! I'm very carefree—I don't care anymore what happens to me Drella I what kind would be better—the bog? Still very rusty—it's also very hot it's still very rusty . . . do you think they're trying to kill me them—are they trying to kill me? Is that enough noise? Here we are at Niagara Falls and Marilyn Monroe is about "kiss kiss me—say you miss miss me" oh I can't go on with these imitations—I'm going to soak as soon as I shut that off we'll be in business . . . who is that boy? Is that Irving uh . . . who is it HOT I believe it . . . it's full of sections, very good oh oh oh I enjoyed the earlier part of today so much like when

when we got to the factory for the first time—
What?
(O) When we first got to the factory we— were wasn't that fabulous? And that silly Steve—he's got really do you know what he wanted to find out? whether or not we were going to the film that's all—this won't get the h—cooler what is the matter with it? Maybe it's the rusty water or something (pause) huh? Is that enough I'm talking very low—I'm talking very low I I oh if it weren't for these legs Drella you I really would have to give up . . .IhopeIdon't sufferfrom overexposure—cut right off in the butt of my career wouldn't that be a terrifying feeling oh welcome to Allen Ginsberg with his indians. Why did he go to India —Was it to find peace and contentment? This is a marvelous bath doesn't he have any little ducks or something that I could float around here—a little duck or an old boat or something.
It's great your ahhh
(O) It's filthy, it's got rusty water, I'm not even gonna let the water sit set in, I'm gonna unplug it now I'll drink all the soap at once.
(?) Ondine I'm throwing that in.
(O) See when I bathe it's like a holy thing with me . . . I like as many bars of soap as possible . . . Drella really you must stop with t-t-thing I'm gonna electrocute myself—it's electric you know—Drella it is so incredibly annoying—what did I do that for? Someone told me my veins were popping . . . and last nite they may have been. Is there a glass in here? Nooooo. Why don't you play some of it back I'd love to hear any of it   most STIMULATING . . . it it would would would be nice to hear Dr-Drella, really would—on days like this . . . excuse me americans . . . (pause) something fucking—this is no private—may I ask you in all fairness—this is no private—it's really not bad at all as a matter of fact it's more or less what I go through every day . . . you know what you do—would you get me a washcloth—
(?) Oh no here what's that for?
It it makes the sound softer—it looks like an . . . you won't mind I'll I'll I'll try it—you want me to shower and get the car out don't you?
I don't know what to do.
(O) . . . . . drink of water if you'll get me a cloth—a washcloth that that washes—no, he doesn't have any rags—ouvrez de la grue.
Hmmmm
(O) Ouvrez de la grue;that's uh I hate to be I hate to loaf
What?
I like activity—I like activity.
You do?

(O) Look, this builds a little dam how many of these do you have in there?

Five.

(O) How many more do you have?

Seven more.

(O) That's not bad.

Seven more hours.

(O) I know, I said that's not bad, we'll be taking off into complete lunatic at the end of it—if they don't put me away before then they never will. That's a very hard technique to grasp—I'm watching the dials the light boy and what else exists.

Really?

(O) I wanna be triple fast and whenever you say fantastic I realize that you mean it . . . what—darn it damn it looks like he's wearing make up . . .

(D) Is he?

(O) I don't think so, but he looks like he is. Uh Peter uh what's his name Paul Myerson is just so nice—isn't he nice, he really is a very sweet man. Drella, what does he do? . . . is he us

(D) He makes his own movies—

(O) He does?

(D) Yeah nobody knows except uh nobody knows except him.

(O) No one does is right—he will not say he's probably very perverted.

(D) Oh really?

(O) Which would be divine wouldn't it?

(D) Do you think so?

(O) He might be which would be heaven—he should be.

(D) Usually people aren't I mean . . .

(O) What? Oh yes.

(D) You know the sicker ones are really the perverted ones—

(O) The sicker ones—yeah I mean I I don't know a lot of them are a you know like the ones who wrote the ones who don't speak well are the ones that that are . . .

(D) Well the Irish are really . . .

(O) The Irish are fanatical about it.

(D) Is Lucky L Lucky L an Irishman?

(O) Lucky L, Lucky L should be gay shouldn't he? He's been acting like that for years.

(D) Oh really?

(O) And he will not, he's not gay he went so far as when I was going out with Jimmy Copper he used to uh come into the bathroom and grab his fly and take it down and all you know we conned it on him we said well you know what the fuck do you want? and obviously he wanted nothing but to do that.

(D) Pretty cock?

(O) I I I I never saw it. I never saw it I never tried to—it again after the the one time cause it we we just I had so much fun with him on his uh mo-motorcycle that I just it wasn't necessary as a matter of fact—it looked good anyway. And and he'd get get his girlfriends to—like in a party where I was the only . . .

(D) How old is he?

(O) About 23 or 4 . . . there would be a party say for a a Halloween party or some something nasty like that and I would go because all of my friends were there and I was like the only one who was gay or something but I wouldn't wear pants and everytime I bent down you saw a tired cock in my ass they just went ohhhh they were really—so one girl said to me "Are you a queer?" and he put it up to her, you know that's that's that's exactly what you know he's really funny I said "Lucky are yo ugonna set her hair on fire or am I?" She got so, then she rode in the car back with us and she was uh terrified, she was she was knee high up to here, she was uh about 17 years old and her name was Linda, and awful stupid.

(O) Now the finishing touch . . .

(D) You're gonna shave.

(O) But the next thing is this doll —hear this dahling? I don't shave, I'll got to rattle in the window—and leave a light burning. Why did you leave with that boy—why why did you I know there was something odd about him—but I didn't know if it were it's it's because he's not gay I think I think I thought the phone answered like Taxine— anybody . . . the films . . . I'm wondering my dear, did you see Buddy in those bags with the oh he was so funny . . . . . Is Buddy Jewish?

(D) Huh?

(O) Is Buddy Jewish?

(D) What? Uhu yeah.

(O) Is Buddy Jewish?

(D) Yes.

(O) Norman is so funny he called the Factory the other day—and he says (muffled) "Hullo can I speak to Billy Name" and I said "Who is this?" he says "It's Norman" I said "Norman, why do you sound like that?" he said "I'm trying to disguise my voice." Henri is the water on yet? "Fuck you" he said "Hullo" but just one line he's so—water is my weakness what's very funny—oh you're Leo that that's a very good planet oh yes there's jupiter that's the biggest planet . . . How many other Leo's around—Leo Slager, Leo Delon, uh sadistic sorrow . . . do I have briarpatch legs?

(D) No.

(O) Can I ask wow I

(D) Aren't you gonna shave in the bath tub?

No.

You're not? Why?

(O) Electric shaver, it's so much

fun cause I only shave one way.

(D) That's all.

(O) That's all I couldn't I would ruin my skin people'd go ACH.

(D) Oh you did so well—does it hurt?

(O) No not at all it's so easy like . . .

(D) Oh it didn't even cut . . . fantastic!

(O) I've got a straight razor, at home, Drella.

(D) Really?

(O) It's so beautiful. I got a leather strop to sharpen it, and uh I sharpened it for two hours and it wasn't sharp, it was still like stubble—and I wondered what the fuck it was, I had to get it sharpened on a stone first I remember, or somebody told me—isn't that marvelous? (*Sink drains.*) Do you remember when I was superintendent?

GLUG GLUG

(D) Oh yeah.

(O) Well that's where I got the bad routine from this Chinese man had died in his apartment.

(D) Yeah what did he give you?

(O) No he left in the apartment . . .

GLUG GLUG

(D) What?

(O) The most interesting things; let's see, like little bags, y'know, little little red envelopes and things just the most incredible things and he had bathing suits tied to chairs, tied, with the straps they were tied to the back of the chairs—it was the most fascinating apartment I'd ever seen . . . and it was all greasy and dirty there and he had the straight razor there it was ivory but it was made to look like bamboo, now why have imitation bamboo? You know isn't that a little silly? Have you given this shirt any thought at all? Neither have I. I don't uh, I can't think of a form for it. I mean a shirt would would be all right if it could work, if if it wasn't inopportune it would be fine. But if it was really good—then then then it would would be worthy of your name. But but ohhhhhh we're a little tired ay dearie? Can you imagine how I feel?

(D) Are you?

(O) I'm exhausted.

(D) Are you? Well I'm so tired that Mr. Mc Gerson Mr. Gerson will give us a a raise I'll scream—

(O) Dahling I really want an obertrol.

(D) What?

(O) I really want an Obertrol that thing Ondine's tired what kind of Pill?

(D) Six hours.

(O) O God, it seems like it's endless, will I ever, will I ever be free? No—luckily I know about it.

(D) What?

(O) Luckily I know about oh Drella oooooo oooooo I'm getting nervous.

(D) Why?

(O) My brain is SNAPping.

(D) Really?

(O) But I wish we could open the window.

Oh I know—please . . .

It's sealed.

OPEN THE DOOR. (*Sighs of relief and music.*)

No it's novel that it's being a novel as a matter of fact—vut what do you mean by a novel? uhhhhhh I know it just . . . there's no other brush stroke. 12 hours of Ondine a novel? qou're not going—are you going to put it in a in a book or what make it be one whole book really and was Steve gonna take some pictures you know I would rather have Billy Name take pictures—or something—he's a much better photographer—god Diane, the picture or her looks like posed French cinnamon . . . . . powder . . . . . refreshes . . . every little spot you look like an elephant I feel like an elephant and an elephant never forgets and it only eats vegetables— really? yeah—did you know that elephants were not meat eaters? no isn't that fabulous? Those big things and they only charge people when they're wounded or sick or tired—a powder room— . . . . . you dahling I feel like a young thing with you thank god I have perfect legs, I'd be sick about it, if it weren't for Higbsib's baby Powder I'd be sick about it, if it weren't for johnson's baby powder i'd be dead—I feel so fresh and new Drella like a million bucks—really like I have a friend at the Chase manhattan—taking a bath with you in the room is something special, and you with that microphone running on, you can't believe I mean people have been driven—they've been driven to peaks. And you've made me a new high, no actually y'know I don't fin dthis offensive, I really don't, honestly, it's very easy too but you just have to reflect for a moment, oh oh oh how, torment and hate. Uh you just have to reflect for one second and do you realize that I or I do any way What? Oh wha ooo who how ooo oh ha hooh a uh pain— uh that I— that that I'd be doing it with somebody else anyway. I'd be driving myself through—I wonder what these are? Oh. One a day —Doctor Belger—it doesn't sound like my doctor. It smells so pretty.

It's Canoe—I once knew somebody who said, "Canoe—that is evil smelling perfume." What does he mean evil? I wish there was some hair cream here. Oh Drella, my face is on fire, fire, fire, oh ohh. It'll go away. Oh feel it, it must be burning— It's cold. I can't believe —it's making me tear or my Open the door. I better get my Dixie Peach Palmette out of my bag—nigger hair cream. Oh really? Oh let me see it—sure. Look at these things, look at them they're marvelous. This is ta few mustard stains. Mustard? Yeah, I was eating frankfurters one day. Mustard? Mustard—look at this one. Where did you get those? Rita. Oh. See the mustard on here, it

smells just uh—I had a black piece of material in here.   Oh, are you
going to wear that today?   Oh no. I've got so much to show you. What
kind of material is this? It's rather, uh, it's a 12, it's a 12, it's a twee, don't
you like those little pieces of . . .   Yah.   It's a new sample. (*Laughs.*)
Let's see, I gotta get my Dixie Peach why why it's for nigger hair cream.

How come?   I went in there only to get my nigger hair cream. Isn't
it heaven?   Give it a bath.   What?   Give it a bath.   Sublime.
Uh it's (*giggle*) give it a bath? Oh, you're—maybe you're right.   Oh
you won't be able to put it away.   What?   You won't be able to
put it away.   Well, if I just washed the outside I would.   Uhhh.
With a sponge. With a sponge. The inside is brilliant gold. Dixie Peach
Palmade. That's the best thing for hair—you can't imagine—it's nice and
thick.   How does it feel up your ass?   Huh?   How does it feel up
you rass?   How does it feel up your ass?   Where—that? Oh please
like glue . . .   Oh—was it terrible?   Yeah—I hate lotions of any
kind.   Really?   Once in a while they're necessary and all but I hate
them—I'd much rather mucous were used, it's the only way . . .
Really?   It's the only way (*pause*). I'm glad my underwear coming
from behind.   They're wet.   I was ju, I was no, no, I was talking to
Rita on the phone and they snapped.   The cord snapped, it . . .
Oh, really?   It just snapped, it it   I said said, told Rita, please get
off the phone, I . . . she was exasperated.   Have all the money you
want.   And in other words . . .   Huh . . .   . . . d-do that.   I
never saw a cock worn sideways.   Well I can't wear it he other way
if it's, it'll break. Like this it should be worn?   No. Sideways.   Well
well sh-should it be like that? Or should it . . .   Yeah.   Sh-should it
b etwo-way draping pricks ins . . '. (*laughter*). Darling, I think it should
be draped that way . . . . . solution.   What is that?   Bad news?
Oh it is?   It's heaven, it's so vile.   Do you make it with water?
Uh, I make this one with iced tea.   Oh.   Do you want some?
No.   It's quite good. I never know the difference. (*Pause and Taxie's
voice in background.*) Do you think I should wash some?   Hmm.
I really should?   Yeah . . . . . (*Laughter.*)   You mean the thing, I
shoudl keep it there?   Yeah.   Dirty.   Open up your pants, yeah
go ahead . . .suitcase.   Yeah, well I live out of it, y'know I mean I, I
have to.   Have you gone home recently?   No, I haven't been home
in two weeks.   Oh really? Fantastic.   . . . . . . insurance.   Insurance?   I need a quick dose of the Duchess's.   I feel terrible that.

Yeah.   Terrible. Sure we can, I'd love to see, I think it's open til,
til 9 o'clock.   Oh.   (*Pause.*)   You can leave any time you like to.

Oh no, I have to see you go into the tub.   Oh, I don't mind. I
mean as long . . .   Hmm.   . . . . .said we could rob him . . . . .

would be fabulous . . . . .   When?   . . . .12:15 and I was talking to you o-over the phone.   Billy was wrong so.   Yeah I know but, yeah but I mean but, the way he, the way you reacted to it really touched me so beautifully that I didn't know what to do. I just—of course I should never have told Walter anything.   Oh.   Cause telling Walter anything is ridiculous.   What did you tell Walter?   I told Walter, I said Drella just moved me so incredibly and y'know he didn't understand and he resented it.   Oh really?   I never was and never will be. Why not?   No, what for? Oh could you imagine. Oh . . .   Where is Walter now?   I hope he's in Bellevue where he belongs. I know I'm gonna be going there if he doesn't get settled down. Look at the bruise.   How'd you get that?   I don't know; I think the Duchess was poking me an . . .   Huh.   Slaps.   Huh huh huh huh (pause). Gorgeous.   You have to, you . . . my hands, I'm so glad I didn't go to the doctor.   Oh fantastic.   It's almost time for the swelling has to go down in about two weeks. I wouldn't let them touch my forehead or anything. I don't trust them because I don't think they know what they're doing. In fact I'm sure they don't know what they're doing. (Pause.) I'm gonna wear a sweater with this.   Oh.   I don't have a tan for it. But y'know it doesn't . . . so . . . mut it's kind of . . .   Oh, it's for Gerard.

It's got an . . .air conditioning.   No.   It's hotter than in here . . . (voices get very low) . . . I don't believe what he stole. I don't mean what he stole . . . . . made out of paper reprief. Your hair is all wrong. Don't.   It's all wrong. Did you ever feel too . . . Is that good enough? It takes me some time but I can't see that it's high. It takes me sometimes three hours just to comb it with my fingers. I mean I could use a utensil to comb it not, I better brush my teeth too. I have a feeling I'm going to my mouth.   Really?   Don't you have the feeling that a whole her-herd of elephants have been charging in here? This is too, this is too garish (sigh. (Ondine whispers something.)   Oh look at . . .

What, what did you say to—the tone of your voice was so perfect, I'd have I'd have to, I couldn't tell him you were staying at the party. Oh please, oh please, oh please, I've never been any party like that. When you, when you the day that the party was filmed?   Yeah.   Oh please, oh plase, come please, I said (inhales) like when I saw the Boson jump in the water I didn't believe it. Did you ever tell me we have to make up . . . petition.   Oh really?   I find it very—somebody explained it to me once. You see I have an astigmatism in my ear and did you ever lose your balance in your middle ear?   No.   I did once.   Oh really?

Oh you can't get up off the, you just, you can't move. And get this, the doctor who came over to check on me, man, I couldn't lift my head off the pillow, said "You're killing your mother and father." Y'know he

meant because my mother said "Oh doctor, what are we gonna do with him?" And I just said to him, "Get out of here before I kiss you." Can you imagine coming over to treat me and telling and getting a psych, uh, psychol, psychiatry lesson? He also, I also went into the office once and he tried to hypnotize me into "stop talking." Really?   He said "Wham" and I said, he said, "You're not going to smoke anymore." I said "Really?" I said, "Do you have a light?" He said, "You don't stutter" and I went, "Duh that the" (*laughter*). I couldn't bear him, Doctor Schwaslinger or Doctor, what was his name, Doctor, Doctor Schlod, Doctor Schlesinger, I don't know, he's across the street and he's awful. Here's another one but this isn't . . .   N-no, what you have on is nice. You sure?   Yeah.   This is too sleezy. You tie old green, I . . . (*laughter*) I owe a billiard to you, you'll feel a lot better.   Put your footsy.   Put what?   I'll take a pill and I'll give you some pills too.
   Okay, good, we'll, we'll make some iced tea.   Oh, I'll get some uh, no.   It's not, it's not a bad solution. Oh all I know is you're (*laughter*) just a toothache. Whew. (*Taxie's voice in the background.*) Ten years I . . . I've been related . . .   Hey, there's . . . didn't saw you you feel a draft.   No, it's all right.   (T) *in background*—It's so awful, he's thirty something.   You'll feel it in.   Who's thirty something? Who's thirty something?   (*In background.*) Is there a way to . . .
   Certainly not the Beatles.   And he said all the knowledge in the world? (*Surfin' Use is background music.*)   I'm meeting the Beatles, Taxina.   When?   Uh, next week.   But, they're, they're not half as interesting as the Stones.   Oh no.   Uh, ever since that, I mean htere's one song on their new album that shows. I think Mick Jagger must be great.   Yeah.   He must be.   Uho, wa, is is he the leader?   Yeah. I really think he must be, and I, I must say I'm a bit bored with the Beatles even though they were great, but they're all taken care of. There's nothing really exciting. There's nothing exciting about them? I don't know, I just uh well like, I thought that Elvis Pres, er Elvis Presley . . .   Oh well Elvis.   would never go out, but he did, he did.   Yeah but on the other hand he's old.   . . . went like this, errgh, I nearly died.   Oh, oh really, oh.   But he's so's   Oh yeah but he, he'll always be famous.   Oh, to me he's really great. Really have you ever heard of hte Stoneheads?   The Beatles are great.
   Oh they were aw.   Nice put it in a bag.   No huh huh huh you're a care job (*Record: recording*)   Look at that, he's bringing it back.   Oh, Ondine is getting so . . .   Isn't it a little bit too Ruth Warwick?   Huh huh huh huh. (*Recordin background:*
)   Put your palmade away.   Oh, if they see that, they'll know I'm ab, not to ruin. (

) Surfin'   We're all wearing hand-me-downs. Mine's a
hand-me-down too.   It doesn't fit anywhere. Air refresher. Prickly,
prickly. (*Ondine sprays.*)   Oh, oh no oh, Ondine.   Where's that?
We'll settle it . . . filthy hole. I make the sweetest dresses.   Huh?
What book are you reading?   Oh, *History of Wit and Magic*.   Oh.
And uh.   You're All Witch?   Huh, no, no, no, I just wanted
to, I was reading about the Jews the other day. I couldn't believe it.
There's one sentence in there that, about them feeding the children to
the guard . . .   Really, wow.   Oh it's horrible. It's frightening about
the germicide. Isn't that better, a little comic relief. (*Pause.*)   What
shoes are you going to wear?   Huh?   What shoes?   Oh why didn't
you tell me that you were going to uh.   Oh, I didn't know, I'm gonna
live in there. I had such a good time in your bathroom. I thought you
were rtying to kill me at first.   I wish *muffled talking* .   Oh really?
Yeah, Billy said he'd be . . .and then he said it'd be all right.   Oh.
So I said . . .   Terrific.   And I have never taken them off.
Oh.   Is that still on?   Yeah.   Don't ever play this . . .   Why,
you coming up?   Yeah, in a minute. I just wanna slit my wrists. ("*Ooh
ooh . . .*   )   What ever happened to Meredith Willson?
I don't know; let's go out on the terrace.   Yes, and thank you.
(*With record*) Marsha, Marsha . . . got a pilly?   Huh?   Let's take
a little pilly here . . . I, I need it.   Let's get some out here. ("*Oh
oh . . . .*") Dhat?   Get a drink of water. Let's have some, like just
zip it up and put my stole on, and then we'll go out on the terrace.
. . . . . or leaving. They wouldn't object, heavenly . . .   What . . .
No one would object to . . .   Moxanne is coming here to meet you.
Oh.   Who's Moxanne?   Moxanne's a French girl whom I know,
who's been in Europe a while and just came back. She's fantastic. She's
very, she's very, got cute shoulders but she's uh . . .   Bulls a or diesel
. . .   She, uh, she has certain, she thinks she's . . . . . (?) but she's
really a nymphomaniac, she's . . .   Oh God.   But she doesn't uh,
she's so bright that you uh . . .   She's no Chicky the Wormgirl?
No, she's really, she's very nice, she's, she just finished a script that I'm
gonna ·borrow.   Did uh, well uh, I mean is there something gonna
happen from any of those two things?   Uh, it's all . . . really happening, yes uh.   Yes oh.   I mean uh, more so in Nite Life than Nite
Life, I'm calling Nite Life Monday.   Why?   Cause they wanna
know about the film. I wanna talk o, find out about it.   Oh uh, they
shoulld, it's bad.   But did you do it once before? You gave it . . . . .
No, it's just a bad scene because they shouldn't ever know what Taxina
. . . like.   It's just like selling you really, it's a bad scene.   Does anybody want . . .   Play play play.   Four minutes of . . .   Oh, you

can, no.   Oh, that's what's taking me.   No, no, no, it varied is it, uh, no.   It's probably.   Huh? Coming in? For pills?   Ye-yes, thank you . . . fine. Do you know where Rotten Rita is?   Here, here, here, thank you.   Ooh huh huh.   Oh uh, oh, who's playing, the Three Sons? or the Four Daughters?   What is that? Beautiful.   Isn't that marvelous?   It's awful.   That's something.   Did you work tha something out with uh, Rink   Oh you can . . .   Wha . . .   . . . talking about the speak . . .   Oh, and they went oh, Drella.   . . . his weekend.   Are you, you gonna be off this weekend?   Darling (*breathless*).   What?   They want us to have some some five minute film things.   I told him that . . .   (*banging noise on door.*)
Well, I can't understand how we can in five minutes. They're gonna get the idea, but also . . .   Y'know . . . they wanna see what's happening.
    Let's go out, you can the film.   So hot.   Huh? Oh, oh is it nice? Can you hold this for a minute, I'll find you a pill. Oh, it's in my pocket? How many?   Two . . . they're very good.   How many do you want?
    Two. Oh, that's uh, beautiful, Twenty more . . . yeah, please, look at the bridge, it oh, but but, before that got stuck in the throat I'll get us a drink. What do you wanna drink? Just a second, what would you like to drink?   Uh, just something.   Uh, water or uh . . .   Oh, Drella, you're out. I thought you'd gone.   Can we have a drink of some knid?   Water.   Water or uh . . .   Although looks like . . .   I don't . . .   The situation is, coresponds . . .
(O) Just spurn me, I'll stand on the terace all by myself with the thing . . . TAXI—No, they mix it.
IRVING—I don't want to be on camera.
(O) All right, then we won't, well then I won't speak to you; I'll I'll go off up here, you just nod, padon me, could you tell me if I can have uh, who, *Otto Preminger* should be put away.
(T) What does Ondine want?
(O) What, I hate that man, I'm trying to block up the sound. Would you please give m something to drink? I don't know where it is, uh . . .
(I) What about a glass of water, Ondine?
(O) Uh, waater, or uh, uh, soda or something like that.
(I) Something non-alcoholic?
(O) Uh, no yeah, this is fine. If there are ice cubes and there are you can s-s-sit there, yeah, but Irving said that he wouldn't talk to us while this was on.
(T) No, I just need my thing and my . . .
(I) Here, this is vodka; I don't know who I have it for.
(O) No, not for me; just plain.
(I) Maybe here . . . vodka, somebody.

RINK—Anybody know if we can go to Europe in he next couple of days? (*Coughing.*)

It's groovy when he said he wouldn't.

Do you know Peter's going to Paris in he next few days?

(I) I'm sure Peter does.

(O) What's in here? What is that here?

(T) It's Coco-Cola.

(O) But look at this, four little . . .

(T) Oh, it's . . .

(O) Spots in here.

(T) It's . . . . (?)

(O) Oh, I nearly died; I thought it was ice cubes. I said, "How did they get those small ice cubes in there?" Drella look at this, a mildew coke. Sugar on top of it.

(I) Well, some of he people I know.

(O) It's mad.

(R) Would you like to spill it out, Ondine?

(O) No, it's so beautiful. Why spill it? It's a fabulous looking thing. (*Music:) I'm sorry, did you get the . . .

(R) She's supposed to be . . . like yesterday. (*Music, slow and drawly:) I have this trick of things where . . . (*Music:). What is this work? (*Music: "Ooooh oooh.   ) It doesn't. (*Music: "That meatball what was it?"* *fads out.   etc.)

(I) Uh, Ondine.

(O) Yes. *Music.* Yes buster. *Music.* What was that? Did you know what that meatball was? That was delicious. That meatball, what was it?

(T) Oh, I don't know.

(O) Mmmmm. very good.

(T) Ondine.

(O) Hmm?

(T) Yes, Ondine.

(O) You're getting strusted, strust, you're getting potted. No, it's marvelous. I wish I could get potted. I feel (pause) y'know, I can't get drunk. (*Music.*)

(T) Ha, ha.

Who's singing?

(T) Ha, ha, ha.

(R) It's the Beach Boys.

(O) Yes it is. Tra-la-la, sha-la-la, d-did Arnold Inoven tell you about meeting me on the street? and going to a place where they played cards? And he kibitzed.

(T) Ha, ha, ha.

(O) He kibitzed! He played, they plaed acey duecy, he sat and said, "How do you play this game?" Well he met me early in the morning and I was going to a drug store to get . . .

(R) Where?

(O) On 45th street and . . .

(R) About where?

(O) Between 7th, between 8th and Broadway.

R—Oh yeah?

O—And he said t-to me, "Come with me, and I said, "All right, I might as well." And uh, we went up to this boy's (*with emphasis*) apartment, and the boy, there was one colored boy and two and two white boys. They they were sitting around playing acey ducey and Arnold sat there and kibitzed.

I—Arnold Inoven.

O—Yes he was . . .

I—How do they play acey duecy?

O—Oh, I have no idea. I, I asked them to explain it to me and then the minute that they started I said, "Forget it."

I—Onesy twosy and acey duecey.

O—They said, no, no. This is three, two cards and they had and you had to be, oh it's impossible to play it; I wouldn't, I would never play the game. I got a headache immediately. I was horrified. I said, "I'll have to go, I'll have to go."

T—. . . This is too much. Uh ha.

O—Leave it all alone; it's a moral security. Mm hm. What do you think this is St. Patrick's Day my dear? (*Taxi laughs.*) Dorothy Lamour at the Versaille "Moon Over Malgiorgia" and it went

out. Come on audience, sing along. They, nobody sang; they sat there. Said, held over for two weeks. And she had an unlimited run when it started. (*Taxi laughs.*) Dorothy Lamour brought back by popular demand. "Moon over Mal . . . (*Surfin' music.*) da, da, da, da, ba, ba, baa. Oh Rita would . . . I wonder where Rita is. She's so furious.

T—Where is, maybe I should meet him.

O—You definitely should meet Rita.

T—I don't, I've always been afraid to because Ondine . . .

O—We're going to the hospital. No, no, we'll meet her at the hospital with the Duchess. She's so

—Rita Hayworth.

No, uh.

No, Rotten Rita.

Rotten Rita.

Rotten Rita, our may-our mayor.

She can meet Rotten Rita at the hospital. Have you heard where she is?

T—Oh, come on, don't.

No, what's her name, the Duchess is in the hospital.

The Duchess is in the hospital.

T—Which kind?

O—The Ethel Roosevelt Hospital.

She has, she has, she's ran, she, do you know what she got away with? The blood pressure machine. She's hiding it in her closet. She—

R—Where'd she get that?

O—3000 libriums; she went down the hall and stole it, yes she went, but how do you take a blood pressure machine? Isn't that fab

. . .

R—The whole population right in

. . .

O—And she's got, now she's got a doctor's coat and a little flashlight and a chart.

T—But Ondine, nobody may be

. . .

R—Rotten Rita or the Duchess?

O—The Duchess.

T—If I meet Rotten Rita I'll know he's fabulous.

R—The Duchess is something.

O—Rotten Rita's divine.

T—Crazy and mad.

O—He's not though, he's terribly gauche and tacky. It's the only thing that saves him as a matter of fact.

T—I just can't. ($1000 too expensive)

O—He's completely silly. You'll love him.

T—I know I'll love him.

O—No, he's absolutely divine. He's got a voice you can't he sings the Empress in Dufraunachap far better than anyone else except Liona Risenick. I've never heard it sung better (Taxi laughs.) He really sounds great in it. Everything else is pretty weird but good though. He's marvelous, he's a great musician, you'll love him. And he's rather attractive uh ss . . . no he would never dare ex-

cept except (Drella laughs) campaign speeches and things. Walter wrote a campaign speech last night.

Oh really?

O—That was so, and so insipid.

What uh, what's the platform?

What's the platform?

If he's elected mayor.

O—Welcoming Red China to our midst and saying thank you for the drugs; you've been so kind. Reducing the police force by two thirds and having that that one third all Peurto Rican. (Taxi laughs.) Heaven and then have

. . .

What all third Puerto Rican?

O—The the the re-remaining cops.

Oh.

O—Will be all Puerto Rican which is pretty beautiful. Gracie Mansion would be a home for the homeless.

T—Ha. Do you realize that that that the police are after me now?

O—There would be no police and he keeps, he keeps, he keeps saying Rot.

T—And my car . . . really have.

Really.

T—We have decided that the car is is worth confiscating.

Well, it's a . . .

T—Because I have a thousand dollars.

R—Really.

T—And then I left it on the bus sotp two days on Fifth Ave.

Oh, did you, ay? I saw it there but I didn't want to say anything except every five minutes you said the bus stop. I wha went around the corner.

T—The policeman came up and said (deepens her voice) "Do

you want your car curbed and turned away?"

O—My God (*laughter*) I thought that was my mother.

T—I said, "I'm terribly sorry, officer, but the car is out of order and I have to have it towed tow-carred to move it at all," and the tow car said, "Well really, it it will y'now" like . . .

In between the two head lights.

T—He started the car and it did run and all that was the matter was it was a little bit—

The batteries.

T—The batteries, that's it. It just needed to be run.

Recharged.

The camera came today.

T—That's all that was the matter. The tow truck was there and everything and it didn't need to be towed.

—Videotape?

T—But I was lucky because—

It's for the new serial.

We have uh, we have monitors and uh

T—About two minutes of announcing.

TV sets and uh, oh, it's really great.

T—The fact that I was transgressing the . . .

—What are the T.V. sets have to do with it?

T—Sitting there.

Well because I got the T.V. set.

T—As well as

On the channel, right?

T—. . . two days, and then he got, oh he was a stitch. He started telling me how Ondine you'll really love this, he started telling me how the car really should be in a párking lot, I mean in a parking bus stop.

Yeah.

T—And then he started tell me if I were in Harlem I would really like policemen.

O—What a cop, the stupid.

T—No but he said it and could you imagine.

O—Was he colored?

T—No, he was with me and he said y'know well, y'know . . .

O—Was he, was was he.

T—Not to be, no no.

O—He was what?

T—What he was is like taking a, he was the policeman bit, he was the.

O—Oh, my microphone.

T—And he he anticipated all the antagonism that authority . . .

O—I don't know why he, why.

T—What it involved.

O—I don't know why he went out to Harlem.

T—Well, that was just to say that like since you're smart and own a Mercedes and you sit here in the middle of . . .

O—Oh.

T—Fifth Avenue.

O—Oh, I see.

T—You can get away with it but my dear if you were in Harlem.

O— *Ondine says with Taxi :* But my dear, if you were in Harlem.) You'd really like the cops up there, that's what . . .

T—Right! Exactly.

O—Yes, of course but I didn't know what you meant before.

T—And he took twenty minutes to say it.

O—Yeah, well that's stupid. That took five seconds and it was a, it was from Norma. (*Taxine*

laughs.) Take me to . . . (laughter). Let me straighten your earring out; it's driving me berserk.

Yeah, it is.

T—They, they really are so mobile
that that there's no way . . .

6 /   1

R—. . . but like to . . .

T—Why not?

R—What, that you're gonna be here? . . . just say so . . . if that's what
you mean, why don't you just say it? (Music.)

T—Oow, Rink that's the first time you ever did that. (Pause.)

O—I thought I lost you, I thought I disappeared and now the microphone is back again.

DRELLA—Why did you do that?

O—I just had wanted to see the rest of the terrace.

D—Oh.

O—The terrace.

D—You should have taken it with you.

O—Huh?

D—You should have taken it with you.

O—But you were fixing it. I saw you on the couch fixing it, so I figured,
you know . . . I mean a moment won't . . .

Oh I have to, I have to really give my new . . .

I—*shouting*—Why don's you come out to Long Island this weekend?
(*Lowers voice.*) I know. . . . Caucus New Jersey.

What?

They need us, they need us in the swamps. Oh my nose, I wish it would

. . .

I—Why doesn't everybody butt in on—

T—Everybody's so . . . they can't see outside their own eyeglasses.

Not, oh I, I'm sorry, I'll take em off. (*Laughter.*)

You said eyeglasses were very . . .

Well I'm just, put them on top of my head and I don't care about anything. Oh she just spit in my eye. What, I just had my . . . open. What
a rotten thing to do. Spilling the poor drink right down my leg . . .

T—Ondine, you have bright red hair.

O—Oh, bright red, they call me Barbaroso. Red, uh uh. Hello gypsy, so
light, let me see, huh

T—Oh Ohh.

O—Huh? Ohh. (*Pause.*) (*In a high voice.*) Look, here they come, uh.
Oh Ondine, Ondine, not too high.

Okay, keep coming now. . . . Let's do it again.

I'll start.

O—(*Giggle.*) The only sound you'll get get up there is a few mynas. But
ah hah hah. I almost fell. This, is, this the penthouse?

Huh?

O—Is this the penthouse? It's very big. *Traffic noise.* What're you star-
ing at, is that the Mercury sign that you're looking at . . . *laugh* so
lovably.

D—What?

O—Drella, what're you looking at like that? Do you see something in the
window that I don't *Joan Bennett?* Is there something going on down
there?

Are all these, all these men looking for the uh . . .

D—I bet the cans don't . . . *Drella's voice is drowned out by traffic noise.*

Oh.

R—You need fore definite reasons. You may be right.

The definite reason is—

R—It looks better on television?

It does, it won't lok bad, it will just uh

What's that?

They want to show 5 minutes of Taxine on television and, from the movie,
and I think . . .

Oh no, they can't do it, no they they can't do it

But, it's like giving the phole point away.

Yeah, I mean it's like cutting the film.

R—That's what it is.

Like cutting the film, n-no they should know that, yeah.

I mean, uh

Keep, keep her in wraps, boys.

R—Right now they think it's a joke.

They don't . . .

Well, if they don't do it now they'll wait til later. They got Ida and they
made her famous.

R—They'll think, they'll think—but but Ida was, Ida Ida is a joke to a
great extent.

D—But she's no longer as much a joke as she was.

R—But we did a . . .

Well, she knows, but

That's what you just said, I mean.

D—She's being used now to perfection.

Her . . . . . is terrific.

O—I saw s—one, I saw some pictures of her in Vogue that were divine. They were divine. Isn't—she in the present Vogue too?

R—I saw her on a T.V. show.

O—Well, Little Ida was bad in person as far as I can see————

R—Yeah.

O—She was just noth—

R—Act . . . she was better in person.

O—I just, y'know, couldn't stand her. She was rather dreary, I thought. Except she she had duh two F-French maids that were just deluscious. The most wonderful women. (Sniff.) That takes talent to hire women like that, but I mean she's . . . oh God.

Somebody's going up to the . . .

O—Frights, oh she gropes everybody that walks in the room. She groped Walter.

Oh really?

O—Yes, and then she came after me, was disgusting, she came after me after that, it was ridiculous.

Well I was . . . joke or something

No, it's no joke. Li-Little Ida's . . .

R—. . . music would be

Yeah, she actually put her hand on your meat. It was a l'little bit much.

O—She was, she was a little bit much. Ida' snot is * * * I don't blame him. There were 15 years old boys, wheee, oh no, not girls.

We got a secretary.

Uh, Cappy Tano. Yeah, she's very sensitive.

R—We've got to give her lots of instructions about how to handle y'know.

But she can only come part-time, like

R—Why don't you . . .

She's, she can she can always make up a—

She started to look . . .

Think about it.

. . . Well then, let's start to write it now.

Yeah, okay.

Just give us big sheets of paper that's all.

R—I, I thought the first ones would be the don't come and call unless you, don't come unless you call or unless you're beautiful. Unless you know it.

O—Unless you have a penis. ($1000) Th-then we'll see who the girls are. Now let's get, does he have any big papers?

Uh, I don't.

R—You be the House, Drella you can be the Legislature, I'll be the House, you be the Senate.

—Rink has paper right there.

R—And, and Drella will be president.

Oh, oh the pictures.

Have you any?

R—You didn't bring me (*Music going*)

Your what?

R—my my—

Surfin'   *with record.*

Your what?

R—. . . remember them, I . . .

O—No, no I mean big paper.

Your what?

O—I have to write.

R—My, my the pictures of those funny people took of us, I wanted one.

Oh.

I, I did.

R—You just never listen.

Oh well, they, they, they'll be in. They're not in? Oh who wants *in Music* MUSIC)

Yeah, ask and then, uh

Where? (   ) Steve's in the kitchen.

No he's in here, he's in here. Oh no no Irv in here (*pause*) in here.

Irving, do you have any big, do you have any big blank paper?

Oh.

Do you have any big paper at all?

Oh, just typing paper.

I—No uh, well I mean just typing paper. I mean.

Yeah. Just doing a stu-studio policy thing.

Yeah, that'll do.

I—Well, Peter, Peter, I have this uh, you ready to eat this food?

PETER—Yeah.

I—Uh, uh, there's an operator . . . . . every 3 minutes when you're calling Greece.

What?

T—We're supposed to be at that place.

I—They'll pick up the answering service.

I—I've gotta pick up the antique show. C'mon, now gather round gentle-
men intending to stall or something. I made an outfit of . . .

T—Is that Ruth, Drella . . . We said we'd meet . . .

I need a piece . . .

I—C'mon, listen, if you wanna have the food.

R—Meet the Beatles and make $100, what do you want? (*Noise.*) Isn't that . . . Rock 'n' Roll . . . (*Music*)

Don't be like that, I just want to get this to Ondine over there then . . . at least. Oh, uh will you uh please, uh Ondine, take care of this?   Sure, sure.   Studio policy, studio.   Studio policy.   Okay, talk to him, tell him, say, say this . . . the radio.   Am I, am I going to do it my myself?   Yeah.   Well, what is she supposed to do? . . . Drella, may I have that pen? And a thing to write on.   You have a pen.   I don't know where I put it. May-maybe it's in my case.   It's probably there. (*Music:* "Oh oh oh oh oh oh oh oh oh oh oh ohh . . .")   Light. . . . (*Hindu music.*)   Oh, I found some (*Hindu music.*) Studio policy. (*Traffic noise.*) (*Long pause.*) We'll start with studio policy, okay? (*Long (Twangy guitar.*) Irving, have you got a light? Or a match. Do you have a match of any kind?   Match? I don't smoke, why?   Oh, but you, I need a light. Because I tried m-most of the lighters don't work.   Well pause.) Here I am . . . (*long pause*) hmm hmm . . . seven and (*extremely long pause*) one . . . hmm hmm (*pause*). Studio policy of factory plan regarding telephone. No phone calls before the hour of 11 A.M. Use board by the phone for messages also, tools for writing. The ability to #3 the ability to let the person who is wantde know whether to bring his or her presence to the phone (*long pause*).   T—Okay.   MMm what? How are you my dear?   T—Miserable.   Why, what's the matter?   T— I'm tired.   You . . . used to be, they're all so tring, aren't they? Every one of them . . . that's something.   T—I'm actually exhausted. You're so . . .   T—And and do you know Rink turned around when I've been trying to understand what he's saying all the day. And then he turns around and thinks I'm trying to attack him, but I never was.

Well, you know sometimes he takes things very personally.   T—But I do too, so I understand it, y'know.   But you're a bit more too.   T— It's like, oh I don't know where to, what can you do? It, I just cannot, if I could let go and say one direction that was not responsible to those millions of draggy people that shouldn't be even bothered about. I'd say there's only one person I'm gonna be with and that's you.   Thank you.

T—And it's true.   Thank you, thank you from my heart.   T— But it's the absolute truth. And . . .   . . . very good.   T—For some reason I still think I can get those people to understand things that they'll never understand. And I . . .   What d'you mean?   T—Prob-probably wasting my whole life.   You will but you shouldn't. They're not gonna expect uh, them to understand. They're not gonna understand anyway. You, y'know? Don't, they will not understand. They will not understand because they can't and because they won't. They'll be in it, in the middle o fit, up to their necks in it and theny they'll understand it. Of course you'll, you'll be . . .   T—Then there's got to be a war, I guess.   Yeah probably and theny you'll be thought of as being this and that and the other thing and uh, then people will see you as uh, y'know you'll have a reputation for being cruel perhaps or mean or or just being uncooperative or being . . . but uh, those few people who know will understand and the rest don't matter.   T—Yes, it's true. (*Pause.*)   Norma and three men.   T—Why do I keep it, why do I keep hanging on about Drella? Because you're so young.   T—I guess it's true.   And it's habit.

T—It's also that I . . .   You can't help it.   T—that I keep insisting that they have to learn and I know that, and I'm right. And you know it.   They will, they well.   T—But you for, the difference is that you forgot you, you just, you knew, and you knew they wouldn't know. And you be just . . .   I was furious, I was outraged, as angry as I . . .   T—You, you left them.   I wha, I, I attacked them too.
T—Yah.   Regularly.   T—But also th-that they lost you and you also lost them. And I'm sitting there trying to, they don't even know what I am and I, they and I'm trying to say what I really believe and at the same time I'm trying to say that, that I'm . . .   That you're somehting else.

T—Something.   That you don't know what you're trying to say; that's what they, they're trying to say to you, what you don't know, what you're trying to be, and say or want.   T—They're trying to put me in the Jennifer jet . . .   They won't.   T—Well, they can't.   Absolutely can't.   T—Unless that's all that I care about.   And it's not fair.   T—And I don't even care about it. STUDIO POLICY, or factory plan regarding telephone use.   T—Oh really?   **One**, no phone calls before the hour of 11:00 A.M. **Two**, use board by the phone for messages and also tools for writing. **Three**—the ability to let the person who is wanted know without revealing his or her presence to the phone needs. Do you think there is any . . . yeah, to the phone needs to.   T— *inverted sigh.*   Not to let people who can best be called kibitzers stay longer than 3 minutes on the phone call. It really, oh y'know.   T— You're so right.   What, look, regarding, en, regarding what uh, entry is uh, admissions and . . .   T—Ondine, what is to be done? Like . . .

Not a thing.   T—But there's no way that . . .   Let it take care of itself.   T—But you know . . .   And you'll be part of it, it will.

T—but.   It'll happen because of many other reasons besides me, and you, and many other reasons besides that, but you'll be a part of it. And it's going to happen; it has to happen, it must happen, and it always does, y'know what I mean?   T—It does. It it just means that all . . .

You must be patient, that's all. You must be patient, and we must die. exactly. We must die. Y'know, but we're all resigned to dying.

T—But I already did die. And then I have to begin again.   I died too.

T—And y'know.   And I have to start again. And each time it, it's a little harder. But each time you have more equipment. (*Pause.*) Each time there's more equipment.   T—But Ondine, you're such uh . . . I'm just the opposite of it too.   T—But . . .   I'm just the opposite of it. As as nice as I am, there's a stupid and unbelieving . . .   T—I know.   Do you know I don't believe in things.   T—Well, you do too though.   Yes, I really want to.   T—It's just the way I don't either.   But I don't believe in things; I don't believe people, I can't and that's, that's what makes me so attuned to them. I don't want to believe them.   T—But, in a few sssituations you really do believe them.

Oh well there are uh, my dear, uh, those people are those people are few; there's even they, you, even you, Rotten is create a whole uh, I doubt all the time.   T—Everything's fine.   All the time I doubt, y'know I mean, I have to stp myself from being so stupid. It's ridiculous, Ihave to stop myself . . .   T—It's just that we've been saying about, it's like the way, I mean, no for you to, there' nothing in the world I'd want more than having to have, y'know you, that you could be there and I could be there and yet, it wouldn't, for me to be able to try and do, work out my own thing and have you there.   You know it wouldn't work.

T—All I know is that, that . . .   Unless it works by . . .   T—You're too much.   Unless it works by itself. Maybe it would unless it is adopting to it, unless it's y'know it has to be.   T—It would that, people that, what what I would, what would want, as far as what . . .   What you want.   T—Not what I want, but what needs to be done if I'm to do anything is to, have you there.   But.   T—But not working. But you must un-understand.   T—You . . .   But I should work because I like to work; I really like to work. I love working, as a matter of fact . . .   T—But, also that . . .   It's rewarding in, in the strangest way. (*Taxina coughing.*) It not only stops idleness but it, it prevents real . . .   T—Yeah, you have to be, but it's all a matter of of you're the the the the 99th dimension.   Yeah.   T—And I'm at the 99th percentile but not the 99th dimension so that we do correspond but . . .   Probably.

T—There's one like I have one step more to go and that's when I give up.   But we have to, we just adjust, my dear, that's all. You know what what that step is and that is acceptance.   T—Except what you chose to do is is the most true in the most beautiful sense, but then it's denying in way, it's it's giving up all, it's you and it's magnificent. That's why I do it. But, but I don't know anybody else could do it. T—Well, that's true but . . . Ondine . . .   I don't expect anybody else to . . .   T—But nobody could.   But I don't want anybody else to.

T—But at the same time, well no, but at the same time other people are dragging up behind and, because you're so great, you're still, you're still, you're you're still a whole incarnation that's one total dimension beyond, and then there's somebody like me, that's sort of half dimension beyond, and half in . . . Ondine, you're whole dimension . . . with the people.

I know what you mean, I know what you mean, but, no, but, that, don't you understand it's a slow and painful process, which removes you from that which you are from and places you into that which you are. It's a very slow process, you, it's you feel it, you feel them sapping away from you, Taxi, everyday. You feel it going, it, you feel them ebbing away, and they and they slowly, the habits that they've given you, the thoughts that they've put in your mind, the routines that yau have are all, and eventually everthing you do will go under your surveillance. You will, you will think about it, you will, you will get it into line, and you will regiment it. You will do away with all that you consider unecessary. But it takes a long time and it is most painful.   T—But Ondine, it's as though you're right, you are right, you've disposed with . . .   Most people . . .   T—I know it's so painful, Jesus, I do know.   It's the only way to live.   T— But it's not the only way to live because I can't forget those people. You, you don't have to.   T—I can't, yes . . .   You don't have to. T—I can't forget . . . I think because . . . I can't, and I . . . . don't want to further-furthermore I don't want, they don't have to be . . . . . . There's no reason that they should be. (Pause.) But they can be rewarded   . But then the n then it's it's best for them that they're forgotten.   T—It's true.   All right, and they, and when they know that, then, when they tell you, no please d-d- leave me alone, blah-blah do what you want. Then you know you've won. You are com—that is a success.

T—When? When they tell you?   When, when they give in. When the submission is over, when they, when thre is no more siege. T—But it isn't, Ondine, it isn't all that.   I know it's not all that. T—It's just that there are not many, there're not many people that are special. There are one or . . .   There are a few, yes, there are more than me. There's . . .   T—There aren't, there's more than you but you are special no matter who else.   Yeah, all right. Thank you. That's beautiful . . . what a lovely thing to say.   T—And that's, that's undeniably . . . and and yet most people, most of those masses of auto machanics would never understand.   And they can't.   T—They can't, I know it.   But they would be made to understand.   T—And yet I'm sitting there screamnig and I just can't.   And they would be made to understand.   T—I know they can't understand and I won't let go.   They will be, but they will whether they want to ot not, me dear.   T—I know it's true, it's true.   They're going to have to . . .   T—That's why I'm screaming, but they have to, even if I don't matter, they will.

Well, watch them scream, watch them scream. They're going to have
. .   T—There will be a war or something that'll change the dimension
of their understanding.   It, it, they will.   T—That they will have to.

They will have to deal with what is obvious to peole whol live in the
present and those are the special people, the people who live in the present. They will have to deal with that and they will have to . . . go ahead
darling.   T—There's a funny thing, this book called, something about
games uh, it's writen by a doctor, and the last paragraph Rink told you
about it, and it was on the, the, when we went to this interview for the
Les Les . . .   Crane.   T—Crane—whatever his name is.   Lester
Crane.   T—Lester Crane *laughing* wherever he was.

O—What is that *Lester Crane.*

T—It was his film, it it's, this du Ball.

O—Yeah.

T—You mean Irving who owns the apartment?

O—Yeah, isn't that Irving du Ball, how gorgeous.

T—Isn't that . . .

O—Dreaming up the same thing.

T—Oh I can't believe Irving.

O—He's too much. He won't let me, he won't let me stay in an-any
    room. He thinks I'm gonna put in in my bag or something or what.

T—Not only that . . . do you know what he said, do you wanna know he
    said to Drella once.

O—He said "please."

T—I had a bad article. Do you wanna know what he said?

O—He's so dreary, God.

T—Listen, he said "Don't forget."

O—We're being overheard, lover. Thank God.

T—Oh. Irving said, "I've been," y'know like, lemme just say what I was, I
    was out of money and I'm the same and I'm struggling, I'm moving
    ahead little by little. And and in the end I get an article in the news-
    paper which I didn't have try to have put in the newspaper; they came
    to me and said, do you know what he said when he saw the article about
    superstar? He said "Don't forget I discovered her." I begged that. I
    begged Irving for money so I could get out of this country when
    Mummy tried to commit me to the hospital.

O—And he wouldn't give you.

T—And he asked, he was drunk, he sat there for three hours and after
    three hours he was so drunk that, with myself and Drella and Rink, he
    gave me about three dollars to live on. A hundred dollars . . .

O—Ohh.

T—. . . not to make a trip but to de. . . .   . It wasn't just, he knew that it. . .

O—That's not very nice, he . . .

T—I've given hundreds of hundreds and hundreds.

O—Y'know Taxi . . .

T—And they're pigs.

O—Either they learn or they don't learn.

T—There's no way.

O—There's no woy, there's no way of bringing someone who likes to see the degradation of a person uh, into, into the realm of o person.

T—Well, he only wanted to sign me up, y'know because some . . .

O—Because what? What could he possibly?

T—For what is absolutely true.

O—Who could he sign you to?

T—And that's what I keep saying.

O—You could sign him to ssomething soon.

T—I already have.

O—You will.

T—Signed him to his role and he doesn't like it.

O—Ah, he hates being stuck there, well he . . . my dear.

T—He is.

O—Because that's where he wallows. And he wallows in it, and he never tries to get out of it and he never sees himself clearly and he never says "Oh well wow, what a fuck I am." He never did any of that, and that's
. . .

T—And wallow knows. *Laughs.*

O—Oh wallow's a heck of an animal; he shouldn't even degrade his names by using that much in, in verb, I mean y'know, he just wallows around in his own pig sty.

T—Yes.

O—I mean when *Dante* place him in the, in the inferno, and . . . he knew . . . he would roll in his dirt. It's true they are like that, they really are. They deserve it. And they deserve the condemnation and what happenes to them because they're pigs or they're alligators or they're hippopotamuses or they're or they're birds or what, or whatever the fuck . . .

T—Yes, well then that rates . . .

O—Buffalo, the buffalo wallow I like. *Laughter.*

T—Drella's gonna try and put us in jail.

O—Drella'll . . .

. . . . . .arrested. I wish my . . . very rough don't it? It's uh,, it's uh, one of the best *Dorothy Killgalens* . . . it, I've never heard of a thing in depth before in my life, it, this, and we're not stopping here, in fact, we better start drawing a diagram for the different levels (*laughter*) of . . . the New York hell . . . or the record.

University.

We made it, a game of it the other day.

It . . . company . . . you know what the movie companies call themselves? Paramount Universal

Laugh.

Interuniversal, M.G.M., Metro Goldwyn Mayer.

MetroGold, well that's the smartest one.

Yeah but that.

That really is the . . .

20th Century Fox.

Yes, 20th Century Fox.

Sly ain't it? Sly . . . they're pretty smart, all right. We're going to do a diagram; we've got to put them all in, oh we can just give a rating, oh we'll just . . .

Can we give . . .

We have to mark it down wh-what they are but . . .

Sounds ridicul. . . .

A crescent moon, right? That's for divinity, that's . . .

Okay oh.

That's the first pleasure on life. I learned these from . . .

I learned these things too.

I learned these things from people who uh, are really great, y-y'know?

You know.

O—Who cares? I like the . . . oh there's a girl here. I think it's I think it's, I think the French girl.

T—Hi Moxanne.

O—You can help us.

T—How are you? Moxanne, you must meet Ondine.

How do you do? How do you do?

T—Ondine, Roberto Olivo.
   Laughter.

O—You can help us.

T—And we're solving the whole problem for you.

O—We're giving uh . . .

T—We're just expressing it.

O—We're riding the whole, we're raiding the scene.

T—It's just such a struggle; you just can't believe it. Moxanne is is fantastic and and she's very . . .

O—She's beautiful.

T—She's beautiful and she's also very practically orianted which which I can't.

O—The first two categories, divinity and second one is stars right?

T—Stars okay.

O—And the third one will have to be.

T—Ondine, I uh, I assure you is is a genious.

T—Well uh, it's only what you can b. . . . . . about on it y'know, because you know, you know about . . .

O—Divinity star, third, what's the next category? After a star is what. Has-been.

T—Ah, no. uh . . .

O—How awful, please repair.

T—Now waite a minute (*laughter*) . . . no no, it's gotta be someplace that does . . . we've got divinity star.

Making up games like golf and, oh please.

T—Something that's that's um, what's next to a star that's . . . the T—No no no, this is closer to divinity is.

O—Mercury.

T—Star . . .

O—Moon.

T—Star, of course the moon is divinity because the whole moon, it can never just have, the moon, or it's a blot of ink.

O—Yeah.

T—And if, and if that's the whole moon.

O—After star, would that be fledging?

T—No no no, gone down from divinity to star to somehow the mockery walks get in, but they get out of it by bottles.

O—Well, we could even, we could make up a game which would be even better. Games are so . . .

T—Well, you know.

O—The only way to talk is to talk in games, it's just fabulous.

T—Ondine has games that no one understands.

Moxi—I'm missing all this mythology behind this . . .

M—You need something that's, you can't see through it, you know?

M—What's this divinity . . .

M—I was gonna say moon but I guess that's it already.

M—Oh, did you ever play that . . . that game that we just started playing, what's it called? something like catch your world of . . .

O—It's wonderful (*Laughter.*)

O—You know, you, you get . . .

O—Dennis who?

M—Do you know Dennis Deagon? (*Ondine* N *Taxine togethers*) Ohh Ohh. (*Laughter.*)

O—Do I remember Dennis Diggen? He's all right. (*Noise of mixed voices.*)

T—I got the next word in . . . I've got a penny pinky.

O—And now we have to make a symbol for it. A round thing with the head of Lincoln in it or a buffalo? What should we . . .

T—Why can't you get . . .
. . . not a penny. No, Lincoln wouldn't be penny gigging but Dennis Diggen is penny pigging, really.

O—All right, penny.

T—Pigging, penny pigging.

O—Penny pig, well then we'll make a pig, right?

T—yes, yes.

O—All right.

T—Penny pigging . . .

O—That's it.

T—Yeah, oh you've got it, I knew.

O—Bravo, bravo my dear.

T—Oh this is the game. (*Laugh-ter.*)

O—. . . . . . .penny pigging . . . that's the best one of the . . . players.

T—Oh we're too much; I don't be-lieve it.

O—Now we have to get the fourth one but.

T—The next, oh uh.

O—That's beautiful. (*Laughter.*) That's beautiful. That's incredi-

M—Did you ever see, it's with all the wor— all the world on it. We've played the game one night and it got so fantastic that every-body's mother and and . . .

M—And we made up and we were playing Dennis, and Dennis made up a . . .

M—. . . Lincoln.

M—No, not a buffalo.

M—No no, it's just too obvious.

M—Make, make a . . .

ble, I've never heard . . . ooh I
. . .
It is, it is, the real and nonsense.

O—Then we're gonna name people
and give them ratings.

T—Real and nonsense put together
into a game.
We're doing a whole number
game and it's just too much.
We've got it all set.

O—Four.

T—Y'know, y'know.

O—I met him twice.

T—And and did you meet Piggy?

O—Oh I just heard what non-personality just said. That could be
the fourth one, non-personality.

T—Wait, wait. We have to see,
wait.

O—You just said that word . . .

T—Wait a minute, I've got it, I'm
almost set. Lemme get this, oh
wait.
Yeah, yeah, I was gonna say . . .
It's just a . . .

O—Insipia you go euh.

T—That were not near to that yet
cause . . .
Yeah, I know.

T—Penny piggi is is uh

O—Genuine.

T—Definitely genuine.

O—That's genuine, like that's real.

T—God save us all but it's . . .

O—God save us all? What are you
thinking?

T—Uh uh (laugh.

O—I love it. Just saying it is good.

T—Now what would, would you
say he next was a non-something.

O—Yeah.

T—Okay.

O—Non-personality, non-being.

T—Wait, wait wait uh

M—Are you gonna make a game out of it?

M—Oh, I see . . .

M—Yes, in a. in a . . . . .

M—In the game, in the game we played on
theother day we would, we would, we
would get t-to the-this points but we would
name it, like the name of the town would
be Insipic.

O—Zombies of some sort.

T—I know, how can you say

O—Yeah.

T—Do you know the word solstice so and shalant, solance how can you make it non-solance? Which is solstice is piece, sholance is indifferent, insolstice, I have to make . . .

O—Yeah but that's, but that's too, that's too spiritual.

T—Too complicated?

O—Yeah, these, this, is this is non-spirit, non-spiritual.

T—But, penny pigging's on- spiritual.

O—Oh yeah.

T—While divinity is . . .

O—But that's, that's kind of a character, a

T—But there millions of them.

O—Yeah y'know, well

T—Yeah, but star and divinity aren't that earthly.

O—No no.

T—Earthly.

O—We're, we're going down now.

T—Yeah, okay, well then let's get to uh . . .

O—Now we have to get to the un-spiritual state. Boy did someone score, the rapid ones.

I—See what happens when my leg isn't going?

O—The village of the damned, y'know.

T—I, he, he he (laugh). Something . . .

T—Uh.

O—Zombies have to be suggested in some manner. Do zombies owe something to somebody? Do zombies have to obey something?

T—They come back to haunt the spirits apparently. Z-zombies are kind of ghosts that are in a way,

M—I think there's nothing more earthly than   a

M—Oh! No kidding?

you're right, they obey.
O—Yeah, well then they can' t be
. . .
T—But in a negative way like.
O—Yeah but. . .
T—They come back to haunt peo-
ple that uh, deny they're, the
truth. You know, they come back
to say that, to defy the situation
that. . .
O—Mm.
T—is existing. The zombies exist.
O—The melevalents, m-e but e-n-
t-s, melevalents.
Somebody sneezes and giggles.
T—Uh.
That's where . . .
T—Again, again it's not quite . . .
O—It's just not quite right. Penny
pigging did it s beautifully.
T—Penny pigging is too much. Uh.
(*Pause.*)
—What are you doing? What are
you doing now? (*In background.*)
Or vacuum plant.
T—Oh, I know what. Uh, the next
one, I've got half of it.
Oh here is a . . . (*pause*).
T—How could you say something
like.
T—No, it doesn't make sense. Di-
vinity star, penny pigging, I was
gonna say schlitz monger.
Ooh, schlameil.
T—No, schlitz monger.
Schlitz monger is y'mean like
T—Which is like shit and
A shit dog.
T—And spit and sh, y'know, shit,
spit, and schlitz . . .
That's right my dear.
T—Which is split as well as the
monger is somebody who, who's
yeah grabby grabby which is
worse than penny pigging. A
schlitz would be you know, would

M—Oh well, I don't know, I just . . .

?—How long have you been here?
M—'Bout uh . . .

be worse than a peeny pig.

O—A schlitz monger's a fabulous word. *Taxi laughs.* I think that should go down.

T—Shall we do it next, it any thing?

Do you want to?

T—Yeah.

Schlitzmonger.

T—Yeah because it's a combination of those things.

But then . . .

T—Both the spit, shit, and split.

O—Do you want to half it between schlitz and monger or one word?

T—Yeah, yeah, we'll see it. Oh, ei, one word, we don't need this, this . . .

O—Yeah, very German, very German. All right, now well, what shall we draw this into. A bottle of Schlitz?

T—No, next, oh ,oh we have the image to deal with I see.

A bottle of Schlitz?

T—Divinity star, penny pigging, schlitzmonger, uh schlitzmonger is uh. Would a bottle do? No, that's to o phallic, you can't have it just that way.

O—Yes, you're right.

T—Uh, schlitz

O—What would you, what symbol would you give to a schlitzmonger?

Uh, sch. . .

M—A schlitzmonger? I don't even know what it is.

T—Think of what it is. It's a spit, shit and split. (*Laugh.*)

A monger is somebody who sells.

Sell, yeah.

M—Monger? What is . . . a monger means . . .

T—Somebody who sells but like it's saying

Schlitzmonger is like saying crap (*simultaneous conversation:* I—Did Drella do that?   O—

M—Schlitzmonger

No, I did them myself. You
know I'm a very, I got lessons
from *Allen Ginsberg* y'know.)

T—Bu it's saying it with spit, shit,
and split which is also divided in,
in, well it's uh ridiculous but.

?—What should we put down?

M—Let's see about uh

T—But we have to think of a sign
because it's a valid word.

O—A bottle of Schlitz doesn't
work.
That three rings would be the
Ballantine thing.

M—No.

T—Or else, what?

O—Yeah, what else could it be?

M—It's got to be Schlitz, right?

T—It has to be like . . .

O—What's that?

T—Well, it has to be se par ated
and two different directions.

M—A glass, no? What about one of those . . .

O—It's insane looking but what is
it? My God.

T—That's
That's not fair. That's not right.

M—Why don't you do glasswork?

O—The the bottle . . .

T—The bottles are too phallic I
think.
But, then I was thinking of eyes
which are sort of things you can't
distinguish in different directions.

M—OH.

O—There's no way to draw a . . .

T—But then there's no way to
draw eyes and like except that if
you do eyes they they could be
like turned and the different directions could be the uh, looking.

M—The person who . . . but make that one
better so that you really see them as eyes.

O—Oh. That's noot bad bad for a
blind person.

T—Wait, wait.
Okay, fill in the other corner.
Okay, that's Schlitzmonger.

M—Fill in the corners completely.

O—Now what is that litle eyebrow;
we should do something with it.

M—Yeah, that's good.

T—It has to go in the opposite
direction.

O—Yeah, she, oh, she, oh, whoever that is. (*Laughter.*) Oh.

T—No, it's fantastic, that's . . . mention

O—Yeah, oh.

T—But then we'll give it . . .

O—Gonna take it right out of the scary.

T—That belongs to the ocean.

O—All right, the next, the next category.

T—What we've given now to the schlitzmonger.

O—A lot of importance.

T—A lot of dimension which doesn't belong to the others.

O—They're, no but. They are the ones that that . . .

T—It's true they do get the dimension (*inverted sigh*). Oh.

O—The schlitzmongers are the majority, right?

T—*inverted sigh*—Oh.

O—. . . The majority, or aren't they?

T—Oh, oh.

O—I thought that the penny piggers are uh . . .

T—It's true; you're right.

O—definitely not the majority.

T—Yeah, yeah, it's true.

The schlitzmongers really get the right to bet. It's true.

Now the next one after that.

M—I think the penny piggers do pretty well.

T—Well yeah, they do but y'know like they've mixed, they're they're mixed to the point of . . . They're not quite as these people are the ones that get the most . . .

Schlitz is is spit and shit.

M—Schlitzmonger

O—Penny pigger, schlitzmonger . . .

T—And what can you get, and also, Ondine do you realize what it is?

O—Even better, penny pigge r.

T—Spit, shit, and split.

M—Penny pigger.

That's two, that's three dimensions.

O—Penny pigger is even better. Penny pigger.

T—Pigger. Oh, that's much better. A million times. Oh wow.

O—Penny pigger, schlitzmonger.

T—That's good, that's a buggy person that has enough power to bug people.

O—A buggy person?

T—Yeah, yeah, The, a pigger. Yeah, that right.

    Pass the pennies and bugs people.(*Moxanne laughs.*) Oh fantastic.

M—That's another category.

O—Oh, but the lice is next.

T—You see

O—Something about lice.

T—Irving's a penny pigger.

M—Lice, cockroaches

O—Yeah, well that's I, all right.

T—Yeah. He's also this.

O—. . . . . . . .the names now.
    Cockroaches oh, oh divine, we should, we should, wha—

M—You can get, you can start getting hung up here from here on. It gets very detailed

T—Oh, it's gonna be so hard.

O—I know, we keep getting, we keep getting the labeling hell. (*Taxine laughs.*) Now let's . . .

M—Insects.

M—So if divinity isn't started . . . it's just the insects. (*Laughs.*)

T—It's gotta get . . . (*laughter*).

O—What's with the insects . . . .

T—How can we get through that middle section?

O—We have to . . .
    Triber T-bow could be the next one.

M—It's all a lot of . . .

    Triber T-bow but that is but that's very like that could be the, something like the Neanderthal . . .

M—Who?

T—Uh, Louis Prima.

O—Lou Louis Prima! T-bo very good, next one. (*Taxine laughs.*) So beautiful. He even looks like a . . . Louis Prima T-bo, oh my dear.

T—OH, I don't believe it.

O—Oh, but what could we do for that one?

T—Touch you cheek.

O—Touch it? More than that.

T—Aa, oh imagery now oh my God. What could we do with the imagery?

O—Oh but Louis Prima T-Bo, oh please *laughs* . That, even hurts. What can we, what symbol can we give him? Yeah.

M—Well, how about a club?

T—Yeah, that's 'Cept that again is, well no, uh maybe it That's right, that's good. That's right. (*Moxanne laughs.*) Got it.

M—Put, put some spikes on it.

M—Yeah, but with spikes on it, it doesn't look phallic.

O—After that it's hard.

T—That's good, that's fantastic, ohhh.

O—After that, a-after that it's the amebas.

T—Right.

O—Right? Ameba and Amebaland. (*Taxine laughs.*)

T—Oh, Ondine.

O—The words my dear, the words are so funny. Oh wait til we get to the people that we put in . . . . (*muffled*). And they'll never know because this, this is just for us. (*Taxi and Moxi laugh.*) But now, but ameba has to be f-framed beautifully. What, what'a the. . .

T—Uh, let's see.

O—Paramecium, a paranoid. Yeah, is that?

M—Paramecium?

T—Yeah, yeah.

O—Oh, that's even be tter. And the ameba is constantly

M—That's one that looks like this and it doesn't change it's shape. This is the kind that you know . . . Yeah, the ameba changes all over and it changes, you look and this is very groovy, you look at it through the microscope and . . . This one, this kind of change isn't so fantastic.

changing, right?

T—Oh it's fantastic.
The, the whole, oh they're really gorgeous.

O—It goes up and down?
Ooh it expands and . . .

T—They're really gorgeous.

O—Oh. Well that's what oh
Ooh, like the blob.

T—They are just gorgeous . . . and and and and when you get them stained with colors, ah.

O—That's, oh no, uh that's too much. I wouldn't have to

T—That's too much, it really is, Ondine. You just don't . . .

O—I'd really haveto break the lens at that point if it looked up at me.

T—You kow about it.

O—You mean it comes up and tries to. . .

T—Oh, that's too much, that's the Those are the ones that the plant life of uh chlorophyll bit. You know like . . .

O—But they're kind of, that's kind of a . . . .

T—It's too much for where we're going now. We have to get to . . . We're not yet at the worst bit.
WE've gotten from s-s-schlitz monger to Louis Prima T-bo and that is a step down definitely.

O—That's like, my dear, that's so beautiful.

T—We have to get down one step down further.

O—Yes.

T—Then we can start the other side I think, may . . .

O—That's gonna be hard. It's gonna be hard. Now, we'll have

M—But this kind of change, it's incredible.

M—Yeah.

M—Three-Dexpansion.

M—You see these things . . .
these things coming up at you in the microscope.

M—What about a euglena?

O—What the hell is a euglena?

M—Oh, those are fantastic. Those are little green ones that go . . .

M—Oh no.

to put the next category which would be . . .

M—Oh you only got anything, oh no what is this people you're doing?

O—Yes.

T—Oh, let's have a pulta glass.

O—Peaple.

T—Lemme see.

M—Things like immovable things.

O—Like chairs or like uh . . . Different rocks . . . oh,, that used to be . . .

M—Like rocks and so on you know.

T—What about a pülter gast? That's good.

O—Yeah, but they're sort of uh

T—No no no you'd only, you don't know what it is.

O—It's . . .

T—I said a . . .

O—A poultry gas?

T—A pülter gast.

O—An evil wind, an ill wind.

T—And what it is is pülter, it's not pulta, I said pülter like the . . .

O—Pülter.

T—Pülter, pülter gast. Pülter geist is a spirit.

O—Yeah from the T.V. spirit.

T—And I have pülter gast.

O—Which is a . . .

T—Ah, ah, the evil essence.

O—Eugh.

T—A pul, pul

O—A pülter gast.

T—P-U-L, I don't know how to spell it.

O—I would like to put an umla in that.

T—But . . .

M—Pülter gast.

But uh, no, pulta geist is really pulta geist. Nobody ever says what it is, they say pulter- geis.

M—Oh yeah?

O—But pul, but pulta gast . . .

T—But pulta gaast is uh

O—Is uh, is an evil wind.

T—Is evil . . .

O—Pardon me for saying it, but, is a fart.

T—Yeah, that's what I mean.

O—That's exactly what it is.

T—S-so that should be the bottom.

O—That's the bottom of it all?

T—Caus we have all the incog names and things, so

O—Oh, all right. P-U-L-T-E-R.

T—Pülter

O—You can't—oh, Do I pet an umla over

T—P-U-L pulter, like the pulitzer pri . . .

O—Pülter gast, P-U-L-T-E-R G-A-S.

It's an unbelieveable . . . (*laughter*). I don't believe it. Oh . . .

T—It seems to me . . .

O—But now, what are we gonna, supposed to draw, vapors? A steamy . . . .

T—A baaped-booby.

O—A baaped-booby (*laughter*).

T—We were saying what can I tell those people when they start asking what I am . . .

O—A baaped-booby?

T—supposed to be, and Dodo said, "All you have to tell them that you're a baaped-booby." (*Laughter*.)

O—She's quite beautiful. I can't . . .

T—She's got it in a bag. I mean it's jus perfect.

O—She has a . . .

T—I want, if I ever got onta any of those shows . . . (*Moxanne laughs*.)

O—She would, yes I'm a baaped-booby.

T—I would just . . . cause I've given them such a serious angle, the I'd get on the show and say I'm a baaped-booby.

O—Baaped-booby what aim is it? (*Laughter*.) Oh what, what could

M—No, you put the umla over the "u."

M—Boy, that's that's really really an inde undescribable.

we write . . .

T—Cause we told them nothing but all the draggy things, that—

O—Can you think of any symbols for the puta gaa, uh pülter gast?

T—Uhh . . . E.

O—I think it should be g-h-a-s-t. G-H-A-S-T. Pülter ghast.

T—Oh, yes, yes definitely, definitely, oh boy. (Pause.) Oh fantastic.

(Laughter.) Oh that's what I meant, that's right.

M—OH, HERE YOU GO, NOW YOU'VE GOT IT.

T—Yes.

O—That's it, now that'll be in . . . simple but it isn't.

T—That's the right, it's the pollution of the gas, polluted, pollution and gas. What do you get?

O—How can you draw polluted gas?

T—Well, it's fantastic. What do you get?

O—Oh.

T—You know . . . from a pülter geist is a, is a spirit unknown, a pülter geist is a sort of mysterious, perhaps evil, but pülter ghast . . .

O— . . . can't escape. Yeah. A pülter, a pülter ghast is a . . .

T—It's evil, it's repulsive.

O—Is a, how can you draw a smell?

T—Uh, perhaps by, let's see.

O—How can you draw a smell?

T—Uh.

O—You can't. No, that that would be letters that you would have to put into it. These symbols are, this is like a pair of some . . . girl brassiere, this has turned into a shrew.

Well, aren' these for uh, aren't they uh.

Oh, the RULES FOR THE

M—Oh, you've gotta have . . .

M—Hmm?

FACTORY?

Yeah.

O—I started them and here's here's, here's here they are but it's only regarding the telephone.

Oh.

O—I'm being very specific.

T—I don't know how you do a smell. That's smell.

O—Oh, isn't it.

M—What does that have?

O—The smell, that's, that has, that's the smell. You could draw a nose.

T—It is, it is the smell. You can tell that's a smell.

O—Doesn't it? (Laugh.)

T—That, oh, I know what we could do.

O—It doesn't look too putrid.

T—Well, I, it's certainly looks.

O—It doesn't look absolutely rancid. (Inverted sigh.) Did you see Irving's Irving's Coke bottle with the rncid coke in it? Did you ever see a coke bottle go rancid? There's little round dots . . .

M—A Coke bottle go rancid?

O—The Coke is like . . .

T—That's too complicated but we can, I mean, the idea is simple. All you do is do the nostrils with the shape of a nose.

O—Nay, no, now.

T—Not only do we have here . . .

O—I f-figured a year ago that scared me. They were like this. The head and eye they were like that, and then a nose and a mouth, but just half of it, and something like that but . . .

Yeah, what's that?

O—But, but it has to be, this is just half of a face. The other is, is over here, but it's so hideous do you know and like it 's just half instead of, I can't do it now.

T—Ondine.

O—Like this.

T—Ondine you, ah . . .

O—Oooh.

T—Look what you did.

O—What happened?

T—That's what you do to me, see that's why I ju. . . .

M—Is it facing from the front or from, from sideways?

O—But the face, straight face, you know like this.

M—Oh.

O—Like it's . . .

M—Oh.

O—You'd only take an angle here like this would be part of my nose and then there'd be half of a curl for my mouth.

M—Oh yeah.

O—And then down again straight and then a . . .

T—Yeah, it's all a uh . . .

O—But there's something sinister about it, and kind odf a uh . . .

T—Oh definitely.

M—You can draw it, then you've gotta draw . . .

O—I dr?draw once, I drew it once, a year ago at the factory and it scared me so much I went up on the roof.

T—I, I used to . . .

O—I really got upset by it.

T—I 'have some pictures that I did in the hospital . . .

O—Ooh, ooh.

T—That I had to tear up, they were so fantastic.

O—Hospital, poor Duchess, the Duchess is in the hospital.

T—Oh, Ondine.

O—And the doctor.

T—I wish you'd teel what kind of hos. . .

O—Roosevelt. She's the doctor of ward B.

T—Oh come on.

O—Well yeah. She's got her own coat . . .

T—You mean she's sh—

O—and she's taking sho, giving people pokes.

T—Oh well then why are you upset?

O—Because she's dying I think.

T—you mean she's a patient.

O—Yes.

T—Well that's terrible.

O—She went to the dentist and they wouldn't let her out.

T—Ohh. Ohh.

O—They said, "You've got to go, you've got to go to the hospital."

T—Isn't that terrible? She went to the . . .

O—Her blood was orange.

T—This is a friend of Ondine's, who's who's . . .

O—THE DUCHESS.

T—gotten herself in such bad shape they've taken her to a hospital.

O—She went to the dentist . . .

T—And they won't let her out, like . . .

O—and they wouldn't let her out of the dentist's office, she was so . . .

M—Oh.

O—She kept falling saying, "Look at the bruises." Bang bang. (Laughter.) Oh she's hilarious you don't know how and and . . .

M—Why don't you . . . . (?) . . . the place and get her out?

O—Oh, that, we were thinking . . .

T—Oh they'd, what Ondine didn't do. Don't be silly. They wouldn't understand him.

O—She said to me, she said to me on the phone, she said, "Ondine you always have a place to stay here," and I went, "Oh!! (laughing). I said, "Thank you THE DUCHESS." She's so sweet. You know she always considers people. She's the biggest bluster I've ever seen in my life.

T—Eugh! Oh Ondine.

O—She's just like a

T—You are a treasure, me uncle.

O—But I still can't get a pülter ghast.

T—Drella said bluster so pülter ghast is a bluster.

O—(inverted sigh) . . . Oh now, let's let's . . .

T—How are you gonna get a, wait, a roumd . . .

O—All right, pülter gas will have no symbol. If it has no symbol next to it, then we know what it is, that's the bottom. There's no more categories. You can't go under that.

M—Under . . .

T—No.

O—A pülter ghast is ,there's nothing lower except m-maybe whale shit. You know you can't do anything with that.

They don't shit.

O—Yes they do, they're mammals. They have to shit. Only mammals shit, I love that. All right, now we'll give the names.

T—Maybe we should, well how could we make pülter ghast worse? We've got to make pülter ghast worst.

O—You can't, no symbol is the best way.

T—No.

O—No, n-no.

T—No symbol, but the words can't be I mean it's too like—

O—More German if you can.

T—It should be worse like, uh.

O—Pülter ghast. Booby. Nothing, can't say that. Look, did you see those categories?

T—Pulaver gust or something.

O—Divinity, star, penny pig, penny pigger, schlitzmonger, Louis Prima Tivo, and (laughing) pülter ghast. Aren't they divine? Louis Pri-Prima Tivo I think is my favorite.

—I think we have to go. They're all . . .

How can you, oh I, I'm glad to be going.

M—. . . Louis Prima Tivo. (Taxine laughs)

—I'm not.

O—I said Prima Tivo and she said Louis Prima Tivo and it was just (laughing) . . .

M—There's only one way to look at it . . .

O—So beautiful.

M—If you're right.

O—I've been saying Primativo, for y'know, since I saw La Dolce Vita. When that, when that (laughing) when, when that poetess said,"Primativo," oh, and

I thought she was so wonde, Ann Savage that was y'know.
Oh really?

O—A very old movie star. That was Anne Southern.

M—Is that the one with, oh the long brown hair?

O—No, no. The short blonde hair who was in Steiner's house.

M—Oh, yeah, yeah, yeah.

O—She was a poetess.

M—Uh,huh.

O—And she would say, "Oh, I gotta go, primativo oh ha ha." She was marvelous. What a great movie. Oh, I wanna see it again.

T—*La Dolce Vita*.

O—I wanna see it again.

T—I saw it while, oh, I can't believe it. I saw it while I was in Del Rio. Ondine, I must tell you. Oh Ondine would love it. Ondine Ondine.

O—. . . . . . .her end is but (*Moxi laughs*). What?

T—I have to tell you what happened when I first saw *La Dolce Vita*. I saw it, I got transported from Summerhill which is a, an open mental hospital.

O—Oh no.

T—In a Cadillac I was taken

O—To see the film.

T—to a theater to se *La Dolce Vitaaäa!*

O—They're so sweet. They are so sweet. They're so sweet my dear.

T—Can you believe it? So I was just seeing people.

O—Couldn't they look back in your case history and—

T—In a Cadillac, to go to see—

O—Oh no.

T—In a local theater from the nut house.

O—Well but, oh here comes the net house patient. Can you, they used to have special masses in St. Lucy's Church in Brooklyn for the blind because she's the patron saint of the blind and that day when you were, I was an altar boy for a little while, and when you would serve mass you'd turn around and you'd see al these dogs in the aisle. The seeing eye dogs and you couldn't believe it and they were all stumbling up t-t-to the altar, it was horrible. Moxi laughs. Once a month, ooh. You know, it's like Helen, going to a lecture with Helen Keller as the lecturer. Beloved Ondine strikes again.

R—Somebody's glass is on the ground.

O—Oh, mine of course, what else?

T—Beloved Ondine is never to be forgotten . . .

O—Oh, it's so primative, these glasses are utterly primative.

T—and or denied, not one ounce.

O—Where's my pillow too? I didn't want to forget that. I've ad such a good time today that I'm going to kill Irving. (*Laughter.*)

T—Where do we go with this?

O—We go, we go in right, right through his neck, honey.

No no no no, no no no no. Don't here.   No, don't go like that, you would, unless you want to break the window, we have to do it with a chair. Aim for about his head.   Any way, it was the wrong room I thought.   I hope, Oh! (*laughter*) Oh please. Drella, I'm a little stoned.

You are?   Yeah, I'm n, it's just. I really sae somebody walking on the balcony out there.   Yeah? With who?   Does it mean? *No, I wasn't walking.* (*laughs*) (*music in background*) We better go, huh? Where're we going?   I don't know. Anywhere. Somewhere, where we're wanted. I'm gonna write on th Ondine, mirror, crippled. There are three things that Piper Laurie wrote.   What?   She wrote, what did she write on the window in "The Hustler?" Crippled, deranged, no, crippled, demented, and rotteness and I don't know, but she wrote three names in lipstick on, on the wall.   Use your lipstick.   I can't.   You ate it that's why.   I ate it. (*laughs.*)   Isn't that strange uh.   What?

Irving—Euh, have you been out on the terrace all this time?   Yes, we were all sitting there.   I didn't even know she was, I was so interesting. (*Voices sound muffled as if the people are speaking in a hallway.*) Oh yes, I think so. I thought it was so inter, (*Irving talks directly into the microphone and so his voice becomes louder.*) I thought was so interesting uh, realest, uh . . .   (*Ondine sings*) Some where over the rainbow (*deep inverted sigh*) way up high. Oh Judy, Judy, where are you now? (*Laughter.*)   Drella—She's sitting right here eating her spaghetti.

O—Oh sing, mmbgmblmm over the rainbow, and the spaghetti falling out of her mouth, oh my God. Come on, have a little drinky with with me and it any any any body.   D—Now?   No, this poor fool uh, uh Judy, I can't stand the thought of her. (*Beach Boys singing in the background*) Oh, are these Beach girls, bags, or the Beach Balls?   D—Is this six Ondine?   I don't know. It mus be. Is it? Is it six? I certainly hope so. (*Ondine starts singing with the Beach Boys.*) I certainly hope it's more than six right now. Let's see. Ju-ju-hoo, a quick step. What's on the bottom . . . what's that Part of a redwood tree?   It's a butterfly.

. . . . . . a butterfly? It's a seed.   A butterfly.   Oh all you people have been on LSD for a week haven't you?   Irving—Drella's gonna get high . . . turned Drella on.   No one turned Drella on. Didn't you, didn't you know that Drella was out?   Of what?   The New York Times has told us so we should know.   Drella's where?   I don't know. They didn't say where he had gone (*laughs*). The just said he was out. What is Al Roon's?   Al, they're foreign.   I keep thinking it's a little Armenian restaurant in the Village with and and it it ain't. Would you do me a favor please and place this, that right here?   Oh, you can't find it? Oh ho ho ho.   I don't know how to treat it.   Oh, I was sitting on it. (*Hindu music in the background.*)   Is there any way of putting his on?   Oh, er're leaving   Way of putting this on.   Yeah but we always, we always.   Just the first aria. Why? Is there a bad, oh.

Is there a bad what?   Is there a bad (*pause*). Maybe I better not, it's such a treasure.   What are you . . . last.   I just have to look at myself in the mirroir.   All right, can I look with you?   (*Singing*) Ah, mirroir, of course. In fact, you can crawl into it with me if you'd like to but Prince Schlameil is on the other sidetoo. Do you have the tales of Hoffman? Do you?   Yes.   Is it one of your favorite operas?   No. Prince Schlameil, what a name for a character. Isn't that beautiful? He's the one who ha dno shadow.   Oh.

7 / 1

(*Noise.*)

?—No, listen um . . . so I'll see you on Tuesday.

DRELLA—Yeah.

?—You get it? (*Noise.*)

I—Ready, I'm ready, let's go.

D—Irv Irv du Ball has your number.

I'm going. . . . . Irving has his number . . .

I—Ondine, thanks for everything.

I hope he doesn't have my number.

—Horse shit.

Horse shit? No no.

—. . . must be . . .

Not horse shit, no no . . . your horse shit, darling. Horse shit everybody.

(*Irving in background: I have paid for . . . more people under my life.*)

(*Deep inverted sighs.*) Iriving . . . that quickly. Irving add a eugh (*inverted sigh*), or else it doesn't fit.

I—Let's go . . . c'mon.

D—Oh you're so pretty, Irving.

I—Hold this just a moment in case you run out of Benzene. Why did you get, why can't, why can't . . . . themselves?

M—It's gonna be open to children.

R—She's really thinking of the Cherry Lane.

Cherry Lane? Long time ago.

R—You're thinking of the Cherry Lane.

M—A lot of close . . . you've stumbled . . . (noise).

R—No children yes . . .

R—No children yes . . .

I—Now how do you expect me to . . .

Oh please.

TAXIN—I must say thank you very much.

But you uh, hm hm. (Taxine in background.) I'd like to have that moldy Coke, I really would.

D—Really? Oh.

It's a beautiful co—oh, isn't it wonderful?

D—Oh I think . . .

T—I just want to thank you . . .

D—He's cominb out with us.

I—I don't————————

T—* * * marvelous . . . well I bet you're . . . the basement.

I—We're all . . .

O—Do you want to see a picture of the Duchess?

D—Yeahs.

O—The ones in the hospital look . . .

I—. . . is Ohio.

O—That's exactly what she looks like Rossini.

D—She rays.

O—She doesn't, she, but she looks like that though.

D—. . . . but she's beautiful.

But she has that kind of a Doctor Barbalo face . . . going to the country.

T—Hahhhahhah.

D—Keep the door open. Oh yes, how does it go?

Turn right . . . here, go ahead . . .

D—Oh, will you h-hold it?

That's all, certainly.

D—Oh.

Of course I will, be, don't be.

D—Oh oh oohh Ondine. . . . . it . . oh Ondine. Oh n-no, no Ondine, n-no, we have garbage.

O—But they just closed the door.

D—N-n-no. They're coming.

T—Ondine, such treasure . . .

O—I never d-d-do.

T—How can you be such a treasurer?

All your friends get so mad at you though, you might as well treasure it all.

O—They hate me. They hate me for being what I am.

D—Who hates you?

Oh, all my.

No, it's true.

Everybody does, but-

No, and I know her-

Oh I know but I . . .

Why should we wait here like this? Oh uh.

O—Why are we waiting? We could wait in the h-h-hall, the lobby and talk with the doorman.

T—Yeah, that's right.

D—Okay.

O—H-hello doorman, how do you do.

T—Don't wait.

O—We're stars. (*Laughter.*)

T—I wanna do it wwith Ondine.

D—We are, we are.

T—But it won't be the, not that people will be able to tell us we're crazy, but that they'll just be so . . . doubt about it.

O—Now we just push one.

D—Yeah.

T—They'll say, "Who are those fantastic people?" They won't say anything else.

O—They're going to say it anyway.

D—Sooner or later, but.

O—My dear, can you walk down the street without having it said?

T—Well.

O—Can you Drella? No—or me.

T—I say like Dodo . . .

O—No, I mean yuh, you can't uh, sooner or or later y-y-you have to

take t-to uh, disguising it or fixing it around. Because they duh, they make, they make it unbearable to live with it. I don't care for people. I don't like them at allll. That's just awful.

T—Oh you kill me.

O—That's just awful.

T—He's a pet.

O—Irving is a real penny pigger. That really is the word for him.

T—That's what I said.

O—Jesus, he's a person.

T—He's a penny pigger. I said he's a penny.

O—Wait'll you hear one of those tapes about IRVING. Ohh.

D—Really?

O—It goes on my head.

D—It's in your novel, it's uh, Taxi's getting the hole bit if we go up for a ride.

T—I'm not doing anything to . . . the . . . is Ondine.

O—What?

T—Ondine's gonna have it . . . and come and talk to me.

O *in a fake voice*—How are we and my dear friends and . . .

T—Except, maybe I should do up today first and then the second day is the real day.

O—Where is the doorman?

T—How many days do we have

O—He's lazy.

T—to do, to make them believe us?

O—Now what are we going to do? Are we going to go. We're not going to the country with them.

D—No.

O—Thank God. What Irv, what does Irving have over Peter? (*Drella laughs subtly.*)

D—I don't know.

O—Hello. What does Irving have over. Nothing? Well why does

Peter take it for?
(*Pause.*)

T—Nothing.

O—I wouldn't endure it for a s-
second. (*Taxi laughs.*)

T—Yes.

O—I'd bust him right in his face.
Immediately.

T—Cause two nothings . . .

O—Bang.

T—Together make another nothing. I think we should . . .

O—What do you mean, you didn't
eat yet? Now d'you want me to
prepare you food or don't you
want me to prepare you food?
(*Imitating Irving.*)

T—Isn't that a fit. See, Ondine
sees it all, Drella.

O—Hmm.

T—And you sit there and say "Aw
no."

O—He sees it too but he's not saying about it.

T—He won't say it, that's all.

O—Why should he? He's having
the, he's really the wise—

T—Yeah, that's right.

O—He's really wiser than us.

T—He's, he's wiser than Rink.

O—Than I am. He really is.

T—Cause he's not putting any
stupid energy into . . .

O—Cause he's ju, he's just enjoying
it.

T—Yeah, and I can't help saying it
though.

O—Can I have a light?

T—Hmm. You want a cigaret?

O—Well I'm going to faint.
(*Drella laughs minutely. Pause.*)
Did you ever see Star faint?
(*Pause.*)

T—They just pass out.

O—You wnat another one? . . . . .
collar.

T—When they faint they just
can't . . .

D—Where's your dark glasses?

O—In my hand.

D—Oh.

O—Ho ho oh oh, I wonder what
I'm going to do. All my friends
have left me; they hate me
and . . .

D—Oh.

O—Well so what.

D—I was doing your day and
you're.

O—So what. I know, but it turned
into my end.

T—Don't let them take you.

O—Don't let the Star. Get in your
eyes (*singing*) don't let the moon
bust your . . . . tarpus?

D—A cigarette's not good.

O—I hate filters.

T—You hate them?

O—Filters. (*Inverted sigh from
Taxi.*)

D—This is the best picture Billy
has of you, that it's great.

T—Oh God, I just adore Ondine
and.

O—She says th . . .

T—It's just terrible.

O—Well I don't feel very kindly
towards you. (*Taxi laughs.*) You
better get (*laughs*) your hands
off me, miss. You're getting to
be, she's getting to be a problem.

D—Yeah, you have to give uh Ondine two days.

T—Two days?

O—Two days?

D—Yeah. In the morning.

T—I jus can har, if I was like, if I
could see Ondine well, could we
do it, like two days?

T—Sure. Because if I see him one
night I can't say.

I know . . .

T—I just get lost.

(*Laughing*) That's . . .

T—Well it's true.

What d'you care about us? We should always be.

I—It looks like we're all moving out, and the funny thing is we're not moved in.

T—That's right. I should be a definite two days.

M—Everybody should . . .

Definite.

T—Ondine, you should.

Tha fell right out of my mouth. I . . .

T—That's it Ondine, two days.

?—Anyone for any clothes?

R—Listen Peter, gimme that.

T—Otherwise I get lost and uh . . .

D—. . . about Monday?

Well now you decide which two days they are, which two days you want. (*Pause.*)

D—Wait Ondine, you can't leave.

T—Y'know you might be busy some days other.

Yeah, it doesn't, no but.

T—But let's say, what day—Tuesdays to Thursdays.

D—Fridays.

T—Friday isn't.

Oh, Friday's a good day to see.

T—Thursdays and Fridays?

Ooh wow!

T—That right?

That's a heavy week-end schedule Taxi.

T—Yeah.

That's pretty good.

T—Tuesday and Friday?

D—. . . . . and Friday.

T—Yeah but if you . . .

O—Wednesday, and or, Wednesday and Fri-Friday is perfect.

D—Yes I think.

T—Friday is perfect.

O—Or Monday and Friday.

D—Monday.

T—Monday, Monday . . . is the mest day.

D—Oh bye Peter.

T—Monday and Friday.

Yeah.

T—And then we'll get, oh that's right, and then we'll get . . .

O—We, we'll get it then, Monday and Friday.

T—Right.

O—I think the best, the best place (*traffic noise*) when you said Friday I nearly fell. It's really perfect. Did you say Friday? It's perfect then. Yes you did say, I remember it.

T—I said Tuesdays and Thursdays . . . because.

O—Oh, Tuesdays and Thursdays and Saturday.

D—Oh really? Oh.

Hm.

T—I was thinking of Monday and Tuesday and Thursday and Friday (*laughs*) when I said . . .

O—Well listen, I'm uh, well I'm gonna walk to Queens. I'll see you Friday.

D—You're not.

O—You're coming with me dear. (*Laughs.*)

T—Are you really going to Queens?

D—No.

O—No, of course not.. Across the 59th street bridge.

I—Bu tha's uh, that's sort of an interesting . . .

T—Ohh.

O—Oh well, I wouldn't give you two twigs for a (*laugh*) I ju, I just, I wanna find Mioca and then I'm through.

T—Oh.

I—We're not going after all, Peter, we're not going are we?

PETER—What?

I—We're not going are we? No, I don't know, I guess not cause, cause . . . like . . . I don't think the jungle girle is going.

D—Oh where. . . .

P—He's so casual about wearing a sweater.

I—Y'know something, I'm so casual, I'm not even there, that car's, that car's gonna pull out of there . . .

(*Ondine says something in the background.*)

I—Well, but why don't y-you wait and I'll load, I'll load the rest of the things in the back of your car.

P—Okay, let's go. Well I have to carry your bag, you can carry my long underwear and I'll

I—No.

P—I'll carry your bag.

I—I-I'll carry my bag. (*Taxi laughs.*) Do you wanna get the car . . . I, I'll, why, why don't you just pick me up here, please.

P—He likes that grand entry where I can.

I—No, I don't like to, I don't like to appear in my garage cause you have a way of . . .

D—Ondine Ondine.

I—ordering gas and . . . (*Taxi laughs.*)

Those three women wanna speak to me.

I—Wait, wait, all rights girls.

O—C'mon, look at their socks. March. Oh they're hilarious. They said they were wearing socks. They have little white socks on, the three of them. Now. . . . . . .   would fly over

to them and say "Go home. Now what do ya mean being dressed like that, you look ridiculous like . . . you look ridiculous, you hear me?" Oh two more. Today is a special night. One is a sailor. Oh, ohh ohhh those girls. (*Taxi laughs.*)

T—It's such a silly . . .

O—And those flats, oh New York is fabulous. The people in it are hilar. . . . it's a collection of freaks. (*Pause.*) I feel transfixed by the micro—am I hypnotized? Will I die like Linda Darnell did, ablaze?

I—. . . . . I mean uh. . . . .

O—Have a nice time, Peter. Nice meeting you, it was. (*Pause.*) That's for you, Ondine I love ya. (*Smacks lips.*) What? (*Drella talking.*) It really is, that's a good, that's good, that's very good but it has an odd and sinister undertone. . . . . . talking about things anymore.

D—What?

O—I hate s-standing on corners. Let's go to Ali Baba. Let's look in the window or something. There must be a belly dancer there.

D—You're on the . . .

O—Oh how Oriental, look . . . Middle Eastern, Ohho. How truly, oh how truly horrid. This was La Ventura last week.

D—Wasn't it?

O—Wasn't it? I know it was. (*Laughter.*) My glasses. I saw something very Middle Eastern in there.

D—Really? What?

O—Tilly Lasch . . . it's ap . . .

D—You know Tilly?

O—No, but I've heard, y'know, but

I've seeeen her in movies. She always dadadances dances the moon. She schroooch back there.

D—Really?

O—Didn't you ever see her, she was wh, what Arabian movie was she in, something like uh, uh, what was the name of it uh, (pause) Oh don't let him go by himself. (Pause.) Don't let him go by himself: Did Irving let him? Did Irving let him?

T—To race cars.

O—Oh, oh, oh well then, oh please, I wanna go to a delicatessen quickly. I get a . . .

T—Can we go eat?

O—a pickle.

T—I wanna eat or drink or so, go home or.

I—Eat or drink and go home and go . . .

T—S-something's the matter with me . . . heh heh hey.

I—Ondine, if you ever throw the side he's pointing at, this is the most passive put-on I've ever seen; as a result of having this, Drella doesn't have to participate in life.

T—Oh is that why he's saying . . .

I—Why he has to participate . . . no, it's amazing, he holds this to all of us.

O—no that's, my dear, this is, he's holding it only to me darling, he's holding holding it o-only to me and he's participates far more than he would without it. (Pause.)

I—How do you know when you run out of tape?

T—He's putting, he's.

O—So there. Now why don't you get done on your racing car.

Thank you Irving, we have a *lovely time*, thaach.

I—C-come up and shower any time.

O—I w—I'll never use your rust-free bath tub again.

I—Is that a promise?

O—A promise, darling, it's not a promise darling, it's a curse.

I—Yes, it's, i's the curse of the . . .

O—And Tilly Larsch dances in there while I curse. (*Taxi laughs.*) Sh sh shh.

I—He's very brave now because he's outside.

O—What d'you mean brave? I got, you're damn right, I got my record.

I—We never even heard it.

O—You're lucky. On your machine I understand it, it would've been slaughtered.

I—I know . . . it's not used to that kind of faithful reproduction.

O—No, darling and it's faithful.

T—Heh heh heh heh.

I—It's the only thing you have that's . . .

O—It's the only thing I care enough to send.
Inverted sigh—SIGH

O—Oh Irving, let's not match wits because you're witness. (*Taxi laughs.*)

I—That's true, huh huh huh, I've given it all to charity when I . . .

O—You've given it all to other people, darling. (*Iriving & Taxi laugh.*) Your wits reside in Judy Garland's.

T—The thing is Ondine is is the . . .

O—Brain.

T—the most witful, th-that it's hopeless

I'm not witful. I'm just s-s-

T—No you're not.

O—I'm just skipping my head above water.

T—You're just an explosion all the time.

O—I've gotta sit dooowwwnn!

I—He's not in the habit of keeping his head above water.

O—Oh Irving. He should know that I bathe eight times a day every place place that I can possibly.

I—Well I imagine I kn-know.

O—I love water. I used to turn blue when I was a child. They would take me out brrrrr, and they would slap me and I'd go into hysterics. I went into a trance as a child.

D—Where are you going?

O—Enjoy yourself Irving, really and thank you very much nnnn-aaaa.

D—Oh oh.

T—Oh that, thank you so much.

O—For a lovely day.

I—Thank you for being all . . .

O—Oh that's okay, now it, you look in the pockets of your coat, you'll find them empty. (Laughter.)

D—Bye Irving. (Laughter.)

O—Oh he deserves it, doesn't he? Oh he really deserves it. What is he pulling . . . . what is he trying to act like Judy Garland? What's this, what is all this pity me routine? Who is supposed to be?

D—. . . . . you.

O—Him. No, y'know what, no look, they're all asking me hah hah hah. I have pissed his . . . . I don't have any friends. They're all after what they can get and blah blah. Oh he says it so many words and

every intuation. Like what he said about you. He's a fool.

D—What'd he say?

O—About that non-participation, is he serious? Is he serious? Does he know what he's saying? No, I guess he doesn't, no, poor fool. Anyway. Hi. (Rink & Taxi talking the background.) I can't stop, I like men, I like . . . of what. No I, no techniques or anything. I could never, was able . . . Louis Primativo, I just did it.

T—The toes . . .

O—La Croisette   That's a silly name for a restaurant. Do y'know I have, I was never able to cruise in my entire life.

D—Really?

O—No. Never able to once. I would burst out laughing or I would have to walk away or I'd feel embarrassed. I can't do . . . huh?

D—. . . . . long story.

O—Oh, wha de when what old story? You mean when I, cause I like boys? Huh huh, I don't know, I don't.

D—I mean when did cruising start?

O—You mean, you mean successful cruising?

D—Yeah.

O—Never, I nev, I don't, I still don't. I have the frank approach. Darling would you like a . . . . ? Do y'know that's it. Hi. I, I don't know why I have to add those little sounds after those, but that really makes the whole thing. Ha ha ha. (Laughter.)

R—Looking at us. You oughta come up at my right, Moxanne . . . . . (laughter).

O—Oh, the A&P. Are you open? Are you open? Are you open? Is

the night crew on? We wanna shop. Oh sell us some things. This is . . . until you can get, oh here we are again.

T—Oh.

O—Where is this, this is 1st Avenue and uh, 57th street.

T—Ondine, where are you going?

O—I don't know.

O—We don't even know, we we have nine, nineteen more tapes (*laughs*) to fill and then we'll be through, uhhh. Personally, I'd like to go home and see mom.

D—. . . . can't.

O—*laughing*—I know. I've given up. Where are you going Moxanne? Where?

M—I'm going?

O—Yeah.

M—9:30.

No, and she said 9:30, where I said, where on earth do you go at 9:30? Oh, let's go to the automat, is there one around here? (*laughs.*) And we can see the people dunk their tea bags.

There's none around here.

There's none around?

There's one down on 42nd street. (*Rink says at the same time*) On 42nd street and 3rd avenue.

There's one up on 57th, right near Carnegie Hall.

Shall we go?

T—I think I'd. . . .

Oh yeah.

R—Look at this car.

Doesn't that, look at that liquor store.

T—Ah ah ah ah ah.

Hello everybody.

I—Oh that's jus twhat I want.

T—Taken our . . . taken our. . . .

M—Maybe he does, he doesn't look like . . .

T—Bye car.

By car.

R—He doesn't look like himself. (pause)

T—It is, it is.

It is, it is, it always will be.

T—And they knew it all the time.

I'm gonna go in there and baaagg.

For what?

My record.

Oh, you have to, you can't go in, Ondine. What? (pause)

I'm having a big blow out. I will, yeah. I think I can buy a bag to cover my record.

What? (pause)

. . . . . have some juice on your bags. It's very hard to buy a bag.

?—There's flowers.

It's just because I'm ripping the cover and everything and I don't want to do that.

They probably don't have it.

MAN—40 cents. (pause)

A what, Sir?

A bag.

Uh, you see I'm ripping it and I just don't want to uhhhh. I really don't and I hate to dirty it too . . . . . oh . . .

MAN— . . . . that's uh, 50 cents.

Oh, they're black though. (pause) Should I take the tape off-

Huh?

Should I take the.

Yeah.

So you haven't got a bag for it, oh well.

MAN—It's the seams. . . .

Think. I wonder what I can do with it.

Uh.

You want a bag fo rthat candy?

Uh, big, big bag s-so that. . . . all right.

The biggest bag is the same size.

MAN—But it is.

Okay.

Oh.

We can tear it.

MAN—The ones that . . .

Yeah and all these

MAN—Okay, 60, 75 cents.

That won't be . . . . . oh, well we can tear it.

Hmm?

If he can tear it.

Tear what?

The bag.

MAN—1, 2, 3, 4, 5.

Oh, these are good.

MAN—and a 5.

Would you.

MAN—I bet you wouldn't have got an opener it you.

You said to him, you said, "Well he can at least like well he can tear it." That must've thrown you. That man is just . . . . well uh, he said that the bag's just, is just no big enough, so all these things and said "Oh yes, you can get a big bag." And he said "But it's not big enough," and he said, "Well he can tear it." And y'know a-after hat point, y-you don't ask any more.

M—You tore it?

Yeah, I ripped it all. What oh, I uhhhh.

Ondine knows. . . .

Oh.

T—Um well, what's the general plan?

I don't have the vaguest idea what I'm doing, and furthermore, 9:30? That's not bad.

T—Do you have an-any idea of where you're going?

M—Because I-I'm hungry. Why don't we go eat something?

Yeah. Why don't we go anywhere?

M—. . . go o us, a drug store.

What'd she say?

(Drella says something)

Ooh, let's go to a fag place. One of those fairy places where, where, where, where, cause they're oh all of them they hate me. (noise) They can't because I, but I am (laughter) I can't bear it.

M—But Irving doesn't like you.

He, he hates me and I'm so glad.

M—He has a nice way of hating people, though.

Irving?

M—He's very friendly about it, I think.

Well he, y'know he he he he's inevitable.

M—I mean he sort of refuses to. About it.

M—He could of refused to argue with you all together.

How dare you.

M—It's so . . . . .   You were witless. Now because.

No, I was gonna get it in before he tried.

Moxanne laughs

He he he already insulted Drella

M—I know.

And he insulted me.

Did he insult me?

Yes.

Why?

I thought so.

How?

By, by, by . . .

M—Yeah, he did. He told you you were ridiculous.

by his current attack on his, or his understanding of the artistic scene. He should be put out of his misery. And that poor Peter.

M—And he comes out with those. . . .

That poor Peter, I really, that boy

is so,

M—That ridiculous murmer.

nice, he really is. And he, he prob, and I can just see the endurance test that he must run. I don't think.

M—Oh come on.

I don't think he's any angel, my dear, I mean, but he's just y'know, he puts up with him.

M—I've seen.

Anyway, I think Irving is just an excuse. He's he biggest.

I don't hink. Arnold Inoven.

See, Arnold Inoven is like God in comparison to him.

R—That was a beautiful remark by Victrola, you oughta, yououghta be.

It's the truth, he is witless. He's completely witless. He's not funny, he's paranoic, he's not charming, he's tastless, he he's just a boor. To suggest that every time a person turns a corner in your house that they're about to,

Where're we going?

that hey're about to flop into something, like into your bag. It's just

Huh?

because they can't find their way.

I have Ondine for a couple of hours.

What?

I have Ondine for awhile.

Oh.

You can get rid of me.

Oh no, I want you.

Aw right.

Are we all gone?

Let's all get in a cab and go over toward Taxi's and then we'll go out and . . . . . (*pause*)

Oh, it's hard to get in.

I just bit my earring with the force of I don't know, Ondine.

With the force of.

And I broke a tooth.

Did you really break a tooth?

It looks like it.

I mean I don't really consider him anything more than. . . .

You were absolutely right.

The first time I met him I think I screamed. I won't make a movie with him because I don't want to, to rec, and what, Drella, y'know it's just his attitude. He's got that silly push-cart attitude. (*Taxi laughs*) I can't push, bear it, yes, it's so boring. Who needs him? (*Taxi laughs*) I certainly don't need his terrace (*laughter*) I certainly don't.

(*laughing*) of, no,

Now who. . . .

Did, didn't you say it was his rust-free something (*laughing*) or other?

Yes, but you should have, you should have seen the bath water that I opened. It looked like a swamp. (*laughter*)

Did you leave it, off the bath plug?

No, I mean but I mean it's not his fault.

It was, the first bad thing was he threw us out of his closet bathroom.

Yes.

What were you doing, what did you wanna do in the bathroom?

I want to go to see. . . .

It's a nicer bathroom. . . .

Oh yeah.

Yeah.

Ondine.

Yet he s-gave us the Canoe.

Canoe. (*laughter*)

Gave us the Canoe, it was he Canoe, that evil smelling thing.

That was just the guest bathroom.

No but, yes I said, no but I've never been so insulted in my life (*Moxanne laughing*) A public bathroom—how hateful.

Ohhohooh-oh.

Y'know one can't us,

It was so embarrassing, y'know because Peter was coming out of the bathroom.

It was nice to see him though.

But you can use the . . .

Yeah, and Peter said to him at the last stop, "Why don't you throw them out of your bathroom?" He's y'know, kinda drunk, y'know how they keep talking. And I take it Peter drinks a lot.

No, he doesn't.

He doesn't? Around Irving he doesn't.

He doesn't drink at all.

That's hard to believe, y'know.

He's worse off than . . . us.

He better, he better then. Irving drinks a lot, doesn't he?

No no, he's worse.

Lester doesn't drink?

Irving was so drunk after thirty seconds.

He wants it. He begs for it.

He slobbers all over the place.

Why do you think he, sa, Judy Garland around? That's his model.

Ohh.

He wanted Divina.

Oh of course, they're gonna fight again, come on, let's have a little drinky, you can sing a little bit but the spaghetti's in your mouth.

You can sing a little bit but the spaghetti's in your mouth.   Oh God, it's just despicable. Oh.   It's a terrible dinner party.   No, but the thing is (*voice noises*)   Nureyev . . . . . spaghetti.   She was at one

time marvelous.   You know Nureyev too?   Yeah.   He he got his
spaghetti that's . . .   I love it, Judy Garland was saying to him coming
down   How come he's so awful? And people . . .   in the elevator,
she was saying, "You filthy Commie spy, you."   Oh really?   She was
(*laughing*) r-r-running around. Isn't that beautiful? (*Taxina laughs*)
What?   What, what Judy Garland was saying to Nureyev on the way
     That's me.   down in in in the elevator.   Yeah I know. Isn't that
terrible?   "You pinko, you filthy Commie spy. Oh," she said, "that's
beautiful."   Is that today?   Oh I love him for that, cause he's he's
he said "Yah, yah yah," or something.   He didn't know (*Taxi laughs*)
     That's a good thing, y'know we got . . .   I was never so disap-
pointed in my life, as when I saw Nureyev.   No but you . . . . . Taxine
. . . . .   Yeah, he'll be using Andy Warhol, and he does use it. What
does he mean non-participation? I really wish he'd keep his remarks to
himself, but it's uh . . .   I told you, Ondine.   evaluation. Oh well I,
y'know I have to tell them immediately that it, what they are, it's, I have
to say that, that they're witless. Or something else of the equivalent, because that's what they are.   Huh huh.   I think Irving du Ball, (*gasp*)
even the name makes me scream. (*Taxina & Drella laugh*)   I'd like to.
     Yes, du Ball, Irve.   That's   No, that's, isn't that marvelous?
     There's something so beach house about that whole place. I like the,
I like the apartment, but it's too beach house.   Y'know were near
hickory dick rosenberg.   It is? I don't know who that is.   It is, it is
hickory dick rosenberg.   It's very beachy. It is y'know.   Y'know, you
expect sand to flow in, to flow in from one room into the other.   . . .
meat ball or something. And you expect a couple of drunks to fall around
and the sand's all over ya.   Y'know a lot.   Wow.   I love. There's
nothing I like better than than than the beach.   . . . than in the
kitchen.   Oh the kitchen. You're not allowed in the kitchen.
You're not allowed in there.   No, because you might get . . .   Oh,
he's he's, h esticks money in there.   Them Ovaltine or something in
there.   Oh, he also refrigerates.   That's Roger Tru-*Trudau* go go
gone berserk.   Yeah, yes. (*laughter*)   Oh Roger said, "You're eating
Taxi's yogurt." said "What? Look, if you say one more thing like that and
I'll throw it at you." (*Rink laughs*) He just said, (*Taxi laughs*) he said,
"You're eating her yogurt," and was just so hurt. I ju, (*laughter*) I was. I
said, "What're you talking about? Roger, are you mad?" And Dodo
Mae Doom just giggled, she (*Drella laughs*) (*Moxanne laughs*) I love
Dodo, I really do, although she's in cahoots with him.   Oh.   I don't
under . . .   She's in cahoots with him.   understand that.   Oh I,
I do, because Dodo's a rather pleasant girl. (*Drella & Taxi laugh*) and she
has to get along (*laughs*) Dodo Mae's very sweet.   Yeah she is.

Anybody would know judas bell for that.   Oh wait wait.   Where're
we going? Uh, do I walk up this street? Is this 63rd street? Because the
doorman in one of these uh, apartment houses.   Oh Ondine. The
police are after me too.   I know darling. But we, we'll hide you again.

I don't know what to say.   Don't worry about it. We'll disguise
you, you put on that Montey Wooley beard.   (gasp) (Drella laughs)

They'll never know. And those big trapper boots (Taxi laughs)
Why is the police after you?   Because they.   Thank God.   They're
writing nasty things.   Oh that's nothing.   about Irving du Ball all
over the, Irving du Ball   Islands.   should be put away.   back to
the islands.   Oh.   Can you see what he's gonna do on the week-end?
Ohh whayum just hang off the sides of the boardwalk.   . . . let me get
hold of it even.   What do you put in drinks like that? I mean if someone drinks and they get like youarenow,that's divine.   No oh.   No,
I mean, th that's nice. But Irving gets nasty and y'know like he gets suspi-
cious and he, and then he does something about his suspicions—he attacks
Wha wha what he thinks is an upheaval attack. (Taxine laughs)
Ondine.   To me he laughs everytime he says something he laughs.
He's like an anteater, y'know I don't like the shape of his lips either
(laughter), or his stature, or his moccasins. I couldn't bear his moccasins
ah, uhh. (Taxi—inverted sigh) Oh I can't stand.   How can anybody
stand up against such an . . . . . Irving du, oh and when he showed me the
picture of Wil-William Inn.   Oh.   He said he looks like his plays.
Rotten. And you know he does, it's a picture of this enormous faggot,
now.   Oh oh oh.   Why did you hit them? (Drella ha ha's) They
were begging for it and if the sniper is there, we'll all fix up. (pause)
There will (laughing) be a sniper one day, won't there? Get, get me as I
come out of.   Oh no.   Oh, I love her veil. Oh.   Wow.   I was,
uh (laughs) I was, I went to Saint Brigitte's Church, and I was I was
coming out of it, hey,   Oh!   Watch out there, this cab isn't insured,
and as I was coming out, a friend came up and told me "Y'know, Kennedy's been assassinated?" I went uhhgh. I promised I would never go to
church again. As I was coming out of Saint Brigitte's Church I heard that,
I couldn't believe it, I mean why bother to go to church? Isn't that awful?
Maybe I'm making a m-m-mountain out of a, I hope you're going to
apologize. (Taxi laughs)   What'd he say?   You tried to kill movie
stars.   She already did.   There's a bevy of movie stars in here plus
producers and directors.   What?   And foreign people. Are you a
movie star?   (gasp) I am sorry to   All I could say is, and foreign
pe-people, for her be, I love her but I don't know what to say.   You're
a, you're foreigners too.   Oh I, may I say something?   Your just so
magnificent.   Am I out of it, am I out of it? I hope. You're out of it.

You just sa, you just said that that   People don't know now, what to say or do.   I'm gonna go sleep in the park again, on the side of the lake with . . .

7 /   2

It was madness, we hallucinated everything. It's fabulous.   That was in that   You're gonna go upstairs and got to sleep.   No body has any yet.   No.   Uh.   You're telling me. (*Taxi coughs*)   What are we going to do w-w-well uh,   Gee, Irving du Ball's the only thing you can think of.   Are you gonna take me to New Jersey tomorrow, or should I rent a car? (*Taxi coughs*)   Oh honey, blow your. Go with Rink. Are you all right? I, that choking, God.   I know, it's   I felt like opening my pockets and giving (*laughs*) ow, that heel was piercing ooh. Oh oow. Oh (*Taxi laughs*) a bloody toenail. (*laughs*) It's the, on the little one, ow you did it so smartly, Taxine, that I can't believe it. (*Taxina giggles*)   Oh, that was,   Well it smarts, that's all. I'm going with an old lady in the Con Edison thing, good night.   Wai-wait-wait,
Do y'know, I just thought I saw a friend of mine hobble out of one of those things ond crutches, with broken arms and legs. He had gone down to give the boys a few, and he he hobbled back up from his crutches and came up . . . I said, "Ben," I couldn't believe his pluck. I said, "I don't believe it. I, y'know, you really are the filthiest things." There he was, craw-crawling out of a Con Edison pit. (*Taxi gasps*)   That looks like Euorpe across the way. (*Taxi laughs*) Imagine, he's so lithe.   Thin.
   Thin and Ben, he's d, he's just too funny. I can't believe him; he's the— We used to get stoned on LSD and he would turn, turn around and we'd like, put whole halves of cheese up (*Laughs*) y'know I didn't used to care for him too much, he was a little, he was a big ballet dancer. (*Moxi and Rink giggle*) All muscle. (*Taxina laughs*) Is there anything siller than a balld ballet dancer?   Huh,huh.   There's nothing siller than a bald ballet dancer. And that's what he was. (*Taxi laughs*) With an enormous, I would even, it was an immen; he was so silly looking I can't describe him to you, you have to see him. In fact, let's go over his house now he'd, he frequently has seizures. (*Rink sorta laughs*) And he gets, he gets even with people by throwing water out of his window, as they leave. (*Ring mutters something*) He's   Like Paris.   L-living on 16th Street?
   Real salt water   and he does dances to the radiator and every-

thing, and the cops are coming. I (*Moxanne laughs*).   Where's he live?
   On 16th Street, it's unbearable. (*Rink laughs*) The thought that he
was doing a dance, he does a dance for everybody, I mean there's no, I
can't think of anything, oh he's so horrid. Listen, the truly revolutionary
spirit in our time. (*Laughing*) He's, he's from Texas, and I know he's
good. Well—   There's a brake. . . .   All there, gracia and buonacera,
that's what, that's what I   Don't you wanna come and have a hamburger?   or something.   That's what a little woman, that's what a
little woman said to, at the, the man that has the ice truck at the Fair.
She said to him, "Do you, do you have lemon ice?" And he said, "No."
he said, "Cherry, pineapple, chocolate." She buttoned the top of her
cardigan sweater and said "Allo there, gracia and buona sera," and off
she went. Then "Thank you and good night." She thought she was a
Jack Benny. (*Rink laughs*) She was a big, fat, Italian woman and she
was lovely. Oh I hope Rotten Rita forgives me.   He made 700 bucks
that . . . that wasn't too bad.   (*Impatiently*) Let's go. Rink keeps,
shall we wa-walk up the stairs?   We can (*laughs*) and then we'll
Listen, we'll call tomorrow and see if you wanna.   Yeah, if you
Taxi, I'll have to call you early.   If you wanna go to New Jersey, remember we're pulling for you.   Uh.   No. uh.   (*tiredly*) Can I
be the mayor?   Yes.   Uh.   All you have to do is kill Rita.
Then it's Ian Coop and Puce Rimmington . . . con, concert that we can
go to af-afterward in Pennsylvania.   Rit's gonna go for New York, it's
   Rita's gonna go, or look at those buttons with the top of it.   That
they would take us and not give us tickets   Oh, no, no.   They took
a neon light.   Well, are we going to uh, it has to be early, y'know.
What what?   We have to get there before twelve.   When?   I
mean New Jersey.   We're going to the Caucus New Jersey.   . . .
has something from over New Jersey, constructive from   For what?
For shows for next fall. And he has to go over and look at them and expect.   I wanna go inna   do do much except.   the park, I'll take
them off, I guess.   But you can't ride over, I'll drive him over, rent a
car.   Oh.   Wait a second, there's no problem.   You have to . . .
it early because he has to be thereby   My aunt lives in New Jersey.
It'll take about an hour and a half to get there.   Yeah.   So uh
It'll be heaven.   Call when you get up.   Okay.   Or we'll call.
Oh what, e, okay.   We'll call when we get up.   I've got   I love
this group.   Well, if you don't wanna go, no I mean, if you don't
wanna we'll think about, we'll get uh   Fabulous. It's the original confusion group.   I mean, if it's uh, if you need me to drive you that's one
thing.   Well uh, it's uh . . . . . Barney Dozier who invited you out.
Barney Dosier?   And Oona with the baby.   And Oona with the

baby?   You know who they are? Well   No.   You like them. Barney Dosier and Oona with the baby sound pretty good.   The ones that invited us.   Sounds great.   Ohh.   That sounds as if they'd like to have a mountain all, all their own.   I'm sure I met . . .   He's the one, the one who had the baby wasdescribingthe interview.   . . . I may, may not.   Taxi, if   Ondine goes.   Taxi.   I know you may not, but you will go.   I may not.   . . . the one who was having the baby and described it to you.   She had   Oh that was good.   it on the side of the mountain. Natural childbirth.   Well, I don't know. Can't you see the woman lying there up, Taxi on the telephone, "I am now having a baby."   You were able to hear it at the other end? Your your your other-er, in your your other poc-pocket.   What? Yes . . . well um.   Good night, good night, my s, wait.   I'll do it if   Good night, good night (*singing*)   Yeah.   (*Singing*) Good night, it's time to say good night.   But I haven't called and I don't feel great, and so I think not.   America to lose you, number 7.   The King family.   A lucky strike extra.   Something, something   I Good night, good night.   I could, I could drive, if you want, if y'know, if you wanta go, it's fine.   Well, it all depends. I might be all over it tomorrow(*Taxi coughing*)   I hope you get over that cold, my God!

Well, it wasn't there almost tall day, but I talked too much. . . . . . (*says something indistinctly in Italian*) That . . .   Get the Duchess, get the doctor to get a pill . . . (*car noises*) Okay, I'll call about 10.   Let me, I'm gonna walk a . . .   Oh Ondine, I wish you. (*pause with car noises and voices in the background*)   Do you think we'll be able to rent a car?   Uh yeah. Just bring identity.   I don't have any. Do you have any?   Like a, like, uh, anything, to,   Well you have your driver's license.   Oh I have a passport and all that.   Oh. And I though of bringing   Let's, c, let's not stand and talk here because the cop it looking at us.   Huh?   So what?   The cop it looking at us.   It's all right.   Well he came over to stare at us.   Oh. . . . unless you're going back . . .   He did come over to stare at us. Yeah. He did. That's why I walked her up the stairs and got rid of it—Oh.   Let's go . . .   Also I told her that as I got, I said to her "Try not to take any nembetols and get some sleep. Watch television and snap out." Cause I really don't think she should take any more nembetols.

Neither do I . . . off the, off the downies.   Just off the downies completely, she doesn't need them.   Off the downies.   Off the downies. Morton and otherwise. So she said, she said, "I," she said, "Y'know I can't sleep without nembetols." And I said, "Put on the television," I said, "and just make your eyes tired and just go to sleep." And she will because she's a little box now. I hope she does because it would

be such a great thing for her. She wouldn't take them like a ninny. She can make accidents so easily.   She can?   Yes.   What kind?
She can she she can accidentally take an overdose with them and not know about it, I mean, really.   She has to give up her.   I mean she really could do it because nebetols and those things are, they're.   Why does, she shouldn't get it, where's she get them anyway? . . .   When she was in the hospital she used to sleep two hours a night.   That's good enough. That's good enough. My mother has nev, never slept more than three hours a night for her entire, her entire life.   I made her sleep for two hours;   My fault.   No, she doesn't sleep, she just has nightmares; she can't get herself to sleep.   Yeah.   And this y'know, like you watch her sleeping, she's so. . . .   I know, I know, I've never been through it but she's got to do without the nembetols, she's got to . . . (pause)   You mean she's got to take the nembetols.   No she doesn't.   No, I mean she's not a sick . . .   Well, she doesn't, she's gonna be fracturing   herself.   . . . what . . . what does it?   That she doesn't sleep.   No, she.   Well, those nembetols probably put her in a very deep sleep and that's what y'know, keeps her   Sure.
Why not? Why don't we all go, why don't we wait until I call Rotten Rita and maybe we can go up there. And have a concert. Rotten Rita wants to sing.   Oh.   Oh trouble.   Oh trouble.   Trouble. Is there any trouble in Tahiti?   Yeah.   Are . . . any good?   No.
What's his name liked it.   Who?   Bill Paul. Oh I like uh, Paul Paul. Oh uh, what's his, he's so cute. Did you really ask him that same question?
No, I asked him about the uh, the other photographer.   Who?
Juan.   Juan.   What, what did y, s, you say . . .   He said, "No."
Euh, he doesn't, I think maybe they're making it.   Maybe.   No, Juan is right into des . . .   with everything.   Is this right?   I don't know, but he was scared as shivers of me the other week. (Dialing on telephone) And the way he said hello to me this week was all, pretty testy, testy, testy, y'know. Oh we can go to the, t, the, uh, whore house. Down on eleventh street. It's always a raucous activities down there. And they'd love to see us. (pause) They'd give their eye-teeth to see us. (pause) I'm getting really tired.   Are you?   Really tired.   Yould you like something?   No. No, I wanna do dicks. Do a thousand.   I know today's a very tiring day for you.   Isn't it beautiful?   Yuh. It's uh, it's different though.   It's very exhausting for some reason. I don't know why. It's not this.   No.   It's just the situations,   Oh.   that occur.
You sound like Billy.   Well I feel uh, y'know, just exhausted. But I don't really. I'm not really tired; in fact, I'm raring to go. (hangs up telephone)   No answer?   No.   Call the hospital.   I'm gonna, shall I?   Yes. It's the Ethel Roosevelt.   Why don't we go into a

place and and I'll call them, like from a delicatess—   Oh no, go ahead.
Oh, all right, but you.   There's no place really.   I keep thinking
that the cops are gonna come come by.   Oh. Will they?   I don't
know. Once there was a fallen one.   Oh.   Her Rink, would you give
mea light?   What?   Would you give me a light?   Give you a
light? Mother of us all.   Yes, could you please give me the number of
the Ethel Roosevelt.   You have it backwards don't you? Or don't you.
Uh uh, the uh, no I'm here, the Ethel Roosevelt Hospital. (*Rink laugh*)
Another match.   Yeah. (*pause*) 5-5-4-7 thousand. Thank you.
Roosevelt Hospital?   That's were uh, the contessa is.   5-5-4-7 thousand. Who do I look for? The Duchess, Rott, uh.   The Duchess.
5-5-4.   Maybe it's Mrs.   Mrs. who? Mrs. Brown?   Brown.
Yeah (*dialing*) Well she's in, she's on, in building G.   I have the num-
ber.   Where?   In my pocket.   The number of her, uh, uh, room?
Really? (*pause*) No I dialed uh, the number of the Roosevelt Hospital uh.
It's G 905.   Wait, excuse, excuse me. I'll uh, call, dial again. I got
information again.   Oh.   Cause I dialed all those numbers.
Really?   5-5-uh.   5, 7 thousand.   (*Dialing*) G 905?   Yuh.
(*Dialing*) I think that the tapes are gonna be, come out beautifully.
We have to find someone to uh.   I got New York City information
again. I just dialed the hospital again and I got information.   Oh, ask
them what the Ethel Roosevelt Hotel, Hos, Hospital is.   I have 5-5-5-7
thousand (*pause*) Ohhh. Thank you.   What is it?   5-5-4-7 thousand
(*Puts in money and dials*) 5, 5, 4, 7, thousand; two,   No, one more.
Put the bag down. Isn't it heavy? Oh I'd hate to have the bag there.
Huh?   I hate those bags. (*pause*) It's probably past visiting hours.
Maybe she's uh, special. (*pause*)   It is past visiting hours though.
She said not to come after 9. And it's   Oh really?   after 9, right
now. Yes, could you please, if possible, get me to, uh, G 905, Miss, Miss
The Duchess's room? Thank you dear.   Oh really? Well they, you can
get calls in. Tell her I think she's adorable.   She is. (*pause*) The line is
busy.   Hmmm. Tell her to get off the phone. (*pause*)   The number
directly is 5-5-4-7   5-5-4-7 thousand.   9-1-5   What?   Thank you.
Huh?   That's her private line, I guess that's a priv, private number.
She wants you to call, that num is the number busy?   Yeah.
(*pause*) Yeah. The number was was was was busy.   Oh well, you
could've hold on.   Where is that uh piece of paper that you had in
your.   What piece of paper?   Th one with the, with the thing on it.
Oh wait, I have. Change it to 5-5- (*pause*) 5-4.   Oh, thank you.
(*laughs*) 7-1.   Well, let's call again. 9.   Yeah, but if it's busy.
Try again.   I just have a nickel. I lost a call on that.   Ask. I don't
know if I have any.   That God-damned woman.   That meat was

great. Kind of stringy, but.   I wonder if this is the building.   Huh?
It must be, it must be the building that, that we were getting. I can't
imagine.   Huh? Yeah.   She's nice isn't she? She's beautiful too.
(dialing)   . . . . . telling her.   When? (pause) Really?   . . . invited her.   Oh fabulous (dialing) I don't blame Rink (pause) She's a
charming girl. (pause) (yawns) Solid. No, it's not. (pause) Hello
Duchess? Hello, it's, is Ondine. (pause) How are you? (pause) Listen
honey, what's happening? Are you okay? (pause) (shocked) On what!
(pause) Oh wow. Oh my. An operation tomorrow Did the mayor come
and see you? (pause)   An operation? What kind?   Oh well t, oh
well t, is there any way that we, I can get in?   Was . . . . . up? (Long
pause)   Okay, good. (long pause) You must've had a lot of people,
yeah. (pause, rustling of paper) Oh my God. (long pause) Oh. (pause)
Oh my dear.   Give her my love.   Drella send his love. Yeah.
Tell her I think she's fabulous.   He thinks you're, huh? He, she
wants t', say hi to you.   Oh hi Duchess. Oh can we come and see you?
Not now, tomorrow. (pause)   Oh. (pause) Huh? (long pause) Is
Rotten Rita there?   Yeah.   Oh hello? Oh I think you're just fabulous. Oh really? What what's happening?   Hem, hemorrhaging capillaries.. (pause)   Oh oh. (pause) What happened? (pause) Yeah, yeah.
(pause) Uh huh.   (whispering) It's so pathetic isn't it?   Oh really?
(pause) You're going to the operation room? Why? (pause) What are
they? (pause) You do? (pause) Yeah, yeah. What is, what're what're,
what is, what're what're, what is capitooshesary ary. (paper rustling) Oh
really? But why do they have to operate you? Ha huh huh. (pause) But
why do htey have to operate?   Hemorrhaging capillaries, what . . . . .
(rustling paper)   Oh. (rustling paper) Yeah, yeah, oh yeah (pause)
yeah (pause) Oh wha-what are they gonna do then?   . . . . . (whispers)
her appendages.   Oh (pause) Oh, yeah; oh, huh huh, oh, hope so. Oh
you should just stay (pause) Yeah, uh, oh, yeah.   What're you doing?
How do you spell hemorrhaging? How do you spell hemorrhaging?
We'll have to do it now.   Hemorrhaging? He-e-, double m,
What's hemorrhaging?   Oh, I don't know, h?   Hemorrhage? or
Hem hem hemorrhaging.   No, h-e-m,   He-m-o-r-   Double r.
Oh   h-a-g-i-n-g.   Huh huh   Yeah.   Double r.   Yeah, oh.
H.   H-a-   Okay, well.   g-i-n-g.   We might, well I think we
might be going to New Jersey or something. We just got, uh, stuck some-
place.   Who you talking to?   She's gonna   Uh.   be operated
on tomorrow, uh, the Duchess.   Who's he talking about?   The
Duchess.   Who's the duchess?   Operated on for what?   Hem
hemorrhaging capillaries.   Oh.   From taking what?   This is just
from th-the lack of, lack of uh   Here's Ondine again.   lack of vita-

mins and uh.   I think you're fantastic.   Vitamins and uh.   Phew!
She's really run down . . . hello, baby, hello, doll.   Well, she's not
sure then.   Okay honey, well no, I'm not scared but I just don't want
you to go through it . . .   See the Kelloge is, uh, . . . dying to run all
the magazines, uh newspapers . . .   Okay.   Oh yeah.   Yeah.
You've been on a trip, everywhere, the duchess, I don't, (*laughs*) You
don't go anywhere unless you go on a trip.   Where is, where are the
capillaries.   I know she   . . . in the legs   In the legs?   Ahh,
honey? I hope I can see you t-t-tomorrow.   She has a pretty face.
Oh really, no   I mean she   Ronal would because   It's not,
Sheldon was up at . . . I just, I just put another nickel in.   There was a
party at Sheldon's like that.   Yeah.   Sheldon's so awful.   Yeah,
I know who she is. She was awful nice to you.   Did you ever meet Mr.
Man, Mr. Man . . .   I just put the nickel in!   Would you be so
kind . . . (*Operator*) Would you please put another nickel in for the next
five minutes.   I just put the nickel in you dumb c-cock sucker. (*Op-
ERATOR*) . . . for the next five minutes.   Operator? Yes dear, hello. Did
you hear that? The operator was out of her mind. Well no, I'm on th I'm
on the street. On 5, let's see 52 or first and uh, Madison.   You'll never
get out. The first, you have the rest . . . and we can never get out.   Isn't
that terrible? We have, I've got to . . .   Oh, we loved it. We ate nothing
but raw meat and salads.   You couldn't get—oh yeah raw meat used to
do that, but steaks, you order steak you can't get y'know they're just all so
bad and . . .   Yeah, why should raw meat be good, and steaks bad?
Because, uh . . .   Marinated or something, or . . .   Because it's not
tough when it's raw. You start cooking it and it gets like leather.
What'd you cook it in . . . the French food is very—   Oh, we have
fantastic.   I know, how about the Duchess? Is she okay?   Eating
hamburgers for the last ten years, you know it's great to have to sit down
and everywhere you have a nice full meal, but if you've been eating nice
horrible meals for a year . . .   Well then let me ask you what I
really wanta ask, uh how are you?   What'd what'd you eat in Paris?
I want to.   Uh . . .   No, no, I mean—do you feel all right?
. . . coupon, because . . .   Baby?   . . . coupons, and uh   Oh, I'm,
you're you're not gonna stay there all night?   We wouldn't yeah, we
wouldn't.   I used to eat at the Coupon a lot, the—   Yeah.
M—. . . steak house, y'know because I used to live . . . they're just all so
bad and—
R—Yeah, why should raw meat be good, and steaks bad?
H—Because, uh
R—Marinated or something, or

M—Because it's not tough when it's raw. You start cooking and it gets like leather.

R—What'd you cook it in . . . the French food is very

Oh we have fantastic.

I know, how about the Duchess? Is she okay?

M—Eating hamburgers for the last ten years, you know it's great to have, to sit down and everywhere, you have a nice, full meal, but if you've been eating nice horrible meals for a year . . .   Well then let me ask you what what I really wanta ask, uh how are you?
Pause.

R—What'd what'd you eat in Paris?

I want to.

M—Uh . . .

No no, I mean—do you feel all right?

M—. . . Coupon, because . . .

Baby?

M—. . . Coupon's, and uh

Oh, I'm, you're you're not gonna stay there all night?

A—We wouldn't yeah, we wouldn't

M—I used to eat at the Coupon a lot, the

Yeah.

M—. . . steak house, y'know because I used to live right around there, so I used to eat in those places.

Uh huh.

M—There's a Chinese place right around the corner there, there are Chinese . . .

R—Uh huh. Ou est the pla-places like the Red Blache . . .

M—La chev, la chevre, la chevre de la gendarme, you know, the conductor gendarme.

R—The one right next to the grocery?

M—Yeah . . .

R—The one right over . . . and then we went

?—. . . sent, but I will as . . . Drella. Certainly.

R—Whadjedda we're gonna get to all these fantastic places, we're gonna be taken to . . .

O—Rita says, Rita says could you loan her two dollars until tomorrow, she's out of bread.

Uh uh uh—oh.

O—What with the Duchess's uh thing . . . H-how are we gonna get over there?

In the subw, not on, I mean I don't know well, I just have enough

R—Look, we got such attention.

Hello? Hello. How'll we get there, over there?

R—I've heard, I call called her

I don't even know where it is.

R—Her sister in Connecticut, she'd say, "I called her mother before."

M—She's gonna haveta the . . . Leo.

R—And I said, uh, I got an address . . .

Yeah!

R—And I sent him a card to Leo . . . place

Of course.

R—to say that we were arriving. And then when, by the time I got there, they said you were in Italy.

O—We'll be, we'll be at your house in an hour.

R—I got, but I

Okay. How many hours do we do we have on the tape?

R—Her mother gave me . . . you were no time in France.

Four or five more.

O—We have four or five more hours on on the tape, so it'll be perfect.

R—You were no time in France while we were there. (*Pause.*)

M—No because

O—No no, we're we're gonna go right through it.

R—You're supposed to˙

O—And fin and finish it all

M—. . . for a whole week and you, while you were in Paris.

R—Oh how awful.

O—I know we should have the Duchess on, but but we can't, y— D-D-Drellr has to go t-to New Jersey tomorrow, he's

M—Oh, I'm afraid of . . .

R—He's an awful . . . cigarette

M—. . . I just ruined his car . . .

R—He, you ran away with his car and left it.

M—And I made a mess.

Whatdya mean? You'll, you'll be home in an hour.

R—Do you remember Alfredo? Tennessee's friend.

That's all right.

. . . we never met him . . .

R—He's

M—No, I bet, but uh

Okay, baby.

M—the morning.

R—Louis Louis thought I was Drella.

M—Louis?

R—Louis Louis, the one who

It's 10:00, 10:00

R—Who's saying, "Give me a post and give me a post exhibition   "

Yeah, eleven.

R—And then he said, ". . . sh sh shh."

Yeah. Bye bye.

M—I went in there the other day and I . . .

Don't mention it darling.

M—was broke and everything and I . . .

Bye bye.

M—said to Frank, he's very sweet (Ondine hangs up receiver) and he told me to go in and have some drinks, and he gave me some money to . . .

R—Oh really?

M—Yeah, and everything—he's really great. (Ondine sighs.)

R—He can't . . .

M—I think a terrible . . . would have been Ron Rico, remember?

R—Yeah.

Ron Rico is, can be an . . . he really ca

M—And then he . . .

O—Ohh, (dialing) I know that by heart. But I always say EL 4, first.

R—Ron Rico always . . . cop . . . right behind him? Y'know the motor cop watches.

O—I don't think anybody's going to be there, watch, Drella, watch. No one'll be there.

M—Starting drunk on the streets I think. And he was, and he was. This yellow light, y'know, and they change red quickly, y'know red immediately, and he went through it, and this whole car full of cops started asking him questions and—

Oh hssh (inhaling).

M—Asking him if he's beating a little boy and

R—Ooh, ah.

M—took him down to the station and beat them up some more.

Really?

Who? How, where, what's wh-what station was this?

M—2:00 that afternoon.

Paris.

Uh.

M—Flogged all over the place and everything.

Oh.

M—Wouldn't let them make tele-.

phone calls, wouldn't let them do anything.

That's a delightful spirit. There's nobody there.

M—One of the . . .

D—Call my answering service, T-R-

M—One of them came up to Alfredo and told him

T-R-

D—6-2-2-0-4 and say you're Drella.

M—. . . button up his shirt.

T-R-6-2-2-0-4

M—Was just sitting there quietly and not saying a word, and he came up and (Ondine dialing) the cop grabbed his shirt collar and got his . . . twisted like that, just for nothing. (*Ondine dialing.*)

Tell her you're Drella.

Hmm? Let's see. This is Drella. Any messages?

R—. . . complete insensibility of the people to what's happening now.

M—And when, when the world is freaky it's gonna be that, we got so scared that there was uh police.

O—Hello, yeah, this is Drella. Any messages?

M—Uh crashed his hands through it . . . the police school came and they started beating it (*laughs*)

O—Pardon me? Okay, I'm holding.

M—like that.

R—There's no real cause, there's nothing to

(*Ondine nasally*): One moment sir.

M—I got a-attacked on that by about sssixteen of them. It was right, right down from Donald. Fringey?

M—came down to buy cigarettes. Who?

M—About two in the morning. . . . All these plain clothesmen

O—R-O-X-Y? Roxy Schawan. Oh.

M—I know. Yeah. They said, "Where're you going?" just like that, and then—

O—M-U, M-U-5

M—You don't want me to freeze. They said, "What're you doing in this part?" I said, "I'm buying cigarettes."

O— -1, 4-1 . . .

M—I said, "If you don't want me to buy cigarettes . . .

O—Anything else?

M—I'll go around the corner." I

started going out, and they grabbed me, and they pulled me into the corner.

O—No, pardon me, this is, this is a different one for the week, yeah.

M—criminal . . . so they can take you to the station and . . . then I said . . .

O—5, 1, 6,

M—didn't go over too well, considering the fact that

O—J-U· ,

M—You know.

R—Huh uh.

O—5-0-

M—So, it was pretty awful.

O—4-0-

M—A whole bunch of

O—That's weekends.

M—By that time I got in hysterics and I said, "I live around the corner, and, please, let me go home. Let me go up to see my friend, let me make a phone call . . ."

O—Will you, will you please do, a drawingf for

M—And the worst thing

O—Yes, uh, I'll hold.

D—Who?

O—I'll hold, I have to hold now, she she got off the phone just as she go tto the name.

M—And they said, you'll have to go, you'll have to, y'know.

O—Would you please, do, a drawing for Walter Thomson, wait wait, Walter Thomson, I hate to to say, "Wait, wait," but I'm uh, make it a

R—What're you doing?

—. . . . . .answering service.

O—Make it a 36? A 36 or 48? Or 48. But, as, big as possible. One moment? Oh, all right, I'll wait.

D—Is there more?

O—There may be. She says, "One moent, please." Roxy Schawan. On the weekdays and on the weekends. And then, who's Roxy Schawan? Is that a girl?

D—She's my agent.

O—She's what a name, Roxy, I love that.

D—She's . . . my . . .

O—Oh. Roxy Schawan.

D—Her name is Rory Silver Schawan.

O—Oh, that's even better. Why doesn't she use the Silver?

D—Well she does, her husband died, no she doesn't . . . the same name.

It's all . . . passion. I know.

Fantastic.

O—Yes. (*Pause.*) Pardon me. (*Pause.*) To say that he phoned.

D—Who phoned?

O—An-anything else? Walter Thomson. An-anything else?

Who? Who's Walter Thomson?

O—All right. Thank you very much. GO-goodnight.

Who?

Now. Roxy Schawan and then

N-no, yeah, I-

O—Will you please do

I know, I,

O—a drawing for Walter Thomson, well, he called.

Yeah, who called?

O—Make it . . . Walter Thomson. Make it uh 36 or 48, but as big as possible.

Yeah. What happens . . .

And then it says, "He phoned."

Who phoned?

Walter Thomson.

He couldn't've phoned.

Huh?

Walter Thomson is a company.

O—Whah, I guess so, I don't know who phoned. Isn't it ridiculous? . . . Here's the, here's the other little thing with the Duchess's . . . in it.

Let's got to the village.

Okay . . . yeah. Sort of, yeah.

Okay.

I have to, uh, and there we are. Oh. All right. Oh wow! I've been down and up . . .

M—Can we go to see the French . . .

R—. . . this fantastic French film maker who doesn't get . . .

Oh really?

Who's that?

M—And the French really take . . . the filmmaker's rise out of the sort of, uh, class that's y'know, class that's . . .

You wa you want a taxi, right?

R—Where we going?

Yeah, I'll take, down the Village. *Pause; noise.*

Thaath . . .

Well uh,

Uh, Greenwich Village, U.S.A.

R—Yeah, just—

O—Uh, let's see. Right in the hub of activity. . . . Aw right. Do you know which which French film I really thought was one of the most beautiful things I've ever seen? Lola.

M—I didn't see that.

Ohh that movie was so exquisite.

Did you like the — — — —.

I didn't see it.

See it. That's it, did you see that singing one with the colors?

All I saw was Lola, Lola, Lola— I'm crazy.

Listen to this, it's great, it's great fun to go to it, it's just . . .

I hear that Red Desert is pretty

good too.
But the singing is, groovy, and the
people are groovy,
I hear that the color in Red Desert
is unbelievable.
I hear it's just, it goes beyond
Well it is.

Into, su-sperness—
I mean if you like to go and watch
color for two hours, okay but I'm
a little tired of Monica Viti
really . . .
It's not really much lolor, it's all
Who is this, the uh blonde . . .

8/   1

And it really worked.
R—They were doing a movie. Be-
cause they got so mad at each
other in the first reel, they said,
"Well, I'm not gonna do this
moovie." *Moxi laughs.*)
And Ronald said—
Then we got mad at Drella when
we screaming over "that toyuaaa."
R—Phoney camera, play Drella.
Paul said, "We're gonna do in
a zoo? Wow."
All the hostility we've gotten.
R—Is that all? And then somebody
decided, let it go like that because
y'know, it kept going and and it's
fabulous.
M—That's fantastic.
After the—
M—If they're really joking at you.
Yeaah
M—They don't think—
Exactly.
M—you're doing it.
After the first reel was was over
everybody was disgusted with it.
We ju—y,—they, he laid down
on the bed and went, "OH,"
y'know, "These people. Oh my
God." And everyone had the look
on their face like "I can't stand

anybody, I wanna g—"
R—I was thinking the thing was
faboulous and then I was thinking t myself, "This'll never make
it."
I went down to Washington Park
because I wa, just, quick had to
get out of the room.
R—. . . or be high, Coke . . . Coca-
cola. I didn't, I didin't even
know he was getting high.
Oh Arnold didn't have, we made
him drink it in one minute he
went, "Chkt," right down, then
he remained immobile.
The funny thing, putting the, somebody, you know how you put the
fingers stiff like this, and put an
egg on, caught on then nose, put
a dab of white color along his
nose *(Moxi laughs)* and inoven's
going, "Sniff, sniff." *(Laughs.)*
Arnoldl, y'know Arnold was so
funny. He really plays as a kib-
itzer.
R—Yeah.
He took me to this hotel, the hotel
Wimpy, and he kibitzed at this
card game that these three boys
were playing. *(Moxi laughs.)*
They said well you do this and

that and he was obviously not listening or wha, he didn't want to learn a thing about it. (*Moxi laughs.*) And I couldn't pretend after a while so I said, "I'll lay on the couch." Then I realized that I had gone out to the drugstore. I had gone out to buy something at the drugstore and I said, "Ooh, I better go back." And so I said, "Goodnight." Oh I sai, said to him I think, I said, "Everybody detests you."

R—I think it's, it's to uh . . . instead of that other place.

"Why? Why does everybody hate you? Arnold. Why do they all say such unkind things about you?" He said, "Who?" I said, "Just everyone," I said, "Everyone just doesn't like you anymore." He said, "Well." I said, I, then as I left he said, "What did they say? Who were they?" I said, "Oh, they say the same things about me." He says, "Oh, no they don't. They adore (*esmphasized*) you." I said, "Goodnight Arnold." (*Moxi and Rink laugh.*) Arnold's really, I don't m-mind him though and I know you don't mind him either,

R—He's sort of likable.

Yeah he's

M—I like him.

R—He's so awful.

Yeha, he's really horrod.

M—Well the thing is he's

R—He takes advantage of of

M—so obviously awful from the start that you don't mind what he does after that y'know.

R—But he takes advantage, all the time.

Billy thinks he's cute (*laughter*), which is really a strain. Billy says—Billy was gonna have an affair with him.

Yeah, he's, he thought he was cute and I thought, whoa y'know really.

M—He's elegant looking.

R—His face looks terribly fabulous, it really does.

Yeah, he can be. Yeah, wha, it must, what does Dodo Doom do? She always . . .

M—Looks like looks like those slicker . . .

She . . . there, right?

R—Dodo Doom she had a frog in her head and she was masturbating his head all during the

Oh that pillow, that pillow, oh.

R—during the, like flicking it like it was the end of, end of a phallus.

M—Real flo, real floss? Floss?

R—No, no frog

(*Hiccup*) Oh, oh pardon me.

R—In the . . . it looked like . . .

M—Oh my God.

I say he's like a cat.

R—The the the the forest . . . people do

I love John . . .

R—You couldn't get them anywhere else in the world.

So it tur, I'm dying to see what what uh

R—We'd, we really need a projector to show things, uh

Mm(that new camera's gonna be divine hah? Mm. We should make our own television serial. (*Moxi laughs.*)

R—"Ondine." Call it, "Ondine."

"Ondine and the Housebreakers."

No, Ondine has the best idea for Alice in Wonderland.

M—It's gonn, it's gonna, ooh, why don't you do something like—

R—They're doing it. I, I saw in the paper today. Somebody's doing an Alice in Wonderland thing. Where?

R—I saw this in the *Daily News.* It was so scary.

Oh, where.

R—Sammy Davis

Oh why don't they kill him. Oh.

R—Sammy Davis and Patricia Camp

Oh, he's just

R—I wouldn't, I couldn't make out whether it was T.V.

Oh it must be.

R—or film, or or

It's T.V.

R—or summer stock thing

T.V.

R—or something like that.

M—Who was that man?. . .

RHappy Tune Day was that.

M—A while ago who was, had this radio broadcast thing and one night scared everybody in the nation, and then the whole damn world.

M, all, you

R—Orson Wells.

you, you mean the pile of garbage, Orson Wells.

R—You know?

M—No. Orson Wells.

Tallulah Bankhead said

M—Well, why doesn't he do a television series like that?

"I thought it was a heap of garbage until it moved."

Uh huhhuh huh.

M—It'll scare all, everybody and 40 million people will have a—

O—Just wait'll they see our faces, darling. We'll scare the entire world. (*Drella laughs.*) I was e, called the la frusa for, sev, the, one year of my, the fright.

(*Moxi laughs.*) I used to walk into a bar and they would just go, "Eugh, the frusa."

It must have been Italian bar.

No, it was, it was this, well, yeah, it was San Remo.

R—I heard that from a total stranger.

That was a beautiful town. Oh, and then one night that

R—I also heard that.

M—It sounds even worse, more like the heebies, is it?

Yeah, it's great.

M—The heeby. (*Laughs.*)

O—One night I walked in and they all stood up and applauded, nd I just went, "Eugh." Norman Organ started it; I wanted to kill him.

Oh really?

I said, "Norman, I hope you die," y'know, "And I'm gonna personally take your life."

Norman? I thought it was Billianboard.

Norman Billianboard, yeah.

R—He said . . . lap but ha ha (*Moxanne laughs*).

M—Yeah. (*Laughs.*)

R—You know Dodo, she was the only one in the world that had no lap. She doesn't have a lap. (*Laughter.*) You tib, you go to put something on her lap and it's not there.

What is Ondine's name for her? I mean her name for him.

R—What does she call you? I don't know.

O—She calls me?

R—Yeah. Does she have a name? She has a name for almost everybody.

O—Yeah, well, I don't know how she talks, she says, "You yeah." I,

I don't know what she, what she
calls me. She's such a doll though.

R—She's

M—Who?

R—She has the Sugar Plum Fairy.

O—Oh, I can't forget myself at that
party though. Falling off the, off
the side of your chair and you
going down off the chair there,
oh. I was so chagrined and then
Taxine looked so beautiful—

R—She's got a . . . in the first place.
Oh really?

O—in the tree and what they did
to that party was so rotten. What
the *Time*, the *Times* covered it
so baaaadly.

M—What was Taxi doing in a
tree?

O—They dy, the gave her a boost
and she was up there and she
was

You gave he a boost.

O—Wha. . (*Moxi laughs.*) D, d,
d, d, did I give her a position?

R—. . . . . there, yeah. (*Moxi
laughs.*)

O—Was I the one that got her up
in a tree? I don't believe it.

R—What is is? You sed . . .

O—I didn't do it.

R—A spare.

O—I tried to get myself up there
and I the who was the first person who tried to get up there?

You.

R—Gino couldn't make it.

O—Somebody who tried to get up
there. No no it was Gino. He
tried to get up there and he

M—Is this in a, in the middle of
a restaurant?

This is the party. No. This was a,
this was the

R—. . . the backyard. *Times* wanted
to do an interview so we, Ondine said, "Let's have a picnic,"
and we all went down to the
Village and had a picnic in his
backyard.

O—This was, this was, this was a
party for, this was a party for
nominationg Rotten Rita for
mayor of New Yor.

But he wasn't there. (*Moxi laughs.*)

No, but she didn't have

GERARD—On whch side is that?

R—Right side.

G—Oh yeah. (*Laughter.*)

O—Ah but she, but she never
showed up for her nominationg
party so we couldn't nominate
her. (*Moxi laughs.*) The hit of
the party, though, was the
schpritzer, that marvelous Brooklyn drink, white wine and ginger
ale. It's so heaven. It's so block
party, it really is. And everybody
was just, that drink. Donna loves
hats

R—UH

O—Doesn't he? Dondon

Right here. That's where.

R—you take a right here but go
one block down.

M—Where are we going?

O—We're going to some filthy den.

R—That's, yeah, we're going to
that place wh

O—That filthy den.

R—Fantastic, the . . .

M—The filthy den?

La Fantastique.

R—It's great. I get ice-cream there.

Oh it, ooh ah, not the Cliché?

R—You don't want to go there?

Ooh, I don't know. I'd love to, I

R—Well it's right here.

Where would I love to go but the
Cliché? I am the Cliché. I would
love to appear in one.

CAB DRIVER—Where are you?

R—Here. Right here. Where are you? Oh wow.

La policia. (*Beep beep.*)

M—This where you want to get off? (*Beep beep.*)

Oh stop it with that quaint horn.

R—People looking into it like

Well why don't you try and just back up and hit those people with that little horn.

CAB DRIVER—Should I?

M—Where is it? Over there?

Good thing. oG ahead. D, d, do . . .

CAB DRIVER *in a gruff voice—* Trouble.

Well just try and

M—But looks like a school window.

Just try and sideswipe the old woman.

Uh, would you keep uh,

R—That's this little boy's mother . . . a place called the

Would you keep 35 out of here. (*Voices in background.*)

M—Yeah.

R—It used to be called, well this is the sequence of . . .

M—Oh, I see.

Would you take 35 out of that (*Muffled voices.*)

The Cliché.

M—That's great.

(*Muffled voices.*) CAB DRIVER—Thank you. Goodnight.

Goodnight.

CAB DRIVER—Don't forget anything now, folks.

Oh I hope someone . . .

CAB DRIVER—Take a look. Got everything?

Everything. Thank you.

CAB DRIVER—Goodnight. (*Door slams.*) (*Helicopter noise.*)

I wanna be a lesbian very badly.

You do? Really?

Oh I wanna be a tigress like some

Who?

Somebody just, some cute thing that, she goes, "Darling, I can't live without you." That happened once to me when I did a Mexican lemon dance. I didn't have a hat so I threw a lemon in the middle of the floor to do a dance around it, and I was a little chubby y'know, I mean I sh, w, and the seventeenth sweet banged down the door, "I must come in to see you." I said, his name was Oolf, I said "Oolf?" He was so funny.

M—. . . pussy cat. (*Little kid talking:* "He said it was okay.")

R—Jeanne Vive's, Jeanne Vive's in town.

M—Anita's in it.

R—Jeanne Vive's back in town.

Oh Anita's in it really?

KID—Aw, they really . . . (*he starts screaming*).

M—Yeah.

I didn't see her.

M—But just, oh she's one of the models in the model scene. She's stand-

ing right in front there . . . (music in background becomes louder—
Supremes).? Here. Hold now, I'll get this table. How many?
R—Three. (Pause.)
Four.
What?
They they, they don't know secretly there are more of us than four. There
are more of us than four secretly. What? We're, are, we we we keep
multiplying. There's secretly more of us. I think your position is the most
difficult one of all, and I really appreciate it. (Supremes in background:
supreme in your) Ohh I, uh. What does Irving mean? No one in
the profession should really be (voice fades out and only the Supremes
are heard).   R—All we need is chairs. (Music.) (Pause.) Isn't it fabulous?   It's all right. I wish that they were dancing.   They dance
sitting down. (Pause.)   Notes scribble on.   What?   The notes
are scribbled on this. (Pause.) The Duchess. (Pause.)   R—I wonder
if we can. We can dance if we're   Let me get to this first. (Pause.)
Should we leave?   A dollar bill? I think you're out of your nickel.   I
know. I think he should be back.   What?   be back.   Come back?
(Pause.) We we're going to . . .   Yeah, they're gonna get the table.
(Music.) (Pause.) Yeah but it's only for two.   It's a table for two.
     Oh . . . (Music.) (Pause.)   M—He likes sitting like that on it.
Why don't you . . . (Noise: music & voices.) (Long pause.)   Oh, do
you want to order?   Okay. (Pause.)   R—I'll see what I like later.
     Anything.   R—Anything.   Anything. Anything. Ugh.   R—
What does that remind you of? . . .   What?   Anything on the full
scale? Is that, is that an insult?   Ha hu hu, it's a slap in the face.
R—Did he mean I don't know if he, did he mean, did he mean you or
me   I don't know what he meant.   R—I think he meant the world
to him.   (In a deep, slow voice)   Hello everybody. Welcome to the
Cliché, ha, wouldn't it be marvelous?   M—. . . and then there's the
fantastic thing about . . .   Darling, shall I head it.   Yes.   R—
Somebody put Arnold in front of the one of the end, the little saying at
the end, it said, "Show me a man with no money and I'll show you a
bum." (Moxi laughs.)   Show me a man with no mo—uh Cliché, beverages, eugh, all cold drinks served with ice cubes—egges, burghers, soup,
pahsterie, prices more or lestt agreed upon by   R—. . . for Drella.
Where? (Pause.) Today?   R—Yeah, but nobody answered.   Probably Steve.   R—Did he sound bood-looking? (Pause.) D—Uh. Youve
got the tape here?   What do you think this is, a christening group?
Oh.   Do you want uh, no, oh here we are, now the second side says
     Black coffee.   Black coffee? Oh have something else Drella, you

must, you're not, y-y-you get sick.   Really, dark.   No, you've had
nothing to eat all day, unless you were at Irving's eating (*laughs*).
Ohh.   I had one rotten meal ball and a clam and it's, oh all and all I
got was garlic buds and some onion soup. D-d-did you eat at Irving's?
What?   D-did you eat at Irving's?   What? Did you eat aat Irving's?
    No.   Well you must eat something Drella, because you'll get very
ill. You'll get ill. Well then have some-something like a malted or some
something, which will take care of your whole thing   . . too much . . .
    M—Where   I'm too fat.   M—But uh, I don't know anything.
He's not gonna get rid of it.   Really?   No, y   Eating less?
No, eating less isn't gonna get rid of it.   M—No.   Oh.   The
only way you're gonna get, to get rid of it is to be—   R—Tell him to
eat something.   He doesn't, he won't eat anything. Have a saandwich,
anything. Just black coffee?   What?   Just black coffee?   Yes.
Just, have a soup at least. Oh Drella, that's silly.   He's gonna kill himself.

O—It's ridiculous! You'll die at a yong age, now stop it. Anyway, I'll have
    the same, black coffee.

R—Oh come on, eat something, Ondine.

O—I'm not very hungry.

R—Ondine.

O—(Laughs)—I haven't had, we've been (laughs), I'm not terribly
    hungry.

M—You've been eating yogurt all day.

O—No, it, that was the day before, eugh. I'm gonna go right down on that.

M—Wouldn't you mind having anything else?

O—Black coffee's fine with me.

. . . . . .pill

O—Can I have, can I have a little more of them?

What?

O—D-do you have one or two more that you could, mmm, with the black
    coffee it'll be delicious. I'd like to go in the back and change. (*Pause*)
    dsh (*pause*). This place is just awful, isn't it? (*Moxi laughs.*)

You're being taken on the town, why don't you go get . . .

O—This place, they're deadly. This place is just completely deadly. Oh
    and the feature players that walk in and out are unbearable. I mean,
    they're real winners, aren't they? They they cluster around the cigarette
    machine because they know better.

M—. . . too . . .

Yeah, like a turnip. Why don't.

M—Hu hu hu.

O—Would you put this record on please, I'd like, they won't put my record on. They wouldn't do it. I found it in, it was from the side of uh, uhhhh, what kind of jar, what's this thing called? What is this thing?

M—It's a candy top . . . yeah.

O—Oh, that's beautiful. Do y'wanna see the record?

M—Hm?

O—Wanna see see see the record?

M—I see, it's Callas, isn't it?

O—Yeah, it's the new one.

M—How does she sing on it?

O—Ohh, so gorgeous.

R—Gary Gordon.

O—You must . . . (*voices become muffled—music starts*) her finest recording.

M—I wish I, she came to Paris.

O—She's so beautiful. (*Noise.*) That's quite a program. And she does it jst so phenomenal. (*Pause.*) It's such a beautiful record . . . (*music*) What?

You want sugar in yours and everything. (*Voices in background and music —Supremes.*) And that's enough to pull on anyone. Look at that (*music*). Oh, categories.

M—Look at the man . . . I mean he's so messy now.

Look at that slob, yeah.

M—Why does everybody keep talking?

O—They kept trying to find out what symbols go where. (*Music.*) (*Ondine smacks his lips.*) And why, I don't understand why they did, did this. In the libretto they put this in the (*pause*).

M—The back.

O—the back of it. It's the picture of the back of a book.

M—Of what? Oh I . . .

O—I don't know, they they

M—Isn't that funny.

O—And in the middle is the picture of the the book.

M—This is nice though, look.

O—Yeah, see that? (*Pause.*) Oh, it's a fabulous record. (*Moxanne says something.*)

Yeah, that's a magnificent book, but I mean, I don't want a picture of it. (*Music.*) Dr-Drella said to connect the dots. (*Music: again.*") I couldn't, I duh, I was going to, but then I thought bet-

ter of it. I mean,. what uh, what uh, what uh, what is she doing? slapping herself?

M—Hm?

O—Is she slapping herself there or what? No, she's, she's admiring herself, feeling and going," Ah, yeah it's me."

M—Feeling herself . . .

O—Yeah, "Ah, it's me."

M—. . . herself and

O—Oh my, oh me. It's such a, it's such a. . . . . .she she she . . . (*music*). That was with the girl in Brooklyn. The girl with the . . . she does but they, I didn't like her. Oh, I thought you would dread them . . .
What?
O—I thought you had the pill out (pillow?) She looks just like—
Disconnected lines? (or Did you connect the lines?)
O—And she even, no I didn't, and she even smiled, she even smiled when we, when we said that she looked like Rossini. She chuckled slightly. (*Pause.*) (*Music:*

) I'm trying to keep . . . keep my coffee 'til they bring me some milk. (*Pause.*) Ooh, a red one, wow.
R—Y'know who, this is the, what game is this? the uh
O—It's the, jus, called ratings.
R—Like like you told me, you pick out the person, a star.
O—Oh whoever you want.
R—And you give a quality to them?
O—No, you just rate them. This is just a rating game.
R—One to ten?
O—Yeah, I've gotta put, put put this up here cause it's
R—How do you rate them?
 —Excuse me, I want to ask you something. I said black coffee, but I want light coffee.
R—How do you
These are the ratings: divinity, star, penny pigger, schlitzmonger.
M—Louis Primoti, oh, Primativo.
R—Louis Primativo? How about, how about Zira Prima.
O—Pri, that's a very elegant young young woman and wouldn't fit

into these categories. She's a lovely woman and a great star in her own right.
R—Well who do we do it with?
M—Oh I got one for for the pulter geist.
O—These are the crumby ones. These are
R—Are those, these are categories.
O—Those are the categories.
R—Yeah, that, nobody has applied, nobody has applied to them yet.
O—No no no no no here here, oh you got a symbol.
M—Yeah, for the pulter geist.
O—Oh, she's got a symbol for them. Thank you.
R—You've got a symbol for the uh.
M—For the pulter geist.
O—Now, could I do something? May I use you red pen? All right now, give me the list of names. (*Moxi laughs.*) All right, shall we start with Irving du Ball?
All right. What is he under?
Nothing. We're gonna rate him as soon as we're through with
M—Irving du Ball.
d-u B-a-l-l?
M—Yeah. Ba l, yeah.
R—ball u irving
All right, the next one is, just give me any names.
Peter Nothing.
Peter Nothing N-O-T-H
Gerard Malanga.
Oh, Gerard Malanga and we all take a vote on these things.
R—He doesn't like Gerard.
M—No. What are you gonna do with these people now?
They're gonna be rated by, just the symbols will appear on the side.
M—Oh, I see.
R—Tokyo Rose.
Tokyo Rose is, goes right down.

(Pause.) Barbara Streisand, Barbara Streisand, bravo.

R—Barbara Streisand.

Oh.

Judy Garland.

Oh ih ho ho ho.

La-Lady Bug Johnson.

It even hurts, Judy Garland. Hey, we're pretty good. (Pause.) L.B., Mrs. L.B.J., is that (pause) Lady Bug? Lady Bird.

How about BVD?

Who's that? B.V.D. B.V.M. is the Roman Catholic abbreviation for Blessed Virgin Mary. B.V.M. we used to call her. Lady Bird Johnson. All right, any others?

Uh, uhhm.

Taxine Taxi.

Patti Page.

This is, this is, Patty Page? (Pause.) Huh. Oh.

Uh.

Would you put some in my coffee, please?

We'll put some all over you.

The noise, no, it's the noise. Do it again; you won't belive it. (Plop.) Oh. It's so vile it's unbelievable. Josephine Levine. (Moxanne laughs.)

Do you know her?

Jonas Mekas, right?

The girl who calls Drella six times a day, follow him all around the world. Norman Billardballs. I'll just put H.G.; I never know to spell it. Uh, Rotten Rita.

You know, you know Rotten Rita

Who's that?

Rotten Rita's the mayor of our fair city.

. . . Rotten Rita.

Well who's Rotten Rita?

A friend of Ondine's, we're going to visit Monday.

Oh, I thought that was somebody and somebody. I thought you said Rot and Rena y'know . . .

Okay, a little bit more, a little more, a few more, Elizabeth Taylor.

Rotten Rita.

Rotten Rita uh.

Elaine Stritch.

Rotten Rita spells his

Elaine Stritch, great!

W-r-o-t, Rotten Ri, Rotten iRta spells it with a w.

Oh Elaine Stritch is so beautiful. Thank you Drella.

Rita, W-r-i-t-a.

Elaine Striich, what a name there, Piped Laurie, I, mmm, oh we deserve them.

How about uh (pause). If you do Piper Laurie you have to do uh . . . Terry Moore.

Terry Moore.

Oh Terry Moore. Aw!

Tony Perkins.

I'll put him right down after this. Terry Moore—oh! All right and then Lisa Gaye. That's Debra Padgett's sister.

Song called "Soul Heaven"?

Souls Heaven or soda?

It's a song by the . . . Christmas.

Roger Trudeau should end it. (Rolling Stones singing in background: So do play with me)

It's something about . . .

Is that enough or do you want more?

how it is in soul heaven. It's all very slow, and it's an hour and a hallf.

Okay.

and the chorus is . . .

Okay, Irving du Ball. Here is the symbols. Which one?

now in soul heaven there are three.

Irving du Ball.

three keys, one for the

Chilldren, you've got to vote or else we'll never come to a conclusion.

. . . key to the soul, and the other one is uh uh

What's better, divinity or star?

Oh, divinity is the

Tie queen . . . tie queen is uh uh better than . . . tie show.

Oh, le, now come on. We're, the first one is Irving du Ball.

The first one is with the prince and the princess is Sam Cooke.

The princess is Sam Cooke?

Yeah.

Irving du Ball. Which one do you think he falls in?

And all, it's all very (pause) very weird.

. . . all the names? Which one of the names?

Yeah. Is he uh duh duh a divinity, a star, a penny-pigger, a schlitz-monger, a Louis Prim-Prim-Primativo.

Oh well. He's much more than that.

Or a pulter geist. No, not really. Chresta . . Mora and stuff like that we . . . (pause). All right then we, then no then we'll I'll, I'll just make this a dinner party that we're having, awright?

Uh.

Invited to a Saturday afternoon brunch.

Did you say what you think Irving is?

Oh, Margaret Truman, I almost forgot. I've got to put that down. What do you think Irving du Ball deserves?

Besa mé muucho?

Andy . . . Andy Russell, what's his name? (*He sighs.*) Besa mé, besa

mé mucho and he has that big, besa mé mucho.

Mel . . . too.

That's Mel Torment. (*Pause.*) Ondine sings: *"Best you is all woman."*) I, but I like the way he sings that though.

I like John Rite Mel Torment.

I think I'm, we're gonna forget this game. It has

No.

just suddenly chagrinned me and why must we be chagrinned.

Why must we be chagrinned?

Uh, that's the timely question.

You know . . . all these awful people.

They're categories.

Well that's it, it's the party.

The party.

The party. What uh wha, what could be a bent bee?

The categories aren't good. I don't like the categories.

Irving du Ball requests . . . pause .

What are we going to do now? The party?

No, no. This is the party he's havingfi requests (pause) the pleasuse (pause) of the following company . . .

Irving's always . . .

On his birthday.

Oh, leave them both.

Gerard

Oh, he spelled it much better than I.

Tokyo Rose.

Oh, isn't that a fantastic movie, Tokyo Rose? and Irving du Ball, Barbra Streisand, Judy Garland, Lady Byrd Johnson, Taxine, Josephine Levine, Jonas Mekas, Norman Billardball's next but ah, Rotten Rita, here we go.

Somebody called and . . .

Elizabeth Taylor, Elaine Stritch is really, Piper Laurie, Terry Moore, Tony Perkins, Lisa Gaye, and Roger Trudeau . . . all lesbians. Request the following company of lesbians. (Pause.) Yes, go ahead (pause) to his birthday party. (Pause.) When, what, what, what, what day was Judith born on? What was Judith's birthday? I think Irving du Ball really should be . . .

Here comes the food.

Is that french fries, I mean are that french fries?

Very hot.

No, that's that's a very good one too. I want one that's not as good, and I want the fat one.

Uh.

(Someone in the background says, "Ooh.")

Oh. Uh. Oh. Ooh. Uh. It's a ho, oh, it's a hot fish, my God. Sorry, I hate to eat like an Oriental, but I'm so unscrutable. (Music.)

John? (Pause.) I wanted you to see the proprietor. He's so sweet.

Match-making again?

John? Are you entertaining? Are you entertaining? (Noisy—Rink continuues to talk.) . . . . change?

Oh. No, nothing on me.

He didn't have it yesterday.

What?

He didn't have it yesterday. (Music.)

He di-

He didn't have it yesterday.

What happened I wonder? What happened to your hand? (Pause.) What happened to your hand? (Rink says something.) When?

(Pause—Rink talking.) Oh. (Pause.) That's very, it must be very painful. (Noisy, muffled voices.)

She looks like Ida Snot. Ho, like uh Ida's not (pause, much noise.)

Hah? Is that John Bull?

That's oJhn Bull. (Noise.)

My brid.

My brid. (Noise and music.) What?

I said the place is being a little lively. Step up and get it. Your hot autographs of Ondine and Drella. Who wants my autograph? You can have it boy. Whoever wants my autograph just come up and ask that's all. I'm not unfriendly. Any reasonable requests will be (pause) dull. No, it's not bad. It's very uh, minature. Isn't it, isn't it minature?

What?

I don't know, it's small something or other.

What?

What is it? It's like a, uh, it's something like a, I don't know what it is like a railroad depot, a dance bar.

Pardon me.

I can't quite take it. (Pause) I will though.

. . . a little sweet.

What are those you're eating? These potato chips are delicious. (Pause.) (Noise of Ondine eating potato chips.) They're very good. (Pause.) They're very special.

What?

I'm talking to the potato chip, excuse me. (Pause.) Very crisp. (Much noise.) Oh Rink I want

to see that picture we took, the three of us—you, Gerard Malang— I hear it's so beautiful.
What?
The picture of the three of us doing this.
Ondine and Gerry and I were dancing in a line and we were out of our minds.
We went intothe toilet and out and then we were
We didn't even put into the picture what we wanted to do.
You should have been at that party it was so beautiful.
Was it here?
No, it was at the factory.
Oh. (*Pause and noise.*)
. . . it was so beautiful.
I saw you smoking something very strange when you came in. It looked like a small, brown cibar.
Were lou smoking something?
No, I was . . .

Oh, I thought it was, I, you know, I was imitating on the terrace, I was smoking, I was, I was imitating on the terrace and I did it so. (*Moxi says something; noise.*) Should we all stand up? Cause Moxanne . . . (*pause*). . . . *Did* you see the split she made in order, t, to get over, she went, and I was asking her at the time, "Shall we all stand up?" I said and she took this enormous split. She's quite a girl.
She's one of the most bodies in the world.
She's one of the most desirable creatures alive. (*Pause.*)
She's . . . body . . . blah, blah, blah.
No, I mean, I mean, she's one of the few children I could (*pause*). She's one of the few female children I could ever have sex with. Wow. She's got some body in there. She's just gorgeous.
What?

God. She's really exciting, physic-- ally. (*Pause.*)
I don't think so.
Huh?
I don't think so.
Oh, I do. Oohhh. (*Pause.*) I'd like to lay her. (*Pause.*) Oh, that's an awful thing to say.
What?
I'd like to lay her, I said. I don't really mean that either.
You should lay Dodo.
Huh?
You should lay Dodo.
Do—!

Robert, Robert . . . on the terrace.
  Robert who?
M—Phizer.
Rink, what makes the person . . .
  compel the image of a hustler.
Oh.
M—He was, I don't know, either it
  was Robert or that other friend
  of his . . .
  . . . some sort of.
  . . . The image of a hustler.

He what?
I don't understand why they . . .
Michael . . .
M—Yeah, no, no. Michael was . . :
  Robert.
. . . yeah, it doesn't matter y'know
  I mean, I mean . . . but I don't
  understand how they can find
  them so attractive.
M—Rifht before I left, Denise was
  living there but . . . supposed to
  work on some play.
Oh.
Anybody who'd want to be a hus-
  tler.
R—No, they would . . .
It's a terrible, yeah, yeah, yeah, I
  mean, but it's just
I really think you're wrong about
  Denise.
What?
Denise Higgins, you don't—
is a is a hustler?
R—I think Denise Higgins.
. . . no, it's like liking Irving du
  Ball.
M—No.
O—Den, Den, Denise Diggin is
  also quite good-looking. He's a

beauty to dig him at uh, no he's
  got this, no this face.
M—He's a fabulous dancer.
Huh?
M—He dances fabulously.
No.
Well, no, he's very—no, he's not
  that good a dancer.
No.
R—Faded good looks, and his
  teeth don't help . . .
O—Yeah, but that's so beautiful
  about him . . . that the faded
  good good looks. (Rink says
  something.) Faded red about the
  edges of his face like the hair
  looks like it's going into a valen-
  tine.
He really changed a lot.
Beautiful . . .
Well, I still think he's beautiful.
So do I. Oh.
But he looked more beautiful when
  I first met him, when he . . .
I understand that Rudy White was
  gorgeous.
Who?
Rudy White.
Rudy White.

O—What a face, like a god. He lives on, he's a waiter somewhere and he lives on eastuh

Here, now in New York.

Yeah.

Well bring him.

O—I'll bring him up to the, to the factory, he's beautiful but he's got, ot's a faded kind of beauty like you know but he but, I understand he was so good looking at one time that he (Moxy says something.) I like the people, who like us, get better looking through the years.

Hah?

O—I like the people, who like us, get better looking through the years. I think we do. I think I've improved. I've improved from what I looked like, and I'm sure you have.

Well you said you were fat. Now you're thin.

O—Yeah. And I'm sure that you've improved too.

Oh, uh

O—Because you keep, you keep pro, progressing. I can see your face. Y'know, like when you looked in the mirror and said, "Tsk," I really wanted to . . . if the mirror cracked at that point I would, if the mirror cracked at that point I would have been, it would have been justified y'know, because you must know that you're beautiful, you must know that because if you don't, you, I don't think, I don't think you could possibly do any of the things that you do. Even if you don't admit it to yourself you really know youare. You have to. (Pause.) See, do you see that

little boy in the black sweater? His name is Jodie. Right, standing up there. And he does, and he's sixteen year old, but hu huh, the word hustler is so funny, isn't it? And he dances like a fool.

Really.

Irving du Ball, I don't think, y'know I mean

Huh?

There's nothing left for Irving du Ball. Irving du Ball is not gonna do anything.

Well I keep thinking he's uh, y'know, will uh, sort of change something . . . very . . .

Well, he can become a philanthropist if he's . . .

No no I mean, no, I mean I always . . . I never see Taxi cry y'know, Taxi aw, everytime Taxi goes sees him she gets a headache but I, I always, you know, I always overlook all those vulgar things he says, y'know I . . .

You overlook that about everybody, and that's very good. And Taxi and I both agree that it was the wisest attitude to take toward him. Like it's the only way to enjoy him.

M—. . . the words to "Satisfaction."

O—Oh, my dear, satisfatcion? I'd like to know.

M—Do you know the words to it?

O—I, no, oh no, it's not that—I mean the feeling.

M—Oh ho.

O—I'm talking about the actual eugh! Y'know.

R—Nothing's happened for four years.

O—I javen't, I haven't climaxed in three and a half years.

What? Haven't what?

O—Since last Easter. (*Moxanne* laughs.)

Climaxed it?

O—Climaxed for 3½ years.

What's climaxed?

O—Cli-climax, pleugh.

Really? Never?

O—No, no, I'm only kidding. I climax every other second. *Laughter.*

M—I only one a year.

Huh?

M—In springtime. (*Laughs.*)

O—That's a very mm, it's very . . . only once a year she climaxes, and it's springtime . . . on a dewy morning, on a particular dewy dewy morning you'll climax.

R—. . . comes on between the rocks . . .

O—With the right vibration and she has to be in a certain part of the park.

What . . .

M—It always goes on during factory week.

O—What, what name could Central Park Lake have besides Central Park Lake?

R—What, what name could it have?

O—It's gotta have a name; Central Park Lake's gotta have a name.

M—. . . so horrible.

O—It's such a, it's y'know such a . . .

R—Uh, Middle Munch.

Middle Manch?

R—Middle March?

O—Middle March—no, that's too nice. (*Moxanne laughs.*) It's gotta really be blah, y'know. It's gotta be called Mayor Wagner Lake (*Mox laughs.*)

R—Mayor Wagner White (Lake . . . White Lake, Okay, let's

O—Or, or Impletitery Lake, Lake Impletitery, Lake

R—Oh, that's great, oh Lake, Lake, Lake O'Dwyer.

. . . he wants.

Mayor O'Dwyer? I always would.

R—. . . O'Dwyer Pond . . . Lake Impelitery.

O—Could you imagine Lake Impelitery? It's really (*laughs*).

R—How about the zoo?

O—Lake Impelitery is this big.

R—How about the zoo?

O—Oh that. Wagner Zoo.

R—Not Wagner Zoo, no, Screvane, no.

O—Screvane (*laughs*).

R—No, how about Zoo Screvane?

O—Oh no, Moses Zoo is very . . .

R—Zoo Screvane.

O—Zoo Screvane is pretty good.

R—That's good.

O—Moses Zoo, or Moses Moses Lake, no. Moses Lake! (*Laughs.*)

R—Moses Maul. (*Pause.*)

O—Moses Maul or Maul Moses I, I (*laughter*). Maul Moses is gorgeous. What are the . . .

M—Oh, what about park? You could do like that too.

Yeah.

M—Park Central.

O—Park Central (*laughter*). Park Central Lake Wagner, Park Wagner

R—I, I, I put I have an envelope . . .

But grant that Wagner Lake is stupid y'know, Robert F. Wagner Lake I know or Robert F. Wagner Park.

R—. . . I have an envelope . . . a little note in it saying

An interview saying uh . . .

R—. . . this is almost a . . . that we were

O—Oh yeah, uh, a friend of the *News,* the *New York Daily News,* where he was in an,he had an ear operation. He had band-aids all around his face. (*Mox laughs.*) He's reading the letter like this, and he's looking at it and all you see is his face, and his face is really incredible. It's it's a complete picture of a . . . he's completely rigged up, he's as near a step to death . . . lobod-omy. He's brainless, completely and utterly brainless and his face is so beautiful. He looks like a hippopotamus or a walrus or something.

M—I think . . .

Oh some of them are so funny.

M—One of the great things too, like . . . on the same day . . . Screvane.

M—A picture of a of a white person carrying out a little Vietna-mese victim.

Oh.

M—And there was one in the *Herald Tribune* which was per-fectly normal, and there was one in . . . which is li e the equivalent of the *Daily News* and it was just ghastly looking.

Oh.

M—They blackened out around all the people and the people were white and the blood came out in big black spots.

Oh.

Oh, aren't they awful?

M—So they made the man tough looking.

Some of those papers are so ter-rible.

M—They made the man tough-looking, and it looked like some-thing else, really.

O—I'm afraid to look in the *En-quirer* because of the pictures that you see. I once turned to the inside of the *Enquirer,* and there was this man's head on a subway track, and it was and I just, y'know, I mean I really get a shock when I see that. (*Pause.*) Want one more pill?

O—No, one is enough for me. I'm gonna, I'm gonna start doing Brazil in a minute with this. (*Drella laughs.*) Y'know, know the N.Y. *Enquirer?*

M—No, I'm not famil—

R—. . . the weird stories.

Oh, it's a, y'know, for 48 years.

M—Ohh.

O—"We we couldn't le-let our daughter out of the house be-cause she had no eyes, and they show you a picture of a woman with a stocking over her face. It's too funny, but they show brutal pictures in it, and one of them was of a man who, who had fallen on the subway track and his head was severed in two places. With that kind of picture y'know, just really revolting.

M—They really show those pic-tures?

O—Yes; they're horrible. The pic-ture they showed of that, of the young boy who died of old age was just so funny. At eleven, he died at the age of ninety seven. The face, from the age of, from the age of 8 to 11, he aged like 45 years, and his face was (*laughs*) was so hilarious that I couldn't, I hadda cut it out and put it on somebody's desk who

I claimed was dying of old age. (Moxi laughs.) It, everybody's moved to this one. I wish they'd push us right on to the dance floor. (Pause.) Why don't, why don't we dance anymore like New York used to be? Why isn't New York nimber one? Why is Tokyo the first city?

First state?

O—Fi—(laughs). First, What'd you say, "State?" No, Tokyo was the first city. It's—

First what?

O—City. It's the, it's the biggest and best city in the world now, and New York is outdated. Y'know, never, not with us in it, but I mean (laughs) I mean, all we need is Rita for Mayor, and we could have all those things done. Central Park Lake—could you see it turn into a marvelous . . . . the last hunting place of the, of the fagots.

When was Rita straight?

Never.

R—. . . Taxine at the interview . . .

M—Yeah, but—

R—and I told her I was a genius, but I, I, when you have genius mentalities what else can you do? (Moxi laughs.) They said I could've, I could of spent all my time sculpting and painting, I

O—She should have said Charlie was just a baaped booby. (Laughs.)

R—But, and I, but I, y'know

That would have been great.

R—and I will, I will paint and write, it's obvious I'm going to paint and write, it's all there is, it's all you need to

Oh.

Oh that's, oh that's . . .

Is that all that she said you need, she?

Oh.

R—It's gonna go . . .

Oh, no.

M—Oh.

Did you, we changed the E sheet.

R—She said that when you go out and you do things, today's the day. She said go out and do things.

M—I read about it.

R—People will talk to you and find out about you.

M—You read something, I read about a beautiful apartment in my house, and sat up all night burning holes with a cigaret out

Ching ching

M—Chinged all night and kept waking me up and asking me how to do it cause she never figured it out.

I thought you wanted that blown out. I was talking to, did you, did you, oh, wait a . . . What was I going to say?

. . . . . . ever really got mad to her in public.   M—You know the first one she ever got? I tell you   . . or you got . . .   D-d-d-do you ever notice something going on?   R—I've been sl, I've been slyly mad to her in public, but never   But never in the proper   dir ection, no. going on . . . like . . . oh   But, what's her name?   It really taught her.   . . . going on . . .   That's something she's gotta learn.   No,

I don't know her.   She's kind of like   She wears this   She's kind
of born up with the idea that you can't learn y'know, I mean . . . she
doesn't even   . . . . . like linoleum skirts, y'know. She thinks (rink
says something) she ran up the stairs in a bold green. . . . . be
super . . .   Yeah.   She's very very good.   Oh!   You know her.
      I met her. I saw her in the street one day.   So wh ydon't you . . .
      Well we changed   M—I only saw her once. She made a U-turn
with . . .   What was she wearing.   Probably what she. . . .   you
know her.   M—She had this fantastic cape on- a big purple cape.
(background; I love her.)   Down to the curb, and the. . . . mid-winter
in winter time   Uh.   M—It's really cold. You sh, y'know when it
gets really cold. . . . (everyone talking at once) . . . long and her hair . . .
and her scarf . . . and she's . . . xx Coupon.   You know her. You know
her. You know her.   M—And I made a U-turn, and just as she . . .
come back and block her on the side of her . . .   That face-a maniac,
but she has a . . . like nobody's business.   She's our closest friend.
Ondine's closest.   Yeah, she's my dearest uh, buddy.   Uh.   Oh
oh oh oh yeah.   She's, yeah.   We changed the E.G.   And after
you can, you get- she's so funny you can't believe it. She's so beautiful,
uh!   What is she doing in the car?   M—Hmm?   What was she
doing in the car?
The way you described her, I could feel the morning air and everything.
  Oh God.
M—No, I only saw her once. I saw her on the street, but he started talk-
  ing about her, so I immediately recognized the person I'd seen on the
  street. I said she wears—she's fantastic. She wears linoleum dresses and
  bones hanging from her fingers, and she said, "Oh, I saw a wench
  on the street," and she described it so very brilliantly.
Wearing linoleum dresses?
M—No, she was wearing a big
A big, a cape.
M—A big, long velvet, a purple cape . . .
Oh.
M—like already you know it's beautiful.
Isn't she marvelous?
M—All the way down to the ground. It was billowing.
And she was in Rome. She was in Rome when we were there.
In the winter was, she was in Paris, too.
M—I thought it was a joke; I couldn't figure it out.
Oh.
R—The goat-girl.
M—Cause nobody in Paris

O—The goat-girl?

M—walks around like that.

O—Mare de Woo, de rig, uh, de, Mare de is her name.

R—Oh . . .

O—They called her Arlene Dolly. It's not so!

R—Mare de Mare!

O—She had four different sets of parents come up   Moxi laughed. and f
and claimed her as their her child. Moxi laughs. Y'know they said
mo—, but your mother. She thought—

M—Where did you meet her?

O—I, me—, or, I don't remember. I just

He uh, part of the uh

O—I met her at Billy Name's house.

Oh . . .

And uh

R—Billy Name has a house?

M—Oh! You mean here?

O—He did have a house on 7th Street.

R—Ah!

O—And she was sitting there, oh no, I met her through Freddy Herker
whom she convinced was a lesbian. She told Friday that he was a lesbian after she injected him strictnin.

M—Ha ha.

Rat poison.

M—Ha ha ha ha ha ha ha ha ha ha.

O—She she she inje, she injected herself with ti too, and everyone else in
the room.

M—Ha.

Did they die?

M—Ha ha ha.

O—No, we all lived. I had it; it was heaven.

M—Ha ha ha ha ha ha ha.

O—Y'know, but she told him that he was a lesbian, and he would put on
dresses—

M—Ha ha ha ha ha.

O—and say, "Y'know, Ondine, I'm a lesbian." I said, "I know, Freddy—

R—Mm he he.

O—I've known it for a number of years."   dow. He made it, shwi, he made
it. He dove out of a window; isn't

R—Ah ha ha ha ha.   that gorgeous? Pause. But she

M—Ha ha ha ha.   tried it too. She tried to escape

O—He recently dove out of a win-   once, y'know we once— And

Ondine, and she took it from Ondine—she took all those sleeping pills, and and uhh . . .

M—Really?

It was the day that the trees were planted on 7th Street.

M—She did.

. . . case of Ondine's uh.

Yes!

M—You, oh.

For two weeks, before she took these plans.

M—Who took the sleeping pills?

O—She took 200 seconals.

Uh, Harry . . .

O—200 seconals is quite a bit. Anyway, it was the day that they planted the trees on 7th Ave., on 7th Street. Have you ever seen the Lower East Side, 7th Street? Garbage cans, and people hanging off of

M—I used to live there.

Well, imagine planting trees. It was that day.

M—They planted trees on

For two weeks before that.

7th Street.

M—Oh.

O—For two weeks before that, she didn't move from the spot. She and she had a page of . . . and she's say, "Oh," she'd say, "I have to go take a piss, but I can't move. I'm working on this shirt." And the shirt turned out to be a watchband and a feather. She said, "Here, your shirt is finished. She handed the shirt. It was so great.

R—. . . feathers on the wall?

What?

R—Feather pillow? Feather wall?

O—But she had, she had, she had hallucinations like nobody I've ever, I've ever known. She dreamed that she heard conversations about, that we had all moved upstairs, and that we were waiting 'til she left the room to rob her. And she wouldn't leave her house. *Moxi laughs.* And she had this old, male cat with one eye out, who had, was all so rotten that all he did was chew the kitten up. He, we heard aaaaaa, and he'd take a bit out of his neck out, and the kitten was frantic that all it did was run around, trying to save itself, and the, the old cat would be killing it. She fed the cats, but she never fed herself. She had traps all over the house, like satin ribbon was hanging and she . . . around a mattress that was upon the wall, so that if it, if you, it would smother you. She had feathers all over the wall and broken glass.

M—Ha ha ha ha ha ha.

O—And she had an altar on one side of the wall to Sergio.

M—. . . traps for people.

O—This was her own trap. She died in her own, she was she was trying to die in her own tomb. It was the tin foil tomb that Billy Name built.

R—My brother's keeper—that's . . .

O—And then he left it. And Mare
took it over and she almost died
in it.

M—Ha ha ha.

O—Anyway, so so, she called me up
and I was on the roof, and she
said, and she, cause she hadn't
spoken to me for two weeks. She
said, "Ondine, you can have all
of my costumes."

All of her what?

O—Her costumes. I said this girl goes nowhere where where where without those costumes, y'know. She's not about to put on a tweed dress
and walk down the, some other city. She's not the type. So I said,
"Where are you going?" and y-, she said, "If you come very fast you
can come; I'm going on a trip," she said. I said, "Ughh!" And I ran
over, and she opened the doors, and her joints weren't there; she was
just like a limp, a noodle, she was taking so many pills. And I said she
had an enchanted robe on, her enchanted robe with a big cross on it.
I said, "You stupid cock-sucker," and I ripped the robe off her, I said,
"If you die, you're gonna die like a pig," and she went, "Oh Ondine," she
said, "You're so intuitive." *Moxi laughs.* And she—

What?

O—Intuitive. *Moxanne laughs.*
She's so divine. She's the most
divine person alive.

But she almost died. That would be
awful.

O—Oh, she was divine. Mare was de, incredible. No one liked here, and
I had to keep er awake and so, u'know I, I then broke her altar to the
de, to the dead Sergio. It was two old bones, some broken glass, a
photograph, and some lace. And she had candles flickering in this
thing, and she said, "There's the a, the altar." I said, "Oh." *Moxi
laughs.* I said, "First of all, he's gotta go," and I smashed it up and she
was just sitting there laughing. She said, "I'm splitting, Ondine. I'm
not dying. I'm just splitting." Aa, haaa, I said, "You fool," and then I
was so furious at her for involving me in the scene, I said because
everything was filled with this mock desard   like flavor. I was beating
the shit out of this girl, shoving a bar of soap down her throat to keep
her up.

. . . call. Did you call the cops?

O—I had, I had to call Bellevue
because I call all of our friends;

nobody would come down and
help me. And she started to
foam.

Oh really? *Moxi laughs.*

O—And then her, and then I had to drag her over to the to the to the
bathtub by her wrists like this, and I called out in the hallway, I
screamed, "Help, co—" Some man finally came in after they hovered
back in the doorway. I said, "Throw some water at her; we've gotta
kee-keep her awake." He sprinkled his hands a little. I said, "A pot of
water you fool." And he took a pot and threw it at her. She goes *Moxi
laughs* , "I'm splitting, Ondine, I'm splitting." Y'know, and she was
just that. For two weeks she didn't eat or do anything, and her breasts
sagged to here. Her whole body just sank, and I ne-never saw her
before, and when they lifted her onto the stretcher her her breasts came
into place, and she was ravishing. Then I thought, "Oh my God," I
said, "If that girl dies, I don't know what I'll do." Y'know, they took
her away, and three days later she was out of the coma, and they tell
her, "You're in Bellevue, and you're never getting out.' So she takes
a walk in the pajamas, and she tells the inmates to crawl out of the
toilet. The only way they'll get out is through the toilet. She had the
inmates trying to get out through the toilet bowl. Oh, she was fabulous.
Moxi laughs!

I never heard that before. We all
thought, we all

O—Oh, she was divine.   was de, incredible. No one liked her, and
then I said, "Jimmy, I will not let her in the house," and and I heard
the voice. She said, "Ondine!" I said "Huh!" I said, "Let her in." And
her nose was all swollen. She said "Aw, awl, all I remember is you
beating me, you darling." *Moxi laughs.* She's so wonderful, y'know
and I, if nothing else, I sw, we all went to Coney Island one day, and
she put her hand out of the window, and she was feeling the air like
this, and she was so happy to feel it, that I just thought, "Ah," y'know.
And she was, she was adjusting her costume to make it look better.
And she finally looked like Buffalo Bill here, and she was perfect; then
no one could attack her.

Billy wasn't there at the time.

She was cau—

O—She was embarrassing until she looked like Buffalo Bill. Then she was
fabulous. Then, then we got married and she fucked me uh uh in the
ass on the street. Hu hu, we had this enormous *pause* she was brown-
ing me. She told the people who passed. *Pause.* Oh, I loved her.

R—Do you want coffee?

O—She was so. She wrote me a letter on Fire Island on toilet paper to m, dear most, to my most unbearable beloved Ondine, my, to the, my most unbearable beloved Ondine, you will never again find another John as generous as I. She said so, the letter . . . on toilet paper and it went on and on. She was so beautifully literated, it was incredible. The way she looked like Buffalo Bill, she looked so gorgeous that just was, I wanted her to fuck me she was so beautiful. *Laughs.*

D—. . . on people it's so funny.

But permanently, permanently.

. . . painted her picture and

O—Well she's so beautiful. The first, oh I know what the first time it was when I met her. I walked into Norman Billardball's house and Dennis Diggen is there and all these people are sitting there—the jet set and they were calling on the phone, "Hello, is somebody there? Oh no? Well then we'll go here." Fro, mi, and the Brazilians are going bluhbluhbluhbluh, y'know. "Dahrling" and I just thought, "Oh my God; I'll go out of my mind." And I saw her sitting there with the staff and she was going like this to me. I said "Get her out of here" and Norman said "What?" I said, "Throw her out of your house," and she went "Who?" She looked *laughs* herself. *Moxi laughs.* She took her staff and went. My, her, I said, "I'll beat the shit out of you. Get out of here." And I chased her out of somebody else's apartment the first time I met her. *Man laughs.* She she went, got, got down and said said, "I love you" she said, "He's divine; he's violent." Y'know it doesn't matter. *Laughs.*

Tell tell her the scene with Jack.

O—Oh she's won—what?

The, her scene with Jack Daniels.

O—Oh well that was the ni-, that was the night of "Norma." We sat there for four hours; it was going ahhh to every line becaus we were full of rat poison. We were so injected with rat poison we didn't know what happened. I said, "Oh Mare." And I was walking up the street and I felt my legs freezing. I went "Eugha." And you know I never lost my timing *Moxi giggles* but I lost my timing on the street. I thought, "Oh my God, what am I gonna do?" And I felt my head going and my extremities. I thought, "Oh!" My fingers were freezing. I said, "Jimmy, we've got to go ho-o-o-ome." And I just lost myself. He said, "This corner, we leave our head." And he left his head back on the other corner. I said, "Jimmy, pleeese, I've got to go home." Yeah, this was before that. When we got to Billardball's we were so spaced that we didn't know wh-, I mean I didn't know if I was dead. I really didn't.

Well, he met you on the corner.

O—I kept going *pause* and I, and then Jack Daniels just sat in the corner was leaping through these things. We made some nasty and Mare would go *pause . Moxi giggles.* I've never seen faces like she made, never in my life. She mad, she made, she mugged like one the, of the Marx Brothers. She was so fabulous.

She was kind of like.

Ohh, I love her.

. . . you know . . . saw "Red Go-rilla."

We used to make life so unbear-able for people; it was just so wonderful.

O—We'd go over to Norman Billardballs house and we'd say, "Norman, we're starving. Do you have anything in the house?" And he said "just macaroni in the refrigerator. Don't touch it please; it's my lunch.: We sa-, we said, "Oh really? Thank you very much," to him. We'de break his sticks and everything. By the time we got through he would be begging us, "Stay. The macaroni just isn't—" We said, "No Norman. You're through. You've had it." *Moxi laughs.* He was ready to die, y'know. *Moxi is laughing.* He, he would anything; he would do any-thing. Sh-, well, we would get outside and screech: we couldn't help it. Oh I miss her; she was so wonderful. *Pause.*

Its' changed. Why?

Hah?

It's changed so much.

What we should—

. . . Mare and Freddy.

Well she said in her will, "Thanks Billy Name; you bored me to death.'

She she wrote that in the will in big, green ink.

She did say that?

R—Brought me to death?

Bored me to.

O—She said, "You bored me to death."

Ohhh, ohhh.

O—She said, I ju-, and so she, I called Billy and she talked to him and she said, "Billy, you bore the shit outa me, and I mean. . . ." She was going out and I said (*inverted sigh*).

M—Who was this? This was Mare's death?

O—Mare to Billy Name and I said, "Oh God, Mare." I said, y'know, what can I do? And I had to put a bar of soap down her throat. She went, "Egh, eugh, oh, Ondine." I said, "No, you've got to throw up." She did nothing but foam. She hadn't eaten for two weeks. For two weeks! She had under her bed, she had under her pillow two loaves of bread that were so rock hard, I could not describe them. The cats ate every day though. She fed them lobster meat and tunafish (laughs). She owes some money and . . .

O—Yeah. Well she's a, her her mother turned her on to amphetamine at twelve. Put amphetamine up her nose. Yeah, she says, "Here, sniff it." And when she went to Mexico after that she lived in the, in a, a deserted Mayan temple. She lived in a deserted ruin and she lived there and she said one Saturday morning a gro-, a group of touristos caught her as she was swinking along the wall and she went (pause) and the animals were hanging around. They just said, "Oh my God; it's unbelievable," y'know. What could they, what could you do to her? When I first met her really good I had to pick up a piece of oil cloth that fell on the floor and say, "Your hem—just fell." She said, "Thank you very much." And it was snowing and I had to go out in a bathing suit because it was so ridiculous. And buy a popsicle and we laughed. The man wouldn't sell us anything; he couldn't believe our outfits. And The Turtle tried to crawl out the fire escape window. He thought he was dead. He really cri-, almost cried he was so—. I had to go—a polo shirt, shorts on and boots and

Oh where, where?

O—Mare had robes on across her.

Where was this?

O—She said "Ondine, don't fuck me up," she said. And she's putting veils on her face, and I, and I looked at her and I said (laughs) "What's the purpose?" y'know. And she said, "See what you're doing? You fucked me up. Now I have to do it all over again." Moxi laughs. And she would put twelve more veils on her face. She had no concern for people—spats in the middle of summer, sweat, she was divine. She came over when I was in great trouble and said, "We're gonna feather your walls." She meant to tar and feather the walls—tar and then threw feathers on it. And she said the word for today is pro-bloom.

Is she now in Paris? No.

O—Pro-bloom she said is the word

Is she now in Paris?

O—for for for today.

M—Pro-bloom?

O—Problem but pro-bloom. (Rink laughs.) She turned to me and she, she could speak perfect Italian and said, "Aiuda." And what can you say to someone who says that? You just have to love her.

I like the mercury bit. Remember the mercury bit?

O—She's so, oh I love her.

Dropping and picking up the mercury.

O—Whe-, oh I don't remember.

We had a whole bottle, she got the bottle of mercury for Billy.

O—We could have died like that, right?

What?

O—We could have died for, like like that.

Yeah.

O—I don't really, it wasn't me. I think it was, must have been Billy (*Pause.*)

Yeah, but I don't remember it. What happened?

M—I don't know. How old is she? About 25 or 30 or so?

O—Oh, she's about uhhh.

M—25 I'd say.

O—About, between, between 25 and 30.

M—Yeah.

O—I mean that's the perfect age, y'know.

M—It's very funny . . .

O—Do you know what she did that day that Jac, that Jack Daniels came? She walked down to the basement and stood there for twenty minutes.

Oh really?

O—She's afraid to go anywhere. She just sits there going like that.

R—Does she look like anybody we know?

M—I thought . . .

O—Imagine injecting everybody in New York with rat poison. What (*laughs*) a feeling was that.

M—. . . never seen anything like it. Never. That's why, I've never seen anything like it.

R—Is she phoney?

M—I took in my car. I ran . . .

O—Ma-Mare has a face like an Indian goddess.

M—I don't know. I couldn't see her

O—Did you see the picture that Billy Name has of this woman in the chair with with staff in her hair like. She looked like Wild Bill Hickock.

Who gave her the staff? We met somebody that gave her the staff.

I don't know.

In Greece.

I don't know. That staff is gorgeous.

We just met. Oh, oh somebody, somebody who met us at the uh studio just came up.

You told us something about it, yeah.

Hah?

I remember, telling us something about the staff.

M—I can . . .

I mean uh.

I reme, I remem, we thought that she carved it.

Somebody gave !it from Greece. Yeah, no, somebody from . . . from Greece. (*Someone in the background:* "Drella, Drella")‚ (*Ondine:* "Mmhm." *Drella in background:* "He went outside. He'll be back. He might as well.")

O *in a whining voice*—Oh why don't we go? We don't we leave, Gladys?

Please, I'm very tir-. He said, "I'm very tired; I'd love to go-o-o."

Why don't you call Rotten Rita and see if she's there?

O—I would like to leave please (*in same whining voice*) Rotten Rita (*his voice changes back to normal*). Oh is there a phone booth here? Is there a phone booth in here?

Yeah. Right over there.

Rink-i-dinky is there a phone booth in here?

Yeah right over there.

R—Right in the corner.

O—Would somebody give me a dime please? I have no money. Oh my God, Oreo. And she, she had to sit on Clair's face because Clair got her out of Bellevue.

Oh.

O—She said, "Oh, I went over and sat on Clair's face," she said, "She's a bore."

R—DoDo Doom"

O—No, Clair Pease, the hideous . . . Clair Pease (noise) well everybody's best friend. (Moxi laughs.) DoDo. (Noise.) (Ondine leaves table.)

R—But Rita is way uptown.

O—Yeah, but one of these days . . . . and then we'll come back. (Pause.) Rotten Rita's just . . . what?

R—I don't want to get caught up with Rita's being shot with all these things, like I . . . when they start taking things I want to take them, but but.

Uh, half an hour.

R—Yeah, but then I get really hung up.

M with sympathy in her voice—Oh.

R—Who knows what they give you. These, I've got vitamin B 12, amphetamine.

Am-phet-a-meen?

R—Yeah, I was afraid I'd get a . . . . . . (pause). Did you hear the way he said that?

M—What?

R—Did you hear the way he said, he said, "You still care."

M—No.

That was only three days ago.

R—See.

M—What did you say? What did you say?

R—I said he said it was a dirty needle they gave me the other night.

M—Yeah.

R—I said yeah . . . pajamas . . . you still can. And then I blah-blahblah blah blah and then three seconds later he says, "That was only three days ago." (Moxi laughs.) Wow! Oh! I mean like, y'know.

Oh, I don't want you to be jobless.

R—Not just yet. (Laughs.)

What?

Not just yet. (Pause.) Well I think we should do a movie about this woman with Ondine narrating it, telling the story.

Uhh. (Pause.) Well, uh.

R—If we find somebody to play her.

I, I always, I really, never really dug her; I don't know why.

R—I mean you don't have to dig her, but the idea's fantastic.

Uh. Well, I never really uh, I mean uh (pause). It's just uh, I don't know (pause) I mean (pause) I mean it was—I just never

R—Nicholls and May. (Laughs.)

Huh?

He was telling Nicholls and May, "You used to like me, but we never really got . . . you to come to my . . ."

No no, I mean.

R—"I like high class." (Pause.)

No no, because uh

M—She's very very strange. She's like a cave woman, y'know. (Pause.) She's a skinny Billy Name.

R—That's really the thinnest person in the world. (*Pause.*) It's like saying she's a fat Fatty Arbuckle. (*Pause.*)

Well she, out of the girl, out of her girl kind of thing she's not like, she's not like, um, like the Duchess. She's, and all the other girls are very tough. And this one is just sort of, just sat y'know, didn't talk much, but what she said, she was very uh, intelligent, very intelligent. (*Pause.*) And pretty in her strange y'know, very really beautiful in her strange, uh, in her dirty way or whatever uh.

R—Telling the inmates in Bellevue to escape through the toilet. I mean that's the funniest thing I ever heard.

What?

R—Telling the inmates that they can get out through the toilet.

Oh yeah, well uh.

R—It's the most fabulous thing I've ever heard (*Pause.*) (*Moxi laughs.*) (*Long pause.*) Hey beautiful?

O *from a distance*—Wait a minute.

R—Beautiful?

M—He's really fabulous—Ondine.

Oh yeah. (*Voices of Rink and Ondine calling to each other in the background.*)

M—Does he go on like that all the time?

All the time.

M—He's fabulous.

R—I know, he, he likes it.

M—Good story teller.

R—. . . for 98 hours.

A T.V. star.

M—Yeah.

R—Yes? Somebody called me?

She doesn't want . . . to run.

R—She, she hired his maid.

O *calls*—Drella!

R—Cause he needed money; he doesn't work and he needs the money to buy amphetamine and he comes a couple of days a week, and now, and he was telling her about, "I came in one day and there he was, Tosca was on, and Taxine was in tears." And he was telling the story of Tosca and she, and she, and he loves Callas; he just adores Callas and . . . I mean know it, and explain it beautiful, but then Taxina was . . .

M *laughs*—Oh she's . . ha ha ha.

R—You know Taxine, Taxine can . . . people . . . and he does this . . . the clock. (*Pause.*) (*Music.*) Can we pick up a pretty boy and deliver him—

Music.

M—I love those shorts!

O—what these?

M—Yeah.

O—They're from John Bacon and Co.

M—Look at tho-

O—They're . . .

M—I think they were a pair of those German shorts. What are those called?

R—leder . . .

M—I think they were a pair of those German shorts. What are those called? Yeah.

Music: long, deep notes gradually slowing down and stopping.

Pause.

Music picks up.

M—Who's that a picture of up there?

O—Our Mayor.

D—Oh Ondine!

M—Well, it's . . .

O—That's our mayor, Rotten Rita . . . (Breathless) Hello everybody! This is campaign headquarters, and we salute Rotten Rita. Let's, I'm trying to think of what, what I'm doing . . . oh do you see this? (Pause.) Billy was throwing us out from Henry's yesterday.

D—Oh.

O—This . . . this piece, I said, "Ooh, let me, let me have it!" That was so (giggle) gorgeous.

D—Ondine, why don't you come down and sit down for a minute?

O—w-I, I, I—

M—Hey, what sorta, where does that come from?

R—Camel saddle.

O—That comes from a——

R—Camel saddle.

O—Yeah . . . one part of it.

H—Camel saddle!

O—Yeah.

M—. . . on the camels?

O—Yeah-up, yeahupp, on the sides of each hump.

M—They're awfully skinny, aren't they?

O—That's a skinny towel cause you have skinny legs. (Music.) (Noise.) (Silence.) I'm taking em . inta Rita. She's go—she's gonna go (Moxi says something.) I can . . . yeah well, she needs a few toys in there . . , do . . . she . . . isn't that a mad thing? . . . I love that. (Music.) Look at this picture.

M—Did you see there was a, there was an exhibition in Paris of this guy called M . . . . . Did you see that?

O—Ohh.

D—Yeah.

M—Did you see it?

D—Yeah.

M—This, there, the, the fantastic heart thing, was, a, the blob was hung on the clock ticking outside and all these neon lights throbbing. It was called "One More Second of Happiness."

O—I think I'm gonna— no.

D—Okay.

O—In there?

D—Yeah.

O—Ooh.

D—And the lights.

O—I tripped over my own bag. (Buzz-buzzbuzzbuzz.) . . . was that?

ROTTEN RITA—I have no idea.

O—Do you want me to ring the buzzer?

R—Did you get the, did you go to the, did you see

RR—Lock the door.

O—Lock the door.
Noise.

O—Uh, all we could get was Vick's. Yeah? Shall I ring the bell? (*Noise of voices in background.*) Yeah, they're right here.

D—What?

R—Whole . . . whole.

O—Here Ri—

D—Oh w oh will you say a few words?

RR—Prick me in a few minutes.

O—. . . tuck.

RR—in a few minutes.

O—How are you Ri?

RR—How are you. Huhoh.

O—I mix them, tha, that! Oh!

RR—. . . well. We have Ethel Roosevelt Hospital on our side.

D—Look at him. He's, he's . . . you look just beautiful, too.

RR—The Duch, the Duchess.

O—They're bathing in it too . . . beautiful process.

D—We've been in two baths.

RR—The Duch, the Duchess is writing (*mumble mumble*).

O—No, because I'm gonna p-put this in the closet. Puh-lease dear,

jus lemme, I'm . . . now who's gonna be at the door?

RR—. . . the police.

O—Well let's, duh the police don't ring three times.

D—Really?

O—Do they? They might. Gimme a coat, doll.

RR—From where . . . it's three rings.

O—Sunshine (*Pause.*) or Billy Name.

D—(Do you think?)?

O—Yeah, it's one or the other. (*Pause.*) You'll soon find out. They'll regret it. (*Pause.*) Oh.

RR—You shoulda seen her—giving education to the nurses.

O—She must, she's quite a fabulous person.

RR—Oh yes, she is—

O—And besides that, she's

RR—. . . I always know there is

O—Huh, she does?

RR—(*garble*) . . . have you taken it?

O—The whatchamacallits . . . it's silly c-cause you'll, you, you'll just get warm.

RR—She said I . . . give the best

O—Shhh!

RR—Pops in town.
Pause. Buzzer.

O—Who's there? Who? (*Pause.*) Who's there? Who's there? If you won't answer, I'm not opening the door.

RR—I heard, I heard, I heard, it's okay. I heard the word, it's Sunshine.

D—It is Sunshine.

O—Is it Sunshine? Oh, good.

RR—Just do me a favor and close the door.

SUNSHINE—Ondine, you're getting more disgusting.

D—Oh, will you come on, come on the, oh oh oh let her in.

O—I will not.

D—Oh c'mon.

O—I will not insulted by that

D—C'mon Sunshine, aren't you coming in? Why not? Oh, oh, c'mon.

O—I will not be insulted by that (*noise*)

S—Is Rotten here?

D—He's . . . what's that? Oh, aren't you coming in? (*Pause.*) What, is this yours? (*Pause.*)

RR—What's happening?

O—Umm. She said, as the door opened, she said, "Ondine, you're getting more disgusting with every (*pause*)

D—Is that yours?

O—It's *Rotten's*, unfortunately I have to pick it up.

RR—Where is she, outside?

O—Outside where the belongs. (*Pause.*)

M—Isn't that . . .

O—Yeah, I got the package. (*Pause.*) I just can't stand her anymore. (*Noise.*)

RR—What did you do to her?

O—Not a thing. What did you do to her? She her how to attack you, too. What a nerve she has. I, all I ever did was love her. (*RR says something*)

O—*under his breath:* Fuck her.

D—She got mad at me too.

O—Oh, let her get, she gets mad at everyone periodically.

M—What's that, lunch?

O—No, this isn't lunch, my dear. (*Music.*)

D—What is it?

O—Medi-wow.

D—Yaahhh.
Noises.

RR—What is the matter with her?

O—I, she's trying to, I think she, she wants to have an ex . . .

RR—I don't understand what happened, what, you were the first cause you didn't hear her say Sunshine. I heard her.

O—I didn't hear, I didn't hear it.

RR—Awright.

O—And, uh, wha, and then I opened the door. I opened the door and I said, "Oh if it's Sunshine, then I'll open the door blah blah blah"—and then she said, "Dear, you're getting more disgusting, Ondine, than ever," and I just took the bag and threw i tdown and I, I clased the door niher face at which, what point he opened the door and said, "Sunshine, blah blah blah the bag's still there," and I said "Unfortunately I have to pick it up," and I did, and I . . . it and I closed the door. I can't see, even be kind to her, Rita. *Ondine, you're getting more disgusting.*

RR—Well, she's entitled to her opinion.

O—Why?

RR—I don't know.

O—Because I, because I didn't hear her at the door?

RR—I don't know why she thinks you're getting more disgusting.

O—What's the matter with her?

RR—She must have her reasons, whatever they are.

O—She does, her brain—

RR—Okay.

O—her brain. Why is she putting herself through it? Unfortunately Ireally love the child.

D—But why should

O—I'm not her mother. (*Pause.*) (*Music.*)

D—. . . get paranoic about this.

O—She didn't even know that she did it. She didn't even know, but she had already made up her mind instead of saying you're disgusting.

D—Yeah.

O—Because I didn't hear her at the door.

D—Oh really?

O—She's completely out of her mind. Anyway, let's . . . (*loud . .music*).

D—Something like that

D—Something like that

O—Something down the drain (*very loud music—trumpets*) (*whispering*) gimme . . . and relax.

D—I never saw Sunshine that way.

O—Huh?

D—I never saw her that way.

O—I've never, listen, she's been, she called up Rotten and Rotten and she said she had Dixie and the other one up there and she's, and they said they don't know why she should come up here and be insulted anymore. And, uh, nobody insulted her. In fact, we went out of our way to be nice to her. What certain people consider insults is their own delusions, honestly, and y'know, that's, I don't have any truck with their own sicknesses. (*Music.*)

M—What does she call being insulted?

Loud music.

O—perfume . . . On-Ondine, it says. D, d, d'you . . .

D—Yeah, I uh

O—Did you s-see it?

D—What is it? (*Sniffing sounds.*) Oh.

O—It's Maria hitting her her, I think it's the end of Il, Il Pir-Pirata, it's just fabulous.

D—Ah, beautiful. Ondine, you're the one that drops these stars all over the place.

O—I don't even have any stars. How can I drop them.

D—How do they get there? I see them everywhere I go.

O—Oh, it's so unfortunate about Sunshine.

D—Oh, she got paranoic about this too.

O—Oh well, that n, no, I think she's jus, she's got

RR—Is that her screaming from the street?

O—*laughing*—Yeah, that's her all right. You could tell that wail. (*Pause.*)

RR—I think we lost a vote tonight, boys.

O—That's all right, we may even have lost a life.

R—She's prob, she's probably down at the end of the city.

O—She's not a lunatic fringe.

RR—She's probably on the roof.

D—She's she's with her dog.

O—The dog must be deathly ill.

D—Huh?

O—Her dog must be deathly ill.

D—Oh really?

O—Fritzie.

RR—. . . go to the ASPCA.

D—She'll never let me in a movie.

O—Wha? Yeah, well so wha? You really don't wanna go there any, anyway. The new management has routed out all the fairies, su-supposedly.

D—Oh really?

O—The only time I'll go there is a (*laughing*) sham—yeah that one, that's the one where I met Sunshine. (*Drella laugh.*)

M—Where is this?

O—The New Yorker, y'know, the one up on 82nd uh

RR—. . . had about the New Yorker.

M—. . . she works . . .

RR—When . . . how are you all?

O—You remember Rink, Rotten, and this is Moxanne, this is Rotten.

RR—Haalohh.

O—Rotten, Rotten Rat, our our mighty mayor.

RR—The only thing we said to her that she coulda been offended at was, she gets very upset about her job.

O—Well, she she should be.

RR—to tell her

O—After letting Bernie in

D—She let Bernie in?

O—Sure.

RR—His manager goes on his lunch hour so we can go to the john and go swimming. Then she got very terrified.

D—Well, there's no swimming yet.

O—I told her that. Rotten said said to her, he says, She, y'know I remember her face when you said it and y'know she did get crazy. She said "g-go swimming." He said, "Y'know, a pool." And she suddenly, y'know she really believed it, Rotten.

RR—She was carrying on about.

O—When did she take LSD?

RR—I don't know. She said she took it.

O—Well, I can't stand that behavior. It's so unfortunate of (*music*) There's no reason for for for her to tell me I'm getting disgusting. (*Sirens outside.*)

RR—What's she doing out there?

O—She must've called the cops. (*Sirens.*) (*Music.*) (*Laughter.*) She set fire to herself down the street. (*Laughter.*) (*Music.*) (*Sirens.*)

M—They turned back the other way, didn't they?

D—Back Ondine.

M—. . . that way. (*Laughs.*)

O—Can't tell, can't tell the Duchess would appear, but you would see, this big and small little beaded black stole the way she has.

RR—. . . very nice. She gave her the tel, uh the address (*pause*) of the most famous veterinarian in th ecity. (*Sirens.*)

O—Ooh. (*Sirens.*)

RR—The Duchess.

M—What's the matter with the dog

O—Sunshine.

RR—Then we found out nothing was the matter with the dog. It was LSD that she took. (*Laughter.*) (*Sirens.*)

O—. . . very strange out there. She's still, she called (*laughter*) (*voices*).

RR—She is very

M—She put all these diseases into the dog.

RR—She's a little crazy about Sunshine.

O—A *little* crazy? She claimed that her mother was banging down the walls, or rather that there was a, that there, there was a prowler. Didn't she give her mother amphetamine? (*Music.*) Her mother said, "What's that white powder you're sniffing?" She was staying awake. She said, "Have some, Mama." And Momma went berserk. (*Pause.*)

(*Music.*) Imagine a Jewish Mildred Pierce.

M—I don't know who Mildred Pierce is.

RR—Joan Crawford.

O—Joan Crawford movie with Ann Blyth.

R—You you you just missed it. (*Music.*) The quick late show. (*Ondine laughs, sighs.*)

O—How is Duch—I hear that you went twice.

RR—The Duchess is just fine, my dear.

O—Yeah.

RR—She saw the bottle of vodka.

O—She must have been in seventh heaven.

RR—She was.

O—I'm glad you didn't give her any LLLSD though, Rotten. (*Music.*) She'd never pass any tests.

RR—I don't want to hurt the poor thing. She would've been killed.

O—No, she might've had a good time, but her tests would've been facious(?) (*laughter*). Could you see her on LSD taking hospital tests?

D—An operation.

O—An operation on LSD! Ooh (*Moxi laughs.*) Oh that's sin, oh that's too much to grasp.

R—Probably pretty good; it slows you down somewhat.

O—Oh no, I wouldn't want to. (*RR says something.*) Do you have her in the doctor's outfit yet?

M—What are those operations when they don't put you to sleep?

O—What's Oh you mean a local—a spinal. (*Music*) They're, they're

M—. . . when they can't put you

to sleep.

O—I know. I had one on a piodonital cyst, but they inject it inta the middle of your spine.

R—Why didn't they put you to sleep?

M—Sometimes they can't.

O—I don't know. They just wanted to

M—. . . or something like that.

O—The doctor was talking to me about the, my my breakfast and everything and he, he took out a football I think from the back of my, from right, right at the edge of my spine. It was an infected coxic tail and y'know that's so painful that every nerve in ya

R—How'd you get it?

O—I don't know. There were stories, were around in Queens that six motorcycle men grabbed me and hammered a pipe up my ass. (*Laughs.*) You believe them and I said, "Let it spread; it's divine." I don't care. But I just got it because sometimes coxic tails get infected. There's no reason for them. (*Pause.*) There's absolutely no reason for a coxic tail to be infected or disinfected.

M—That's . . . in the . . .

O—Yeah, that's the very end. That's hair too.

RR—You didn't kick her out, did you?

O—I just closed the door in her face, that's all.

D—She just got mad. Ondine really didn't do anything.

O—I just

D—She just threw the bag at him.

RR—What's the matter with her? I don't know.

O—She's, Rotten, what what is it? She's hard up. And she thinks she's gonna force our hand. Ah haa, she might force our hand to around her throat.

RR—She might get, she might get something besides our hand.

O—I mean, y'know, why not accept friendship? Is, is that right or wrong? I mean y'you seem to me to be a pa-particularly level headed-headed girl. I really mean that—completely so.

RR—A large part of me.

O—Is it, is it?Not you, darling; you're all woman. I've, but is it, is it impossible to accept friendship from a faggot? Huh, I mean, no is it impossible for a girl to just accept riendshi.

M—Yes, very.

O—But it's not ofr y, no on our, on your case it's, it's not. What have you done? What seeds have you taken?

D—Well, you have to let that thing   use friendship.

O—I beat her up when she was a child. I lived with her. I b-beat her up because she was a Jew. I nearly killed her.

M—Did you know her for a long time?

O—We grew up in the same neighborhood.

RR—I don't know what she has.

O—I never knew her then, y'know I mean, I just hit her once cause she was a little Jew.

RR—The three times that I spoke to her on the phone

O—She's unbearably mad.

RR—she was crying. All she did was cry. Aaaah.

O—Well she should've.

RR—The first time I saw her I just came home to get some food and I can't get back to the hos-

pital after 9 o'clock. I said, "Goodbye, I'll call you from there." I called her from there. "Aaaaaah" (crying) she said

O—She's

RR—I can't stand that.

O—She's crying at the box office, right?

RR—She says, "Hang up," she says, "I'm watching television." (Ondine laughs.)

O—I don't blame her.

RR—She's going . . . keep going up I said.

O—Oh well, that's, that's the Duch, the Duchess is glamorous.

RR—Higher all day.

O—She was going up ah ha ha ha oh can you see her? My God. Where did she have the blood pressure machine? In her closet?

RR—On the wall right over her bed.

O—Ooh! For all to see.

RR—She took Ondine's blood pressure. She took my blood pressure. (Lafter.) I heard the nurse came in to give her a pill and she says, "I know what that is," she syas, "That's nothing," she says, "that's vitamin C."

O—And the nurse, she was right.

RR—She said, "I know what they all look like. I know that chart," she said.

O—She had a book!?

RR—I think she memorized. She said, "I," she says, uh, "I requested my pharmacist's index. It'll be brought up here tomorrow," she says.

O—You believe the Duchess? I can't.

RR—She said, "I know nebutols and obertrols and escotrols and tuonols and ob and blah blah

blah blah. Even I can't tell.

O—No one can. The Duchess has been studying this since twelve.

RR—She's had relationships since she was like and she says, "Aaah," she says . . . she says "And besides," she says, "I give the best shots in town."

O—She does too.

RR—She's got that little girl look on her face.

O—Oh I can't.

RR—She says, "You know when I first got interested in this?" (*laughter.*)

O—Isn't she, isn't she a fiend, God bless her. (*Laughter.*) No, she's fabulous. Was she checking the ward out though.

RR—Yeah.

O—She she she didn't.

RR—She was in the room all by herself in the corner.

O—I know, well she, she's got a private phone too. (*Music speeds up.*) (*Telephone rings.*) That's Sunshine. That's the Duchess. (*Phone rings.*) (*Music is very fast.*) (*RR laugh.*) She sounds like somebody else I know.

HA HA HA *Ring Ring* HA

RR—Hello. You couldn't believe what just happened. Oh, this is a beautiful story. I was in the bathtub

O—It's the Duchess.

RR—and uh, Ondine and Drella and uh, company all came in and uh, and uh I was still in the bathtub and the bell rang. It was Sunshine. (*Pause.*) Do you know what? Ondine opened the door and she said, "You're getting more disgusting every time I see you," and flung the bag at him. (*Pause.*Q What do you mean,

"What bag?" *The* bag. (*Ondine laughs.*) Not the bag of seeds, the bag of pot, the bag of tea.

O—She's all right.

RR—the tea bag.

O—She's much better. The tea bag?!! She's all right though, the Duchess.

RR—And then Sunshine fled.

O—Fritzie was with her.

D—Is that who called?

O—That was Sun, uh Fritzie was the dog.

D—Oh.

O—Unless Fritzie Green is the person that called you.

RR—. . . coming over?

O—Who's what! Oh, please. What has she done?

RR—The Blue Circle answering service?

O—Oh ho ho. What has she done?

RR—She's called up the Blew Circle answering service and they're all coming over.

O—To her hospital?

RR—Her hospital tonight.

O—She hates to be alone; I know that. She's so funny, it's unbelievable.

RR—She's so serious.

O—She's so beautiful, she really is great. When you compare her to Sunshine she makes Sunshine look like a silly fool. What is Sunshine acting like that for? Pe-pe-people are bearing up under it. She's not. Wha-wha-wha-what are they coming to her hospital room for?

RR—Is she, she using their service?

O—Obviously, she's going to drill them. Hey, your food is green, ohw come? . . . paint.

RR—The whore house.

O—Ah! The whore house. Oh I

left my powder there.

R—. . . take this there. You never did. Can we go there now?

O—Certainly they're always up.

R—Bardell's is nothing but twelve-year-olds or something.

O—Well, it's changed a little bit. Three's nothing but my name all over the walls now. (*Laughter.*) (*Music.*)   (*Pause.*)   (*Voices.*) (*Music.*)

R—. . . blood pressure . . . hospital . . . Do you want to hear a fantastic rock 'n' roll song? I just thought of this, this

O—I guess she's she, hello, hello there darling (*gasp*). Don't put that like that, I'm gonna go, an, I'm gonna swallow that Drella.

R—I'm from blue circle.

O—In fact, you are blue circle.

R—I'm heavenly blue circle.

O—I'm heavenly blue circle. (*Ondine bites the microphone.*) I had to, I had to eventually.

R—She's telephone and telestar and tele the Duchess.

O—Ah, telephone, telestar, and tele the Duchess (*gasp*). Awright the Duchess. Remember she's sick—tomorrow and operation. Don't push her. Those capillaries are exploding all over the place.

RR—She said she's gonna get into the operating room.

R—The Duchess's gonna set the place on fire.

O—(*blows into the microphone*) It's not, oh, not the last exit, Medea.

R—She said she's gonna burn up the blood pressure machine. She's taking, she's gonna see what the blood pressure of phosphorous is.

O—What's gotten her so excited?

R—She's gonna, she, y'know, how blood runs through the

RR—Everyone's crossed her down there.

O—She's gotten crazy.

RR—Everybody's crossed her at the hospital.

O—I wonder who? I bet, bet it was the night nurse.

R—She's gonna wrap, she's gonna wrap the matches on your leg? Oh, the blood pressure machine. Does it stretch that

RR—Yeah I know cause I mean we should be able to hear this.

M—Yeah.

O—Oh, but those hearing things you could hear.

D—I have one, I have one, I have one, I have one.

O—You have one?!! He's got one!

R—She's finished the box.

O—He's got a hearin' thing. Oh, how gorgeous. Indivis—all day long we've been out of our boxes. He's got a nice bag there.

R—Come to the inner blue circle.

RR—Drella, that's fabulous.

O—Oh my goodness! To hear the Duchess's voice booming over the room. Yes please. Oh, he's plugging it right into his ear, plugging it right into his ear, plugging it right in.

D—Where where does the sound come in?

M—There.

R—Okay, they're coming in the room. She's fighting off the nurses.

THE DUCHESS—Exciting movie on television (*interference*)

R—It's a girl in prison movie she's watching—fantastic!

DUCH—Oh (*interference*) the fights not (*interference*)

R—Oh are they? Is it um

DUCH—Spring Byington.

R—Spring Byington is the matron?

DUCH (*her voice is sugary*)—No, who, who's the matron? The one that was in that divine picture with

R—Hope Emerson?

DUCH—Joan Fontaine. Y'know, God who played, oh shit.

R—Uh, Mary Astor?

DUCH—No no.

R—Oh, everybody's a matron when it comes to

DUCH—I don't care who they are.

R—You can't be too guarded about letting out who the matron is.

DUCH—Yeah, watch, my dear. This one I've never seen before. Shelly Winters is in it too.

R—Oh Shelley Winters should stay in it.

DUCH—No, I'd much rather have Kim Stanley in it.

R—So, yeah, well. (*The Duchess laughs.*) You think, you think, you think we'd put them in the same show? I don't know.

Duch—No.

R—That's, that's like uh

Duch—I don't think so.

R—That's lake-river water.

Duch—They're too much alike.

R—Hm.

Duch—Yeah.

R—Yeah, one gets away with more, that's all, and one used to.

Duch—Yeah, I agree with you.

R—Yeah, it's just uh, it's flying a (*silence*) (*pause*). Won't a liquor store delivery close by?

Duch—Perhaps not, but the problems, sweety, is that I'm not supposed to, that's the last thing I'm suppose (*silence*) (*pause*). Well, I've been drinking.

R—Get out your guide. Look up a vodka pill.

Duch—I like vodka and (*interference*)

R—That's how our, that's how our bottle's labeled.

Duch—Tell em I've taken all the tu-ease　pills and I've smoked the joint.

R—Tu-ease, smoked the joint.

Duch—Um, Oh God!

R—And Oh God. Yes, smoked the joint and oh

Duch—Now I . . . together with my stash and strength will have to appear like—

R—You were supposed to keep it till tomorrow? You've gone through everything? Anything left?

Duch—Well, everything's at home cause I didn't. You see, when I went to the doctor's and they brought me over here, I didn't go home to get my clothes

R—Oh.

Duch—and thank God my stash bag was there because

R—Everything, everything

Duch—here, my dear, with that straw bag of mine there'd be enough trip, but I need a bag to take everything home because when I go out of here—what I'm not gonna take—the blood pressure machine's going (*laughter*)

R—Oh wow, she's got a spool proof plan for smuggling out the blood pressure machine when she goes home.

Duch—And my dear the (*interference*)

R—And she's, oh wow, she's got, she's got, she's going to make Roman vases out of the urine bottles. (*Laughs.*)

Duch—And the shit. Tell tell Rotten that the shit containers are perfect for for elephant turd for Patty.

R—Shit, the the shit containers are perfect for elephant turd for Patty. (*Interference.*) Got a moan from Ondine.

Duch—Oh tell her, tell tell him I'll save my soft-boiled eggs for the rest of . . . my dear.

R—He needs, you mean by way, by way of epiderm, epiderm turds, he needs, he needs, he needs telephone of two boys, uh, the telephone number of the boys who want.

Duch—What?

R—In, he needs the telephone number of the two boys in want.

Duch—They want the tea?

R—Yeah.

Duch—Hold on a sec, hold on a minute, I think the doorbell's ringing.

R—Holding on a minute and the doorbell's ringing.

Duch—Yes? Come in. Come in. Another hallucination.

R—Just, no, there was something there. It was an, a-a-nother hallucination.

Duch—It was one of the nurses, my dear, that I told that I knew more than she did.

R—It was a woman in white. Have you got a meric guide up there or something?

Duch—What?

R—You've got the meric guide.

Duch—No, I don't have any guides up here.

R—The pill guide.

Duch—What?

R—That's the mer, meric company puts out that, the pill guide.

Duch—I've, pill guide?

R—Park Davis.

Duch—Well, baby, I've got the physician's desk reference.

R—The physician's desk reference.

Duch—And ask Rita what that is. That's every pill listed.

R—How, how do you keep up with the new listings?

Duch—Baby, I get them. I get every sample.

R—Oh, how do you do that?

Duch—I'm a doctor. I'm a doctor. Strangelove they call me.

R—I know you're doctor, but I mean the the the

Duch—I get everything.

R—What would the posts o-

Duch—You ask Rotten—do I get what I want or not?

R—Does she get what she wants or not? This is inner blue circle three reporting. Uh, I'm asking does she get what she wants or not. (*Pause.*) Confirmed. Confiermed.

Duch—so yeah. They come out with the new one, what are they?

R—All is resavado to you.

Duch—They're speckled or they're round or they're oblong, but they're still the same.

R—What are those white, what are those marvelous labs called, the one with the blue speckled light one.

Duch—Uh, those are parca-damage are called adasap.

R—Adasap. What's, is, is, that uh, what's the

Duch—Madam Phetamine-Hydrochloric.

R—Mada-amphetamine. Oh, I'm stuck with these

Duch—Which is, which is the same as the zoxin.

R—Yeah, I'm stuck.

Duch—It's the brand name.

R—I'm stuck with these 20 milligram bi-phetamines, but they make we feel funny.

Duch—Oh, blackbirds.

R—No, they're, no they're red and black.

Duch—Oh, they're red and black for bi-phetamine T 20.

R—Is that better than the blackbirds?

Duch—Uh, no, not really. They're longer action but they they have uh, tranquillizers in neprospek.

R—Oh they do?!

Duch—Neprobe, meprobo, be

R—No wonder!

Duch—Yeah, that's why I don't take them. They're big red R.J.F.'s.

R—Red and black.

Duch—Yeah.

R—And they're

Duch—They're red and black the same as the blackbirds. The blackbirds are super strength and then

R—Black is 10, 10 milligram

Duch—Yeah, and then comes the red and black but the big, the black and red is much, much fatter capsule.

R—Yeah I have.

Duch—And it's the black and red, my dear, has tranquillizers.

R—Oh what what, how awful. No wonder I feel funny.

Duch—Oh baby, stop taking blackbirds. Stop taking biphetamine completely.

R—What should I do?

Duch—Because it's, you know something, it's not a goof, that stuff.

R—Hm.

Duch—I tell you, I mean cause I feally know the trip of the pill. I don't take uppies anymore. I just take my pokes (*sigh*) I'm finished with pills.

R—Uh huh.

Duch—Uh uh uh they give me heart palpitations.

R—They give you heart palpitations?

Duch—Yeah.

R—You mean permanent, or just as you go?

Duch—They're they're, it's not that they make you frantic but they give you, don't you feel sort of a little bit of a short breath on them?

R—Yeah.

Duch—And you get up a little.

9 / 2

R—Those are double blackbirds?

Duch—Well, I don't particularly goof on any of the pills.

R—No, well I just have to stay awake so I can work all the time—I mean write things.

Duch—Who is this?

R—This is inner circle blue three, suc-successor to Sue's answer phone, now dead, kn- also known as the last ring. I'm what happens when you decide to plug in.

Duch—I, here, will screw you, Peter Rabbit and tell me your name.

R—I'm a, a screw you Peter Rabbit? They don't give me, they don't allow me a name. The people I work for don't allow me a name.

Duch—Well.

R—It's part of the deal.

Duch—I'll tell you what you take.

R—Hm?

Duch—Um.

R—Um.

Duch—La—oh, lavender lilies.

R—Lavender lilies?

Duch—I'll have to get those because those are . . .

R—Oh, you have to get me lavender lillies, well they make, I want . . . you see, I'm a genius, and its, and I'll

Duch—. . . jargon.

R—Oh.

Duch—I, dexies, they don't do anything at all. Do you know what I dig?

R—What do you dig?

Duch—I dig those round ones that I gave Rotten—the pink ones that are geigy which I think

R—Round, pink, geigy?

Duch—Yes, that's prelude.

R—Prelude?

Duch—Indirect, they're kinda wild.

R—I thought they were anti-pregnancy pills.

Duch—Oh, don't, are you kidding?

R—Prelude.

Duch—I do, I do, prelude, my dear, that's endomyn.

R—Prelude, pre, pre, that's endomyn, oh that's right. Pre-pre-prelude, it sounds like a ritual; it's a vulgar ritual.

Duch—It's the one uppie there is that doesn't, it has none of the amphet-amines in it and they say, you see, I started taking it years ago when, when dexy was making me too frantic.

R—Well what puts you up i the prelude if there's no amphetamine in it?

Duch—Well, my dear, that's the trip, my dear.

R—That's

Duch—Just take one of those.

R—Oh.

Duch—And they're supposed to not make you frantic but they do.

R—Oh wowfi I, I, I want to be just completely concentrating like on the head.

Duch—Tell Rita to give you a poke.

R—I want to be the pin thinking about the number of angels.

Duch—Come over here tomorrow and I'll give you a poke.

R—A poke, a poke doesn't always do, I mean, I uh, I uh, I'm not sure about pokes, whether that's, that's, that's the answer.

Duch—Well, that's the way baby.

R—Poke.

Duch—A poke, a pole is the, is the biggest, is the most beautiful up there is, is the most, well not intravenously because I was on it for two years, I was on meta-amphetamine.

R—Meta-amphetamine, I.V. huh?

Duch—And also amphetaimne sulphate and amphatamine hydrochloric and the only thing bad about I.V. amphetamine is it really makes you a manica. I mean, right after my shot I get

R—Each time?

Duch—walk and shop. I have to leave the stores, the stores aren't open long enough for me to do things I want to do.

R—You want to shop after you get

Duch—My poke in the fannies are beautiful, I mean.

R—You gave me a poke in the fanny the other night.

Duch—Oh, well who the hell is it?

R—Who the hell is it? Now you, now you're, now you're getting, dog-gone it.

Duch—You, you weren't one of my patients.

R—I was one of your patients, that's right. Now, now you're my doctor. I was one of your patients.

Duch—Did you come up for psychiatric treatment?

R—No, I didn't come up for spychiatric treatment. I sor-sorta do my own. I'm a doctor, too. (*Pause.*) I'm an existentialist psychoanalyst. Which I—

Duch—This is Billy! . . . No it isn't.

R—Did you get that, Ondine?

Duch—No it isn't.

R—She said, "This is Billy." (*He laughs.*) After all that, my, it's—it is Billy, I'm Billy.

Duch—Billy—

R—Billy who?

Duch—Oh fuck!

R—Thin Billy?

Duch—Are you the guy in the white shirt?

R—Am I the guy in the white shirt? From where?

Duch—The older man with the grey hair?

R *excited*—The older man with the grey hair! (*The Duchess laughs.*) The older man with the grey hair? (*The Duchess wheezes.*) The guy in the white shirt? He's here too. Maybe you, I don't know, maybe you don't know, maybe you

Duch—. . . came up for somebody else and I . . .

R—That came up for somebody else . . .

Duch—And I gave him I think 28 of something ob-oh . . .

R—Oh now no no 28 of something—

Duch—What did I give you? Just a poke?

R—You gave me you gave me a poke in my, I did I did have a little *muscle* pain the next day. Is that usual? Or am I sens—hyper sensitive?

Duch *whispering*—That's nothing.

R—Huh?

Duch—That was in your head.

R—That was in my head?

Duch—Oh come on, tell me.

R—I sit on my brains, I admit, but the pain wasn't in my head. (*He laughs.*)

Duch—Oh pleaese now. I'm lying here, I'm in the hospital, I shouldn't have things in my head, and I have so much on my mind.

R—Who?

Duch—I'm going out of it, so don't let me go out, acuse I, I'll think about it all night.

R—Oh no no no. You *do* remember. I was in the studio when you came up the other night, with pizza.

Duch—Ohh! You're—

R—And you were writing notes to Ondine . . .

Duch—You're the blond.

R—Yeah, I'm the blond. Je suis blonde—toujours.

Duch—Oh yes, I was writing notes to Ondine about—

R—Je m'appelle, je m'appelle père, backside.

Duch—Last night. I was on another trip, my dear.

R—You were on another trip? You do a lot of travelling.

Duch—Oh god. Oh, yes. Miles and miles.

R—What do you think of, what do you think of of space orbit? Are you are you willing to—

Duch—Space orbit?

R—Are you willing to land?

Duch—Sweetie, I've—

R—You take trips, but are you willing to land?

Duch—Of, course.

R—Really?

Duch—I landed yesterday. When I came in here.

R—You landed in the hospital. Oh—that's very clever.

Duch—Darn right. I left space, but I tell you one thing is that I've been there before.

R—You've been to the hospital before? Or space?

Duch—No. space,

R—Space. What spaces did you find when you left with that trip?

Duch—Well, I y'know, followed Glenn around.

R— . . . Is it more like Mars?

Duch—What?

R—Is it more like Mars? With the trip like—had?

Duch—Well, I don't go anywhere with that kind of space. That's not what I call space, darling.

R—Something—

Duch—I think the whole idea of space is not where there's—capitols flying around, and, uh people are, I can't even describe it, but I think where we have to go is the there.

R—Is the bear?

Duch—Is there.

R—Is there.

Duch—Space.

R—Space, but what is space? I mean where, y'know . . .

Duch—Space?

R—Yeah.

Duch—Well, I'll tell you what it is. Right now, I'm sitting up, and I'm sort of

R— . . . poke.

Duch—The other whole side of my bed, and I'm looking out the window, and I see two buildings around, I see sky . .

R—We, uh, our space line has been jammed by by uh . . .

Duch—It's dropping, and the whole scene, y'know, is closing in on us, my dear.

R—Oh.

Duch—It's just all right out there where there's nothing else. Where there is space.

R—The Duchess.

Duch—And there's not much space for anything in this town any longer.

R—The Duchess there—

Duch—Let's go there, darling.

O—The Duchess, baby—

Duch—What?

O—This is Ondine. I was just in the bathroom and Rotten gave himself the most perfect poke I've ever seen.

Duch—Oh that, that makes my heart sink.

O—Not a bit of blood. That makes your heart think?

Duch—Oh, I want him to give it to himself perfectly, my dear, but don't advertise it. Y'know, because I do like to give people pokes.

O—I know, but Rotten gave himself—

Duch—And I don't like everyone to turn themself on giving themself a poke.

O—D'you know Rotten, that she said . . .

Duch—Then who will I have left to poke? And that's my hang up. Not the poke, my dear, but the pokee. (*She wheezes.*) You Know? I told every nurse to, oh my dear and yesterday . . .

O— . . . herself her own poke.

Duch—And the intern came in and he got my name and my age and my history. And he said, and he said, "Do you diet?" And I said, "No, I drink about three quarts of vodka a day," I said I don't eat regularly, and he said, "Do you take any medicines, at all?" I said, "Yes."

O—Darling?

Duch—I said, I started, I said, "Oh, about 5cc of amphetamine a day, one cc of   , one cc of B-12, mercanhydrate dehydration, and then I went on another, and then y'know all the pills, and he looked at me and he said, uh, "Have you ever seen a psychiatrist?" I said, "No, I can't confide in psychiatrists." I said, "The first time I was in this hospital, 12 years ago, I fell in love with my resident, and then I went home to my family and I decided I was leaving home, so I called him up and I said, "Dr., can I come and stay in your apartment, I don't, y'know, I've had a fight with my mother," so he said, "After six years of practicing internal medicine, graduating from Cornell and . . . one of the finest diagnosticians in the country, he switches to psychiatry, then he tells me he's a homosexual, so I said, "No, I haven't made the psychiatry trip, my dear, because I don't have the . . . that any of these nuts, y'know, are gonna fuck me up . . . because I am, y'know, that have problems, y'know that are gonna send me over to the hydrator across the street.

R—Oh wew.

Duch—Then this big, bold type doctor, Dr. walked in—

R—Dr. Bernard?

Duch—Yeah, a resident also, and so good that you wouldn't believe it, and she walked in and she said, "Ha, I'm Dr. I'm Dr.," and I said, "Very nice to meet you, doctor." And she said, "This isn't patient contact, or anything, but could I bum a cigaret off ya?" "Sure, I have a cigaret" and she sat down, and she'd heard about the medicines I'd taken, and she must've been very hip because she said, she looked straight in my eyes and she said, "You must be higher than you head twenty-four hours a day," and I said, "Dr. I'm right there," and I said, "You know, I go to bed and I sleep, and do you know that every night I do go to bed I lie there and I say, "I'm too old to start, y'know, really going to medical school," I said, "You could be there," I said, "Think of where you could be." And I said, "Don't tell me that it ruins your health or any of that, I don't think that anything that I have ever taken —it's from vodka, but it's not from anything else.

R—What'd Dr. say?

M—Does it hurt?

Duch—Ask Rita what I said to the colored mammy nurse that walked in tonight and asked me if I wanted a backup. Just a-ask Rotten.

R—Wh-what'd she say when she when when the colored mammy nurse asked her for a backrup, Rita? (Pause.) What'd she say when the when the mammy nurse wanted her to have her back rubbed? Did you say, "Shove my mouth?"

DUCH—No, I did not, I told her about my pokes. He brings up these. Who's he poking?

R—Uh, a French friend of mine, a girl from uh, from uh—from Madagasoa.

DUCH—Well, you know something? I don't, I'll tell you something,

R—Yes—

DUCH—Uh, I'm a doctor, you know.

R—Yes.

DUCH—Uh, a very ethical doctor. I have not been busted for malpractice yet . . .

R—Uh-huh, uh-huh.

DUCH—Or anything else, but do you know what's terribly important?

R—What is?

DUCH—I don't believe in mixing the amphetamine bother up. I like mine sealed, 30 cc bundle.

R—You don't like the mix.

DUCH—Uh, no I don't. Because it clouds up.

R—It clouds up.

DUCH—Anything, y'know, that is not clear, y'know, I saw a piece of tobacco in it, in that bottle of amph . . . at . . . the other night, I saw, uh, maybe a little bit of tea floating around in it.

R—Oh no.

DUCH—And me, I just don't like that.

R—I don't like it either.

DUCH—And I get—

R—Everywhere everywhere "pure" should be the word.

DUCH—And I never . . . . have never been touched.

M—But I *am* bleeding. She did?

DUCH—And I don't know. I I just think mixing, u'know, you mixed the other night for me . . .

R—Oh, but they've been chasing me with that . . . but I didn't think that was me.

DUCH—Well, that that doesn't well, that didn't work for me.

R—I don't like that crazy kinda mixed up high.

DUCH—That could be terribly dangerous. You could put two c per whatever it is, if you put the powder of the tuinols with something, it's just terribly terribly dangerous.

R—Did they just, what's dangerous about the tuinols?

DUCH—I get very *high* and I don't know many I'm taking. I keep forgetting that I've just taken a pill. So I pop another pilly in my in my mouth, and you know, I I used to—

R—I I did, I didn't get high the other night when I took one.

Duch—Well I may—

R—The Duchess my doctor's telling me not to mix.

Duch—Darling, in Mexico last year for nine months I did not make an ippy for nine months. I didn't take a poke, I didn't take a pill, nothing to put me up. I took 38 e-gram tuinols a day.

R—Oh wow! 38 tuinols at 3 grams, wow.

Duch—But I took them, there's a way to take them.

R—That's 104 grams of tuinols a day.

Duch—It takes me 7 to go to sleep.

Rotten Rita—Hi darling.

Duch—Hello.

RR—I've just poked myself and two other people . . .

Duch—Yes.

RR—And everybody is okay.

Duch—All right, well uh, you're my you're my—

RR—I am very very sorry that I had to do it.

Duch—You are taking over my practice while I am away.

RR—There is nothing else I can do but carry on the on on on the tradition.

Duch—I know, because you're just taking over while I'm away, but I'm resuming practice the minute I get outa here.

RR—Oh well, you know.

R—She's afraid about losing her practice.

RR—You're resuming your practice toworrow at the hospital.

Duch—Listen Rotten.

RR—Yes.

Duch—Listen now, darling.

RR—Yes dear.

Duch—Those needles have got to be sharpened right away, right tonight with emery boards, not with nail files but with emery boards, and right tonight they have got to be sterilized and not with uh, uh, what d'ya call it, machtes.

RR—Yah, yah.

Duch—They've got to be boiled.

RR—Uh huh.

Duch—But don't put the plastic in or you're gonna have nothing left.

RR—Yeah, I know that.

Duch—That's not terribly important, but those needles now they're really getting dull.

RR—I've taken care of everything.

Duch—Have you have you nail filed, I know you haven't done that yet, I know it.

RR—No, but I have taken . . .

Duch—Do you know how you do it?

RR—Yes, yes of course, but I will tell you what, what this—

Duch—No baby, you don't do the point at all.

RR—This is a drill.

Duch—You do it straight up.

RR—Yeah.

Duch—Everything has to be straight up.

RR—Doctor, you're fabulous (*The Duchess laughs.*) Straight up it will be.

R—Straight up it's gotta be.

RR—It's gotta go straight up.

R—This is a manual.

RR—Doctor . . .

Duch—Yes.

R—Emmanuel.

RR—How are things going down there now?

Duch—I'm swacked outa my wick.

RR—Did you finish the vodka?

Duch—Yes. I need more. Can you bring some more tomorrow?

RR—Yes, of course.

Duch—Bring, you'd better bring me a quart.

RR—I would've brought you a quart today if I wolda had the bread, but I got the pot tonight, so I'll get some bread now.

Duch—Yes, because, you know, I don't, I, I, what is this you brought me anyway, it's more than a pint, isn't it?

RR—It's Majourska.

Duch—I don't like, I don't like Smirnoff.

RR—I know you won't like Smirnoff.

R—Do you like the vodka with the buffalo grass in it?

Duch—I like Majourska.

R—You don't like buffalo grass.

Duch—Majourska's my trip, y'know.

R—But Zbit, Zb . . . . . .

Duch—You know, I'm very—

RR—The Duchess, The Duchess baby, you should be here and I want you to know that you belong here and I do miss you very much.

Duch—Um, wait just a minute, I'm very high and I might be sneaking out soon, so will you wait a mintue, I . . .

RR—I'm hanging up now because I have things to do.

Duch—I wanna talk to—

RR—I'm listening, and I'll hear all of this again.

Duch—talk to my patient.

RR—Okay.

Duch—Uh, hello?

R—Yuh.

Duch—Let me tell you something. I'll tell you why I like Majourska. Well well, y'see, my trip, really, I used to be a very big Gentry girl, and I drank nothing but gin.

R—I hate gin, I hate gin.

Duch—Well, I love it, I still, I always loved gin (*her voice is garbled*). I love Beefeater's, I, but my husband was sort of, uh, well, I don't get drunk on liquor.

R—HMM.

Duch—He was something else on gin. So, I absolutely had to stop having gin around. Because, y'know, it was dangerous, I got poked with electric drills, and um egg beaters, and flower pots and everything else, the lousy Beefeaters, so we stopped that, and I said, "Oh my God, I'll never be ableto drink that lousy vodka. So I started drinking vodka, y'know occasionally, and I began to dig it. I don't really dig vodka, I like vodka and water, just a little.

R—How is Majourska on the rocks?

Duch—And I love, d'ya know, what, d'ya know the only thing that hens makes me high, I'm a weary y'know, I drink, I could drink scotch, or gin or anything, I mean, I just dig my booze, but my trip now, has got to be Dubonnet Compale.

R—Hmmm.

Duch—Because nothing gets me more skulled, that beautiful high. I get so str. . . . . and vodka. Y'know vodka, I never get drunk, and I drink y'know a qu—I'll tell you I drink a quarterly quart of it a day. I'd die for my liquor. I really do. I sold those ten obetrols the other night for that bottle of gin.

R—How does, doesn't your stomach sorta never come back? My stomach would, y'know, if I was on nothing but rom for a whole six month period, and my stomach went to pieces, and then I, uh . . .

Duch—Well, y'know . . .

R—Coudn't digest the rum. Wouldn't even digest the rum, needless anything else I would try to put in it on occasion.

Duch—Well, y'know, how's it gone with me. I can, I could drink y'know if the bottle is there, I woke up one morning at Rita's and he'd taken the vodka, Walter had the night before at Joe Dingle's

R—Oh, terrible . . .

Duch—And I woke up in the morning and I didn't have my bottle of vodka, oh I hate him.

R—Joe Dingle's the bitter end.

Duch—Oh, I can't stand him. He's such a aa, years ago I used to go over there and—

R—He's gotten worse, he he he's un on the verge of, on the verge of schizophrenia now, he's on the verge of . . .

Duch—I get tons of tape, though, mobbed on him but well.

R—Oh, wonderful.

Duch—Because I wouldn't sit in that god-damned place with these fucking purple curtains and not get high, and sit there and not poke. One thing is digging me, baby, opera I love it the most, but I'm not gonna sit all evening and shut up, y'know.

R—He never stops.

Duch—There's time for that. What?

R—He talks all the time.

Duch—And the machine, that—

R—He asks me, he keeps giving me "mickys," he's pas, y'know, micky finns. He puts, y'know something in it, I don't know what, in the gin.

Duch—Darling, he started very very uh recently.

R—Ohh.

Duch—He used to be such, so many, I can't tell you, I've known him for years.

R—Oh, he's still mi . . .

Duch—He would never, a joint, my God he's still, I'd go up to the little balcony, y'know, upstairs, have a joint downstairs, I don't, I don't really have to have a joint, I just have to have my . . . three things I dig; my vodka, my poke, and my pillys.

R—Hmm, ummm

Duch—And I mean I can even do without the pillys, I dig, I mean I can dig, I dig being very frantically up.

R—Yeah, so do I.

Duch—Well, do you remember the other night I came over, and I, I didn't have any grub with me, and I had, what was it, ten obetrols for that bottle of Fleishman's.

R—uh huhm

Duch—Oh my dear, and I carry it around, and they call me, and I always have to have it around, oh my God, Joan Fontaine was in that.

R—Joan Fontaine, wel—you even mentioned her in passing before. Joan Fontaine is is is the other side of ugly.

Duch—She's a great friend of mine—I love her. I don't think she's ugly at all.

R—Ohh—you haveto, she's not ugly, she's just something else. She's Olivia de Haviland's sister. (*He laughs.*)

Duch—Do you know something? Uh, I, well—I think,

R—She got married again.

Duch—Yes, I know, but I think women that look, well, I don't know

R—She smiles so much

Duch—I tell you, it's my idea of the most beautiful woman in the whole world

R—Is what?

Duch—Is Ingrid Bergman.

R—I, I, I think, I, I knew that, it came out of my mouth at the same time, I didn't try to say it because you were talking, that's fantastic!

Duch— . . . is my idea of a beautiful woman.

R—Yes, that's, when I was eleven, I was.

Duch—Number two.

R—I went out with her daddy for three years, he looks like her now.

Duch—A friend of mine I went out with, my dear, I was engaged, her for her daughter's ex-husband.

R—Oh, the insurance man. The insurance man.

Duch—From . . .

R—Oh, I knew, I knew, I knew Journey when she was Pia.

Duch—Yeah.

R—And pia and, I went to school in Beverley Hills, in a little grammar school.

Duch—Well we were, great friends. Uh, she, Jane and

R—B-beautiful little girls

Duch—Sophie Churchill and myself . . .

R—Ohh. Did you ever, I didn't, I didn't, after a, I ran into them in the Hotel Sc . . . in Rangoon, on her honeymoon.

Duch—Oh, wait a minute.

R—And I knew her by her mother's walk.

Duch—. . . . . number two.

R—Huh?

Duch—Wait a second.

R—I knew her by her husband's walk.

Duch—It is, wait a second, wait a minute, unmber, well . . .

R—Is she married again, now?

Duch—No. She gets number one, actually, along with Ingred Bergmanis a, I think, the most beautiful woman in the world.

R—Uh, let's see if we're getting some message on this one. Uh . . .

Duch—She made one of her first trips, uh, I'll give you a clue:

R—Somebody, a more recent figure?

Duch—She made one of her first trips, and her greatest sensation was La——.

R—Uhh. Wh wh, what's her oh ohohohohohsim, Simone Signoret.

Duch—Right.

R—I don't know her, I, I, it's hard for me to tell whether that's fantastic or awful.

Duch—I think she's so beautiful, I really do.

R—I love her too, in that, and in . . .

Duch—Oh and that scene I'll never forget

R—I like some weird nobody else likes.

Duch—Who?

R—Valley. (*Pause.*)

Duch—Rudy Vallee?

R—Hmm?

Duch—Rudy Vallee?

R—Hmm? Nooo. Not Rudy Vallee. Y'know Rudy Vallee is not one of the three most beautiful women in the world. (*He laughs.*) I don't care. Hmm?

Duch—No. Rink.

R—No, Rudy Vallee is from the THIRD MAN and the and the Paradine Case.

Duch—No, No.

R—she she . . . and after that she, she's only done the Vie de Carmalese   but she's not, she's not the same anymore.

Duch—Hold on a minute.

R—Vallee's through ages has been ennundated and eroded,

Duch *in background*—Can I have, listen, nurse—can I have . . .(*pause*)

R—Hi.

Duch—That was a trick.

R—No nurse, no . .

Duch—She came in and I said, "Can I have a pill to go to sleep. . . . ."

R—She's giving you something to go to sleep?!

Duch—I think so, but I don't want to go to sleep. (*She giggles.*)

R—Well, you can, you can fight it.

Duch—. . . gonna be out there all night. I'm on a high journey, a . . . ride.

R—Oh wow. All the night nurses are.

Duch—Do you know who else get's a prize? The girl who was in, I think was divine, was it uh Goldfinger, not Goldfinger.

R—Pussy Galore? That one?

Duch—No, no I get, I get all those movies mixed up.

R—Oh, you mean, you mean Ursula Andress, Ursula Andress.

DUCH—The Swedish girl, yes.

R—Yes.

DUCH—I think she's divine.

R—She has a body.

DUCH—Oh, heaven.

R—And . . . Yes, mmm. There were some . . . There's a Chinese star that not many people know who's named LILY Huah. Who's also one of the most beautiful women in the world.

DUCH—Suzie Wong.

R—That that Suzie Wong was a bitch, I was I was in Suzie Wong. I was a sailor in "Sizie Wong." I was livink in Hong Kong then.

DUCH—I, I, I like I liked

R—Oh, she's so awful, Nancy Kwan, she's two feet high. She's half English to boot. And she's a bitch, and she reads bad comic books, not good ones. I mean, you know. She's somebody who could actually rea—

DUCH—And I get very brashy if I haveto see Susan Haywood.

R—I like Susan Haywood.

DUCH—But my biggest trip on Susan was with her pearls and her white gloves.

R—Oh yeah, she's fabulous.

DUCH—Wasn't she beautiful, I think

R—I think Susan Haywood's marvelous, they just never told her she was marvelous, in the right way, so it never . . .

DUCH—. . . . . and I love that movie, that John Gavin, well, he's something else.

R—Y'know, I love

DUCH—A male actress will go . . .

R—Joe Sorrell . . . something beautiful now called "Bombole," four short Italian movies, in which Gina Lolla brigida was in one., she's she's she's the wife of an innkeeper. And there's, and I can tell him off as a priest-and John Sorr, John Sorreal is the one I mean, he's so beautiful

DUCH—I never get to them.

R—I can, I can just as well leave as take Alan Delon,

DUCH—Do you know what movie I went to see the other day, and I went right off my rocker? And I'm not much for the Broadway great big large production.

R—You're talking about *My Fair Lady*, what're you talking about?

DUCH—No . . . "The Sound of Music."

R—"The Sound of Music" I don't know.

DUCH—Well, I dug it.

R—I can't dig, I can' dig niceness.

DUCH—I don't know whatit was about that movie

R—Julie Andrews? She just

Duch—There was something in that movie

R—She's too right, she's too Mrs. Right.

Duch—Something in that that was not very me at all.

R—If that's the sound of Music, I wanna be deaf.

Duch—That picture, I came out of it, and I was sorta divine.

R—I mean, you know, I was so sick (*Duchess says something.*) Ohh! Fantastic it was . . . . picked me up in a dancing bar in Berlin. (*Pause.*) Oh really? Then I walked out with him in the morning on the street, and everybody . . . . abotu two.

Duch—John Wayne, too.

R—John Wayne is exciting. In his newest movie, called, uh, what's it called, that big one . . . . I don't know, he's

Duch—I think, I think he's fantastic

R—No, I like (*long pause*) . . . You see he was, his son is, I saw his son in "Ride the Wild Surf."

Duch—Boy, I mean, I've always dug

R—Ondine, way to the left, way to the left of center

Duch—Oh yes but I

R—You saw, you saw, how about Robert Mitchum? Everybody

Duch—I adore him.

R—Did you ever see Kate Field?

Duch—Yup.

R—Wasn't that fabulous? He played himself.

Duch—I adore Robert Mitchum.

R—Oh, Ondine just, Ondine just Sancho Padrez . . . to the to the picture, "Don Quixote."

Duch—I dig the, uh, who is it, oh my dear, I'm trying to think of people I like, I can't think, (*Pause.*)

R—Wow.

Duch—Oh Robert Mitchum I think is beautiful, I love Kirk Douglas.

R—You like Kirk Douglas

Duch—Yup. I love that chin.

R—Ohh.

Duch—I dig it at the end.

R—Umm.

Duch—Jane Russell.

R—Jane Russell.

Duch—Not Jane Russell, Rosalind Russell . . . . on television.

R—Who are they gonna cast in the "Ondine Story?"

Duch—In the "Ondine Story"? (*Pause.*) Normal people.

R—Very normal people. I liked his last picture. Very normal people.

Duch—Who am *I*, did you say, "Who am *I* gonna cast for the Ondine story?" Audrey Hepburn.

R—Audrey Hepburn. Oh, wow. Oh. Wait, I'll have to Should I let them poke me with that mixed mess?

Duch— But be sure it's up on the upper right quarter.

R—Upper right quarter?

Duch—Yes! In the hip darling, and not in the fanny.

R—Oh, okay.

Duch—And make sure he does it high.

R—Andylwants to say now that Inner Blue Circle is signinfi off. We'll we'll we'll be back tomorrow, about lavendarand about, uh

O—Come over . . . for lunch and dinner, and you know I just ordered.

10 /   1

Duch— . . . gear is kind of

R—That's the

Duch—the island around 5 o'clock

R—To join the, the great white way

Duch—and that's gonna be a trip and Ultra Violet.

R—Hm? Little Ida

Duch—Then we're gonna have a scene.

R—Oh fantastic, they're inventing a flying

Duch—Ultra's bringing me over come campy things. She says she has a present for me.

R—Oh, I love the name Ultra. Is Ultra a nurs too? They've invented

Duch—Oh Drella mustn't ask to hav the answer to Ultra Violet.

R—Do you know, do you know Ultra, don't you, Ultra Violet. Uh.

Duch—Thank you. That's, I think that's (*Rink blows into the microphone*). Wait a minute.

R—Oh, a fly they've just invented a flying nurse here for the great white way. Do you think, do you think a nurse could fly?

Duch—Hold on a minute. Drella won't kill me.

R—Oh.

Duch—Wait a minute. I, I

R—That's, that's an important question without the sound.

Duch—What?

R—I, it, I think it's uh, it's important, we're trying to figure out, if you join Nurses Anonymous, and join it's the Great White Way and now they want

Duch—You know what I just got? (*She whispers.*)

R *he whispers*—What?

Duch—A big nebutol.

R *he shouts*—A big nebutol just flew into the room.

Duch—Shhhh.

R—A big nebutol.

Duch—Big, colored, black

R—O Dig, a big black nebutol

Duch—Shh. (*Laughter.*) No, a big yellow, a big yellow black nebutol, darling.

R—No no, a big spade brought it in. A big, black person brought her a nebutol.

Duch—A big, black, colored maid from down South just gave it to me . . .

R—Oh.

Duch—Now, that's just gonna put me more up there.

R—They think they're gonna put her to sleep with that.

Duch—I, I just wanna

R—The big, black nebutol.

Duch—You think, you think so, they think they can put me to sleep, ha.

R—The spade's gonna get a real . . . .   We're gonna

Duch—My dear, I'll be out of doing something else around that desk, ha ha.

R—You're gonna do, you're gonna do the dance.

Duch—Already they, u'know, well they know me so well over here. I spend my life in hospitals, my dear. I'm always in them and the operator that I called the other day said, "Yes, this Miss Brigid Polk, oh you back in Miss Brigid Polk?" I said, "Yes."

R—And you're back in; I love that. It sounds like a cell block to

Duch—I was nine months in the hospital last year.

R—Nine months?

Duch—I love them; half the time I go for my diet.

R—Nine months in the hospital. Oh wow!

Duch—Well that was last year for my diet.

R—For you diet, you had a nine month diet.

Duch—I did that in Mexico.

R—Oh, you were in, you were interned in hospital.

Duch—Well, I went down therebecause I heard of a fantastic thing where they put me on

R—Don't you think that's pushing hospitality a bit too far?

Duch—No.

R—Nine monthe Don't yo uthink that's, Ondine?

Duch—Heaven.

R—Nine months a year in a hospital. Don't you think that's pushing hospitality a bt far?

Duch—My God, I didn't even have a baby, can you imagine?

R—Ooh wow.

Duch—I thought, y'know, I was on that diet, I lost 112 pounds. At least I should have a baby. I gained 60 while I was at it.

R—Oh you should have a baby.

Duch—Stark.

R—. . . . . an amount of nebutols.

Duch—The Reese brothers.

R—Get a wind-up baby from Schwartz.

Duch—No, my dear, do you know where the wind-up babies come from?

R—We're gonna bring her a wind-up baby.

Duch—The wind-up babies, darling, the real beautiful wind-up babies come from the Stork Club.

R—From the Stork Club?

Duch—Yes, I've been there, my dear.

R—Oh, the wind-up babies

Duch—They, my dear, have the smiley cry and laughing ones.

R—Oh fantastic.

Duch—But I think that while I'm here in the hospital I think you can bring me a real, live uh whatchamcallit, you know to put right in.

R—Debbie Danridges   comes to the phone.

Duch—Now they're going to make me turn the television off

R—Oh.

Duch— . . . taken a sleeping pill. They say, "Now you must rest."

R—Blue circle flying out with the nurse, I've got, I haveto give it to Dorothy Dandridge.

Duch—All right.

R—Cause she's craving.

Duch—All right.

R—Okay, I'll see you tomorrow.

Duch—All right.

R—Okay.

Duch—Bye bye.

O—Hello?

Duch—Hello.

O—The Duchess?

Duch—Yes.

O—This is the strange man.

Duch—Hello darling.

O—I'm telling you that . . . and Angela Rapberry's speared to the wall.

Duch—Oh, I've always been told that before my haircut, my haircut, my dear, that's the first time You told who I looked like for years, Angela. Did you hear what I did the night.

O—Yes, I did.

Duch—Of the opening of of of Arthur's, I put Sybil in a condition, darling

O—Sybil Burton?

Duch—Yes, I, well I'd been to the opening and I stayed twenty minutes because I thought it was such a bore and I went back home.

O—Oh.

Duch—And I was with this friend of mine and I put of the eulogy of Richard Burton from Camelot.

O—Yeah.

Duch—The record player and I called up Arthur's and I, and I asked, I said, "May I please speak to Sybil Burton." And they said, "Who's calling? We're terribly busy." I said, "It's Miss Angeline Lamberry, awfully important," I said, "I've got a wire from England and it's necessary that I speak to her immediately." And they said, "Certainly, Miss Lamberry, we'll be . . . . and I . . . . a nedle on my dear and I went (*in a very deep voice*) "I demand to have her on."

O—Ooh.

Duch—And she, oh she went off of her wig. Is that beautiful?

O—Duchess are you alone in your room?

Duch—No, yes, I am now but I'm not alone my dear cause I'm with all of you.

O—Oh of course and listen darling, do you know that your voice has been recorded during this entire conversation?

Duch—By whom?

O—By Drella, you're on tape.

Duch—Well, I haven't been talking to him.

O—He's just plugged you in.

Duch—Plugged me in?

O—You are now . .

Duch—Oh well, my dear, if if if I'm gonna be plugged in over there some one can come right over here and plug me in.

O—You've been plugged in over there.

Duch—Well I would liketo get really plugged in right now.

O—I know, well maybe, I wish we could take care of that.

Duch—You know what I mean?

O—I know what you mean by being plugged in, my dear. I'm not blind, deaf and dumb.

Duch—My bill has been in the cleaners for so many weeks. Madame Levek, my dear, she charges a fortune to get those.

O—Would you like to speak to a gorgeous French girl?

Duch—Of course.

O—Of course, I knew you would.

Duch *in a French accent*—I love French women.

O—This is—*long pause*
Goodbye from Ondine.

Duch—Au revoir.

M—He's losing his dress, Ondine.

Duch—Bonsoir, comment va tu? (*Good evening, how are you?*)

M—Mm?

Duch—Bonsoir.

M—Bonsoir?

Duch—I'm very high, oh my.

M—Tu . . . .

Duch—Oui, je pense a sa fontaine.oui.

M—Je pense que c'est mieux parce que si je parle anglais tu crois ne pas je suis francaise. (*I think it is better because if I speak English you will think I am not French.*)

Duch—Oui. Mais um.

M—Tu est très high. (*You are very high.*)

Duch—Oh I'm so high so-, I can speak French really very well but I can't speak it right now, I'm so high.

M—You sound very good, what you said.

Duch—I keep thinking, I keep thinking in Spanish.

M—Do you know how to speak Spanish too.

Duch—Yes. Spanish I much

M—I can't speak Spanish.

Duch—Oh yes, but Spanish is much fresher in my mind. But you know in Mexico last year and I speak in Spanish all the time.

M—Where did you go? In Spain?

Duch—No, oh yes, I, I went to school you see, in in Switzerland.

M—Mm.

Duch—For a year in Levan . . . and then I was in Spain and Madrid for a year and then I began to learn Spanish but I picked it up really last year in Mexico.

M—Did you go back to Spain last year?

Duch—No, I was in Mexico for the whole year.

M—Oh, in Mexico.

Duch—I lived there for about ten months.

M—Where did you live in Mexico?

Duch—In Mexico City and I have a house . . .

M—Is there a place in Mexico that's really called uh Port . . . . . stapa

Duch—. . . . . stapa?

M—Yes.

Duch—I never heard of it.

M—Probably it doesn't exist.

Duch—Well, I don't know.

M—A little fishing village, somewhere.

Duch—Perhaps, y'know, you you y'know

M—On the Pa-, maybe it's an entirely fictitious name. I just read it somewhere.

Duch—Uh.

M—You getting operated tonight?

Duch—Hm?

M—You getting operated tonight.

Duch—Maybe, if if my, if these black and blue marks don't go away by the end of the night, but, my dear, I don't think they will after what I've had to drink and what I've taken this evening. (*Moxanne laughs.*) I'm um, I'm all

M—If you get operated they'll give you a lot more.

Duch—I don't give a shit, y'know who cares if I get operated, it'll be done in the morning and then visitors come. I'll be back and I'll tell them I'm to be y'know, not, no recovery jazz, my dear.

M—You have, you have to show us all your wounds.

Duch—I don't even care if they do it with . . . . . . I can, just y'know . . . . they give me a quart of vodka. (*They laugh.*) I said they'll take me down there and let me come up there by myself, right?

M—You're gonna come up by yourself?

Duch—Of course.

M—With your, with your, your wounds are going to be all open and everything.

Duch—I don't care.

M—You don't care. Your're gonna walk up all by yourself back to your room.

Duch—I was, oh, no, I don't mean that, my, walk up by myself to my room!? I, I I won't even walk out the shower, my dear without a wheel chair. (*Moxanne laughs.*) You know, I get terribly, you shoud see the nurses I carry on with absolutely like crazy, I am the most difficult patient.

M—Do you make them do everything for you?

Duch—Oh. I ring ring ring twenty-five times.

M—You know what's the hardest thing to make them do?

Duch—And it's all you see, darling, an intercom on the wall.

M—Oooh.

Duch—I just can't get used to talking to an intercom on the wall so they

M—You've got every single machine in there, don't you?

Duch—Oh, you can't imagine: the television set and my executone, and my room is so

M—Executone, is that your telephone?

Duch—No, my telephone, I've got a direct wire right to my room, you don't people you know

M—Yeah.

Duch—even know my dear.

M—. . . . what's that, that's the executone

Duch—when I check in, you dear? with my agents and what have you, I don't even have to tell them I'm in the hospital.

M—Oh.

Duch—Not that I have any agents, just undercover ones.

M—My dear.

Duch—Wait just a second, you just keep talking to me , but I just will have a little more vodka. (Fading away.)

M—Oh, we should, is it too late to come visit at the hospital?

Duch—Well, I tell you som thing, I don't know what, so they throw me out. All right, listen.

M—Why are they gonna throw you out tomorrow?

Duch—Well, because

M—They're gonna operate you.

Duch—Well I told them this afternoon, oh I went on a trip with the doctor this afternoon.

M—Where?

Duch—Before everyone arrived, y'see . . . . the whole group was here

M—But they told me about it.

Duch—And uh, uh, because . . . get mad at me because I can't, uh, you know . . . I hope I have some water left for my vodka. I don't give a hell about the grapefruit juice—

M—What about ice?

Duch—Oh, I don't like it with ice anymore.

M—Oh, just water and vodka.

Duch—Dear, if it's vodka, it's drinkable, I don't care what's in it.

M—Oh, what about the campale dubbonet, I heard you mention it. eh, mixed together?

DUCH—Oh, be-because nothing gets me drunk, y'see the thing is is that I'm one of the few people that really likes to drink along with pokes and pills and everything else. I have to have the booze.

M—That's sensible.

DUCH—I really do, I don't care. I like my booze, I like my drinks, y'know, so why the hell should I stop it, that's the reason I'm in here, that's why I'm black and blue from head to foot. But who gives a

M—Head to foot? I thought it was only your legs.

DUCH—Only my legs and arms.

M—Oh, and your arms, too.

DUCH—Yeah.

M—Oh, and you're losing all your circulation, now that's about the capillaries.

DUCH—This is hemmorrhaging capillaries, and mal- nutrition, which, when you meet me, my dear, you will look at me and you will say, "Mall-nutrition!, andyou're gonna laugh your head off.

M—Malnutrition? (*Laughs.*)

DUCH—Malnutrition, well perhaps it's so because uh, Rotten'll tell I never eat . . I y'know, really, I just drink ,that's all.

M—Oh.

DUCH—And here we are so let me raise my glass to you (*clonk*) and my whole family up there (*clunk*) and tell right now (*clonk*) while I'm here on the phone tell hi mtell him that I'm raising my glass to that (*clonk*) house of ill repute and to that T-shirt around the pillow.

M—Rita, Rita, she's raising her glass to the houseful and to the T-shirt around the pillow.

DUCH—Listen, I've just thought of something, you know what?

M—Rotten wants to speak to you.

DUCH—Wait a second, I have a fantastic idea, now listen to this.

M—Wait Rotten wait.

RR—Oh, I'm sorry. Tell me when I can pick up. (*Hangs up.*)

M—What should I do?

DUCH—I have a fantastic idea. Do you know something? I don't know why the hell all don't get down here but you know the one trouble is?

M—We can't get in the door.

DUCH—You see the trouble before of hav, of y'know, when I, when we I wanted them to come before and Ondine is Ondine listening in?

M—No, he isn't

DUCH—Also is he except y'know, Ondine's a trip my dear for the for the nurses station.

M laughs—Ondine's a trip for the nurses.

DUCH—For the nurses station.

M—Oh wh-, is that downstairs?

Duch—No, that's on the floor.

M—Oh yes.

Duch—You pass that to come to my room, I'm the corner room.

M—Hell we can't pass thateither.

Duch—Well, well wait a minute, how are you dressed?

M—Oh all right.

Duch—But you don't look like a bnm, do you?

M—No, not at all.

Duch—That's good then uh, well Drella's fine, Rotten Rita must change his

M—Drella's got this funny shirt

Duch—Well, he can take that off. Rotten must change his T-shirt because it's dirty.

M—Yeah, Can can you take the shirt off to go by the hospital?

Duch—And you, well they may come back up here but you know what I'm doing? I'm going to call admissions now and I'm going to reserve the whole, you see something? You can have friends stay here with you

M—Oh you can have friends stay in the hospital with you.

Duch—I'm gonna reserve the whole goddamn side of the whole.

M—You're gonna reserve the whole wing for us.

Duch—Not the, one floor and everyone will stay here and in the morning we'll have a lovely brunch sent up from the hospitality shop 21 delivers lu- yo, food over here.

M—Twenty-one will deliv-deliver fod to us for brunch tomorrow morning.

Duch—Of course and we'll have Steak Diane for breakfast, tell them that, and we'll have

M—Do they have milk shakes?

Duch—Oh yes, coffee malteds.

M—Mm.

Duch—We, wait a minute, I'll read you the

M—Can, can thye bring costumes?

Duch—Oh yes, because we're gonna have a costume party.

M—Costume party.

Duch—And cocktail party tomorrow night is gonna be from 5 to 7.

M—Mm hm.

Duch—Because I may have a test tomorrow between 7 and 8. Now wait, let me tell you about the milk shakes. Listen to this menu. Now this is quite chic I think: Hospitality special, sliced white meat of turkey, imported ham, swiss cheese, tangy cole slaw, "tomorrow's slices," with Russian dressing, crispy potato chips, well I, forget the potato chips my dear.

M—Hm hmhm hm.

DUCH—Three decker club, combination corned beef and cabbage on rye bread with potato salad, horse radish, mustard, *hot* English mustard, now where the hell in, Rubens doesn't

M—Cole-Coleman's mustard.

DUCH—Darling, Ruben's doesn't even have English mustard. I

M—But everybody has Coleman's mustard.

DUCH—I carry it around in my pocketbook.

M—Ha.

DUCH—I do. Cause I like it mixed up with catsup or chili sauce and it's like 21 sauce, it's divine. Turkey salad club

M—But they don't need to have it.

DUCH—Now listen to this.

M—Hospitality has everything.

DUCH—Choice boneless sirloin steak, tender choice steer filet mignon, loin lamp chop

M—Well now, lamb.

DUCH—with mint jelly.

M—Now you're getting elegant. What's that with jelly?

DUCH—A loin lamb chop

M—Mmm.

DUCH—mint jelly.

M—Green jelly.

DUCH—Broiled half-chicken served with French fried Idaho potatoes or whipped potatoes. Well I, I've changed that, I've called them up and told them to get baked potatoes with (*Moxi is talking in the distance, not through the phone*) with uh, creamed spinach on the bottom and sour cream and garden fresh sallad and then, you see, this is rather divine, they say, "And your waitress will suggest specialties of the day." Hello!

M—Hm hm?

DUCH—And the milkshakes, my dear, are deli-, aren't delicious, but they're delucious.

M—They're delucious, delucious milkshakes.

DUCH—Your favorite flavors; an old-fashioned double scoop ice-cream soda

M—Ohh.

DUCH—skillfully blended with finest syrups, sparkling cold soda water, and two scoops of ice-cream.

M—Now that's mine.

DUCH—And super-sundaes made with three scoops of your favorite ice-cream, delicious fruits or syrups, well make a stop please at Maison Glace and get me some, you know, marons, or something like that.

M—To put on your uh, ice-cream.

Duch—Get some melba sauce.

M—Melba sauce. That's . . . . . sauce isn't it?

Duch—No it isn't, it's, it's raspberry.

M—Oh.

Duch—And it's sort of pureed raspberry sauce, I love it. And pure whipped topping and a cherry, even get a cherry.

M—How about, how about honey too? I think that would be a good idea.

Duch—Oh, I like honey with bananas.

M—Mmm.

Duch—And horse radish and sour cream.

M—Horse radish and sour cream.

Duch—Now heaven, but just, just a twist of horse radish, love it. My bananas are divine, my dear, stuffed with chop meat, and peanuts, and uh rum, baked, it's heaven.

M—And you stuff them with chop meat.

Duch—Chop meat.

M—How fantastic! But do they, oh they still must taste, bananas taste like bananas anyway.

Duch—I'm a gourmet. Tell them my dear that I'm a gourmet and not only of pitiful meat.

M—Of pitiful meat?

Duch—No, I'm a gourmet

M—Yeah.

Duch—And not only of pitiful meat.

M—Oh, I see. She's a gourmet and not only of pitiful meat. She wants you all to know right now. There, now they know.

Duch—Well listen

M—Rotten gasped.

Duch—Now, let me tell you something.

M—Ondine lost his dress again.

Duch—I'm calling Cary-Cary Car to send up a car for you right this minute. If Cary won't charge, now called Buckingham or Esquire.

M—Esquire's going to call us?

Duch—Oh Buckingham. Tell Drella that will pick him up in a Rolls.

M—Drella, she says, will pick you up. Is that right? He's gonna come and pick us up here in a Rolls. Is that right?

Duch—Because, uh Cary I'm signed out with. It's a mopped up Roll but it's something. It's a London taxi-cab, dear.

M—A London taxi-cab, oh those are fantastic. Those are the most wonderful cars in the world.

Duch—Right. So.

M—That's the doorbell. He's gonna pick us up.

Duch—I'm calling.

M—Are you talking about, he's gonna pick us up here, isn't he?

Duch—Yes, and you're coming down here.

M—And you're coming down to the hospital.

Duch—Now, all right, now you have one chore to do.

M—Does, Rita keeps wanting to talk to you, I think.

Duch—Who does?

M—Rotten wants to talk to you. (*Pause.*) Everybody's life here, ohh, hey, are you there?

Duch—I'm having so much fun tonight. I feel like I'm there.

M—Ondine's got this beautiful black sheath dress on now.

Duch—Oh yes, with the side hold-up thing.

M—He's got it all wrapped up around him, it's so beautiful.

Duch—Tell him he thinks he's very Norell, my dear.

M—He's very Norell?

Duch—He thinks he's Norell.

M—You think you're Norell, don't you? Do you think you're Norell?

Duch—Norell.

M—Morell.

Duch—Norman Norell.

M—Norman Norell. (*Voices.*) No, he doesn't think he's Norman Norell. He's got the hugest belly button I've ever seen.

Duch—He's got a huge something else, too.

M—He does?

Duch—Oh, I think he's, he doesn't, he's too dirty for me.

M—Why?

Duch—He's dirty.

M—Physically or or or

Duch—Did you just meet him

M—Yes.

Duch—Well, you know something, I met him for the first time, oh a couple of years ago and it was a little bar called Dinko, on Second Avenue.

M—Yeah.

Duch—And he was with a girl that was, really scared the living daylights out of me. She was a witch.

M—She was a witch?

DUCH—Her name was Oreone de

M—Oh yes.

DUCH—And my dear, fingernails, ooh, she really scared me. I love crazy, campy people but I don't like weird people.

M—You don't like weird people?

DUCH—No.

M—Why not?

DUCH—Shut up, he'll hear you talking.

M—No. He doesn't hear' he's busy talking.

DUCH—Very very strange people, I don't dig them. I love fun, wonderful, crazy, mad, you know, divine human beings but somebody that's very strange and odd, I, I, I just do-, doesn't come to meet me at all.

M—But he's so, he's so wonderful a man, no?

DUCH—Ondine?

M—Yes. He's very human, my friend.

DUCH—He doesn't hear.

M—No, he's very busy. He's playing Batman now.

DUCH—Darling, he's a trip. He he he ca-, he can drive me to the point of insanity. I can't take it.

M—But what do you mean he's dirty? Is he dirty physically or mentally?

DUCH—Oh God, dirty physically-

M—Physically?

DUCH—He carries that bag he brought down here the other night a bag which you know had bunch of shits in it that he had from the baths.

M—From the baths?

DUCH—The baths, where the boys go, my dear.

M—Oh God.

DUCH—And y'know he kept the sheet in an old green bag and he lives out of that baf he's got. Oh he's filthy.

M—Oh.

DUCH—But I like him, but I just can't too much of him and certainly, I'm that kind of a person, uh fun is fun and nobody, my dear, nobody in the whole fucking world is wilder than I am, really, I mean really carry on.

M—You're wild but you're not weird, is that it?

DUCH—No, I'm not weird at all.

M—Oh.

DUCH—I'm, I'm crazy, I go on trips

M—You mean that makes the di—

DUCH—I go for someplace inda-, in wi-, in hi-, in complete high drag, my dear, or in something else.

M—Well that sounds, I mean that's not weird actually, you know.

Duch—No, I come in with maybe my Battaglia blazer on and my polka
dot ascot and my Dunhill shirt, y'know, and tapered khaki pants or
something, y'know, polished loafers, but that's it.

M—What you wear may be weird.

Duch—No.

M—Oh, that's too bad you know.

Duch—Are you weird?

M—No, I'm not but I like it.

Duch—I, uh, you know something? I used to, years ago and I just, I I
went through it you know?

M—Hm hm.

Duch—I got bored with it and I I found out I you know, I used to, Oh
God . . . . people, day really I mean I always had an entourage
around me seven days `

M—Who are you talking to?

Duch—You.

M—Oh.

Duch—Now I don't like it anymore. Now I really like to be just with the
people that I believe are really right there. And I do, I admit it, I love
uh, you know, they've just got to, you know, their heads have to, my
God I've got to get off this telephone.soon cause I have to call that
answering service back

M—Why do you have to call them?

Duch—Cause I went over to meet some girls in the answering service
yesterday, finally, y'know, after five years of talking to them on the
phone.

M—Hm.hm.

Duch—And one has a problem and she wanted me to call her back at
12:30 and my God, it must be 2:00 now.

M—Oh let's see. It's 1:30 baby.

Duch—I'll call back there in a few minutes, all right?

M—All right.

Duch—All right, then I'll talk to Rotten Rita when I call back and I'll
call a car.

M—Okay.

Duch—You're coming by, all of you, all right?

M—Okay, well take care.

Duch—All right. I, I'm calling back.

M—Yeah, you call back.

Duch—I'm not going to, you think I'm going to bed, are you crazy?

M—No, don't go to bed before tomorrow morning because you'll be

Duch—Darling, I never go to bed.

M—They might operate you in the night.

DUCH—Sweetheart, the more downies I take the upper

M—The upper you get.

DUCH—Right.

M—Okay, you said that.

DUCH—All right, be sure Rotten takes care with my his, poke because darling, I showed him how to do it.

M—He's very good.

DUCH—I showed him, darling.

M—You showed him.

DUCH—I'm the pro. I'm the, I'm the doctor.

M—The doctor.

DUCH—I don't like everyone taking away my practice, but Rita's all right.

M—Rotten's pretty much taken away most of us right? here.

DUCH—I don't think so.

M—Not a drop of blood.

DUCH—I love Rotten very much.

M—You do. You like Rotten, he's not weird.

DUCH—No, he's Rotten's divine.

M—Rita's divine.

DUCH—He's railroad master from a French French station.

M—Oh, which one?

DUCH—I don't know.

M—You don't know.

DUCH—Chamois or something.like that

M—Oh ho.

DUCH—I've gotta get off the phone.

M—You call up the answering service.

DUCH—All right, I have to call her up, what's her name? Alice Cavers, 12 12 1

M—Ca-, or well, skip it.

DUCH—Cavers, Plaza 11700, well darling I'll call back within about 15 minutes.

M—Bye then.

DUCH—Quickly. All right, chow. (*Click. Pause. Zap. Static and voices.*)

M—No, she didn't like it and she doesn't like weird people.

        D—Oh really?

        M—And she says she likes only
           wild people.

        D—What?

        M—She likes only wild people,
           who doesn't like weird people.

That's a very strange distinction of wild and weird. It's not strange but I've never thought of it before. She said he's very wild, she said nobody's wilder than her and went on describing about a lot of clothes and nothing but clothes, y'know the different kinds of clothes she wore to different places. I said yes and I said, then she told me she went for, she used to like weird people.

D—Oh, Ondine.

R—We're playing records. It's your life.

O—Oh, here I am again.

D—Come on o—, can you do this over here, Rotten?

RR—Can I give you what?

D—Can you wrap wrap wrap it over here, no, wrap it over here.

RR—A librium?

O—A librium?

D—Wrap it over here.

O—Wrap it over here, wrap.

RR—wrap it up. Okay, wait a moment. She's a little quick for me, this—

O—Oh, the Duchess is tucked away safely in bed.

M—No she's not, she's calling back.

O—She's taking people, oh . . .

M—She wants us to come down there and she's gonna rent up all the rooms . . .

O—Take the phone off the hook.

M—Of the hotel.

O—The Duchess . . .

RR—Oh she's crazy. Y'know she really is. We can't go down. We couldn't possibly take a, I mean I wouldn't—

O—I I wouldn't go down in a minute.

RR—I would, no, I wouldn't hesitate but as far as I'm a board director she stands a lot to lose. She's a little terrified down there now.

(*Static.*)

O—I'm putting the microphone right here.

RR—Body is fantastic.

O—Isn't it? Bo-body by Wrap.

RR—It's the perfect, it's the perfect, the perfect—

D—What . . . on that?

RR—the perfect thing for Ondine and me to work . . .

O—She doesn't have to eat. (*Static.*) (*Static.*)

M—. . . is rough.

O—Here he is, Rotten Rot, nuuuhoop.

M—Uh oh. No.

RR—Of course he is.

M—Now he looks like—

RR—He's he's, no well my dear, he's not doing opera tonight, he's not doing opera tonight, he's a young, Italian, woman, Prima Donna—

M—He looks . . .

O—Right, he's right darling, he's right.

RR—As a painter, lover . . .

O—Besides, he knows what he's talking about.

RR—or a husband.

O—He knows what he's talking about.

RR—And who at this very moment is (phone rings)

O—There she is.

RR—You get that. (Ring.) Who has a young painter lover . . .

M—Hello.

RR—for a lover.

O gasp.—Um, wait a minute, who's Johnny?

O—I am Johnny.

RR—Oh yeah, somebody called.

O—It may be my m-mother. Is it a woman?

M—I don't know.

O—Mother? You're not Mother.

RR—Who are you?

O—Mrs. Schwartz! Mrs. Schwartz! (With enthusiasm.) D, d, oh how have you been my dear?

RR—Turned you, turned you.

O—Oh I'm being, they're ruining me here, it's disgusting. They're putting me through the mill, my love. How are you darling? How've you been? Wait a second, I have two, okay, come over

here. Hello. How are you drear? Oh I'm being, I'm being taped.

RR—Who is that?

O—And I'm being mummied.

RR—Who is that?

O—Johnny Cool. Oh, I, Rotten Rita just told me that you called earlier. Ohhhh, you're heaven.

RR—Ask him if he likes . . .

O—Huh? Nothing. Why? What, what are you you you doing?

R—I'm writing Chinese scrolls.

O—Oh well don't you see that he never picks it, ever drinks it. You don't want any marijuana or any-thign. He doesn't, he can't take them, he goes crazy. He's com-pletely . . .

RR—Tell him the best place for him is a movie house.

O—You spoke to my mother? What did she have to say? Isn't she fabulous? What did she say? Euuugh. Mrs. . . . . yeah, she's marvelous. (Drella and Rotten are talking in the background.) (Pause.)

D—Oh.

RR—To wake me up. And she, she . . . made this work.

D—Oh really.

O—She called you and you . . .

Voice on the phone—No, oh she said, "Don't get smart."

O—My mother said, "Oh shit, don't get smart?" Oh go on with this, this is—

On phone—Get smart and I said well uh, I'm sorry, but I'm, I'm, I'm, this is Johnny Cool. She sadi "Who?" And then she spoke her grammar, I said Oh, she said "I'm terribly sorry, I thought it was Johnny Cool." And she said we sound alike on the telephone.

O—We do.

JOHNNY COOL—She thought I was, she thought I was, uh, putting her on.

O—Oh.

JC—And it was really so funny when she said "Don't get smart." What? (*Laughs.*)

O—Isn't she too much?

JC—It was just too much.

O—She she she she she's an absolute meagre.

JC—It was just heaven.

O—If I could see you in a while, I guess I see you later.

JC—Where will you be?

O—Oh well I y'know, I'll keep popping around twin brothers untli I see you.

JC—Oh shit.

O—Okay?

JC—Yeah, all right.

O—Well does it, well, when I, I'll probably be up here unless I'll be somewhere else but I won't—

JC—Well, how long are you gonna be over there?

O—How many more hours do we have on this?

JC—About an hour.

O—No, u-, two more hours of tape.

JC—About an hour.

O—Hm? (*Voice in the background.*) Yeah, yes it is enough for Norma. Yeah, no, about two hours probably.

JC—What the tape?

JC—Yeah, the tape.

JC—So look, I'll be over there.

O—All righty.

JC—What's the address? Is it too much though?

O—I don't know. I think you you you you may faint.

JC—Oh really?

O—Sunshine ran out of here this evening and she said to me, "You, you're everytime I see you, Ondine, you're more disgusting."

JC—Oh I see.

O—You know how sick she is?

JC—Where is it?

O—It's on West 85th street.

JC—Hm?

O (*Clears his throat*)—West 85th street.

JC—West 85th.

O—Mm.

JC—Ah so.

O—You see, and it's on Columbus and all that.

JC—Ah ha.

O—And you you tell, ah so, my dear. You tell me what to think. I have a dress on . . .

JC—Well look, you're gonna be there.

O—a black and white, I look so, what's her name, uh, who's the wo, who's the woman in movies?

JC—I need some diversion darling.

O—Oh well listen, I'll divert you.

JC—All right.

O—Then you'll . . .

JC—You're going to be there for at least two hours.

O—No no no no, no no, we have two more hours of taping. We'll probably only be here another hour.

JC—And then where will you go?

O—Then then where will we go to? The factory? (*Drella answers.*) To the factory I guess.

JC—To the factory!

O—Yes.

JC—Uh, look when I get off work I'll call there, I'll call there, where—

(*Phone rings three times.*) (*Opera in the background.*)   O—This is my life. One day in my life I should way. (*Ring.*) (*Opera.*) I should of. This is gonna be my really big day. (*Ring.*) Hello. (*Ring.*) Adio (*Opera.*) (*Ring ring.*) (*High note.*) (*Dial tone.*) I'm calling Gramercy 3 (*Click click click*) (*Pause with occasional notes from the opera*) (long pause) (*loud opera*). Yeah, 2 8. (*Ondine starts singing.*) You can hook it back here, can't I?   D—No put it up here.   O—I wh—   —Do you feel less born?   O—Like Doris Day. (*Noise.*) I could never be . . . . except in Calamity Jane. (*Music.*)   R—Try on, come all . . .
     D—He put out the hook.

O—I, don't want it on the hook.

RR—Gee I'm glad nobody's talking to me.

O—So am I.

Opera and voices.

O—Oh how hot. I wonder how this reproduces the voice. Can it do it very well? I mean like uh

D—Yeah.

O—Like uh (opera)

RR—Drella . . . . . . (voices) (opera)

O—1953

RR—Callas

O—Baby, you could, at one point like just about now could could we see how how, like could you put it to the to the best kind of possible reception? And we and we just one sound of this and see if it catches those little—

D—Yeah.

O—Like like like

RR—And I'll be the echo.

D—What do you want? What do you want me to do?

O—The echo, the echo.

D—What are you gonna do?

O—I'm trying to think, I wonder

how well this picks up singing. Very very well?

D—Yeah.

O—Great. It is. (*Opera is loud*) I mean God or heaven? Ech, or censorship.

(*Callas.*) (*Callas Callas.*) (*Voices are faint.*)

O—Ternamente Maria Menegini Callas. He. La regina del mondo. ("The queen of the world.") Oh n o,no no. I'm talking right into it like this. I'll be superimposed, la regina del mondo, la superbe di gratcio di Dio)"superb by the grace of God"). Maria Menegina Callas, e molto ("She's too much.")

R—Ah ha ha.

O—Wagner?

R—Rotten.

D—What do you call him?

O—Rotten? He just called you Rotten. He said, "Rotten," He he ha ha ha ha ha ha he said Rotten

R—Say it again.

RR—I want you to say

O—Call our mayor.

R—Call the mayor again.

O—Mayor Rotten, mm hm, Mayor Rotten is divine. This enternemente Maria Menegini Callas hm hm hm. That's better, that's mono, that's it. Perfecto eternemente Maria Menegini Callas he he he he. Et meme si cordially. Hm? Oh. If he plays that piano he'll sing. I wish you'd play for us if possible.

R—Oh please.

O—Yeah, he's right, it's much too . . . . . (voices) . . . . . I have to read into the microphone.

R—Yeah.

O—Let me read it into the microphone.

R—You can't you can't read my writing.

O—I can read your writing. I'm, I'm a wiz.

R—Start here.

O—What's this?

R—It's the first line, right here. It's called Not So Funny, the poem.

O—Oh Not—, your writing is strange.

R—I knew I had

O—You're writing is calligraful. Calligraful? Is that a word? Yeah.

R—Calligraphic.

O—Calligraphic, but no no, calligraful is, must be a

R—Something like colorful.

O—No c-, (pause). A poem, by Cristine Rosetti hm hm hm hm.

R—I want to read it. But I I read very poorly. I'd rather have you read it the second time through. If you would listen to it you might be able to do it.

O—All right.

R—reciting—

Are there any Jews in opera news?
Do you have a wayward daughter?   —

You get, are you up?

O—Not for me. What was that last line?

R—Do you have a wayward daughter?

O—No not that one. I mean the one after that.

R—Are there any blacks, don't sing the blues? Don't laugh at the pygmy slaughter. Sixty girls

O—Listen to this, you've got to stop, the texture is all wrong. No you must stop, it has to be done with no interruptions for a backgruond. I must understand it.

D—Oh you mean what? You can't hear the poem unless the music's on?

O—I can't

R—Can't hear the music.

O—Go with Maria Menegini Callas all over the place. Maria makes me faint, I get sick, I wanna throw up.

D—Well you gonna read or not read?

O—Red or not read (*inverted sigh*).

R—Mayor not Rita.

O—Mayor Rotten, no, but Mayor Rotten. Mayor Rotten.

RR—Rita.

O—Ma-, Ita?

R—To be or not.

O—Someone just ripped my dress in the back room, uh.

R—To read or not.

RR—To read or not to.

O—Mayor Rotten.

RR—Yes.

O—I have a question.

RR—Any question?

O—Yes, Mayor Rotten, one question.

R—No politicians get high filuted especially if they're rotten, have rotten ritas.

O—Is that the next one. Are you reading li, now see you

R—My worst kind of a night.

O—You're worst time of the night was, oh, no but something else in the cab in the cab.

R—Mayors get high falutin especially when they have rotten ritas.

O—Would you hit him with the butt of the microphone now, quick, sharp, and right across, right over here. If you miss we're all introuble. Hm hm hm. But if you hit the mark we're saved (*inverted sigh*). Please please, now listen to the background. It may b esomething entirely sphinx-like. You'll have to change your whole face.

R—What's the background?

O—I don't know, well she's got it in her hand.

D—Well, there's nothing in the background.

O—What do you mean there's no background?

R—Drella you're

O—With this dress you think I don't afford a background? This is not cheap shit. Why do you make your f's like that? They look like Chinese temples. That looks like

R—That's cause I'm used to writing Chinese characters.

O—You're very inscrutable, aren't you? You are. You're very orien tal in your own right. Oh ho ho ho ho, that's a Mae West line if I've ever heard one, you're very oriental in your own right.

R—She made right sound like a tea house.

O—Mm hm hm, the tea house of the east rite.

R—Doesn't it? In your own right.

Here I was, sitting in my own right.

O—I wish the cat would come in. The cat come in with the right.

D—Oh really?

(*Music.*)

O—Oh. See that, that's a background.

R—Something gay.

D—Oh read read.

R—Rotten, is it all right to read?

O—Sure.

R—Can I read now?

RR—Listen, do me a favor, if you'd enjoyed . . . . . before the election, don't just say Rotten, say Rotten Rita.

R—Oh.

RR—Only, no, not because, not because I mind, but i-i-it, we've gotta get the name across.

O—Yes, Mayor Rotten would

RR—It's gotta become a household name.

O—Mayor Rotten would just be ro-, y'know, but Rotten Rita, well listen there's a lot of vot-, y'know what?

D—What?

O—On every new piece of plaster that we see setting, Vote for Rita

RR—Do you have any matches, Ondine?

O—or Rotten Rita for Mayor. (*phone rings.*) No darling, I have no pockets in this outfit. Rotten Rita for Mayor would be sweet on every fresh plaster. (*Ring*)

RR—Hello.

O—The Duchess.

R—I thnik I should write a new poem.

O—Don't write a new poem; I like the other one.

RR—Hold on a moment, just hold

on a moment. Yeah, I wanna go inside

D—*Bright* lights.

O—That's Hollywood. That's

D—That's not Hollywood.

RR—Get away from that—

O—Who was that?

RR—That was a curse.

O—Who was it? Was it her? I thought so, the bitch.

R—What'd she say?

M—Oh no. Did she hang up?

O—What was the curse?

RR—That's what she said, I really forgot.

O—Well, my dear, I wish you would repeat it, or remember it because I'd like to know what that witch has to say. And who she's cursing.

RR—My curse.

O—Well, it's Sunshine's curse.

D—Let's start with D.

RR—No.

O—She's not that immediate.

RR—She's a very involved person.

O—Oh what did she say? What could she have said?

RR—Oh who cares what she said.

O—Your mother wears Army shoes? What could she have

M—Why are you so worried about it?

O—Because she's such a wonderful person.

M—Oh.

O—I love her and so does he. She's marvelous and she's quick and aware, and bright and tortured.

D—I've never seen her like that.

RR—She has been tortured and

D—I never caught her thing

RR—ever since we met.

D—brought it up y'know like six months later. She made me take it and I didn't want it.

RR—She's a, she's a funny girl.

O—She's got a problem.

D—What is her problem?

O—Her mother.

D—Her mother?

O—Yeah.

RR—Yeah.

D—What's her problem?

O—She thinks she is her own mother.

RR—. . . her left side.

O—God, it's really ridiculous. She, her mother stood outside the box office at the New Yorker and waved to her.

D—Oh yeah.

O—She didn't want her to be lonely.

D—Ohh.

O—I mean really, that's very ill.

O—She went with her mother?

O—No, her, she went without her mother. She worked as a cashier nad her mother stood outside and waved in to her.

D—All day long?

O—They started, yeah.

D—Every day?

O—Not every day, but either to do it on Sundays is unbelievable.

D—What, Sunshine won't talk to her mother?

O—Sunshine talks to her mother and begs her to leave her alone but she won't

D—She must have told her she was working there.

O—I told her to go down on her mother, or try to and watch her mother fly. Her mother ne-, Sunshine said she stayed. What? (*Moxi says something.*) She'd stay, she wouldn't fly. Her mother wou-, she'd stay. I said well then . . . . . and, she should stry anything. I think that's their whole problem. Sunshine wants to have sex with her mother. The only way to find out about her is to go to bed with her. Ha ha do it yourself.

D—What?

O—Do-it-yourself kit.

D—Would she be better on her own?

RR—She'd be better off if she had a kit.

O—A kid?

RR—A kit, a do-it-yourself kit.

O—Yeah, she really would too. She had three of them already.

D—Kits?

O—Yeah. She had lots of kits but she gave them away. She gave the kits away. (Laughs.) No, I'm just kidding.

D—What happened to Rod the Rod and her?

O—They nev, they never never they, anything but next door neighbors.

D—Oh really?

O—Are you serious? Rod the Rod with the ducks in his . . . ohh ho. He's really too sweet. Ducks in his belfry.

M—Does she live near here?

RR—Oops.

O—No, she lives on Suffolk Street.

RR—She doesn't live, this is probably why

D—186 Suffolk.

RR—Anybody who would mail me that pot of shit she got me.

O—Barbra Streisand's story in uh, telegram.

RR—She mailed me two telegrams and a note this week in the mailbox.

O—Rink, may I try and read your writing again?

RR—One telegram was about four-teen pages.

R—Uh.

O—May I?

D—She mailed this or made it?

O—No, she mailed it.

D—Oh how funny.

O—This is the continuation, huh?

D—Oh.

O—But that sign is gorgeous, Rotten.

RR—. . . . . and this was in the envelope.

R—. . . beautiful . . . something

O—That's so beautiful.

RR—Look in the envelope, Drella. It says Hotel Delmonico, Please Do Not Disturb.

D—Oh.

O—It's the loveliest piece. Isn't it a lovely sign?

R—Hotel Delmonico?

RR—It's really a joke.

O—It's really nice.

R—I have one from the Minza about a year ago I went down to Vestida and I have Vestida baths.

O—It's really quite nice.

D—Hey, this is fantastic.

O—I know, but the story is

D—Was this really sent to somebody?

O—I guess.

D—Or did they just make it up?

O—Yeah, originally it was.

R—Too kthem a long time ago.

D—What?

R—It's a picture of something.

O—Doesn't have any

D—What took so long?

O—It's the story of Barbra Streisand. I don't know, let's look at the ending. It's a continuation. (Voices.) Time Incorporated, it says.

D—Oh it is . . .

O—Mm hm. Listen, oh God, the

last line is unbelievable. Somebody tucked away an ear.

D—gasp.

RR—Who wrote it?

D—She she, this is a real telegram.

O—. . . sent to Billy Name. Look
what's in there.

D—This is a real telegram!

O—Yeah.

D—From Barbra Streisand's agent.

O—Barbra, listen, you invited me
here, I didn't invite you.

RR—Billy, uh Jimmy, I mean Ondine.

O—Conversation with Mickey
Rooney, David No-

RR—Ondine, this is sent, it says
send to Billy Name.

O—I said, send to Billy Name. Uh
huh. Barbra: I can't get in the
movies. Why not? My nose.
What's wrong with your nose?
It's different.It's a lovely nose. If
you look at it from the right
angle. Most people don't like it.
It's a different commercial market. Listen, I'm going to Rome;
there, they like big noses. Ivy
Snow, Time Incorporated.

D—Wow.

R—This is from Barbra Streisand's
agent.

O—This is from Ivy Snow.

D—Barbara.

O—to Barbara. Bar-ba-da.

R—. . . about nose.

O—Well, did you ever see Boxi's
nose?

R—Yes, but I mean she mu-, I
mean she shouldn't talk about it.

O—She obviously thinks it's her
prick, in which case she's mis-
taken.

R—Ha ha.

O—She she does, that's why she's
got it.

M—Is it a huge nose?

O—It's not just a huge nose. She's
got this nose like Monica has a
nose, y'know, that is a prick nose.
She's got it in the middle of her
face and it acts like a prick. There
are people that have faces like
that. They can't help it; they
keep doing it. Barbra Streisand's
such a funny thing, though. Isn't
she awful?

R—She's the most awful talent in
the last century. She's not even
bad.

O—One, no, she's really ooh ooh,
noe thing is really beautiful wi-, I
thought when I first heard, it
was

R—Happy day?

O—Yes, that was so lovely but that
was just

R—The first the first one.

O—Everything after that was just
disgusting. (*Singing.*) Aah, the
great one. (*Singing: "I love you
now. I want you now."*) Mmooh.

D—When did she work with *Time*?

O—Mine. No, it's Rink's, I'm wearing it.

RR—Gee whiz, maybe I can get
away with it.

O—You look it. The sleeves fit you
perfectly, darling, look.

RR—Gee whiz, now I can go down
and join the crowd.

O—Look at how nicely the sleeves
fit him Drella.

D—This is fantastic, oh.

O—Look at his sleeves, doesn't it
just fit him perfectly?

D—Oh yeah, perfect.

RR—That's all right. I'll wear my
white pants which is even dirtier.

O—It looks absolutely gorgeous,
darling. It's yours. It fits so well.

RR—Hey, is that, is that that

O—That's Canoe.

RR—But I think it's Bundy.

O—It's Canoe.

RR—No, it's not Canoe.

O—Yes it is, I put it on there this afternoon.

RR—Well.

R—. . . Something to eat?

O—Why should we eat?

D—You should taste one, it's fantastic.

O—Ooh, I have to read it now. What? (Laughs.)

RR—It tastes very . . .

O—It does, I told you so.

M—Who sent the telegram to whom?

D—. . . doing a story on her for Time magazine, so I guess the people who work there do it:

RR—She's Mary Birdie.

O—Ha! Sunshine?

RR—Of course, they two go together.

O—Oh my dear, they'd die. In one week.

D—They're constantly holding hands.

O—Ho, Mae West is great. Woww (singing). She was really incredibly shaped. Do you remember her shape? Stuffed.

RR—Have you seen her in movies? Did you ever see her in movies?

O—Her movies are perfection.

RR—Her movies are a little too much.

O—They are not. Not "We're No Angels." (gasp.) Aaahhh. They love this letter.

R—Why do you take yourself so seriously, Barbara? I don't. You really don't know me if you say that. Walrus says, you focus almost exclusively on yourself.

O—I's true, it's true, who knows

and who cares?

RR—She spends, she says all her time with her little uh . . . or something.

O—Yes. LOUUD. Mr. Criswell. Do you ever read the NY Enquirer? He predicts in there. I predict that Boston will be overrun with rattlesnakes. No, don't darling. Enough. Now go burn . . . with. Drella, why don't you have some marijuana?

D—Uh.

O—Drella, won't you have some marijuana?

D—It'll make me very sleepy.

O—No, this one doesn't. This just makes you confused and horrified.

RR—You're getting a little jumpy.

O—Tomorrow? Okay. All right. Oh how do you do it? May I look at your writing again? I would like to see if I could read it.

R—Should we try the one we just did or should we go back to something that seems to be

O—Anything, I just like to look through it and see and see if I can understand.

RR—All right. Is that part of it?

O—Yeah.

RR—That's nice.

R—That's a tough pron—first, that's with, the first one.

O—Yeah, with lots to o-overcome?

R—Uh huh.

O—I can't, no it's too small.

R—Begin.

O—I can begin to write of you . . . . . and

R—Chance.

O—Chance.

R—No as, the s is crossed off.

O—Oh, for chance (singing) s . . .

R—S, yeah it's gonna be s Jews . . .

O—Yeah, rendezvous and if firmest? Belief makes all

R—Makes allowance.

O—Makes allowance.

R—Only

O—Only for the present. Five years into my majority.

R—Uh huh.

O—Through many lines

R—Wives

O—Wives, one lived as another

R—As any.

O—As any other.

R—As any another.

O—Excuse me, as any another. I thought that said another.

R—Mm hm.

O—All or any another, all

R—No no, as any another, that should be

O—. . . see

R—That's all.

O—All

R—All, comma, that's right.

O—Thank you for write, rewriting.

R—That's all.

O—See more seeking.

R—No no, no that's not see, that's all.

O—All.

R—Read on.

O—What?

D—(Reading) There's a . . . . . the victim who says Gertrude . . . mother . . . I'm sorry I'm not a fag, I'm lucky I'm not a fag.

O—Oh.

D—That's fantastic.

O—Who's that, her husband?

D—Yeah.

O—She's Mrs. Sherman?

D—No, Mrs. uh

O—Mrs. Allen, Mrs. Jane, something.

D—No no.

O—Allen Jane. Oh all m, more seeking than circumspect. Fun and flavor.

R—Mm hm. Cross, there's a t.

O—Pirouette?

R—Mm hm.

O—On marble sadness, a thousand.

R—Lying.

O—Lying.

R—Heroes.

O—Heroes. Zing.

R—No that's

RR clears his throat.

O—Oh, there ev, uh, a, very

R—A thousand . . . . . confess

O—Uh, are you writing on the room?

R—No, I don't know why, I just like to.

O—Testing challenge witness, grointing?

R—Equals.

O—Equals.

R—Groint.

O—Grointo, growing to

R—Growing to a stop.

O—That's, you're using something else there, right.

R—Yeah. Ground to a stop.

O—Ah, my dear, you have to write, you have to take up typing.

R—Testament challenge witness, growing to a stop, haltingly it got to identity.

O—You've got to find a way to make it more legible. Braille. This is my life so

R—In this milieu, vague and reverential there is refuge in confirmation (*piano starts playing*). Ah ha. (*Music with voices.*) Moxanne plays but she doesn't listen. (*Laughter.*) Maybe Moxanne and Rot could play together.

RR—Moxanne if play the piano in any way (*voices and piano*)

M—Oh.

RR—Can you sight read Moxanne?

M—Nope.

R—You can too.

M—No I can't.

RR—Oh nonsense.

R—I should think that if you can do anything you'd be able to sight read well. I know your type, you sight read well. (*Moxi says something.*) Oh really? It's no fun to sight read. (*Piano.*)

M—. . . go through all these tortures (*piano*) look at the keyboard (*piano*) (*Moxi alking*)

O—Oh stupid.

M—Dumb. (*Piano.*) I hate . . . . .

M—I heard of this boarding school in Canada where (*piano gets louder*)

O—Ah. They waited?

M—They just wrapped them very tight. (*Piano.*)

D—Oh wow.

O—Ah ha. Hey Rotten, hey Rotten, if you don't want that letter, I'll we'll, I'll

D—Yeah, do you want this uh

R—Is that Western Union?

RR—Well I read like one half way through in the taxi cab last time, I haven't had a

R—A day in the life of peoples mumble mumble (*piano and mumbling*). That's that's Barbra Streisand's houseline . . . Barbra, come and get your ch—

O—It may be my life but this is not—

11 /   1

O—Do you know how many tapes he's he's got?

D—Uh, another day.

O—Yeah he's, cause he's he's gonna play them from the beginning. (*Piano.*)

R—She hides and waits when his back is turned she pounces on him? Oh wow.

O—Who is that? Oh Barbara's a lunatic. She's a lunatic.

R—They're like a couple of lovesick . . .

O—Send to Billy Name, gee, see how sneaky that girl is. (*Piano.*) We'll all be afire.

R—. . . in the evening, Streisanr hides and lays in wait for him and when his back is turned,

pounces on him.

O—Ahhh. (*With the music*) Bum bum bum, this is what Patty F. should sing When you said when you come back here yo-you'll sing the violin concerto. Then, she went, she must have died. Who is that? Richard. (*Piano.*) Who is that male?

RR—It's . . .

O—Oh.

D—Why'd she do it?

O—She loves Billy.

D—Does she?

O—Yeah.

RR—She loves people, that's

O—She and Billy are palsy walsy.

RR—. . . loves rice and she was amazed . . . . .

D—She . . . look is nice.

O—She looked like

D—. . . sweet and happy.

O—No, she's always sweet and aa, no darling, you understand her . . .

RR—She she she can't, she's . . . . .

O—Why is, why does, it doesn't mean that much. (*Piano.*) It is not off. No, it's on. Is it on? I knew. (*Piano gets faster and louder.*) Tss tss tsstss. That was not Mayor Rotten Rita speaking. That was her ugly transistor. (*Laughs.*)

RR—Clorinda Rita.

O—Clorinda Rita. That's (laughs) Clorindarata.

RR—Clorinda.

O—She's now going to the bathroom. (*gasp and noises*) glub glub, oh that's so beautiful. Sunhsine eats shit, boiled shit. Sunshine said she put a pile of shit outside of Dodo's door. (*Piano.*)

D—Who?

O—Because Dodo stole her stole her boyfriend. Now I

RR—What if she comes up to strip tomorrow right here?

O—Oh, she's gonna oooooohhhh, darling, ban them.

RR—. . . since she took LSD she's all screwed up.

D—Oh.

O—She should give her mother LSD. (*Piano.*) Bum bum (*Piano.*) I, I think Peter & Gordon gave it to her, right? He should be killed for doing that, it's dangerous. No, who gave it to her? I don't know. It doesn't matter, she has her own, lots of sources. She's Miss Drug.

RR—She's uh pushing . . .

O—Yeah, unfortunately, yeah she's laughs

RR—Ha ha ha ha ha.

O—You're damn right. But she always has that cocaine source which she'll never let out. You can only get one week of cocaine.

RR—If you could only hypnotize her.

O—That that that's easy enough, just mmmm (*laughs*). It'll be brutal darling, but you deserve it. She does deserve it. How dare she talk to me that way. I wasn't being brutal to you, Rita.

RR—Oh. Oh well.

O—It's all in the way you look at it. A-as I was saying, being so philosophical. Can Sunshine eat shit, dog shit if she can get it. Y'know, I feel sorry for her.

RR—Oh forget it.

O—Because, no I won't, because I really, I really like her, and she disappointed me here, she disappointed me here so much that I, I'm disgusted with her. No I

RR—. . . for the last few weeks if you know it.

O—Because she saw me

RR—. . . New Yorker

O—Oh no, my dear

RR—She came here in the afternoon and that's all she spoke about.

O—Because she doesn't believe me when I tell her what happened. She didn't even see it. She's upset over nothing. The management never knew I was her friend.

RR—No, that's, you're right, but you

O—And we made this point two weeks ago too.

RR—I knew; she told me that.

O—She has no right to talk about

that.

RR—She said, "I wanted to say . . ."

O—Again and again, the dumb, Jew broad. I'm gonna slap her right in the mouth if I ever see her again, if she ever dares say hello to me, I'm gonna knock her teeth out.

RR—Wait a moment.

O—I don't wanna hear, why?

RR—She says that you have a

O—I just discovered her, I just discovered her and I'm gonna smack her in the mouth the next time she opens it. Oh, she's a gross insult to my entire way of life. (*Long pause.*) (*Humming noise and piano.*) (*Voices in background.*) (*Voices become louder.*)

R—Barbra . . .(*they argue*)

O—Filthy, rotten . . . and she always wears . . . . . Oh y'know, we never finished the poem, we just did the telephone . . . (*Humming.*) What's happening now? (*Moxi says something.*) I think sensory, oh she . . . beheaded. (*Rumbling.*) (*In a loud voice*) Death to Barbara, yeah but it's not. (*Voices in background.*) Aaw. (*Music.*) (*Rumbling.*)

M—Who's she?

O—That's Cinderella, darling. (*Gasp.*) (*Gasp.*) (*Music.*) Here we are. That's the ve, Cinde, Cinde, Cinderella's bathroom (*music*) where she just sat on the pot.

D—What?

O—And she sings her last aria. This is her on the pot; she's thinking over the day's doing.

R—Let's read that . . .

RR—Wait, we have

O—We have, haven't we?

RR—. . . . . a bit more to the . . . . . two years ago . . . . . and when I go . . . . . T.V.

O—Oh. (*RR talking.*) She's fabulous.

RR—and I heard her saying . . . (*music*) my dear . . . wonderful story of Snow White.

O—Ah ha ha ha.

RR—Seven, seven, oh how beautiful Snow White living with seven dirty old men in the middle of the woods. The Joyce Brothers went on and on and on.

O—She does.

RR—As I remember. (*Rumbling noise.*)

O—My dear, it's so professional. (*Noise.*) Like lovely bouquet (*gasp*)

RR—The Russian Embassy. (*Noise.*)

O—The Russian Embassy. Lovely bouquet of flowers.

RR—You talk about bugs.

O—What bugs?

RR—We've got such a beautiful bug and he's watering it. Could you imagine a nice little . . .

O—Hey, what happens when you burn yo-, a rose, do you, do we get a . . . (*music is loud*) (*voices*) don't forget where the bug is, Drella, right here.

D—Gasp.

(*Opera.*)

O—What's? Oh, New Jersey. I'm getting very involved with myself and too much subjectivity (*crash*) and it's no good. A very painful thing; people with whom I was acquainted say you won't know it when you're famous. (*Opera.*) If they say things like that, no I wouldn't, I can understand stars being temperamental. I think temperament and talent go together. (*Opera*.) People who meet me never look at my eyes. (*Laughs*.) They're afraid I'll reject them or something just because I've been on T.V.

D—She's been to the factory, you wouldn't let her in.

O—Bravo.

D—She was coming up the stairs . . .

O—Oh Drella, stop lecturing. Hm? (*Voices*.) (*Opera*.) Why? No, that's yours.

RR—You know who did this?

O—Paul Bunion. It's uh, let's see (*opera*) (*voices*) I didn't invite you. (*Opera*.) Come and say to me, come and say to me. (*Opera*.)

RR—Will you blame me for not reading?

D—Oh. (*opera*) (*voices*)

O—Oh, this especially is dull. (*Opera*.) Darling? Now, I'm going to make a phone call.

D—Call at the studio.

O—I'll use the phone here.

D—Did you try it again?

O—No but I, ah but, I'm gonna call the . . . office.

D—Oh.

O—Okay. Because do you want the . . . brought uh, brought

R—No.

O—Yeah?

M—What are they?

D—Bring the phone over. (*The phone rings*.) (*Opera*.) (*Ring*.)

RR—Hello.

O—Hello you, SMACK. (*Opera*.)

RR—Okay.

O—Y-o-u, you, how do you spell? Like that? Oh (*smack*) that's p. How how do you spell (*makes a noise*) would you spell how. What would you, ps? (*Opera*.) W, w

M—W. t-w-o-o.

O—W. (*opera*) Who?

RR—Billy Name!

O—Oh! How divine.

RR—Do you want to talk to him?

O—Yes.

R—Yeah.

RR—Where are you? (*Opera*.) (*Voices*.)

O—Oh we can get.

D—Where is he?

O—Where is he?

RR—The factory.

O—This is a male whore house.

RR—What do you want? (*Opera*.)

D—He's at the factory?

O—No.

RR—I don't know. What? Do me one favor. What time is it? Oh. (*Opera*.) I'll call you in five minutes . . . . . (*Opera*) all right . . . . (*Opera*) okay?

O—Shh, he's at Henry's.

RR—I certainly will. (*Opera*.) Okay? Okay dear. Thank you very much. (*Opera*.)

D—Oh oh

O—You, I, no no, he's probably arranging something in his own incredible grain. (*Laughs*.) I'm serious. He's gonna call him back in five minutes. But that's that's that's good. No, it's mine.

RR—Okay, my dear, we'll speak to you soon.

D—Oh don't hang up. Ondine wants to talk to him. Don't you want to talk to him? (*Opera*.)

RR—If I don't have a, what?

D—Where's Billy? Ask him where he is.

R—He's where Ondine first said.

O—I told you, I mean yeah.

RR—Okay? (*Opera.*) Okay dear, bye bye.

O—Bye bye darling.

RR—Byyyyee.

O—Bye Billy.

RR—I've gotta call sickness downtown.

O—Right right right.

RR—I think

O—Then we'll get him back on the phone, Drella, as soon as he calls back. (*Opera.*) (*Voices.*) She's doing . . . that's a good pair of sunglasses. (*Ondine sings with the opera.*)

RR—Bye bye. (*Boing.*)

O—Let's plug it in.

D—Here, hold this. (*Opera is very loud.*)

RR—Lift it over to the side, the other side. That's the telegram. (*Noise.*) (*Opera stops.*)

D—Don't put in on too loud Ondine.

O—No darling, I won't. (*Opera starts.*)

D—That's loud.

R—Oh that was so bad . . . . . . to do it. (*Music.*)

D—What?

O—This is a campaign speech I think.

D—Oh really?

O—Yeah. These are quotes from people. Here's one of my quotes. (*Pause.*)   Really?   (*Pause.*) (*Boing.*)   (*Boing.*)   (*Rustling paper.*) Isn't that great? (*Long pause.*)

D—Huh? (*Voices muffled by opera.*)

O—It's so, I know

R—I mean disguised it as a sphinx . . .

O—No, I mean to make it look, but as a musical, it has no chance.

R—What do you mean?

O—I mean as a musical comedy.

R—But rock'n'roll.

O—No, not as rock'n'roll, a musical comedy, broadway, theatrical musical.

R—A rock'n'roll opera.

O—It could be made.

R—And they'll have movie stars.

O—Oh no, it has to be something else. I keep thinking of the bossa nova and her walking through it with y'know, just that, with the same plaintive theme, and it would be very good. (*Opera.*) She's marvelous. I can't go any faster, my throat is out. (*Very hoarse*) My throat went out. (*Very very hoarse*) Let's play with the ice to refrigerate . . . (*static*) Just one more hour? Then we're through? (*With joy*) Then we're through, Drella? You're no shittin' me, are ya?

R— . . . just remeber that it was.

(*static*) (*bong*) (*cough*) (*static*)

O—Duto duto duto duto. (*Static and opera.*) Un umbriago (a drunk) (*gasp*) umbriago (*little laugh*)

D—You have the, uh, cord for this?

O—Yeah. (*The opera is very loud.*) This is the climax of the opera, this is the very end of it and the aria finishes, she . . . (*bong*) the opera ends; isn't that beautiful? Ts,s,sh, she's so

RR—Jerry?

O—That Jerry Max? (*In a rough voice*) Oh Drella, I'm so tired, I wanna go home.

D—Really?

O—I wanna go home, back to Atlanta. (*Snores.*) (*Gasp.*) Drives me crazy, this here.

D—Drives what?

O—This is the one that drives me mad.

R—Hamburger.

O—Cinderella.

RR—I don't know how you do it, not allowing yourself to listen to her.

D—Sing some.

O—No, I can't, I-I'm really listen, listen to it.

D—Just a . . .

O—I can't though, because it's, tired . . . (*In a rough voice*) and my throat, darling, is so hoas from ri din' all over the fields. This I love . . . oh that, hat . . . marvy mouth

D—What marvy mouth?

O—oh oh oh, the one who' singing, she's so gorgeous, oh she's singing the tele, the telegram now, great (*Singing*—ahhhhh-aaaahhhhhaah ah ah o eeee aaahhhhhaaaaahhhaaah oh oh oh ohhhhhhheeeeeeeooooohhh.)

D—She's got every kind of thing she's been doing.

O—She's lethal.

D—Really?

O—Yeah, she's lethal. She's puttin' me away again, I think. She's puttin' me away again.

D—Why?

O—I can't believe it.

D—Who's putting you away?

O—That fuck on the victrola.

D—oh.

(*More singing.*)

O—I can't go on, she's dri, driven me (*more singing—louder*) oh (*the finale*) she's, she's unbelievable, who ever (*starts saying something in Italian—it sounds as if he's crying.*)

D—Don't look at it.

R—She screams her way out and then

O—Listen to this.

D—Play it again, Ondine.

O—Yeah. Rotten do you mind if I place it on from the beginning?

RR—Not at all. You can put it louder or softer, I don't care. (*Ondine laughs.*)

R—Did you interview Drella for a French paper or something? Talk to him in French.

D—. . . French after we do it in English. How many uh, how many uh, how uh

R—Twelve hours. (*Pause.*) Five hundred pages? Oh really?

D—Fantastic! Come back Ondine, you've got a hundred more pages to go. Come on Ondine.

O—Why am I so gay? (*Laughs.*) So gay.

D—Oh.

O—May I have that that other piece, honey? The one on your shoulder?

D—Oh.

O—May I?

M—No but, this is a book.

D—Something like sixty pages, uh, not thirty, I mean

M—If um, three minutes

D—Sixty.

RR—Minimum.

M—Twenty.

D—Oh that's not very much at all.

M—That's 480 pages.

D—Oh.

O—(*he blows into the microphone*) That was me.

D—Tell me.

M—280 pages.

O—What are you talking about? All these numbers.

R—The Ondine Story.

O—Oh the Ondine Story cannot be put in one book.

D—Well then, well then

O—Eat Treat, the . . . cereal.

D—(*laughs*) hu hu hu hu

O—And as the . . . . . of the year

M—140 books, 100 pages each.

O—Imagine punishing 140 million people. (*Laughs.*) Each week, oh how gorgeous.

M—I bet it will sell too.

O—I don't mean it would sell, what do you mean, I'm established. I'll establish a new high in Ameircan living. I haven't because I'm

RR—What are you talking about?

O—That my, they wanna put my biography like

RR—Hello, this is Rotten Rita, your new mayor, I don't think I know you.

D—Uh.

RR—July

O—No Bob.

RR—I said . . .

D—Do you like Bob?

O—I've always liked Bob. Wait a minute, she's she's going to Rome. Oh you little cheata, Rita.

D—You're losing your voice.

O—(*unintelligible garble*) I live here . . . (*garble*) I thought maybe you wanted to speak . . .

D—Oh really?

O—(*making noise*) Did you see him?

R—Not today.

O—We passed him on the street.

D—Oh.

(*Noise and voices.*)

O—(*gasp*) Hello darling, how are you?

(*Opera is drowning out the voices.*)

R—Did you work for him?

M—I was going to . . . . . . (*opera is extremely loud*) right now . . . (*Ondine is grumbling into the microphone.*)

O—Even if, put your bottle down. Do you want your tie like that? Put your hand there. (*Opera.*)

M—Completely bankrupt y'know. (*Into the microphone*) Seven rooms, he's got a beautiful place. He used to redecorate it every week, make all the different rooms change them all the time and he had to sell it because he went bankrupt. Now nobody trusts him in Paris anymore. So he can't publish books; that's why he has to cometo New York but I don't think he'll make it. Not even the . . . trust him anymore, evidently.

R—Is he publishing anything?

M—Hm?

R—Is he in publishing?

D—Oh yeah, terrific.

O—Huh?

D—Yeah.

O—That so.

D—Oh Ondine, On Ondine!

O—Wait a moment, I'll just stay there.

D—Ondine! You're not allowed to talk on the phone Ondine

O—Of course not. Is he talking on the phone.

D—Ondine!

RR—Ondine, you don't have any money to talk on the phone.

D—Oh. No.

RR—And he's in there too.

O—Can we go with the receiver now (*opera*) . . . . the receiver. (*Opera.*) (*Silence.*)

O—Someone just yelled.

R—Out of your light.

(*Voice on phone*) What?

O—Who was that?

(*Phone*) I have a record on of Buffy Sainte Marie.

O—Who the hell is Buffy Sainte Marie?

(*Phone*) She's an Indian folk singer Canadian Indian.

O—Oh.

(*Phone*) She sings "The Universal Soldier" and "Codeine."

O—Codeine?

(*Phone*)—Yeah it's a song about it, addicted to codeine.

O—Codeine. (*Laughs.*)

D—What?

O—Codeine. Oh I'm so stoned forget it. (*Buzz.*)

(*Phone*) Okay.

O—I'm coming down. Bye bye (*Sounds of mouth bow from record*) (*Hangs up*) (*Dial tone.*) (*Beep.*) A-A (*Silence.*) Having trouble with it. (*Ondine is making a call.*) (*Phone rings.*) It's like a wart on the other one. (*Click.*)

BILLY NAME on *phone*—Hello.

O—Hello dearie?

(*Phone*) Yup.

O—It's me.

(*Phone*) Hello.

O—How are you?

(*Phone*) All right.

O—You mean you recognized me even with my deeper voice?

B—Well, it's not really deeper, it's just uh hoarse. More uh, like a peson's or something.

O—More like a person's?

B—Yeah.

O—You mean do people talk like this?

B—Yeah, that's wh, it's y'know, quote, people, unquote.

O—Sunshine made a disgusting pig of herself this evening.

B—Who did?

O—Sunshine. I'm ashamed of her.

B—Where?

O—Right in front of Rotten's door. I'm ashamed of her.

B—How did she do that?

O—Sh-she just became rude and boring. I'll tell you all about it when I see you.

B—Okay.

O—Horrible and I'm upset with her.

B—I was thinking of getting in touch with her, earlier.

O—Well do, please Billy, she's very upset, she's very sick about her scene.

B—Are you still at Rotten's?

O—Huh?

B—You still there?

O—Yeah, we're at Rotten's.

B—I we-, I just called and I was gonna ask uh, line was busy, but would you bring a quart of milk?

O—What?

B—A quart of milk?

O—A quart of milk?

B—That, at that silly store I guess it's still open.

O—Is the silly store still open?

B—Yeah.

O—Okay, all right.

B—Make sure uh he doesn't forget the—

(Voices and noise.)

O—Hello Emily, how are you darling? Oh you cock sucking . . . .

RR—. . . . . 81st street.

O—Oh you must. Eek! Don't you dare.

RR—I'm just going there for about ten minutes.

O—Oh Ro- I was just swallowed the microphone Du du du du, Ondine just swallowed the tape recorder. (chwt)

D—Ondine please.

RR—Do something.

D—Please Ondine.

(RR is talking) (someone is making a pone call) (voices in the background)

O—. . . too much.

RR—Well all right then, that's all right, that's that's good enough.

O—Who who who you calling?

D—Uh.

O (makes noise into the microphone)—There's no one there Gerard Mala, Malanga's off fucking with his tillies.

D—Oh really?

O—Yeah, he calledthis girl Tillie, he said, "A chick, mmm." Ridiculous.

D—Tillie.

O—Tillie, what what does he mean? Cartoon strip of what?

RR—Yeah, where should we

O—Got it all crazy, that whole (gasp) something fell out of my dress, it's a pearl. My dress must've made it. It's one of my

teeth silly. Uh ugh uuuggh.

RR—. . . . . . I have to do something.

O—Let me do it. I'll do it right now. I ma-, I can't keep it in my mouth. I wanna pair of plastic teeth. I want Cass Daley teeth. Let me talk to the law like that, hello officer. I'm Cass Daley. D-did you want to see a score of . . . .

D—Oh well not now, later.

O—Hey Rotten.

D—Oh not now, no no later

O—No no no no no, but I mean

D—When we're, when they, when they clean it up.

O—Yeah, but he'd like to see it if y'know

D—Well I, no, only borrow it.

O—It's on the piano.

RR—It's on the piano.

D—Well, when we need it, we'd like to borrow it.

RR—Okay.

D—Ondine, Ondine. . . . . . .

RR—. 22

D—Oh

O—Send it to, oh yes that's right.

RR—I got this for only two dollars.

O—Someone just squirted himself with wa-

RR—. . . picked up 22.

D—Do you want it to be in your light?

O—Don't you hate me, Drella by this time? You must be so disgusted with putting that thing in my face.

D—Huh?

O—You must be so horrified with just, m, looking at me with that microphone. Jesus, to think you had to ggo through Irving du Ball this evening. God, you shouldn't be bothered with people like that. He's a bad influence on you, he's a bad influence on you. (*Drella laughs.*) (*Pause.*) Oh drop the curtain. (*Pause.*) Yes baby.

D—You don't haveto . . . . . .

O—Well I'm . . . . a joint and I can describe it perfectly, it's so beautiful. Wait, Rotten (*music starts*) (*light piano*). This is what's beautiful. I won't speak while I'm. . . . .I want to hear it. (*Piano.*) (*sniff*) (*whispering*) Amunition y'know (*piano*) (*whispers Loudly*) Amunition y'know. (*Piano is very loud*) I I'm just

D—Alice in Wonderland.

O—Gorgeous mo-, certainly perfectly, Alice. (*Music*) (*voices*) okay, we need a piano. (*Piano*) In fact we could use two of them. Hey (*very low notes*) Oh God. (*Ondine screeches into the microphone*) Mmmm. That was a slurp darling. (*music*) Aa oom.

D—What are you eating?

O—Chew, that's cough drops.

D—Oh wow. Describe a joint.

O—Describe a joint, well it's a long and thin (*music*) The joint that The Duchess doesn't like to roll.

D—Really?

O—Called baseball joint. She likes the brown tobacco.

D—Oh.

O—I like palmers. More conviction?

D—Yeah.

O—Then watch out.

D—But how can I put a piano, a piano in the uh

O—Very easy.

D—How? I mean in the uh, book.

O—We can probably scan somebody else's piano. What do you mean, how are we gonna put a piano in the book? All right, let's talk about the book.

D—We'll talk about uh

O—Oh we can talk about the (*Music*) (*Della is talking*) What do you mean transcribe this?

D—What?

O—Well why don't we make the book a tape? We can make a tape book, y'know so that, so that you can only play it on a tapere-, yeah you're right.

D—When it comes out.

O—I hope the book will work. I think it will. The book will work. Uhh, I think Ondine would be fine.

D—Ondine sounds, it could be uh

O—It could be but it isn't gonna be. I mean what else can it be called, Sunday at the Races?, what, A Day At Stark's?

D—a.

O—A. (*Laughs.*) Then we'll go on to B, right? oh perfect.

D—What?

O—Then we'll go right on to B.

D—Yeah.

O—Why call it A?

D—Well there is no B, but A.

O—Well we can't, A, B, C, D, E, F, G, H. . . . . . . .certainly. You can't give them more than a sixth of the whole thing. . . . . .role as teacher.

D—Teacher? What do you mean?

O—And she hates your little people?

D—What?

O—That's nevermind

D—She hates?

O—You influence people.

D—Oh.

O—That's the present thing, to influence people.

D—Why shouldn't I influence?

O—. . . . . . . she hates, she's jealous of . . . .

D—Of who?

O—Of Ke, oh pardon me, Mayor Rotten Rita. Don't believe a word I say; I'm a hopeless lier. Isn't it marvelous? I'm a hopeless lier. You know I don't lie. (*Piano.*) (*Crunching noises.*) It's duce. (*Piano.*) It's duce, it's it means. . . . . . .in Barcloniash.

D—Somebody ate it.

O—Hm? He may, but you notice how softly he's playing, that's because it's great. He's not (*piano*) aach, ish, ah (*piano*) chewing gum beautifully, more people should chew gum. You're doing a good job of yours too, Drella. Put it right on top of this. Thank you.

RR—This is the perfect role for her. She should do it.

O—Idioot, do you remember how beautiful that thing was last time.

RR—I never realized.

O—It's the perfect thing

RR—If this is the next role, this is the role for her.

O—It has to be. It has to be her role

RR—Should I write to her?

O—Cinderella. Can you imagine her in a fairy tale?

RR—First of all, the idea of her in a Rossini opera is enough to drive you crazy.

O—Yeah.

RR—Second of all the

D—We could call Maria Callas .

O—How?

RR—It was about Cinderella.

O—You mean just call her? What'll we tell her? We could call the book Maria Callas.

RR—And then

O—Or Chenderetella, Cinderella.

RR—staged

O—Oh, that would be so beautiful

RR—extraordinarily very hard, y'know how, I don't know. It's gotta, y'know it's gotta be done like the real old-fashioned fairy tale.

O—It's gotta be done well.

RR—It should be put, she'd, she'd look so awkward in it.

O—I'm trying to think of her as a spinning wheel. She certainly would beat Cinde, she'd she'd

RR—That's not Cinderella, that's Sleeping Beauty.

O—No, I saw Ci—a picture of Cidianata at the sleeping, at the sleeping world.

RR—See, you don't even know what you're talking about.

O—I saw a picture of Cirianada at the spinning wheel and she looked like

RR—She looked like Rotten Rita

O—She looked like Imogene Coca. She had the funniest face I've ever seen

RR—She looked like Rotten Rita and Imogene Coca.

O—Oh I hate her. What a face, that buck teeth and the way she sang. I said to you it was much more than a nickel.

RR—Give me the rag.

O—I said to you take it, leave two handfuls out.

RR—Can you go to the opera tomorrow?

O—I don't want to go; I have to

go to the ballet.

D—When is the opera?

O—Please.

RR—Tomorrow night.

O—So late at night. I don't know what he's talking about.

RR— . . . performance for . . . with with with with various guest artists.

D—Oh you mean outside.

RR—No inside.

O—It's in an old house. Outside Drella in the chicken fire.

RR—Oh in the chicken fire, that right.

O—I'm leaving, excuse me, pardon me, would you please have my bag sent?

RR—We will, yes. How many?

O—Three, just

RR—Leave that with George and we'll send it.

O—That tape recorder, whatever she's wearing (*laughs*), the television

RR—The television, we can't.

O—We should throw it out the window my darling, you should take the tube out of the back. I hate the television.

D—We're running out of power.

O—(*in a rough, loud voice*) We're running out of power (*growls into the microphone.*) Did you hear that?

RR—Ha ha!

O—Power. Aaa (*let's out his his breath.*) Power, you speak to me of power. euhh (*sucks in his breath*) the queen of freedom (*laughs*) what did that? That Ralph called me the queen of . . .

RR—Is that Rotten Ralph?

O—Ooh I wish it were.

D—Where's the, Ralph

O—That's the one we're talking about. He's married in Lindenhurst happily. (*Drella asks something* You're kidding?) No.

D—To who?

O—To some girl. (*Phone rings.*) (*A lot of static.*) I didn't mean to drop it on your toe.

M—Hello? Oh. Yeah. The Duchess?

O—It's The Duchess.

M—She's got a long letter for you.

O—Ugh! (*Static.*)

M—Are you felling better?

RR—Ask her if she had the operation yet.

O—Has she gone under the anesthetic yet? Is she all right? Did she eat the dyke in the back of the room? George, she, uh no (*breathes*) almost spit up the whole thing, aaaaa aaaaa laaaaa aaa

M— . . . from the dealer.

O—Hello.

RR—I didn't take the phone of the hook; Sunshine took it off.

D—Ondine.

RR—Yes I spoke to her.

D—Okay.

RR—Would you hold on a moment?

O—Take my dress off?

D—Uh yeah.

O—Leave this on and take my pants off? He

D— . . . I haven't seen you.

O—Uh, I went to the bathroom once in that place but, and I pissed.

D—Really?

O—I went and pissed.

D—No you didn't.

O—When did I piss?

D—Remember at the studio you, oh I'm sorry.

O—Oh I pissed at the studio.

D—No you didn't.

O—Yes I did.

D—I was watching you.

O—Not all the time.

D—Yes, I was there with you.

O—I pissed somewhere, I must have.

D—Here.

O—Don't tell me I have to piss.

D—Here.

O—Did I piss here? I don't know. I may have.

D—We-, where, oh, I know where you pissed.

O—Where? In the in the cab.

D—No (laughs). No. You pissed down at the uh

O—At the Cliché.

D—Yeah.

O—No I didn't, I just washed my hands.

D—(Gasp!) Really? Then where did you piss?

O—I didn't I guess. I must be all full of water.

D—Really? (They laugh.) (Pause.) Ohhh, that's nice. No but it's nice with the buttons on the other side.

O—These are nice, aren't they?

D—Yeah.

O—This this this this way is.

D—Yeah. Oh, yes.

O—Isn't that beautiful?

D—Beautiful.

O—I wonder if I should say beautyful. Do you think I should instead of beautiful? Beautyful?

D—How would you spell it?

O—(laughs) Spelled, b-r-o-o-k, that's nice, too much.

D—Oh.

O—Muh. Just because, uugh.

O—How about Gordon

O—Who's Gordon? Ot the little,

oh no, I don't know anything about him, what I like is someone like Michael. I just took a look at these face, I can't read . . . . of Drella . . . . . anyone . . . like that

D—Oh really?

O—Even in her hand, yeah.

D—Really? When?

O—Uh, oh, I don't remember, in 1950–57.

D—Oh. How?

O—Look at her teeth.

D—Yeah.

O—Her hair, like a mad woman.

D—Oh. Where?

O—At the Met.

D—Oh really? And he got, she really . . . . to him?

O—Yeah, there's a big picture of her and him, somewhere around.

D—Oh.

O—It's fabulous, it's called when noses meet.

D—Oh.

O—J, d, d, see his nose come long and and hers and they're both looking at one another.

D—Who took the picture?

O—Uh, hetook a lot of them . . . took lot and these are, there are his, these are, these are his references y'know . . . (pause).

D—Hey lover.

O—Yeaas. (Laughs.) Can I help you? (Laughs.) Oh. Ah so, my dear. Oh. You know what will knock me out of . . .

D—What?

O—Ah so booko and I wanted to just stab them that wasn't funny y'know. And now it's become a word; all they say is ah so booko, ah so boo, what does it mean? It means neither uh

D—Does it?

O—A piece of veal

D—Oh is that what it is?

O—Yeah. It's calf.

D—How do you know that?

O—I, a?aate it.

D—Oh.

O—Because . . .

D—Look at those beautiful legs?

O—The legs are perfect, there's no question about it, and thinking it over, I don't even need to think about it anymore. (*Laughs.*) My voice is gone.

D—Is it?

O—Listen to me. I sound like Bela Lugosi's mother. Why don't we sit down for a second, I'm so tired it's an effort for me to say I'm so tired.

D—What're you doing now?

O—I'm dressing.

D—Oh.

O—What am I doing?

D—What?

O—What am I doing? (*In a funny accent*) I hate t' bea just like this. Once again I have to get back to-, oh Jesus, put your hand through my hair, you won't believe the feeling of it, like straw going through

D—Ohh.

O—(*laughs*) Nigger hair, right?

D—Yeah.

O—But I made it that way.

D—Really?

O—Yeah . . . . . . strange old women in the 70's.

D—Ha ha.

O—Just put it on going where the wild root's going.

D—Hah?

O—You just plan on going where the wild goose goes, darling. I can't belive you with that microphone in your hand, it's it's it's

D—What?

O—Uh, it's a vision I don't see. (*Laughs.*) No, it's not bad, but uh (*gasp*) can you imagine how much more irritating anyone else would have been?

D—Who?

O—Oh just imagine if you didn't have anyone else to . . . . I'd faint . . . . so are you. Irving du Ball, darling. We have to do something about him please. He used to be, kill him!

D—Oh.

O—There's no question about it, he must be poisoned this week —arsenic.

D—All right.

O—See, that's what Rotten's got.

RR—Ho ho ho ho ho.

O—Shall we put him on Joanny Sullivan's list for murder?

D—Yes, how many are on the list?

O—Rotten and myself, no no, just Rotten and myself . . .

D—Oh really?

O—and uh Irving du Ball. Who put you on the list?

D—Uh.

O—No one put you on the list.

D—Uh. Joanny did.

O—Just, oh yes, Joanny did.

D—Uhha ha.

O—That's right you were, no, but he can't write who he wants to; he's gotta write the people we tell him to.

D—Oh.

O—He can't be

D—What's he been doing now?

O—Just practicing gun tar, gun range.

D—Really?

O—No, you (*laughs*)

D—That's not so funny. (Or On-dine.)

O—I know it's not, but it should
be, it's . . . . .wash her feet
with the cat. I do a lot of weird
things, Drella; I'll even wash
them here. (*Running water.*)
That's water. (*Running water
and Drella and Ondine talking.*)
(*Ondine screeches—sounds like
he's choking.*) A dead man.

D—Like Maria.

O—I'll be worse, my dear, worse.
I can't, no, she's patient, hard,
hard working.

D—Really?

O—Yeah.

D—She probably didn't see anything.

O—She, what do you mean, she's
gone? Cause she's miopic, completely.

D—Oh ho ho.

O—She can't see a thing you know.
She can't Drella.

D—Oh really?

O—She's completely blind.

D—Oh.

O—She has to have everything
marked off

D—Really?

O—so that she she

D—Oh really! What color?

O—Well white, white chalk?

D—Oh. Oh I'm sorry Ondine.

O—What for?

D—I'm walking on your clothes.

O—So what, it's only my dress and
my dress is your dress and your
dress is, your name is Drella
isn't it.

D—Yeah.

O—(*gasp*) That's beautiful,
dreaded whe, Drella.

D—That's supposed to be, gotten
the biggest laughs.

O—Wh osaid Drella?

D—You did.

O—No but I mean who made it
up?

D—I think you made it up.

O—I sa-, I heard it that day for the
first time.

D—Oh really? I thought you were
the one.

O—I think, I think Rita made it
up.

D—You think so?

O—Sure.

D—Oh.

O—Why wouldn't she?

D—Well maybe DoDo made it up.
DoDo's got a name.

O—DoDo's witty.

D—Yeah.

O—True.

D—But you kept saying it.

O—Because it was so great, Drella
Drella Drella.

D—How do you spell Drella?

O—D-r-e-l-l-a.

D—Oh. That's beautiful.

RR—Prella.

D—What?

O—Prella.

D—Oh Prilla.

O—No, Prella, P-r-e-l

D—What is Prella?

O—Prella the woman, the shampoo
woman.

D—What?

O—Prell, the shampoo, Prella, the
shampoo woman.

D—Oh, that's not Prella.

O—I know but I just called it that.
Pretalini, candidate for U.S. Sen,
Senate. Hah? Why?

D—Hah?

O—Why?

D—Uh.

O—Yeah, no no that's okay.

D—Want another pill?

O—I don't know, do you think it
would would work?

D—No.

O—No I think I'm ready to start moving.

D—Yeah. Should we go down to Billy's for five minutes?

O—Call him. Oh but she's sa sa . . . . . . How much more do we have of this?

D—One more.

O—One more.

D—Con we got to Billy's just for a few minutes?

R—I-I'm calling him.

D—Oh you are? Oh well we just have to finish it off.

O—Well then do you want to go? The whore house?

R—Same place?

O—11th street, no no.

D—Oh, it's 2, it's 2 o'clock. We've done twelve hours; we started at three. I don't understand.

O—I know. We can do twelve more. It's heaven down there; you'll love it.

D—Where?

O—Down at the m, at the

D—Oh I hve to get up early in the morning.

O—Would you like to go? Rink?

R—Let's go to the whore house. Yeah, Drella's gotta go to a whore house.

O—Well duh, he he won't come.

R—Tape at the whore house?

O—All right, I'm gonna keep my mouth shut so that he has to come.

R—He has to come.

D—Okay, where is the whore house?

O—Hm hm? (*Pause.*)

D—Where is the whore house? (*No answer from Ondine.*) Downtown. (*Drella laughs.*) Oh that's a pretty hairdo. ᴀPause.)

O—(*feebly*) Where's pretty hairdo. oh. (*Pause.*)

D—Ohhh. Ondine? Please talk about that hair.

O—Huh?

D—Please talk about that. That's the first time I ever met you with with uh

O—What can I tell you about Billy? I've always lo—

D—Oh no, it was Billy.

O—Oh yeah, of course, I, I knew you before I knew

D—Yeah.

O—We've been t, sort of together for a long time, my dear.

D—Yeah.

O—And I keep, I remember when I, what did I meet for the first time?

D—Yeah.

O—And today was like an anniversary. Cause it's been fifteen minutes. (*Laughs.*)

D—Wasn't wasn't Waltre terrific?

O—Yeah, but I thought I was better.

D—Yeah. (*Ondine laughs.*) You were better.

O—You know what? I'll tell you the truth, everytime I see that movie of mine, there's an applause. Those two queers, the first time you showed that film, applauded (*claps*). Joe, Joe Johnson said, "It's a horror show, it's a horror film." They applauded, I have o wet this, come latement, mon cher, please.

D—Oh no no no wait wait.

O—No.

R—Are we going to the whore house?

D—Yeah, but where is it? How far downtown? What?

O—Uh, A.

D—Oh way over there? Huh? (*Running water.*)

O—What are you doing Drella? (*Noise.*) (*Running water.*) (*Voices sound hollow.*) Darling . . . . . control the Greenwich beat list.

D—Uh, thi morning I had a corn.

O—A gorn?

D—Yeah.

O—What the hell is that? It sounds like a

RR—Is that what's bothering you?

D—A corn.

O—A corn. What?

D—Corn.

O—A piece of corn? A head of corn?

D—Yeah—shaped nicely.

O—(*laughs*) Drella!

D—I took it from the cat.

O—Shaped na ha ha ha ha. My dog was one.

D—Oh really?

O—Don't step on that dress.

D—Hah?

O—I said don't step on that dress, it was alive.

D—Oh no no Ondine.

O—Please shut it off, I'm so horrifying.

D—Well you don't have to talk. No one can sell the . . . . . . ice cubes.

O—We have 'em.

D—What?

O—(*makes noise*) The hair is combed, the hair is combed, now leave me alone. We have to do (*laughs*) we'll just go bats if we don't.

D—I know.

O—No, we're already bats. I'm not going anywhere else. I'm not going bays or anything. Oh-h. That's a bug on the floor, come

bug. (*Drella laughs.*) You can keep it on the door in here.

D—Really?

O—And then, and record in doorways and all. Hey, but there's something you wanna hear in the . . . . call me.

D—Really?

O—Telltale pair of shorts.

D—Uh hu hu hu.

O—They must be mine.

D—W eshould have spent a lot of time in the bathroom.

O—Oh cause I like them.

D—You should take 'em back.

O—I I oh, oh, I (*laughs*) 17 over, besides when I go downtown, I'll take one, no two. I take 2 downtown, 3 uptown. Rotten's on the phone. I feel like a truck driver, I just had a cup of coffee and a penny.

D—Oh really?

O—Ooh that's a, no, that's that's a truck driver's meal. (*Pause.*) And they use colored uh, hair (*screech*) dis a peach. Then I wear the veil on the street cause you never want to get your hair messed, or a stocking, just a plain, simple stocking, a nylon haa haa, well, I'm colored. (*Pause.*)

D—Ondine, listen, I like you.

O—Hah?

D—I said I like you.

O—To, to be colored?

D—No, running out.

O—Who's running out? I'm walking slightly over there in time with the music. I think they call that dancing. Babe, where are you?

D—Who's that?

O—That Herko.

D—Oh.

O—The dear, dead virgin. (*They*

laugh slightly.) (Pause.) This is that girl's, I got that

D—Where?

O—Petticoat, Brooklyn. She's not getting it back. (Laughs.)

D—What girl?

O—It's hers.

D—Oh.

O—I'm not going to part with it. (Mumble mumble.) Oh ooh, my callas, oh ho.

R—Your calls. He's worried about his callas; it can't even sing.

O—My callas is hurting me.

D—You can sit here and all htroughout the whole day.

O—I know I can't help it and I repeat it and but, Walter would say if he were referring to his foot, dip is swelling. (Singing) You can help me hold my dress, mmmmmmmm, you can help restore my dress, mmmmmmmmm

D—Ha ha.

O—You can push me in the dress, mmmmmmmmmmm, but remember it's my mess. I'm going from here to that bause that's really the Italian word for mess. That really is the Italian word for

mess because I think it is. The musical stuck?

R—(singing) Stuck in the name of love.

O—Stuck in the nam eof God. (Laughs.) That could be one of Christ's songs.

R—Stop in the name of love.

O—What is that, is that that same thing over and over, that haunting melody? I don't know.

R—Stop in the name of, haunting me. (In a high voice) Haunting melody? Haunting melody?

D—Ha ha ha ha

R—(in same high pitched voice) Haunting melody, come to the, how about (singing) come to the casbar and dance neath the rasbar doodoo

O—Dance neath the rabar? and give you the rest . . .

D—What was that? (Pause.)

O—What embago. Ribumba RIBUMBA. I want to ribumba you. Ri who you want.

R—Boom boom boom boom boom boom I wa wa wa

O—Li di cuma nu na na (singing)

R—Boomboomboomboooomboooomboom.   O—Remember when everybody saw Carlton Carpenter in the museum?   D—Ohhh.   O—The day we were goingto the museum of of   —DOhh.   R—(in a high voice) Blah blah blah blah blah blah blah said the monkey to the chimp.

O—(in a whisper) Let's go go, that all guy.   R—Blahblahblah said the chimpy to the monk.   D—You haven't had a scene today.

O—Huh?   D—You haven't had a flight.   O—With who?   R— (in a very high pitched voice) All night long they'd chatter away, all day long they were happy and gay.   D—With anybody.   O—Well it's boiling toward an invisible   D—Uh hu hu hu hu.   O—No, why should it? This is one of the most peaceful, hellish-like days I've ever seen.

D—Oh really?   O—I'm in perfect torment, my throat's gone.

M—Let's go.   R—Yes, we need air.   D—Oh.   O—Just leave . . .

D—The whore house is all the way down avenue A.   O—The

whore house is pretty eery.   R—So what? You led us astray. If we've got to go to the whore house we might as well   O—Just leave young man leave duh.   R—What did I say?   O—Nevermind, get out, get out I tell you, before I put you out. Don't get smart.   R—The wailing wall.   O—Cause I don't want to talk, now. I feel terrible strong about it.   O—Besides, it's over.   D—hu hu hu hu hu.   O—It's over, it's just, that was the end of A?   R—Let's all go to the whore house.

O—No more tape than A.   R—Let's all go to the   O—He's (RR says something from background.) The Duchess its either The Duchess or the Duchess.   R—It's either The Duchess or the Duchess again. (Laughs.)   O—The persistent mental case.   R—The Duchess of. . . . .   O—She isn't breaking capillaries, she's breaking brain cells. Couldn't you see her brain cells popping? Isn't she w-wonderful though? Isn't she? She's marvelous. She's, she's fabulous I mean, y'know, but she keeps going to . . . . . . .I think. She's gonna put us right out of our thing. She wants to buy the General, she's gonna get us the General Mills.   D—Oh really?   R—Is she?   D—. . . . . . . .the Hedda Hopper column.   O—Who? I think the whole thing. The General Mills would be nice. I just wanna do the Catholic column. I wanna get the Catholic column in the General Mills. I wanna get them once and for all.   D—Hm?   O—I wanna get the Cath—

12 /   1

(static)   (music)   uh uh, I can't, oh no, we're going.   Wel we'll see you there.   We're going to go.   Well, I'm going home then . . . well I'm going home; I'm so tired. I'm going home. (pause) Okay. (pause) Bye. (voices in a hallway) (noise) Five minutes, we're coming away from downstairs. Wanna hold it here?   We have no choice. Oh really?   Push the button.   Hold it open. Where is open? (much noise) Oh I'm so tired, wow. Are you tired?   No, not really.   You look tired. (crash) Oh what time, what time are you coming in tomorrow?

Hm?   When should we plan on going tomorrow?   Would you call me and wake me up?   Oh, early? You mean like ten o'clock What?   Ten o'clock?   Oh would you call me then?   Yeah. Then you have to come down first of all, so that we can rent a car. All right, where can we rent a car   Unless we, unless we   Nobody's going to use it.   Huh?   What?   Let it close cause nobody's going

to use it.   D—Where is Rotten? (*Bang.*) I guess you have to press 1.
R—You wanna go down?   D—Yeah, don't don't   R—Huh?
D—Let's wait.   R—He's, how long are we gonna stay at Billy's?
D—Uh.   R—Or Henry's?   D—Uh.   R—Henry'll be there
too.   D—No no, Henry's away.   R—Oh I see. Well what's at Billy's
that they wanna do?   D—Uh, we have to bring him some milk.
R—Oh. (*Pause.*) I'm hungry.   D—We haven't even eaten, oh you had
a hamburger.   R—Yeah, but that's like nothing . . . . . gee . . . . . the
other day, three hours early, that's the first time I was early.   D—Well
I, y'know you're learning, because uh it's   R—It's not a question of my
learning, it's a question of being able, being able to tell, being able to have
her know how other people are thinking. Well she can handle herself
perfectly.   D—But she has to play everything very cool and you can't,
I mean you just have to pretend, I mean y'know it's it's not working, you
have to work hard for these things. They like you whether they like you
or they don't, you know, you have to work at it.   R—Uh.   D—But
Taxi puts everything into it and it's, you do a little bit sometimes too.
R—But they, all all you would get then if she, y'know, if she, otherwise
if she sat there and just been sort of charming and everything like you
told her to do it they would just uh, first show wouldn't even, wouldn't
have called her back,   D—Yeah.   R—Cause those people were afraid.
They weren't interested in giggling. They didn't want Ida Snot.   D—
Yeah.   R—The second person he would have liked, probably liked a
little bit more . . . . . most people they get on those shows sing, dance,
do something.   D—Yeah.   R—Like that they wanna show   D—
But they always are looking for a girl to uh be charming, and be with the
boys like that.   R—There were two other people that were supposed
to be interviewing but they kept telling, kept sending them away.
D—Oh really? Oh.   R—She was supposed to Aspeaks *very quickly*)
be through with us after about fi-, thirty-five minutes we were there an
astrologer walked in and came over and said. The guy said well I'll be
right over . . . . . fifteen minutes later the guy came back and said, "Well
aren't you going to come and interview me?" And he said "Well I'll be
over." The third time he   D—Oh oh. Which one was this? Night
life? or   R—That was the Merv Griffin.   D—Oh. Taxine.   R—
But I mean Taxine doesn't know she's hung up in justifying herself.
D—Yeah.   R—Everything she says. So when she   D—Tell you what
they would pay or anything?   R—They haven't even y'know, they
haven't even asked about the show yet.   D—Oh oh.   R—It's just
that   DRE—That's the kind of thing she asks   R—What?   DRE
—Y'know, I mean, I, it's, you bring . . . professional, I mean, that's the,
her being professional, I mean, everybody's supposed to be professional

O—. . . . call. Do you act as her agent?   DRE—We should . . . . .
she'll have to . . . agent . . . right away   O—Oh. (*Pause.*)   R—I don't
want to be Taxine's agent.   DRE—We should, ... (garbleọ. . . .
R—Why don't you be Taxi's agent?   DRE—All right. . . .   R—
Somebody has to do it. They tell you what they pay . . . there's a set fee
for the show.   DRE—Yeah.   R—You oughta ask them what they
pay you, before they wanted me on. (*Pause, sounds of walking and doors
closing.*)   M—. . . go outside. (*Pause and traffic noise.*)   DRE—
Huh? . . . . . huh?   R—. . . get's so miserable without even trying
. . . her natural, it comes from not getting anywhere.   M—Why don't
you . . . . .   DRE—Yeah, well, I . . . six hours. Ondine really is tired
. . . the worst day I've ever seen, and we really weren't doing anything.
. . . It is, uh, well he's been up for a couple of days.   M—Oh . . .
this would be an ordinary time then.   DRE—Uh, he's usually a little
more, uh, bouncing, y'know when he has, when he is a little more higher,
then he would just be out of his mind.   M—Well that's all right. I
like a certain tiredness in people.   DRE—Yah. (*Pause.*)   M—It
sometimes makes them forget about where they are and what they're
doing.   DRE—Yeah. (*Pause.*)   M—There's a great picture of um,
Paul McCartney in, um . . . . . it's a French rock'n'roll magazine.
DRE—Oh.   M—On the beach in in the Bahamas. And I guess he's
got a sun tan or something very red, he's all wrinkled, he looked really
great.   DRE—Oh really?   M—Very tired looking.   DRE—Oh.
M—Bags under his eyes and everything. Thy usually always make
him look like a little boy. (*Pause.*) The same magazine had a picture of
George Harrison all in green.   DRE—Oh, oh. (*Truck goes by.*)
M—Looks like a double   Cause you see half his face is lit up with a
green light, and all the rest is very dark and pale . . .   DRE—. . . . .
took funny pictures of all of us, Paris Match, and none of them really
came out.   M—Did you really? They take a lot of pictures.   DRE—
Oh, they just, all of the same thing, they're all funny, I mean, the four of
us always in bed.   M—Which magazines came, do you know?
DRE——. . . Paris Match, Vogue, and . . . Adam   M—I didn't see
anything in any of the   R—I know, neither did I. Adam, maybe.
DRE—. . . and English Vogue, and then they let everybody . . . except
me.   M—They were supposed to do a big article on Deborah, and
that never happened either. She went over there one day and gave them
a full interview. I don't think they really know what they're doing. They
used to come down to . . . . . very often, and take thousands of pictures,
and you'd never see them.   H—Except I saw one (*noise of a truck
going by*) saw the magazine in Italy had printed an article on it. (*noise*)
DRE—Wasn't Paris Match terrific, we had all these round-ups

(*rabbits?*) and, really great.   M—Do you mean they brought in things? DRE—Yeah. They hadda bring the rabbits. Wel.   M—That musta been great, yeah. (pause) . . . . . people. (pause) I don't know, the Match usually makes articles like that.   DRE—What?   M—Match, Match usually doesn't make articles like that, doesn't usually do articles on people like that.   DRE—Oh.   M—They usually do very straight things.   DRE—Oh.   RINK—On pop art.   M—Not even, really. They do the old artists . . . not even . . . it's the young artists. (pause) (*Lots of noise*)   DRE—Uh, just . . . . . uh I think, yah, yah,—oh I had a, whole page, oh   R—I had this whole thing by David Berry. DRE—Yeah, he took pictures of all of us, but then they left them out . . .   M—Ohh. (*noise*)   DRE—Oh, why? That's a very good idea.

R—. . . . . fantastic thing I ever . . .   DRE—Do you think we should leave them, or tell them or   R—Maybe we should just go. DRE—. . . we can get a cab.   R—They wanna go, they're gonna go to Billy's anyway and we'll go to Billy's.   DRE—Okay. (*noise*) (*voices*) Huh? (*noise*) Oh.   R—. . . like that . . . the whole idea of kids organized in the house, wow. Ondine went into the house and . . .   M— Did . . . . . tell you about that fantastic network of gang land that we broke into in Paris?   DRE—Where?   M—In Paris.   DRE—Oh yeah, oh, they were broken into? or   M—No, we did.   DRE—Oh yeah, oh yeah, we heard about it.   M—. . . . . Rosie is the one who started it all off.   DRE—Yeah.   R—She started the gang land? DRE—No no.   M—No, somebody picked, started talking to her and said do you want to got to a party and then Ron Rito was along and then he called me up cause I wasn't doing anything so we all went. Went up in the middle of the country somewhere and walked into a house full of about fifty people, old and all naked running around. And then we kept seeing the people over and over, over again.   DRE—Oh really? M—I remember the place. And this one man took uh Dominic and I to another one   DRE—Oh really? Oh.   M—Then we wanted to go and then some other time, then somebody took us to a hotel (*traffic*) DRE—Oh that one's coming? Did he pick somebody up or (*traffic*) I can't feel like I've spent a whole day, I can't (*they're getting into a taxi*)   (*cab driver*) Going down, right?   DRE—Yeah.   R—We're going down the river.   DRE—Spent a whole day, wow. Ondine could be so tired of me that it's probably better.   M—You've been carrying it around all day?   DRE—Yeah. (*Moxi says something*) Yeah. (*voices*) No, I'm doing that, I wanna go and get . . . . . (*noise*)   (*cab driver*) Y'know what I mean, it's gettin like stuck cause I just came from the highway, y'know the West Side highway and it woulldn't pick up, y'know what I mean.   O—Oh wow. I mean, anytime we're liable to go a

thousand miles an hour.   (cab driver) Go ahead, tell me you're ready.
O—We're all, we're ready now.   (cab driver) You can't even see it
with those glasses. You must be takin' goof balls, you hear what's hap-
penin'?   O—What's happening?   (cab driver) Well it's, the mo-
mentum it's it's droppin' dead like, y'know what I mean, it's takes, it see
O—Oh I see.   (cab driver) See see, I got it all the way down
right? The thing should be in seventy miles an hour by the time it gets
started. See the way it's like dyin'?   O—Yeah.   (cab driver) Ya get
it?   O—You're losing some pressure.   (cab driver) I'm losing some,
y'know what I think happened?   O—Yeah the   (cab driver) No, the
gas pedal, y'see . . . steps on the gas pedal?   O—Hm.   (cab driver)
There's two hinges on the inside that holds the pedal together. They might
be a litle loose, y'know what I mean?   . O—Maybe they should be
tightened. Y'know what I mean?   (cab driver) In other words the
thing that ya mash on the gas pedal goes   M—No.   (cab driver) to
the gas.   R—Oh.   (cab driver) Do ya understand what I'm talking
about?   O—Yeah, I I I've had that happen to—censored. Not in the
same area. (pause) What?   DRE—Do you live around here?   (cab
driver) I'll take the battery.   O—Doesn't s, doesn't seem to have that
feeling—weak battery. You can always tell the way the car runs on weak
batteries.   (cab driver) See, I got my foot all the way down.   O—
Batteries, weak batteries.   (cab driver) It should be out like a light.
(noise) The other one.   DRE—Wow.   O—Oh. It's the junior bobsy.
    (cab driver) Well I mean it's stupid. People don't scare. Couldn't
hit him if I wanted to.   M—Where is this place, Dukes?   DRE—
Uh, it's in the Village.   R—In the Village.   M—What does it look
like?   R—It's it's, has jazz records in it.   M—Oh.   O—. . . in
big sort of cubes . . . . .   (cab driver) Cubes?   R—Cubes, yeah.
(cab driver) What da ya mean, ice cubes?   O—Sugar.   (cab driver)
Sugar cubes of what? (pause)   R—What?   (cab driver) What are—
O—They're cubes.   (cab driver) What da ya mean cubes? I don't
understand.   0—Menus.   (cab driver) Cubes is menus. Sugar cubes
is menus.   O—No, wood block cubes.   (cab driver) Oh, made of
sugar.   O—Made of menu.   (cab driver) Made of men-, I don't
know. I don't know that's . . . . . wood block cubes is tells you what to
eat.   O—Wood block shoes to walk on and also to eat.   No, you
prob-, wooden block, with cube, lots of salad and I'll eat and I'll eat
(cab driver) I went in places with saw dust on the floor but this tops 'em
all.   O—Well you, yeah, but you can't order from the saw dust you
say, "Sawdust   (cab driver) Yeah, no, on the floor.   O—I'll have a
Coke and sawdust," well it might as well be flour . . . (cab driver says
something) What?   (cab driver) Y'know the   O—French, French

drive.   (cab driver) Let me see, I'll go down 7th avenue, right?   O—Yeah, that'll that'll hang in there. (pause) Oh, it's a cube menu.   (cab driver) Well what da they serve?   O—Cubes. No, they have anything you want, you name it, you want, you want   (cab driver) I got cows brians.   O—Uhhh, they even have bulls' balls if you want it.   (cab driver) Aw, now you're being fresh.   O—I'm not fresh.   (cab river) Cow's brains happens to be a Jewish delicacy.   R—Well bull's balls is a Spanish delicacy. (pause)   M—That's true.   O—Don't put me on with all these specialties, it's bull's, these these these the Spanish have y'know a taste for the killed bull.   (cab driver) I never heard of it, ordering   M—Some people eat uh, female donkey's ones.   (cab driver) I never heard of ordering that in the red bull's balls.   M—Not female donkey (*all of a sudden they all start yelling*)   R—. . . in the part of Spain there, they have ballsy bulls, whatever.   (cab driver) Uh (*mutters something*) but do they have the cow's brains?   R—Yeah, they have the cow's brains.   (cab driver) (*yells out the window*) Hey, did you ever hear of bull's balls being ordered in a restaurant? (*they laugh inside the cab*)   (someone outside) What?   (cab driver) Bull's balls.   (outside) Yeah.   (cab driver) That's ta eat, is that true? (*They're laughing softly*) Well, get inside. (*Person he's talking to says something*) It's a Spanish delicacy.   M—And where is that street? (cab driver) From Spain.   (*Drella says something to Moxanne*) (*Rink is laughing*)   (cab driver) If you can get it anyway.   (*Rink mumbles in a high voice*)   R—The . . . . . said you can get it anywhere. M—Ha ha ha ha   R—He said you can get it from anywhere. He's full of shit.   M—(*hysterically*) Fantastic.   R—Oh.   M—Oh. (*They're both hysterical*)   O—Believe it . . . asking the next guy if he's ordered, ever   (cab driver) I wanna, I wanna verify the   O—He said, "In Spain?" and he said, "No, not in Spain, everywhere."   (cab driver) You can get bull's balls anywhere. I'm gonna ask my wife for some bull's balls.   O—Ask him how to cook 'em. Ask him what's the best way, roll donw your window there.   (cab driver) (*yells out the window*) How da ya cook it?   (outside) call mountain . . . . .   (cab driver) What'd he say?   —It's called mountain orchids?   (cab driver) Mounted orchids.   O—Mounted, oh.   (cab driver) Mounted orchids.   O—We should drive up to him and say "mounted what?"   (cab driver) Orchids, he said.   O—Hey, mounted mountains, ask him ask him, here he is, right here, roll down the window.   DRE—Oh oh oh oh.

    R—Yes!   DRE—Oh.   O—Roll down the window. (*Yells out*) Mounted what?   (outside) Mounted orchens.   DRE—Orchens. R—Ohhhhhhhhhh.   M—Mounted orchens? What's orchens?   O—Make me nauseous, he said.   (cab driver) Mounted orchens, *he said* shit.   M—Orchens?   DRE—What'd he say?   (cab driver) Mounted orchens.   DRE—What are they?   M—What's that?   (cab driver) That's bull's balls. That's the name they call it, give me some mounted orchens. I think he's nuts too. I don't know. We're all buggy over this one. I thought you're puttin' me on and he's comin' along with stuff. R—No.   (cab driver) Boy, I'm tellin' you, live and learn, mounted orchens. Lemme ask someone if they know what mounted orchens is. We'll find out for sure after this one.   O—. . . . . bull's balls.   (cab driver) I'm gonna ask that cop what mounted orchens is.   O—He'll think it's a Canadian policeman.   (cab driver) We'll pick up a chef. (They laugh.) Mounted orchens   O—Mounted orchens.   (cab driver) Boy you really . . . . .   O—Hm?   (cab driver) Got me goin' now. I'm ready to believe everything after listenin' to that.   O—Mounties order, mounties, mounties in southern, in southern . . . . . would get them all for Iberian jet.   (cab driver) Mounted orchens, mounted (traffic) And he was serious; he wasn't kiddin' around.   O—I s'pose. Looked that way. Nonchalant policemen, midtown has the most nonchalant policemen in the city.   (cab driver) Nonchalant til they shoot somebody.   M—Did you see that Harlow?   DRE—No, we want to.

R—No, I didn't see that Harlow. That other Harlow.   M—The ad, the advertising on the radio for it is great.   R—That other Harlow, it was lousy cause remember how we (honk) bad it was.   M—Jesus, what's that?   (cab driver) . . . horn.   O—Yeah.   M—Is that your regular horn?   (cab driver) Yeah.   M—Oh.   O—You've heard of rider horns.   (cab driver) Vibrators, y'know.   O—That's, oh wow, ... wow . . . . .   (cab driver) We're gonna turn over to the right. (pause)   M—Somebody smashed this tonight.   R—Aren't you tired of talking Drella?   (cab driver) Tired who? Her or me?   O—No no, your name's not Drella, your name's Stanley.   (cab driver) Oh oh. O—Drella, Drella.   (cab driver) Drella he's not.   O—This is Drella.   (cab driver) He's not, he's involved . . . right?   O—Here, yeah. (cab driver) He loves himself.   O—That's a good question. (cab driver) Do ya?   DRE What?   (cab driver) Do you love yourself?   DRE—Uh, no.   (cab driver) Huh? What were you thinkin' of? You were in such a deep s, trance. Mounted orchens, that's a good one.   R—What were you thinking of, he asked you what you were thinking of.   (cab driver) A secret. He was thinkin' of the flame of desire.   O—The birds ever so whitely wail.   (cab driver) Desire!   O—(singing) It's burning, it's burning, my love overturning. (cab driver) Better get over to the right before he   O—(singing louder) My love's . . . burning, my heart, desire.   M—What's that?   O—That's my new song. It's about him. I can write a song about anything. Just about anything.   (cab driver) Y'know we're on sixth avenue now. I don't understand it   M—Oh ho ho.   R—Say, ya heard (traffic)   (cab driver) Y'know we   O—Rotten for Mayor.   (cab driver) Where is seventh avenue? Y'know, there's no seventh avenue here.

R—What?   DRE—We can go down Fifth anyway.   R—Uh, he can go down, yeah you   M—We're still only at 31st street.   O—Yeah, it's a long short ride down here; it's very funny.   M—Cause we started from like   (cab driver) Where'd ya start from?   O—(sing-ing) Rotten Rita's, Rotten, Rotten Rita's. See, Rotten Rita's running for Mayor. If you get a chance, Rotten Rita's gonna   (cab driver) (yelling out the window) Hey, what's mountedorchens?   (they laugh quietly)

O—It's straight, it's a straight, the other guy.   (cab driver) It's a delicacy, is that what it is?   O—You can tell him now. With that kind of sad look in his face, I'm so embarrassed.   (cab driver) No, he's too sick lookin'.   M—(laughs) He's just had them for dinner.   (cab driver) He looks at me like I'm crazy. I'm askin' the question. Can't ask people questions. See what happens . . . I wouldl leave them in the dust an hour ago.   O—Hey, a horseback ride. (traffic)   M—What's the name of that building there in the middle.   O—Boolding.   M—What?   O—Boolding in the middle.   M—Boolding, no.   O—Uh uh, it's the Empire uh, it's the um um something empire, the Empire job.

O—Which one? The one up there?   M—The triangular oone. O—Oh.   M—Right at the corner.   O—It's the s, it's the   (cab driver) It's twenty to four.   O—No, we're talking about names of buildings.   (cab driver) I know.   O—That building isn't called 20 to 4, that building is called 20 to 4, that's what's got, that's what. DRE—What?   O—That Building over there is named 20 to 4. M—No.   O—This is the, the uh   M—We passed 239 someplace else.   O—. . . . . say 39 someplace else, you should know that. (cab driver) Now, lemme see where Fifth avenue, stay to the right there hah?   R—Yeah.   DRE—No, right down to the (traffic) (talking)

M—Did he say you said . . . . .   (cab driver) Can I ask you a question, I mean, I'm, I wanna be regular with ya, awright?   O—Fine, yes.   (cab driver) But no no, no offense or anything, y'know, awright? Don't you feel   O—There are no offenses.   (cab driver) No, but don't you feel uncomfortable not takin' a haircut in this hot weather? (tarffic noise)   O—No.   (cab driver) Y'know what I mean. O—No, it doesn't bother me in the least. First of all, I love hot, tropical climate, I don't mind being hot, I'm not, by nature, a sweater, I'm not, by nature, a trouser.   (cab driver) I often wonder why some people don't take hair cuts.   O—Because some people look better with long hair. In fact most people look better with long hair, most people   (cab driver) (*yells out the window*) Hey, what's mounted orchens?   (outside) Mounted?   (cab driver) Uh, orchens.   O—The boy next to us is very pretty.   DRE—Oh.   (cab driver) He's worried about the fare, we're gonna get information out of you people.   O—Yeah, he put you on in here and then, then killjoy.   (cab driver) Huh?   R—Some people get   (cab driver) Aw, but tha, at least if he didn't know it, I'd tell him that's bull's balls.   DRE—Sounds like Taxine, this whole bit. . . . . . enough nagging.   R—You had enough nagging, you had enough nagging. (*They lauh.*)   DRE—Well, I had my thing yesterday. O—Dig you. Dig you.   DRE—Well we take turns.   (cab driver) Uh, now what? M—Where did you go with Ondine today?   DRE— Uhhhm, well he was very sweet; he waited, I was very late, I mean Gerard was very late so I had to wait for Gerard.   (cab driver) What should I do now? Keep goin'.   O—Go straight ahead.   DRE—Then he met me at 86th and Fifth avenue and we uh, went to get some bouquets and there weren't any, it was closed, so we went to Stark's and uh   R—It was closed.   DRE—Wee Carter-Pell was there and he was closed because he was talking to Bedroom Billy.   R—He was closed.   DRE— So we had some coffee.   R—Bedroom Billy.   DRE—and then I had to call in because they were gonna deliver the camera and when I called in it was three o'clock and they said they would send the camera right over, so instead of, well all along we were calling Rotten Rita because we wanted to go to the hospital to see uh what's her name.   M—Barbara.

DRE—Not Barbara.   M—Duchess.   DRE—The Duchess. And we weren't, went down to the studio and we got, the camera came and then we were gonna leave but then Gerry wasn't there, Gerard.   (cab driver) Make a right?   O—Make a right.   DRE—Then Rink came.   (cab driver) And then a left?   O—And then a left.   (cab driver) Right.   O—Then a left. Uh, I think   M—Then you went to Irving's.   DRE—Yeah. I'll finish this up by calling Billy and I'll leave my thing there and then it'll just happen.   R—Uh huh. Irving. Yeah.

M—I met somebody once who lived in that neighborhood.   (cab driver) What street do we go in, MacDougal?   DRE—Uh, no, go straight up this street.   R—Yeah, we'll go down this street.   (cab driver I'll let ya out right on the corner.   R—Right on MacDougal.

DRE—Turn left here.   (cab driver) MacDougal, right?   DRE— And two blocks down.   (cab driver) Right, MacDougal, and what's the other one?   R—Oh, Bleecker.   (cab driver) Aw right. Lemme ask ya somethin', hah?   DRE—Oh uh.   R—He won't, he won't know. DRE—Please.   (cab driver) What's mounted orchens?   (someone) Mountedorchens?   (cab driver) Yeah.   (someone) Um, are you kidding me?   (cab driver) No.   DRE—Oh.   (cab driver) He says

it's a delicacy—bull's balls.   M—The light screen.   DRE—Oh uh.
(someone) Mounted, that's very good.   (cab driver) (*laughs*) You
got me, got me goin'. I hope it's the truth, I'm gonna find out anyway.
Call up the *Daily News*.   M—All right, get back in the car.   DRE—
Huh?   (cab driver) I think this is trouble here.   O—You look like
you've broken   M—Hm?   O—I said I've never known you to uh
eschew the crews.   (cab driver) But he said that was a dirty word and
he laughed, he laughed, he laughed   M—I was joking.   (cab driver)
He laughed, he said that's a good one.   O—Should we get off here and
walk that block?   DRE—Uh, uh, what is this?   R—This is, well
there's one by uh, the next one.   DRE—Oh it's straight down   O—
Yeah, one more block down.   (cab driver) Right down here.   (*Rink
and Moxanne are talking.*)   O—Fantastic night.   DRE—Oh wow.

O—Oh wow. Well, she sounded, sounded nice.   DRE—Would
you turn up uh, left again?   (cab driver) Okay.   DRE—I think we
should get out here.   O—Yeah, I think we should get out here. Let us
off at this corner.   (cab driver) What street is this?   DRE—Right
here.   O—This is Bleecker Bleecker Bleecker.   DRE—Have eight
dollars please.   (cab driver) Okay.   R—Bleecker. Let's pull up right
there. (*Sings.*) Rotten Rita.   M—Oh I wanna hear some music, decent
music too. Oh, it was hot there.   O—You heard opera?   M—I guess
I don't like opera.   (cab driver) Well, have a good time.   DRE—
Thank you. (*They get out of the cab.*) (*Noise.*) (*Voices.*)

12 / 2

(*Low voices.*)   O—Huh?   (*Low voices and buzzing.*)   O—
What?   RR—(*on the phone*) went home at night.   O—What?
RR—Billy went home at night.   O—Uhhh.   RR—You want the address?   RR—Oh no no., 9826614?   O—Right   RR—Okay. Oh,
mixed up, oh you were When were you there?   O—Uh, somtime last
evening.   RR—Oh, because I called you there and that's why, we had
called you all evening there.   O—Oh . . . . . answer the phone . . . I
was uh . . .   RR—Huh? Oh Ondine and me (*humming*)   O—If you
get him and he's there   RR—Yeah.   O—Would you ask him to
call me and let me know.   RR—Okay.   O—Okay.   RR—All
right. I'll call you. I'll tell him to call.   O—Okay.   RR—Bye.
O—Uh, think you'll have time?   O—No, just all that stuff came, and

Taxine had all her appointments. (silence) (dial tone) (silence) (voices in between static) (dial tone) (Drella's making phone calls) (Phone rings) At the tone the time will be 6:27 exactly. (Beep) At the tone the time will be 6:27 and ten seconds. (Beep.) At the tone (click) (buzz) (silence) (busy signal) (click) (dial tone) (dialing) (phone rings)

B—Is Ondine? Yeah.   B—Oh, fifty minutes of tape. Are you on the phone?   O—Yeah. Will you talk to me for fifty minutes?   B—Oh, of course. Okay, I'll take the, right here.   O—What?   B—I (silence) (clicking with voices in between)   O—. . . at Dukes, we waited for you so (click)   B—If I walked out (click) she's too much.   O—Oh. B—Y'know.   O—You were tired anyway.   B—She's as bad as the Duchess. Oh no!   O—Huh?   O—Weren't you?   B—No, God no. O—Oh.   B—Are you serious? It's hostile occasion. .   O—Yes. B—When she gets operated on we're lucky she'll die.   O—Oh really?   B—Oh no.   O—There's a lot of her.   B—Wait'll Rotten marries her.   O—Oh yeah.   B—Then we can have the General Mills for . . . . .   O—Oh fantastic.   B—Oh ho, we can sort of   O— Huh?   B—We could start another Spanish American War. Anyway, y'know what what what, I guess you (click)   O—No, I just came from up there.   B—Oh, I called, baby, after you called.   O—Oh.   B— So it was y'know.   O—Cause Rotten said you had just left.   B—I had a bath there.   O—What?   B—Thats the old Roman baths. O—What?   B—That's y'know with broken glass bottom.   O—Oh. Anybody working?   (Interference.)   O—Uh, I don't know.   B— You mean (clicking with voices cut off) I don't know what you mean. (more clicking)   O—Oh ho ho ho ho.   B—What? Y'know I (click-ing) (laughs). You're not really?   O—Holding it.   B—Oh.   O— . . . you've got . . . . nice   B—When when are you free?   O—What? B—When when when are you gonna hear it?   O—I heard a little bit of uh, it's fantastic.   B—Did you hear the very beginning?   O— Yes.   B—Is that with (click) fabulous, isn't it marvelous?   O— Mmhm hm.   B—I didn't know what (click) I thought. Oh my God, I lost the whole thing.   O—Mm.   B—You were (click)   O—How did you know that? Oh really?   B—Ondine (click)   O—Really? Oh   B—D-D- Duke Cassidy, C-a-double-s-i-d-y.   O—Is he there too?   B—No, he's not here, he's lac ck in Lake Ronconcomi.   O—How do you know he's there.   B—No, he's not here.   O—Oh.   B— Gerard is in uh, on, is aw, is uptown, I guess.   O—Oh, he is.   B— I mean (click click click) Joycie.

O—Joucie . . . . . . a lot of time there . . . they throw up a lot there. DRE—Oh.

O—They take LSD.

DRE—Really?

O—(*click click click*)

DRE—Oh, I didn't think.

O—Oh Gerard was so funny the other morning, I came in and I (*click*) funny . . .OH

DRE. . . . . in his ass?

O—Yeah.

DRE—Really?

O—And the face he made was so beautiful.

DRE—Oh, what was it?

O—Y'know, confused . . .

DRE—Oh really?

O—Yeah.

DRE—You mean he liked

O—Well no, but just (*clicking*)

O—Gerard is too much.

DRE—Yeah I know, he has to go.

O—Oh (*click*) said that.

DRE—Oh really?

O—He will.

DRE—How can we train him?

O—Oh, well he's got, I don't know, it's hard.

DRE—Mm.

O—Gee how can, he just won't learn, he's lazy.

DRE—Really?

O—He's lazy.

DRE—Yeah. I guess that's what it is.

O—Is that what it is?

DRE—Yeah, he's lazy.

O—. . . . .when it first started and he was lazy.

DRE—Yeah.

O—Yes, is he still

DRE—Still lazy.

O—Now I am too. Ask me some questions, anything.

DRE—Uhhhhhhh, tell me about the world situation. What do you think of VietNam.

O—I think, Viet Nam?

DRE—Yeah.

O—Uh, it's . . .

DRE—Really?

O—It's one of the best we-ve ever had and I think, coming from San Francisco.

DRE—Really? Oh.

O—one of the hot points

DRE—Uhh.

O—Do you want to talk to anyone else here?

DRE—Uh.

O—There's Robert and Tommy and Clare and Jean.

DRE—Clare and Jean?!

O—Uh huh.

DRE—Then how can it be a whore house?

O—Well listen, those girls don't care.

DRE—Is it a whole house.

O—It's a whole house.

DRE—You're kidding?

O—No, it's just three rooms, oh and Susie, the dog will be here.

DRE—The dog?

O—Drella she . . . . . you can't believe it.

DRE—Oh really?

O—It looks like

DRE—It's not a girl?

O—the dog

DRE—Oh.

O—It's a girl dog.

DRE—Oh it is!

O—Who wears a leather strap for

DRE—Oh really? Hm.

O—. . . . .she doesn't give anything, and Boots is here too.

DRE—Who's Boots, a dog?

O—No, Boots isn't a dog, Boots

DRE—Mm.

O—a young man.

DRE—Oh.

O—And who else . . . (click) it's fabulous, tell me, I'd love to go.

DRE—Mm? No, I was just gonna

O—Oh go ahead Drella, please. It'll be a scream.

DRE—Would it?

O—Oh, I'd love it.

DRE—Wou you wo, uh . . .

O—I'm uh, what?

DRE—They should be your agents down there.

O—I'm to report to Stark's this morning.

DRE—Oh you are!

O—And to stand there in front of (*laughs*) in front of the . . . . .

DRE—Oh the bedroom.

O—Bedroom Billy. Well I enjoyed the day.

DRE—Uh, Billy said . . .

O—Oh he did?

DRE—Yeah.

O—No. I'm not going.

DRE—Oh you're not.

O—No.

DRE—Why?

O—I don't want to go.

DRE—Why?

O—Because he said that he was sure that whatever Sunshine did was right.

DRE—Oh! Really!

O—So I said . . .

DRE—Oh. You didn't do anything.

O—I did open the door.

DRE—Yeah.

O—Open the door.

DRE—Yeah.

O—No, but Billy will say to you, "I'm sure he did something to her."

DRE—No he didn, I'll tell him. Maybe, what?

O—He won't say anything.

DRE—Because I have the tape recorder maybe she got paranoid.

O—She said, what what were her exact words? What she said to me.

DRE—Yeah, I don't understand.

(*Clicking and voices.*) (*Static.*)

DRE—How long were you uh, up there? At the, is Rotten Rita there with you?

O—No.

DRE—You mean you left alone?

O—Yeah.

DRE—Oh Ondine.

O—Oh I got, well I can't

DRE—How'd you get down?

O—Oh well that's, I borrowed . . . from Billy.

DRE—Mm.

O—Drella?

DRE—Mm.

O—Fifteen minutes are up.

DRE—Ten minutes are up, yeah. You've got twenty moreto go.

O—What?

DRE—Hu hu hu hu, we can always quit any time, I just wanted to finish you off.

O—No, that's all right. You *have* finished me off.

DRE—Have I?

O—No, not yet.

DRE—Maybe we could start like.

O—I have a divine idea, a divine idea.

DRE—What?

O—The minute that this is through

DRE—Yeah.

O—I'll meet you in front, in the front of the little house.

DRE—What little house?

O—There's, there's a little gazebo.

DRE—Really?

O—In the park.

DRE—Oh.

O—And oh, such lecherous activity is going on.

DRE—Oh you're kidding. Really?

O—Shwwww

DRE—At what time?

O—Oh but very early, at the cr-r-rack of dawn.

DRE—Oh really? You mean . . . the crack of dawn.

O—Oh they just uh, stand around the rocks . . .

DRE—You're kidding?

O—No, it's fabulous. It's utterly divine.

DRE—Really?

O—It's a nature's paradise of temptation.

DRE—Oh.

O—The wonderland.

DRE—Mm.

O—And right next to Mayor Wagner Lake like it is.

DRE—Oh really? You mean over there?

O—Yes.

DRE—Oh I used to go over there to . . .

O—Oh.

DRE—All the time.

O—No no, I mean right in the middle of the west side.

DRE—Center Park.

O—You you know the filthy section.

DRE—Yeah.

O—Where all the dirty people are.

DRE—Yeah.

O—Well right there.

DRE—Well they wouldn't let me interview you there.

O—They don't, are you serious? They

DRE—What?

O—don't know what's up your sleeve.

DRE—No, yes they do.

O—No they don't and whn you're there . . .

DRE—No.

O—Well I can conceive of you . . .

DRE—It's smaller than you cock.

O—I wouldn't want to get, I'm supposed to hide it under my balls.

DRE—Oh wouldn't it be fantastic.

O—(*laughing*) the microphone.

DRE—That would be very strange.

O—(*laughing*)

DRE—Or put a rubber on it.

O—Wouldn't that be, with a rubber on it, Drella . . . ah.(*Laughs.*) Under your balls.

DRE—You have last minute words to say?

O—My last, no, should I should I?

DRE—I don't know.

O—IRVING DU BALL

DRE—Oh.

O—That's all. What a nerve he has. And a lot of people have the nerve. I even got off the phone angrily with Rita.

DRE—Really?

O—Well Rita and I are always yelling.

DRE—Oh your line was busy, was that you and Rita?

O—Yeah.

DRE—Oh. Wish I could keep that.

O—Darling, she said it's very annoying.

DRE—Why?

O—Because she's just so tiredsome.

DRE—Oh.

O—Y'know she has to go over things 12 times.

DRE—Really?

O—I said yeah, I said, I said you're . . . she said, "Well I don't have to go to sleep, I don't want . . . . . I said . . . . . with you she said auww . . . . . I said well . . . she got very annoyed.

DRE—Oh really. Oh.

O—She she she . . . . . .

DRE—Yeah. Oh well there's so much more tape but we can just call it, say say your last words.

O—Baby, whenever you want to tape again tell me.

DRE—Okay.

O—Tomorrow.

DRE—All right.

O—Let's see, my last words are Andy Warhol . . .

DRE—Okay.

O—Goodbye.

DRE—Bye. (*Click.*)

13 /   1

(*Loud voices.*)

Is that rain? (*Loud voices.*)

. . . wait until I lock the door?

Oh. (*Moxanne and other people talking.*) (*Shouting.*)

Oh I go down.

Well we're leaving.

Do-Do, I'm going downstairs, this is my tape, get in this elevator now!

But we're leaving Rotten Rita's. (*Gasp.*)

Well it's your . . . .

I know it's kind of . . . . right there please. Yeah.

(*A woman's voice*) It's too late.

Wait I'll talk to them.

(*Woman*) Will you stop it, you're (*Gasp.*) Can you believe it?

Hu hu.

(*In a high pitched voice*) Here I am, darling. They tried to prevent me from getting to speak to you. Are you all right, honey? This girl kidnapped me. (*In a very high voice—almost screaming*) Who are you? Who are you? Do-Do Doome would, . listen

Barney we were just on our way out. (*Pause.*) (*Someone speaking in a high pitched voice.*) Yeah, no no, we'll be downtown in a couple of minutes. I think. Yeah, hey hey, are you at Sloppy Joe's? (*Voices in the background.*) Look, come down in half an hour, please?

(*Someone with a very high voice*) Yeah please. Oh please.

In fifteen minutes get here.

(*High voice*) Please please please come, please come.

Bye bye chow.

Who's Johnny Cool?

Uh.

You know Johhny Cool, he's always

He's in the video film before "The Eating Chinese Food"

Oh DoDo, I'm frightened, I'm frightened, I'm scared as

Look at this.

He's very nice.

Paul and I decided that we should use up all the video tape and then tell them that we need more.

Uh hu hu hu.

Oh Billy do you have a raincoat or something that I could wear?

Oh fuck you.

You can take it back here, honest.

Oh I know it.

The rain!

I can not only take it back with me I can not even give it to you.

. . . give me give me . . . drinks Would you mind?

No, uh, this is mine. I don't wanna be selfish but you very rarely get a Dorothy Lamour gift.

Gee, it's raining very hard.

It's raining cats and dogs.

If we wanna do something uh sort of. . . . . .

(*DoDo is talking*)

I don't want them.

I wanna see the animals.

. . . or the other ones y'know I thought it was already used.

Yeah.

But then if we don't use them they might ask for them back and you (*Do-Do is talking.*)

They won't. No they're ours. (*Do-Do Mae is talking loudly*)

But where did these bags come from?

Oh darling, your hand must be tired.

Ohh oh oh oh.

Let me take it. (*In a funny voice*) Do-Do Mae Doome is trying to kill the sugar plum fairy. She's trying to pervert his life and make make his life a misery by giving him babies, sugar plum babies, I mean sugar babies. (*Someone asks him a question.*) No, we're only to Sloppy Joe's. (*A little laugh.*)

Oh oh (*shouting*) Bella Donna. I'll go out and get a cab.

Uh huhhuh.

Be right back, oh (*slam*)

My God! (*Lots of yelling.*)

(*Shouting*) Oh no you Ondine, of aal people you, no Ondine we need you.

. . . . . really is brave cerioso

. . . . . waiting

What's that word, it's not mesigination, it's uh

Precipitation. Precipitation.

. . . two?

Yes.

Two. But not all of them. Massages then precipitation (*Silence.*) S-sleep? Sleet. Hail.

No no no.

See a whale.

No no no. (*Pause.*) (*Rain.*) No salutations.

Why is it raining? I don't see why Why.

. . . . . . party, is that Ondine?

I don't know why it's raining.

No, oh, no no, oh there he is.

Water's on strike. (*Someone shouts "Open the door."*)

(*Rain.*)

Oh Ondine.

(*Cab door closes.*)

. . . like a jeep, like a jeep, thank you, thank you.

Well done Ondine Ondine, Ondine well done, oh Ondine you're so good, you're so kind.

Oh, wouldn't he be an Italian.

Who's Italian?

Mr. Mecurio. See, he appeared like, that was really good, God sent, oh, perfect timing.

(*Cab driver*) Where are you going?

Where are you going?

Oh uh uh

Waverly

Waverly Place and Sixth Avenue, Sloppy Joe's, U.S.A. Does anybody have a cigarette?

I believe I have weeds on my person.

Do-Do, if you continue to talk like that I'm going to report you to the National Retarded. Wasn't that marvelous? I never expected to see a cab.

Is this good enough?

No, that's a teacher's cigarette.

Kent Kent Kent, listen, don't accuse me of being a teacher, I mean people . . . . it's just so unfair

You gotta tell me where, about

Stop acting like one.

Yes exactly. You better tell me about uh, this, the reason why you think that Selly Clark and Michael Mis. . . . .

Solly Fine.

So, yeah Solly Fine wouldn't be good for uh

Sonny Parkes?

the

I'm a Solly what's his name fan.

Solly Fine?

Was that the singer's name?

Larry Parkes.

No. Stickers all over New York I'm a, I'm a so and so fan.

Oh no no no no no.

I'm an Allan Dale fan.

No, that was something else.

No, not Allen Dale?

I'm an Andy Warhole fan is what the sign said.

You should have been in the Esquire California uh, who's is

Oh.

Because everybody's been from California.

Yeah.

You're not from California.

No.

O—Are you from California?

B—No-oo.

O—Oh, you're from Keysport aren't you?

DRE—No ho ho.

O—You're a New Yorkerf, aren't you? You must be. Or if you're not, you're from the East somewhere. .

B—The East? How about the mid-East?

O—Where are you from, Drella? You must tell me. Please.

DRE—The Bronx.

O—The Bronx? (slyly) What part of the Bronx?

DD—Say something Drella.

O—He didn't know. Drella would ge-

DD—Who's humming?

O—Please tell us, Dre-

B—It's all in Who's Who in the East?

DRE—Well Billy's my son in Who's Who?

Your so-, real ly?! Are you serious?

Yeah.

(Gasp.) Oh well then I'll, I'll (Billy says something) Gerard and Ondine . . . . . (laughs) Would you like to be uh, would you like to be interviewed Mr. Mecurio?

(Cab driver) On what?

O—On a tape. This this this is the, this is a novel. It's a uh, so far it's gonna b uh, 18 hours, it's 18 hours in the life of Broadway's yougest star, namely me, and uh, we'd like to interview you, if you wouldn't mind. Nicholas, n, no D. Mecurio. What does the D stand for?

(Cab driver) Dominic.

O—Dominic.

(Cab driver) Yes.

O—You're Italian of course.

(Cab driver) Yes.

O—Uhhh (pause) I can't figure out the part of Italy you're from, from Mila—

(*Cab driver*) Brooklyn.

O—Oh I know, so am I, but y'know my name means I'm right from the middle of uh, Catsanzaro.

(*Cab driver*) Yeah.

O—Are you Napoletan or what?

(*Cab driver*) I'm Sicilian.

O—Sicilian?

DD—Yoooooooo, watch out.

(*Cab driver*) I'm half Napoletano.

O—You're you're you're not only that, you're half . . . . . too. . . . . you can't go . . . . . half . . .

Oh.

(*Cab driver*) You know I was born in the states. I was born in Brooklyn in fact.

O—What part of Brooklyn?

(*Cab driver*) Uh, uh, East New York.

O—Oh East New York.

(*Cab driver*) I live out in Sheepshead Bay right now. I mean I was born in East New York.

O—Oh Sheepshead Bay is beautiful.

(*Cab driver*) Yeah.

O—I was born in Williamsburg.

(*Cab driver*) Williamsburg.

O—Yeah, Franklin and Myrtle, y'know?

(*Cab driver*) Yeah, I know the neighboorhood.

O—We're trying to distract his . . . (*voices all at once*). Uh, let's see

Oh Ondine, would you like a ring

Oh I'd love a ring, not that diamond ring, oh he's giving me presents.

(*Cab driver*) An aquamarine and silver ring?

Yes.

He gave me a ring yesterday.

Do-Do, you shouldn't be telling people what they can and can't do.

I'm not.

You least of all, in love with a hopeless fairy.

Yes, a hopeless fairy.

You are in love with a hopeless fairy.

A hopeless, beautiful fairy.

Beauty has nothing to do with my dear. The only reason why you dig this beauty is because you admire things that are dated.

He's reading it.

What, he's meaningless?

He's meeting us.

She has a dated smile about her

Of course he's meeting us.

like a river sad Renaissance mirror

Keep your hand off him, will you?

He's over, oh.

Oh c'mon, now Jim's been around, dear.

And my hands have uh been around.

And Billy's hands have been around too.

But not around you.

O—I, as a matter of, no I thought I recognized you for for one second from a block party, but it's not so. My last name is Olivo. My first name is Catherina. (*They laugh.*) La Fabiola and also la lagga conda. I saw a movie on television the other night with with Anna Magnani called "Pedlar in Society", and she was really, she is the funniest woman alive. What's my second name?

B—Xavier.

Xavier.

Savior? Savior!

Oh now don't get crucifixtion complexes, it's not Savior, it's Savorio in Italian.

DRE—I thought you were Hungrian.

O—I'm part, part and I'm part Croatian, I'm not Polacrauasian, I'm only half Italian.

I'm only half Italian.

My other half is uh

My other half is uh

Yugoslavian.

Uh

See that, he always does that; isn't he awful?

My other half is

Isn't he terrible? Wouldn't you think that I would hate him

My other half is

Secretly

. . . cluster in my soul.

Look at the ring they just gave me. Isn't it masculine?

Got the gypsy in my

It's terribly masculine, isn't it? Where where wher'd you get it, at Marcroche? (*Laughs.*)

Someone gave it to me.

Oh God.

As 't were.

Did you hear what he said, Howard gave it agh. Billy, oh you know, it's a genuine zircon.

Genuine.

Isn't it?

I think it's a genuine gem.

Oh Do-Do, I have to put that right on your chin, now I put on ash on your own bag. (*They laugh.*)

Don't pick on me Ondine, I, you hate me don't you?

I don't hate you, I'm just trying to help you.

C'mon Ondine, that's just what you did to Sunshine.

Aw now, c'mon now, that wasn't

fair, you know how I love that kid. Do-Do, there are few girls that I meet that I would really take home to mother. I hate my mother you know.

And you were just. . . .

You're the only one I wouldn't know. (*Do-Do keeps talking.*)

She's making life a misery.

You had another big scene this weekend, did you?

I had the crise of all times my dear. I had the crisé this weekend.

I heard I heard. I heard.

The children?

Is it true?

Is it what they say about, it is.

Oh.

Jesu, ma come piove(?) See that's alitalia they say, Jesu, ma come quiove.

(*Cab driver*) Yeah. . . . . .

Who's on that motor-, it looks like Capt. Shovealove. Whatever his name is, yeah, Captain. Yeah I think (*noise*) Captain.

Oh that's not Captain.

Oh you're making that up. You're making that up. (*They're arguing.*)

Capt. Shovalove . . . years ago, he's riends now.

Yo uweer ilving ith one another.

No, they're were good friends. Practical.

For heaven sake, I-

He walks the dog in the morning.

Who walks the dog?

Capt.! He does the house dress, oh, but oh

That dog is not a dog.

Well what is it? It's really the dali lama right?

All over the street.

She has, how tired I get holding this thing. Can't imagine how lowly I am. I am lowlier than the lowliest person. (*Do-Do is protesting.*) What d'ya mean, Lent?

A weak paw.

She's a, she's beat.

I didn't say a weak wrist

Well what do you mean by a weak paw?

A weak paw! If you got so tired holding it . . .

Look at it, my dear. That was bitten by a human being. Wouldn't you have a weak paw? This was all scarred, my career brought to an abrupt and brilliant end.

(*yelling*) Well listen, tell me

By a Pepsi Cola bottle.

Tell me about Ron Rico's arms.

I don't know about Ron Rico's arms.

Well you went on andon all afternoon, wh-wh-what

They look like arms.

I mean, were they all swollen and

No, don't be ridiculous, you are talking to the sugar plum fairy.

We saw Larry . . .

Yeah, I had a scratching fight the last time.

We did. Drella I can't thank you enough, the ring is overwhelming to such degree that

Johnnny cool is gonna be very envious.

I'm very envious of my my my own finger. Don't take the shit off . . . very seriously. She'll leave you tipped in Georgia and nowhere else. She's an a one-woman crusade that'll wind up in Tip . . . Georgia, or bust.

What is Tipten Georgia? You talk

Who knows? Death I think.

No, you tolld me; I don't recall.

She's been after death for years.

Yes, that's right.

And I will say, I

I personified death.

Dorothy, I, I, like I think so much of Joe that if he wants to die, let him. And Billy, that really true.

I go to his bedside daily.

Ohhh, what for?

Were you there? No. No.

What'd you weep for?

I thought . . . was going to die.

Did you see these beatniks? They're vry strange looking.

They're not beatniks, they're British.

Oh they're (*Laughs.*) It's true. Ow! Oh excuse me, this interview has degeneratd but you see with wha, I, this action I have around me. The only prson who is (*Do-Do protesting*) Be quiet Do-Do, or else you'll be banished in the trunk. (*Billy giggles.*) Uh, the only person who uh, who has respect for uh, is is Drella or (cab driver).

We saw a lady with elephant . . . . didn't we yesterday?

DRE—What?

I said you don't but in and, in, and uh uh

Who had elephant . . .

You-hoo is a perfectly great interview with uh, a charming cab driver.

Who ever heard of a teacher in a trunk?

O—I'd like to get her in a trunk ugh. See, they divert me. (*Pause.*) Oh well, here we are again. . . . . together. Suddenly, I'm tired. I am exhausted now, since Saturday. I could sleep now, now that I have the tap recorder around me.

B—You could sleep, you could sleep when I first came to the factory the other night.

O—But did I?

B—Did you? You did not.

O—I sat down, you rip up boxes immediately.

B—You stayed up and bothered me.

O—And I urged you beyond belief. But that that was that was better than sleeping. We'll have to admit. (*Singing*)
freight

B—I feel better.

O—going so fast,
going so fast-, look what you've done, you're so sloppy, Do-Do.

B—Let me see, let me see, let mesee.

O—I did not do that Do-Do, you're hallucinating too, it's awful.

DD—Ondine did it.

O—Mm mm mm. . . . . .I'm not picking up anything.

DD—. . . . . .everybody else should hear.

O—Oh.

D—Why can't Ondine be in the movie?

O—What what movie?

D—The one on Fire Island.

O—I heard Stan was su, su supossedly naked with with me . . .

D—What! You lie you lie you lie out of your mind.

O—I don't want to be in Stan's movie; I don't trust him and anybody who lives in the pines is definitely dclassé, my dear, definitely.

Billy, will you be in the movie?

B—I certaily will.

Fabulous.

B—I've been waiting around for my contract. . . . . .

O—Well, I was *going* to be in the movie

B—I was calld on the phone last week

O—Sam asked me and was vry nice.

B—and told me to sign exclusively with the Warhol studios.

O—Just because you're so smart.

B—And not to make movies with anyone else

You sound just like Ondine.

B—And I haven't heard a word about it since.

O—Well I don't blame him.

B—Don't make movies for anyone else I was told

O—And I am exclusive—

B—That was two weeks ago and have I heard a word since? No.

O—This big boy.

I—I stand around and make video tapes.

O—And darling, weren't we supposed to make a movi with wha, with one another?

B—Yes.

O—(*with haughtiness*) W are the oldest stars in the Warhol studios. The oldest! And perhaps the gayest.

B—We're the most vintaged.

O—Wasn't that right?

B—W are the most vintaged.

(*Pause.*)

O—Would you, oh I didn't evn think of eit, would *you* lik to be a movie star?

(*Cab driver*) No. (*Laughs.*)

Why not?

I mean do you know the advantages of being a mmmovie star? You could go anywhere.

B—I obviously know the disadvantages.

O—You see them right in front of you. (*Drella laughs.*) Uh, look at those people holding the . . . . . . But why why wouldn't you want to be a movie star?

(*Cab driver*) I don't know. It's too, it's too late.

It's too what?

(*Cab driver*) Too late.

It's too late. No! Don't be si-, he says, it's never too late. Any way we asked you.

(*Cab driver*) Make it down this block now?

Oh (*laughs*). Imagine, just now imagine being married to Ethel Merman.

(*Cab driver*) Holy shit.

That's the reason, that's enough to not be a movie star.

(*Cab driver*) 2 270 west. . . . .?

Thirty six days.

(*Cab driver*) Thank you.

Really?

There's the longest . . . . . Uh, there we are, this is the new

Our destination.

This is the new . . . . . . deli.

Oh wow.

This is the new commissary.

This this is any old llama.

This is one of New York's

This is Sloppy Joe's. And if we're lucky, we'll see the freak, Zoppa Patoukas. (*Voices.*) I have I have

Should we get off?

Yes, no let's standhere all night. (*Noise*) (*They get out of the taxi.*) (*Yells into the cab driver*) Well listen, you had a chance in a movie career.

You missed out, I, you

Drella, Drella, Drella, get out this way.

Okty. (*Door slams.*)

(*Cab driver*) (*calls out to them*) Buono appetito . . .

Goodnight uh, Nikolai. (*Pause.*) (*Noise.*) (*Voices.*) Well I have every one's bag in my hand, you horror. (*Voices.*)

What? (*Voices.*)

Oh we'll never see . . . (*voices*) (*they're all talking at once*)

B—Does anyone know this is your shirt. They're gonna say, "Oh there's a fellow with Ondine's shirt."

No, no one. That looks like a television for a second, but it's only a Belair ad.

DD—That is the bride of Ondine.

O—The bride of Ondine. (*laughs.*) (*Noise and voices.*) There's only one little table that's stuck in the back and it's very stuffy. (*Gasp.*)

Ondine, do you see yourself? (*Voices and noise.*)

Who are you?

I saw myself again.

I gotta fold this blanket.

D—Why do you gotta fold the blanket?

Because it's so cumbersome; I've been dragging it everywhere in the street.

That doesn't look like beads around your neck; it looks like a cord.

Well I don't care.

Beads?

D—(*gasp*) Oh it's whatis it?

O—I found it over the phone; I don't know whatit is or who's it is but it's so pretty.

Oh.

Somebody's line, somebody had to do a line over the phone.

O—Yeah, a lot of people hand me a line like, Ondine would you like to go to Fire Island; I want to make a movie

D—We're going, we're going. Do-Do is arranging it.

O—When?

D—Uh, three Saturdays, from now, two Saturdays from now.

OO—Weekend after Labor Day.

O—I'd love to go, it would be beautiful up there then then, that would be nice, that would be heaven.

We're looking for a John.

. . . . . w-wouldn't that be sweet?

What?

Vicious Vivian.

He's going to Paris.

That's all right; maybe we could convince him to, not to go.

What a great idea.

Fantastic? I've been, I've hear-heard Vicious Vivian for a, and now I don't know how to stop myself from talking to that man and so Vicious Vivian finally . . . (everyone is talking at once) I'm glad . . . he only gave us one. Oh you know John.

Didn't Billy . . . . oJhn?

No no.

Yes yes.

No no.

Yes yes yes.

No no.

Well you can't be a John.

No no well I can't either.

Yes you could if

If I had money I could.

. . . the oppurtunity to be a John.

You be a John. I mean you would scare away pricks . . .

I have no money to be a John.

We'll give you money for that week.

Oh I hate (gasp) . . . marshall, I could even limp a little bit, ohhh.

All you need we'll give you for that one day. How much do you need for one day to be a John?

One uh, one uh, oneuh oneuh oneuh.

What does it take to be a John? What what what

White enamel.

Where? Where do you put it?

Poreelin, you put it around your rim sur—

Shhh! White oJhn, y'know what he

Don't get carried away.

Don't get carried away.

Yeah.

Do-Do

You're taking back your invitation.

I'm not.

Oh no she wouldn't dare.

No, invitation take her back.

Not not

How how how

But . . . . Ondine be a John?

Not now that I'm invited.

Oh oh, oh that oh well

Make Arnold a John.

If you could get, we would just love to have Ondine.

No no no no Arnold is truly rich and that would hurt him. It would be a slap in the face to rich people.

So Drella is falsely rich if uh

Well then it wouldn't be any bag . If you could oh no, no no no no. no no no, his whole vi-visage is different. I think Jim Beam would be a better John.

No, he's aging, he's our star.

Oh he's no star darling, he's the John.

He's not a John!

Do-Do, you're in love with him.

DD—(nagging) How could he be a John? How could he be a John? Just take a good look at him.

DD—Oh stop it Honey.

Take a good look at when he . . .

his money, baby.

DD—I mean you always, you always have been so blunt . . . (*she goes on*)

I don't know why you're using the term anyway, it's like saying why did you come out, y'know?

O—Oh Do-Do, now listen

DD—Oh no no no no

JOHNNY.COOL—Yes.

DD— No no.

O—Do-Do, stop acting like a woman.

DD—No no no no no.

B—Well actually Donn Harper could as well.

DD—No no no no. He's too st, I don't know Donn Harper, John talk about a John John John.

O—John McDuff.

D—John McDuff. John McDuff.

O—would be perfect.

I remember some some

O—Wouldn't he? We *all* agree.

JC—If he can't do it nobody can.

O—Oh he would be fabulous Johnnny, thank you. They just said, they just said me.

JC—Oh no.

O—Or, and Drella, he definitely isn't and and then who who was there with the sugar plum fairy, which really is.

JC—Who's the sugar plum fairy?

O—Jim Beam, Jim Beam

JC—I don't know him.

O—You know the small intensely 1930 looking boy?

Drella you're gonna hafta choose what you want.

Okay Drella, you're gonna hafta *choose* what you want.

D—John McDuff or Irving or or Vicious Vivian.

DD—. . . no.

D—Vicious Vivian.

O—Vicious Vivian would be best.

DD—No no, no no.

D—Vicious Vivian?

JC—John McDuff in a serge, a serge black suit and a black padora

D—John McDuff would be great.

JC— In a clean shirt.

O—Oh he'd be really divine.

JC—Now a smack of rice powder, we can have

And you would have the perfect John.

Oh yeah, rice powder would. . . . .

He really would be fabulous. You always have the, a-

Is that what it's all about, Johnny Cool?

Have you two met each other formally?

Not before rice powder.

Have you two met each other informally?

How do you do? I'm Johnny Cool.

I never met him before that remark.

We see McDuff very frequently.

I see your mouth on you Do-Do. You have to go under thetable and leave, and quickly.

How did you get down here so fast?

We still haven't decided, oh we caught the wonderful cab, we still haven't decided what you want. When he comes back

What can I have?

Wha wha wha (*laughs*)

D—What's good? Tell me, I can't even read these things. (*Noise.*)

Do you do you do you want to eat?

Uhh (*someone singing—ooooooooo in a high voice.*) Eggs.

Eggs, potatoes and stuff like that? That's awful.

Well youh cause that's the only

thing I ever have here because it's

Oh.

What what what would you like?

What are you gonna have?

What do you want?

Uhh.

I really don't know because I can't read, I can't see a thing

number 5, its

Yes, it's a very famous piece. Would you leave us alone while we read this? (A huge kiss somewhere.) Oh God I'm glad you stuck it in there, heaven.

A radio first.

(Another kiss.)

Oh we had a better one today

What are those? Surping in fat. Microphone.

Yeah.

Oh I had a few of those at the baths.

Oh really? When?

The other morning. Yesterday morning.

Oh. Really?

Oh. It just snuck up on me. did you see that?

What was so different about it?

It was nice and big.

Really?

What would you like? Do you like cream cheese and jelly? No.

Imagine Billy . . . (all voices together)

Oh it's a gas, isn't it?

Oh stop it!

Oswald gave me this.

Michael and Joey were

Oswaldo.

Is there anything new?

What? Yeah. Learn anything new? I mean any new tricks?

Yeah.

Well there's the humming busi-

ness, you put balls in, and you go mmmmmmmmmmm. (Pause.) I promised I'd do the costa dia for Felicious Ruger.

Who's, ot you . . . Louis and . . .

Drella, he's coming back; I sense his, I feel his breath down my back. Would you like a fried egg sandwich

Ohhh.

How about a cup of coffee?

How about a cup of java? (Drella laughs.) Are my stockings on straight wait. I'd like a blintze put right in that woman's hair, please. Strawberries and cream are terribly gay. I think I'll, I know, what are their hamburgers like here?

Horrifying.

Have a west, have a western uh

I think Do-Do said a western and what?

On toast.

And

What?

Three Russians on toast and a Coke.

Three Russians?

Westerns on Coke, toast.

Oh. What are Russians?

I don't know.

Occidenatl.

Yeah.

Three Westerns?

Yeah. tUh. Yeah.

Who are you to say if we can go or not?

When did you come out, huh? When did you come out?

I came out in 1956 and I was in the glass slipper. I was born (gasp) pardon me.

I thought you came out of a pumpkin.

There must be Johns out there.

Cause ooooooo, Johnny cool.

You girls have to move in.

Oh ho ho ho ho.

Move in now.

Move in now, c'mon.

Hey.

How are you?

How are you?

Do you, hey would we all like a little table cloth. (*Pause.*) Johnny is, move do-do; get your bag out of there, give it to me.

Yech!

Isn't Johnny isn't uh, sugar plum fairy coming now?

(*probably* johnny ooo) Yeah.

Sugar plum fairy will have to sit over there where she belongs.

No no.

Who would make a perfect John?

Who would make a perfect John?

Someone we know?

Yes.

Someone I know who would do a John, John who (*dishes crash*)

No uh, you know, a John that, a rich, uh, a consumer. (*waiter says something.*) No, I'm sorry, wehaven't . . . no no, but that's just us.

I'll have a western on toast and a coke please.

(*waiter*) Western on toast. (*music —the Supremes.*)

Isn't that a gorgeous

I said Jack Keaton.

But that's just us, that's just us.

Oh. (*much noise.*)

I haven't even looked at the menu.

(*Waiter*) You want me to come back?

Would you please? I mean

Egg salad, bacon, lettuce, and tomato, number 7.

We're waiting for somebody else, that's why we must stay here.

What does he want, the movie?

No.

Do you want her to leave?

Light toast. (*Supremes singing.*)

Mmmmmmmm.

Did you run that take again by the way?

I hadonly seen it that one time. (*Music.*) Mmmmmmmmmm.

(*Waiter*) I'll take your order when I get back.

In the mean time you can get nine going. Take care of me; forget the rest.

Johnny Cool think of the people we know—the studio people.

Yes.

The people that have been up there, I mean think of who would

Oh, what's his name?

Who?

James Cagney.

Uh, oh you (*gasp*) John McDuff!

Yes.

Oh no.

(*Waiter*) A western on toast

Make that two more. That's three westerns.

(*Waiter*) Three westerns on toast, one number 7 on toast.

What is a western?

And, yes I'll have a chocolate, no, t-two Cokes, a chocolate malted

And a grill cheese.

Non, I just ordered you a western on toast.

Well that's all right, we'll have two.

Oh all right, that's all right and

And you're having a westren.

Yeah.

You're just having a western.

I'm having a chocolate malted.

(*Waiter*) Let me just check this back. How many western omelyettes?

123.
(*Waiter*) You want a grill cheese.

No, I have a western, too

There are three, that's right.

(*waiter*) There are still three? Do you want at grilled chesse sandwich?

Who?

And then thre's, what did you order, Billy?

And a cup of coffee.

What did you order.

Number 7.

Oh and number 7 for Bill—and then I ordered two Cokes and a chocolate malted.

(*Waiter*) Two Cokes.

O—And a chocolate malted.

(*Waiter*) That's three Cokes also. Let me just read this back so I can be sure now.

Yes.

(*Waiter*) I got three westerns on toast, one number 7 on toast and a grilled cheese?

D—Yeah.

A-, but Drella, what else?

D—Oo.

(*Waiter*) Now I have three Cokes, one coffee, and one chocolate malted.

The chocolate malted.

JC—Oh it's yours, I mean it's mine. You ordered it.

Yes.

O—Wha wha, wait, that's darling. Do you mind if we put it down? Our own table cloth, we have our own plates down here. Did you hear what he did?

D—What?

O—Ordered three, we ordered an enormous amount

Oh really?

What is a western on toast anyway, that boob.

What is a western?

O—Is it a pice of leather or what?

D—Do-Do, what's a western?

DD—It's it's an omelette

B—It's an omelette with peppers, chopped ham, onions.

DD—With vegetables and things like that.

D—Oh.

O—Oh perfect.

What?

No I, don't mind. DoDo sounded so intense about it that I doubt it

What happened to the ring I gave you? Did you give it away?

No.

Oh. I think it really is, however you say it, lapis lazulli?

Is it?

Yeah, lapis lizulli. How do you say it?

Lapis lazulli.

Oh Drella, may I wear your sunglasses now?

What?

May may I wear your sunglasses for just a minute, my eyes are tearing my head out. They fell on the floor and broke. Did you see them fall? That was the third thing that broke that night. Didn't you, oh they're i-, ohh nooo, it makes it worse. Oh bears, I know what I need.

What?

I don't know what it means.

Oh it means uh

I always know what I mean.

Political . . . . . . meaning that he didn't either uh, he didn't fully reproduce . . .

You know every time I think of you holding that mike and then you trying to get it out of your hand, that cracks me up.

Where is it? Where is it? When? When? Uh, not these two.

The Ritz Brothers.

Oh I know what you mean, uhhh (*pause*) Stephen. You've got to see that tape, Drella, you've got to see that tape. It is so well done and so beautifully timed, it's so fabulous.

What

The tape that we made. The one where your finger is discovered.

What finger?

His finger. And IRVING puts his finger into action

Who's finger?

. . . . finger technique.

You ruined that shot you know you

bitch.

Oh you think so.

Yes.

I think I made that shot. You didn't make it at all.

As it turns out you did.

You didn't you didn't.

As it turns out, as I turned it out with my finger.

Good. That's only sheer coincidence, nothing planned, nothing perverted, just perhappen. Did that cab driver try to take something?

What?

Don't mind me, I just lost my marbles.

Ondine, what are you bu-

13 / 2

O—. . . . . . tear. Get your hands-, yes, thank you, one two A—No, I don't want a Coke. O—I ordered you a Coke and a western. Oh that's all right, I'll have two Cokes. A—You'll have two Cokes. O—I love beverages. B—Do you have a frosted? like Do you have coffee ice cream? (*Waiter*) I have coffee ice cream. B—Uh, so uh, chocolate frosted with coffee ice cream. (*Ondine is smacking his lips.*) (*Waiter*) Chocolate frosted B—It's called . . . D—Oh yeah. O—Yeah. (*Waiter*) You ordered coffee didn't you?

D—Yeah, but I'll have the same thing too. (*waiter*) Chocolate with coffee ice cream.

O—Oh, I- (*little gasp*) B—I'll have

my coffee now please.

(*Ondine clears his throat, growls into the microphone.*)

O—I may, yes, the Baroness Karon

Von Bixen, I'll have my toast served by western-, don't bother to bring the coffee now.; bringn ti when the order's ready JC—Yeah, but I want a coffee please. (Noise.) O—I, I'm stuck my dear, I'm stuck. I need help. (Noise.) Oh, it's so tiring being in this company, it's unbelievable; these people are crazy.

JC—What'd you do today?

DoDo Mae Doome—When the room gets . . . . . leave Ondine. Now you . . . . stay here.

O—Now DoDo, you know you are not Joyce Brothers.

D—She's a prop.

O—She *is* a prop.Look at her, *she's just a paper mache woman in love with a paper mache fruit.*

DD—Oh fuck off, I mean fuck up.

(*Johnny laughs.*)

JC—Oh bravo.

O—She said fucko fucko. She can't even, she slurs even the word. Darling, would you put the mike away here, I have a secret to tell you.

D—What?

(*Ondine whispers*)

(*Waiter*) Grilled cheese.

D—Yes.

(*Waiter*) And a number 7.

O—Number 7 looks like it's, oh for Rita Hay—, (*he whispers— Obertrols*) That's with Eric, Eric passed, Eric Ambler.

D—Oh really?

O—Did you see him amble by? No no

D—Right here.

O—Ooh.

D—Just one.

O—Gratcia.

Johnny Cool—What is it?

O—It's a ten milligram ampheta-

mine pill to help the digestive tract—eugh grilled cheese . . . (*funny sounding words*) Una frug. (*pause.*) Do you really have to read now with the camera and everything and these eating . . . let me look at it while you eat. (*Pause.*) With, oh yeah, which one is DoDo's, oh there it is.

JC—Pass the cream.

(*Pause.*)

O—It's poison.

JC—What is this thing with John McDuff? What's with him?

O—This John business.

JC—This John business.

D—DoDo's a new scenarian.

O—Ohh.

DD—Drella you see how much he loves (*jiggling glasses*)

D—Who?

D—Look what I found in my drink.

O—I put it there to poison her.

DD—Look what I found in my drink.

O—Everyone knows that when a, er, that that uh, a ring disolves my dear.

D—This

(*Waiter*) Western.

O—Yes here.

D—Well, it's a sandwich.

O—Yeah.

DD—This this, I mean this proves we're engaged?

O—No I wouldn't marry you on a bet. Throw me the catsup please.

B—Wanna bet?

O—Oh, he was hiding behind Johnny James. Why are these people so typical? Are we doing anything strange?

(*Noise.*)

O—Ooawh!

DD—Oh, my God!

O—Now, now sh's gonna claim

that I put that in there too.

B—. . . . . popped off.

O—She ripped the ring off my finger my dear, and threw it in her own glass. Now you know. DoDo, you've done everything now.

D—Oh the poor polluted Coke ah!

O—(laughs) Poor polluted Coke.

D—Oh-, ohh.

O—Eat it quickly, it's tepid.

D—Well, what happened to my sandwich?

O—It's coming.

D—Oh.

O—No . . . a western sandwich.

JC—How is T . . .?

O—You mean Tita.

JC—Tita.

O—He's not, he's in Masapequa.

JC—Masapequa.

B—Masapequa Point?

O—Ma, there's no point in Masapequa.

D—What?

O—I wonder if he forgot. (Pause.)

D—What are you reading?

O—Ano-, ano-, another western's coming, right?

D—Yes.

O—Oh good. Drella, have have a mine until

D—No no no.

O—yours comes.

D—No.

O—Then I'll have yours.

D—No. Oh, it's over here.

(*Waiter*) Western.

D—What? Coffee?

B—Yeah, with chocolate ice-cream

D—Oh.

O—Why don't you whip off one of those, but darling, because yours is coming and then I'll have the other half.

D—No no no.

O—Please. (*Pause.*) (*In a high voice*) Bllless you. No, are you serious? B-bless you.

D—Hah? It's salt and pepper.

D—Oh, aw, aww, I'm sorry.

D—That's all right.

O—I didn't mean to make you sneeze.

B—That's a dirty Italian movie.

O—I bet you that the uh, Sugar Plum Fairy doesn't show up.

B—If you do that with . . . around they'll think that you're uh.

D—Oh really? Oh.

. . . Italians go around.

O—Yes, they're very, they're really get insulted by (*Pause.*) Well, it all depends on how, y'know, on how superstitious they are. (*Pause.*) Dorothy, why did you order this, bubblegum? and, what's the matter, are you bleeding I hope?

There's a . . .

Mmm. (*Pause.*) Would you like some Coke? (*Pause.*) Yeah. (*Pause.*) Unbeliev—

Oh, that's my chocolate.

Yes.

Which one? Oh, thank you darling, thank you; how sweet (*Billy says something.*) A minimum? Oh.

What's that?

Oh. (*Pause.*) We're certainly gonna be on that.

. . . . . . we have thirty-five people.

I'll bet the SUGAR PLUM FAIRY doesn't show.

Who's the Sugar Plum Fairy?

Jim Bean. Wantsome Coke?

Jimmy grew up to be Jim, hah?

O—How, how do you like your western? Do you want salt and pepper and m, uh catsup on it?

East is east.

What? The Jews are like that?

And the wrong one I have chose.
(*Singing.*)

O—It's, it's, already done. It's so listless like that darling. That's not the Sugar Plum Fairy. That's some man who turns my very existence.

Is it?

Early, so be it.

D—Ooh Ondine!

What're you doing? What're

D—You hate Norman and me?

O—Norman? Why would I hate Norman?

D—Why'd you see that word?

O—You mean another Norman.

D—No.

O—Norman Schwartz

D—Yes.

O—No, I don't hate Norman Schwartz. Why should I?

D—Norman, Norman said that that Solly had a . . . . . . to you.

O—It's not so, and don't start trouble.

D—And I said I didn't believe it.

O—And don't start trouble.

D—Well, he said that to me and I said I don't believe it.

O—DoDo, this is not a situation for uh, that I deserve particularly on uh, I duh, I think that you've just gone over the bounds of the past . . .

OO—DoDo exclaims in a high pitched voice—Ahhhhhhhh.

O—I don't think this is a scenarian idea.

D—I don't thing it's funny at all. It's why did he say it?

O—It's a slap in the face.

D—Why did he say it?

O—And a disgrace . . . . . (*Ondine makes a funny sound.*)

What?

O—I couldn't even say the word.

He didn't say it. He didn't say it. He knows better. Why would he try to make trouble?

JC—Ha ha ha ha, is that what he's making?

O—I mean don't I talk to you openly and frankly and brutally?

O—I think it's what's his name that's trying to make trouble.

B—Candidly.

O—Norman.

D—No, Sonny.

O—Yes, that's what I mean, why would he try to make trouble?

D—He always does.

O—. . . . . are you sserious? Are you out of . . . If you're serious, I'll go over there and whack him one.

JC—(*laughs.*)

DD—Norman told me that. Now I certainly trust Norman far more than I trust Solly Fine.

B—I don't.

O—Why?

B—Whad'ya mean? Whad'ya mean? Huh? Huh?

D—Because experience has proved that he's more thoughtful.

B—You mean you can rely upon him.

O—I think we need an impartial witness.

B—I'll be the impartial witness.

O—Noah has, it is ARNOLD INOVEN who was there?

B—Noah?

O—Uh, he knows what was said about Norman.

D—I don't know anything at all about that because Norman was by himself when he said that to me.

O—What did he say then?

D—Well

O—Norman said that Solly said

that I hated him. Oh what an awful thing to say. I said I loathed him. That's better.

D—You despised him?

O—Despised is very easy.

D—You said you loved him.

O—I do love him.

DD—You don't hate him.

JC—You don't hate anyone.

O—How could I?

JC—I thought you loved him.

O—This western has burnt my tongue right out. Oh I don't think the Sugar Plum Fairy ever shows up.

D—Oh.

DD—If it doesn't bother you, it bothers me.

O—Mr. Lamore has been taken care of. The sugar plum is very decadent.

JC—Say that again. D—Is very what?

O—Is very decadent.

DD—Decadent? So are you Ondine.

O—I'm more than decadent darling. I'm a centaur. Mm oah oh aw, that restroom is so horrible, isn't it awful? No no, it's deadly. No I haven't seen . . . (*voices*) Johnny because of you mumble mumble the only reason we came down here is because of you.

JC—And now that I'm here, what shall we do?

O—When you're so blood-thirsty for us.

JC—Sugar Plum Fairy.

O—No. *John McDuff.*

JC—Oh, is that the only one I like?

O—No, but you would be amusing.

JC—Who?

O—You. You came down here in the rain. DoDo . . . ti-, a duh, completely to the DoDo DOOMe.

That's speech pattern, delivery, attack, everything.

JC—Did you just get up?

O—I haven't slept. Why, do I look sleepy? I thought I was terribly alert. (*Pause with voices.*) Oh. It's still on me.

D—What's on?

O—That drop. Uh, meet at that apartment at uh, where Gerard Malanga's staying? (*Someone says something.*) No. And you know why? Ursala Beat? There's somebody named Ursala Beat.

D—. . . old things over and over, now you're uh

O—Do you know what Gerard said to me on the phone?

D—What?

O—Because of his relationship with Buffy, the one who's dragged down from Cambridge or whereever.

D—Why What's he doing?

O—And he has no relationship with him.

D—He doesn't?

O—It's just jealousy, y'know.

D—Is he having an affair with Duffy.

O—No! Gerard is not, Gerard isn't capable of that thing. But he says to me on the phone, he said uh, he said, what is that person looking at me in that manner for? I know I'm gla-more-iss but I mean, no but he said to me on the phone, he said uh, duh, "can you go somewhere else this evening?" I said, "You realize I'm staying with you." And then then he he said, "Oh no he didn't. but he did because I'm sure that Dan had told him.

D—Oh.

O—So when I got there I apo-, I

did an inceedible act.

D—What'd you do?

O—Meanwhile my bag had been stolen, and it was the bag that Taxina gave me.

D—Which one was that?

O—That marvelous brown bag with the pouch.

D—Oh.

DD—She gave you a blue bag.

O—No but this was before that. I don't call a Pan American bak a bag. That's just a piece of uh, they can't get over it, whatever, we are they cannot get over it. (*Dodo is talking.*) Oh viva la, viva la. (*Dodo is still talking.*) (*Ondine laughs.*)

DD—I mean I asked Dodo what

O—Listen to this. Dodo was . . . . . that was beautiful.

JC—Would you please recite that again?

DD—No, we can't speak . . . . .

JC—Oh bullshit, c'mon.

O—Listen, lift the magazine away from him and read it again. You mean your memory is that bad?

DD—(*in a loud voice*) Searing mentality, blazing intellectuality.

O—I'm not your reality.

DD—What?

O—Inter-reality, bla

JC—Blazing intellectuality. No?

DD—Yes! Blazing intellectuality.

B—This talks about it; go ahead.

O—Lazy emotionality into a (*Dodo protests*) Lazy actuality inter reality I sa-, that was, that's what it was. Oh everybody's having a good time. Would you like more of this?

D—No.

O—Drella, because I, I don't want it. Oh, what a lovely woman. Ug it. Oh, what a lovely woman. Ugly snob. Drella, why so pensive? Are you plotting something?

D—Hm?

JC—Ha ha ha ha.

D—What?

O—Now c'mon out with it. Oh, my husband. Who told him to meet me here?

JC—The Sleeping Beauty?

O—No, it's my husband, darling.

JC—Oh. Is it the Sugar Plum Fairy you're waiting for?

O—Yeah, we're waiting for the Sugar Plum Fairy but she won't come.

DD—She won't come.

O—*THE SUGAR PLUM FAIRY DOESN'T VISIT ANYONE IN THE RAIN. SHE'S AFRAID OF MELTING.*

BS—How about the Rose Adagio?

O—The Rose Adagio was danced last night at a, at a bar called La Pompiai or something, it was most atrocious.

DD—Who was there? Who was there?

O—Jim and I. We got so

DD—You were there last night? You know that's what ruined everything.

B—Ruined.

O—What do you mean ruined everything?

B—I mean ruined.

DD—I mean just stop.

O—Why?

DD—I mean you invited . . . filthy, hustling bar . . . . . didn't you?

O—Yes because he had

DD—You lid! Then you did.

O—Sugar Plum Fairy's package, my dear.

DD—Yes you did. Yes, yes. Sugar

Plum Fairy's package yeah, what do you mean, Sugar Plum Fairy's package?!

O—(*In a slow voice*) Sugar Plum Fairy left a package at the bar, which he—

DD (*sarcastically*) A package of what?

O—Uh some shirt that he bought uh some uh

DD—I don't believe it, a lie, a lie on you.

O—Dorothy, put your face in your own western and shut up. A lie, how dare you.

DD—A lie, a lie.

O—Ondine non mento. (Ondine doesn't lie.) No, he had a package of bras. No, whatever it was it looked like a shirt, a package of, it looked like a, a tie package, he must have bought some terribly horrid tie, you know and he left it there and he was worried about it before he went to sleep, so I called up and said, "Come over," which I had forgot about.

DD—That's why you said you hadn't invited him.

O—That's why I said I hadn't invited him, because I didn't realize

DD—If you could have seen the way that person attacked the Sugar Plum Fairy.

O—Well, if you could have seen what the Sugar Plum Fairy did to that person.

DD—What do you mean? What did the Sugar Plum Fairy do to that person?

O—He delivered our drinks and the Sugar Plum Fairy immediately put her hands right down into his pants.

DD—The Sugar Plum Fairy . . .

O—But she said to him, she said, "I

don't care if it's not hard." she she, she said, "I like it soft." She said, "C'mon c'mon, you've shown it to me before." "Oh," she said, "Ondine is big and fat." She went on and on this poor creature and the creature never moved, but the creature kept getting hard ons, getting had ons, the Sugar Plum Fairy, look at, watch Dodo's glee and delight now and then listen to her say that she loves the Sugar Plum Fairy. (*Silence.*) Notice, wretch

DD—No, I want, I want . . .

O—You've been found out at last. But what she did was the best thing my dear, was when she pissed.

DD—Who?

O—The Sugar Plum Fairy came out and on, on 3rd street and 6th avenue she said, "I have to piss." And she

B—Oh . . . piss . . . and open up eh

O—Listen, and she, and then, these women, it was, Billy, it was a (*Billy-says-something.*) All right, then she says, "I'd like to pull it." And she kept pulling it. I said "Jim, the police." And she said, "I wanna pull my thing," and she kept pulling it.

B—Who did?

O—Jim Beam, the Sugar Plum Fairy, that filthy doll. I could barely wheel her into a cab, the cab driver was really demented. We kept changing our destination. First it was 47th street, then 23rd, and she, then she said, she

B—That's not all of it.

O—The Sugar Plum Fairy had everything in the bars when she went out.

B—In the bars?

DD—What?

O—Every, she had every person in the bar.

JC—Ha ha ha ha.

O—She she bumped into everything. She was really fabulous. Oh I, she was really, I've never seen the Sugar Plum Fairy so (someone says something) I just gave him that. Cause I got, I got two Cokes and one of those, I didn't order any of it. I don't remember coming here. But certainly you can have it, he didn't. Would you believe that? How considerate people are; he ordered it for me because there's a minimum here.

D—Oh.

O—(with food in his mouth) Which of course they

JC—It doesn't apply before 2:00.

O—It doesn't apply when he he doesn't have one word straight on the menu, not one

D—Why are you putting napkins in there?

O—Oh am I? I didn't meant to. I could use that. Aw. You don't want to hold that

B—Oh oh oh digadigadigadigadig

O—What?

D—Oh, I have ano-, I have a

O—What is it? They won't answer. They won't answer.

D—Hm?

O—Well what did he

D—What what what?

O—(gasp)

BS—I've, I've been

O—Everytime we pick up the sound.

JC—Ohhhhh.

O—Can Dodo pick up the sound?

You want to do, four?

D—No just . . . all right. Would you

BS—Dodo, Dodo, you're so lovely.

O—Osa mason, oh ooh, osa mason.

D—Oh I know uh, she was uh (Ondine burps) Oh pardon.

DD—I didn't know Marseilles.

D—She was

DD—All I know about Marseilles (Mersay?) is M . . . . . is at the purple cat.

O—What was that for? What she said, Mersay is at the purple cat?

DD—. . . had a purple cat.

O—You see how people . . . the Sugar Plum Fairy's stories out? They just tell. Don't draw pictures for that tired soul; she's had it. That's why she was sniveling.

B—It's all right.

O—Did someone say Betty Hutton? Didn't you enjoy Rita's this evening?

D—Rita?

O—Yeah. Wasn't she marvelous?

D—Fantastic.

O—Oh and the Duchess you know, what a telephone conversation, wasn't it though. And Moxanne, isn't she beautiful?

D—Ohhhhh, yes. Oh.

O—I, oh, y, so she, she she's going to summer stock isn't she?

BS—Yes.

O (Ondine sucks in his breath.) (Everyone is talking at once.) Fisherman, picture Al as a fisherman.

DD—Yes.

O—Oh . . . in hr new movie, "Western On Toast"

D—"Western On Toast"?

O—. . . a new movie. Oh yeah,

most of it. The western was un-believable.

JC—I'll have some water.

O—The western was unbelievable. I never tasted anything so incredibly . . . I almost couldn't eat it; it was fabulous. Plastic and rubberbands. (*Dodo is talk-*

DD—I knew that there was one *ing.*) Wha ha ha ha.
too.

O—An-anyway, as I was saying, blah blah blah blah.

D—He didn't eat anything.

O—He he doesn't want it. No, he has a very very touchy stomach. He can't eat certain kinds of . . .

D—Oh.

O—He eats incredibly, he eats incredibly. I never heard of anyone who eats like he eats. Oh, no thank you, I've just had two Cokes and a malted, I, I really. Yes but, no, you, I'm sure you know the reason why he cooked like that.

B—or—

JC—No who? He cooks like that all the time.

O—His ex-roommate.

—He cooks like that all the time.

O—Who was your last lover? He's like uh . . . I've never known any of your lovers. I knew of one almost-lover of yours last year at Fire Island when you said to me that you had to make the great decision and you did. And you were about to enter into a love affair and you decided against it. I knew you were making love just to divert me, but it was a charming doy, mm hm. (*Drella says something*) What's the matter? . . . For hte world of me I can't

remember. (*Johnny Cool says something.*) No. It's it's, if we make the Hedy Lamarr thing? No, no, I want to see Lana Turner in anything. . . . Hedy Lamarr.

D—Who Who—

JC—Hedy Lamarr redid it?

O—Clark Gable, Madame, (*Drella says something.*) Madame X.

D—Are you sure?

O—Certainly. Certainly. It was Madame X. She was a spy, a Russian, of course. Uh, what was I going to say?

D—No, it was Comrade.

O—Comrade X, you're right, you're right, thank you.

JC—The original was called Madame X.

O—Where did we run into Dodo? For the world of me I can't remember.

D—In the elevator.

O—Oh that's right. She was coming us and we were going down, yes, I wouldn't believe it.

D—And Billy.

O—Oh listen darling, he was under the table all that while, imagine.

JC—Who was this?

O—Billy, for two hours he stood under Rotten Rita's table and we didn't know a thing about it.

DD—What the hell? What what

O—He was there all that while.

B—What's that?

O—Did I know that you were there

B—When?

O—When when Moxanne, myself, Rink, and Drella stopped in to Rita's? No, no.

B—Where?

O—At Rita's. Oh what's where where where?

D—What happened to Rink?
O—Oh yeah, what did happen to
Dink? I think Dodo killed him.
B—The movies I think.
DD—Tonight?
D—No no, he was with her.
O—He was with us.

B—And I was under the table.
O—For two hours or more. If you
don't know where you were for
two hours Billy, I mean you must
have been a little stuffy.
B—I called you all on the phone
from the extension under the
table? Is that where I called you
from?
D—hu hu hu.
O—Oh listen, he's trying to be
humorous, isn't that sweet? Anyway, forget it dear, your memory's certainly short. I can't believe it. You should go to a doctor. As for Dodo Mae, she's trying to pretend.
D—What?
O—She's, she can't talk you know.
I saw her push him down the in-
cinerator thing. She stuffed her

in quickly. That man's making a
sound like Pachukas.
D—Huh huh huh huh huh
O—Do they know T-oppa Pachukas? They're making a sound like
him. (Sound in background—
Toooooo) Oh please! Oh I want
he book. Oh! That's a little better. Now get it out and walk it.
(Gasp.) Bravo senore. As I was
saying, how—, Rita looked a little
peeked (piqued?) didn't she? I
mean being mayor must be a
drain on her.
JC—Did you do anything after I
left that day?
O—No. We made a chow mein
movie, a chow mein movie with
the television shot.
D—Really?

O—Which was marvelous　　(Dodo and Billy are singing together.)
D—Well!　　B—At this moment (singing) there is no . . .　　O—
Drella, I'm sorry, I'm sorry . . . at Rita's (Dodo and Billy are still singing.)
(Dodo is reciting something very quickly.) The reason I'm not saying anything to stop it because I want them to understand what they are when
they hear it.　　(Dodo and Billy together) . . in my own.　　O—All
right, you're both gonna love yourselves when you hear this. (They keep
singing and reciting.) Oh, now this is the part that . . . (They're still at it.)
(Between the singing Ondine is trying to get Dodo's attention.) Drella.

D—What?　　O—Talk to me. It's been so long since you've talked
to me.　　D—I know.　　O—Tell me something interesting.　　D—
Uhh.　　O—Oh, some man came up to all night from California with
David Bottom.　　D—Where?　　O—To the factory.　　D—(gasp)

O—And David showed me some of his swimming movies. And they're,
the three of them are lovely.　　D—Oh, Andy was supposed to do something.　　O—He was supposed to sign it.　　D—Yeah.　　O—Well,

Gerard signed it instead.　　D—He did?!　　O—He signed Andy's name.
　　D—Oh he did?　　O—Yeah.　　D—And did the boy—　　O—The
boy said y'know anybody could sign it if if if they want to but　　D—Is
he a cute boy?　　O—Yes, he's marvelous, and he's with, he's with a girl
named Regina.　　D—Who's Regina?　　O—Uhh, she's the queen of
uh, God knows what. I don't know, but he's wearing a wedding ring. Not
David.　　D—No. Who?　　O—David wants to put Walter on the
Brooklyn Bridge.　　D—He does?　　O—And walk him right across it
nude.　　D—Ohh.　　O—Wouldn't that be fabulous?　　D—Yeah.
O—Of course Walter would die by the time he got to the middle.
D—Why?　　O—Cause Walter would have no choice. (*Pause.*) The
Sugar Plum Fairy has not shown. Typical. That's your love darling.
B—Doris Day, Latin Lovers.　　O—Ooh bravo darling, no but—, no
there's some-something else that I said before. He's a very nice boy, oh
and C. W. Post came up.　　D—Why was C. W. Post　　O—And his
wife Bauxite . . .　　D—What time were they there?　　O—They were
there the same time around 8.　　D—They brought a camera?　　O—
No. They brought . . . concert or whatever it is.　　D—Oh really? Oh.
　　O—She's very dreary. (*Pause.*) Oh.　　O-p-a damour　　D—O-p-a
damour　　O—Ho. How can you tell when it's over? Philips is the new
thing y'know y'know, it's it's a really new tape, record company, everything, Philips. The people who make—, do you remember what you
thought about the movie before you saw it? About the tape? What you
thought it it would be like? Your preconception while it was being filmed
and the reason wha-, where, which led to certain actions. This is the same
thing . . . this turned out to be so fabulous you cannot believe it. (*Everyone is talking at once*) Aren't, aren't the tapes marvelous? Everything,
every single thing, every mwuoss　　Why do you hold it so close?
Because it's a micro-, we call it Connie Boswell and her gallant struggle to
fight infantile paralysis. She may be in a wheel chair but she's still (*pause*)
the New Orleans song . . .　　(*pause*) What must I do? What do you
want me to do? Eat it again? (*Slurp slurp.*) Here it goes. Oh I'm dipping
it into Coke now, Mr. America. Oh please don't. (*Hollow sound.*) Did
you figure it out?　　Yeah.　　That was a Coca-Cola bubble bursting.
Once more. (*Hollow sound again.*)　　Joan Crawford.　　Joan Crawford's rival just put on a pair of sling pumps. Da da da dummmmmmm,
look, French toast, ooh, have French toast, all that food (*laughing*) the
look you make. You know I couldn't make another one. Oh no, oh. Dodo,
you want some more of a western? Dodo must be from out west, isn't she?
　　What are they doing?　　They're reading. Oh. Are you leaving?
Oh.　　Why? In all the long years I've known you I never met you on

86th street before in my life.   86th?   86th.   Johnny Fatts
Johnny Cool   Spanish Eddie

———

14 /   1

O—And   D—8, 8   O—8, 0, you know the one I, the one we—, oh
I love to see that just breathe. Number thirteen?! (pause) Y, U n-, oh
we're on again?   B—YU 9   O—9-880. Why don't we do something
very sacred now?   D—What?   O—And go to church.   D—All
right.   JC—Where will you be tomorrow?   O—I'm, either there or
or at the fac-, more than likely at the factory, I think, oh no, I may even
be-, okay, more than likely at the factory although there is a banding together needed for different purposes. One is Gerard Malanga's imminent
a-and quick education; he needs it badly. Well look, y'know not necessarily, if he, if he can, if he can ship up uh, then won't have to shock
shap, I mean no, what is it? If he shapes out then he ships shape. No, but
he can't go around lying in Andy Warhol's name; that's despicable.
D—I've only known him for a couple of years.   DD—You can't go
around lying in anybody's name.   O—Exactly. Well that girl was us-,
has a complete necklace of tuonols.   D—Oh ho.   O—And maybe it's,
she has   JC—Chow chow.   O—Chow down. (kiss) Bye bye Johnny.
Thank you for McDuff. So long. Johnny Cool is the   B—Johnny Cool
with one leg.   O—is the essence of the dance.   D—Huh?   O—
He's the best dancer I've ever known.   D—Dancer?   O—Yes, classi-
cal dancer.   D—Well how come he said uh . . . . . or uh   O—Oh
no, well he's uh, he's always like that y'know, he's he's very solitary, he's,
his habits are very very very solitary and and he has an incredible uh
image like   Really?   To what he, what he, what he, focuses on is
insane. Nonetheless, he's great, just absolutely great. He's the only person
I know who absolutely terrifies, terrifies, terrifies Rodney the Rod.
Oh really? Why does he terrify him?   A, eu, oh, I don't know why.
Rodney the Rod just is terrified by him. Rodney the Rod is just terrified
by him. (pause) Gerard Malanga, Drella   What?   I, I, first of all, I
want to ask you this question. Did you tell Gerard Malanga that Jim
Beam was not to come to the factory anymore? (pause) Well why did he
tell me that then? Y'know I heard him last night, I heard him last night

tell the Su, the Sugar Plum Fairy that. I mean with my own ears I am witness to him saying that Drella said, he said, "Drella said that the non-participants (pause) (gasp) I didn't even think about it, it's a Lester Sturgis word, it's an Irving what's-his-name word?   du Ball.   du Ball. (laughs) Irving du Ball. It is! Irving du Ball and Jean-Jeanette MasDonald are the same person. They're Jeannette, Gerard Malanga!   Jeanette du Ball.   Jeanette du Ball is really, mm, I, really, I am overwhelmed by that fact that they both use the word non-participants for, to describe different people.   Anybody who'd use anybody else-, Gerard Malinger, ohh beautiful. Gerard's Malinger.   Gerard Malinger—   Gerard's.

O—is such a, I mean that's really elegant though. It's a little too elegant for him. I think he should really maybe maybe maybe, y'know leniency should not even, Drella what what could you do with him? I mean because you're so kind y'know, you're so kind and and and you don't like to hurt people and I know you're not gonna say anything that's gonna dement him. What could you say say to him, what, did you tell him, you're not gonna do that Drella, you know you're not. We could do it. We'll put big masks on and go ooooo. Tell Gerard to bring his own replacement; he's through.   Ondine, would you please hold out your hand. (pause)   Roger?   Yeah.   Is that his or is it just because he's   He really believes that he can get away with things . . . . . and that people will help. He really is sick.   I think it's mo-, it's more, I think he's malicious.   No, he's not malicious because he uh   I think Gerard Malanga is uh, is is is pitiful at times.   . . . . . that someone isn't gonna be able to figure out what he's done is sick.   He doesn't really think that does he?   Yes. He does, he thinks that he can get away with having something happen and that the person . . . . .   Oh yes he does.

Frequently with people (they're both talkingo . . . . Dodo, I don't want it on this finger; it's too smawll.   Well where do you want it? He gave it to you.   You're torturing me.   He doesn't think that people are anywhere beyond him.   Yeah but he, then then then why does he always try to figure out where people are at?   If somebody tries to figure it out you can tell right there where they're at.   Yeah. But Gerard *has* figured it out, right? And *he's* left behind. Well why does he, what has driven him to these measures? These measures are   Relax!   Oh of course, if you figured it out accurately but I, but I'm, I'm presuming . . . . . or analyzes at various times when he's up or something what is going on in this particular situation or that particular situation and never gets beyond the relative points.   You must tell me Billy; what has driven him?   Figure it out.   to such (pause)   Oh I don't know, something much more central   than I'd be able to, to materialate.

No, it's it's, it's as simple as fear or terror or   It's very essential.
What kind of position did Gerard have before this?   Oh, he was born;
that's enough right there.   But do you know what he was born into?

The same thing we were all born into.   His his, he told me the
other night when I was there that he slept in his mother's bed until he
was ten.   I slept . . .   But I, but he he used that as an excuse for
having a rash. (Billy says something) Yeah exactly and he should wise up
ship shot, I mean sha-shape shot or eh eh and then, no it's not pleasant.

What?   Oh you're yawning. I thought you were so tired wh-, are
you tired darling?   O If you wanna go to sleep you can postpone this,
and us, I mean we've gone already 26 hours, how long is it? (Pause.) You
don't believe what story. (Pause.) Gerard Malanga is 22 because Gerard
Malanga is a perfect product, he's the, he's the worrying war baby, it's
unbelievable.   B—Our degeneration.

O—(with emphasis) Where is the Sugar Plum Fairy? Th-, ooh, the Sugar
    Plum—

DD—THE SUGAR PLUM FAIRY

O—appears. We were sure you wouldn't come. (Pause.) We were sure
    that you wouldn't come, Jim.

D—Are you here by yourself or not? What?

O—You're with who? Who are you with?

THE SUGAR PLUM FAIRY—No one. I'm by myself, myself.

O—Ameria, meet Jim Beam, otherwise known as FPF. Ooh!

D—SP

O—Dodo, eat your western!

DD—It's not mine Ondine.

O—Well it wants you.

DD—I don't want it.

O—I think it was Drella's but Drella left quickly in this fell swoop.
    (Pause.) And who expected the Sugar Plum Fairy?

SPF—Can I get something to eat?

O—(gasp) Say you must be starving Jim.

SPF—You haven't been to sleep?

O—No, of course not, you know I haven't. The Su- these straws ar eall
    wet. (Pause.) (Gradually his voice gets lower.) Happy birthday to
    yooou. (Pause.) That sweater is heavenly. You should be nude under-
    neath it. Oh, Sugar Beam, here is your food. I just asked Drella if
    Gerard, and he said no.

B—I inquired about it more discreetly.

O—Don't be a-, Sugar, we can't be discreet about this; you must be
    exploded. Oh Jim, stop saving someone's skin with—(they're all arguing)
    how is he supposed to grow up (arguing)

SPF—I was drunk y'know, I mean and I and I deserved exactly what I—

O—*I heard him say to Drella* that you were not allowed in.

SPF—He was pleasant with us once I got there.

O—I don't care how pleasant he is; you don't lie in anybody else's name.

SPF—He was very pleasant.

O—Well do you withdraw the charges, Sugar?

SPF—N-, he just said that I shouldn't—

O—Do you withdraw the charges?

(ARGUING ALL AT ONCE)

O—This is played tomorrow for Gerard's mother. (*They laugh.*) As she boards the bus. She's a poor lady at Barton's chocolates isn't she? No, I don't know what she is. God forgive me.

B—I've spoken to her a number of itmes. (*Everyone's talking*)

DD—I hate you. I hate you. I'll kill you dead.

B—Oh, you feel the same way I do about people, huh?

DD—What?

O—May I look in the American Record Guide Billy please? May I look at the American Record Guide please?

B—There's nothing in it.

O—I'll decide that for myself!

B—There's only one thing that would interest you.

O—If you wish not to show it to me, if you wish not to show it to me, say no.

B—There's nothing in it at all.

O—I don't need your editorial comments. I want it yes or no.

O—Hah! Right on that smart tie my uncle gave me. Ha ha ha ha ha, that was divine. Drella that was perfectly—

SPF—Are you on drugs?

O—No, it was a ring; it knocked me out, I mean I was so over-whelmed (*inverted gasp.*) Look at this.

B—I'll read you the only thing you'll be interested in.

O—I wanna read it myself, I wanna be quiet and read.

DD—. . . cause cause if you read

B—You'll just be forced to tear it up.

O—No I won't Billy, I'll just, I'll read it in your hand. I just want toread through it. I want some-something to look at besides you three.

SPF—Why don't we, why don't we go to

DD—Oh let's.

O—Is it still open? Oh, we can dissolve there.

A—Why?

O—Because that was the last night where you took us . . whacky whacking . . . that is, it's right on 3rd and Thompson, it's the, it's the most, Le Pompier.

DD—Do you know what that means in French?

O—It means, it means, pumper.

DD—It means cock sucker.

O—Oh everything means cock sucker in French, Dodo.

SPF—Is it Pompiere or Pompier?

DD—Pompier.

O—It means the pumper. (*Voices.*) Oh may I? Oh let me see it. Please let me see it.

D—What was the word that uh Rink and I, that I asked what Ondine meant, not Ondine said it was Ondine or uh, it means boredom.

O—What means boredom in French?

D—Ondine.

O—Ondine means boredom? No. Ennui means boredom. But it's a kind of a real pushed kind of boredom. Fiorente means spinach.

D—D-D-Dodo?

O—But the Callas (college boards?) is now unfortunately a frayed rag. (*Laughs.*) Isn't that heaven?

D—I wouldn't be surprised.

SPF—You know what they are?

O—Taquila Margueritas are the only drinks to drink. Quantro and a few dashes of . . . . . Oh Drella, it was the most divine thing ever. I, I was (*voices*) We, we we we we we (*voices*) when I said a half hour we meant a half hour.

SPF—You didn't say anything like a half hour.

O—We said a half hour; we're leaving now.

SPF—Did you see how Dodo scratched Ron Rico last time?

B—Well that's too bad.

D—What!?

SPF—Dodo decided that Ron Rico should stay out of the service.

O—She otld us that she would con-

tribute.

SPF—That she'd keep him out, y'know, of the service.

D—Oh.

SPF—So she scratched his arm.

O—How evil. What a feeble excuse for sadistic action.

SPF—Isn't that the truth.

DD—His arms were all bloody and scratched.

D—Oh wow.

SPF—And she did that on the pretext that that would keep him out of the army.

O—What I lik is the way she lied and told us that you did it in your sssleep.

DD—Who did what when? Cause he wants to get away from me.

O—Oh yes you can get drafted; good.

SPF—Yeah, I, I'd like uh, two poached on whole wheat.

O—(*inverted sigh*) Oh pardon me.

SPF—And lettuc and tomato.

O—In God's name.

SPF—No potatoes. Lettuce & tomatoes.

O—Lettuce and tomato, no potatoes.

DD—No potatoes cause you're getting so fat.

SPF—Whole wheat toast yeah, and uh, a very light coffee.

DD—Obesity is not—

B—Well what do you want him to turn into, a prune?

DD—No, just a lovely plum.

(*waiter*) Anybody else want anything here?

O—Pardon me?

(*waiter*) Anyone else care for anything here?

O—Have you any sherbert? (*Pause.*) Well, then nothing. I love sherbert.

B—Another frosted.

DD—Ondine's not fat.

SPF—He's not fat?!

(*waiter*)—How many scoops do you want?

DD—Ondine's not fat.

B—Three.

SPF—He was thin last year.

(*waiter*) How about one chocolate and one coffee?

D—One chocolate and one coffee.

O—You're appearing by grace on my tape.

SPF—You were thin last year darling.

O—Remember that.

SPF—Uh, uh, Ondine, you were thinner last year.

O—Point, point to the witch (which) room and then talk, don't, not me.

SPF—But you gained weight. What makes you gain weight when you'r on-

DD—Why don't you stop picking on me?

O—Your face. Your face, your very presence.

SPF—No really—

O—Yes, I trink a lot darling. Ondyne? Listen Sugar Plum, don't call me by my first name, Sugar Plum. I dring everything from Wink to seltzer.

DD—I've never had any Wink.

O—Wouldn't it be heaven if we could get, we have to drink, the best place you have to drink it in is in the baths. There's no other way. We could have had breakfast at the baths.

DD—You went to the baths? You went to the baths? Did you invite me to the baths?

O—DODO, I, I went to the baths.

B—Ondine, you and Drella should

retire.

O—We we we have been re- for years. We've been retired for just generations.

SPF—Where's sweet Stephen? Where's sweet Stephen?

O—Let them. They all wish they had it.

D—Oh really?

O—Oh well, no one but-

SPF you're a sadist. (*Everyone is talking.*)

O—She's an incredible horrid sadist.

SPF—She's always pinching and scratching and gouging.

O—I threw her down a flight of stairs at the factory once just to stop her.

SPF—She's got big balls I tell ya.

O—It's a dick she has.

SPF—No really DODO.

O—Wait darling.

?—I'll wait.

O—No, don't wait, do whatever you will, but don't take anymore frogwomen pictures please.

B—Have you seen me take any? Are you going to start calling me thief soon? Huh?

O—O.T.C. is O.T.C. Is.

B—I'm not a frog.

O—Yes, it's Leo Gorcey and I don't like it.

B—Well that's there with it.

SPF—I've never even seen the—

O—He's the best photographer I know.

DD—Who?

SPF—Where is Steve?

O—Billy NAME.

DD—Why are you so interested in Steve?

A—Yeah he really is.

DD—Yes you are goddamn, I mean you really, you are so vaunt

O—Oh he's divine.

DD—and loathsome. I mean corrupted.

O—Oh, well you think Stephen is a, worth saving?

SPF—It's remarks like that, DO-DO, that keep you out of Tiptin.

O—Yes, I told you you were going to Tiptin, Georgia whether you're wanted or not.

DD—What is this? What is this all about? What is this all about?

O—It's Kill a Negro weekend in Tiptin, Georgia. If you can bring a live Negro down there

SPF—Tiptin U.S.A.

O—my dear, in the back of your car you get the town and one week with Susan Hayward. You know it. I told you you were on your way to Tiptin, DoDo. You wouldn't believe me, and now you know that I see and tell all. (Singing to the tune of "California Here I Come") Tiptin Tiptin, U.S.A. That was somebody's birthday. That, that, she's the disgusting eater. It's horrible when she goes to a restaurant, embarrasses you right in front of everyone. That's a delicious looking lunch.

SPF—Isn't it?

O—Is that for your weight problem? DoDo, you're going to love Tiptin, Georgia, you're going to love it. (SPF laughs.) Can you imagine trying to pick out which one is Jim and which one is Ondine with the sheets on their head? Which one is Jim? (SPF laughs.) The questions rolling around in your brain.

SPF—That's a poem.

O—There's Ondine, I see a twisted, I see a twisted sheet. There's the Sugar Plum.

SPF—What time, what time are we gonna pick you up?

O—Oh well, oh well we'll decide that when we get there.

SPF—Do you know what Roger Roger Roger said that, that you weren't really gonna go and I said of course he's going.

O—Roger thinks he knows everything.

DD—Roges is so sick.

B—Roger's another little boy.

DD—Who cares what Roger says?

O—Roger's never been to Tiptin.

DD—When are you going?

O—We're going to Georgia on Sunday. Will you come with us? Would you like to come come with us and see her go up in flames?

DD—You've got to come back in Tasa Caloula. Get him to come back in Tasa Caloula.

O—Well if you

SPF—I'm not even coming back.

O—Well how am I supposed to get back?

DD—What doyou mean you're not coming back?

O—You told me, "Don't bring any money; don't worry about a thing."

DD—What do you mean you're not coming back?

SPF—I didn't say don't bring any monye for Christ's sake.

O—The first words out of my mouth were, "I have no money." You said, "Don't worry about that darling,,' you said, "don't worry about—

SPF—You're out of your mind. I never said any such thing.

O—Well then you go to Tiptin by yourself.

SPF—You said you'd get money money from your mother.

O—Sorry sorry sorry that I have to mess your plans.

DD—What do you mean you're not coming back? What do you mean you're not coming back?

SPF—It's the death set.

O—America, America, I'm going to—, you're damn right it is, for you if you go without me it is. Uh, America, I'm sorry to have missed DoDo's crucifixtion but, well I'm no-, I'm not going to Tiptin. (*Pause.*) This all has a bit of reality about it somewhere that's scary.

D—Uh huh huh huh huh.

DD—Well could Drella make him stay up here for the movie.

SPF—Oh you oh, is that for the record Ondine? You're not going to Tiptin?

DD—Hey Sugar!

O—Well I have no way of getting back.

D—Sugar, you're the star of our movie.

SPF—I-I'll try to get you back.

DD—You're the star of the movie.

O—Can I make money down there?

DD—Yes.

O—Make a movie with us in Fire Island please.

DD—Why do you have to fuck up everything?

O—Even our careers, our faulty little worlds.

SPF—DoDo, would you keep your foul mouth down?

O—Her mouth isn't foul; it's her soul that's foul dalring. As for the other parts of her body, I-, I didn't think she had any til I saw hed in that charming dress

this evening. By the way, you're tailored exquisitely. You almost look alive.

DD—You told me I had no lap. You said I had no lap.

O—You really are the lapless woman. Irving du Ball as a young woman.

D—Huh huh huh huh huh.

O—Just pinched   (pause) Zzzzzzzzzzzzap! Who's your chicker (?) Hu hu, gasp, ooh! Again. What's happeening? My throat's being taken over by somebody.

SPF—DoDo, will you pay the price for—

O—She'll, she'll pay the price for anything. You just have to ask her and she'll

D—No, I mean does she really, has anybody really really

O—She's a professional price payer.

D—Oh really?

O—Yeah, she's a rap taker.

D—A what?

O—There is, there are a group of people who uh, who uh, there are a group of people like that called rap takers. They will take the rap for certain crimes.

DD—Rat takers?

O—They will take the rap.

DD—Rat?

O—RaP takers. They'll take the rap for certain crimes and get paid for it and get paid for it, now, mind you.

(*Waiter*) Coffee over here.

O—Yes, n-, uh, no no, I'm not having anything anymore. I've been told off and no uncertain terms all over town. Why don't you pour the coffee over the egg?

DD—All right, I'm bar ely sorry.

B—Barely sor ry?

O—Imagine that, bar ely sorry she says.

B—Par tly sor ry.

O—Oh God (*as if exhausted*) Aren't you comfor table Sugar? You look like you're having a mar—

DD—Appar ently no t, I'm ver y ve r y sor ry I did it.

O—Don't be, Dor othy, we're sorr ier. (*Pause.*) Ohw (*as if in pain*) she's got me, America. Mr. and Miss Amer ica. I-, I've never, the her shoe is shar pened to a point, and o n the end of it is a-, my de er , well what do you have on your toenails? A li, a la, a s pike?

DD—You should see what I did to Don Rico.

O—You t old me Jim did that t o his ar m.

DD—I d id that to him.

O—Ohhhh, where's my Breck to damaged hair?

DD—What do you have in your book bag?

O—Br eck, for damaged hair.

DD—What e lse is i n your book bag?

O—I have a few piec- ar -ar icles of clothing. I was going to change thi-this evening. cause I was, I was r eading a-

DD—I heard that you've been changing all day long.

O—That's all I can do on some days is keep changing—

DD—Oh. Miss Dior I was thinking.

SPF—What, are you gonna do a dialogue thing for blowjob?

O—(*gasp*)

SPF—Or is it going t o be jus t sound ef fects?

O—Who's vulgar mouth is upsetting you?

SPF—That's an art film.

O—You've turned and so has Do-Oo's vulgar mouth. You've turned an entire table around; the way Blowjo b blew off a woman's hat off in the factory. Did you catch that, Billy, on the camera? the woman's hat going off whoooooops. Does anybody have a match? (*Cash register rings*) Oooh, like that; I know you have heart. Oh nevermind, here's a light. Thank lou, oh music! Beautiful. Just what we needed. (*Rock'n'roll emerges from the background.*) Now can we dance? (Have a pie honey bunch)

DD—This is the Sugar Plum Fairy song.

O—Ohhhh hohhhh DoDo (*a lot of noise and voices*)

SPF—I was talking to the girls that typed that thing.

O—Yeah, Risilee and uhhh

SPF—Rosilie and the other one.

O—Cappy.

SPF—And Cappy said uh h, I said, "What are you doing?"

O—In a rather, her faulty voice (*he raises his voice*) she said "It's worse than Henry Miller."

SPF—She said you hired her.

O—Yes.

SPF—And she said, there've been three of us working on this

O—Billy, may I please have a match again? Do you know what the thir one's name is? Brooki.

SPF—We only have three hours done; there's nine more to go.

B—Are you looking for a match again?

O—I need a light. I have to, I have this in front of me.

SPF—And she said something about Drella paying us.

O—She never said that, trouble maker.

SPF—She said—

O—I admire those girls because they were (pause) complete slaves.

SPF—No, she saidthat Drella said that "he'd take care of us."

DD—Take care of us?

SPF—But he, she said, "I can't imagine him taking care of us for this."

O—No, now don't say that

SPF—I swear to God.

O—because the girls even gave me a little crayola present.

SPF—That's what t hey said.

DD—A little caryo la pres ent? They made for you ?

O—The third one's name is Brooki.

DD—I don't thin they're girls at all.

O—They're not; they're dwarfs.

SPF—No, there was a boy that came with a handbag the other day.

O—A boy that came with a hand-bag?

DD—A beanie handbag?

B—It was one of their girlfriends.

O—Sure it wasn't one of their handbags ? Shoulder bags have become very stylish.

SPF—Who who was there last night?

O—Anybody hat-, DoDo, your be is relentless.

SPF—Who was there last night?

O—Where?

SPF—Was that Iris last night?

O—I, no, I du h I had o go to, I had to go o Rot ten Rita' s wih wih Dreltla and uh uh, uh Rink and he other one so I hadn't, and

who was i t, Moxanne and so uh, excuse me

D—Oh no no no no no no no no no no. (*Static.*)

O—Oh I have to ell them; we can't really.

B—N o, just speak in retrospec that's all to tell them.

O—How can you possibly speak in retrospect; I have never been there. DoDo, don't hide now.

SPF—I just lost the whole, the whole stream.

O—I, well I'm not going to explain it again because it's so bor— James, take my word for it, this is July 1966 and we're on West 86th street, this is Bickfords and you are sitting with

SPF—Thank God it's not Rotten Rita's.

O—I know, we just got out of there with our lives. She was about to push us into the bed. She's a mean mayor. (*With sarcasm*) Lake Impeletari indeed. Mmmmm-mmmm mmmmmm mmmmmm, pardon me darling, I was just humming my own Crotion na-tional anthem. Mmmmmmmm mmmmmm. Well, where to from here? All o-, how-, how much are these these tapes? They're very very expensive, hah? What price? What price? Ca-cause we may get a donation. No that is a lot of money, but we may get

DD—You're well worth it, On-dine.

SPF—I heard another tape, On-dine, that said that you were one of the founders of the mole as-sociation.

O—I was the president of the mole people for for a long time. You are one of the original moles you really are.

B—Oh I'm not the founder.

O—I was known as the president of, but Norman BILLARDBALLS is the

B—I don't want to be the founder.

O—No, you're not even a mole anymore.

SPF—What ever happened to Norman?

O—He's retired to the lower east side and he is painting billiard balls.

SPF—Still painting billiard balls?

O—Yes. He'll be painting, my mother's, my mother talked to him on the phone and thought that he painted the numbers on the billiard balls. She said to him, "Oh, I thought you pai—

B—When I first heard I thought he painted real, true billiard balls, that's his profession.

O—That's what she thought. Y'know I saw part of the album leap on your lap. (dishes crash)

SPF—Just like, you mean

O—Like Stanley Shell. It's getting so sickening in here I feel like I've been in a swamp. Oh here's your book back, thank you Ge-, u h uh uh, uh uh uh uh, Moxanne (pause) You got a little headache, huh? Maw? Got a little headach e? DoDo, you'd make an ex—

SPF—She's most

O—Low.

SPF—In the morning.

O—What an array of beauty.

SPF—Did you did you g et caught in the rain ?

O—No.

SPF—Jesus, did i t come down.

O—Ye ah, we h e ard i t, p itter

patter, pitter pat ter.

SPF—Splish splas h.

O—Pitter pa t te r pit ter patter. No, what's t h at, khat's the rain by telling you.

DD—That's t he dance of th e fairy prin ce.

O—Oh! That's the sound of the microphone dropping from Ondine, otherwise known as Barbarella's hen.

DD—Yes, Barbarella, Barbarella

O—That's Gerard's.

DD—You're Barbara and he's Drella.

O—Yes, the mother of Barbarella.

DD—Yes. Drella is the mother of Barbarella?

O—Yes, and ancient step sister or something.

DD—Drella is Drella.

O—No, you're not my mother Drella. You're the mother of all of us, but you're not, you're not mine. You're Ices, the new goddess.

DD—You're ices? Who is . . .

O—So are you dear. After drinking that coffee you're the one who looks sick.

B—No really, I said Ices, I said?

O—I said Ices. Listen darling, you're next and then-, all of us are a little said dear, but that's the price we pay for true fame.

B—True slices of life.

O—(laughing) True slices of life. (Gasp.)

DD—True slices?

O—Yes. Ohh, that's a new magazine, "True Slices of Life," the sado-masochistic true confes sional.

SPF—Can I have a cigarette please, out of my pocket?

O—Have one of my crunched

ones.

SPF—No, I might as well have one of mine—my crunched ones.

O—W. Sommerset Maugham presents Rain, no no no no, darling don't ruin your rouge; it's only a trick.

DD—My God, what is he doing?

O—It's hhot pepper, caliente caliente.

SPF—Those are the kind of things that get you kicked out of decent places.

O—Caliente.

DD—It's gonna go up in flames.

O—(screams) Aaaaaah, eeeeeek, oooooh, have you ever seen steel or glass burst into flames?

SPF—A malatov vocktail.

O—With a Russian dres-, imagine the next pepra isn't that divine? That's one of the nicest things I've ever done. I'm so pleased with it, oh - don-don't take it out Jim, please. It's so simple.

B—Right, the only way it is

DD—What?

B—Well you know the way it is.

O—You've just ruined another trick. (*Sniffles.*) My new tobacco pepper is—

SPF—What are you doing oh ow ow ow tonight?

O—Something that you'll ruin obviously, like you just ruined that effect. The next person to come here would have really gotten it, Bill.

14 / 2

O—DoDo didn't even have a lap. You expec ther to have rashes? (*DoDo is laughing—sounds like baaaa baaaa*) Listen, can we get out of here?

SPF—Yeah.

O—Cause I'm getting depressed.

DD—Where are we going?

O—To the church around the corner. We're—

SPF—You should have heard Ondine singing awaay last night at the piano bar and said, "Play something chic, play something chic."

O—He's talking about himself. I sat there and said, "I can't sing my part." You said smart.

SPF—I didn't say smart. You said smart. And what were you singing?

O—And he he played something that-, is that Taylor Mead or a young assistant? I see a . . .

SPF—Monkey . . . from Savanna he was singing.

O—He was playing a vamp that was particularly uh, archaic and Joe went into a review and "aaaaaa," I said, "Play that again." The guy played it again and he screamed and it was the man's first night. (*Everyone laughs.*) Oh it was really cruel.

DD—Oh, do they have new entertainment there?

O—Ohh, it was his first night and we really christened him.

SPF—He had never been there before and the waiter said that he was horrifie

O—He was gree-, he was green when we started making . . .

DD—What did you do to him? What did you do to him?

O—Well Jim did a couple of acts that were—, the the the big finish was the big roller skater. He had this enormous roller skate and skated right around the piano top.

B—How did the Norwegian sailors at the uh, did you ever find them?

O—And wthe waiter sang very very loud, "They're not chicken; one is about 37 and the other," ooh *everyone laughs*). It's really one, that kind of place you know and Jim was throwing rose petals at them every minute. "What are they drinking?" he said.

SPF—Oh what beautiful roses.

O—"To begin with," he said, then the waitress came over and said, "Well, they're very tired my dear," and Jim Jim Jim said, "Let them buy us a drink."

SPF—I didn't ask for a drink.

O—No, you said, "Let them buy us a drink." Them.

SPF—Who?

O—No darling, please you're confused. Now don't worry about it. I've got everything right in my little brain. Didn't I get you, didn't I get you to Solly's last night? Get get you corn on the cob which was rare?

SPF—I remember that.

B—Rare corn on the cob?

SPF—Did you cook last night?

O—I certainly did.

DD—And worse and worse and nothing but cheap tricks. You got that too didn't you?

O—What cheap tricks? Y-y-you, do you mean happy? That wasn't cheap. There's nothing cheap about happy.

SPF—He was all but the state teacher's college. I tried to impress that upon him, DoDo.

DD—And he thinks that society is a standard of quality.

SPF—But the bartenders.

O—Bartenders are okay.

SPF—And he's a nice looking boy isn't he?

O—Well, a sorta, that that that (pause) that happy look.

DD—Well I see for advanced age you can't be too fussy can you?

O—He's not what I call completely and utterly class.

B—New Paltz is better than Albany.

O—New Paltz, Betty Nahser has her own farm. I'd love to visit it.

B—Grow sweaters?

O—She grows big brown sweaters.

SPF—Betty Johnson.

O—Betty Brownsweater, an enormous girl.

SPF—You aren't speaking to us tonight.

O—You're not speaking very little. She just holds, she's a non-participant ala Irving du Ball. Do you want to leave a cig-, what a question to ask a person who's leaving. (*They laugh.*)

DD—Did you jay for your food?

SPF—No, I didn't.

O—Well then you're—

DD—Yes?

O—I tried to pay for mine; here's my dollar and I wasn't, I wasn't allowed. They whisked me off. Oh, I love this feather boa I had. I've got a folder, I've got a folder.

(*Someone says something.*) No, I want mine now. Like Callas' voice.

DD—My God, what was that?

O—It was my mother's wedding dress and I thought I'd bring it along to Tiptin. Tiptin's never seen a wedding gown like this. This is a sacrificial garment darling, This is the thing that Doo will go up in.

SPF—That's fruital　cloth?

O—No, it's the amazing plastic woman. I wish my sunglasses hadn't broken. I'm thoroughly terrified of facing the night without sunglasses.

SPF—A dollar sixty-eight!?

O—Yes, you're n-n . . . dear.

B—. . . ice-cream.

SPF—Oh I see.

O—Oh. So actually he's paying for-, here, take a—

B—Joe's paying for everything.

SPF—What's this?

O—That's, that's it!

SPF—Oh no, you didn't have anything.

O—That's all right. I had things before.

SPF—No, there's nothing on here.

O—James there was another check before you got here. Now c'mon c'mon.

SPF—Yes but you

O—Your jacket your jacket, don't forget it. Where should we go?

SPF—I don't know.

O—What should we do? It's steaming hot out there like a plant.

D—Oh, isn't it?

O—It's lifle a clam shell. You suddenly be a-. I'm not going into any other place like a donut mart or a barge bin. Let's go to Le

Pompier; that would be fabulous.

DD—You want to go there?

O—Oh my dear

DD—screaming and carrying on?

O—They couldn't believe us.

DD—But do you think they'd let you in again?

O—We could wreck it, let's go.

DD—Do you thing they would let you in again?

O—Of course. They wouldn't dare let-, they c, how could they say no?

B—(*curtly*) No.

O—I mean I'm all grubby and my toenail's are-, I'll rush into the bathroom and get it all done (*pause*) quickly. I'll bathe in the sink. (*Honk, honk.*) Uggh! I broke a fingernail.

DD—Do you know who called me up yesterday?

B—(*imitating*) Who? Who called you up yesterday?

O—Who?

DD—Earl.

(*D, B, SPF and O together*) Earl?

B—(*falsetto*) Earl?

O—You better tell the Sugar Plum Fairy that. She knew Earl better than any of us.

SPF—Do you know who she went to bed with?

DD—Oh! Don't don't don't

O—Oh yes, yes.

DD—Don't don't don't don't don't

SPF—DoDo I'm sorry, okay, I'm, oh, I I, okay, awright awright awright, I'm sorry.

O—(*in a low voice*) Now you'll have to tell us, now you'll have to tell us.

SPF—I didn't mean it that way. I once started with her (*They're all talking at once.*)

O—DoDo, now that's not fair,

DoDo.

B—If, if I have an interest, if I have an interest you have to cultivate a . . .

DD—He repeats everything.

O—You tell us DoDo, please. You heard everything that there is to hear about me.

B—by showing all aspects.

O—I make it available. Will you please tell us now and spare-, in wide embarrassment tell us please. I-I-I would be delighted to.

DD—I'll tell, tell my good friends. I don't care.

O—Tell.

A—Really? Is it all right?

O—Yes.

A—No no, don't tell, I won't tell.

O—She doesn't care, please.

DD—Al.

O—Al?

D—Is it all right DoDo?

DD—No, it's all right because the two of them were standing and watching.

O—Oh Al! The one in the Air Force.

B—Now what's so terrible? I think that's terrific.

DD—He's the one in the Air Force.

SPF—He's not in the Air Force.

O—Oh, it was one of the Sugar Plum's uh, room mates. I knew that months ago.

B—Is he the one who came to the factory and brought me lunch?

O—Oh, well then you can, you can answer this question. Is it IBM or isn't it? Is that Miss Iiddy Biddy Meat?

SPF—You should have heard the way she . . .

(DD & O) What?

SPF—He said, "I thought I was being nice to your friends."

O—Well he wasn't; he was rude.

DD—Wasn't he?

SPF—Look at the way they left the table.

D—Oh, we didn't, we didn't leave anything?

O—Uh, poor table, poor table.

SPF—Well I hope not.

(They are all talking at once.)

SPF—I don't know. There's a madame, there's a madame in there. (They're all talking again.)

O—Let's go to Le Pompier. Uhhhh

SPF—There's a madame inside with a care   transplant.

B—(singing) There's a madame waiting for. .

SPF—And his name is Arthur Adventure and he's had a . . . . . "could have lined up a few things for you," and I said I'm not in that business anymore, thank you.

O—I'm opening a shop in Tiptin darling.

SPF—He's sitting, he sitting with his back to you.

O—Tell me about his house needs. Was it big or small? Sugar? Big or small? The one that DODO Mae went to bed with. Did he have big meat or small meat?

DD—I didn't, I didn't go to bed.

O—She said to ask you about the size of his meat.

SPF—Transplant of what?

DD—I didn't I didn't know he was, did you know he was house boy?

SPF—Yes!

DD—How did you know that? Did you know him?

SPF—Yes!

DD—Oh I didn't, you didn't tell me that.

SPF—or

D—Transplant of what?

O—Hair.

SPF—Oh, all right, ear   did you know that? Did you know that?

O—Oh let's—move on! Why must we stand in front of the dive?

B—Yah.

SPF—Yah.

DD—You didn't tell me that. Why didn't you tell me that?

O—(gasp) It's another rambling ambulance . . . Shall we go to Le Pompier? (pause) Oh isn't that dog cunning? . (Honk.) (Traffic.) (Under his breath) . . . I'm sure he doesn't know, I-, the tragedy of his life was lack of meaning; it would have to be.

SPF—Ondine!

B—   Woof woof.

SPF—Ondine!

O—What?

SPF—Ondine, are they made well?

O—What?

SPF—Uh, the, the uh

O—Here? They were heaven.

SPF—Mar-Marguerita.

O—They were heaven they were heaven. I had one this afternoon. The man, do you know how the man tried to put the salt on the glass?

D—Yeah.

O—He took the salt shaker and was trying to pour it on the rim. I said cannot make it like than and I had to take the salt shaker out of his hand.

SPF—He was shaking salt on the rim?

O—This was this afternoon at this bar over here.

D—Well do we take a big cab or uh?

O—No no, we just go to 3rd and Thompson; let's go.

D—Oh.

O—Yeah, oh, yes, heaven. Nice, quiet.

SPF—I love the park.

O—I do too, under its—

D—Ondine, you have, you have no idea, you have no idea, you don't know what's going to be.

O—In Tiptin?

DD—No, coming back from Americas.

D—Oh, you can't go because you're in, the star of the movie. We have

SPF—No, I'm not a star.

D—Oh, uh

O—Oh Sugar, stop it. You know damn well you've been a star for years.

D—We have Ondine in it.

O—Here, take my ring, I—, you can have my ring, honestly, please take. And here, take this this too.

(Bum) It's on 49th and 3rd avenue; it only takes ten minutes from here.

SPF—I don't take all that.

O—Would you.

SPF—No, you've never been there before.

(Bum) It's where I live, 149th and 3rd avenue.

SPF—Well it doesn't take ten minutes.

B—Well, why aren't you home in bed?

SPF—Here.

(Bum) Mister, I wanna thank you very much.

SPF—Sure. He has a pretty ass.

O—. . . that boy's need. Written all over his face. I had to give that ring, the ring that I treasured.

B—You know what I'd do? I'd give

him a subway token. Then he can't do anything.

O—I slipped him. I hate bums.

D—Huh huh.

O—I hit a bum on this corner once because

D—He aws a dope addict.

O—because the man asked me, he said, "Do you have any money?" And I said, I gave him my most contemptuous no, I said, "No-o-o", and he spit at me.

D—(*gasp*) Oh.

O—And an enormous oyster was hanging off my coat. So I had a package with me and I hit him on the side of the head with the package and he fell down on the floor. It must have really connected and I, I said some incredibly archaic line like, "Now you'll abide by . . . (*Dodo is laughing.*) Oh.

D—Uh hu hu hu hu.

O—That is the entire second floor of Barton's chocolates. Oh, who's in here? (*Singing.*) Go to sleep and

SPF—Wouldn't it be funny if there was?

O—Oh y-, the Bowery is hilarious; they're tucked in under hydrants and everything; they're very exclusive.

DD—Cuba.

O—Peuter? Who said peuter?

D—Look at that. What beautiful eyes.

O—Who Jim?

D—Yeah.

O—Sugar is a glorious body. It's a pity all tha-, all tho-, all that, that whole standard went out.

D—Uh huh huh huh, what standard's that?

O—Oh, st-, human turd!

D—Where?

O—Fertilizing their plants with shit. Oh my God. Oh! Nauseous. (*Speechless.*) I had such a fainting spell.

D—Where do you get your uh, Sunday Telegram?

O—Balls.

D—Mh hm hm hm.

O—Where do you get your Sunday Telegram? From Western Union, where—

D—No no no, where do you, Billy?

B—What about my Sunday Telegram?

D—You have, you you, you have two Sunday Telegrams.

B—I, I don't have any.

D—No no, the Sunday Telegrams.

O—I don't have any.

D—You know, the uh, the uh, the London *Times*, the *Telegrams*.

O—If you people put me in the bins after these tapes

B—Oh, you mean the weekend magazines?

D—Yeah.

DD—Ooh ooh ooh ooh. Look look look look.

SPF—Hanging up i the wall.

O—What?

D—What?

B—The guy who was at the

D—He brought those two and that's all?

B—He gave me one to show me what the magazine was like.

D—Yeah.

B—Then I . . . lying around.

O—If you Drella, people com-, if you people after after this tape is finished, put me in the bins I'll be very (*laughs*) you're sopping all away with you magic name I'll be very annoyed.

D—What?

O—I don't need the bins.

D—What bins? Hold it.

O—This is the Swichidio Hotel. This is where, do you remember you walked Erik around the park —you and Curt, right?

D—Yeah. Oh, did you hear what Curt said with those magazines?

B—What magazines?

D—I don't know.

B—What did he say?

SPF—He said how awful America was.

O—Oh how colored. Oh Curt needn't be so ridiculous about it. (*Talking at once*) Who Curt? (*Music in background.*) Who was playing with you when you were asleep?

DD—That bartender from New Paltz.

O—Darling, I fucked with you when you were asleep.

DD—New Paltz.

O—New Paltz State Teachers, we're all for uh- (*voices*) exactly.

SPF—You know that DoDo is right.

O—Certainly, you would be too if you saw people try to take your life. Gerard's not really frightened though; he's just mean.

SPF—It's called that as a russe.

O—Charlotte.

DD—You've never been known for your perception.

O—You've never been known for your percetpion she said. (*Singing.*) I stroll through the wood where it would do us good. (*Pause.*) Oh, doesn't the park look divine with the mist coming up over the elephant house? (*Someone . says . something.*) Sure.

D—You are?

O—Yeah, as long as you walk with me.

D—Oh really?

O—Yeah, as long as you're not sick   or anything.

D—Who said that?

O—But there are different groups that just don't pay a bit of attention to it. Yo uthink someone might take us for a strolling paper or something?

D—Huh ha ha ha ha.

O—A wandering, a straggling newspaper. Oh well.

SPF—It's not even funny Ondine.

O—I know, but what do you do? I like to pretend.

DD—. . . why would Ann Sullivan say?

O—Lower your voice darling, you're in a public park and the elephant house is on th ehorizon. If you speak too loud you can spend a week in front of the urinal there, they smell so unbearable. Now don't pull too quickly DrEL-luh, because my entire left tit will come out and mars will be—

SPF—What is your home town Drella?

B—   Shirley Maas.

O—Kingsport, Pennsylvania, y-, my gra-, my grandmother and-, he knows

DD—. . .   falls.

O—(*reprimanding*) Chagrin falls! Chagrin never aflls my dear; it only drops. Tiptin! Pennsylvania. It only drops.

D—Really?

SPF—Yes.

D—Where?

O—Tiptin, Pennsylvania. Hello Connelville   Is right outside of Erwin.

SPF—Uh, is fifty miles

O—The limit.

B—Didn't . . . call?

D—Oh.

O—Did she?

B—I think so—recently.

O—Yeah, she she she did, green eyes. I'm so glad she went.

SPF—It used to be a coal mining town. I think al lthe coal is gone.

O—What about Olga Troscova? (Drella laughs.) Did she finally die?

SPF—Who?

O—The woman who p layed Joan of Arc. (Someone is going ooooo-oooo.) The pha— (laughs)

DD—She, all of a sudden she died.

SPE—Y'know what, y'know what I want to do to make us some money?

D—Yeah.

O—No one would like us.

SPF—We could do a musical play from uh

O—Of what? My Pustural? What did you say? Of who? A musical version of what (Someone mutters something.) What is-, oh don't be ridiculous, musical? Who would write the music? Oh! I just stepped in something soft and slimy. It was Dorothy's drapes. (Laughing.) Dorothy's draper.

D—Why don't you walk through the john?

O—Because we wanna get that lovely aroma while she's. We want all of Amer-, we want all of America to, DoDo, DoDo would you do me a favor darling please and let me wear that and save my life? Cause you don't need it cause you're covered beautifully. That's it. Ugh! all

over mud. Oh! What a horrid feeling.

B—(imitating) Oh, guys, what a horrid feeling.

O—You're not allowed to un-un-undress in New Jersey y' know y'know. You're not allowed to, we've been, what country, where what? Let's get a place to country, let's take them with us.

D—Uh hu hu.

SPF—Hm hm hm.

O—That's the special riot squad and we're all under arrest. Dorothy fir-, of course everybody is.

DD—You have a chance of getting

O—I was spose ta live in that belfry.

D—Ohhh.

OJust over here for one second honey, I wanna splash in this puddle. (Sound of water being stepped into.)

D—(gasp)

O—Oh heaven.

DD—Are you gonna make it again with your your smart, your your your your, for your fantastically intellectual bartender.

O—(gasp) Oh now don't get snied   about Catholics.

DD—He's not very fussy. I mean you can't. . . . .

B—   You better give up that act, DoDo.

O—If you do, if you do, DoDo, you'll never see that rising over here in the morning like the sun. Wha-, open up we want NICO's autograph.

D—Uh huh huh. Oh no, does NICO write anymore?

O—Yeah.

SPF—Sure.

D—Oh yes?

O—He forges. He doesn't write

anymore; he forges.

D—Oh, shall we get five more dollars or?

B—Yes.

O—All he does is buy LSD capsules with it you know. (*Everyone's talking at once.*)

SPF—. . . . . Church of Christ, what kind of a

O—I was supposed to live in this belfry.

SPF—You *have* lived in it.

O—No, I wished I had.

D—. . . downstairs.

O—Oh I lived downstairs in it for a while yeah.

DD—I thought you lived in the belfry.

O—Yes, this is where you drove me one day. I was gonna live in the belfry with Oreo.

DD—Because you're a bat.

O—I know you love bats. That's the only, that's the only thing that attracts you to me.

DD—I'm mad about bats.

O—It's open I think, Billy. It's, I wonder if it's open. DoDo, try the door quickly. (*Pause.*)

DD—It's open.

O—We could go and sit in the Judson lounge and cause a RIIot. They would ge so sick. Oh, you should see the inside of it; it's just a hell hole (*laughs*). You should have been into some of those dances. Drella, you should have been to the last dance.

SPF—. . . description of

D—What?

O—I'll give you, no, I'll give you, I'll let you see the copies of it. That's all I can do is that. Uh, you should have—

D—What did you bring back to Pachard Gappett?

O—The Pachard Gat . . .

(YODELING IN BACK-GROUND: O LAY-DEE-OOOOO)

D—Oh cannons?

B—Barry Corn

O—Barry Corn

B—Yeah.

O—So it is!

(*Voice in background*) Who is that?

O—On-, Billy NAME, Ondine, Drella.

(*Voice*) . . . Billy NAME

O—An entire art movement.

D—The Sugar Plum Fairy.

O—The Sugar Plum Fairy and the murderers.

DD—The Sugar Plum Fairy.

O—Ennui! (*Laughs.*)

DD—You said ennui, Ondine?

O—They're coming out after us darling. They can't believe it. What? Oh, well I'm being the domestic again.

D—Aren't they?

O—What's with it? DoDo, you horor, here's the rag I gave you to protect yourself with.

DD—Oh that's. . . . . .on the grass.

O—Well, that's as blue as you think of it. (*Pause.*) (*Billy is singing.*) (*Ondine singing.*) Here's the bag I love so much. There's the bag my mother wore. And here's the bag that grandma-, hm, there is le Pompy-A.

D—Where?

O—Over heea. And that's over there.

D—We have the light, Can we take a cab?

O—It's right there!

D—Oh.

O—Right next to ,right next to the fire hydrant.

DD—What makes you . . . . . Drella. So it is.

O—It's a fire hydrant! Look! An op car.

D—An op car?

O—Yeah.

D—Where?

O—Op. (*Laughs.*) Oh, it's oh, my dear, I have faulty vision.

SPF—Listen, this is a very posh place.

O—Well, we're very posh people. (*DoDo laughs.*) I mean we're very (*softly*) posh.

DD—We're . . . important don't you think?

D—Is there too much noise there? Oh, there's a lot of noise.

O—There's a piano. Oh and it's

D—Is that all?

O—Yeah.

DD—I don't think we can get into this place.

B— . . . had a fire would the firemen come if they knew . . .

O—Everybody knows me. They look at me coming in and go, "Oh yes, he's very," I hate you too, but this place . . . ruined! 'Well we'll go in and if you don't like it we'll go right out.

SPF—Just turn around and walk right out.

O—Go ahead. Yes, it's never like this. (*Door squeaks open.*) (*Voices sound hollow.*) I don't hear a noise.

DD—Go ahead Ondine.

SPF—You go first; you're a girl.

D—You go first. (*Pause.*) (*Squeaking.*) (*Music emerges.*) . . . . . .

O—It's not too loud. Where's my other bag?

D—Where's your bag?

O—It's on my shoulder. It's not too loud. (*Pause.*)

DD—Ondine,

O—*There's* Drella, ha ha. Shall we have a seat?

DD—Let's not sit there, Billy.

O—Let's sit up there or over here.

SPF—Why not just sit over here?

O—Good. Come over this way. Come then.

DD—Ondine—(*Music starts blasting.*)

O—There's only four chairs there. (*Music: Beach Boys*) (*Above the noise*) Don't press me—just drink. (*Lots of noise.*) *That's* Andy Warne (*voices*) *It* was sort of nice of him to, you know uh, be . . .

SPF—What did they say?

O—I think it was a charming remark.

D—Really?

SPF—Do you know Gino's gallery?

O—Darling, would you tell me how this thing is recording?

D—Huh?

O—I think, I think I pulled something out. Is it all right? (*Pause*) It's okay. Tell me tell me . . . (*Music*) DoDo, I love you.

DD—I love you, Ondine. (*Music*) (*Noise.*) I want you to wear it.

O—Darling, it s . . . . . I don't want anything . . .

DD—What?

O—I don't want this underneath it.

DD—Take it off. (*Music*) (*Fades.*)

O—Oh zzzaa. Say a few words? All right. A few words, Must that juke box

SPF—Shhh.

O—Did you come over last night? —Yeah.

O—How are you? —Fine.

O—Happy, this is Drella and

DoDo.

DD—This is such a momumental repeating knife.

O—Don't mind her; she's a terrified murderess. (*Music.*) By the way, that's DoDo Mae Doom. This is Happy and this is Drella Happy.

O—Happy, what's your name?

HAPPY—Darling, I'd love it. They were gonna let us do it.

O—What's your name?

H—Happy.

O—No, you're real name.

H—New . . . Paul . . . Saint . . . they used to call me.

— . . . state, N. L. U. and the New School.

O—Darling, you're

—And a whole semester at Columbia . . . (*noise*)

O—And Billy, this is Happy. (*Four Seasobs*)

B—. . . my nose, and he said "Which nose?" and I said, "The right nose," and he leaned into the darn bureau and said, "Uh, how do yhey say in America, uh, uh, I don't know," and I said, "I'd don't know either."

DD—Who was the man woh down and see it. Take your clothes off and dance up here.

O—All this grovel up here. (Four Seasons) Hold this like this cause then. . (Ondine singing shrilly with the F. Seasons) Is it plugged in?

DD—It's not plugged in.

O—It's plugged in, DoDo.

—She knows Bobby. . . . .Fire Island, , ,to write you. .

DD—Listen, you know everything you hear you, ...and, I mean, you are so audal (?). They did *not* go out together, and you

know damn well they didn't.

—I didn't say they went out, I said they're going out.

O—You said they went.

DD—You said they went.

O—DoDo has a tendency. . . . . . (Four Seasons with sing alongs) . . . .DoDo.

DD—What are you *doing*, Ondine?

O—. . . .does not stretch all the way, i must have. . . .take these

DD—May I come?

O—Really, would you? We'd really appreciate it. . . . .(Billy and the Four Seasons)

DD—. . . . . .big enough?

O—Yes, it's it's going to working. Oh, Arnold Inoven ?—. . . . . . they turned him away. O—Lady Birth Defect. DD—They turned who away? O—Lady Birth Defect. (laughing) —Lady Birth Defect. Oh. D—Oh. (In unison) Oh. DD— (*Squeals*) O—. . . . I didn't. . . . it on you dear, —I just tripped over somebody's —Mine doesn't have any salt. DD—Spit on it. ?— Voila. _—Mine doesn't have any salt on the ribbon. DD—Now you see this was a long song and dance you told us about last night. O— Oh, if mine doesn't have salt, t-through a snit fit. —Salt. O—Oh please, you mustn't (*Herman's Hermits,*

—Don't look at me so guilty. I just order the drinks and they come to me.

—Well, tell her . . . go to the bar.

O—And a little sauce. I'll do it, I promise you. Please just do. I can't do it with a bit in the glass. ?— You do it . . .O—I can't. . . .I can't, I can't- —I don't know. . . . . I don't. . . . . O—Take my advice, ... —XX I'll tell you

what, ... (*Hermits and noise*)
lights be going down. O—Why
must I be disputed with? I said
you can do it like thois. I *know*
what I'm talking about. . . . . .
sure I do, my dear, and no matter how you argue. . . . You will
not convince anyone. . . . .oh

Gerard Crow and look at the
plastic pants, you'll not convince
a *soul*, but you know. . . .DD—
Ondine! O—Shut up, DoDo before
I belt you. DD—All right, it's all
right, I, I, I'm going to fix it for
you. O—It's done. No, it's done—
and she really did a nice thing.
Give me a kiss, I'm sorry. But
you know I hate to be made a
fool of in my own backyard. . . .
. . .very . . . . they should be kind
one and all. (*Hermits*) Is the
tape over? (*Hermits*) Oh God
bless you, bless you. DD—Ach!
(*like quakk*) O—Oh my God......
that. —No that's all right. (*Baby
baby,*
beat?) O—You're an angel. ?—
What happened to all those glasses
you said you wanted another glass,
didn't you? O—Oh no, just one
glass. —Just one glass, in case anybody else wants to pour this. . . .

uh

how's that? ?—These are marvelous
machines. 625 people. D—Oh.
(*clink*) 25c. I'll give you 25 cents.
(*noise*) 25c . . . . . Oh heaven....
salt, it doesn't taste good without
salt. Oh Drella you *can't*. I refuse
to drink it if you. . . .without salt.
Della please, ... it's delicious.
oh. . .drink it without the stuff. Oh
Drella you must, for *me*, well I
won't drink mine then, I just won't
drinkt it. All right, I'll have it with
salt. All right, you're gonna sup
this as though its' . . . . . . pleeese-
All right all right okay okay ALL

RIGHT I'll do it I'll do it Sugar
give him one. (*Music*) no no *Now,
hold it, now give me That's it,
now give me the glass. Wasn't
that* Delnnos van. . . . .? What?
Severin-s-e-v-e *music* in J. Church

15 /   1

O—Are we recording? . . . This is on?

BN—Yes

O—DoDo, shut up. You were expecting a head of us a minute ago

RN—(*muffled laughter*) D-DoDo, shut up

O—I'm leaving, I don't care if you aren t. I-tsa. . .I ftel likean Asshole. Compleer-. .

DD—It figures.

O—Whaddya mean, figures?

BN—Whyda. . .Why don t you see if you can get the taxi driver to-uh. . . come to Henry s?

O—Well, he. . .wellhe. .Well, he said he Wo-oo-ould

BN—Chow mein, isthat his name?

O—Whatsisname?

BN—Chow. . .peterpottermane. . .Chow mein. Sparafucile

O—I don t know about the taxi driver—he looks like a cop.   . . . There —we're at Henry's C mon in. DoDo, . . .

BN—Lets do it again

O—ALL right, let s go b-back dow-dow-down. . . HERE weare down-town, . . . at the—whats the name of that place, the tu-the Twelfth of Always?

BN—(*Simultaneous with last part of Ondine's last statement*) . . .posi-tuck . . .

O—An, now yhre back at hen-Henry s again,, well, here we are

RN—Well. . She s baked cookies.

O—And now we re at the factory. Good heavens—this is fast

BN—Hey, Ondine, you can tell that we we re really right up There, the way we re talking

O—We re talk-. . .We use speed. ... We use Speed, don t we?

BN—Ye-e-e-eah, ..an I mean that

O—I guess it s nat that good, huh? I don t particularly like the way I m talking or feeling right now

BN—(heh heh) I feel ve-eh-ery, unh. . . . .

O—I feel bored—mundane—horrible

BN—The word that s frequently applied to the Youth of the Nation

O—What?

BN—It s notaword I could use

O—Lost?

BN—No

O—WHAT is it-uh. . .

BN—Uh, a lack of-uh. . .

O—Oh, PURPOSEless.

BN—Naaoooo, it s. . .it s one of each. It means-uh these. . .type. . .family words. It means uh. . . . .a certain kind of, uh. . .

O—WithOUT. . .apathetic. . . .

BN—withOUT EMPATHY. . . .I have no EMpathy

O—Th-That s what your feel--you feel una-. . .

BN—Unempathetic?

O—You feel Unempathetic, right?

BN—No. I think it s a different word. That s thy WORD?

O—I dunno

BN—whoKNOws? Nuh-nuh-nahpathetic?

O—Duh-duh-Does it mean. . .? Do YOU mean to convey that you feel empathetic? Not empa-..

BN—Not empathetic. Non-emptahy is not empathetic.

O—Yeah, I thought so. That s what I mean, you...

BN—But there s no word for that

O—I KNOW, zut you isa-...

BN—Well, whatISit?

?

16 /   1

D—What?

O—I never said anything like that. C'est la guerre.

C—. . . the ney Salon inn.

D—What's that?

O—Welcome to Bombay and he's just in time for the tidal raid.

D—What is shini-suck?

O—Shini Town, Jew town.

D—Ohh.

O—He's, he's he, you know he's . . . politely he's a dwarfed Shini sucker. He's a sense of glee, that's what . . . (*loud opera in foreground*)

B—Are you going to have an exhibit at the Jewish Museum or not No.

B—. . . painting at the Jewish Museum . . . I used to work for him . . . 85 ft. painting at the Jewish Museum.

DD—It's done by the guy who did the, uh, spaghetti.

D—Really?

Yah.

DD—I used to work for Sambo.

D—Oh really? Oh.

DD—He's very stupid.

D—(*worried*) Everybody's taking off their clothes.

DD—What?

Everybody's taking off

DD—I'm not gonna take off my clothes.

JC—Did you do this?

D—No. (*Opera.*)

DD—NOT only are they taking off their clothes, they're looking at themselves in the mirror.

JC—Is that painted?

D—No, that's a print.

DD—No, from a comic strip or—

D—No, it's just technique. It's Roy Lichtenstein.

DD—But what's he do to it? I mean, how does he make it?

D—It's uh, it's his way of doing it.

DD—No, I know that, but how, how, how but hoe would you do this if you had to do it?

D—. . . did it with a, with a mask. Whyn't, whyn't ya tell us about this? Do you know anything about this?

O—This is sownisdownat the Jewish (*with laughs*)

D—Oh, oh, you don't know anything about these.

O—No, I have never had anything to do with this, I, I, don't know anything about that. I just know about the Andy Warhol's that are around.

D—Oh . . .

O—Mucous?

D—Mucous.

O—Becau . . . noise . . . it's the greatest film ever written and we're the greatest stars of all times—we are the great stars of all time. Do do . . . all right. (*Opera.*)

DD—I think this is terribly beautiful.

O—It's gor-geous. (Opera.) That's not bad. Shut up you skinny fink What do you think this . . . Isn't it fantastic how all these places look like how all these places look lige Atlantic Beach . . . (voices drowned out by music.)

DD—What what?

O—I am.

DD—YOU are—

O—. . . I jump. . . in my shorts (laughs), imagine having shorts (Opera) and I don't wanna. . .   DD—You what?   O—. . . . be very close to . . . . all the time- (opera) (Ondine muttering)   DD—Oooh. Don't be so serious.   O—That's not even Enid. Just listen a minute.   DD —What?!   O—. . . . . . look look look look! I want you to hear tht voice.   D—What?   O—I want you to hear . . . . voice. (Opera). . DD—uch . . . . such . . . friendly.   O—Since, since, she's a past-.

DD—Oh really? On the informant of what   O—Do you, do you ever hear . . . . Ann . . . . (Opera) . . . to expresion- watch out there, now. (Music) . . . with those shoes . . . Is that for Heaven Streets . . . I don't care.   D—It really is, isn't it?   O—It's a feminine under garment.   D—Is it?   O—Let's discuss . . . getting fat.   D—Huh. O—She's . . . fat . . . terrible, everybody . . . . Do what? . . . . I don't want to.   D—You laughed at your face over the weekend.   O— That's, that's because I'm terrified, just terrible.   D—Why?   O— And then those three come in and at what price.   D—Oh, well, I don't really care.   O—One price.   D—Uht, uh, how come . . . . with uh, well how can you still eat; y'know, like, I mean, doesn't it now make you hungry?   O—I have, I have organic . . . ooooooohhhhsamea D—How do we get Billy back at the factory?   O—He's, he's back already.   D—But how can we make it look like this?   O—We have to get rid of sloppiness.   D—Oh, yeah, oh Billy . . ! (opera) Please get rid of sloppiness at the factory   O—And that means Gerard Malanga. D—No, I can't . . .   B—"i thought, without . . . people who just come in   D—Why, how do we do that?   O—By a very strict, uh, code of rules.   D—No, I can't . . .   O—I know, darling, you want, I don't know what to say, Drella, except that, the only thing that will happen is that it will really be just better for Jerry- and his poetry, too. B—I'm going into the colset door-   O—You belong there- No, I'm serious,   B—All right.   O—Because Jerry's poetry is less than he even thinks it should be. That's that's a pity, because he wants to be a poet. All right, if he wants to be a poet, let him suffer. There's no poetry without suffering.   D—Oh I know that's true . . . . told him   O—Nonr- you can't walk up to somebody you can't walk up to somebody and just suddenly say,

"Oh hello, I'm a poet." D—Yeah. O—And that's that. D—Well, it has to be the other way, or so, , well it has to be so the other O—Yeah. D—But he isn't. He's really not suffering. O—But he is suffering. D—Is he? O—Yeah, he's being, but he, but the but the torture that's torturing him is the tarture of the businessman. D—Oh yeah, oh. O—It's not the torture of the man who sees his fellow man in torment. D—No really, Ondine, cares so much that we can O—I love him. D—(*quickly*) Wh- can we what can we really do with, I mean let's find his career. O—Okay, I'd love to. D—What should we do? I mean, how can we really, uh- O—What can we do? D—. . that's a pain. Yeah, ho, how can we really, uh. O—Help him? D—Yetah. I mean, what kind of poetry do you think he should write? O—I gave him amphetamine, I gave him amphetamine one night, when when D—Recently? . . . O—I first met him. D—No no, a long time ago. O—and he was a frightening poetry D—Yeah, but O—He wrote poetry that he hadn't preconceived. D—Yeah. O—He wrote poetry, he wrote poetry D—It scared him very much. O—It scared him, . . . D—He's been on LSD,and uh, pills and uh every O—Baby, it doesn't matter. D—It doesn't matter, well well- O—Why why why don't yo have to take pills? D—Huh? O—Wht don't you have to t-t-t-ake drugs? Why isn't it a necessity for you to take drugs? D—Oh. O—Why, because you D—Well, no, I O—You're high as you are . . . Hello? WhO's caluing? Buchess oh, Duchess lover, it's Ondine. D—Tell her that we . . . before. O—On come over, Duchess it was so sweet, it was so swe t talking to you like that. When we called you the last time. Don't you remembre it? Oh, it was, come over! Oh, please come over. (*pause*) We have tons of Chmampagne. D—There's tons of champagne. O—There aretons of champagne, Lots a shit, come over- okay, byebye. (*hangs up*) Now that was a bit of fraud- I don't even D—Is she coming? O—She may come. I don't know, she's very (blah) uhhhuhh, oh, her Rotten won't see her. D—Oh, Rotten(s coming. O—Rotten couldn't be contacted the last . . . . minutes. Did you get the cigarettes? D—No. O—What can we do for Garard Malanga is really in essence, what can Garard Malanga do for himself, this phrase,—(Sings with record) it's so ,(*opera*) gorgeous. D—Uh, what what can we really do, for, uh, Gerard? O—Uh, I on't think, I, I, I, don't think. We're we're not seen to be stupid. I don't know what can be done for anybody, really. And nei-neither do you. You know you and I think alike in so many things, and you know I just got to know you so recently. The first tije I ever got an inkling about you was when I told you on the phoen about that silly occurance with . . . . , and I understood you, really humanly forthe first time, and I couldn't believe you, you overwhelmed me. You just zapped me out, you just—you really zapped my m-mind, I couldn't believe anybody withthat much humanity and sympathy and understanding- I mean it, and you're also just the exact opposite too, but that's- you must be the exact opposite of yourself, if you're not, and Gerard is not. Gerard's not the rose poet of the world, he's not the greatest poet in the world, he's just mediocre—   D—Yeah, but,   O— . . . he's gotta see it himself.   D—Year out, what what y'know   O—The fact that he couldn't see in the haiku, *Day is Breaking*, was excessive. And, day's dawn, and day's beginning ir day day begins, or day com, y-y' know Did ya hear her—on the stage (*noise*)   D—Is that the rag? O—It's the rag- oh, the old rag- Isn't she ever, the old rag, *de la Frugula* This is the- the- . . . . vella, for, a Italian Jewess named Judy de Pasta. D—Really?   O—And it was written in about two weeks. Pasta's career lasted for about five years. Anr she was the original Norma, the original Sa. . . . . .   D—Oh.   O—Can you imagine that? . . . no. 1831,32. Incredible woman. The rest of her life was spent, her, she spent, she just worked for five years and the rest of her life she lived off her earnings from these five years. She's an Italian Jewess.   D—Oh really, oh. O—Her name is pretty severe, too—Judy de Pasta—(*whistles*) (*Opera.*) Hello? Yes, who's this? Hi, baby, how're you, honey? Why? . . . Oh well I thought that, I didn't know, Rita, Oh, I'm sorry, we she said she might come, but I don't think that she will. Oh well then listen, then then she's en route then, then. What should we do then, quickly —is there something that we can do? Can we turn the lights out or something? (*pause.*) Oh God, Rita, and I want to see you so bad! (*pause, Opera.*) Well listen, hhe would be, she, of course (*Pause, opera.*) It's reunion night. Aright now? When? Don't answer. (*Opera.*) Not Billy (*Opera.*) She's looking in the garbage pails, right? That son of a bitch. D—Who is?

O—(*Sinisterly*) There's a plot for her. Is she taxiing? Is that Billy? She's Not taxiing, I told you wouldn't. (*Pause, opera.*) Darling, she didn't sound like she was coming. She . . . (*pause*) Yeah, that, this Rita—The Duchess called from his apartment.

D—Yah, she ran out?

O—He haid, "Do not," he should have told me before not to invite here here.

D—Why? Why?

O—CAuse he's trying to get rid of her.

D—Oh.

O—Cause she

D—She left already?

O—Yeah, and he was describing, her, her progress; have you got the bug?

D—What bug?- Uh yeah.

O—Get it get it get it.

D—Really, oh, okay.

O—Hello, I'm- she's standing waiting for a taxi. Was, well she's taxiing, then. Tell me when she gets into one, cause she won't move to far. Yeah. (*Pause.*) Yeah. Oh, Rita, no one's ruining your life but you, but, uh, she's a dandy instrument. (*Lots banging.*) Yes, you told me, but baby, don't forget to watch out, and see if she gets that cab contact. Have a . . . is right. She's . . . (*music*), oh, she's getting, is she— loafers? . . . (*Opera.*)

RR—She has both bags in one hand and her bags are empty, the cock fucker.   O—Her bags are empty?   RR—Yah.   O—Ohh.

RR—She's on her way down there, turn the lights out, turn the music off.   O—No.   RR—Cool everybody when she gets there. Have, uh, you go to the door and you say that I, I, really have no right to invite you cause Billy, Billy   O—And Henry is still at home.   RR—Henry came back. Henry is here. Y'know, she thinks Henry is gone.   O—Now baby, don't forget to allow the time.   RR—Well, she's on her way now.   O—Okay, well then, good bye—   RR—No, I wanna stay on the phone.   O—Huh?   RR—I'll stay on the phone for it.   O— Okay, good. But who should I hand you to?   RR—Uh, give the phone to Billy and He'll give me a commentary. Turn the lights out, and O——Billy Billy Billy! (*Pause.*) Go get Billy,quickly quickly—hurry, quickly DoDo, quickly.   RR—Lights in the front room out.   O— Hold on, this is divine. Billy, quickly Billy. Open the closet door, DoDo, open it. Open the door.   RR—God bless you, Ondine.   O—Hold on.   RR—God bless you. (*pause.*)   D—What, what?   RR— Who is this?   D—Oh, this is Orella, what?   RR—Oh now, you just   D—Ondine what?   RR—Turn *Belaina* off   D—Oh, he's in the dark room, he's exposing film.   RR—All right, that's okay. Turn the phonograph off.   D—Okay. Turn the phonograph off. Turn it off. RR—Oh, this is outrageous, Drella,   D—Oh, which, what happened? RR—Oh, I just got rid of the Duchess, baby,   D—Yeah, oh and she called.   RR—She's been on my ass a whole fucking night.   D—On. RR—And she called and she's coming down now.   D—Yah.   RR— And I was waiting for her to split cause I was coming down now. And she called and Ondine said, "Oh my love . . . " and mahwahah- and he8s gonna pull a- I just watched her get into a cab.   D—Oh, akay, maybe she won't come here.   RR—No-   D—Oh, we have all the lights, and everything. Oh, did you ever arrange that thing with that guy? RR—Um, I'll tell you, Drella, tomorrow I'm doing it, I've been having

trouble. It's my day off.   D—Okay, it's okay, there's no rush.
RR—I'm home, I knew there was no rush. I'm home tomorrow.   D—
Oh, tomorrow's Saturday.
RR—Oh, that's right.
D—Can you still do it Saturday?
RR—It's Friday.
D—OH, tomorrow's Friday.
RR—Yah, that's right.
D—That would be just terrific.

RR—and I just can't find the time to sit down at the office in front of . . . and besides, I don't want anybody in the office to know what's going on.

D—Yeah, okay, then that'd be fine. Ondine went, uh, he's in the dark room, so he'll be . . .

RR—Is the bell ringing yet?

D—No no no not yet.

RR—Tell everybody to be quiet.

D—Yeah yeah, we're all quiet.

RR—And hide—

D—Yeah, we're hiding

RR—Oh, well you're all hiding.

D—Yeah.

RR—Where you hiding?

D—Uh, we're all hiding because all the lights are out.

RR—Uh, ah, baby, this is what this is something you should be filling   for Christ's sake.

D—Ah, yeah, oh yeah.

RR—Ohh . . .

D—I don't hear anything yet.

RR—you will, you'll hear King Kong, my dear.

D—Really?

RR—Coming through that door.

D—(Pause.)

RR—She put on loafers because it rained a little tonight.

D—Ohho, Ondine? (Pause.)

O—Hello, RR?

RR—Yeah?

O—All is in readiness. Ow! I al-

most fell. It's so dark in this room.

RR—What's she doing? She must be blowing the cab man.

O—If she's blowing the cab driver we're through. Darling listen, I'm gonna open the window.

RR—Are you up front?

O—Sure, this here. (Whispering) . . . oh yeah

RR—So open the window so you can see her come out. I want a commentary on everything—her arrival. You're divine, my dear. (Pause.)

O—Billy's coming out of the dark room.

RR—Oh, he's up—not that, we haven't time for the story.

O—Huh?

RR—Rita's coming down and she's gonna give you your poke.

O—The, the uh, bell? Rita?

RR—The bell?

B—Do you just not want her to end up at your place?

RR—No, baby.

B—Because I'll keep her if you don't

RR—No, stop it, stop it.

B—I'll make sure that she doesn't.

RR—No, stop it baby, I'll tell you.

B—Yeah.

RR—She left here finally,

B—Yeah.

RR—and she called Ondine down there,

B—Yeah.

RR—and Ondine said, "Come on down," and well, I didn't want that, baby, cause I'm getting down there.

B—Well, yeah.

RR—So Ondine's gonna give her a story now.

B—Oh, all right.

RR—She must not get in the house.

B—Okay.

RR—Open up the window Billy, so when she leaves the house you can see which way she goes.

B—Oh, I can.

RR—Is he talking to her? I must have a commentary.

B—Uh, well he's around the uh, he went, the door is the other way. I can't see her from here.

RR—Can you hear what's going on?

B—Commentary please.
Shhh!

B—DoDo, uh, give a report of . . . uh doing (*pause*)

RR—Billy?

B—Yes.

RR—She walks into the room, I, don't let her know I'm on the phone.

B—Oh certainly not.

RR—How did things go at the drug store?

B—Fine.

RR—Good.

B—Yeah cause don't you remember I saw you, occasion, in uh, in front of uh—

RR—. . . nothing for Ondine I hope.

B—Oh no no no no nothing at all.

RR—Very good. Well, someone just came in. Somebody come in?

B—Ondine came in alone.

O—I told you that Henry returned between the time she called and got here, and I said, "I don't know what to do." I wouldn't let her in the front door. She said, "Let me sit down," she said, "I don't know what to do with the cops and everything, and the big bag

O—and knowing that

RR—The big bag is empty

O—I know, I know, I know—you told me previously.

B—She hasn't come up the front door or anything.

O—I'm going out in five minutes, and I'll tell her Henry asked me to stay, and "Duchess, goodnight."

RR—Well, what do you mean is she waiting for you know?

O—on the front stoop.

RR—Why

O—Because I, I, I said to her, "Duchess sit down on the front stoop and relax for five seconds.

B—She has, she must be in the lobby- she hasn't gone outside.

O—Well then she's inside the, uh, lobby—she hasn't go—Which means either I or Billy will get off the phone. We'll tell her that she can't stay but that I'm staying.

RR—Ondine, my love—

O—Yeah?

RR—You are the one to do it.

B—Yeah because I haven't spoken to her yet.

O—Yeah, bye bye.

RR—I'm waiting.

B—I'm still here.

RR—Billy?

B—Yes?

RR—Can you see the stoop?

B—Yes. She's uh she hasn't gone out yet.

RR—When she gets out on the stoop, I must know in which direction she goes.

B—Uh huh.

RR—If she heads back up here—

B—You mean, if she goes, uh, east, she's going up there?

RR—I don't know

B—Oh you, oh you mean which way she goes when she gets to the avenue?

RR—Yeah.

B—Well, in any event, you shouldn't com down uh Colubbeus, you should com down Amsterdam.

RR—I don't care, but, I mean, I don't wanna come down there with, and walk; she's gonna catch me or she's not gonna or she's gonna catch me not here.

B—Well why don't you want her to why don't you want her to uh, run up to you?

RR—Baby, because I've been with her all fucking night. You were here for a half hour tonight, Billy, d'you know what I'm talking about?

B—Yes indeed.

RR—And she's not after you're fuckin' box.

B—Mm.

RR—Just think about that.

B—She didn't talk about my meat. She talks about yours, though.

RR—Just think about that.

B—Oh, I don't want to. I know a word, uh, I think Ondine just went out again to tell uh (breathing)

RR—God bless you all.

B—(singing) God bless Ame—

Kate Smith keeps coming into this.

RR—Ah, God bless Kate Smith.

B—Oh, Duchess—the return of Kate Smith.

RR—She's coming in?

B—No, The Duchess, no (pause) (Singing) ai che musa, ai che musa. Oh don't, don't mention farther doctor uh, the doctor.

RR—Huh?

B—In this conversation don't further make mention of the doctor.

RR—Duchess's name you mean?

B—No, not The Duchess.

RR—Me.

B—No-o-o.

RR—Doctor David.

B—Yes, that's the end of him for this conversation, okay, please— S'il vous plait.

RR—Well yes.

B—Oh yes.

RR—I mean, of course.

B—Absolutely for this conversa-

RR—You know I don't even question you.

B—Yeah, I know. It's not a matter of integrity or any tthing personal, I'I'm just saying, I'm just saying

RR—It's just a matter of-

B—Wait, I'm just making a point —I insist we stop doiing this conversation for practical reasons.

RR—Exactly, and I tell you

B—For practical reasons

RR—Without even knowing or even, you know, and I would always want to know what the reasons were I obey.

B—Yes, thank you.

RR—Without even knowing, or even, because the word comes

from the hierarchy.

B—Mm hm.

RR—(*laughs a little*) What the fuck is he now? Is Ondine hung up out there?

B—Ondine has gone out again.

RR—How manytimes has he gone out? What's he giving? A——?

B—Darling, this is his second time. He told her that he would be back up in a couple of mnutes because Henry had returned to let her know what the story is.

RR—Yeah?

B—And now he's letting her know what the story is. And I just see her going . . . down these steps uh, accompanied by Ondine who's probabily going to get her a taxi. (*Pause.*) Yes, Ondine is walking her to the corner.

RR—Oh. Now wait, this is Ondine.

B—He'll be able to report specifically what has happened.

RR—When they come back I'm gonna start getting dressed.

B—When they come back I'll call.

RR—I, and I'm gonna fill up a needle. Do you want a poke?

B—Oh sure.

RR—Ondine must want a poke.

B—Oh, undoubtedly.

RR—Okay, adio mio filio.

B—Okay, I shall call you as soon as he returns.

RR—Blessed. Blessed.

B—Okay.

RR—Bye bye.

B—Bye bye. (*Phone being hung up.*) (*Silence.*)

(*After a pause voices.*)

B—Well it's just a matter of uh that Rita has had to, been uh out an hour the most.

SPF—What do you mean he had

to? What do you mean? All he has to do is say, "Look get, get out."

B—That's not all he has to do. He has to do a number of other things starting out with basic elementary factors like breathing, eating, and stuff like that which go up into various other activities like

SPF—Well I mean if he doesn't want her to be there.

B—. . . has something to do with the same activities that we all have mutual uh

SPF—I, no all I'm saying is that

B—relationships. You can't just say that all he has to do is this or that. He has to do other things too.

SPF—What I'm saying, Billy, is that of he doesn't wish her to be there

B—I heard what you said though.

SPF—If he wants to get rid of her all he has to do is say get out.

B—That's not all he has to do.

SPF—You make such simple, such simple things so complicated, you see.

B—You can do that with turds but you can't do it with your fingers.

DD—Drella do you tap the telephone?

No uh, just for uh

B—JIt's not tapping (*with anger*) DoDo! It's taking advantage of it.

DD—. . . the telephone up in the studio.

No.

B—It's for an epitome.

No no no uh

SPF—(*says something*)

No, we're not uh, tapping anything.

B—We're not doing anything dirty.

I guess you can't prove anything anyway.

DD—I just wonder if you did it.

No, I, no I, uhm. I did it at home for a little but just once in awhile but nothing, it's just, well we have, we have

DD—It's never, it's never . . . (Do-Do and SPF talking at once)

No no no, we have a two hour conversation with The Duchess that's unbelievable.

B—You mean you were an intern first.

SPF—Yes. (Pause.) Why did everybody take their clothes off?

What?

SPF—Why did Ondine and Billy take their clothes off?

Uhhh, there's something about something that Ondine has to take his clothes off and try put other things on. Well Billy does at hime I guess.

(DoDo says something.)

I always take my clothes off at home too.

SPF—I was tired, I was tired and I wanted to go to sleep.

(DoDo says something.) (Pause.)

DD—Billy don't jump.

B—(a little laugh) (says someing)

What?

B—I said it's . . . film in it that isn't developed yet.

Oh,

B—That's what I was doing in the closet, putting film in the can.

Are you doing all, are you doing all the fi-, oh maybe next month I'll

buy an enlarger. Oh!

B—But I'm not in a hurry because first I have to match with this.

Oh Stephen uh, wants to rent the thing if, so he'll probably bring down all his enlargement stuff, shall we?

B—Oh you mean he'd like to use the one.

Yeah, I don't mind Stephen because Stephen and I could control.

B—Oh, I don't mind him either. So you know that way.

Yeah.

B—Where's the uh

Do you want him to do it because I'm sure he would.

B—Sure.

Well I'll tell him to uh.

B—He'd probably like to get out from under his father's thumb also.

Oh yah, yah. And he said he would pay the rent uh, y'know using it.

B—Mmm. Which will pay for the supplies and everything.

Yeah, oh terrific.

B—Do you know where the remote control thing is that goes on by itsellf?

What rum, what? You mean the T.V.'s on?

B—It goes on by itself.

Uh!

B—Here it is.

Where? Oh, oh is that what it is? I thought, oh.

SPF—Did did Andy paint this or is it silk-screened?

Yeah.

SPF—Silk-screened.

Yeah.

16 / 2

B—You can tell if it's perfect by reading where it says Kodak plus R safety film and the numbers. If it's under or over exposed you can tell by that. Like I've had some prints come back from the, negatives come back from labs where it wkas totally black and you couldn't see anything and others were very pale and you couldn't see anything, but these come out perfect every time because of the way they have arranged it so that you mix the chemicals in a certainsequence so that you can't make a mistake. So there's nothing to it. But that's the . . .

What? Yeah.

B—It's better than having somebody poor.

Yeah. Oh yeah, so shall I tell him uh it, because uh he comes around anyway so, and uh he won't be a nuisance.

B—Yeah and when it comes to uh, printing it's not that easy.

No it's, he'll really teach you how. I think he does it beautifully.

B—He's just been doing it for

Yeah.

DD—Does he have a dark room at home or what?

No he, they have a big apartment so he uses uh, the extra bathroom.

SPF—Who Gerard?

No, Stephen.

SPF—Where does Gerard live, in Jersey?

No, he's uh from the Bronx.

SPF—Does he have. . . . . . ?

No. (sounds of an opera in the background)

SPF—That's what I gath- I got that impression.

Well, he, he's uh, he's sort of uh, tries to keep people away.

SPF—Why?

B—(from the background) When Ondine comes back—

Uh, well I don't, I guess he likes me but I don't, y'know, I mean that's all.   SPF—Well, y'know I can understand why people like you but not to keep. . . .   Oh well, Gerard is   B—I think it's best we better be calling Rita agai if you like.   Oh okay.   SPF—Does Rita, is Rita aware that   D—. . . . . . . .gone out without his clothes?   What?

D—Did Ondine run out in the street without his clothes?   I don't, I don't know. No. (music)   SPF—Rita's aware that I. . . . . . (opera) Do you think, you don't, if you could take an obertrol.   Yeah.

SPF—Or five obertrols and have the effect that you want and then just

turn it off.　　You can do that.　　SPF—How can you do that?　　Well
you, you then take a uh, tranquilizer.　　SPF—Yeah but I　　Or a drink.
A drink sort of pulls that down.　　SPF—But I don't have any tranquil-
izers.　　What do you drink?　　SPF—Of course I don't have any tran-
quilizers.　　Well a drink just brings uh, you can, uh, take this and then
drink and uh, it's like drinking water. It has no effect on you — but then
it cuts down the obertrols and you (deserve?) just normal.　　SPF—You
mean alcohol neutralizes this sort of thing?　　Sure. . . . .it has　　(slow
music)　　SPF—(yawning) No one smokes pot anymore.　　Uh, —
no because pot makes you tired.　　SPF—It doesn't make me tired.
Really? Oh.　　SPF—I love it, y'know, like I'm so, like I'm up all the
time.　　Oh, and this brings you down a little.　　SPF—Yeah, and it
makes me relax.　　Yeah.　　SPF—And it makes me enjoy what's going
on around me. I actually enjoy it. Otherwise I'm so nervous my balls are
up in my stomach all the time.　　Really.　　SPF—I'm, I'm very nervous,
y'know. I'm extremely nervous.　　You don't look it.　　SPF—Well I
am. That's a Jaquard shirt?　　What　　SPF—A Jaquard shirt?
What's a Jaquard shirt?　　SPF—What you're wearing is a Jaquard
shirt.　　What shirt? (opera)　　SPF—A Jaquard weave, that's a
Jaquard weave.　　Oh.　　SPF—J-A-Q-U-A-R-D.　　How did you know
about that?　　SPF—I don't know- I must uhm, what are are all the uh
little pin holes for around there?　　Uh, I don't know.　　SPF—I mean,
most tape recorders just have a hole and you just stick it in a hole.
Yes, but there areall these other gadgets you can use for it and you can
use a typewriter and and stuff like that.　　SPF—A typewriter?! You can
hook it into a typewriter?　　No no no, but I mean you can put one of
those foot pedals on and and work with a foot pedal.　　SPF—This is an
extremely expensive looking thing.　　Uh, (music)　　SPF—Like a hundred and fifty dollars.　　It used to be that much; now it's coming down.
　　SPF—Are you coming down? From all those drugs you take?　　Uh,
I don't, I don't take anything, just Ondine. I don't take drugs.
SPF—You don't enjoy eating?　　Uh, it's just that I get fat so
quickly. No, I really do.　　SPF—You're soft.　　Huh?　　SPF—You're
soft. What's all that?　　That's baby fat.　　SPF—You're not fat
but you're soft. How old are you?　　Uh, (long pause) uh　　SPF Very
great silence.　　Yeah. . . . .uh, talk about Ondine.　　SPF—Nah, why
do you avoid this problem?　　I'm really doing Ondine.　　SPF—Well
there's nothing really to say about Ondine. I mean I've known him for
years and years and years, and he's always been the same. He hasn't pro-
gressed from anything to anything.　　Oh.　　SPF—Uh, I knew him
when he was 17 or 16.　　How old were you?　　SPF—or 15, 16 I guess.
No, I was 16, he must've been about 15. God, I can't imagine Ondine

being that young really. But he must'have been about 15 or so.   Oh
really?   SPF—Yeah, and uh he was exactly the same.   Oh really?
SPF—He didn't take his clothes off.   Oh really, ever?!!   SPF—
(*laughing*) No, I mean he didn't take his clothes off the minute he arrived at someone's apartment. But he was exactly the same; he was always
on stage.   Oh really?   SPF—Uh hum. And he was aware of his
importance at an early age.   Yeah.   SPF—Uh, I think he was aware
of his destiny too. I remember when I was very young and I said, "Ondine,
you must go to work."   Was his name Ondine then?   SPF—Yes.
Oh it was?   SPF—Yes, and I said, "Ondine you must."   Ten
years ago.   SPF—Twelve years, fifteen years I guess, I said, "Ondine,
you must go to work," and he said , uh, "I'm searching for God." (*pause*)
Wow I mean I didn't even know what he was talking about. You know,
I mean, prim, primarily I'm a square. You see. And Ondine is not. He's the
in crowd. (*laughs*) Yeah, he's in with the in crowd. I mean he is the in
crowd. (*opera*) Y'know, as far, I mean he's always been that way. It's always been that way and his mother has always been that way too.   Oh
really?   SPF—Yeah. He doesn't change. I change constantly. Do you
change?   Uh   SPF—Do you develop?   Well,   SPF—Looking
back on on y'know, fifteen years ago, do you feel you were different?
Yeah, uh, no. I'm still the same, but I I've learned more.   SPF—I mean
you knew what you felt fifteen years ago and you feel the same?   But I,
SPF—But you didn't behave in a way that was any different than today.   No, I   SPF—You didn't do things then that you, that you uh
wouldn't do today?   No.   SPF—Really?   Yeah.   SPF—I've
changed enormously. I used to do things constantly that I'd never do today.   Oh really? Like what?   SPF—Oh like all kinds of obnoxious
things.   Like what?   SPF—I'm I'm, I still uh, still do things today
but in a year from today I, I realize that I won't do those things either.
Well, like what? I mean   SPF—Obnixiousthings. I mean, uh I
used to take my clothes off.   What?   SPF—I used to take my
clothes off.   Yeah.   SPF—Well I mean like last night, jacking off
in that bar.   Yeah.   SPF—You know, that was a pretty obnoxious
thing to do.   In the bar or out in the street?   SPF—Well I did it in
the bar too.   Oh really? Where? In front of everybody?   SPF—No.
In front of no one.   Oh.   SPF—I didn't see anyone there, there
might have been people.   Ondine must've, someone must've   SPF
—Well Ondine was there but I don't think anyone else was there.
Oh.   SPF—And uh, I called the waiter over and I said, "I have a
present for you," and he said, "What?" and I said, t"I've got it in my
hand." And he didn't see it because my dick isn't that big so he put his
hand down there and I dropped my dick in his hand and I, that's a pretty

obnoxious thing to do.   What'h he do?   SPF—He played with it.
Huh.   SPF—He played with it.   Well what's, what's wrong
with that?——SPF—Well, it's just sort of an obnoxious thing to do.
Really?   SPF—I mean it's an attention get gift pick, (he laughs)
(opera) Oh dear. What do you like to do most in the world?   Uh.
(opera)   SPF—Paint?   No.   SPF—Go to the beach?   Oh.
SPF—Why do you avoid yourself?   Huh?   SPF—Why do you
avoid yourself?   What?   SPF—I mean you you almost refuse your
own existence. You know-   Uh—it's just easier.   SPF—No, I mean
I like, I like to know you (talking very quietly) I always think of you as
being hurt.   Well I've been hurt so often so I don't even care any more.
SPF—Oh sure you care.   Huh.   SPF—Sure you care.   Well
uh, I don't get hurt anymore.   SPF—Well maybe, of course you get
hurt. Everybody gets hurt every day.   Yeah, but uh I can just turn it
off and on.   SPF—Really?——Yeah.   SPF—I don't know if I'd like
that or not.   Really?   SPF—No, I think, well I mean like being hurt,
in order to be hurt, you know I mean, it makes you realize that you feel.
Uh, yeah, but then uh, but if you keep on, like uh, you can make it
up.   SPF—I mean, it's very nice to feel. You know.   Uh—no, I
don't really think so. It's too sad to do- (opera) And I'm always uh, afraid
to feel happy because then uh. . . . .just never last   SPF—I'm happy
occasionally, but I find that uh the happier you get, I mean uh, it's like
the worse you're going to feel later.   Uh well-   SPF—You certainly
pay for it.   Huh.   SPF—You certainly pay for it; it's a dear price.
Well I just now find that if I staye with. . . . . .it's easier.   SPF—
Yeah, well it's easier, but but it's not, it's sorta dead.   Huh.   SPF—
It's sorta dead.   Oh well, it's it's a nice feeling   SPF—I suppose
but what do you really like? Do you like drives through the country?
I like everything.   SPF—Do you ever, do you ever do anything by
yourself?   Uh no, I can't do things by myself.   SPF—What uh do
you mean. I mean if I ever called you up at uh ten o'clock in the morning
and said, "How would you like to go for a drive in, uh New Jersey, or
or. . . ."   I'll do that, yeah.   SPF—I mean could you just simply sit
in the car and look at the scenery and and stop for a hot dog or something, or or are you always doing things?   Uh, no.   SPF—Making
silkscreeens and photographs and, do you consider that work? I mean does
he get up in the morning and say, "Mon, I have to get down to the office,
the studio."   Uh, it seems to be that way. You know like uh, it's getting
up and going someplace, but it's not really work. (opera.)   SPF—I
mean you don't have to be there at any time.   Well uh,   SPF—But
I mean are there days when you just don't want to go??   Uh no, I like
it very much.   SPF—You do? That's fabulous. I never found . . . a

thing that I like to do when I knew that I had to be there.   Oh really?
Oh.   SPF—that I didn't find some reason for not going.   Oh really?
What is that?   SPF—Well because if your job was to go to a party
every night of the world with the people you loved most in the whole
world I'm sure you'd decide tht you wanted to stay home and read.
Oh, well you- well I, I justthink it's nice to get to a point when you can
do whatever you want to do whenever you want to dot it.   SPF—Then
you never know what you want to do.   Oh yes. Oh but I mean you
know, like (pause) well yeah—that means you can do anything whenever
you want to or if somebody calls you up and says, "Do you want to go
out for a ride?" then you can do it.   SPF—Yeah, but you don't know
what you want to do, do you?   Huh? Uh (pause) Well then maybe I
guess I don't.   SPF—I mean I never know what I want to do. I never
know whatI want to do.   Well I want to get to the point where somebody will tell me what to do.   SPF—I mean I sit there and I say, well
(pause) and y'know the phone rings, that's all and someone says, "Well
let's go" and I say "All right." If the phone doesn't ring I say, "Well, I'm
not awfully happy doing what I'm doing, but then I don't know anything
else to do.   Uhh.   SPF—So I'll just sit here y'know.   Really?

      And sleep or drink or   Oh.   SPF—or go out and pick somebody
up or something.   But you seem to have the ability to be busy all the
time for some reason. I don't know why. You look like you—(opera)
SPF—Yeah, I'm always doing something but I'm not awfully happy doing
whatever it is that I'm doing.   Why don't you do something you like?

      SPF—I'm only happy when I pretend entirely.   Oh.   SPF—
And that's the most, well it's horrible.   Oh, wha-what thing?   SPF—
Oh, I don't want to discuss it. But I mean, but but I, I think that it's
fascinating I think about you y'know? And I think about your mother
and I think about that house that. . . . .and I mean it's just simply fasci-
nating—the whole thing. (opera)
(noise) (voices) (silence) (crash)
  —(rough sounding) Surely surely (interference) Doesn't have any place
     to go. Where can we send her?
(Strange sounds—like a space craft conversation.)
O—To Bellevue.
SPF—No, why don't send her to uh uh Kitty Kitty Kitty route.
(A woman's voice.)
B—Um, the wrong person's on the phone.
O—Pardon me?
(Buzzing.)
B—(laughs)
O—No, that's me.

B—Yes I know it's you. Yes, but that suggestion makes the whole thing just out of hand.

O—It gets worse. Yeah you, please Billy.

B—I know I, uhh (pause) Well I really don't know what you, what she, well I guess she can't go to Johnn's huh?

O—No, she can't go to oJhn's; she can't go to Jerry's. (Buzzing.)

B—She just left Rotten's house.

O—Well she can't go back.

B—No, she can't. (Buzzing.) That's not her hollering is it?

SPE—Ondine, where are you?

O—I'm in the subway at 8th Street.

B—That's not her hollering is it?

SPF—In the subway?

O—No, that's the ticket agent.

SPF—What the hell are you doing in the subway?

B—Thying to get rid of The Duchess.

O—It's the only phone booth that works.

(Buzz!!)

SPF—You're trying to get rid of the Duchess in the subway?

B—Excuse me! Uh, Ondine?

O—Yes.

B—I have to have you two help me. I'm working in the kitchen and I need help and and she just can't come and you have to.

SPF—Ondine?

B—And you promised me that you're gonna help me.

O—Well I wanna help you.

B—I can't do all that heavy work by myself.

O—Billy, I wanna help you.

B—I can't do all that heavy work by myself. You told me you were going to. Now The Duchess is uh uh older than I am even and she should be able to establish herself somewhere. She's uh from influential uh tidings and families and all that stuff. And I, I mean what can I do, what can you do? We can't sacrifice our continuity and existence uh.

O—I don't wanna; it's not that Billy. Listen (roar) it's Billy, it's not that.

DRE—(pleading) Oh, Ondine?

O—What?

DRE—(pleading) You've got two more three more hours.

O—You know.

DRE—(pleading) Oh Ondine, three more hours.

O—You know that I will.

DRE—(pleading) Ondine.

B—C'mon, you promised. You said you were gonna . . . come back and uh and uh (*pause*) that's all there is to it.

O—I firmly intend to.

DRE—Ondine!

B—Just tell her, just tell her the pracical facts of the situation Duchess baby. Uh I mean she's not gonna fall aslepp anywhere. She, there must be someone she can go entertain and have fun with. Can't she go to Times Square or something? (*Laughter.*)

DRE—(*pleading*) Ondine?

O— . . . with the, with the, with the fucking caps.

(*clicking*)

DRE—Ondine?

O—Yeah.

DRE—Three more hours.

O—I know. (*Laughs.*)

DRE—Oh ho ho, Ondine.

B—C'mon Ondine, don't put yourself on the spot.

O—What am I supposed to do?

SPF—Run out.

B—You're supposedto come back here and help me like you told me you were (*pause*) going to . That's all there is to it.

O—I can't come back and help you.

DRE—She can go back to Rotten Rita's.

B—She can't go right now.

O—Rotten's got a trick. Fucking Mayor has a trick.

B—She has to go to the East Side, that's all there is to it. Ship her East. Listen Bob, I don't know why, I don't know why you uh are . . .

(*The operator comes in*)—5¢ please.

O—All right operator; I have it in my hand.

(*Operator*) All right.

B—Don't continue to put yourself on the uh, in a situation for her.

O—I'm—

B—How come all of a sudden you're being uhm, sympathetic toward her?

O—Well because I-

B—Towrads she.

O—No well uh, well uh, look, all right, I'll come back, I'll come back.

B—Yes.

O—I'll come back. The Duchess, what should be. . . . .

(*Pause.*)

Can't you bring The Duchess back?

B—He can't right now.

Oh.

B—Uh, the, in order for her to go places now there has to be someone

there who will swear to God that they're gonna take her away with them when they leave. But even that, even beyond that she can't come now because Rita's coming over and The Duchess just spent hours at Rita's and Rita sent her away trying to get away from her. (*Pause.*)
(*Ondine talking to The Duchess . . . "and Billy's right."*)

B—(*laughs*) I just can't do that work alone. (*His voice rises as he speaks.*) And I have to get it done. (*Ondine talking*) And the fresherds

O—I'm sweating like a mother fucker in this place. (*Opera.*)

DRE—(*pleading*) Ondine.

B—Listen, I hafta, I have uh, film that I'm renting and I have to go to it.

O—Okay.

DRE—(*pleading*) Ondine?

O—Listen.

B—Drella's gonna stay on. I have to go back to my film.

DRE—(*pleading*) Ondine.

O—Put DD on the phone.

DRE—(*pleading*) Ondine.

B—Who?

O—Put DD on the phone.

DRE & B—Who?!

O—DoDo.

SPF—Oh, she's asleep.

B—Oh, she's not asleep. Here she is. DoDo! DoDo!

O—She'll have a—

B—DoDo's asleep.

DRE—DoDo!

B—DoDo's aslepp.

O—DoDo—

B—(*falsetto*) Dorthea! (*Opera.*)

DRE—(*once again*) Ondinne?

O—Drella's talking.

B—I haveto go to my film.

DRE—Okay.

O—Okay.

B—Drella, just get him to come over here without her.

DRE—Okay, all right.

O—I'm coming!

DRE—(*pleading*) Ondine Ondine!

O—Drella please.

DRE—Ondine.

O—Drella.

DRE—(*pleading*) Oh Ondine Ondine.

O—I didn't know that you were back there.

DRE—Ondine Ondine.

O—Drella I tell you right now.

DRE—What?

O—I'm coming. Darling.

DRE—Okay. When?

O—I promise and I'm coming. I told you that I'm coming.

DRE—Oh but-

O—I just want to see Brigid off safely somewhere where she'll be happy.

DRE—(*desperately*) Oh Ondine.

O—That's all.

DRE—Oh but y'know like I'm still going on. Ondine, please come.

O—I'm coming back now.

DRE—Well, right now.

O—Right now.

DRE—JThree minutes.

O—Three minutes.

DRE—Okay.

O—I just wanna get the Duchess on at least an East Side bus, because I don't want to worry about her.

DRE—Oh, give her some monye for a cab and I'll give it back to you.

O—She has money.

DRE—Oh, well send her on a cab.

O—But wh-where, with the cab to where?

DRE—Uhh, the East Side. (*Pause.*) Through the park.

O—(*talking to the Duchess*) Will you want to go . . . (*still talking*) okay. Bye bye.

DRE—Okay. Bye. (*click*) (*buzz*) (*click*) (*silence*)
Yeah.

B—(*says something*)

DRE—He's coming, yeah.

(*noise*) (*pause*)

SPF—Have you seen this?
Yeah, it's a nice box. It's an Agnes Martin. Do you like it?

SPF—It's nice, yeah.

(*opera*)

SPF—I love it.
Do you ever thing of doing art?

SPF—I don't think I have much to offer.
Oh.

SPF—I mean I would never do anything except for myself y'know. And then if other people liked it I'd give it to them.

Oh. (*Opera.*)

SPF—I, you can't sell it.

What? All right. Yeah I know it shouldn't be so . . . . . (opera)

SPF—The whole idea is that you have to make money.

Yeah.

SPF—Y'know. (*Opera.*) It's like y'know you have to work with the sweat of your brow?

Yeah.

SPF—The Waves! 1963! Eleven inches square.

Is that what it is?

SPF—That's what it says. No, I mean y'know, it says that side: 11 inches square. I mean like who the hell cares.

Well because every inch counts. (*Pause.*) In this kind of business.

SPF—I don't th-, I don't see how you can do it, y'know.

What?

SPF—But you must have a soul that can stand it. Y'know, money and and talking to people that own those galleries and things like that and Mrs. Mrs. whatever her name is that had her photograph taken.   What photograph taken?   SPF—You know that one that showed you sitting with that woman.   Oh yeah, isn't that terrible? I know.   SPF—With all those photographs? Doesn't she hate you? (loud opera) Sends it back?

Yeah, we have two fights each year.   SPF—Wha'd you mean she buys it and sends it back? What does she think it is, a dress?   Yeah, that's what she thinks it is.   SPF—I don't understand. (opera) (voices) (silence) (buzz)   B—Have you got the thing on?   Yeah.   BI mean the attachment. (pause) An opertor said, "Hello, 2–5–8–7," and I said, "1–8?" I said, "Yes?" You know it didn't ring or anything.   Yeah.

B—I just picked it up and she said, "Just a moment, a doctor is trying to get you."   (man's voice) Hello.   B—Hello.   (operator) Go ahead doctor.   RR—Thank you very much operator.   B—Oh, is this Dr. Earp ?   RR—Yes.   B—Ah! I'm glad you got through.   RR—I was reallu concerned about you.   B—I'm glad you goth through.   RR—Hah?   B—I'm glad you got through. I had just picked up the receiver to call you and the operator told me that you fere trying to get through to me.   RR—Did she say Dr. Wrapper is trying to get through to you?   B—She said a doctor is trying to get through.   RR—Uh huh.   B—The Bridge has been set to cover 11th street and Ondyne is on his return to here now. He called from the 81st street subway.   RR —You put him on the subway?   B—And he's sending her down to 11th St. And he's coming back here.   RR—he's ding wonderful things then isn't he?   B—Yeah! He was sacrificing himself.   RR—She's after something big, baby. Keep you eye on her. (laughter) See ya soon.

B—She's not a stork.   RR—See ya soon.   B—Okay. Bye.
RR—Bye. (*click*) (*pause*) (*opera and noises*)   SPF—Drella!
Yeah.   SPF—Did you ever paint trees?   When?   SPF—Any
time.   Huh?   SPF—No, please don't, please.   Why?   SPF—
Don't put that in my face.   Oh. Why not? It's part of uh, I have to do
it, I really have to do it.   SPF—No, but really, you don't want me to
talk about you, do you? You want me to talk about Ondine; there's nothing to say.   Uh.   SPF—I'm fascinated with you, not with Ondine.
Uh. Yeah, I, I paint trees.   SPF—No, I mean when you, when you
first ever held a paint brush in your hand wha'd you paint?   Uh.
SPF—. . . . . .cans.   No-ho-ho. Uh, movie st-, uh Hedy Lamarr.
SPF—You painted Hedy Lamarr?   Yeah.   SPF—You know the first
think I think I ever painted?   What?   SPF—In my whole life?
What?   SPF—Well I don't mean in school. I don't mean in the first
grade. Not in the first grade. No, I mean I painted in school, y'know,
drawing y'know with crayolas?   Yeah.   SPF—I painted monkeys.
Oh really?   SPF—in a cage, yeah. Monkies in a cage and then the
next thing after that I painted uh, trees.   Oh!   SPF—Green trees.
DD—Did the monkies. . . . . .in the trees?   SPF—No, I painted
mon-, uh green trees, uh, green and yellow trees. But but I couldn't understand why all the other kids made their trees round,   How'd you
make your trees?   SPF—Uh, just sort of all over, y'know.   Draw
one.   SPF—No, I mean I can't draw, I can't   Why?   SPF—I
can't can't draw.   Well, I mean draw the way your trees, I mean, they
must be-   SPF—No, I mean my trees just look like trees.   DD—
Well if they weren't round what were they? I mean lots of trees are round.
SPF—No, I mean you know how kids paint trees.   DD—Yes.
SPF—Big round grren things on brown stalks and I didn't paint my trees
that way.   DD—What did they look like?   SPF—Mine looked like
trees.   DD—Well what do you mean. I don't know; big? tall?   Well
then you must've been good.   DD—Phallic-looking trees?   SPF—
No, just big trees with holes in them. (*laughs*) I mean trees do have
holes.   Yeah.   SPF—And I painted-   DD—And there were no
monkies in, oh.   SPF—No no, I didn't paint animals. I never painted
animals, never any kind of a moving thing.   DD—Well I don't see
why you didn't put the monkies in the trees.   SPF—'Cept I used to, I
used to paint glamour girls.   Oh.   SPF—I think every young gag
paints glamour girls. I mean I really do.   Yeah.   SPF—But I I' I,
I put like y'know, like their arms came out like this (*pause*) and then they
had a dress on like this.   DD—Are these the monkies or the glamour
girls?   Those are the glamour girls.   SPF—And they had tits out
like that. (*laughs*) Their tits always came out under their arms.   Oh!

SPF—I could never figure out, I said now I know that women don't walk around with their arms sticking out like that but, how, where, how do you do it? I couldn't figure iut that they were in the front. I always did it under their arms.   Well, well finish; what else happened?   SPF— Well the rest of it was very ininteresting.   No, well finish the whole thing.   SPF—I, I, I didn't like big skirts y'know.   Well no uh. SPF—I always put tight skirts on them.   Yeah.   SPF—Yeah. (*He drawing.*) Like that. (*pause*)   That's a long skirt.   SPF—Yeah, I always put them in long skirts. (*much opera*) And they were very sexy girls as you can see (*bursts out laughing*)   Oh. Oh, I think that's just terrific. Wow (*Dorothy is laughing*) Is that really the, the way they really looked or or is it just   SPF—Yeah—to me.   Oh, no, but I mean is this the way that you did then before it looked like this or or uh   SPF— Well I mean I don't think it looks exactly like.   Or no no, oh   SPF —something that I might have done in another age.   Oh.   SPF—I mean you can't forever do anything twice the same way.   DD—Oh yes you can. No no, but I mean like now you did it fast and and like SPF—Yeah (*with emphasis*) Oh mine were monumental.   Oh. But I mean in this kind of proportion or or or   SPF—Yeah.   Oh. SPF—That sort of proportion. But it doesn't mean much I don't think. But neither did girls to me at the imte. I, I always had trouble with girls from a young age.   Really? Whq?   SPF—I used, I, my friend y'know was a a boy that lived behind me and uh, he used to play with me. And you know what I mean Dorothy.   DD—Mm hm.   SPF—And uh, so I decided that it might be fun to play with his sister. And I invited her into the house y'know and I said I would give her a bottle of perfume which I did and she snatched the perfume and ran out the back door. (*laughs*) and and, and then

17 /   1

SPF—What thing? (*noise*) Oh, it's Rotten on there.   DD—Where the hell is Ondine, cause Ondine has just simply disappeared.   He took the Duchess, he took the Duchess and . . . oh there you are! Oh!   O— Did you see George's photograph of the Duchess?   Ohhh.   B— Isn't is gorgeous? What happened to The Duchess?   O—I sent her in a cab to 533 E. 11th St.   And are they there?   O—No, they're not there. Who knows?   Aww.   B—Well, will she be back up here?

O—No, no-no, no . . . Bobby and, Bobby and   Oh!   O—Isn't
that a camp?   SPF—A camp, it's beautiful.   It's beautiful.   O—
Yeah, it's beautiful. George is a great photographer.   George who?
DD—Who is George?   SPF—I've never seen the Duchess look so
good.   O—There arepictures of her that make this look tired and old.
    DD—Who's George?   O—George is Roger's friend, the one who
writes those scenarios.   DD—I don't know George.   O—You know
George. You must know George.   George.   O—Oh, I'm so warm.
I just ran out in the fog.   Take it off, take it off, take it off.   O—
But it this a nice outfit to go out in?   Oh yeah yeah. Pretty sweater.
Oh! It looks great. Yeah great.   O—Oh look at this outfit.   You
have earrings on.   O—Yessss!   Whose?   O—The ones that Taxi
gave me.   Oh!

O—N-oh! Hi, howare you?

(*cab driver*) Hallo dere.

Weird. (*Pause.*) Funny. Do you thnk he's a cop?

O—Drella, this is our taxi driver.

DRE—Hi.

SPF—Are you really a cop in disguise?

O—He's really a cop in disguise and that's Jim Beam and DoDo Mae
    Doom (*insane murderess*)

(*cab driver*) Wow, it's big.

O—What's big.

(*cab driver*) It's big; it's nice.

O—It expresses a lot.

SPF—Watch out you don't express yourself on it.

O—I'm going to take my pants off immediately. I'm so warm; I just ran
    that fat thing around the park.

Ha ha ha.

O—I trotted her like a brewery horse around the park. And it was no easy
    job. (*Maria Callas and Giuiseppe di Stefano are singing the* BND *Act
    Duet from Rigaletto and are obliterating parts of the conversation.*)
    That's our taxi driver.

DRE—It's so weird.   O—It's a camp? Did you know that he'd come
back?   DRE—No.   O—Well I did.   DRE—Really?   O—He
just couldn't believe it. Didn't you hear him say I wish that I could take
you to different places. Vscitene means go way.   B—Congratulations.

    O—But the way she does it she says   DD—Vscitene.   O—This
is Rigalootto isn't it? Should Taxi be called or what?   DRE—Oh-eh-
she's coming right over.   O—Oh my perch is gone.   SPF—That's
Franco-American you know that.   B—Oh! Congratulations.   O—
Thta means French American doesn't it, Franc   SPF—Doesn't Franco-

American sound like Campbell's?   DRE—No. We're going to change his name to Joe-Joe Camp.   O—Jjd. The bead woman attacks. DRE—He has a wedding band on.   O—It doesn't matter.   DRE— Oh.   O—Not only that . . . (*garble*) I'm I'm I'm I'm I'm I'm gonna take a shower or a bath and and and and make him hold the tape thing.

DRE—(*laughing a little*) All right.   B—You know I had better pictures of the Duchess.   O—Like the one of me . . .   DRE— Watch thee speaker.   O—Oh sorry darling. Billy sug-suggested that

DRE—I think he wants your   O—(*walking away*) Well now that I have intermission. Okay. . . . . . heaven (*DoDo says something.*) George who?   DRE—George.   O—George Borden, Roger's friend. DRE——Which one's Roger's friend?   O—He's the California-ite. I've gotta, I'm gonna go.   DD—What's the   O—Noooa! the thing that keeps Roger alive is (*opera*) Oh what I had to do with that fat truck horse. I had to run her around the park three times.   DRE— Ohh.   O—Oh what I had to tell her—a packet of lies and bullshit.

DD—Where's Rotten Rita?   O—Rotten Rita's on her way, the Mayor is coming. I'm dying to see the Mayor again; I haven't seen him in so   DRE—Oh, is this the first time you're seeing him?   O—No, this is the sec-second time.   DRE—. . . . . take a bath or what?   O —Hi Dougie! How are you? What's on his hand, got a ring on it. Oh, it's one of those new, smart, Schlitz rings, aren't they heaven? I'm gonna run my bath. (*Noise and opera.*)   DRE—Oh you have to take all that out?   (*water running*)   O—I just wanna gather my pitiful belong-ings. But I really would liketo take a shower and rest for a minute. DRE—All right. Have him come in and hold the tape recorder.   B— . . . . . . record.   O—Which one? (*Billy ansewers.*) Are you serious? Oh Billy, no, I didn't know that.   DRE—Oh this would be a marvelous sceen on tape.   O—What?   DRE—Oh you have to do it because it's just   OJ(*whispering*) I think somebody else should. DoDo should sing this thing.   DD—Can you play some of that back or is the . . .

O—It can only be played back inthebathroom.   DRE—Ondine, get him in the bathroom.   O—See, it I get him in as . . like he would be, he won't stay.   DRE—What? (*Water gets louder.*) What?   O —If I get him in he won't stay.   DRE—Really? You think so?   O— He'll find some excuse to . . .   DRE—He might.   O—He might; he is adventurous, and he did come all the way up here.   DRE—Yeah.

O—He must be interested in something besides fares.   DRE— Yeah.   O—Is he interested in art at all?   DRE—What?   O— Art, the artistic way. I'm starving to death all of a sudden.   DRE—On-dine, you can, you can, you can; do, do, do, oh no, no, don't do it. O—There is no room. A cigar would be better.   I'm not as cute hah?

(?) I'm starving. (*Opera gets terribly loud.*) Darling, we hadn't been in a room. I had to get him in the bathroom. (opera opera)   DRE—Uh. (opera) (opera ends)   B—Floor.   O—Oh I'm sick of that. I'm so sick of doing it all myself.   B—You've got a hand.   O—I— where? Oh no I can't; I'm too embarrassed.   DRE—No, it's very simple.   O—DoDo should do it.   DD—You think you're more embarrassed. than you are.   O—I'm too utterly embarraseed.   DD—About what?   O—About asking that man to go into th ebathroom with me.
    DD—What?   O—To ask that man to go into the bathroom with me.   DD—Do you want him to?   O—I'm wondering how the tape would work. Look at DoDo's face. She's just so delighted. She can't believe it. My dear, this is filth. No.   DRE—Ohh.   O—I can't because I'm very clean at heart.   DRE—Huh?   O—I'm very honest and sacred. I need a cigarette very badly.   DD—I hate this part.   O— Yeah, you may hate this part but not the way this is done. This is this is the woman who's been locked in her heart for fifteen years. (*Music in the backgorund is very sentimental.*)   DRE—Who?   O—And suddenly hears those, the shield is insane.   DD—Ondine, it's Ondine.   DRE —Oh Ondine, Ondine! There's no troube. He really looks like a girl.
O—Of course. I love this picture.   DRE—Show him the art uh, in the bathroom.   O—What art? This?   DRE—Yeah. No, just tell him, take him into the bathroom and show him your art there.   O—Well then I should take the tape with me right?   DRE—Yeah.   O—Stick it in my pocket and make it look unobvious.   DRE—Yes.   O— Right now with the hole pointing.   DRE—Hu hu ha.   O—This, oh but do you   DRE—That's all right.   O—When do you have to replace it?   DRE—I-I-I'll be in. (opera) (voices) (*Ondine approaches the cap driver*)   O—. . . .would like to show you some of their new— ow! I got mud on my foot. You should step on the white spaces. Here, step over here, on the white space, and then come this way. (THE SHOWER) Yes, come in. Yes come in. The slowest tub in the world. (adjusting water) Now.

(*cab driver*) I like to hear a . . . if possible.

O—You see see when this runs out there shall be about ten minutes before you . . . removing it . . . no noise like that. (*Turns off water.*) (*Dripping.*)

(*cab driver*) Can I see 'em?

O—Now this.

(*cab driver*) I know; I used to sell them.

O—Is this a very good one or what?

(*cab driver*) Well, it's a farily expensive one! It sells for

SPF—Ondine, hwat are you doing in here?

O—Taping. Taking a—what happened to your neck? I still don't know about your operation.

SPF—Well I wasn't a pretty sight, Dougie.

O—Neither are you.

SPF—But do you see this, see this, see that. Isn't it pretty.

O—It looks a little like Elizabeth Taylor.

DD—Ondine!?

O—What?

DD—Ondine Ondine Ondine Ondine. Ondine?

O—Yes.

DD—The Duchess is outside.

O—Well, you'll have to take care of yourself from now on.

Dougie—his crazy little thing sells for around $200.

O—$200? No, I'm not going outside. Can you imagine?

SPF—She must.

Dougie—Uh yeah.

O—Yeah.

Dougie—You can leave it open.

O—No no, please please, they're just gonna plague me about the Duchess. We just got rid of her, the Mayor's doctor.

Dougie—The Mayor is doctor?

O—Or so, she's so called.

Dougie—Well what is she?

O—(opening door) With a coward's Rita! Is the Duchess out there?

RR—Are you the cab driver?

O—Yes! Is the Duchess out there?

RR—No.

O—Well then, why then lie to me?

RR—(in a very deep voice) Nooo.

O—They just said, "The Duchess's out there."

B—My apologies Onidne.

O—This is your Mayor. This is your Mayor. This is your Mayor, the one and only Ro-, the honorable Rotten Rita.

RR—You know what I brought fellas? I brought some records in case you, I brought along It Tirata, I brought along Parsifal, and I brought along Lucia.

DRE—Oh wow.

RR—Join me. I'm going to sing them all for you.

O—Oh' I've gotta show you. . . . . . .oh. . .is outside so I have to.   RR— Now don't say that.   O—I know. I sent it to the children.   SPF— Yeah.   RR—They're a psychiatric institute.   O—. . . . .with open arms and won't they?. That is the goddess singing.   RR—Tonight was the first night. . . . .because I had her in my clutches from 7:00 on. Empty bottles. Let me tell you. Uh   O—Well you warned me Rita—OW! ow ow.   Ondine come back here.   (*people shouting*) Ondine. Ondine Ondine.   DOUGIE—How, far away can you pick up sound?   DRE— Uh, well I, it's supposed to be really very close.   ONDINE—Yes of course. I like to be very close to you at all times. (*in the background*) Where's my pictures?   DRE—Huh? Hah?   SPF—How long can it run?   DRE—Huh? I don't know. Why don't you take a bath so we can have   O—Oh I just let the water out but just, I, I   DRE—Oh uh, oh, all right.   O—I can't fix, I can't adjust the water.   DOUGIE—How long can this tape run?   D—half an hour   O—Where are my pictures? DRE—Oh, I'll get them. If you uh uh say things.   O—When will this be through? How much more time on this? A few minutes.   DOUGIE— When do you turn it off?   O—Oh my God, look, do you see that? This is number 16, this is the 16th hour. Do you know what this whole project is?   DOUGIE—Well, it's fairly simple to figure out.   O—No, I mean this whole thing that we're doing, the whole tape.   RR—Where are those records?   O—This is called, it's gonna be a novel. Oh thank you Drella. I think George is so talented.   B—Yes, he's got creative fervor.

O—I think this is nice of The Duchess.   B—Oh, I've got better ones of The Duchess where she looks like I was made.   O—Doesn't that look sweet?   B—I've got pictures of The Duchess that look like someone had just finished making her.   O—Ohh God.   B—And I don't mean making—making out, I mean making—putting together. O—I was going to tell him what we're wu. Would you ho-ho-hold this please. Uh, what is this 16th, 17th, 18th or what?   18 hours.   O— This is number 18 now. This is the 18th hour, right?   Yeah. (*Music!*)

(*through the music*) O—That now   DOUGIE—What are you gonna do with this?   O—We're gonna write a novel. It's a novel. It's being transcribed by three girls.   DOUGIE—What is it all about?

O—Me!   (Rita laughing like a face in the fun house)   O— Look at The Duchess; the next one you won't believe. (*music is drowning the voices*)   RR—Oh me, oh me, oh my, corpuscles (?) both of you come over here. Good. I just wanted to know one, oh I shouldn't ask you anyway. Ondine, may I just ask one question. Is it cool to uh, to take out, to take our drugs and shoot and everything in front ofthetaxi-driver? O—Certainly.   RR—Oh how wonderful.   O—Certainly.   RR— Does he mind?   O—He better not. I'm gonna go in and do the test now. Come with me, come come with me; this is an official arrest. Oh, Rotten, Rotter uh. The Mayor and myself both are, we we think your spirit is marvelous. This is a rather unusual group to stumble into. Can we see something that will prove to us that you're not   RR—The police.

O—the police? Or J.F.K. is disguise or something. Do you have, I'll take your word if you say that that's all we have to take, but we're going to take drugs here and rather vilently.   (*laughing*)   Dougie or SPF—Are you gonna tie up?   O—No, I'm not gonna tie up, but I don't like zane business, but we're going to give ourselves pokes. So-called. I'm sorry, don't let this cut. Keep it under your hats, darling.
RR—Innoculations please. Stretch that out. Innoculations.   O—And if you witness these things your promise not to, it doesn't offend you does it?   SPF—He's getting terse.   O—You don't have a two, may I see your radio, I mean your wristwatch? May I see it?   RR—Now he not only has us, but he's got us on tape which we don't stand a chance. You and your big mouth; you just put us up for six years. You cock-sucker.   O—He's calling Officer Joe Bolton.   RR—I fired him. He's okay.   O—I think you're all right. All right Rotten? I'll take you on face value, but don't get upset if one of us,   Dougie—Face?   O—I, no, no no, not just face alone. Faith. They have trouble understanding. But they're new. Oh well, all right. You're not going to arrest these two innocent children are you?   B—What's wrong with those two?
O—Dorso is, this is a murderous Negress. Now watch out for her. SPF—She's an Indian.   O—She's not an Indian. Sugar! Sugar! Go in there and fuck them up. Don't let them get upset.   SPF—I'm not let-ting them.   O—You two are, by the time we come in there with pokes you have to be ready for them.   (*Finale—applause*)   D—Oh On-dine, where are you? Ondine? (*music*) (*Ondine talking*) Oh Ondine, pleeese.   O—Let me try it.   D—Oh I no no, but you hold it. Huh?

O—Listen Rotten, I know it's awful to ask you to hold the, would you? Cause Drella's been holding it for so long and he's just, he shouldn't have to. That's not the needle. That's the vitamin B 12.   Dougie—My attitudes towards narcotics   SPF—Narcotics!?   O—These are not narcotics.
SPF—These are not narcotics.
O—Do you call vitamin B 12 a narcotic? But keep this next to your mouth when you speak. Rita, are you all right in there?
Dougie—Avenue D.
SPF—Isn't that funny. I was on 6th street and Avenue C.
O—Suddenly a tear came to my eye thinking of my first experience on the lower east side.
D—Really?
O—Oh he does *so*; he looks like Brooklyn too.
SPF—No no.
O—Oh he looks like a New York boy.
SPF—Do you know the last couple of nights what we were up to?

O—Dear, you were in the midst of a festival night. We were down, they were beating drums and singing about Pan American Day. That's how the lower east side, but the lower east side was, Brooklyn was different too. I mean. What do you think of us? Is'nt it wonderful to find such freedom in the midst of New York City? Did you think that Wagner would permit such nonsense. It's really that Rita is our Mayor. Do you see that silence? Isn't she a gorgeous creature. Isn't she divine. You'd never know that she was so foul.

D—Isn't Billy 24?

O—Billy's twenty-f-, no he's 27.

D—Oh he is?

O—I don't know. Billy, aren't you 27? How old are you? Oh. He's 25.

DD—Tea bag?

O—She thinks you said tea bag.

B or RR—Yeah!

O—May I say one thing From what you said you have a tolerant attitude.

RR—. . . get some chicken and turkey sandwiches; that's a wonderful idea.

O—No, you said; yes, that's a delightful idea. Dodo, would you hold this for me for a second? And with God's help I will put it away. What do you feel about me? Isn't there a twinge somewhere? I doubt— How do you feel about homosexuality Is it permissable?

Dougie—I think if it's one's prerogative to be homosexual, fine, but everybody does not have to share his beliefs.

O—Don't you see Venus being contacted (A *succulent inverted sigh.*) Look at this, a hand-maiden, a gorgeous Indian maiden. I hate them; I live next dor to them.

Dougie—Is a drug that's supposed to give you a charge.

SPF—Yeah.

Dougie—Um, I think it's something that one becomes addicted to. I think it's something that one has very little control over after a certain period of time.

SPF—Yeah, well that's not altogether true though, because I mean lots of people are addicted to a lot of things they have no control over. In fact, they don't even try y'know?

Dougie—Like smoking?

SPF—Oh well like eating chocolate pudding every night.

Dougie—Yes but

SPF—Do you know my stepfather ate chocolate pudding and ground chuck steak every night for years and years and years.

Dougie—You mean he lived to be a ripe old age?

SPF—No, he's, I don't know. Well I mean he was addicted to that y'know, he really was. And he decided to stop, but he couldn't, he couldn't. Say an addict decided to stop.

Dougie—Well let's take chocolate pudding and narcotics. And you take both of those men; strap them down.

SPF—Did you say pot head?

Dougie—No, narcotics.

SPF—What do you call narcotics?

D—Ondine.

Dougie—Narcotics.

SPF—What? What's a narcotic?

Dougie—To me a narcotic is a man who takes drugs.

SPF—Any kind of drugs? I mean aspirins are drugs.

Dougie—Takes drugs to feel high, takes drugs to feel no pain, takes drugs to make him do what he really wants

SPF—Narcotics are opiates. Aren't narcotics opiates?

D—Oh, I really don't know. I don't think about it.

SPF—And opiates are addicting.

Dougie—I'm not really deeply familiar. I have never read on it y'know.

SPF—Narcotics are opiates and opium nerivatives, and they are addicting like opium, uh, methadrine, heroine y'know.

Dougie—Yeah.

SPF—And then you have a few other things that are addicting like cocaine, that's addicting after awhile. But the rest of the things are not narcotics, like pot or amphetamine are stimulates like benzedrine; they are not addicting and yet people do take these things.

Dougie—Yes.

SPF—And pot's not addicting you know.

Dougie—No, not pot.

SPF—And I'm scared shit of needles. Do you like needles?

D—Uhh, no I

SPF—The whole thing about needles upsets me. I think very graphically of muscle tissue and the cold steel forcing it's way through and the blood, skin, and. It's frightening.

DD—It's a good thing that you couldn't see yourself.

SPF—Why?

D—When?

DD—When you were filled with

SPF—Filled with what?

D—Needles.

DD—Needles.

SPF—(walking away) I was never filled with needles. I never have had a needle in my life.

DD—I didn't say filmed, I said filled.

D—Was he really very serious?

SPF—I was never

DD—I was too! But it was a good thing you couldn't see yourself.

SPF—I was unconscious and I did'nt know about the needles.

DD—It was a god thing you couldn't see them.

SPF—In a hospital you see I don't mind needles. I mean they're slightly unpleasant in a hospital, but you know when you tie up

DD—I never had any experiences.

SPF—and the eye dropper and the fountain of blood rushes towards y'know it's all just a little bit afraid. Have you ever seen anyone want to gouge their vein? I mean searching for a vein?

DD—No, I have not. I have not.

SPF—Gouging with a safety pin?

DD—No no, but you have your junkie friends that are here.

SPF—Have you ever seen that? Gouging themselves with a safety pin and stuffing the shit in their arm?

D—Oh I

SPF—You know that's frightening! I mean it's not frightening to them because they realize what's happening. They associate needles with pleasure. I don't associate them at all. (*Conversation and music.*)

SPF—I mean sleeping pills are the greatest test because with sleeping pills you just fade out. I mean you've gone to sleep and then. I mean if you are gonna do away with yourself I think an overdose is *the* way to do it—*the* way to die.

D—Oh I uh, I actually think just uh staying up and getting a heart attack is the best way.

SPF—Heart attack.

DD—Staying up? But how long do you have to stay up?

SPF—Don't you realize how painful that is?

D—What? A heart attack?

SPF—First of all, you have a stroke which means that you can't talk or walk.

D—Not all the time.

SPF—For twenty-five years.

D—Not all the time.

SPF—Twenty-five you won't be able to walk.

D—Oh Ondine! what are you doing?

(*Delightful music.*)

D—Oh, tomorrow's Friday, oh.

SPF—I worry about you.

D—What?

SPF—I worry about you.

D—Oh.

O—Are you going out for sandwiches you think? I, ooh, OW! Oh, I'm
sorry.

RR—Listen, I would like to order. I think we should get Reubens on the
telephone.

O—Yes, let's.

17 /   2

O—A liverwurst civilized. Yes, and no music. Oh my dear, no, I would
like that. Is this the last hour?

D—Can we do it here? The music's too loud.

O—This is the end of the mad scene now so (*Maria Callas is singing the
mad scene from Lucia. It is the Mexico City performance.*) (*The end.*)
The way she sings that (*applause*) I can't believe it. Just a second; as
soon as he injects Billy. The thing that I love most of all about her is
that it truly is the most healthy thing in the world. Look at this. (*Applause.*) Yeah, he could use it. It's the pit.

RR—That's very strong isn't it?

O—For use in the treatment of pernicious anemia. Now it's, it's, my dear
that means incurable anemia.

RR—I hope you hit a high C.

O—One cc daily decreasing to one cc weekly as improvement is noticed:
For inter-muscular sub, sub, subcucaneous?

D—What?

O—S-u-b-c-u-c-, subcucaneous or slow intravenous use. Oh the ampules (?)
Ooh they're so beautiful. Can I just take one out and show them? I
won't break it. They're special, they're divine. The Duchess will come
to reinveta

R—I'm sure.

D—Ooh.

O—Do you see the line here? Oh but don't open it. You want to shake it
all the way down. See this is why Rotten makes the best doctor I've
seen. And then then you break it up through the line. Then you inject
it. This is 20 milligrams of dis-oxine which is—

RR—That was the first time.

O—Afternoon concerts. It was beautiful too. No one wanted The Duchess here. No one.

RR—I'm not getting involved, I said . . . "You know twice as much and that's why you're dangerous."

O—Billy, your injection's ready. Billy! She is very dangerous. That girl is terribly dangerous.

RR—I called the operator up, I said, "Operator, this is Dr. Wrap," I said. I said, "Get get on that phone," I says, "and crack into that conversation," I said, "and I want to speak to Ondine or Mr. Naine," I said. "It's Dr." She said, "Yes doctor." (*Billy relaying the story.*) I told her she could check if she liked.

O—That's the thing—you never can. (*Finale and applause.*)

D—What?

O—Yourself. You can never run away from yourself.

D—Why should you wanna run away from yourself?

O—Well, my dear, who knows, who knows why. Jim has a lot of problems like that. Everyone else has y'know (*applause*) Jim. Oh, who's these . . . darling he's a mother fucker.

D—Is he really?

B—Oh certainly.

D—You're kidding.

O—Are you serious. He's divine, but he's mean. (*Applause.*) Billy, your injection. (*Very loud applause.*)

D—Turn, turn it all off.

RR—I got on the phone an I called up information an I asked for the telephone number of my drugstore

D—Yeah . . . Can we not hear any music for a while?

RR—So he heard . . . he heard me ask for it, so he got the name of it, right? Location, then when like we got to the drugstore I asked for my man and he got that guy's name and I asked him for certain things. Then we got hung up around the apartment for a couple of hours and it got very late and I decided that I'm not gonna go down tonight, I didn't need any thing, but at Igor's place I could pick it up tomorrow

INTERLUDE

He left my hourse—and went

down to the store and said, "Mr. Effort sent him and picked up the package and delivered it to me—nothing wrong with it. But he diddtha- . . . did that to meet the guy

BN—I said, "Tell (Rita) Mr. W. WRop I-uh . . . give Mr. Wrap my order."

RR—So the guy said to me,and the guy was very . . . this guy's very (mutters) . . . He's a family guy —he would never give me anything that would-uh . . . he would never— . . . ya know what I mean . . .

D—Yeah.

RR—He always watched out—he wasn't like one of those mad characters who'd give you anything**ya know what I mean? (Pause.) He asked the guy down there, the look . . . Bob asked me now if any girls came in an I said Oh Yeaah—he's OK—You can . . .

BN—. . . let . . . use your . . . up . . .

RR—I said that. He went there 5 times. The 6th time he went there he brought 2 tokens with him, sat at the luncheonette counter while Joey placed his order, and as soon as he paid the man, the dicks came over and busted the drugstore. Two licenses were involved—he had obviously . . .

D—You sure it was him?

RR—You bet—the drug was strong.

O—Yeah, he's always been . . . and Jack, he . . .

RR—You know how I exercise, I . . .

D—. . . told me once he didn't do it.

RR—You can't believe he didn't?

D—No no—he said he didn't do it. He brought it up today or something like that

RR—Well, you know what he said to me the other night when I saw him for the first time down in somebody's house? He said: I really went to your drugstore. He said he . . . I mean, there is all the evidence—we know he did. That's why he left town—that's why he went to Florida.

D—Oh.

RR—He had, probably. Not him, I think it was Pete who got in trouble with the police—that kid he was going around with at that time, or he still might be going around with—got in trouble with the police. And, yaknow, theyy worked out some kind of deal whereby-uhh they would go easier on him, ya know, if he would do something like that. And you know, the drug store, of course, was very severely hurt—they didn't sell to kids, they didn't sell pills to people who-uh . . . who look out of their minds or demented or like regular junkies or anything like that. No, y'know, they just did family favors Oh . . . did you poke yourself?

D—Oh-uh, mo

O—Did you get . . . oh, by the way, where's-uh, where's . . . ward is being paged—uh. Do you know, Rotten, that our telephone conversations tonight were also done on the thing, so that the Duchess' escapade is entirely intact. From the inception of the plan to its execution.

RR—I f you can find it, I wanna hear the part that took place at my house between me and everybody

O—The girls are going through it

RR—That's not so important, but I wanna hear the part with . . . uh, what's her name, the Duchess—

D—(*inaudible*) . . . (Is this Parcival?)

O—No, this is *War and Peace* . . . *War and Peace* . . . He's—because he's . . .

RR—Because *Parcival* is so fuckin dull . . . it's fabulous

O—(*throaty O*) (*again*) Uh huh, I know, but*uh . . . Billy, your injections.

BN—I can't do it

RR—What were we just talking about?

O—About Jim.

RR—No . . .

O—About *Parcival*.

RR—Oh, no, I said, yes—that's, yes

D—Oh, and-uh . . .

RR—Yes, that's very good—

D—I'm not sure . . . I'm nit sure I have that

RR—Because I haven't spoken to her, and I didn't speak to her today, I spoke to— . . .

D—No, I'm not sure I have it . . .

RR—You DO—You hadda pick it up.

O—The thing was that . . .

D—No, uh . . .

O—. . . when-uh, when we-uh went to the door, we heard the bell,

and then we went back immediately. We didn't hear the bell before this. And, then.

RR—Just picked it up.

D—Well, I'm not sure I had it on, but*uh . . .

O—Oh, yes—you did, darling. I'm sure of it. Because it was too explosive a moment.

D—Well, uh, we*uh, yaknow, it was just—

RR—It was a fabulours moment.

O—The gods took care of us, it's there—it's there . . .

RR—Well, Drella, I'm sure you picked it up—

D—Well, if I see it, then we'll play it . . .

RR—Because everything

RR—Because everybody else here in the room during this whole thing was silent.

D—Yeah, but-oh, but but, butI, but—no, I'm not sure I had it on, because—. . .

RR—. . . I have a whole world to take care of.

D—We're . . . we were going from closet to closet and stuff like that . . .

O—Yeah, but, yes, that machine has . . .

RR—Billy!!

O—How much. told me she is worth? Two hundreds dollars and a self-portrait. That's what that boy said.

D—What boy?

O—Uh . . . Rotten.

RR—What was that?

O—Rotten, he said that—that's a $200 machine.

D—Oh

RR—Where did you pick up that taxicab driver?

O—In, tonight, well, wait—we were

coming out of the restaurant.

RR—He fled, too.

D—Are they coming back?

O—. . . (giggles) . . . I hope they come back with turkey sandwiches.

RR—Hope who come back with sandwiches?

O—That group is so sweet, it . . .

RR—They wouldn't, though—they just don't do things like that

O—Sugar left his tie here, too.

RR—Uh huh

D—Oh, he did

Uh huh

RR—Gee, he has god ties, too. Where is it? (Giggle.)

It's in the other room . . .

RR—You know I wear those string around me T-shirts, right down aroung here—they look like . . . (flapper days?)

Angel, when you see him tonight in the restaurant—you wouldn't need it.

RR—He sleeps in the restaurant down there?

He grabbed his tie, and it went like this—WHOORRSSHHH (rip), and Sugar's face went—

(muffling laughter) Why?

He couldn't believe it?

(again with laughter) Why?

Well, Sugar . . . but Sugar is all— . . .

I didn't sneeze . . .

Sugar a lot of time is a very prissy creature—

RR—No, Eddie, now please be faster

Well, tell me more about him—

BN—Doctor, forget about the . . . (fade) . . .

(opera.)

Well, I'll take it . . .

Tell me about Sugar

RR—I have a practice

Go right in there, darling, and give it to him

RR—I am—I have to atke care of . . . I suppose it's bad enough, but when you have to chase the patient out of the fucker's room . . . I'll get him

We're right here . . . It's up to

RR—I'll be right back, hold it—

We're holding the fort, Sugar (laughs). I've-uh . . . I've known Sugar for fifteen years, Drella.

Oh

And, of course, he's evil

Really?

O—He's rotten, he's . . .

Why's he rotten?

O—Well, he's mean, like evil—why, like, well, everyone is mean, ya know, really.

D—Well, how's he mean?

O—Well, yaknow, he's . . . he's playing a love scene, too. Like, everybody who . . .

D—Really?

O—Anybody who makes up to the mirror . . . with people falling in love with them is, ya know, uh sick

D—What?

O—Sick. I mean—yeah, (and never completes the scenes). Never, except if he runs across a mad woman like me who, yaknow, waits till he pretends that he's asleep, and then, just—

D—Oh, really?

O—Oh, what I do for him

RR—Sodium, sodium bisodol (to Billy)

O—They don't pay for any thing

RR—Those pink pills

O—Those are the ones that are raised a*uh, a little bit. I've-uh, I've been having . . . having them

RR—You have. Well, I called the doctor up last Friday—I said I need that prescription, too. And he wouldn't give them to me. Sodium bisodol.

O—You gave me one at your house, my love.

RR—Aren't they, aren't they great? . . . Sodium bicarbonate . . . tranquilizer . . . (*Fade out with music.*) Am I a tranquilizer? . . . No. A stimulant.

O—Drella, and this is a compliment I'd like to pay you—like I said earlier, . . . (*inaudible*) . . . eleven to . . . She's worried about her dosage.

RR—Listen, would you please get her file out?

O—It's right here—I brought it*uh . . . I brought it along

RR—She belongs on 24. She's trouble . . .

O—She's always running the water in the toilets

RR—I want an immediate review of the Name case.

O—It's-uh . . . it's all right . . . it's right here. It says, "American boy gone awry"

RR—Those-uh . . . are those her fingerprints?

O—They're all over everything, including the tie.

RR—The tie?

O—Now, now that boy, ya know, really, was absolutely—absolutely nothing, but the Lower East Side.

RR—Taxi cab driver, couldn't even make it.

O—Couldn't believe it—

RR—And he didn't want to show us his wallet

O—But he didn't have to, really—

D—But, still, it was Sugar . . .

O—Of course, ti was Sugar who interrupted the scene. I dragged them away.

RR—It's always Sugar who'll always do things like that. That's the liar he is.

O—And we'll both agree he's divine and he's gonna be so much better once he's cured—

RR—He's gonna be part of the wax museum right here

D—Really?

RR—MmmmHumm

O—He is fun

RR—He's on the boat that's going across the river. Oh, you're all ready!

O—Ward 4 calls in

RR—. . . stand in the door . . . hello, hello—stay there. I'll get it

O—Oh oooohh WARD 24 uh Ward 24 doesn't answer.

BN—. . . get my . . .

RR—Ohm really?

O—Sugar is . . . Sugar is oh so very (*en francais*)

D—Very what?

O—(*French again*), considerate. He's very—kind, and very beau— . . .

RR—Would you take this thing? This is from Marco Polo

O—Oh, I'd love them

Voice—Marth's Vineyard?

O—He's—uh . . . he's a paint; I'm sure there's a better word to describe his particular type of sickness which is, but I don't know what it is . . .

RR—Billy, you just say . . .

O—But the point is, overinvolved with those things—overinvolved with the hustlers, but-uh ego reasons . .

RR—Just wait a moment

O—And, I don't want to make judgments because I don't know

RR—Because I don't want you to have a dull needle. I'm changing the needle/I've decided not to give it.

O—have some . . .

D—I don't . . . uh . . .

O—It's delicious . . . oh, it's the compliment I wanted to pay you my love was that I know that you are one of the only people I know who do not have to take drugs.

RR—Nobody sit on a paper bags, because there'd be a lot of breakage.

O—Do you know how long it takes to understand a person that doesn't have to be placed anywhere?

O—Like when . . . when Sugar spoke to you, what would . . did you do when Sam came to you? That's a question I'd liked to have asked you, too, cause, ya-know, I wouldn't have the . . .

RR—I would not do anything but taking an appointment Monday

O—The honesty with which she asked you, I . . . I thought that . . . that you might've answered

in—but you didn't

RR—. . . you won't even feel this . . . the ear . . .

O—Because you have such a matter of fact way of saying what you did before, Drella. Usually, I . . . I use . . . wait. Wait. I'll UH! AH! Help me! Please. Take it out.

RR—No, no . . . I want that one changed

O—Oh, do you want it in? Oh, all right

RR—(Shriek)

O—Right into your middle—is it okay?

B—. . . World's Fair pictures?

D—Oh you are, wow!

BN—Would you like to see these pictures?

D—Oh, really? Wow

O—Yeah, you do have a lot of them

BN—I'l give you some. I've got about 24 rolls

O—Rita, what happened?

RR—. . . . sat on the coat again . . .

O—I keep seeing Oscar LaMocha in my window again

RR—. . . animal in my house,

O—You do.

18 /   1

RR—Yer sucha fuckin fag, talula, you a-a-are more than Frank Sinatra . . .

(Overwhelming distortion.)

O—I've n-never done anything so ridiculous in my life—why am I taking drugs? I need them, that's

why. We're just coming, and you'd never know it . . . You're so Smart, you're like Hildegarde. Dahling, je vous aime beaucoup, je ne sais pas WHAT to do . . .

BN—Ya wanna drink?

RR—No. He doesn't drink pineapple shesti deah . .

O—Well, ya live a little . . .

RR—. . . especially the ashtray.

BN—Whaah?

O—(*gasp*)

RR—. . . at this, this 15th century . . .

O—I just turned to . . .

BN—Fuck off

O—. . . Traum, clang, und rhyd-dums

BN—Hey, Mars, Bars

O—Why don't you have one, darling? Before we put you under.

RR—Billy, I think you really need a . . .

BN—I spend all my time trying to U-U-UP, an then when I get up, you . . .

RR—Dis-cum-bob-u . . .

O—Thank you

RR—Here, my dear, take the tranquilizer for us, who love you

O—D-d-Don't go . . . I'm frightened . . . ah-duh-I I'm so far up

PR—Ya mean, you mean that's not jus working?

BN—I have . . . I haven't been so . . .

O—Oh, my dear, I'm SO far up, I'm frightened

BN—far up since-uh I was very . . .

O—Thank you

BN—Way out on a test of LSD that was . . .

O—OOwuss zapzap dago?

BN—. . . so loaded that the guy would go out and buy more, an I went outamyhead. And, I wasn't frightened—High was my friend . . .

O—What're you gonna call the-uh

D—Huh

BN—. . . parts of my head

O—Have Y/yuh-you-oo decided?

RR—. . . exploded . . .

D—Ha, Mars . . .

BN—Anything that can frighten me, I like it

O—Ohhh. I keep doing this Peter Hartman jess-uh . . .

(*Mara Callas singing KUNDRY from Parcival in Italian.*)

Look: I k-keep doing this Peter Hartman gesture

D—Where IS Peter Hartman?

O—I hope Orio strangled him. Ya know, he's the one—he introduced us to Amphetamine

BN—Has Wilba Toast gotten in touch with you lately?

O—(*gasp*) Wilba Toast—that fucking name again

D—Shall I call him up . . . uh, uh . . . Should I call him back or . . ?

BN—No, don't call him back—he'll be around

O—ass-Ask him over. Ask him over now. Tell-tell him to bring his dirty pictures.

BN—He's a Li-Little bit-uh

O—Listen to this: this is the way Wilba Toast tells every- . . .

BN—He's a little bit passe

O—. . . body he's gonna do it

RR—There's something inside.

O—About Onassis and Callas?

BN—. . . he's a little bit Village Bard, ya know. He told you or the Duchess told you?

RR—HE did. Right there

O—Ooooo—I've gotta get something to wash that down

RR—Ya know what? Me, too—bring some here.

O—OOOOooohhhHHH, God.

RR—. . . Onassis was sitting there rolling joints. He said that he hadn't . . .

Maria Callas interlude.

. . . he hadn't done that since he

was a waiter. When was he a waiter?

BN—Wilba Toast?

RR—NO. Ona- . . .

BN—Onassis?

RR—Yeah

BN—As a young . . .

RR—Tha was years ago, probably.

BN—boy?

RR—Well, thass what he said, he was . . .

BN—On the boat, on the-uh boat

RR—She was-uh . . . she was Right out of it. And, she said-uh heshu uh, ya know, it's surprising He s-uh, as much as he adores her, he's never seen a performance of hers, an he told her that . . .
Maria Callas.
An, she said, WELL. She made arrangements for him to go to one of the Paris NORMAS, an he said: WAAOOW. He said there's no VOICE. . . .
Maria Callas.
He doesn't know How she does it.

BN—Yeah, I'm sure—I really-uh wish I didn't hafta miss the-uh . . . I should have gone down . . .

RR—Ondine. Ya gonna bring me in a glass?

BN—*inaudible in background*

O—Here. Oh. That taste is still in the back of my throat

B—Oh, you know, that REALLY looks like art.

BN—Yeah, I been leaving it hanging because I like the way it looks. . . . There's not much black in this place—there's a lotta white.

D—No, that's nice
Opera chortles: hahahahaha HA-AAAA ha, etc.

RR—Do I jus pick this up like that?

D—Yeah
Three muffled simultaneous conversations.

O—Drella, do you have any gum or anything on you?

D—Uh, no.

RR—Ondine. Do you know where the needle and thread is?

O—No

BN—I can get that right know. I just-uh . . .

RR—Now, you just take your time.

BN—It's too late, Reet. . . . I mean I'm already all ready to do it.

SPF—I'm rushing for them

RR—What did you throw all these things on the floor for?
Sound of objects trickling to the floor.
I really think he's losing his mind. The only thing to do is to be overly kind. Treat him overly nice,
COUGH
LISTEN TO THE FAGGOT whine. . . . I'm telling you—I hadda come down there tonight because they really are in trouble down there.

BN—Who?

RR—Billy an Antis . . . an the other three
Maria Callas.
Drella . . . I hadher around the-uh . . .

D—What does thing mean? Dona-uh DO NOT RESTERILIZE

RR—Wha

D—Youcan T-uh . . . You can't use it again?

RR—It says don't resterilize?

D—Yeah

RR—Well, I'll tell you why, be-cause-uh . . . the-uh . . . Oaaow—

is there one in there?
Maria Callas.
OK. I'll tell you why, this I've sterilized, and I'll tell you what happened.
RR—Dissolved plastic-uh . . .
D—Oh? Even the needle?
RR—It's all bent, see. I've gotta know how to do it. See, I can't get off. It's jus-uh . . . What I use is like a fork . . . (*inaudible*) . . . that's if you go right ahead into the vein
D—Oh, really?
RR—and, if you're gonna start doing things like that, then you're in trouble, an you gotta go through all those hang-ups
D—Oh . . ?
RR—Just intra-muscular—that's why it's such a long point . . .
D—Oh, ya mean . . ?
RR—Just intra-muscular-uh . . .
D—What about . . . the-uh . . . Your-uh . . . when you're doing the-uh—what do you call them.
RR—Popping?
D—Uuhh-no
BN—Veining it?
D—Nonono-uh . . you know, uh, . . . putting on the designs, ya know—tatooing
RR—Oh, Tuh-when-uh Tattoo? Oh, yes, that was vrey bad—that's why they-uh. That's why they made it illegal because the-uh . . .
BN—That doesn't go into the-uh . . .
RR—There was a big thing about-uh hepatitis. Well, not—that's because the used the electric needle
D—Yeah? What does that mean?
RR—And-uh, it means that they use it on you. They used it on me after they used it on you, and

they didn't clean it. See? And-uh, they-uh . . . that's Bad.
D—Oh
RR—Because you might have hepatitis.
D—Oh
RR—And you'd give it to me through the needle. That's how I got my hepatitis.
D—Oh, really?
RR—They—ah—I had inFECtious hepatitis, which isa hepatitis in the bloodstream. You can only get this through getting into you . . . by injection
D—Oh
RR—I wasn't into anything like this when I had hepatitis
D—Oh did you get it?
RR—I had a series of warts, on my face . . .
D—Yeah
RR—. . . and the doctor gi-uh DID each of them with—not an electric needle, but a regular hypodermic needle. Then he placed it down . . .
D—Yeah
RR—and he drilled, and he-uh scraped it off with an electric needle, and he just—ya know, back and forth with the same needle
D—yeah?
RR—We traced it to that. All the doctors that I had spoken to, and I had-uh . . .
D—Oh. Well, how did they? Well, but it was . . . , But it was the same needle being used On you.
RR—Yeah, it was, but-uh . . . it was resting someplace, and-uh . . . those Hypodermics—that's why you don't find doctors using hypodermics any more
D—Oh. no.

RR—Do you see any ruh-doctor go ahead and Boil, and boil . . .

D—Oh, well. Then, can you use these over again. . . ?

RR—These are disposals. Of course you—yeah, you can use them over again. Uh . . you can use it with the s-uh with the SAME effect. At lea-easily six times. 20 cents, anyway.

D—Oh . . .

RR—It's a hang-up, though—the disposal stuff

BN—A havoc?

RR—Oh. Uh. You don't have the dark thread?

BN—Fraid not

RR—Only white?

BN—I'm aFRAID that's allIgot

RR—(carrying through BN's somewhat Slavic dialect in the last comment) Yuh got enny (babble) siiize trea-uh-duh?

Maria Callas overcomes all replies.

O—(inaudible) . . . silk thread. Oh, Heaven . . .

RR—What's that, Ondine?

O—A Tuonol gets stuck in your throat, you're dead

RR—Where did I get . . . did you just gimme these? . . . Oh, thank you.

BN—Thass quite all right

RR—I just figured—the other one you gave me is too . . .

O—(inaudible—simultaneous with Rotten)

RR—I just figured—the other one you gave me has been marvelous

O—Do you have a taste in your mouth?

Maria Callas.

SPF—Wanna do some—?

D—No. What is-uh . . .

RR—(inaudible)

D—Oh, it IS?

BN—Yeah

RR—It is

BN—. . . when it gets to the white surface, you can seeit. Look: the Orange Bowl.

assorted aaahhs

yeah, it's a ilttle bit faded because it was-eh-uh. Because it's a . . . long time ago

O—Oh. . . . Fuck. Fuck

BN—. . . and it's been in Ondine's book

O—AMERICA—O beau-ti-ful for spaaa-cious skies, for am-ber waves of graaaaain, for pu-urple mountains

Billy and Rita converse in bacground; they become audible as they walk near microphone.

BN—. . . It's just that—I accumulated. . . .

RR—(simultaneous) HA. HA.

BN—it seems, allof a sudden

RR—(simultaneous) You're gonna lose a few chihuahuas, my dear, lemme tell you right now . . .

BN—And I didn't want—I didn't want to put them into Modern-age and-uh . . .

O—Lower the boom on them . . .

BN—have them just mill around for five days . . . (fade with microphone distortion)

Maria Callas and distorted microphone.

O—Oh, God in Heaven, and Rita's lost his jug . . . We'll put the boom down this way . . . The boom's coming down on ih- . . .

RR—apresionae . . .

O—Cmon—I'd like to know one thing, please, before I-ah . . .

RR—I'd like, before you do anything, I'd like you to fart, because I'm sure the bottle's up yer ass

. . .

O—I'm gonna cought it up (*Bill-woough*)

RR—Look uh-everybody—I HATE them, all those lousy, miserable . . . punks . . .

O—punks . . .

R—. . . they're only doing this because we hate each other . . .

O—You oughta know . . .

RR—And we hate them, too, don't you think? And as soon as I get into a suh-, and believe me, I'm getting in there, all those cocksuckers are gonna go.

Ondine raps in background.

RR—my firsht act is gonna be ta go ahead and get the power to put them in the Hudson River.

O—(*very raspy-teen*) BRAH-VO!!!

RR—Then, let them crowse, an I'm gonna kill them jus . . . like they were Jehovah's Witnesses.

O—They are the REAL Jehovah Witnesses; the cunts . . .

RR—(*inaudible*) . . . are RITA's witnesses.

O—. . . Rita, The ceiling must be razed—whoo whoo (*warning whistle of wrecking crew and/or a sign of the awesome power of the unknown Rita, whoooOOO-OOOOOOOOOOOOO*) . . . He COMES . . . (*Rita doing Gregorian chants*) Rosilie—Capry—and Gookie, mark—that Voice (I'm speaking to the girls) That Voice is the Voice of your Mayor, girls . . . . . (that's right girls—d-e-a-t-h).

RR—The . . . that Voice is my Voice, and I'm a madwoman. But I know how to use my madness.

O—And she's more ma-a-an than you'll ever marry, my dear.

RR—I-uh . . . (*long pause after which Rita reassumes normal voice*) . . .

BN—(*in background*) . . . and-uh, a lot of things that individually . . .

RR—She'll take aver for me. Or you, perhaps . . .

O—(*continues ghoulish voice*) The Mayor now goes to- . . .

RR—(*background in normal voice*) The mayor now goes below the floor to find the bottom of the . . .

O—The Mayor desc-e-nds . . . blu-uwa-wa atasoah.

RR—The Mayor now stands . . .

O—Dejects the entire crowd and screams: WHATCHAWANEN-NYWAY?

RR—I may get to the bottom, but I won't speak to either one of them

O—And you'd be wise not to.

RR—O, Kay . . .

O—They don't care about yo-oo-ou,

RR—I don't like the evaluations

O—I don't like-uh Judgments

RR—And I don't like the plot against me

O—You know about it, then?

RR—Mayor Lindsay, man—I can tell

O—I don't like the idea of the ethical vergedie

Operatic interlude

TO-day . . . ethical . . . Drella Whole is a nice man, mut he s—he's not BROADminded enough, th-that s what it is is. Drella Whole is non-permissive. (Tee hee) Drella . . . Drella . . . I just said the you're non-permissive. He does allow things to happen—he's so reactionary, it's unbearable. It's due to him that *stifling things* happen. . . . In fact, I think he's Yiddish. Dyou know what he said?? . . . He turned to me and said, he said: sheneese . . . shenee . . . oh, i dunno what the next word was, but it was heaven . . . The Mayor returns—this time with an urgent petition. . . . Awwwww—the Mayor is always asking another beneficial act. The Mayor (*muffled laugh*) . . . The Mayor smiles and breaks wrists

RR—Yeah

O—Who's that??? Is that the Duchess? . . . WHO??

BN—I've known her longer than even Dodo, an . . .

O—WHO???

BN—Devars-uh

O—Helen Devars is an evil man. Would you stand over here by the lamp. Behind the 8-ball, darling?

RR—DREL-la. In the eight—. . . pocket number eight

O—There's a big—there's a big thing there, and-uh

RR—They've got everything up there

O—O—K

RR—An, let's get this thing . . . I wanna get that aeroplane up here . . .

O—All right, darling—x We're gonna make a little basket, and a little dart
Ondine's and Rita's conversation muffled by opera.

O—She shoot the hell that way out . . . She's parading to the shit house, and to the garden?

RR—(*voice fades out*) . . . darling . . . darling . . . one shot in 6 hours . . . (*becomes inaudible*) . . .

O—Your glass bottle?

RR—Yeaah, Ondine, I-Uh . . .

(*fades out*) . . .

O—Oh . . . uh . . . Besides that, you're FIGHTING for your very existence

O—. . . with this cock-sucking bunch of . . .

RR—VE-EH-ERY existence

O—Yes, but you've made the-uh . . . I-da-ina- Indeed not tell you that Evelyn is a moron if it weren't for you . . . (*paper rustling, Ondine sighs, rustling*) . . . I'm dropping a bag, hoping that someone will find it an give me help . . . (*rustle rustle*). Some one picks it up and rejects it— Instant Rejection. They think I'm Joey Benjamin. Billy Name goes on . . .

BN—*mumbling in background*

O—A marathon in himself—he's talking forever

BN—*more mumbling*

O—Paranoid. I don't even know what the word means

BN—*mumbling*

O—It's the first time eitheroneofem called Ondine Bob . . .

BN—*mumble*

O—Rosilie, Cappy, and Gookie, Mark well: . . . This is Your Life.

BN—*mumble*

O—Who would sigh God is violent?

BN—*mumble*

O—They're speaking about—. . . WHO? . . . God bless my-uh *Michael Katzjammer*.

BN—*mumble*

plop plop plop plop plop plop plop

O—The Mayor didn't like That, but . . .
Male falsetto warbles in the distance.

O—I'm tryin ta kill the Mayor,

Mother . . . Chshooogh—I got her in the neck, boy . . . Is this a piranha? . . . You should put the—the entrance onto . . . Do you . . . Do you hear the wholena? Nonono—I unnerstan, Rotten. With hope, With hope and love, my love

RR & BN answer inaudibly

O—. . . because if that's a mistake, . . .

RR—Because I called up his old room, and-uh . . .

O—. . . then more people . . . What?

RR—. . . where it is . . .

O—Oh, well . . . Nonono, in fact, do you know, Rotten? It's a mistake that we called that a mistake. Cause that's not a mistake to-uh . . . evaluate human . . . Be higher.

Operatic solo warbling.

I wish I could join you—my throat doesn't permit me . . .

BN—(*very indistinctly*) . . . exACTly where I think . . .

O—She's taken another thing in her whole heart. But I think—it's a LIFE-saver where she's hanging . . . when she's handing to the tenor.

RR & BN WARBLING

Sing to Drella . . . Hey-yus . . . Dya know you sing, my dear, and there's a nuh- . . . Drella's hair. Naaaow. Ya talk about . . . Rita —he's here

Screeching

that's a privileged fact. That's a very prof—Drella, it's right here. Problem? . . . I almost fell down the stairs

More screeching vibrato

LISTEN. Aaaoow—Drella, Rita sung, and you were the . . . that

means the last test was passed. You are dEFinitely A.W.

D—Why?

O—Rita sings only for all women. Rita sings for all women—Oooh, *Rita!* Cmon RIIITAAAAA.

Tumultuous applaus.

Stop em

Applause absolutely out of control.

Sonali Das Gupta

BRAVOOO BRAVOOO

I'm going swimming now, darling.

BN—Why don't you do that

RR—If you find that glass bottle

O—I don't know which glass bottle you allude to

RR—You know the one I want . . .

BN—The one I gave you that you sort of gave aside . . .

RR & BN warbling.

RR—I-uh . . . I found the cork . . .

O—Something tells me . . .

D—(*inaudible*) . . . the Bottle?

O—Something tells me I've done something iwth it

RR—Something tell us All that

O—I RAN OUT WITH YER TACK

RR—You ran out with it

O—Where'd I put it?

Chortling opera aids the search.

RR—(*wicked laugh*)

O—I've come after the expensive young Maa-an . . . do I look like I—. . . Not even nodding out on the bus

RR—You're tired as you say, how can you . . .

O—I look a little weird.

RR—howkin you mittinahdeece

O—I look a little weird, Rita

RR—Thass true

O—I look a tiny bit weird, baby. I wouldn't be except for the sky falli- . . .

D—Did you find the . . .

O—Yeah cuzheleftit ovah there. Now where did I put there? Next to the record

BN—(*at a distance*) Rather than-uh . . . rather than . . . risk a situation of having to go to-uh . . .

O—Aaaaaggh . . . (*a commentary above and upon BN's simultaneous words*). The currents on—listen to that one rap.

BN—. . . make it easier , , , or something like that if he spent more time . . .

O—OK, virginia—bACK in the shock room. You've talked enough for two months rations—

BN—. . . and, and after . . . after all . . .

O—You're all yer gootsatungginn

BN—. . . Once ya come down to it,

O—Ahuugh!! (*gasp*) Ooohhh . . . AAaaaow . . . Two at ONCE. Since you were gonna come down to it, what can you do?? That was three (*haha*), that was three

BN—(*continued*) . . .can't you see . . . I think that . . .

O—Another Name throw-home . . .

BN—(*continued again*) . . . as it is, he has an apartment that you can go to a room when she wants to be alone, and . . . (*continues*)

RR—(*beginning inaudible*) . . . do you?

O—Huh?

BN—. . . Because she told me that one of the things she . . .

O—Oh, Thank you, prithamps. Thank you

BN—. . . And, uh, I was seeing them for a little while, and . . .

O—Imogene's gone mad again

BN—(*continues rapping in the distance*)

O—Doesn't anybody love me or want me? I mean, it's MY tape.

RR—. . . because he's moping . . .

O—It's my tape, and will you stop talking, because you're inSULting. It's my tape.

D—Why did that cab driver come here if he really-uh . . . ?

O—Cavenaugh?

D—No, I mean, If he was-uuhhh . . .

BN—Because he's . . . he's . . .

O—Forgive them everybody, they don't. . . .

BN—. . . the cab driver, and he couldn't settle for being the-uh profession he originally those, so, uh . . .

O—Have you ever seen any Jewish person who-uh didn't want to sop up culture?

BN—. . . but he's-uh, G-uh-rrovie enough to want to . . .

O—Groovey, my ass.

BN—Well, he's not groovey, but he s . . .

O—A Prick, a stupid prick . . .

BN—. . . slick enough to be able to sense . . . sense

O—Fat prick . . . TORTURE THEM

BN—. . . she's . . . some fun for something . . .

O—I'm coming, darling, right . . .

RR—(*inaudible*)

R—. . . do sucha thing . . .

BN—. . . I mean, went out on special word, and . . .

O—(*rustling paper*) That'll tell you where you're at

BN—MMMMmmmm . . . lubadaaaaahhh

O—Listen, darling—I . . . ya know, I have certain observations that I would like to make. These are called ONDINE'S OBSERVA-

TIONS

D—. . . all that about the cab driver, or just-uh . . .

O—That cab driver is . . . is . . . I've never known a Jewish person who wasn't culture-seeking. Duh. Uh . . . That's part of their grooviness, and part of their un-grooviness, that they sop up culture. They're in the HEARt of every cultural brink.

BN—Right. So they know what . . .

O—. . . ihihihih It's a helia

BN—. . . a cultural . . . in fact it's eviden . . . it's everything But . . .

O—Cultural wanting.

D—nonono, it's scared on this-uh

O—Would you please give me my dress back . . . I . . . I want you to witness an outrageous act done . . . in the name of progress, which is the first bad act that the Mayor has committed. Rotten, weave that fabric . . . Weave with it//it's soo Beautiful. You'll love it.

RR—Aaawww

O—It's the best thing I ever had. Lookatit//go it, go ahead. Jim Beam? Jim Beam really poses a serious problem too EVery body. His mother died—do you know how his mother died? Carrying in the Thanksgiving turkey

RR—Waaaooow

O—Isn't it inSANE brr-ooo-oooo

O—Are you all right, dear??? You all right in there?

BN—No tongue there please

O—The Bill is cleaned . . . from the floor

RR—From the floor.

O—She was just walking home with

the Thanksgiving turkey about five years ago

D—Ooooooh

O—And she had a heart attack, just as . . . just as she crossed the corner with the bag-uh, the turkey, and everything else. Boomboom in the street—I would have died. That's really a laugher . . . That's a laughing . . . that's a laughable situation/

BN—hahahahaha hahahaha (*mimicky laughter*)

O—*garbled conversation*) . . . She pissed

RR—When this thing gets played back, Ondine, you'll realize how CRAzy you are

O—Naaaooow . . . You've been charming . . .

SPF—You see what I mean??

O—You need turning . . . you need . . .

D—Yeeaah

O—Darling, why don't we play . . . Hey, Mary, who don't we sing some I songs?::: IIIIIII LOVEA PARADE . . . I love you, all those. . . .

VOICE—You are a ninny.

O—You would be, too, if you were human. Unfortunately, you're not

V—Ya know, really, Ondine, I don't think you love much of anything

O—You, weeaall, you never did, darling

V—Yeah, when I knew you as a young boy, you liked things . . .

O—YOUNG BOY . . . ? They didn't call me that at that time.

V—You gotta kick out of it

O—Never called me a young boy when I was a young boy—he'd say: aaaooo, Hi, Ondine . . .

V—You used to get a kick out of

tricks

O—I used to get a kick out of champagne, darling

V—Noo, out of tricks . . .

O—(*begins singing*) AaahhIIIIII get no . . . All those nights he asked the boy in the bar: Why don't you plan on getting no kick from champagne?? All those songs to ask, and then that guy played the rotten vamp

V—DADADADADADADA dada-daddle, DADADADADADADA da da da

O—He went on and on and it would . . . just drive him into hySTERics

SPF—(*hacking laughter*) That *is* hysterical.

O—Ya know, Sugar sometimes makes me feel TERrible . . .

D—Really?

O—But yuh-you didn't know that he was ostracized ow-out of Queens

D—Why??

O—He used to sing in a church choir, and he went out with the notorious faggot in Queens called Lorelei . . .

D—Lorelei??

O—. . . and he was denounced from the pulpit on a Sunday afternoon

D—By the priest?

P—By Reverend Flare.

D—Who told him about it?

O—He knows about it

D—. . . and what happened?

O—Uh, I dunno—I was never a Protestant. I don't know. He's a Protestant.

D—Oh. How d'you know that?

O—Ooo, muhwella, I was told, I mean, unless they were lying.

D—Oh really?

O—Do you think people lie

Opera interrupts.

It's getting coldness up here . . . I wanna tell you something. Do ya know (*word or name is inaudible*). Ya know, that's not there, but TAXINE would do at this rate. And, but . . . and Why is it that she doesn't understa-a-and? And-uh . . . she was Better when she was on just the amphetamine, but with the barbiturates, it causes her complete confusion, and it doesn't bring her out of it. It makes you . . . not under- . . . Look at the Mayor's ranting . . . The Mayor is en-RAGED. . . . No, she's digging it—pardon me.

SPF—No, you see, if I take pills, I won't be able to . . . operate for the next few hours . . .

RR—Then you take downs . . . obviously.

O—When Jim Beam takes amphetamine, he's at his most beautiful

D—Oh, really?

SPF—(*in background*) . . . sleeping pills . . .

O—He gets . . . he gets very ridiculous, because he begins to be-LEEve

Rotten Rita, Billy Name, Sugar Plum Fairy continue coonversation in the background.

O—(*replies to BN*) . . . Not me, you're not . . . Not ME yer not —I'm just here for tricks

SPF—Have a sip

O—Thanks, pearl. . . . There's nothing in here but a bunch of shit—doctor Schooll's corn . . . corn remedy.

SPF—I . . . I couldn't enjoy it because I'd be so frightened

O—Well, then, give it back here . . .

Rotten continues urging SPF to

indulge.

O—Rita—don't PLEEAR, Rita.

SPF—I mean I would . . .

O—Don't plead for progress

SPF—I . . . in some other way. Watch them push a hard at me . . . watch them push a hashish at me . . .

O—Darling, those things are wonderful drugs—I love them too—but, you cannot the-uh . . . you must . . . I mean, no matter WHAT it is—down ta drinking yer own piss—you've got to be reCEPtive to it. If you AREn't, you're not an intelligent human being

SPF—whaddayameEEan? Yer not intelligent if you're not receptive to EVrything?

O—E-V-E-R-Y-Thing tha- . . . Everything that ever exists or happens

SPF—But you say . . . No—you gotta reACt to everything. I react, I don't accept it

O—(*simultaneous*) You've gotta be reCEPtive . . . I didn't SAY accept it—I said to uh be reCEPtive to it

SPF—I'm receptive . . .

O—No, you're not—you have preconceptions about dru- . . . the needle

SPF—I can SNIFF as much amphetamine as anybody

O—*I* can sniff more than YOU or anybody else that ever LIVED

SPF—The thing is that you don't know how to HANdle drugs

O—. . . Oh, those WORDS!!!!! *Laughter from Rotten and Billy.*

O—Ondine faints . . . (*more laughter*) . . . Dirt thanks if one of your friends just told me off and on in n-n-no uncertain terms

with your very words.

BN—Irate words spoken . . .

O—Yes, he said: (*mimics SPF*) You don't know how to handle drugs

RR—I speak with forked tongue.

O—I knooaaooow—. . .

SPF—heh heh heh heh (*almost a tee hee*)

RR—I said that, didn't I?

O—Yes, you did, you cunt. . . . That hurt

R—. . . you took me out of context . . .

O—That hurt so badly, but what hurt was when she took the Yeh-uh Yehudi Menuhin record off . . .

Rotten Rita and Ondine converse simultaneously—Rotten only audible occasionally.

RR—. . . she went nuts . . . she cooled it when Uh . . .

O—I wanted to just . . . smack your face—PPPSSSHHHEEEW. Like that, I said, you silly cunt

RR—I couldn't say anything but that, and I couldn't say anything

O—MY dear . . .

RR—Well, you . . .

O—You made your fatal mistake that night.

RR—You know what you said to me?

O—You made your fatal mistake by taking that Japanese—that indigeno—. . . My dear, why, what a slap in MY face. That Indian music bore . . .

D—*a completely separate conversation*) Is it?

BN—Yeah.

D—Are you sure?

BN—I musta just woke up

O—. . . I was really enjoying it, and you just went over and whacked it right off

RR—I musta just woke up

O—No, you didn't. Yes, you did. You did

RR—But, uhhh, you were . . . (*simultaneous with Ondine's next few* comments)

O—But it was an evening of— RHONDA—it was an evening of . . . I'm so mad at you

RR—You know where you said to me—you said: you're hallucinations . . . you're hal-lu-ci-nit-ting

O—I said I don't need a Light to take them; I said you're hallucinating on WORds

RR—You were divine the other night when you called me up on the phone and said: You-you-you Fuck, can't take dru-u-u-ugs . . . you-you-you . . .

O—I said: You cock-sucker, you

R—. . . you sock-sucker, you . . .

O—I said I hope you're ready to die at that speed . . .

RR—I mean . . . But it seems like you popped the pill to NIGHT, my dear . . .

O—No, I didn't.

RR—I know . . .

O— HEAAARD . . .

RR—you you you . . . oh, Ondine, ooooo

O—I said, you can't over dose

RR—Yeah, . . .

SPF—(*to Drella*) . . . and then the green

RR—(*continues to Ondine*) . . . . You're getting traumatic, thank you

O—. . . I TRIed . . . hard, ya know, because I was watching this filthy television program—oh, come on, darling—I used to go

SPF—What is this called, a (*word muffled by continuing comments*

from Rita and Ondine) machine?

RR—You want to do something? Drella?

D—What?

RR—This is very funny

O—I got this one . . . THEY don't want to hear: all they want to do is talk about pleasantries.

O—. . . who's got the knife and fork? Who's being the new Crespan de Los Angeles (*slurp, slurp*)?

RR—(*very muffled, intentionally*) Here: taketaketaketaketaketake

O—Who can or can't have . . .

SPF—Who's the new Crespan de Los Angeles???

RR—. . . (*to Drella*) who stick them in themselves and keep them there for hours . . .

D—Oh, really?

O—Is that a name. There is a singer called Montserrat Caballe

RR—Am I gonna get bo . . .?

O—. . . otherwise known as Boredom on Toast

RR—She has a triple B-flat

O—. . . and all the fairies say: You should hear her, my dear boy, Milanov in her youngest days. (*Sniiffff.*) You can barely FEEL this

SPF (*mimicks*) you can barely FEEEL this

O—C'mon, it's Groucho time . . .

SPF—. . . Look at a shirred . . . shirred boroff

O—She's all . . . All fraud, my dear. And he said (*simper*). And I said: She's DisGUSTing, blablablah. And, he said it's Crespan de Los Angeles. Well, week later, the College Record comes out, and doesn't Crazy Mary come over and say to us: ya know, that Is right Lu-Lucretia Borgia

RR—(*some inaudible question*)

O—Wal-ter. Lips of Callas, my Mother

SPF—weeaaall . . . you're just no . . . (*fade*) . . . recording, my dear . . .

Ondine, Rita, Sugar Plum, and the rest in a fiery, simultaneous, and therefore totally garbled conversation).

O—(*the only resulting audible, semi-coherent statement thus far*) . . . you, watch you, walking through the park, and you had some lovely, beautiful thing—you're not a great artist. But not a great artist. I've been a great artist, marriesta my communion.

RR—I thih . . . I think it's time we went to the hall.

O—No. *I'LL* put the time we go to the hall, my dear.

RR—I'll go back to the hall this time

O—YOU're ready, and I'm NOT.

RR—I'm—OH. awright

O—I asked her for coaching a long time ago. She's done nothing but accuse me of mishandling my drugs. She's robbed from me behind my back, spreads FILthy rumors infrontof behind my back.

RR—Behind my back

O—She's made stand with the biggest lih- . . . Hey, that cleah—sort of clears the air. Didn't Didn't you frauds want an honest opinion?

Operatic interlude.

SPF—. . . bouquets

D—Oh, really?

SPF—Yeah

SPF—Don't—I wanna pick it.

O—You see that? He will not take a needle, but it'll pick yer pimple. I-I-I'm going to BURN it

D—No no no.

SPF—I can't

D—No.

O—Only if you can make your heel first, like this

SPF: Why can't I pick it?

18 /   2

O—Don't put a submitch to it—I I want the pimple to come to its own natural head I reFUSE to have that blood . . .

SPF—Put your needle right up . . .

RR—It's what you deserve, baby . . .

O—If you wanna fuck me, darling, then fuck me, but don't pick my pimples

RR—. . . If you chose to uh . . . the operation, . . .

SPF—. . . a pretty fucked up the-

uh . . .

O—I wanna be fucked on a table, under it, in Macy's—I don't care where-uh . . . I . .

D—. . . it's a half hour, aaah, . . .

O—. . . in front of my mother . . .

RR—Not by any of us.

O—Oh, I'd love to be fucked for more than a half hour

RR—. . . Don't think I'm not spreading that around town

SPF—(*heh heh*) You're spreading syphilis around town???

O—DARling, she's the one who GAVE it to me. (*Pause.*) What can I say, ya know?—I mean, her needles aren't good.

RR—(*not very appreciatively*) HA-Ha-ha. You'd know it

O—They're not leaving—they're just changing position. No Exit, my love

RR—Wha?

O—I'm Estelle, the baby sitter—Aaaahhh.

RR—I . . . I . . . I'm astou— . . .

O—I'm trying to-uh . . . Quiet my . . . beeceeves up

D—Oh Oh Oh ohoh:

O—DoDo Doom

D—DOOOO-DOOOO!!

O—He's a very great acrobat, you know, . . .

RR—DOOOO-DOOOO

O—He's a very great (*interrupted by Rita*) . . . on the rope

RR—Do me a favor, my dear, give me a (*interrupted by shrill operatic shriek from DoDo*)

RR—Hand me up one of those big pillows . . .

O—You may have just a taw Henry ahnono . . . tha wihwihweah you may

RR—(*babbles inaudible to DoDo in the background*)

O—Like, you know, my dear—. . .

RR—Oh, naaoow, stop it—it's no big trip.

DoDo—Fuck you.

DRELLA—What's the zipper doing up here . . . Ondine?

O—It's a little zippity zipper.

D—zipper

O—It's a pho-o-ony one . . . it's a poopsa.

Indistinct conversation between Rita, Sugar Plum and DoDo.

RR—I wanna ask that moron an-

other thing . . .

O—She's colored, besides

RR—Oh, well that settles it

VOICE (*probably DODO*)—meeee meeee MAAAAAAAAAA

RR—She's (*inaudible*)

O—Who threw that?

RR—I dunno

O—Yeaaah

RR—That's not so

O—DoDo says that she likes me because I resemble a bat

RR—She likes you because you look like a . . . a . . .

O—I look like I'm in a belfry

RR—a . . . a . . . Big Sam

O—Who's Big Sam, darling?

RR—(*muffled by strange warbling in background*)

O—Oh Oh—when she gets into her David O. Saznick periods, I hav-ta go out the way

RR—What?

O—This-this was one of the original Scarlett O'Haras, my dear.

RR—I saw it.

O—They AAaaall tried it.

RR—But Susan Hayward won.

O—Do you know Susan Hayward really LIVES Scarlett O'Hara now?

RR—Do you know that Susan Hayward really is in the movie, not Vivien Leigh? . . . (*fades*)

O—That's the greatest make-up job in history. Not only did Max Factor work on it . . .

D—How are you sitting?

O—I'm in a strange position—my pimple is propping me up.

D—(*exhausted laughter*)

RR—AH. She's telling hm now that I remember his kiss . . .

O—Drella, this character—this character comes through and he says: What have you heard from my mother? She said: I just passed your cab, and then she was dying. (*Haha.*) And then she just laughed, and goes back into the thicket, and—ah.

Opera: Aaaaaaaaaaaah . . .

O—She's just a CHARacter. . . . Because, in Italian . . .

D—Wha?

O—. . . La Scala in 1962.

D—Who?

O—Callas.

D—Oh, really, oh . . .

O—You haven't . . . OOOOHHH. God forGIVE me—I suh . . . I didn't MEAn it

Maria Callas overwhelms any attempts at conversation.

SPF—That's all

O—Look at the reindeer—it's heaven

D—Doesn't he sleep up here any more?

O—He must die of suffocation if he does.

D—Oh, really?

RR—. . . some of us . . . used to come up here occasionally . . .

D—Who?

RR—. . . and sung out. Mitzi Divits . . . Mistletoes

O—Mrs. Dennison, don't get up-stairs, and would she saaa—OO-oooooo

RR—Is there a match in here?

O—(*very Tough*) No, baby, there's only-, some, ah, Flintstones, and a few . . .

Background noise to complete crescendo.

O—(*shouts*) DOOO-DO, doya—have you got a match??

DD—on-DEEEEEN.

O—I'd like a match DoDo.

RR—She's standing there waiting for that order—you can tell the

way she hasn't said anything

O—DoDo—a MATCH!!!

SPF—Where ya all planning on going to?

O—Never mind, DoDo.

RR—Set it on fire

O—I want her to get some exercise in her legs, because obviously go-ing to die of . . .

RR—Bless you

O—Thank you, Do Do. . .you ve been more than scholarly—you've been abrupt (*yawn*). What's this I dah hahahahaha. Drella—two. True I'm funny, but I'm—I've also got a heart. I mean, I'm not just a clown—I'm also a clown with a hole. Ie mean a heart. But that's the one. . . imakine that I hate is Pagliacci. I deTEST Pagliacci. Why does the Pagliacci just rrrruin me, Rita—I HATE it.

RR—Well, first of all, it's because . . . (*fades*) . . . an Italian girl.

O—Nedda?

RR—I dunny . . . (*fades out, over-come by opera*) . . .

O—Because I want Drella to get . . .

RR—She's really. . . She's the only one who's been able to give Pa-gliacci the feeling of bereavement . . . where it belongs.

O—Yeah, but I HATE the charac-ter of Pagliacci

RR—Yeah, but you like Nedda, though

O—I think she's—OOOh, Nedda's diVIIIIIINE

RR—When Pagliacci's on the stage, Nedda. . .

O—Pagliacci's a frau-aw-aw-aud. Am I right?

RR—Of course—it's with her or *Borise*

O—Yeah

RR—And she goes: ——— =

O—Ro-Rotten doesn't ever sing. She says: Reject me?? She's toooooking in it, and we rejected her. . .for the Holy Grail. It must It must have been a gas. . .

RR—Who cares. . .she decides what's a gas. She tried. She says: I got yer mother's kiss for ya

O—I've got your mother's kiss for YOU. Isn't it beautiful, this— Maria Calls continues Parcival . . .And, at the end, she-she fails, but she sings it to the thicket

RR—(simultaneous). . .the elements.

O—And she ends by singing it to the thicket, the-. . .the magician calls her back because she's failed in her attempt. She said a lulla-lulladishtowell. . .My head is in the most uncomfortable it's ever been in my entire life. . .No, now I'm dead. Jim Beam wanted to pick my pimple, and God, I didn't let him. Forgive me, God.

RR—(very muffled and inaucible)

O—I know That. heh heh. I didn't want him to dirty my insides, because he was so. . .

RR—You're not doing it right— I mean, first of all, ...

O—Ohh, would you? Isn't the Mayor sweet? All your duties, and you still have to cauderize the patient

BN—. . . your pimple?

O—Oh, really, listen to her go back into the thicket. . . . This is Baby Maria

D—Oh, really? When she was young?

O—She was about twenty. . .ssix?

RR—No no no—in 52, she was 14

O—Listen to her jump—

Maria Callas jumps.

O—I think she mm-. . .Wagner especially
Maria Calls in very frenetic part of opera.

RR—She says ferma, ferma: Stay, Stay. (Rita translates the opera.)
Maria Callas: feeeeeeerma. . . FEEEEErma

O—. . .someone who gives that much much to uh-ah/the-her . . . performance . . . should be dead . . .

RR—Yeah, well-uh, but I don't like this opera at all, and I jus. . .

O—I never did before her . . . sss-a-llopppy Mayor

RR—That's right, and playing this duet, I listen to this recording and Wagner's . . . . . . and a few other people.

O—TH-duh-those misconceptions just completely turned around . . . .

RR—Wuh-what I really loved . . . when she sneaks into the thicket and sleeps

O—Yes, listen to her go. . . . Listen to her seeka-sink away. . . Listen to her sink away—she sinks INto the thicket, she goes YEEEE-AAAAAAGGGGGGGUHHHH, and she returns to the mud, where she comes from

SPF—C-ca-kin thi-. . .

O—SHHHHHHHHHH. . .This it it. Listen. This really is import-uh. It's important
Male voice in Parcival.

O—Ya can't come into a theater, an expect to be heard immediately—WAAAAIT
Rotten and DoDo begin their own musical interlude—Rita: HeeeeeHEEEEEEEheeeeeeeeeeee-heeeeeeeheeeeeeee

DODO:EEEEEEEEEEEEEEK
BN—What happened therere?
O—She went back inta the mud
BN—It's frOOoH-ze
O—Kundry—that heavenly Italian.
Knudry may be the most de-
mented character in all of opera.
In AAALL of it. She is SOOO
SIIIICK.
RR—She's just-uh. . .she's just
smothered in her own garbage.
And there's a lota garbage. . .
O—Do you think she lives on the
Lowes East Side?
RR—No, I didn't mean That.
D—What opera is this?
O—Parcival
D—Parcival. It's parcival—it's only
eaten on special holidays
RR—Yes, huh huh
O—And it contains parcel, and uh.
. . .
RR—Small parts instead of big
parts dih. . .
O—Sugar would you like us to
leave?
SPF—huh?
RR—Look, if you want us to go,
I'll go.
O—Yes, if you wanted to leave. . .
RR—Just say the word
O—Will you come to Titsin Geor-
gia with us?
RR—(*simultaneous with Ondine*)
. . . and I'm doing some more for
. . .
O—Let's get together in Titsin
Georgia.
RR—. . .early morning workers. . .
O—Would that. .would that set the
town on its ear? It's a twisted
face, my dear. Twisted. What
kind of a face is that? DYou see
what he thinks he spots?
RR—Thatsa. .that's a face from
the twenties

O—Sick—Sugar, you're sick. I can
only pray to the reindeed goddess
SPF—Others have said the thirties.
O—ALL should say the thirties—
that's the proper era. You are
The Aaa-AnTITHESIS of the
thortoes—you are IT. You ARE,
my dear—your face is so perfectly thirties it's incredible.
SPF—This is an album—this is an
album called K-K-K-Kriwn Kland
un W-e-e-thaus.
O—I TRIed to read that before,
but no one would listen to me
D—hahaha
SPF—. . .and it s-uh
D—hahaha
RR—Ooooo, Ondine, you know
that there I was looking out the
window when a Police car went
in front of the house
SPF—. . .it inncuhludes-uh. . .
RR—and they were going so
S-LLLLLow, baby, you couldn't
beLEEve it, and the cop who was
driving had his arm out the window
O—It was full of needle tracks
RR—. . .full out the window, with
his short-sleeved shirt on, and I
wanted to just th-r-rrOW a
needle down and jab him in the
arm. Wouldn't that be good,
naaow, I couldn't do it, though
O—But you cahcah cahcah—you
gotta have a long finger, you
know—that's eight floors, yaknow
RR—Eight floors, and (psheewat)
—jab him right in the arm
O—You could do it with a blow
gun—pssssssshhhhaaaaaap. But
it has to be poison, my honey,
it's hafta be curare
RR—Well, let's put some poison
on it

O—. . .Or, uh-uh. . .Others that kill like that. . . .This is my reH-. .This is my reverseH-. .This is my REverence time—I'm going in to pray to the staute of ST. Francis Xavier

D—(*laughs to an inaudible comment of Rita's.*)

SPF—Do you remember, Ondine, when you-uh told your mother for the first time that you were searching for God?

RR—Now wait a moment, I've gotta go. . .

O—I THINK I remember, vaguely, but I'm not sure.

SPF—What was her reaction?

O—She jus gatve me a flashlight, widasall.

D—hahaha

O—What else? I don't know—my mother was always tuh-treated God as a. .a very. .uhuh. .Like she's very. .a very. .Like she's a very dogmatic, but she doesn't follow the dogma. Yaknow? Like she s—she s—she goes to church because she wah. . .

SPF—But what was her reaction to Your search?

O—Aaaaooow, Her reaction to MY search was—no—invalid, . . .invalid completely. She doesn't be-uh-believe that ah-uh—— am searching

SPF—I mean I KNOW you're not searching, but I. . .

O—YOU may think I'm not searching, and HE may think I'm not searching, but I'm searching. WHO. .Wih-which one of us isn't searching for God?Gah-. . . God is a ten-inch dick, or a it's a-a piece of shit with a fly on it—who KNOWS what God is?

SPF—I read the most FABulous pornographic story the otherday —It was 28 pages long. . .

RR—uh uh—there he goes. . .

SPF—and on the last four pages, . . .

RR—I-uh-ah. . .I've heard that line before.

SPF—on the last four pages, he was saying. . .

O—(*mimicking in a high affected voice*) nyaanyaa nyaaa, etc.

D—Oh, really?

SPF—. . .really his father.

D—Oh, really.

SPF—And he said, Oh Dad? Dad your 13 inches are so beautiful. It's not like Kip's. Kip was a. . .

RR—. . .an asshole.

SPF—Kip only had. . .Kip's was only eight and a half inches

RR—. . . .who cares about his . . .

SPF—Only eight and a half inches, but it was fat.

O—It was fat? Now I'm going. No one has a fat factory instead

SPF—(*giggle*) No, can you imagine—he only has eightandahalf inches, but it was fat.

D—heh heh heh

O—Well, so?? What that Daddy's or the kid's

SPF—No the kid s

O—Sugar, if you re doing this just to provoke me and make a holy mess of my life, forget it

SPF—he said . . . he said, Oh, Daddy—you may slap me across the room for this, you may think I m shit . . .

BN—. . . keep on doink that violence. . .

O—He still poked m

eSPF—But thre's one thing that I've always wanted. . .and that's to have you, and he too his father, and. . .

O—I've never turned around about what Sugar just said.

SPF—And . . . and the took his father, and the father

O—It takes you sexuality and just twisted it in one. . .

SPF—No. And the father

O—Look at what he's doing now. He's divine, because he, because h tantalizes you beyond belief

SPF—No. The father pushed him away. . .

RR—From his heart

SPR—. . .from his piece, and the kid said to himself, God . . .

DD—SHREEEEEEEEEEEEEEK

SPF—God, what's in store for me now?

O—Good night, darling

OOOOOOOOOOOOOOOOOOOO
OOOO-OOOOOOOOOOOOOOO
OOOOOOOOOO-OOOOOOOO
OOOOOOOOOOOOOOOOOOO

(attempts to drown out *SPF*)

O—Besides, cookies are waiting. . .

RR—Oh oh oh, Pleee-ase, Oooh oh oh oh

O—ha Ha Ha Ha HAAAAAA

RR—Oh oh oh oh oh

O—AAAAAAAAAAAA AAAAAAA
AAAAEEEEEEEAAAAAGH

Eeeet s only a seee-ga-rrettee *absolute confusion*

O—Wha di—Rotten, what did you sa-uh. . . ?

RR—. . .from Me.

O—DiVine. Nonono—it's not taping; now it's stopped. I pulled it all outa the machine.

ALL—AAAAAAAAaaaaaw

RR—. . .And I just told the one about Lady Macbeth

O—I *Heard.* I thought you were sending a teletype off to her.

RR—. . .walked right in, and . . . they called her the forMIdable

task—and she's Lady Macbeth

D—Oh, where is she?

RR—She's the forMIdable woman

O—Oh . . . really.

RR—Yes, indeed. That's-like . . . That's like saying: You're a machine, Ondine

O—I AM a machine. The Machine Ondine presents: HOT TIT

RR—mmmm, Hot Tit.

BN—Hot Tit.

D—Hot Tit?

RR—What's this. . .? A roach. . . a joint. . .or one a those Pall Malls. . .??? It's a Filter, icccghh

O—Are you going to bed? . . .No, you just reLaxing

RR—I'm going to fix my pants, if you don't mind

O—Can I do it FOR you?

RR—NNNNoooOOOO. You can't do anything for me—you know that

O—I can do this for mySelf. . . . Stop him—the filthy bondage that I was borne in——Aaaaaah, FREEdom at LAAAST. To the guillotines—C'mon, Ginsberg, Dylan we-w ere all going down for a Dip

RR—If they're going in with you? you'd better turn them off for a little while

D—No no no

O—He has FIVE more minutes on the roll

RR—Then turn the phonograph off

O—FIVE more minutes

BN—Don't mess the fulcrum with my agitator. . .

O—EEeeeeeyuch (*Beats the machine.*)

CRASH

D—Disposable. . .

RR—That's the wrappers, ya dumb cunt

O—I Know THAT

RR—That's not disposable

D—Oh . . . you look so RrrrrRoman

O—Huh?

D—You look so Roman . . . You look very Roman

O—I feel very Doman. . . . I just felt so stupid in making that

RR—First of all, ya hafta say hello to yer Father and mother . . .

O—Hey—my father's a bread driver, Drella

D—Really? You're kidding

O—No—what da yis it? Friday?

D—Yeah

O—He hates me, though—he HAAA-Ates me. He's be so- . . . Drella—stop the thing and we'll go get dressed, and we'll get the last few words of my father. Oh, come on, Drella

D—We've got four more hours. . .

RR—He doesn't hit the St. Louis and the Puerto Ricans. . .

D—We'll finish it off some other time

O—Ah . . . Well, wouldya like to meet him?

D—Yeah

O—I introduced the Mayor to him once, an-an-an-uh said, Get a Loaf of Levy's Jewish

D—hahaha

O—I mean-uh, Silver cup Jewish . . . and we got it. Myy father's very-uh. . .uh, Cheap.

D—. . . a mailman . . . ?

O—Huh?

D—Isn't he a mailman?

RR—(complains in background over the continuation of the taping)

SPF—ya got blood on yer boots.

D—Where?

O—Let s go way, darling

SPF—Ya got blood on yer boots

D—Where. . . . . .Aaaaah

SPF—Dya ever take yer clothes off? ya know, when you come in a place. . .   Do you often, . . . or ever. . .

D—No. .

SPF—. . .take off your clothes, wear leather shorts, or chains. . .?

D—No. . . .do you?

SPF—Not all the time. Although one of Ondine s friends came to my house one time, and got into my bed, . . .

D—yeah. . .

SPF—. . . .took off his clothes, and all he had on wasa bo-. . .

WAAAAAAAAAIIIIIIIIILLLLL

SPF—. . .Was-uh, . . .boots, n chains, n things wrapped around his penis. . .

D—Oh, really. . .

Ondine and Rita rap in the backgorund.

SPF—. . .hear like some. . .athletic types—ya know

RR—mmmmmm, Rock. . .

SPF—That was kinda ghastly

O—. . . .I wanna be alone for a moment or t-tuh-two—this is reverence time. Believe me.

SPF—Who was that person who came to my house with chains wrapped around his . . .

Tape goes out of control.

O—(continues, several sentences after malfuction) What was it? That he took his pants off— couldn't believe her

D—Heh heh heh

SPF, RR, D, and Ondine: NAAA-AAAAOOOOO. . I didn't know (in dissenting unison)

O—He took his PAnts off—you filthy sheehneee

RR—Wail of protest

O—Oooooooh, that word again—

Rotten.

RR—(*screeches dissent*)

O—Buh-low all Jews—Jews, falstity, charity
Loud background, lew by Billy Name, obstructs.

O—A/a-a-Aqueduct
Opera is turned up to drown out all possible conversation—Curtain Call.

D—Nonono—it s almost done. . . No, there s time for it. There s just time fo rit

O—This is the-uh. . . . Oh, well, this harp soloist will take care of that time

D—Oh. O.K.

DD—(*inaudible comment*)

D—You don-. . . .

O—I don't wanna s-speak to any of those people out there with their-uh . . . values

D—Why?

O—. . .with their fucking values. . . . I mean FUCKINg values. Oh, no—c mon, darling

D—ah, no. . .

O—Darling, I wanna tell you something very secret about the Sugar Plum Fairy

D—Oh . . . awright. Oh, lookit— . . . aw, c'mon. . .aren't you going to fuck for five minutes with me? On tape? Now, Just on tape . . . ?

O—No no no. . . .I wantcha to—
. . . . . .

D—. . . .why not. . . ?

O—(*hushed*) go. . .let . . .

D—Huh?

RR—. . . let my voice in the ELEVATor. . .

O—. . .let the Sugar Plum Fairy make love to you

D—What?

O—. . .and make love to him—he's diVINE

D—Ooooh, uh. . .I don't wanna do That. . .

O—But . . .Oh, come On—he's diVINE—he's HEAven. He's HEAVEN. You will enjoy it immensely.

RR—Is that thing working? Is it taping? You got a couple a nice things here.

O—No, Please, Billy—five more minutes, an then this is going on Billy, PLEease.

RR—Billy, this is a special request from a. . .

O—This is a special request from a Nazi/. . .Drella, your-uh, . . . your Prussian tactics have led to nothing but. . .

BN—You wanna. . .Clear. . .five . . .kithout background. . . ?

O—Oh, OK—clear for five, and then you can p-puh-put the spot on me. While you're over there, you can put the spot on me. HIIII, America—Welcome to the 1966 Chevrolet.

VOICE—. . . jellybeans in the gas get em free

RR—Now, wait a moment

O—That's John D

D—WhaT?

O—That's John D

D—What's he doing in the other room?

SPF—He's pressing that button, releasing the gas. . .

D—What gas—he's not in the stove. . .

O—No, but he's sitting on the ta-. . .

RR—Oh, you are Aaaall right. . .

BN—(*Munchin voice*) thatanElectricstove

O—I think there's smoke—. . .

RR—I-uh, ah. . .

BN—Right, you're sewing up your

hole, there, heh? You know how
many times ya come, and had to
repair your pants. . .

SPF—They've got it

BN—Huh?

SPF—They got it. . .They got the
guage on

RR—Be quiet

O—Now in real madness, things
happen—They've got to lifh . . .
(*hushed*) what is that ball thing?
*Three simultaneous comments
from RR, BN, and DoDo.*
They're playing it like it's a game,
and I laughed. . .

D—What?

O—They're playing it like it's a
game in there. That Ball game—
I don't know what you call it,
the psycha-. .the Psycho- . . .

SPF—Psychedelic

O—. . .the manic depressive Jesso
—I don't know, I'm not sure
what it is. The BLUE WAVE
—The blue Wave, that's it

D—Well, that's just the Blue Wave

BN—Now, wha. . . .you call it by
the name of the ar-. .Now, what's
her name?

D—uhhhhh

BN—. .The woman who made that
box. . .

D—uhhhhhhh

BN—That's what you call it,
though?

D—Yeah
*bounce bounce bounce plop plop
plop*

O—Now I wantcha to try it this
way—I am a good ball, I am a
plop plop
good. . . NO: Iam a good boy,
I ama good boy—she. . .she. .
walks in as says, . . .

PLOP

BN—Agnes Martin

O—What is this? I ama good boy
. . . I ama good boy . . . I ama
good Girl. Uh uh uh—what is
this? You are expelled . . . and
your Father with you, now get
Out. Come on, you two

PLOP PLOP PLOP

BN—(*inaudible*). . .last night,
Ondine?

D—When did you learn to talk like
that?

O—I never talk like that, darling
—I stopped. I talk the worst like
that, darling
*Tape speeds up to Munchkin
chatter.*

OHey, Sugar—. . .and DoDo, . . .
If you would both appear here at
once, we could question you both
at the same time

BN—(*singing*) On who, silly girl?

O—(*singing in very nasal Jerry
Lewis voice*) . . .So what's new?

SPF—Say m what you think of me

O—Hey, whor're you calling

BN—Yeah, we got Wink—we're
gonna have Wink sandwiches

O—Ooooo ooooo

RR—Ya want me to make it for
you?

SPF—Dya wanna Wink sandwich?

O—I'd love a Wink sandwich

RR—I'd . . . Like . . . A . . . WINK
. . . Sandwich

D—What kind of sandwich

RR—. . . a pair of peppers

O—I like it, unnnnnnhhhh . . .
unnnnggghh

D—What kind of sandwich?

O—Wink

D—Oh, wink

O—Every time I bought a baw-oh-
bottle of Wink today I/da -I geh
it turns out like this—. .

RR—Hey, you haven t questioned
anybody—you haven't said any-

thing
O—Oh, O.K.
O—Here, youwa lohveid
RR—. . . afternOOOOn?
D—Oh, no—I think the thing's broken
O—But not the playback. Can't we play it back?
D—It s yesterday. ///(fades out)
RR—. . .play this. . . .Athe next few remarks were uttered simultaneously and are largely indistinguishable.)
O—Say, can you play. . .
BN—This. . .this HAppened
RR—. . .I kicked the letter off of Rose Kennedy, and I think. . . (continues inaudible)
D—. . . Uh, uh—Paul there? Uhhhhh, welll . . .
BN—I was trying to work it.
D—He was trying to workit, and-uh. . .but-but I'm sure it's broken.
O—Rose is a great woman, by the way
RR—Exceptional
D—Yeah. Oh-uh-uh . . . I like a little bit of you I saw wuh-w-when you were talking
BN—Well, what I was doing was saying what Ondine said 'immediately after he said it.
D—Wuh. . .Yau have an idea what movie we could do. . ? I mean, we-uh. . . .
SPF—Let me see. . . .
O—Not Lu
BN—Not any particular ideas, . . .
RR—Oh, Lu's a lecher.
BN—. . .but I that sometimes. . .
O—Oh, I would love to make movies with him
BN—. . .that-uh . . .started DINner. While the dinner is going on, the whole thing. . .
O—That is FABulous, and we woo

wedjusee—It's BEAUtiful. You must see the glaw-. . .
D—Who was there?
BN—It was me, and Ondine, and Paul, Steve, and Larry. . .
O—He called it a crookinLa
BN—. . .it was me, and Paul—do you see?
D—Yeah
O—We s-s-ssand Leonora in triplicate—my dear, we were diVINE
D—Well . . . .
BN—. . . again?
O—. . . just BEAUtifully. . . . We made two tapes. . .
W—Yeah
BN—OH, I don't think it could be repeated. . .
O—. .on the tapes the thing that you Must see.
BN—. . .that can't be transferred
D—Well, then I should really ssssue goodwih-. . .do things like-do things a tthe studio, like
BN—Well, Paul and I really started that with-uh. . .
RR—I want the Oooooold. . Duuuuutch. . .cleanser
BN—. . .doing taping sessions as frequently as possible,. . .
D—Yeah
RR—(in background) old dutch . .old dutch. . .old dutch
O—Your mind
BN—. . .because they were gonna take it back before Too long. . . .
D—I-uh. . .I m-uh, I m-uh. . .
O—Repeat me backit
RR—Yeah, well maybe that's what . . .
BN—. . .that's what I need. . .
D—Yeah, well, I. . .
O—. . . .they don't keep that thing. . . .

Conversation between D &BN, and RR & O become indistin-

guishable. PAUSE/*simultaneous lulls*

BN—But what we could have. . . .

O—Yeah, now that's called badd-ggio.

D—What?

O—Replace the thing that's in there with a little substituteof your own. . .

BN—That's base-uh. .

D—Yeah

BN—I mean, there are a lotta terrific people there

D—Yeah

RR—Neither but else is. . .

BN—I-uh I guess I haven t seen any sh-showing of the-uh. . .

D—We cant. .Wedon t have . . .(*fade*). . . . We just don t have enough . . . . (*fade*)

O—(*discreetly i nto microphone*) She LIES.

D—. . . this-uh. . . .

O—No. Wuh. No, You. No. Like.

BN—. . . finding out what he's going to do with the sound

RR—. . .it couldn't be. . . .

D—. . . Yeah, but I mean for television and things.

RR—He's beautiful. He's there only because I. . .

D—. . .Yaknow, like uh. . .

O—YOU LOve me only because ya can space me

D—. . .and I just don't say anything, . . .

O—. . .and ya know I belong to you

BN—Well, the thing that he does is—instead of sending a finished statement . . .

RR—I know who you ARE

O—Oh, yeah?

BN—. . .he presents his. . . . .

O—I think it must be over, baby

RR—I think it's Morris

BN—. . .three weeks, and. . . .

O—MORRIS. The hell with Morris. GLEEDaidugahhuh

Ondine crashes the tape recorder

O—Awwwww. HELP, Morris, please Morris, close the-y circulit. Morris, I m really down. SHREEEEEEIK   (DODO DOOM)

The murderess appears—Come in here, you. We have a few questions to ask YOU.

RR—COME HERE

O—COME OOOON

RR—COME HEEEERE

BN—Actually, if I. .If I didn't say . . .

RR—BRING YER WING IF YA KNOW WHAT'S GOOD FER YA

BN—. . .really clean. .a lotta people, I would be good to say things, but I frequently. . .

O—You say things better than anlbody I know

DD—(*sqwaaK*)

BN—I really. . .

O—You shouldn't talk to THOSE people. Ya know WHY? Because they irritate YOU, and you sh-sh-show it all over your face and in everything you do. You just canNOT TOLerate them. Listen you—stop bringing parrots in this room. The bats are dead.

DD—The bats are DEAR?

RR—. . .at the bus stop

BN—Listen, I know how it is, . . .

O—AHHHHHHHH-CHCHCHC-OOOOOO It's the barber of Sahville, the barbara rusefeldt. OOO —OOOOweeeee. It wossh me up because I'm getting worried. . . I'me getting ready. (*Sings*) I'm getting ready in the mor-. . .

BN—You're carrying John, and gonna go on and on. . .

OOndine makes a rather gremlin-like exclamation.

BN—Oh, where re you going?

O—I wanna split, Babs. I've gone all the way, but this town istoo much far fe, You're sick . . .

BN—OK, Ondine, what're ya gonna bring me bach-uh? A plane, dad, huh? Ya gonna bring me back somethin—aaahooooooo, Ondeeeeeeeen. . .

RR—OOOOOOOOOaaaaaoooooo, onDEEEEEEEEN

DD—ONdee-eee-ine

eeela, eeela, eeela (raucous lam-pooning from RR, BN, and DoDo.)

DD—Whatsamatter with Ondine?

BN—Someone simulatae Ondine.

DD—Whatamatter with Ondine?

BN—Simulate Ondine for the (voyeurs)

DD—I'm being off us.

General confusion

SPF—How many hours will this be?

O—Oh, approximately 1–2–3 hun-dred.

D—What?

O—Darling? Ya didn t have a Times. I went out taget it, I had ta ·get it

D—What for?. . .what for?. . .

O—Who shot 84?

RR—Dollar Bill

D—18?

O—Morris, if you don t get over-uh. . .over in the car, I ll faint

D—Oh, NO, this is twenty.

O—Morris—. . .DoDo, get me something to write with, please, darling

DD—(sings) OOOOO—ooooooo oooooooo

BN—I thought this was the end of you, ·baby

O—No it's not

RR—Besides, ya got four more

SPF—He has 5 minutes

D—No, you got six more, yeah.

SPF—Six more?

O—And now that we're all gath-ered together, I wanna tell you. Hey, Gram, Aunt Helen, Doro-thy

D—. . . Taking over?

DD—LOOOOK

BN—. . .which speech is that. . ?

O—Would you like to join me in this comfortable chair, darling?

D—One and-uh. . .

BN—One and what ever it is speed?

D—Yeah

O—O—Do. . . . .DoDo, may I borrow your necklace for amo-ment?

DD—. . . . .weird bee-EE/eads?

O—No, I just wanna try it one place, and if it works, I know just what I need. Just. .just take it off for one second. . .And put it right here.

BN—. . .oh, it s a cartridge

D—Must be a threwer.

RR—It would have to be taken out, and then you wouldn't be able to use it again.

O—If that works—. . . .

DD—What's it mean if it works?

O—I listen to something. That's good.

BN—B is at A-standard speed, one is at. . .

O—I just wanna see it for One minute. . . .

D—Then I can put this on . . . but this is number 5. , , ,

O—Oh; DoDo—this is it. If I can make go with it. Tiiisss warm. No, it's too much—it looks like braids. On your neck, it looks lovely, and magnificant, but on my . . . it looks a . . . . . .

DD—Huph? Who does?

RR—Primara shiss coaowd

BN—He-heh-Here comes my Impérial waltz

D—What s coming off?

BN—My entire heel

D—Ooooooh.

BN—Do you ever wear jewelry?

O—You ve been eating Pretty Feet . . . . It gave me a ridgin. .

BN—. . . very finger,

O—Oh.

BN—My toe and heel

O—It makes me so sick when people are in pain.

BN—Sicak and tired, huh?

O—Well, ... Find a better place for it—it s just a little. . . . .

RR—Hey. That s. Good.

O—It s good, but it just could be better.

BN—You look tike a (fades) . . . Lois-uh. . . .

O—Lois Pitkin

RR—Lois Blowus

O—Loze Blows. There—uh, Nuh, Now it s not bad

BN—Wanna down?? Take one of these?

O—No, it's not bad, but it hangs off the seam like this. He's got-he's got a magNIficent body. May I have something to write with, Please? liddeyiddle yoodeeyahda ah. ah. ah. Ah, the remarkable is it. Ah—I'm rushing get it in one second.

D—Is it finished?

SPF—Didjou. .Did you. . . .

D—All right. . . . What part do you want?

O—We don't want that do we?

D—No

O—We're here to pull the thih-

wih. . . c'mon, there's—. . .

RR—I/duh. . .I just. . . .

DD—Billy, you are wrong. . . .

O—Yes. . . . Yes. Did you want something, darling? Probly. .do you want me to renew my Muh-mah-mah-MILK order. . . ? They're talking about M-uh. . . they're talking about me ag-eh-heh-ain (fakes whining.) Come, Man, I take ya to the shit house, an (hoodlum gang dialect)

D—Huh?

O—Put-the. . .Put the water on

D—What?

O—Mah-mah-mah-mah-May I take it into the Tearoom, and. . . .

D—No, it's almost finished.

O—Ah-I'm going to sit on the toilet and talk to it

D—No, no no/ It really is-uh. . .

O—Oh, alowah. I'm gonna play shit house now twelve times—Rosilie—shit house—Cappy—shithouse and BrrrrrrOOOky-shit house. Now I'm mustin. . . You girls have been so sweet during this whole grueling mess that I wantew to say the tenderest words in the whole English language SH-SH-SH-SHITHOUSE. Shi-it-tHOW-ouse. Or you could say SHEEThouse. Or you could say sheethaus.

SPF—I think you oughta wIIInd it up on a grand scale

RR—I think you oughta. . . (distortion)

O—Did you hear what he just said? He said. . . You stuck me with this filth. All right, give me some of your ideas, Curly. Whaddya mean: Wind it up on a grand scale? Whaddya want me to do —get my. . . ?

SPF—(inaudible)

O—Yours. . ?

SPF—(*very hard to hear*) Yes, play on the Haw-. . . .

O—Whose harp?

RR—The horse. . .

O—Who on the horns?

RR—. . . . .up by Riverside Drive, . . .

O—Doya want me ta pu-. . .Do you want me to clean your pipe, Baby, on-on tape? Whip it out, honey, you're on.

RR—. . .Not on. . .

O—I'll make such noises that these thu-three girls will be RIGHT into. . .I can't do it unless it's real—somebody's gotta do it.

DD—You look so SAD, Ondine. What s wrong?

O—I'm trying to think—Oh, that's just your BRAIN, Baby, don t worry about it. Don't worry about YOUR head. What? . . . What? . . .bah bah pahdeece

BN—YEA Bob, Yea Bob. Yea Bob Bob bob bob bob very very very very bob bob bob bob

O—Ondine? He does what he wants.

BN—Here s the weather report. . . .

O—Well, Rita—I LL even shut the light off.

DD—It s ONLY . . . (*fade out*)

O—DoDo—you and your TIMEly questions. Look at her—secretly deLIGHTed by the actions of a BAT. Try???? Oh, I KNOW I m gonna make it

Overture to Bellini's Il Pirata.

DRELLA—Hello.

ONDINE—He was born in America?

PAUL—Yes, Japanese. Udah.

O—Oh c'mon.

P—Born in Udah.

O—The first thing is Billy have you any amphetamine?

P—Hah hah hah

O—Billy.

P—Oh what's wrong with that?

O—I would like a sniff of a schnorrt. Wait'll he comes in off the window; he's checking the Railroad.

D—You have your hand on it.

O—Oh, what's wrong with it you mean.

BILLY—I'm I'm. . .

D—Talk louder.

O—Talk louder, *Billy*.

B—*Bobby*.

O—Have you any amphetamine?

B—I just turned it all down.

O—Could I have a snort? Oh, you ffinished it.

B—I just turned it all down. It made my ankles ache and everything.

O—O———kay, that means this'll be snortless America.

—Now. . .

—An American concentration camp?

P—Does that help a cold?

O—Where?

Girl—In Utah. It's Japanese.

P—In Utah.

O—In Utah.

It was a Japanese concentration camp established in the United States?

P—By the Americans.

G—Jesus.

O—By Mormons or what?

G—By Americans. They shoved the Japanese into little fenced areas and say there you know.

RON VIA —They don't like colored people.

Boy—We're at war with your people. ?

O—Oh. . .

It sounds like it. . .It doesn't sound feasable are you sure that this isn't pod people? We were never at war with Italy. Italy was at war with little Ethiopia but that was all.all.

Ff th

B—At war AT.

O—Italy, they really didn't bother you know.

P—They were the ones who were financing Germany.

O—They may have started it// they didn't finance Germany, they merely gave them the ideal like they've goven, they've given everything German the ideal// for everything. Germany's just flailed, eh the Germans have flailed Italy. Since the beginning they've nothing but ma-ma-mechanics. The Italians are the originators//always. Sempre sempre sempre. . .Italia.

P—Giggle giggle heh heh

O—That's il Papa and I happen to be Jewish by way of my mother's Croatian marriage.

P—Giggle giggle

O—Irish by my Uncle Bickford.

P—Heh heh heh

O—My Uncle Bickford is Irish.

P—Heh heh

O—Er ah only in the morning. Oh the Germans are really tacky— the only people in the world who could ver have fallen for Hitler.

P—A-heh heh

O—-heh ha the only ones.

P—Heh heh heh

G—I BEG your pardon.

O—He is the dreariest moron I've ever heard about—even Mussolini though he was a laugh.

G&P—Giggle giggle

O—Oh Hitler, he should have been raising uh oh my God he should have died where Lorenzo da Ponte did in Hoboken.

P—Heh heh

O—Oh what a horror show.

D—Who's Lorenz Lorenzo da Ponte?

O—Dutch ah Mozart's librettist also he was the first

P—He died in America?

O—Yes, there is a statue in Hoboken to Lorenzo da Ponte and he was the first pushcart salesman in the United States. Wh ou e who is it?

GERARD—No, I just wanted to know.

O—Didn't get smart Gerard you asleep.

P—Giggle giggle giggle

O—Germany. First of all their diet is wrong.

P—Yes.

O—They should stop with the potatoes. Potatoes this potatoes that —all out. Right? Beer. Oh no, no. Beer is all right cause it can be healthy. Someone peeed in my jacket—and I didn't know how ha heh they did it.

P—Ohyehreally?

O—There's a feeling of pee in my jacket. Anyway, Southern Germany should be saved and the rest should be extinguished.

P—What s Southern Germany?

O—Phewst Bavaria—the rest is sshhweest Blow it all up/

B—When I was there

O—Blow it all up. . .

Girl—Serious.

O—And it's ah the crowning glory of Germany.

P—heh heh

O—Northern is nothing but fish industries, my dear, fish industries and more Protestant churches.

P—Yeees, let's get rid of them.

Girl—Huh haa. . .

B—Sounds like Paul too.

O—Ehh Potestant churches will be abolished eventually but we're working on it it's a very slow and subtle policy.

B&Paul take prer der MW .. ....

P—Yes.

O—We're enjoying the infiltration quietly—if they start.

P—Did you ever know a Protestant you liked?

O—Yes, the Presbiter of the Presbiterian Church. This way to the Presbiter, you know like some in some in my God that went on for days. Oh, someone take the microphone out of my hand I feel like I'm on the spot.

I realize that everything Isay is going to be

(whisper —used against us.)

D—Heugh

B—Well, that s your realization if that's what you want—realism.

O—A HAHA

All right name, I'm down on the card to say that.

P—Is Rotten's trial?

O—The German's shouldn't have purified the Jews.

O—In that manner—ridiculous—if yer not gonna do a job don't do it at all.

P—Heh.

Don't do it halfway.

O—Eleanor Roosevelt is a

P—Heh heh

O—Obviously Negroid said Hitler Look at the shape of her lips. Huh hunh huh. What a brilliant man.

P—Wasn't that

Girl—Oh, Rotten Rita's trial.

P—Did that ever come up?

D—Rotten Rita's trial . . .

P—Yeah heh

O—Rotten Rita's trial will come

down soon.

I dunno no no they he was indicted which surprised me but It seems that, ah, that was discussed, you know—anda

P—Wha bout those cops, jever see them again?

O—Oh those pigs—are you serios?

D—The fat Italian one.

O—The fat Italian one stopped hitting me because I was Italian —oh REALLY.

P—Hah hah

O—Really— You mean Vincent Impolliten's neice?

P—Heh heh heh heh heh heh

D—When did he . . . when did he find out you were Italian?

O—Wen did he find out. He says, Ondine, yah Ondine Schwarz, hes' famous.I said my name is you know, my real name is blah blah . . . He says, you're Italian? he says

P—Hah heh heh heh heh

O—He says, you dumb bastard you. What could I say? Ho hum, nothing. I said, yes,isn't it gay?

P—Heh heh

O—I says, I don't wanna ho ho ho. I said I will cooperate, officer— you're so brilliant—is this part of the six hours? six hours, and THIS is the memorial to Joe Cino? Braaack

P—Heh heh

O—Part of a raspberry,darling. Paul Paul eggs me on to all of this. He is the one who planned those slaps, you horror. You know Paul, you really are responsible for that nonsense   e

P—Huh huh huh heh

O—He kept telling me during the filming, hit er, hit er with the tambourine, hit er with Bob Dylan, hit er with the wibb wibb wibb

Ooooh—I'm used to it, you see any anything (from afar)

B—Oh I'm not responsible for any of that.

D—What happened to Joe Cino?

O—Joe Cino killed himself quite un quite glaringly at the PEAK of his career Ummmm ummmm

P—Uh huh shusj

B—He suffered the after effects of electric shock.

O—He saw Orio's hair before she washed it.

P—Heh heh heh

O—It was quite a shock, quite a shock—it's TOO ea wha down No he

P—Heh heh Did anybody go the the funeral?

B—I didn't go.

G—Is Billy here?

B—Who wants to know?

G—Weiss.

O—Ha ha

B—Why didn't you take it Ondine?

O—Okay, YES, tell tell Lion yes.

P—Go for the phone.

D—That doesn't go with the

O—Hullo, how re you? No,it's Billy. No, it's it's Billy. Eh, this is Billy Name.

B—The last time I talked to him.

O—He's not talking to you, he told I don't care what's urgent darling, he said to get the message. PAUSE. He doesn't want to talk to you.

Billy, he says you do wanna talk to him.

B—Well.

O—He says it's urgent.

B—Don't don't.

O—ed deh uh what.

WEISS (*on phone*)— . . . im to the

phone, get him to the phone any way you can.

O—Trick him to the phone?

S—Bring him to the phone.

O—Well, he's in his darkroom and he's being particularly dif . . .

S—I want him to come out. Tell him to come out of the dark, right now.

B—Did he say

O—Can't you tell me an' I can tell him?

S—No, no, no. Lemme speak to him alone.

O—He doesn't wanna TALK.

S—*Make* him want to talk.

O—MAKE HIM WANT TO TALK? YOU BULLARD.

B—That's it.

S—My name is WEISS, will you get him out o fthat dark and to the phone.

O—If you raise your voice I will not.

S—I didn't.

O—Pick up the phone the next time you call it

S—Ondine, the next time you come to my house, I won't be pleasant.

B—Tell him it's hard time.

O—YOu haven't been pleasant to me, Jimmy, since I've seen you in the street when I picked up a garbage can and found you under it. Now listen to this, Billy doesn't wanta come to THE PHONE.

B—Don't make things up.

S—YOu do it for me.

O—Are you coming to the phone?

B—No, but that doesn't mean I don't want to.

O—He says no, he does no.

S—Will you do it for me?

O—Well what?

B—Imean I didn't answer it.

S—I want to—I want some, oh . . .

O—Tell me.

S—I wantcha to do a favor for me.

O—Yes, what?

S—Call . . . MARE'S . . .

O—Yes

S—. . . find out if Jimmy's there and if he's there I want you to have him call me.

O—I know he's not

S—He's not there?

O—I just left there.

S—Where is he?

O—I have no idea where wha I I've been with Orio for the past— week
no no no no no She's been long with and very very divine
Yes it is. I have laryngitis though. Ah Oh Yeaa Jacky Seven's not there.
Don't know where he is.

S—Sohe 's not there?

O—No, he's not there. And he hasn't been there either.

S—Jacky Goldberg

S—Oh oh I uh no I just have a feeling that he was there right now at this moment.

O—Eh, I don't think so.

S—Would you do a favor for me?

O—Sure, whaduyawant?

S—Would you call there right now and wait cause funny tho I think he is there—I think he just arrived there.

O—I ah well if he did arrive . . .

S—If he DID just arrive, I want you to do something for me, would you?

O—Tell me what.

S—Just wha talk just uh I'll call you back in around ten minutes.

O—Well what the hell am I supposed to do—call there

S—And tell

O—And SO WHAT?

S—And I'll call you there in ten minutes.

O—Jimmy, will you listen to me for wo for one moment?

S—Yeah.

O—First of all RUDINE is not home.

S—And

O—Because she's walking there— she has no money.

S—Ondine.

O—And she left the factory in a huff.

S—ONDINE (plaintive)

O—Are you even listening to me?

S—Is this ONDINE?

B—Violation.

O—Yes this is ONdine.

S—Is this

O—Yes it is, IT'S NOT ANNA MAE WONG, my dear.

S—Ondine, you're too serious, hang up.

O—If I say I am—I am.

S—Why do people crawl on the floor at Dennis Secco's?

O—What does he look for on the floor at Dennis Secco's.

B—Ha ha ha

O—Who the fuck are you talking about?

S—Who am I talking TO?

O—You're talking to Eric, the boy with the shit throat.

S—Aargh, grod.

O—You DUMB BASTARD.

S—You FOOL, you moronic FOOL.

O—YOU DUMB

S—Shut up.

O—Fucking idiot you. Do yoou a favor—I should shoot you.

B—Mirror drop?

O—My God. now that's a typical phone call from one of your

friends.

What the hell is that moron up to?

B—You've been talking to Eric Brunn?

O—Did you hear no I told him I was Eric—huh? He said do me a favor I finally had to get the I hope I got hi got him on the thing. He said do me a favor and call and see if *Jimmy's* there and then tell him I'll er hmmmmm

P—Hah hah hah

O—You know?

D—Who's Eric?

O—Who's Eric? Eric was one of the first suicides. I think he was the *first* suicide.

P—Heh heh

B—He was my introduction to art and aesthetics.

O—Yeah, he was, he was a very great friend of Billy's, a good friend of mine, a very beautiful boy—he sl he slit his throat with a Schick injector razor.

P—What for?

O—My dear, whadaya wanna he wanted a shave very bad.

P—Accident.

O—I don't know why he did it. Why do why do people do things like that Paul? He did he did it well though.

P—Just once.

O—I guess just twice. I don't know —he did it every week. I think or he tried to—I don't know what his story was except that I wasn't involved in it.

P—Who went up to Buffalo?

O—The whole Springfield troop/

P—Huh huh

O—That phone call depressed me.

P—Who's this person calling?

O—Johnny Weiss? Oh, he's a journal square rat.

B—That's what you get for being

P—Heh heh heh heh heh heh
What's Journal Square?

O—Journal Square's a place in Jersey, you know.

P—Ohh

B—Scully Square's a place in Boston, you know.

O—It's not quite North
Oh, I hear a car idling—I think it's Mr. and Mrs.—heh, IT IS.

B—Oh hi Miss hi Misses.

O—Whee. Oh. just think, they've come all the way down from Dusinbury just to see me.
Oh, I'm depressed no so I'm gonna feel strong Oh yes I HATE him.
What does he mean calling me like that? When it wasn't even me he was calling.
Why don't you take your own phone calls like any one.

B—That's space not my why.

O—Uhhhggh.

Gorl—Jibber jibber

O—*John McDuff*, he's still making a movie.

B—He just went out the door. I said I don't leave like that. Did you hear what he said to me in the third person? He said I speaking Billy and I was right there in the room.

O—I know you were right there in the room.

B—I know you knew I was right there in the room.

O—You di you di da you didn't have a good chance to move. I I said I'd be right back.

B—I had any kind of a chance I wanted.

O—I said I'd be RIGHT back— and I wanted you to stay.

B—I know—I heard you say I guess I can see when I'm not wanted.

O—Whatever happened to Taxine and the movie she was supposed to make?

G—Who?

P—Taxine.

G—Who the hell is TAxine? Taxine?

P—That's her name.

G—Oh, there's no such . . . you mean you mean the whore?

P—Taxine.

?—No, not Maxine.

P—That's Taxi's name in the BOOK.

O—I didn't know anything about any book called TAxi, Taxi. Maxie. Slaxie. No.

P—Taxine.

O—Wha?

P—Taxine.

O—What the fuck is Taxine? Is that is that is that a vaccine? What is it?

P—HEH heh ha heh Taxine.

O—Tax—I've never heard of it.

B—It's a literary nom de plume.

O—I've never heard of it.

P—To the Roman it's

O—Gloria Graham Cracker is the name I was gonna give Taxi in the Mack
Ha ha or Erik Arick.
What did she say what if you he's got the insidious suggestions that one back there—Billy—all of his in suggestions.

P—You don't know what name di dis huh

O—No, Vicious Vivian was not a friend of mine.

B—Oh well you know somebody named Vicious Vivian.

O—No I didn't. I mean don't know anyone but I'm sure that somebody in the

B—You can be packaged and merchandised.

O—What?

B—I could never get anywhere.

O—Just in a package I could not.

B—No no no no you

O—Maybe maybe I have a package back there. I'm going to see.

P—Heh.

O—I'll be right

P—Heh

O—Did I leave a package there Billy?

B—I'm going to leave you alone.

O—Wha what did you say to me?

B—I said you can be packaged.

O—Oh, all right oh fine thank you.

O—In other words.

B—It's totally uncharacteristic of the way I'm behaving.

O—In other words, kiddies, Uncle Ondine

B—I'm really not, you know

O—Could be Aunt Ondine in Chapter One.

P—Do you ever run into Corina?

O—Oh, that weird cross-what?

P—Eever run into CORINA?

O—Once in a while—she's a pig.

P—Huh.

O—With those big blue eyes of hers doing that twelve year old little act always and taking people off for amphetamine and their jewels. She's a scream—Mare hadda finally throw her out of her house.

P—Yeah

O—She didn't even want her there in the first place.

P—Recently?

O—Yes, last night or the night before.

P—Hah. Hah.

O—How dreamy Corina is. She

says Ondine, please give me a shot. Well I gave her a shot. She says I'd like a-another one

P—Haw.

O—Immediately you know other people have to go and another—doesn't care I said she says (cutely) and save me a little for the morning please.

P—Huh huh huh huh huh huh huh

B—Just like the boys.

O—She's a very sweet girl. If you like reform school—she should be in a reform school.

P—Did you ever know a friend of hers—a great big tall guy named Marinni? He used to hang out at 57th Street?

O—No, you asked me something b-before I was pulled off—into—look at him—look at him back there—the wa mysterious huh

B—You know I was just gonna say Paul don't mumble.

P—What was the youth in the package?

O—There was no youth in the package; he says I can be packaged.

HONK HONK (car horn) I guess I can—like Nabisco Swiss cheese.

P—They don't make Swiss cheese.

O—They do so—Nabisco makes everything—including Ann Page.

D—What happened to Joe Cino?

O—Joe Cino died—he killed himself.

P—What's his name in the book?

O—Yeah zz well I—Joe Cino will be Joe Cino.

B—It was more of a scissor blend.

O—He was a scorpio saggitarius cuspra—a you know—birth

P—He was a cusp

O—He was a cuspridor.

P—Cup a da

O—He was a very dear sweet boy.

P—Coffee cups are cusps.

O—Who uh figured it was all over in the theater for him.

R—Said that all of a sudden behind a coffee machine

O—Oh, one of my old friends said last night to me, at the bar, said a very good thing—he says, the rest of the Chelsea Girls may have been good movies—I don't know he said because I don't care, he said, but you're always good theater.

Heh heh heh heh

P—Heh heh HEH

O—Ha ha I thought that was funny hah hah and that's quite a good observation to make because it's TRUE.

D—It's true?

O—He said he said no but I was always good theater

Oh oh he says you've never been less than grand and then I figelt

P—You must went to a lottla plays when you were young.

O—The thought—I didn't go to PLAYS.

P—Huh huh heh huh

O—Whadayou-I *was* a play—whadayou mean I went ta plays. Abbot and Castello meet the Bazooka Boys. Heh heh heh are you

P—Heh heh

O—Serious. I grew up in Red Hook, Paul

P—Heh heh heh

O—Now that's not the play area.

P—Hyuk hyuk hyuk hyuk

O—That's hardly what I would call the play area—I was

P—What did the kids like in Red Hook?

O—Wasn't as imaginative as my

decoder ring. A heh heh that really got me going.

P—What were the names of the kids of the neighborhood?

O—Biggy, you know, they, I named them after their pricks zeh zeh it's as simple as that—I was over-stimulated. Oh, I had such contests.

P—Did they have gangs?

O—Bangs.

P—A hih hih.

O—Uhh uhh, I had a good time in Brooklyn, but going back to Brooklyn is really really terri

P—You musta liked it.

O—They were all right—my only really true b-friend I mean you know like ya have a friend—this was one of them, his name was Dominic Peorio and we used to —that things found radium didn't it—I heard it, and we used to get the chema-chemistry set and laugh and produce things in school. We hadda be separated heh heh not drugs quite, but he was a friend you know. For one year we were really good friends an—then

P—The physics class

O—The physics class—No no not in high school; it was in grammar school; it was the 8th grade, 7th grade, the year before the last.

P—How can you remember so

O—What? Oh, that's not that far back. Certainly look at look at Elizabeth Taylor—she can remember last week.

B—Don't care has no home.

O—Why does it why why why does it a heh heh what? You know, really, he's evil. So I am homeless, so what?

B—You mean you have no quarters.

O—I have no place to ha-hang my ha-ha-hat. You horror. I guess my hat is ob (clunk)

P—Oh oh come come

O—Mu my hat's an open book but Doris Day eats rrrmm ooohh

P—Didja ever see
Tingle (telephone coin)

O—What?

P—Dya ever go to the movies at all?

O—The movies I never bother with.

P—I didn't see that—it's funny.

O—An I—I don't even go to the movies to cruise. I can't go to the movies—are you serious? Warhol's ruined me for all time. I ca- I can't go to the movies now either. What could I see?

P—Ya ever been ta Detroit?

O—Cartoon series perhaps. but that's all. No I have an Aunt Norma in Detroit.

P—Really

20 /   1

O—Norma in Detroit is her name —she's Northern DEtroit—no she's Yugo Yugoslavi

P—Italian?

O—Think of something more homespun. Paul don't interview

me let's interview the young man there—Peter.

P—Peter, what's yer last name?

O—Peter, what's yer last name?

PETER—I need a translator.

O—No no it's just an int—

P—It's Billy's book.

Peter—Oh it's an Italian name.

O—If you don't mind that is

P—We'll change the name

O—Do I MIND?

Pe—I have to ask her—do I mind?

O—Never mind, he doesn't have a last name.

P—Heh heh

O—Zzhzzh take it away Virginia Dare. Do I mind? I wha-tha now really. How can she say

Pe—Night owl

O—How an she say will you mind a

Pe—It's a night owl

O—Nnnh nnnh it must be. Well, I'm glad that interview's closed.

P—Heh heh

O—Haah BACK to the suburbs. As we left our little bus circling it was cir cir cir cling Queens. My family didn't live in Ridluk— they were a slice above it. My father ran the grocery store, you know, which was a slice above it. Yes, of course I was always doing wa

P—You always had soda

O—I had everything I wanted including
telephone rings
typewriter types
telephone rings

O—I'll get it; No I won't

P—Did everybody hang out at the store?

O—No my father's store was a regular grocery store and they respected it as such.

P—Yeah?

GERARD—Orio .

O—Is that on the phone Or-i-i-O is on the phone
Orio
Hello

ORIO —Hello

O—Yes, is it you? What happened to you? Where did you go?

OR—(*on phone*): I'm home.

O—Oh, you louse you—you know who just called here? Weiss.

OR—Jacky Seven (*inaudible*)

O—He called there. He says call— you flew out of there my dear. I was getting my nickel. (*Type-writing typing.*) What did I do? I didn't do anything except
Oh don't be silly—Ah, I'm glad yer home though. Izzs everything hunh hunh is everything all right? Well, don't bother with it. No en ne newa welll, listen, well my dear I know that, it's a terrible attitude
Listen you—
Listen you—
You called, didn't you? You're divine (*typewriter typing*) not net. There is no PHONE (*Type-writer typing.*) No, it's not too new—there's no phone. As you ho (*tap tap tap tap*) You know don't you realize what what happened? Λ*tap tap tap tap*) NEM BU TOL.
It. wa— Huh—are you serious? Do you know what you get ma like my dear and look out your attitude right now (*tap tap tap tap*) Well, that's your attitude with Nembutol (*tap tap tap tap*) Well, I never wanna see you again I didn wanna see you again 3 years ago I didn't wanna see you ever again (*tap tap tap tap*)

B—She didn't wanna see you again

about 2 weeks ago.

O—And I couldn't care less about you—you louse (*tap a tap tap*) I dunno how you can get there OK if you can get th—Run fa fa fer a cab (*tap tap tap tap ta ta tap*) Good, what did he do? (*Tap tap tap tap*) Have you heard a NOW Have you have tap tap

TAP TAP TAP

have have you heard from a Richie? (*tap tap tap tap*) Oh, darling, well he didn't know what to do he didn't know where you were (*tap a tap a*) and I was trying to make the phone call (*tap tap ta tap*) Well, if you wanna be alone—fire. Yeah Wh just listen You sound very bad. (*tap tap tap tap tap*) Well you should—you are horrible.

OR—Hum, I feel

O—Yuh huh Whatya mean— you're not as horrible as you feel? YOu're being recorded heh hah if any listen

OR—Eeaugh

O—Da wa wa what did you DO? Listen, I was asleep, you forget darling, I was asleep, I didna I was not awake during any of it (*tap tap tap*) I was asleep. Well listen, don't ever ca jl ju ju class me with any group of people. Iwas asleep, and when I woke up I went out and when I came back you were out-outraged. It had nothing to do with—my at- titude was one of a person being confronted with nothing but yell- ing. Well all I did was go an make a phone call my dear and then lose my dime (*tap tap*) I mean that's not a bad attitude With your head . . . Your head

is not demented hah? Whadju- say? Tanks tahnks—you need help all right. Yeah ha What? I detest your very existence, you rat

OR—I hate your guts, you rat

O—Right. You won't heh Okay, gabye darling A heh

D—Let's do a monologue.

O—She's marvelous. Orio is just the most marvelous person in the world.

D—Do monologue.

O—Yeah, it seems that no one is really equipped.

B—Ethel and Albert—that's who you are

O—Ethel and Albert Monster.

P—Where is Orio ?

D—No, he's gonna do a mono- logue.

O—Where is ORIO . Orio said that you—your attitude, Billy, was disgusting. She says she hated loathes and despises you. She hopes she never sees you again and she said she doesn't care if you burn.

B—Ondine, if you're gonna tell me a story don't tell me one that's SUPPOSED to be the original of everything . . .

O—She doesn't understand them wa well either

B—She probably

O—Anyway

B—Anyway

O—That was the voice of Billy Name, heh, you'll never hear it again.

D—How's Octavio?

O—Octavio? I don't know. Who is Octavio? Oh, you mean Oxydol. She stopped by there and he wasn't there

D—And what happened last night?

O—Oh, we had a marvelous time, Drella, we had a really good session and that thing has been promised for a long time yer just the ordinary ah kind of a-ss oo how about a phone call with an amour?

DRELLA—What happened last night?

ONDINE—Oh, we had a marvelous time, Drella; we had a really good session and that thing has been promised for a long time. Yer just the ordinary ah kind of a-sse—oo—how about bout a with an amount?

tap tap tap tap
tap tap
tap tap

Something very cute.

BILLY—Any old amour?

O—Any old amour ahh mour aaghh mour huh huh. A little stale but so whaaat? Homosexuals have the right huuh heh—don't they. . . . Little sticky around the I don't care I don't care. I'll waltz if one to the thing awright? Oh, I—I—I hope he's home. He's beautiful ih wi

D—Who is he?

O—His name is Lou, he's tall, he has a blonde moustache and beard and he looks like a—wa-a-wa a-a—ri—a riflleman. He's he's swzz just divine Uh Alan MIDGETTE you look so divine. You do whtsamatter? Do you feel badly? Why?

ALAN—What?

O—You won't talk about it

A—I'm tired

O—O wa Oh. Jesus but ahh don't you feel a little angry?

A—No . . .

O—You look so saad—I don't know what a

B—You can turn the volume on on that can't you

D—What

B—Can't you turn the volume on while you're recording?

tap a tap tap tap tap a tap

O—Gee, I've never seen anybody look like this/that sad

B—Tohear what's being recorded

A—I'm very tired. I can't change the station lately

B—On and off if it's because I am and I started a long time before you

D—Ohhh

O—You look quite beautiful

D—Oh, Gerry, do you have to type, or—

GERARD—What?

O—Oh that's alright. I'll just talk very close to it

B—Yes, you decide, Bob. You the one that really knows.

O—Uh, I think I threw the wrong section of thenote away

D—No you

O—Ohh NO . . . I did

tap tap tap a tap tap a tap

Oh I ate the wrong section. Oh, Drella, really I did it. She called up; She said I hope I never see you again Ihate you. I said I hate you too. She's marvelous

tapping tapping

I love Rudine—but she really does get a little too outrageous. a daa I threw the thing awa MY own true lover, like Calamity Jane I who wmy OOLeeoh What did I OH Gee it's a pity he's like that

D—What?

O—(*gasps*)—isn't it?

D—Yeah

O—Isn't it

D—That's it

O—That's a terrible to see he's beautiful

D—He's beautiful

D—That's it

O—We—hell. . . . . I'VE GOT IT . . . America (screech) Jane Meadows phone number—He's 21 I think he told me and he's so so beautiful—I keep falling

D—(*heavy expiration*)
tap a tap a

O—and he's just unbelievably—I don't know.
Who's next—Oh, that's it? I'm a little groggy. you know because I'm stoned
Coin tingles phone box.
93 I think this is 934, 924. Lemme see—does that say 924?

D—924

O—924 (*dialong phone*)

D—12 holes like 2895

O—2894?—2—8//aphew. Does this record well in the phone? heh?
Phone ringing on other end.
Oxydol's not home . . . no
tap a tap tap tap tap tap tap
tap a tap a
arla great love affair lovers mirappen. What could shehave meant by Billy's attitude was so bad? I think she's just been happening thing from the Nembutols you know cause that makes you tight aye—aye—there's nobody there darling
I'll try Oxydol's again. Oxydol—I//I—anyway I knew Oxydol for a long time. I knew him through the jet set.

D—Really?

O—Yeah. The first group with NICO and all those—and I thought that he was just a real wasted, you know, but SOO aw-

ful, too, and so fag-fag, but he's not, he's quite marvelous—at times—he's got a uniqueness to him that's good he's ba ah and he's good looking—you know, in that way/. *Coin tingle*
And I don't mean that Brazilian way. I mean just that that way that if you're good looking once you'll be like that always. Like you to bring thirty-two. You know most people are attractive to me—I don't have heh-hah any trouble with types *tap a tap a tap A TAP A TAP* even some women are—but rarely you know. Usually I-I- very attractive women are beautiful to look at.
Hello, Oxydol?—ahhh. This is Ondine—is this PALL?? *Hi . .* How're you, Pall.

PALL—Hi, how are you

O—How are you

P—Fantastic

O—Okay. We've been calling you sort of all day

P—I know, we haven't been . . . we had to

O—You have—not been answering the phone, right?

P—Nah, nohnohnohnohnohnohnoh nohnohnoh (*becomes inaudible*)

O—Been a little better . . . Oh, jesus. That's alright

P—There's a BETTER way to do it than that

O—Oh, man, that was fabulous, why didn't you tell me? Oh—would have loved to have gone with you.
Oh I would have gone
Oh it would have been great
Oh, well, too late
Ahhrrgh

P—Aaahah

O—What can I say?

tap tap tap tap

It's only fair to say you're being recorded. I'm a-ah—I'm at the factory YEAH—I'm at the factory—YEAH—I wondered what you were doing—YEAH—uhhuh nothing . . I have nothing ta-to do, Rupine and I are not going to be-uh with one another right afte rthis—uh, she got-uh She was insulted.

P—Who?

O—Rudine. Well, you know if you take a certain amount of Nembutol—you get insulted by no matter what happens.

P—Wha she insulted about?

O—Oh, who knows—some ridiculous affr—I was-Iwas asleep when she got insulted/—it doesn't matter. You-you know it's just her way of saying uh-hello, I love you. You know at home in 9 on 94th Street. When-uh, so? in other words, I'm noh-I'm not going—I want to be with er—and-a I'm notgoing there and What're you doing?

P—Well, . . . I'm in a fog (*inaudible*)

I haven't taken it yet.

O—What did he say? Have you taken a Thorazin?—you'll never be up if you've taken a Thorazin. Oh, are you going to? cause that's a real crippler; that's a bad drug. I hate that drug—really.

P—MumumuI think my (*inaudible*)

O—Well, if you'd like to hear—if ya'd like somebody to hear about it, well—I'll listen. I may be able to help you, too.

P—Well, I-I-I-(*inaudible*) I hope a bite on methedrine.

O—On you mean it's impossible to talk now.

P—I'm all out of everything. I'm— I mean I don't even know what happened

O—Yeah

P—You know, I don'know why— and a—Rudine—that trouble— outa my head—how the fuck does anybody

O—Oh sh

Oh yu

Well, she's a-she's a little too much

P—. . . . . everything, you know, ev-ry-thing, you know. But what happened, I dunno what happened last night I really dunno what.

O—I know, neither does she, really, but she knows that sh-she knows that she came out ahead.

P—Yeah

O—Let's put it that way she knows that she had a real f-field day.

Wha-an you know like anybody who gets involved in those kind of things should realize that that's what they're involved in and it's nothing more than that

P—Yeah, but you see-uh

O—Betcause like nobody wins or loses

B—Anybody who gets involved in anything doesn't realize anything about what they're in

P—. . . . . lost ah
. . . .

O—Not ra now, you couldn't have lost, you gained—

How did you gain? Probably by losing. (*Paul continues speaking inaudibly*)

B—Aha, so it's speculation, hunnh?

O—Exactly, that's the see-see, you know. What the fuck did you win or lose, you stood 8 hours in the corner of a room or in the doorway or you on or a or a you continued to exist—doing ehh-ahh. Whatever it was that you were doing and a—it doesn't uh—ma-ma-matter what you thought you did, what you actually did was the same thing.

P-B—(simultaneous, talking unintelligible)

O—Then WHY do that??

B—Not very imaginative.

O—Is only a clue to your physical body.

B—The same thing about the same thing then he's not very imaginative at all

O—Fuck your mind, baby.

P—Where, where? Ah-what point? What happened—what did she say?

O—What happened (coin drops inside box) did you get a physical reaction?

P—Yeah, sort of—I dunno wha-a-what point.

O—Nothing, she probably bored you to tears. You know she goes on talking after a while can, you can get bored with it.

O—She's amusing, amorous, divine, delightful, desert, witty

B—How can you say to him that she probably bored him to tears and him not say whether she did or not?—

O—Well, did she bore you-ah. No, well then you did. Wh-I-I-I guessyou—I don't think it's that.

B—You're not—

O—I don't think the problem is understanding—you see you shouldn't bother to try to understand.

B—Stop standing under

P—Uh. Whata minut-ah—

O—Listen, I-yeah

P—Whataya want a lemme—talk to Oxydol

O—Yeah, but I but-but-a-but-but I don't wanna discuss this over the phone anyway cause it's important not-not to talk about these things over th phone—they don't ever get talked about . .

P—Oxydol. . . .

O—You know really right . . You deserve to be . . Okay.

Oxydol—Ondine?

O—Hello, darling

OX—Hiya

O—How're you

OX—All rright

O—You-you freaked out

OX—Uh, yeah . . .

O—What happened?

OX—Nothing bad

O—You're being recorded

OX—Aaahh?

O—You're being recorded

OX—Oh, really?

O—You know, you learn. Oh, if I had known you were go-go-Going to the baths I would have weeped and wailed and mashed my fuckin teeth out—I would have loved to have gone

OX—Oh, I had a great time

O—Didja have a ball?

OX—Had a ball had a doctor

O—A doctor?

OX—A doctor, my dear, a young doctor who licked my ass like

O—Sounds divine

OX—Sno tomorrow

O—heh heh heh heh. That sounds very good—a young doctor

OX—A VERY young doctor

O—Sounds particularly good

OX—avery young doctor
a very young doctor who

B—Marone

O—Yeah, as Billy just said, marone. heh heh heh heh heh

OX—Yeah. Where are you?

O—I'm at the factory

OX—hmmmm

B—Factory

O—You know, 47th . . .

OX—Yeah, so—

O—East 47th

OX—Didja freak out?

O—Well, you know, I went to— wh-we went back to 94th Street and bathed and everything—wa

—and then we sort of freaked out there because—well—they made their minds up that they were gonna get an hour sleep which they knew they wouldn't get, and . . .

OX—Yeah.

O—So, I just said fuck it—I'm not gonna get any hour sleep. I still have that same bottle of liquid stuff around me without the spike of course. You know I don't know how to get to it.

21 /   1

OX—So how's Rudine.

O—Rudine just freaked out over the phone. We went aah we c. . . .

OPERATOR—FIVE CENTS . .

O—Owwh, 5¢ how—could you call me back, Oxydol?? Yeah a L El-dorado 5/ninety-nine forty-one.

OX—Eldorado 5-9914?

O—Yeah

OX—Sure

O—Bye-bye

clank clank (hanging up)

O—Ahh. I didn't know which one was which—Paul I think lives there but I'm not sure whi

B—Paul who?

O—I don't know his last name— I think he's Italian . . . Oxydol said. Oh, I had a young doctor he said at the-at the baths who lickedmy ass it was just divine He's-he's fabulous.

Telephone rings

Oh, Oxydol

Picks up receiver

Hello. . . . . . Oxydol . . .

OX—Yes

O—Gay—now tell me. Oh, yeah, te/. . .

OX—Yes

O—Uh—Rudine-uh you know we-we came down—we went to the Gymnasium to see uh-the group and evreything—and uh/uh the-there was another Armenian wed-ding there—it seems on Saturday nights the hall gets rented out to Armenians who hold their wed-ding services or whatever they do there, there, that night.

OX—So I heard

O—And we had just enough cab fare—so we got there. We were a *little* bit wierd and slightly slightly Nembutolly, you know, and it was a little and a very a-well what can I say—we were very stoned and . . .

OX—Eeeyeah

O—Anthen-and then we came down heah—and/a Rudine kept getting offended.

OX—Why?

O—Oh, well, who knows, you know? Because no one responded to her particular brand of-of-a clowning around

tap a tap tap

Bill, you know, once in a while she can get on your nerves—as-uh a matter of fact there are times when you would like to strangle her

a tap a tap a tap

really yaknow the best thing you can do would be to greet her with a

OX—Really, was she carrying on about here?

O—a sixty-foot boa constrictor

No, she was having fun and sometimes her having fun means that she runs around in hip boots and bangs and yells and screams y'know . . .

OX—Ooh, yeah, I know

O—She-she just makes a general nuisance of herself at which point I ca-call her Barney. She-she-she's still heaven, of course, but-but then, if no one responds correctly she's uh-uh she's offended.

OX—Yeah, uh, so-uh she's in bed at home

O—Yeces. She says, no. I hope I never see you again, you piece of trash.

OX—heh heh heh heh heh heh heh

O—And, my dear, you know, my dear, the saddest thing in the world is that she *is* that piece of trash—she rolla—I think she's got something cooking though

because-eh uh-two minutes before that phone call there was another phone call from *Jimmy Weiss*, who said

O—Is Jacky Seven there up at Rudine's? and I said I didn't think so cause I didn't even think that Rudine was up there. She told me that Jacky Seven had just called there

tap a tap

Now I'm sure thy're probably together again—which means NOTHING to me except that there'll be a little more cheap

OX—Isn't that her boyfriend?

O—Well she this series of friends, I don't know, who-ah—I think this is her conductor, I'm not sure ther he makes her—he makes her all-ters fall and everything hmm hmm, yeah?

OX—. . . . . nothing, she'll be all right tomorrow

O—I-eh-ah listen, she's not gonna, oh, of course, you know, I mean she's fine

tap tap tap tap

I adore her—I d'know who doesn't adore her, isn't she great? and I hope that she didn't blow Paul's mind

OX—Naaow

O—Cause she's very funny, ya know.

OX—Oh yeah, naaow that's

O—I'm sure that sh shi-she had a good time

OX—Well, I mean, like, you know she put on a royal big

O—Eggsactly. Na sh played it with A general huh huh

OX—Yeahss, she played the roll big bet

O—Well, see when she came in-uh ta-ta her the house this after-

noon Richie was leaving and
Richie wouldn't say a worrd.
Richie just said I refuse to and
walked out.

OX—Oyeah

O—and so, you know that-that kind
of fucked up Rudine.

OX—Ahh, but she's. . . .

O—Oh, yeah, ya know if a—wel—
so what?

OX—Seen Rita?

O—Ahh. no, I haven't seen Rita, I
didn't stop o-over there, I didn't
know-uh—Why, I just didn't, ya
know, I can't?uh—I—ee—I
wanted to go there earlier but it
didn't happen and then—ah-eh
living with Birdie establishes certain rules with Rita, you know,
like he has a-an ordinary—dinner-
dinner cALL an all that. Of
course her house is open any time
at ALL to me, but I don't do anything about it

OX—Yeah, I know-uh

O—You know, when she like when
she dosen't answer her bell I
don't care to ring it a-guh—twice,
or go upstrais and stand and stare
at the door

OX—She doesn't have a phone?

O—No she I now I think that may
be a blessing—her not having a
phone is a blessing otherwise she
would never be off it . . . you
know

OX—Right, she—

O—Aaaaaah

B—It's no different

O—It's-uh like

B—It's no different

O—It's no different, you're right, I
guess

B—Having it or not having it

O—Eeeyeah, I don't know what to
say—did you want anything in

particular from Rita?

OX—No, honey, no

O—No what wha wha I . . . the
mike now you just confuse, deah
Drella good I had fromoral on
the phone—heh that's what telling her I would say I would remember t-that you had said give
my love to Rita

OX—Yeeass

O—Umb I ambu slipped

OX—Yeah, that's what I said

O—Where's a two my b-be yer yer
yer a bed yer yer yer alone both a

OX—No we had a great time

O—You had a BALL, darling, it
was heaven, and there was a moment in the bedroom where you
. . . Uhhh—oh you Oxydol, that
poppa was great—do you know
Stefán?

OX—You di a

O—Well he has some of the world's
most incredible pieces of meat—
just beautiful big and delightful

OX—A boy named Stefán, darling,
I don't know who you mean

O—Heee's glorious. Oh-eh ah-I
don't know, I think he may be
Hungarian—I'm not sure but he's
just perfect

OX—He's a friend of whom

O—Oh ah I dunno—he said He
was friends of little Joey and a
friend of the other one—Loito or
whatever his name is—uh you
know aih I saw seven people
didn't know last night

OX—Ron

O—Ron Via

OX—Ron Via

O—Oh no no no no no en no no no
not him

OX—Oiyeah he's that bay that was
standing

O—The boy with the plaid pants

OX—Yah, that's the boy with the big cock?

O—Y-yes

OX—Oyhis name's not Stefán

O—What a is his name?

OX—Ahhh—Steve . . .

O—Oh, Steve, welll

OX—Steve Crockers

O—Yeah, he's nice

OX—Oiyeah, he's an old friend of mine

O—Yeah-uh ah you know he sa he seemed like he would—would he he's marvelous, but anyway-ah that moment in there with tha poppa when you—we all Called for you, you know please break the poppa bah-was at the point when we realized that there was nothing we cd do—I hadd go down in im

OX—OIYEAH

O—The gu-the guy he was with couldn't do it . . .

OX—Yeah, but you HAD to do it

O—Of Cour-ourse

OX—And if you are not there I have to do it

O—Bring it wa ha hah

OX—Are you kidding?

O—An whats-his-name Lou was

OX—. . . . . that boy, Ondine, You would not believe it

O—I know and I been faking get home

OX—His—. . .

O—EEOAP—he's a LITTLE too good

OX—I haad, Yeah

O—He's a beau-ah—you're going to sleep

OX—Yes, honey, I took, you know, little ah-Doradin, honey—. . .

O—Oh, God, the pill. Mystic pills are heaven

OX—Yeah-eh-duh—. . .

O—You'll feel very strange

OX—Somebody

O—You should read the Ouija board an then go ta sleep

OX—But, look, Ondine

O—Yeah . . .

OX—When're you gonna call me?

O—Well, maybe next week

OX—THIS week, this coming week

O—Yeah ah-ss, ah-s, I suppose, I don't know, you know

OX—A-Yeah, let's do something

O—Okay, of course, you know

OX—Get together

O—Ds-does Paul live with you?

OX—More or less

O—Because he's belief

OX—Oh, yeahss, very

O—I mean he's gotta fu ah a ffffrantic way of looking at people

OX—Yeah, adorable

O—He's he s-a-he s yeah he sam AND, I like to speak with him—he seems demented

OX—Ohh Po

O—Anyway, duckie, a sleepwa, sleep well

OX—You too take care try to get some sleep

O—Oh, WHYYY????

OX—Well, because next week we're gonna see each other—the middle of the week ah me . . .

O—Yes, we should wha the middle of the week is right

OX—It's so important it happens beforre Friday ev-ry week I don't know-uh

O—Oxydol, you know, your home is divine

OX—You liked it? . . .

O—Ooo-ooh please, my dear

OX—Good-th-I'm glad you liked it

O—Itsa little-Itsa little what I would call advanced, you know—

fer-a-ah fer many of the citizens

OX—Yeah

O—But it's dah it's doh it cut the shit out

OX—dis it clearly

O—Oh, it's heaven, it's the end—romper room, it's gre-hea-hea-heat.

OX—Right, dear

OIt lets the shit hit the fan, my dear

OX—Riiight

O—I know doubt about it

OX—Well, we must get together—this week

O—Nun an I never know with Rudine, what's what—I don't think she'll be——really staying in after Monday, I think she'll probably be going to Rio

OX—Eeeyeah—. . .

O—I hope she does

B—Well, which that which what what now what . . .—/

OX—Yes, she's got

B—What

OX—She's got supa system verve

O—Mmmmm

B—Which what-what which what

OX—San Francisco's the birds

O—Mmmmyeah

B—Which what what which what

OX—Go to bed

O—Okay—y-y-y-you have no idea where Lou is, hah??

OX—Wy I—din't eh

B—Nyah

O—Okay, baby. Does he sleep long hours?

OX—Long?

O—Yes.

OX—Yes

O—Di-de-should I/uh ring the phone in you know, like wake him up, ring it, you know erratically-dzje sort of-eh to get him up or should I just take—Take a

hint after a couple of rings an hang up

OX—Ring a while er two and then talk

O—Right . . .

OX—Because-ah he's ince he sleeps like a log

O—Ah, he probly is asleep I know woulda bin

OX—Well, you

O—He was SO beautiful last night GOD he was forgeous WHAT a

OX—Oiyeah??

O—OH he was a su-such a body—he said somebody said he was a dan hewa he he he was a dancer and I said OH not with not with that BODY I said your too beautiful you know that body is REALLL

B—Sigh

O—An he says/yeah wa wa he s a swinger

OX—Oh, that was funny

B—chuckle

O—Oh, that ASS is the most divine thing live eh huh well, you know, Ste-an-Stevens ass wasn't so bad either, darling

OX—Ny but it . . .

O—No, but I mean ih nothing in comparison to LOU . . . LOU—has an ass that is like out of the-out of the cave of the gahds.

OX—Nozier, neefar in a vow

O—It-is-the-most-divine thing-I couldn't oowah-an after a while I just kept mou-mu murmuring to him—sit on my face I said boos in a mum

OX—Ondine . . . . . asshole

O—Ahuh huh I was under my head with im. Ace was divine

OX—Honey . . .—(*inaudible*)

O—I know I live it

OX—Till there's no ass left in the

world—I-I dint start

O—There's something about the position above

OX—An I meant really you know and so I went to the baths

O—euh-huh. Very few can do it really

OX—You can an

O—Ducky, a young doctor, hmm

OX—I remove the pillow from my head since I lay flat and I told him to hank onto the bed, you know

O—Oh, stOP IT, Oxydol

OX—an just sit on my face and run it in, baby.

O—Huh huh huh Oxydol, stop it

OX—I think he looked right back at me I stuck my tongue ahalf a my tongue up his ass

O—I'm sure thatchour da I'm sure that your chin that ahw

OX—I gotta hard on an uh tongue I really got it inside which is very difficult

B—You know who used to talk to me about Oxydol

O—That's vehh?ry hard to do, my dear

OX—That's very hard to do

O—You know it's very hard to simulate that kind of fe-ah-ah

OX—Aihh it was so beautiful

O—Once, once at the beach at Fire Island on the bay side I got that but that was a long time ago

OX—Eeeyeah—I got that three times this month

O—ONCE . . .

OX—I was surprised

O—Well, I had been rather eesin uh eh

OX—Well it was so beautiful cause I ate ass two an a half solid hours

O—I love it (sigh)

OX—Of one number alone

O—What's it like there

OX—Nothing goes

B—I love it I love it (like Cheetah spot ad)

OX—I just at his ass and ate it and ate it an

O—Ayeah ate

OX—Nose up it

O—Ahah Huha

OX—I put my finger in an then I LICKED IT

O—How heaven you are

OX—THAT was beautiful. I love doing that

O—Sleep tight my dear

OX—Talk and then a talk. You talk to me tomorrow

O—Allright, I'll call you tomorrow, what time?

22 /   1

OX—Anytime after two cause I might (inaudible)

O—What about Freddie, what's his scene?

OX—Fred??

O—Yeah

OX—Oh, honey

O—He's a doll but I feel SORry for him though.

OX—Yeah

O—Cause he seems like he ca he de he's not row he doesn't

OX—I din't know what

O—What happened

OX—Know what a

O—Yeah he's-hes putting himself out of it, why??

OX—Yeah, I dunno, I dunno—I tried, you know, I tried

O—That's hard, you know, that's a *hard* feeling cause I saw him doing it last night and I felt very bad

OX—Yeah, yeah, I know

O—It's like that he yu he yu he pulls himself away from you

OX—Right that's something

O—Ahhh—well maybe it with Sam er whatever his name is

OX—Yeah the—freak

O—The fuck. Good-bye, darling

OX—Okay see ya tomorrow

O—Sa-sleep tight. Bye-bye

OX—Bye.

O—That coversation was sO good —what, darling? What, darling? Of course, I'd love to—hold on for one se—what a gr- . . .

D—What?

O—Nasty conversation

D—Really??

O—That was—he said he loves he ate 2 hours of ass and after that he

D—What??

O—. . . said he put his NOSE in it, then he said he put his FINGERS in it he said to- . . .

D—In what?

O—In his Ha-in this guy's ass an he said he LICKED it an he said SIT ON MY FACE (*gasps*) he goes ON—Oxydol went oN and he knew he was being ree-a-recorded, so he didn't care, you know, he mustn't of cared—this yeah this THIS should also be subtitled something about assholes ASSHOLES in breakfast or assholes for tea or assholes Alone haha hah heh heh whatever— anyway, it was GREAT—gee, did you turn that tuh—?

Boy—No . . .

Girl—YES . . .

O—How long was the conversation on the ph- I'm sure that you heard every word of of—his cause it was coming very clear

B—It's AYY very clear, Bob.

O—No, but I mean of Oxydol's p-part—oh—WOW—ah, I think, should I get something A LITTLE

P—Warmer?

O—Yeah, like some-something else

P—Yeah, yeah

D—Chilly? Is it really?

O—I don't think I'll be much colder than this—I would like to do something about these shoes, like extinguish them huh huh hi don know what happened to them, their sorta

P—Orio's shoes are all falling apart

O—Well, Rudine's falling she juz

B—See those fires?

O—See, his fly his falling apart— ah wa—*there* you are—they thought that what's his name was your friend. . . . and I said NO, he wasn't, he wasn't your friend at all—George, you wah me to hol that

tinkle of telephone bell

UH Oh (*sniff wipe*) HULLOOH

Voice on phone—Hell, is Paul there?

O—Paul who?

V—Paul Paul.

O—Who's calling?

V—It's Jackson

O—It's Jackson for Paul Paul— YES, he is

P—(*underbreath laugh*) Yeahello yes hello

O—Did he say no—that he didn't wanna talk to him?

D—Yes

O—Oh, SHIT, I wa I di—who did that?

P—Yeah, I guess so

O—It's sorta nice

P—Are we gonna go up there . . .

ALAN—A nerve slips up

D—No, tell him to meet us at Sxam's.

O—We're gonna go to Sxam's.

D—Oh we have them, oh, yeah

P—What time is it now?

O—Two,two

P—Ten of one

O—Who? Who fa who

RON VIA —Spend twice as much money on A instead of tape an we'll map out a plan to revolurevolutionize the world

O—Bette Davis? Oh, no

D—Bette Davis, oh, no

O—The last parts-a alone that other life by Bette Davis

D—Oh, it's a great book—it rally is

O—I know, she's a marvelous woman, you know

D—Did she write the book?

O—Well, she ghost writed—she ghost writ it

D—No no no no no no She did NOT . . .

O—By herself

D—Yes

O—Heh heh—no, she's beautiful

P—No h never came back—he wa

D—I lost my breakfast

O—Isn't that strange, Oxydol said certain

D—Your hair is different COLORS ——

O—It's 3 or 4 different colors . . Yes, there's a lot of gray in ih-it,

a lotta red in it,

D—No, it has light brown in the background

O—Well certainly and then this goes into RED—aalll red over here

D—Well, did you do those things?

O—No, that's the way it grows—I was a BLONDE at birth then I turned into a redhead

D—(*inaudible*) tie by nie . . . . .

O—Sure

A—Can you remember the details?

O—Hey-whA-k-oh. Duhya—Duh-you wahme to carry the mike??

D—Oh, no, that's alright

O—Cause it seems unfair—oh, now where's the book—you-uh you were giving me—Ohh the man from pansy

D—Oh, Billy, WILL YOU LOCK UP?

O—No one took anything else??

B—Yeah, lock downstair

O—Is Billy coming with us?

D—Nooo

B—Hah no no no no no

O—WHY NOT?

B—Ohh, no

D—Is the elevator working? C'mon (*door sounds*)

O—Well (*singing*) here we are

B—Here WE are . . .

O—You know b red

D—Paul wants to go to Newport

O—Always the latest but me, I-it seems I'm going somewhere for a minute an then I (*door sounds, jabber*)

O—Ve-ry strange

D—Huh?

O—YOU're something else this evening, Alan

P—Yah had yer coat this morning

O—Ohhh—I mean, you're very WILD looking

B—Hah

O—Are we going to one? Yes, close pulease. Gubye Bill (*singing*) Happy Holidays, may the mis a mis

B—C'mon back soon now, hyeah?

O—Go fuck yahself ya rotten . . .

A—It isn't working

D—h ya hafta lock. . . .

O—happy, may yer evry dream come true . . . Oh I took the tape—

D—But there's no need to be claustrophobic about-uh

O—Who's, who's CLAUSTROPHOBIC?

GERARD—I do

D—Bcause ya can get stuck, but it's —airy

O—Oh, it's so wonderful to get stuck here you can-uh see the memory of Pepper

D—uh ho ho ho ho no no

O—Reciting the Hail Mary's

D—UH, Roger Trudeaux

O—Or Roge rTrudeaux

D—A Night in the Elevator

O—STILL with the withe withe cheepest room in the Irving—Oh, I can't BELIEVE his room is so funny it really deserved a medal of acre

G—He still has a room there? Oh, his father probably owns the hotel

O—WHO'S Roger's father?

G—I DON'T KNOW

P—Trudy Trudeaux

O—Tru-Trudy WHO-who. Trubudy Trudeaux . . . (*All giggle.*)

D—Ahh, lock th door downstairs ahh lo-lock the door down here (*general gabbing*) Gerry, make sure the door . . .

O—Trudell—Trudy Trudell be Roger's parents—uh, father

D—Gerard, can you see if the door is locked?

O—But those were the moments when I really think that you're at your best, Paul, is when you're completely inconsequential— you're greatest then—thatwa-that was lovely. O, you know, I came off like such a pompous ass wha-when we talk like this—I bu-Because you know I know so much about myself (*screech*) ardda hah hah

D—What er those girls doing there?

O—Oh, they're tryin ta heh give thi-those boys hand jobs—I cah-han't stand this night trade— Look at this arrgh pieces a rubbish

D—Umm

casual walking footstep sounds

D—Oh, Gerry has his cute pants on

O—Hey, hello Gerry

G—Hi, sweets. Kenni tape yah?

O—No, when

G—Lemme tape ya

O—Didja—chew ya. Whadaya mean by tape? Tape me? Oh, yeah, buh put it uh-in that K-ow, that's not bad—they went ta-ta the baths and Oxydol said he had a JYUNG doctor—doesn't that sound fresh??

sound fresh?? eh heh heh heh heh heh knife . . . Yeah, he had a young doctor—doe noe whadee meant budid sounded good. whada you aaoow uhn. What do I look like uh uhh. Now don't get smart. Garage in time to find me a corsage. Trudie Strudel?

P—A-heh

D—Oh ah—Taxi . . . Well, ah

G—Who's gah—are you going to the Dom first??

D—No

Well uh oh why doncha get in uh Ondine's cab—so you can guhhh —an I'll give you a dollar down there? OK? Ah wha we're going to Sha-Sxam's—oh—

O—That was quick work, what?

D—Huh?

O—Seeyat Sxam's

D—Oh uh

P—ahh

2 car doors slam shut

O—Hey this thing is—

P—Pocket

RON VIA —Yer gonna tern him into an egomaniac

O—I AM an egomaniac. That thing is HEAVY, Paul

P—Ja play it back?

D—Huh?

O—This is the same set as the other one, right?

P—Didja play it back?

O—But this is ah ah in a different uh-uh-size thing (gasp) you mean it has sheets that enter it—no— uhhh—ah, it doesn't enter like the other one did

D—Yes it does

P—The little bitty one

D—Oh nah nah

O—Ya mean—oh, the little bitty one

D—No nah

O—Was so beautiful

D—Yeah

O—hahhhhh—What's our driver's name—SPARAFUCILE?? . . . Jesus—GOD . . .

P—Huh huh

O—VA . . . Oh, Sxam's. Uh, sometimes it's Chahrrmink ah other times it s-a-mu

P—Doesn't it remind you of Kansas City?

O—I sat outside once I usually

RV—Only Mickey

O—I usually sit in the back, you know, I sat outside once an it doesn't—it didn't work, I felt miserable an horrible—except for Ronnie, who was just so divine that night, God, NO? you were, you were greatness itself. I walked in with Barney and uh . . .

P—Barney??

O—Barney—Rudine.

P—Who's Barney? That's Barney?

O—Barney . . . Well, when she gets in that mood her name has to be Barney—nobody else let's see, we were with Barney and Gabriel and we were—she was babbl . . .

P—Is Gabriel Indian really

O—I don't know what Gabriel is, I think he's a jeweler ahahhah I'm sure Gabriel's a jeweler. Gabriel's nice, but boy he's a—and is that thing really an emerald? —that light green shade? I thought emerald's came in a clear kind of deep green—it's a- whatever stone it is it's one of the mo

RV—The bitch did get it of—

O—It's one of the most beautiful stones I've ever seen in my life, but what I wanna

RV—(continues talking simultaneously with Ondine, but unintelligibly)

O—Know is that really an emerald?

RV—Yes, Yahp

O—Cause I thought emeralds just came in one collah and onecolor only

RV—No

O—A clear deep emerald green

RV—Gabriel before he starts hallucinating he does lay out a few bit odd chuckles

O—Hmmmph—a because EM-

ERALD is my collah emerald is my STONE too. I love emeralds more than anything (*boop boop*) I think everybody likes emeralds more than any other stone— Why? There s seh

RV—djyaget through the sex?

D—Uh—what's uh tantric yoga?

RV—Yogi and yin-yins

O—No, what I wanna know

G—Ya got it?

D—Yeah

O—Tantric? ta-ha-han-tric

PAUL PAUL—Tantric yoga . . .

O—At's a new flavor they have in Dannon—Tantrum

RV—It's a it's spiked out a Shaman a Shaman

O—Tantrum yoga

RV—Bonsah

D—What?

G—Eeeeachh (*softly, to the one who isn't beside him*)

RV—And wha-what this cat, Oxydol, is doing, he is running a tantric temple and . . .

O—Buh ebbuh

RV—And shakti and bhakti worship only he doesn't have any bhakti, it's all shakti

O—What's bhakti, woman?

RV—Yup

O—Well—then that's his preference, then it's his right

RV—Yeah, yeah, and there's that happening, you know, like in India also

O—It's eyeah eyeah it's right, too

RV—It's-a it's-a mah and some people should live their entire lives doing nothing but fucking, sucking, and carrying on

O—Yes, I should—

RV—No criticism of it

O—I'm one of them. I'm one of them

RV—And, you know, this is why I LOVE you, baby, because you're into it and you know you're into it an it's no BULLSHIT

O—Ahhhh that's a

P—Huh HEH

O—I know, I can't DO it

RV (*simultaneous with Ondine: indistinguishable*)

O—But you know how frustrating it is, my dear, when you come across people who don't understand it. I spend most of my time EXPLAINING to them that-uh I can't do anything else, but it's gotta be quick

RV—You're full-grown monster, th-therefore I think we can talk it—we can discuss it and be very sensible about it.

O—Paul-Paul is a fiend, darling.

RV—Paul is . . .

O—YES, but there's—uh like he's —uh a little devil brROOoding behind the eyes. He wants this mystical, uhh, faraway, un/ . . .

RV—Yeah, but he could turn into a sex maniac

O—Well, we shouloot him. YES . . . He's a psychopath—I can see it in his eyes . . .

RV—I know, and he's such a masochist

O—Well, listen, Ya-you know— everyone has his own role. Yo-yu-you're also a peace mover: I don't unnerstan that. I don't unnerstand why we want to prevent psy-psychopathia in ANYbody.

RV—Sentosatho; kj

O—Heavens, that's all

PP—What's a peace mover??

O—Ohh, ya know, people who arch with the peace people.

P—Where'd the parade start?

RV—I wandded to blow up police

stations, but . . . (nobody will give me dynamite) . . .

I'm in lots of trouble already, otherwise I would

O—E-eH/Everyone wants to blow uh-duh-up police stations

O—Duh-dUH/Doea that make any sense to you—thesepeopappeople who-uh-ehah would like to

RV—(blah blah blah) I can't think of a cool way of doing it—

O—Th-thOUsand of peo-people who just have this wild sexual thing about cops, and they're just SOOO dreary and dumb—wh-whoo could
. . .

RV—Yeah, uh

O—He bothered with em

RV—. . . against uniforms and things that would reverse tha . . .

O—Ah-Eh/ I . . . mean . . . I . . . have . . . yet . . . to . . . see . . . aaa . . . COP that really turned me on. I mean they're All a little too wise guy f-for me . . .

RV—Come walk along the park with me on an August night and-uh . . .

O—Well-uh Well-uh Imna Imna I'm not talking about Greek caps, ya know. GREEK cops I'M so beside the pitted olives

RV—I've seen them breaking people's feet, man, cracking backs, and they're beautiful when they do it.

P—Break their feet—whaddoes that mean?

O—Don't t-talk to the wall, Paul

RV—(a simultaneous mumble)

P—Well??

O—Uh, oh, that's their form of torture

RV—The Byzantines, ya know, its its-uh question and answer time.

D—Uh-oh, I thought you could park along here on 42nd Street . . .

O—(indistinguishable) ya mean the plouzz around heah. . . .

RV—(simultaneous) that would be wild were really bad ya know. . . .

O—. . . . . restaurant—ughh—what kinda cooking? must be Italian . . . (chuckling) (chortling) how disssguhsting . . .

P—Grease, ya mean grease . . .

RV—. . . I oughhdda know, staigguh fignewton; we'll start a new entertainment

O—Ya know . . .—I KNOW. That's what our driver's name—his name is Spartacus . . . Hello Ron
muffled laughter from one and all

O—Ya know, driver, dahling, it's so happy being us. Weee-uh Um (fadeout)

Driver:

O—YOU DONE LIKE COPS EITHER? neither do I (driver laughs)

Driver: Are you KIDDin? I ged robbed by em

O—No,, an I-uh . . . you get RoBBED by cops—REeeally?

RV—(*indistinguishable*)

Driver: (*garbled*)

P—(*insignificant rapping*)

O—The fUNny thing about l-last night was . . .

PP—You hafta pay the cops off when they arrestem?

Driver: I sometimes . . .

O—OF COURSE not . . . cops c-can't do Anything—Paul . . . unless you aLLLouw them to do it. An nobody knows how s-serious that is. That's the truth. Cops are merely your servants.

Driver: No no no: when ya drive a cab ya fine out where . . . heh heh

O—. . . you can become their victim if you want to, but what-uh ah yer-uh. They're paid for your protection by you, so you should use them, and use them well, or make them ih-eh-ineffective. Cops can't do ANY-thing unless YOU give them the weapons . . .

D—Can you make a right-uh-left turn?

O—Yeah, an-uh a right into the glass window? whyntcha (hahaha)

P—We wanna go ta . . .
   unanimous mumbling

O—You can make a U-turn, cantcha? . . .

D—Well, can you go down the block and turn, you know, well, how far is . . . . .

O—What goes down with this tape recorder is HORRRIble . . .

RV—That's when we put the callidin

Driver: I can't do it— its very bad

O—the verge

D—Well, no, then you can go down another block and then turn

SNNIIFFFF

O—Anyway-uh, uh-when you give

RV—C'mon I'll carry you in . . .

O—. . . the policeman a bit of information, a bit of information, you're giving him the only hold he has over you

RV—Allah Allah

O—ANY bit of informAtion . . .

P—Whaddya

O—ANY i-information, no matter what it is . . .

RV—That's all they NEEED

O—No, notcher name. You have to give your name at times

RV—That's all they need

O—No-if-ifa-cher. NO. You can Ooownly give them the truth if they ask it, nothing more, like if they ask you yer name, you have to give it to them, but . . .

RV—The first estate/that's a mistake

O—Listen, don't fuck it up, Ronnie, it is NOT the mistake

RV—It is

O—Only—never mind

RV—. . . . how they had . . . . .

O—dinclosed. You're WRONG—there is a way to deal with the Police that EVRYbody should know about dididih you DON'T need lawyers, and you don't neew anything else. You just need knowledge, and that is to d-deal with them effectively, and that is to P/Puh-Precisely tell them nothing, nothing at Aawll. Except . . . . . (ape garbles)

RV—When will you be going back to Sunnybrook Farm?

O—As soon as ReBECca gets home—you know she's on vacation, don't you? . . . . . you can't s-say (besides she's baking cookies). You HAFta . . .

RV—I'm so embarrassed that I'm with Emma Bovary here tonight

O—You hafta give good-uh . . . You HAFTA give good-uh. . . . I have some change, Drella

D—Nonono I have about two . . .

O—You hafta give yer goo-uh R/Right name if the cops ask, because if you give them a-uh phony name, you re a-uh fu-uh fffool. They've got you on two raps then. . .

RV—then you hafta have a phony ID to go with it, and a phony life to match it . . .

O—. . . go around cashing checks. Why don't you go into a-uh police station and ask them to cash your check?

RV—I-uh-I'm gonna sset one up as ssoon as I can

O—This isn maki—do you want me to cuh-carry a tip? . . . Thass OK . . . Paul is so fast . . .

RV—ouch

O—Thank you
   shuffle shuffle
   shuffle shuffle
   shuffle shuffle

O—Sugar cane. Sure we can. Of course we can. I know and its marvelous. I must really go upstairs. I must really go upstairs.

P—Didja go to the Peace March?

VOICE—Yes, an it was . . . . . tooka picture . . . it was great an

O—Can we sit upstairs?
   Faluouble. OK, an there's just four of us
   Drella? Paul?
   clomp clomp clomp (up the stairs)

Oh, pahdon me
I found this in the cab
jangle tinkle tinkle
it should be quieter up here
I don't know—Paul hasn't even fffainted
general cacaphony
he's probly talking to someone
I think we'll go an get some of this. yeahhss
BUSBOY—yeah, we'll take some chairs from over her and yadeeyadeeya
(*sounding like a social director*)
D—I dunno—uh, ah, maybe they stopped downstairs
VOICE—well, we're ready for you up here
dissonance
stomp stomp stomp stomp shuffle shuffle
D—They coming up?
P—Oaaaoow, it's NIce around here
Yeah

23 / 1

O—(*indistinct*)   D—Huh?   *ding ding ding*   O—I thought I was being stuck in the can . . . um spah/hah-uh um rrrr Oh, Yeah. knocked out . . . I hadta go to the bathroom so much, dropped out on this side an go???   D—Nooo, don't go   O—But I have to   D—Nooo: you can wait a little while   O—Owh, but I have to   P—Bring your tape recorder   CRASH (*glass breaking*)   O—(*sigh*) no, wait a second, I want to put this cord . . .   (RENE)—Rodney fucked up. . . . O—more cord in here an more cord in here annd more cord in here and then like this   D—(*Something or somebody*) fell   O—Good, I would have hated to have lost it   ALL—uughhh   D—let's get a table—another table—out here   O—Can't they expand tha booth? Uh, would you-uh I hafta get my-uh   G—Ya getting a chair??   O— But I hafta have-uh; I need-uh a sss. . . .   P—ha!!ha!!   O—Sitover . . . sitover . . . what?   ha hah ha   O—aninastah aninastah   Is Al here?   VOICE—no   O—Is anybody else . . . ?   G—I'm gonna go downstairs   O—Gerard's going back downstairs   G—Can I get out? O—Can he get out, please? He has to go downstairs   GIRL—Oh,

sure   O—. . . .dance—the top of the fly dance . . . Lou   P—. . . a
week before.Not Last week, the week before. Lou an . . . . . an extra
check   O—I know I'm not allowed to go to the bathroom, but . . .
D—Gerard, aren't you coming up?   G—Yeah, I'll be-I'll be back
O—Do you suppose that . . . Hey, Paul, uh . . . uh, Lou? Who else? Who
else would have it? Who else would you do?   Lou—He was here now
O—If somebody comes in . . . . . WE'VE ran into another Armenian
wedding, thank you   L—Oh, was it going on AGAin?   O—It certainly is, and they don't know—they don't know Warhol at all, they said
no I don't know what it is—I think it's one of the Ed Sullivan shows
L—Ya gonna eat anything?   O—Yeah, but he left plenty of . . . in
the oven. He looked so glittery I couldn't believe it   P—Do you have
a pen?   O—I have one   P—I don't need tha now   O—Heah—
help yourself to mah jacket . . .Oh, wow   Lou, howanya   Whatsa
matter with—uh.Aaaow, she's gotta pen back there. I thought she had a
pen back there. That dress is so . . . yabbadabba . . . It sounds like you're
taking off material and going out of your thing. I CANt get nooo . . .
(satisf-). What're you doing this evening, Lou? What're you doing this
evening. Hey, Maddy. Lou, what're you doing this evening, what're you
doing?   L—(mumble)   O—You're not going theAH? To the-uh to
the Ah Gymnasium? are you.   O—Since about 11—I don't know-uh
what time it is now, so I wouldn't. Two hours of tape so far or wha? Or
an hour?   D—An hour   O—Just about an hour   D—Is Jackson
coming here?   L—What happened in . . . (indistinguishable)   O—
A lot. A lot—you should have come   P—Uh   O—A lot—I was
waiting for you, and then all of a sudden . . . I realized that you weren't
there, an, uhhh, woaow—whddifhe had come? An I said: whew (whistle)
It was a little too much. Look, maybe you could get up—I been sitting
here for a while. Unless you've been sitting here for hours an hours. Oh,
well, nevah mind nevah mind. I thought maybe Lou's here. Huh . . .
Oxydol's rese-uh electrifying; he really did   L—Who showed up?
O—Uh . . . the RIGHT people   L—Rudine?   O—An everything
. . .   L—(indistinct)   O—Whaaddya mean? Yer book? And-uh . .
uh uh ooh—I had it. And-uh whatchamacall-uh And all of a sudden I
went out-uh. . . . (fades out)   P—At the Gymnasium with the Velvet
Underground which they didn't get paid for   O—And I was going to
the gymnasium whether I like it or not, so Rudine went, And-uh with an
amphetamine mixture, and she gave me the proper amount, but-uh behind
my tongue-uh, back there, and it got me up—Boy, did it ever get me up.
wheeh (whistle) Now-uh/ah, now . . . have we gotten a thousand a day
yet, noo   P—A few weegs ago-uh . . . last week   O—It was-uh . . .

it was-uh. It was-a . . .the night that the shit hit the fan and-uh cleared the place. It was a very important night, ya know, and-uh. In as much as the people who missed it missed it; the p-people who didn't miss it were rrrrriGHT there. heh heh. Not that that means anything—its a clever . . .

L—Crux and Nee Co. and everybody were around here-uh . . . uh Nico . . . uh . . . Before   O—Nobody heard the bell . . . Nobody heard the bell   L—Oh, is that what it was . . .   O—It was ma/a/aD after a while, I'm sure. No one heard the telephone, an I unnerstan it had been ringing all morning. We didn't hear one phone call. Alan, you know that all you do in-uh. . . . *(fade)* . . . is take some sleep   God, you were-uh. I mean, thatsa   DISTORTION: about five simultaneous conversations

Oaow, what's tonight at the Gymnasium? The people who do gymnastics were havin like a year-end final. *(ha)*   Ah. When the curtain opened, and you saw them all in their-uh ah-electric blue shshsh-s-s/sweat shirts. 1967's champions. They were rather-uh . . . oh, Jesus, they were awful—the place looked like a BAH-arn, it was lit so strangely   What did they have that a . . .   They had Like-ah crepe paper, and-uh The SONG OF BERNADETTE . . .   I . . . nihnah . . . they didn't even HAVE songs . . . I'm beginning an abcess on the side of my arm . . . It's delightful: I mean, I gave it to myself so-uh-ooo level. Anyway, wha happened   We went to this thing called Pennisiffic-uhsociation . . . and elevated after our exposure   Oh: it must be daown Park, divided by four. It's so-uh scary, you walk in, and it's marvelous . . . *(Ixsam's own particular variety of distortion)*   O—IT CAN STAND UP . . . No, it can, ih can, you can POINT it   UNIDENTIFIED PERSON— Rodey was saying that he likes her using the earphones with it. He said that he thought she should use it throughout the entire show   P— Broadcast THAT part? are you sure??   O—Barbara . . . truly Barbara . . . uh, laaah   L—Did we tell you about the song Ondine's gonna do on the . . .

Oh, really?? On the next album?

Look what went on?

It's on the upstairs jukebox

Isn't it divine??

It's such a . . .

It always was

The Vlevets song

The Velvets are so good . . .

It's so poor

It doesn't matter maybe you hafta be bridges. You're so beautiful . . .

Loud grunts from adjoining tables

You're Winston Churchill

Where was that creep who was supposed to audition today? He didn't
show up

Notice the level of the conversation that just went—did you hear—didjou
hear what those

O O O I forgot (*jingle jingle*) Did you see this thing?

. . . started to talk

Then Maxim's is great

Didjo see this?

Oh, that's good

The Mad Hatter

Oh, thATS THE Night Tide scene? Is that the same one I was in, Paul?
Cause there was a view from the book in-uh *Night Tide*? Oh what a
great title—that book—it's just fabulous. . . . It's my-uh, my-ah, my-um
uh uh uh I mean I wasn't exPECted to react to it.

It's so TRUthful

I guess my charm, lively, my ac . . . Paul Katzjammer: I see Paul Katzjammer every minute. I see him everywhere. Each time I look up . . .

He was DeMENTed last night

He SHOULD be. That was a very groovey party—a great opening

He wanted to come back down

O—Another night like that, and-uh . . . . . (*fade*) hahaha . . . You could
step on them as you went on the stage—that's how you got up there.
That kind of vagilation. And-uh, listen: if it comes to that, accept it.
Why refuse to make a person a USEful part of. Society. I mean, don't
be ridiculous—don't judge them, step on them

L—This week: if, or tomorrow afternoon, if you rehearsed your-uh your
noises, the noise songs

O—I sorta have the noises in the right place. I did a few noises of Ravel's
Boleros that afternoon that were-uh INSANE. I mean, because Ravel's
Boleros are sooo   that it almost, ya know, you hafta have noises that
are-uh so right away that, so THERE that you hafta have noises that
are funny inna way that-uh—not funny, but—that if they work, they're
almost what I want. Inna way, and they work—I love them. Well,
LISTEN, I duh-uh . . . I uh-ah I went Last I went Last I went this
evening to see you, and I got the Armenian wedding the second, now,
and that's it. That's a fate worse than death. Plus, when we got outa
the taxi, there wasn't a cent left, and an Armenian wedding—I mean,
REally. We couldn't hav acted oriental as the cops had just threatened
us three or four phone calls—deLIGHTful threats, ya know. "We know
who you are—you gotta whore up there. We know whoya are, ya pimp,
you" A little tired

L—We're gonna have some new stuff. We're bringing the tape recorder down with the tapes

P—Ta play with the movies?

L—Yeah. We got this one tape—it s absolutely incredible—it all happened by mistake, Because the tape rcordr didn t work

O—Oh Rodey . . . . . Rodey

L—These things don t work, Rodey . . . (fadeǫ

The tape recordan did absolutely EVErything wrong

P—Peculiar sounds?

L—No, I mean, we could never get a tape like this. . . .(fade), . . .I meAn, four trAcks, . . .

O—I gotta rip in mY pants. The tape recorder s off-key. . .like, when yer springs on if there s mattress. . .

D—Oh really?

O—But lookit. It's soooooo. . .Yeah, it s always pinching, yaknow. Oooo, I feel like going to tha bathroom so badly, Drella. Can I PLEEEase go to that bathrroom. Do you realize this—that I am not allowed to go to thw bathroom. . . .I ve gotta go. I could take it withme

D—Naaow. . .I could take it with me. I mean I must go—Ireally must go to that bathroom I hafta PISS I mean, andI m not gonna pull down my-uh. . .

P—(indistinct)

O—Sure it is. .OH, Paul, donna—it s MY voice—you know it all record it It's gootta record it. . .ihihihihihihIt has no choice. Drella, if you strApped it ovah my back and give me your-uh the microphone, I ll go to the bathroom. .I WONT PISS OVER IT I KNOW howta put it aside—I ll talk while while I piss even if youll let me. PLEEEAse let me go take a piss. I r-really must. I really must—honest. I don wanna piss on the microphone, unless, of course, uh uh. I WONT mayforna, dahling. All right, somebody can come withme Does somebody wanna come WITH me. I could us use HEIP with it, I mean. If somebody wants ta come with me, they can, a-a-a-nd I would be GLAD foah tha help. Ah-ah-I would be glad to have an a-p-p-ointee, you know? W/E/ell, yes, but-uh . Who? Would someone come to tha bathroom with me and help me hold the tape recorder? a-a-and the microphone.

UNIDENTIFIED VOICE—indistinguishable

O—NononONO thanks. Ta hold tha tape recorder and the microphone? while I take a piss—(oh, pahdon me) while I (heh heh) U-R-I-N-A-T-E?

UV—(unintelligible)

O—That s not an outlloof—thass an INlay. . . . . . I don t hear any volunteers. Awright? you all get dooOONK-uh haha. American citzenshipp— you fAIl, and can t bear it any more. Would you halp me, LEu? Thank you? I really HAVE to go to the baathroom. Yes, guys hahahahah (nyah nyah): *LEU* will help me go to the bathroom. Now heah now . . .Assign us our de-

MSASH CRASH (*glass breaking*)

O—An I want my jacket, too, becawuse there's something in it. Mainly my lipstick.

SILVERWARE CRASHES, some sort of hassle

O—Could I have my LIPstick in here. .

P—LIPstick in HERE?

O—I can moveta thaw. . .I m so loopsy. I be right back. . . .Drelladeah— PLEase don t look tha way at mEE. I mean Ive done this bfore

D—Really?

O—Yes, but its more a machine that Ive gotten. . . OW. . .

RV—Sure

O—Aaaow—we almost gaa—A real miscarriage gave Rodey a haircut

JUMBLE JUMBLE

Oh, uh—I couldn let myself-uh always cuh. .But he's too-/but he s too-uh such-uh Uh. Didyoo notice that?—Idunno..(*fade*) . . .the night it was opened. Ut, that one or the other one—I don Know. I ll just wet my hands. . . .(*fade*). . .if I had any amphetamine ya know whaddI di OR I lost

L—(in bathroom—indistinct)

O—Normal. Drella got the most the most worried look onhis face as if the microphone would nevah come back. He s so fUNny. I don t what or where re ya going after this?

L—I dunno. John an Crux are downstairs—they should come upstairs

O—Yah—Joehn and Crux ar wonderful—The WhooOOOle thing it divine. Those peopleare so beautiful. On the stage your gorgeous—very GOD you re beautiful

L—Ellis Socks dropped his

O—I mean that was there the last time. . .

L—I sawa good one the other day. "Give me liverty orgiv me meth"

O—Now lemme see if I have veryth-. . .It s not here. Not here, not here, not here, and the only one that I do have, if thissisnt it, it THIS, and thisis. And this—i is has. .I hafta have a spot to get it out. mmmm

L—I got some desoxin. . . .

O—Ohhhh. . .Desoxin's a bore, really. I look a little like Nanookof the North, if you forgive me. Naaow—I m not gonna even take thatpill. . . I hafta get it back on so I wouldn t waste the rest of it, I wouldna do it. Iwould do it, but if I did it, I would just WAaste. .ruim the rest of it

L—Io got some Desoxyns

O—Ooaaooow

L—De oxyn never does anything

O—Desoxyn s a bore, rEEally. I look a little like Nanook of the NOrth, but forgive me. Naaow. Im not g-gonna even. . .$ doan hafta do anything except wash my self an face. And geddit b-buh-back on so I wouldn t wuh-w-waste the rest of it, I would DO it.

L—Yeah

O—But if I do it, I will just waste th-the rest of it

L—Oh, thats.IK

O—But-uh-ah, I-uhah woodhuahoinm. There was dEEFinitely gonna be a spot in our future That BOOK got wet

Gurgle gurgle

I really-uh

L—That's good

O—That was MONstrous. Look at it. Umuhah. I mean, *really*

L—Oh, that thing on Ondine hahahahaha

O—This is beautiful

L—It's REALLY great

O—Yes, it s your picture to have. I dunno—it's so great, it's really good

L—Welllahs, it's really good

O—What was I gonna say? uuuuhhh. I dunno. I've lost it again. Uh. You re so beautiful on stage, it's NOT to BEE beLEEved. Especially when you get into playing your instrument. You're just. .So. . .there s that

SLAM

extra loveliness, that extra beauty, only uma ama amusician h-has. There s some very innocent. . .

hahaha

SOooo Gorgeous. Last night I s-saw that reflected on a couch—s-s someone was looking up at me, with a blonde moustache. That innocent, Johnny Appleseed goodlookingness he had. . .

L—Yeah, right

O—and I went Out Of My Mind. Oooh, I sort of screamed at him—he s *such* a beautiful bot, and that. . . My hair s combed, isn't it??

L—Yeah. Uh. . .Looks good

O—Rudine came to the factory an jus got offended an went out. I d-don t know WHAt she s doing. She doesn t have lowanathisasuhsphere. Now one more check we ll If uh-ah-I recall having it on me Ooooh. And Danty when your people is the MOST beautiful, even if. . .

L—Yeah, I wish mo. . .

O—Even if it is SSOlo. Even if in my case it gets to be a Marathon an I go out of my mind

L—That s when it's the most fun

O—Yer—EXACTLY, but-UH

L—Blowing your head

O—And, when uh-I g-got up on the stage, I I it's just like you ALL said hello. It was just beautiful, Anyway, you re a great. . .

L—Aww, we were so happ to see you

O—AHHHH. Every night. You're not gonna be happy after three months. . . . Everybody will ge a bit of annoyed. There, alright. Thank you. I don't think I

Slam slam

did a thing in there.

step step step step step (amid general confused noise)

these things should go Rrroving through sxam's.

crash

Oooo—I almost got it. Oh, Sorry. Doesn't that sound as if I re-re-really didn t know if I was sorry?

Johnny Rivers   FER ME

well, wait, lets let them get—. . . Oh, awright. Jus move in, move in a little wid

PP—Did everything go awright??

O—No. No, I was tapped

D—You were tapped?

O—I was having a spinal tap, and i just (heh heh, no no. I just—the cut . . . the cut on my hand is really annoying me. And-uh Lou jocked . . .

P—issbiddleiddleEEE?

O—. . .he coulen help it, though. I mean and-uh he. .Us-As a matter of fact, he threw it. hehehe. for anothr discourse. He said he-uh never again. . .all 17 tracks. . .

P—hahaha

L—Who? Since when

O—Nouhaha, itsjus his hands sweadding. It s sweatiy—I don t blame him

Voice: You can't break witha joint. .

O—Aah, a join—. .I hava John Ford. I feel OOOWWW. What do you do to deaden the pain in something like this. Yaknow, paper burns, or uh mattress burn really alarm me. You take the proper durg—well, uh
. . . .

That s what the D stands for—DRUGS— Are you from Detroit?

Voice—no.

O—I have an aunt in nothern Detroit

giggles from table

I do—I love her for it.

P—An aunt Norman.

O—No, heheheh. She s a charming lady. I m spinning withing the spinning wheel. Yeah. Athing of mine—I don t know, I think it must be be-

cause of my astigmatism—but I look away, an when I look back, I-uh
feel like Im gonna face us. . . . .

OH, and THERE's the Reverend-uh. ˙ .HI, howereyou? Whatre you
doing with Veronica Lake?

D—What're you all dressed up for?

O—Detroit's a strange city. I imagine you hafta be Vehhry. . .

DETROIT—It s very-uh. . .

O—Well, outside of New York City, there s not much

P—Eighteen Alabama sons. .

O—Do you suppose they re pouring it on lower Brooklyn? I don t know
California aat all; I hava feeling I would never. . . .they would probably
kill mr in it—smuggle me into the inside of the Chine. . . .OOWW.
Thre s hours of periodic reminders of the-uh PAAIN. .that I m feeling.
The infinite of the llaaAAH. And I guess I m feeling a little sorry for
myself rightnow. Ah-I AM; I don t wnna use them any mor because
they re a Bore

P—Yeah. . .

O—I wanted to give them up six years ago, and I on the way to-uh. .doing
it. It takes a while, very boring it off,. It s a long experience—My with-
drawal is very long

P—HEheheh it certainly is
HehHEHheh

O—What it this?? Is this the meny? Aoow: Smax's—*STEAK LOBSTER
AND CHICK PEAS*

L—Wait a minute.

O—Yes. . .

L—So WHAT did happen last night?

O—When??

L—At Oxydol's

O—Oh. A LOT. . You know, it s one of those thingsthat

L—Who was it—you, Rudine, Oxydol . . .

O—Uh. .Uh. . Rudy White, Steve Romiah, uhhhh, Mark Dale, Uh/Eh-
It's hard to get these back with golden. Paul Someone,

L—(indistinguishable)

O—Yeeaah, a drag queen. A REEal old fasmioned platinum drag queen
(chuckle) A very nice girl. I nevah haddher typed. All night long. I
went BESERK the minute that Rudine started to sleep—FLLed the
room. —And-uh, Ron Via

L—Vail vile Vial

O—An, theres-uh-who els was there??—someone named VOIL, I think.
Voil Val//I dunno what her name was, but she was ill-equipped, and
I would say—. . .and then there were visits

L—Somebody named Tinkerbell

O—TINKERBELL. . . .

O—. . .TINKERBELL. .? ? Yaknow, Peter Pan's jersonal fairy

L—Chingle Bell

O—What did Tinkerbell—we don t want Tinkerbell, so we said, ya know, why dontcha stop eating so fast or I ll have a heart attack. Was it? She s LYing.

L—I wouldn't give her a. . .

O—Ya know, GOOD. You had one popper that was therest of the. . .I took four nem nem Nembutol by mistake, was going off to sleep when Rudine came in with rishavalushki and said, put it undayour tongue and-uh Youll-uh Revive. And I did, Sh-sH/She said Ya wont try my grain? Heheheheh I hada try it—look whaddI said, ya know, the dear thing, but it got me Right Up. It got me Right Up. God, it was beautiful. And THEN, . . .then it was the staginguntil the one popper, an the one popper had ta go at one point, the point I described earlier, and-uh ended on the table, and I will describe it to you properly. I doan think it should be really overlooked, althought maybe I can whisper it to you Well, BernAHRD. Bernard Moler, or whatever his his hishishis thing, . . .(indistinct) . . . . DOWN at this point, and. . . . .(chortle). . . . .I cant say, anyway, it took a popper to do it, and-uh the whole room was ppullingfor him

P—Tha mightnot be the cause

O—IT MAY NOT be, I hope it isn t. Right. It shall be owend back to 7P.M. It shoul/-there IS a lot of static in Sxam's, that s cause they won t open the windows. Imagine. Is that—. . . This girl wassomewhere in on . . .last night

L—Where was she?

O—Oh-uh. .At the Gymnasium. . .You looked to beautifullast night. When you were. . . . . . .So divine. All I could think of was marking paper—I couldn t see anything like it. Ah-too Ah/Too: do yo-you mind if Ihave totell you that later abouttha. . .

L—NAooow, that s coll

O—Because, its its/a dirty, filthy. : .and it doesn t fit in a clean place like Sxam's. Ooooow my eyes are spinning again. Back to back. SEAFOOD AND. . .ROAST PRIME RIBS OF SEAFOOD AND SXAM'S SEAFOOD

D—It s pretty

O—It is wonderful. They all mean something, don t they. What is your red red red. .what is your red riding for? Paul?

P—Eh?

O—What is your red necklace an. . .

P—Actually, it s the Morocco

O—Oh, for heaven s sake, then it s MINE—I lost it, I m jus saying that
. . .aw, cmon now. What does it mean??

P—You don t . . . . .

O—NOO. It s BEAUtiful.

P—I'll take it off

O—Don t you like it?? you been rEEeal. . . .

D—The last Ingrid was terrific

O—ooooah ehohnfdjk Yer SICK. .You wanna see someone who looked
unhappy—did you see *Allen Midget*???

D—He s tired

O—My God, He looks like he s sooo sad

P—Allen—doesn t he look sad?

O—I-ihme&anuhbuh I mean, I waana CRY when I m with him

P—There s one white one in it

O—Instead of what?

P—There s one white one among the many

O—That means that purity is still there, an you better. . .

P—Allen looked so depressed

D—Waht?

P—Last night. . .oh, Yaaaah

O—Yeah, at that new place. That place must bemarvelous

L—Oh, its really great when you re up there when Ilook down an. . .

O—There s nothing I want

L—. . .look up. . . .

P—sort of with-uh the Velvets at the. . . . Cheetah. . . .

D—What??

ONaaow . . I have nt seen any of them. Lou Reed doesn t bother showing
he does things. He just does them to an album of his very own. . .That
is so funny—God. I wished you hadn't offended Paul, really.

P—Ya mean tha day with Rudine.

O—Yeah, he made her, I dunno, some nasties thatwere VERYnasty.

P—Bounce it up now. . .

O—Oh, yes, yes, I Saw-us S . Its awful having faces as-uh a . . . .

P—Wha??

O—It s awful having faces because they showeverything. Ya know whaddI
mean? God, I mean they re so emotional, it s unbelievable. It sso
marvelous to see the corner of his eye a little happier or a little more
mischeivous or eviller. It makes me so depressing, I mean: lookadhim.

P—Uhhhhh. .heheheh

O—Gerard. I mean I liste . . Tell us about Gerard

D—Gerard??

O—Gerard, the Spanish wonder. . I dunno what to say, but I m glad to see your faa—I m glad to see yer face in present condition. You look-heavenly. Why?? You didnt get any sleep—you re not rested.

Voice—Yes I did

O—Thats//there s a little bit of evil returningto view somehow. HATE, my DEAR—hate, my dear, is something that moves the world, something that gives a cheer to everyone s lips. CRUElty is a real beauty. Cruelty isthe act of a considerateman.

D—Someone who loves a lot?

O—A love a lot?? I hate as many people a day as Ican possibly crowd into it. . .Hate is a GREEat function. It s like taking a Sssshhhit. It essential —muh-muh-must be done. If it isn t done, you re a liar. I love as little as possible, I mean, it usually leads to suicide. I can t be bothered with it. I wanna a love that ll grow into hate. Start from love and build into a crescendo of hate that is sooo overpowering that by the time IVa Iva I ve fffully realized all the hate in my puh-puh-uitiful little body, well, then, it llturn automatically into SUPER hate. There should be a character called SUPERHATE. Naaoow, SUPER what?? SUPER DISS

D—SUPER DISS???

O—Superdiss. Ohh, Drella, if you point that another way, I ll take it right . . .I have a special cross I got for last night s wo-or-ork (hehehheheh). A St. Bernard—whadda retriever. .

L—Was it a big as yer hand-

O—Dahling, it was bigger. I have never seen anyting like it. . I could put my head in my mouth, are you s/s/serious??? My rising sign is Taurus, you forget. That means: the Throat. I have a large collar. I m a collar tycoon. . . . Now that I know what I m really like, I don't mind being heh heh publicized. I like to be known as the biggest. .hahaha. Now that I know what Im like. Drella?? I think—no, it was bigger than that.

D—Really?

O—Yes. Aoow, are you serious?? Elwood was 13 inches, darling.

Shriek—ADELE . . .

yeeaahhss. 13 inches, darling, and at least the circumference of-uh. . .it was UNbeLEEvable. There s a trick to all that business, you know, you have this kind of a throat; certain positions render it able to be used for anything. Everyone can be a sword swallower, it s j-just a little technique. You hafta tilt it the right way or you ll lose yer tensions back here or ya getthis an that, but there s no difference between a sword and you YOU KNOWWHAT. : P blank blank blank. K. There s no difference, except, perhaps, swords don t get soft (hahahahaha). If they did, darling, you would have something to do with them. And it s as easy to swallow. . .

L—That s a good song title

O—What??

L—Swords don't get soft.

O—They don't. Not that I know. And-uh I dunno—I m not sure. Maybe they do, somewhere in the sword, having swords go soft all over. I don t know, but anyway, there s this. Everyone at this table—if they were properly schooled in the throat movement, would be able to do as much as possible.

RV—Thank you for that inspirational message

O—JWell, it happens to be great. . . To knowthat you can neverchoke to death. . .is HEAVEN.

RV—Chip that one in stone—just don t record it, yaknow, like they're putting. . . . .

O—Isn t that the truth?? I mean, you can never really choke todeath, and allthat g-a-g-g-i-n-g business is a lot of nauseous nonsense. It s only you and your-uh confessional

RV—Said for a. . .

O—That s right, if I m a realist, darling, I read that paper—that Village paper—*The Realist*, and Ive-uh they ve taught me how to bery realtied about my life

RV—We re having a flaming faggy Abby Van Buren. . .

O—We ll have him filling in for a manhole—what re you serious?? LOWLIFE PRESENTS: SERPITUDE. That michael frond became omnious and then I started to address it. And there re so many things you can do with your throat—to start with, SING. then, you can make nininKnots with it. And if you re lucky you can really turn out a good pair of shoes in three weeks. Does the waiter ever come here?? Or do they ignore you purposely?? Did they place us hre because we re on some sort of. . .

DETROIT—Are they painted this blue

O—I don t know, aren t they nice?? I love them. I thought theywere very-uh. . .and the feel of them is even nicer.

RV—(*indistinct*)

O—Yeah

P—. . . . . .beeeds. . . .

O—BEEEDZZ. They re from Sid Caesar/Imogene Coca (*singing*) YOUR SHOWOF SHOWS. You look tired. I know, I wish I had—why don t you godownstairs and see-uh. I ll go downstairs with you.

L—Naaow

O—Al Coa will have. I don t want. . .Thhheeey missedit. THEBADSEED

P—*The Bad Seed*—didja see that?

O—Naaoow. I-ah-I couldn't. I-ih-it was filmed on location in New Haven.

I hate that town. I would never go there. Its an evil tow// New Haven is an Evil Town. I wouldn t go there. Yuh-ya/You know, Ionly just picked it outof the air. I d LOVE to go to New Haven any day of the WEEK and see Ann Baxter's corpse.

P—. . . .it s charity—a terrible picture. .

O—Charity begins alone. You don t like Sxam's any more.

Girl—Hmm?

O—You don t like this place any more.

Girl—No, I mean the song. . . (Buffalo Springfield for what it's worth)

O—Oh, I don t know it

L—The bass drum on this song is. . .

O—Sounds like it s got a message. Does it?

P—It does.

O—Well, then it s bullshit. What is it about? OurBoys, or what? Saving the boys, or what?

P—Savin the boys an money.

O—Oh, Liisten—SOMEone s gotta save them. Just think of all that Money, darling. All that lovwly warm money. Thay created this ridic-ulous chop suey just for their war money, and that s what this war should be called: CHOP SUEY.

P—. . . .peace. . . .

O—I wouldn t go ta that peace sit-in

L—. . .songs. . .

O—Whaddya. . .ya con t make a ring out of this and get away with it. .

L—. . .on the radio it said that it was the largest. . .

O—I m gonna piss on this

L—. . .peace congregation in history.

O—You were there? Oh, I hope there s a lotta peace. Ssomething effective, ya know, give up your United States citizenship if you object to . . . .

L—. . .I didn t want to hear Martin Luther King. . .

O—. . .but don t tell me I can t stand it and then support it. Liars. They love to be seen and walk around

L—Really.

O—They'll pop their own bubbles soon, too. Why don tthey just lay themselves-uh. . .

Unidentified, undistinguishable comment

Goood, that was an act of God. That was an actof God, darling—he told the mto disperse before it really gets them. I m not saying that the war is right, but a hyprocrite behind the peace badge is wrong.

RV—Who s a hypocrite

O—9/10 of those marchers are. Or show-offs. I mean the majority o that march is a bunch o ullshit

RV—(*mumbling*)

O—Including you. You would of been a bunch of bullshit if you had gone there.

RV—My insanity interfered.

O—Anyway. Anybody tells me about peace and doesn't give up their US citizenship is a liar. Simple and honest—I believe in WAR. any war. Its usually essential for the economy of the country. This was forged somewhere by a policy made somewhere in Eleanor Roosevelts's t ts, the nettle of the night. when she was traveling to meet Madame Chiang Kai-Shek. . Ooh. . A waitress. Thisis a Is it time? Do the dancing girls come with the poodles??

Waitress—now, yoo are having salad

D—Just four

O—Four?? How dyou know, I mean, nobody asked me if theres four here. Was she here when I was gone?

DETROIT—Uh-Yes.

O—Well, you ll have to start aall over again, darling, and I mean it. She s not gonna pay any attention to me—look. Nonono one. . .

L—There s a lot of people who are so pretty, but-uh

O—Who? Sure they re pretty, but I like to look atthem to, but that peace business is bullshit. They shouldn t hava m-M/message.

D—Salad?

O—No, I don t know. Yeah, I guess—Idunnoo, I don t have to eat. There s about it.

D—No no no—You can ask for a bowl.

O—Oh, I d love a bowl—A BOWL PLEASE (*giggling*). . Wow—that would be really peculiar. Noooo, except that—is everyone gonna eat the same salad dressing?

L—The cops said that there was a hundred thousand people, but there. . .

RV—There were about 300 thousand.

O—Ah, sooooo

D—Were there that many?

O—Like I couln t have gone to that Easter thingin Central Park.

L—Oh, that was so good.

O—I couldn't have gone. I coudn t have gone

L—Is was to gooJask Billy about it—

O—I know, but I couldn t have gone. I just couldn t have been with all those people.

L—No one wanted to leave. Nobody should have left. We shouldhave just cAmped there forever and stayed there.

O—It wouls have been so marvelous if it happened, but it didn t happen. It s no so—it s a lie. And I don t mean to be-uh uh anything but the way it is, but why pretend?? That s for Saturday morning.

RV—OK, so we get some dynamite and we blow up a police station

O—Who blow up a police station???Just give up your citizenship. I don t wanta do anything. I LIKE war. . I like it—I thing waris great. I love the dead VietNamese. I love millions of the dead Vietnamese. I d liketo see them lined up, row by row, the more the merrier I say. It creates a largeamount of us. It purifies the Southeastern Asian coast, and the Chinese are getting toofast. Do I wear this? Drop the Maizell. The Koreans are punks.

RV—Three bowls, baby, that s all I can say.

Waitress—Now here s forks and knives

O—Oh, the inscrutable Pepsi Cola

P—What about the scrutable West?

O—The scrutable West is even less scrutable, Imean, before oJan Crawford is alive, you hafta gte. I lik this as a bracelet with a hanger on it. I am just against any kind of a business of saying that we re haveanycontrol overthis business at all.

'O—We don t.

RV—Who doesn t.

O—We don t.

P—Would you vote. . .

O—I wouldn t vote—are you serious? After Kennedy s murder, does a guy Vote??. Oh, don t be an aa-ass, I mean, thatsatsa. . .

P—......dead murders. . .

O—I would not vote unless I could vote for Him again.

P—That s true

Voice—Why vote for him if he s responsible for it. . . ?

O—He s responsible for a-an- invasion. I think War Is a Necessity. That every politician just admit what he knows, or admits or reveals what he has to Reveal, and so he s bla-a-amed for it. But po icies go on aaall the time, and everydody knooows that this war is essential, and who cares about dead bodies—I DON T. REEEaally, I missasouncallous but I don t, It s ghoulish. . .It s ghoulish. Peace? Bullshit; it s ghoulish. It s the death worship that makes me nervous.

P—. . . .the marijuana march. . .

O—AAAaaaoww—the Marijuana March, an tha Heroin Hop, an the uhuhuhAmphetaimne. . .What? Ascot I suppose. No, I can t do those double sans. . . . I don t beLEEEvethe people who walk. I KNOOOW that most of the people who walkin the walk are PHONIES.

RV—How do you know most of them are phonies. . . ?

O—Because I KNOW them. Everyone I ve ever been in contact with who IS involved in this IS a phony. If you re the exception, well, then, I m sorry, but everyone else has been These millions of Lowes East Side Village make me Sick to my Stomach.

RV—Listen, dig, the chick that laid out ten grand to get my ass outa jail an spending like all of her time an gangs of her bread on that scene. I wantchoo ta meet her.

P—Id LIKE to meet her

RV—A nice girl who is like doing Something.

O—Very good, allright, fine

RV—She s the exception

O—Awright, she maybemaybe the exce-. . .

RV—There s three others like her, ya know, like-uh

O—But I don t take anybody s word for anything—I can t say that she s the exception

RV—What are they sposed to do? Take Lady BirdJohnson. .I ll rip her limb from limb

O—I m not saying that. Just put yer sign down, and do something aboutt it if you really want to

RV—What? Lay on thethe railroad tracks?

O—Give up your United States cisisisicitizenshipp.

RV—Go where? You can t get a passport

O—Anywhere—stand in front of the United States embassies screaming. THAT s giving up your United States citizenship. If enough do it, the war will stop. Be efFECtive, in other words, not just merely a pretense.

RV—I m willing. Any time

O—Well, I told you How

RV—. . .(*indistinct*). .on my passport, baby. . .

O—Give up your United States citizenship—that's not givingup your citizenship, baby. That s a different story

RV—I ve gotta trial coming up. . .

O—GO into a foreign land and howl in front of the United States embassy: I HATE THE UNITED STATES

RV—People are doing it—they re burnin draft cards, man

O—And they re burning themselves, too. They re using Benzene, or whatever they have handy

RV—OK, well, what else do you want em ta do?

O—I d like them to choose a barbecue pit, so that the HUNgry of Asia don t go unnotices. They could eat it afterwa-. . .

RV—Sheat it off the war effort.

P—hahaha

O—That a BUNCH a Bullshit. Half the reports you get aren t true. You don t know what you read, an. . .it s ridICULous. . .PLEASE. Johnson —is if he could possibly direct a war

RV—He IS directing the War

O—He s direct from the helicopter with the twitching arms. . .

RV—He s directing it very well, like gangs of people are being done in, I mean, whadelse doya want him ta do?

O—Well, then there s there are times when. Time to go.

PUSHIN

(song from jukebox)

I don t wanna give up things. I don t wanna shuffle offto Buffalo because I think s-someone s being done in. I really don t. I used to, though

PUSHIN

I used to think, Oh, my God, the wrathe of God, the Unite-. . .the world is a horrible place, but it s Not. It s ALWAYS been a horrible place. Never specially horrible

RV—Tings get worse then get better. . .

O—Naaooo, they just become affected more or non-affected. Theyre used and used well, then everything s all right. There are different levels of mediocre-ism, right? ahuhaha An, it s not funny, because it is itsuhitsuh-itsa it s a tantrum. Ih-i-It s a mess to realize that what you ve been. . thinking is going on has never, ever VAGUEly happened. Ha. That your breath has been planned before you were born

RV—Ih-i-it s a thing with, I happens to be in LOove with acouple of times. Ya know, like, you were like next door

O—I KNOW that people feel it greaatly, and-uh I . . .

RV—. . .and if THOSE people feel it into it, then. . .

O—. . .and I understand that, and I don t Mean to insult you, but-uh I

RV—Uh-I m sorry, but it makes me crazy—it really does

O—Really, it SHOULD make you crazyfi but-uh. . .

RV—. . . .But it does, and-uh. . .if you really loved, then you d hafta bein love witha couple of Vietnamese

O—Nonono, I understand, but-uh I don t wanna get involved PERSO-anlly

(completely indistinguishable simultaneously aggravation)

. . .Probably very well, but-uh and I say you maybe. .you may be a person who is what you say you are, and I think you are. .That person, and that I m sorry, but-uh you re STILL should break down dishonesty. And don t join forces with the hypocrites, cause they ll just weaken you. You ll turn into a Love Mist. A luh-luh-luh. .a WAD, talking about Love on a lawn somewhere. Sould be put down—should be REEally but. I mean, that s some kind of a Catholic function in the middle of the afternoon. The Mrs. Jane Wyatt. . . Yes, and-uh J/J/Jane Wyatt s mother is the most catholic woman in the world, ya know. She s worse than Clare Luce, darling. . .Yaknow?. . . .That business is a lotta bull-shit. Loretta Young was agood fairy

RV—. . . much more interest YOU, since you have a a a name thing. On the bah-. . .what YOU put on tape. What YOU think of something. . .

O—He s not that stupid (heheheh). . . . .

Your. . . . . . .gonna get emBROIled in one a these things.

Drella. Leave him alone.

RV—Yes, that s fun at the settlement. I don t know if you re Leo the Thirteenth or not.

O—Nonono. He s Leo. . .nonono, that s the Sun King, darling

RV—This is beside you people

O—That s the Sung King all right. Naaow I know nothing about French history

RV—Would you like to be Mdme. Pompadour?

O—Nooo, but I like to read Dorothy Lamour. Or I was Dorothy Lamour. (*indistinct flights into assorted memorable jungle scenes*). I ve-I ve *bled* on it—you can really tell. It s sooo red. Oooo, I hope I sound phooooul-ish during that one. Particularly evil. A panel show: WHERE'S YOUR CORPSE? No. You bring yer corpse to the television studion, and the panel has to identify what land thecorpse. What land the corpse is from and how it died.

RV—What about those fiber cuts —what is that?

O—I ll call. . .

RV—I'll call the audience right in here. . .

O—Of course, when it s on the color television sets, it s veehhrry intricate. . Dihv-. . .a large amount of the judgment depends on her judgment, her color, her shading

RV—Listen—with the late-late non-necrophiliac audience, I have another pogram in mind, we ll discuss that

O—What is ·this?? . . . .What is this?

Garbled reply

Oh. Excuse me. Go ahead, right now.

RV—I ve been planting petunias lately, and I

O—You ve been talking t-to Orio. She's thinks everybody s against her

RV—She s one of the sensible peo-ple in the world

O—Oooorrr. . .Practical, I d say. . .

RV—Seriously. . .

O—Certainly, a 450 dollar apart-ment in/nin/nin New York City is certainly a sensible idea.

RV—Mmmmmm

O—. . .definitely, right down the line—she couldn ty have gotten anyth-thing cheaper ANY where else. Iiiiii Telll you sh-sh-she s about as sensible as a COW inna

RV—She can do what she wishes to do. . .

O—She s an IDIot

RV—she needs aahh. . .

O—SHE NEEDS NOthing but her own area, an she can create

that on BROADway or Bleeker Street for 15 dollars. 450 dollars a Muh-mmmonth rent.

RV—Shes gonna. . . .

O—She deSERVes to go down like this, because it s ridiculous. Come on—Huh Ronny?

RV—Orion go down??

O—Orion s going down with the apartment, and you know IT .

RV—You think she s that tight, Man? Ya shoulda seen a some grease, baaby.

O—Ah. . .Uh. . .I think she s going dow-. .

RV—On FIRE

O—I think she s going to admit, as she usually does, that she s wrong. She s WRONG. Period. She s happens to be wro-. . . I seem to be against you for some reason, and I don t know wh-why. An I don t like it. . . . . What I wanna know, dahrling, is what woul appeal to me

RV—It s not on tha menu.

O—Yeah, I know tha-bah/. . . Why:eh-wou Would I like a spot on tha floor or something What s that, Paul? What s that, Paul. . ? . . .What IS IT?

P—Want some?

O—No, but I would like to know what I could have.

Miss. . . .Lass. . . . .waaaaaaa. Thass one a those sounds aaah she s terrible. Maaah. Her name is. Her name is Pigeon-toed. She's a retard. Ah—doya know what people get angry at is my delivery. Oh, God, it s the Kih-. . . . Aaaaowah thisismisthofooSmith? Who is the lovely girl in the black slicker?? Uhhh. . .Helene Curtis? Ingrid still is an egnima ding ding ding ding ding

She's the tuh-. . .I can t believe her. I wish she could have bedin the salad bowl—I don t know liah. Ingrid, go away hahahaha go away. You know what?? She was caught under the wheel of a car. She was ffixing it. Ingrid. . Ingrid—why do you Ha-ha-have th this BO problem? Why don-choo move away.

That s one of my lovely little ways of saying, Hello, Ingrid darling.

INGRID SUPERSTAR: Are yoo up theah agen?

O—No, darling, But-uh I jus better be, because the uh circulationof your armpits is-uh revolting. I wish you d move

RV—Those Lesbian tendencies of
. . . . .

O—She sai-uh—ya know what? An audience of mine an I m doomed because everytime I see her hits me for drugs or comments on my body odor. Obviously, she has n-no nose, no purse, r sense. An-uh-ah I ssstill like the girl despite her many ffailings Uh. I wish she d go back ta Jersey until it s all over, an then . . . If you say BO to me one more time, Im gonna put yer head in water. Because you re rude—ya know, just very rude. Well then go down before you-uh. . .

INGRID SUPERSTAR—If you don t like me. . .

O—I Don t dislike you, Ingrid but I'm telling you something. We went there too, deah—an Armenian wedding, Right??

O—So, off we go—into the wild, blue Henry. . . . Let Us Go (Gasp) I can hold my breath longer than you. . . . No, I can t.

Gee
BN—(*cackle*) Ha HA . . GEE
O—GEE . . . The next is *H*. It's
11:15.
BN—It s till early

O—It is as early as it can be——
OOOOOO, no, non-empAthetic
BN—Mightwork then, ya know.
O—Oh, Boy, am I tired. (*Yawn*)
Pause.

24 / **1**

OND INE SO LILIQUY
O—It's not supposeo to be meth, though
BN—Oh yeah?
O—Supposed, supposed, it's just amphetamine—you know? I don't like
This is a supposedly long m-on-o-logue about whatever it is that I talk
about uh—I 'm no brain—and I never have had a brain—and I don't
want one; I dun no what else to say—this tape should be finished—I
wish I were a brai-n. Twelve bri?dges t o roll abate—uh—I've—
ih name a v ero its J. Fallow, fath er an d gay, Mr. Picwi ck's aunt—
twelve—thir ty—n d all all a al l al l all—u ch. It's not funny t o
when you're takin g amph etamine and you want to go t o sleep. I should
wan t to stay up. I don't! I feel h ead achey—aroun d the eye s I als o
feel log-uey around th e log ue . I h ave a ter rib le t aste in my
m u th—and I'm con temp latin g sui ci d e . Well—what's lef t? I
always say . Fil t h y b aske t . Relig ious , re ligiou s relig iou s, like
b leg h tribes. Ut, th at's th e f irst ti me I ev e r heard Billy course. In,
I really neve r have he ard hi m cu rs e b e b or e. Inat s u th ing?
He 's workin g l i ke a d e mon! (*roll bang clang a oll bang*) *Yes,*
those are n oi s es (*crang*) an d th ey're inten se noise s of Wi liiam
Name Alle n I th i n k we n t t o s leep. Gerard is still dan cin g with the
people ou tside. I'm
re cordin g. Drella ju st went someplace on 42nd Street. Rotten Rita
wen t to the dent i st. The art patron s just left. Mari a Callas is still
alive—and here 's this is t he stop, f ootstep of Dr ella—uhh, noh.
Hu uh there's the ph on e an d f or m e—No one ev er calls he re f or
me—' cause I d on't li ve he r r an ym ore. No on e eve r knows
whe re I'l l be. Twelve filthhry trolove ? No, No , d ona be s i lly.
It's har d when you' re readin g Sherlock H olmes fro m beginni ng
to e nd , very , very relig iou s—y es, religio usly . Hello .
He llo may. I'm makin g love t o th e tape record er. Hehh Hehh Hehh
I don't kn ow wh at to say to i t . Uhh—religiou s.

(clo p Clo p clo p)

DRELLA—Are these t he pict ure s, B i lly?

B N—Tho s e are t h e one s t-that have bee n ther-e .

(Clop clop clop)

O—Religiou s s—r e l igious—re liGIO US—re lag o us—real ly gr oovi ous.
—rili gaus—have a n i ce time

(clo p clo p cl op)

H eech—He uh (tatte r ed voice) Have a n i ce time ! Feebla! Feeble!
reeheck

Alright, have a swell time—No ! They'll have tha t later .

Well. . .f or o ne the y're not gonna have an yth i ng!

(clo p clop clop clop clop CLOP clop clop clo P clop cllopp)

The y'll have so meth i n g o r othe r—whate ve r it is—it doesn't matter.

B—Does Su san look g ood in thi s or does sh e look t oo f at?

) (cl o p clop clop clop)

D—It' s —uh —it' s in t erest ing

(clop clop)

O—Makes it l o ok like Rene ? He y, the-thank yo u , Dre l la.
Dre lla. Dre lla, that real ly co mes in han dy . Th-thank you.
I was just wo ndering t o my self, I sa, how am I go ing to do it, and
t hen, t hen it was do ne for me . Oh ! ah I l u cky. Lucky am I.
Oh. Oh. Oh . Oh.—Oh .—Ar thur Co nan Doy le! Let's see.
Lif e wit h out a l over is a bore. Life with a love r can be—
I fe ar it's imperati ve that I do somet hing o n the st age—
I need pu bli c acclamat i o n, and I ne ed it qui ckly. I want the ad or
ation o f uch—cr o wds. (BANG) I want pe op le—cheering, le ering.
Must be t he r e always (Cr ack Br ack) e h —Bi lly , yo u look g ood.

B—Oh, yeah.

(ZIP)

O—I feel li ke a mi llion bu cks !.! I s aid. We ll, whe rever theye're
going, I'll be so mewhe h e else! The y've always be en so meo ne.
All—t ho se—t h i ngs. I s aw th em in my t ime when I was a child,
a long time ago , in a por ch so mewh e r e in red clay. Re d clay
No rthwes t Nebr aska. Po h nny twe lr th—twel fth th i r te en miles
from f a thering A—is th i s is tr ue! H i s true. I was ve r y y ou n g at
th e time of course but—I sti ll k n e w en ou gh—then—that I cou ld
decipher what was what! What? It was whatit always ie? whate ver it is.
Eh, what is t h at? What i s th i s? What is th o. Whachowhat. Public
aaclamati o n —it came to me e ar ly. Ye s, t h at's ri ght. People
s tarted cheer ing when I we nt to scho ol. Scr e aming an d cheer ing—
Hur r ay! Ray! Xay! Ray !

I'll n e ver for get t h e r inging—of —their voices in my hair .

O o oh what a th r illi ng day w hen I he h eh fir st e nt e red
kindergarten uh h uhe .Yes, it was rathe r s st e r l in g.
My e yes ar e cl o sing t he l ids are so he av y that—the y have closed—
And , I swear I' m asle ep! I must b ! I cou ldn't jus t be hanging
he r e like th is. Hajhabi jd. To be hnging her e like th is—wo uld
be wo rse th an fate—fatae' s s cr u e l e st blo w—ughh! ughhh!
Those ar e breaths. Ugh! Ughh! Ughhh!
I have to make sou nd wi t h th e V e l vets. Ughh! Ughhh!
I wonder wh at I' go nna do . T om o r ro f is th e fir st r e hearsal.
At th e gy mnasiumor so . I hop e I ' m good. I kno w I'll be di fferen t.
Eve n—extrao r din ar y per haps—but I h o pe i t 's good.
I ho pe it ' s (*sigh*) I re ally do . Well—we ll, we ll. Still dialing
t h at nu mber . Hu h! an d some voice! O u e st la vo ice. Ish the most
inane —y ou!—th i s is t h e mo st i n ane t ape I' ve e ve r taped.
I feel h um an ly r e spon si ble f or it! Alt h ough I don't l ike th e
id e a o f bei ng all too h u man. I st i l l res e nt the fact o f
b e i ng human at all.
Susan (*on ph on e*) Re ally! (*ac i d t on e of voi ce*)
O—REALLY! wh o e ver th at g i r l was—she re al ly is u pset.
S—we ll . . . . '
O—Sh e 's l ay in g so m e b ody out. ahh—I he ar d he r. The
f allin g ray. She onl y me ant to p r e te nd—d e v i ous and slleevious.
Sh e's just co pp in g ou t . I'm as lee p I 'm t e l ling yo u—I'm
j us t asle ep. I jus I just t h ou gh I bit my tongue whi ch wou ld hava
bee n a di sast er ! S My t ongu e is no t bi t able. It' s to o
swo llen. Oh h—if you ' ve eve r had a swolle n ton gue yo u kn ow
what I mean. I t' s n on s e n se !
PSQUAA—I als o h ad a d ev i ate a s e t a th i s plug. What el se ?
(*g`oer ve l*) als o I h ave —I have my o wn imitations, yo u kno w—
I mean—t rul y —I—kn o w so met h i ng's happening. A h u rdy -gu rdy.
The cost of ch anges—can ' t se e peo ple in my mi nd, can t hey?
In my m in d we r e t h e go peo ple? Huhh—who kn o ws?
PSNEUGH—Whe neve r I he ar the apple sauce, I th in k of me ,—and
I' m b rou gh t h er e — (*3 slu mbe r in g br e aths*) do n ' t let that
sugar bend—t he y' ll be no wo r k f i ni sh ed he r e ! The war sre
giving (*he av y br eaths*) N oe w /. (*H O N K*) Eh theisioeuvegen!
SNORE / SNORE / SNORE / SNORE / SNORE / SNORE
SNORE / SNORE / (*Pr elude t o sn o ri ng*)
SNIFF / SNIFF / SNIFF / Sniff / Sniff
That ' s It ' s en ou gk h at hat (*8 s n o r r e s*) What inek?
H o woo utthat. What? Wh o ju st walke d in ?
Oh Please !.! ' D o e y par ry po obydin. That' s all. Ha Ha (sl ur r ed)

Wh o cares? H owbout ha? SNIFF. It *IS* gr oovey !

WH O WALKED IN ? Wh o walke d in? I' ll n e ver f i nd o ut this way!
Neve r!———————

Ye ah! What abou t *me* !? Huff fe— fo r me ! Sniff— f or me! f or me
' snapping t o fr o m no d) cle chh— Sur e whay n ot—or r eha,ah.—

Who?———————Ih si ghthguitar.———————

What am I magic n umbe r (

24 /   2

O—I don't KNOW It. The word for—. . . . non-empithy.

RV—. . . . . superfluous

O—No, that Not it.

RV—That's not the word.

O—That's not applied to the tithati ti ti ti ti ti tithagih (smack) the
present generation

RV—Oh, well, theyere not big presences, they're. . . . .

O—War baby. You feel like a war baby

RV—During the day, I feel . . (*slurs out*)

O—Jason Robards, junior.
sound of Jap bombers in the distance

O—What is that—a Jesuit priest.

RV—(*rather Gregorian chant*) Aaaaaaahhh—Hooooooooo
short interruption by Jab bombers and background noise

O—. . . . groping.

BN—. . . with a nice view. Awright, where's the next place to go?

O—The factory, to the (*blip/censor*). . . . If he has one page that says
Hallucination Ma- Monologue, . . .

BN—Wadath? Ya mean the one that ya done, or-uh . . .

O—I've hallucinated going to Henry's. I'm not going there at all

RADIO—The Arbor is opening the hour with. . . .

O—And then, Ronny, ... Oh, Ronny, I wish you would talk with
your-yeryeryer . . .

RV—Balloons.

BN—Ba-looon-na-na.

O—This place is hallucin-na . . Hallucinations.

RV—Hallucinations are a way of. . . .

O—. . . hallucinary . . . Oh, that's kinda cute—an Hallucinary Mongoloid

RV—. . . . loosen their minds. Do the life B- . . . .

RADIO—From GARDEN CITY comes . . .

O—THATs an hallucination. This clearly what it is—it's a ribbed fabric.

RADIO—. . . and I'VE decided to DROP you PEOPLE a line, because
. . . think the YOUNG sound is GREAT, and I. . . .

O—Look, Ronny-

RV—(*muffled, inaudible*)

BN—You're waiting for some-. . . .

O—Cipro KEEn?

RV—. . . lie down there? . . . glas to a piece of china. . . .

O—(*name is muffled*) . . . was up there.

RV—I Know.

RADIO—. . . . MEN'S WEAR, head to foot, . . .

O—OK, that's my hallucination (*beating of the microphone*) . . . . full of
pennies.

someone beating out the microphone obscures the next few statements

RADIO—THREE for eleven eighty FIVE, and. . . .

O—Empathy . . . Non empathy

RV—Sock it to me . . .

O—Sockit to—do you feel sock it to anything?

RV—NO

BN—(*grunting*) You can't say the WORD. It's always usd.e WhatisIT?

O—But I- . . . I don't know what thy call them

BN—What is the Youth of the Nation when it s—

O—(*humming*) hmm.Hmmmmm-HMMMMMMM

RV—Piteous

BN—No. When it has no care or feeling or means of association or a
definition.

O—Lost.

RV—Owwwhhhh, uh, mmmmmmm Mmmmmmmmm MMMMMMM
beating on tape recorder and continuous drone of Radio announcer

BN—Straighten out that piece starting. Nayasee what I ME-EEE-EAN
short speechless pause

> BN—THAT's apathy
>
> O—(*muffled laughter*) I KNOW
>
> RV—. . . . makes a lot. Makes a lot,
> that fucking male.
>
> RV—. . . . . . ALIENated. . .
>
> BN—NO-Ooooo
>
> O—No.
>
> RV—Able, that's what it IS.
>
> BN—Sorry, sorry, that's not it at

all. You didn't have any empathy
set up
O—(simultaneous with Billy) The
reason is . . . he's an Ilitera-
illegitimate. You Said it before.
RV—You said it before.
BN—. . . . you've added/edited it.
O—MoNono again. Orio . . . Am-
phetamine. . . . (heh heh ha)
RV—Yes, it's naanaaanaa
O—No, it's lkanooo mooooo
(CRASH) That was it.

BN—There's a word in depositor
form. . . . .
RV—I ONLY wanna talk about
sex and drugs—if you're not
gonna talk about sex and drugs
I'm not gonna talk.
O—OW-UH-mmmmm. I dunno
what the wor dis. Oooooo-mmm-
mmm misennis, ... but I didn't
get to it.
BN—Wah-uh-welll, . . . Here We
Are.
O—This Aw-all . . . ? This is every-
thing . . . ?
BN—My head hurts.
O—My head hurts (all mumble
off). -ments with the Emperors
of China.
RV—(inaudible)
O—You DID.
BN—And you laughedafter you
said it.
O—No, but he was a head
RV—I could he was RAIsed on a
dioc. . . . . (fades) . . . approach.
O—He was
BN—He had to go up-uh a stair-
way. . . . O, hmmmmmmm,
hmmmmmm
WHISTLE: Screeeeeeeeech
O—That was the factory whistle.,
We baly goff
BN—Weee blay go. . . . Joe Bang
is it? Weebedda go

O—No. We parta coff
BN—We carta co
O—Ah, the name's . . ah . . the
same?
BN—Are they bigger than . . . uh
. . . a breadbox?
O—Are they frozen bed boots—
are they bigger than ever?
BN—(shrewish falsetto) sssiiiiix-
teen tuonols
RV—(half-singing) What is this
thing. . . . . this thing. . . . . .
O—Are we recording Now . . . ?
aGAIN. . . . ?
BN—uh-GANE.
O—. . . . . . bedbugs (low whistle)
Uh-oh. Whoopsie.
Female Singer—. . . . somebody
else. . . .
O—I wonder what music we're go-
ing to hear now.
BN—Oh yeah. Ya see, I've discov-
ered I can play the radio AND
the mike at the same time
O—Non-suggestive
BN—Non sequitur
O—Nazis. Prussin—your Prussian
Tactics
BN—You're losing the tempo of
your soliloquy
O—I know, but it put me to sleep.
BN—TEMPO—
O—PRESENTS . . . temp. Ronnie,
RV—What?

O—I think we're gonna go, I tell ya. I think, Billy, that that's done, right?

BN—However, it's the last opportunity to include things in the book that you want to make sure are in it.

O—What?

BN—However, it's the last opportuntiy to include things in the book that you want to make sure are in there

O—AWRIGHT. Let's see—what other group? I wanna really get rid of people. . . . (YAWN) Ho. HUM. Well, if it's not in the book now, it never will be. The Book.

BN—THE Book.

O—Well, its about timetogo-GBYEEEEE. So, it's nice to see you again, Billy. OOOOOO, welcome to Henry s. Ciao, queens

BN—Ciao Queens.

O—Ciao, Staten Island, Bronx, . . .

RV—More, more—you never know how much is enough until you've had too much

O—Ooooooooo, he's leaving.

RV—Nothing succeeds like excess. Sock it to me.

O—Spock it to me.

RV—Oh, more of these immortal words.

BN—Doctor . . . ?

O—Fay Blows. Well, so long, I'm off to Henry's.

BN—Oh, no.

O—Oh, yes.

BN—Not you, Bob.

RV—That's the end of the spotlight for this hour.

O—Heh-heh . . . this hour. Hey, Billy—here's a picture of Henry.

BN—I Know. Oh, no—not THAT one. Out of the garbage, into The Book.

a: A Glossary

by VICTOR BOCKRIS

a was the first book Andy Warhol wrote, although not the first published. That distinction went to *The Index Book* (Random House, 1967). *a* was published by Grove Press in the fall of 1968, a few months after Warhol had been shot by Valerie Solanas. The novel purports to be a recording of twenty-four hours in the life of Warhol superstar Ondine, but actually it was recorded in four different sessions. The first twelve-hour session was recorded in August 1965. Thereafter, there were three separate taping sessions in the summer of 1966 and a final one in May 1967.

The book then found its own voice, taking on a life of its own when the twenty-four one-hour tapes were transcribed by four women: The Velvet Underground's drummer, Maureen Tucker; a part-time Factory worker and Barnard student, Susan Pile; and two high school girls hired for the express purpose of transcription. All four shared a disinclination to spell correctly or apply the rules of grammar. This was due in part to the difficulty of transcribing tapes in which many voices were talking at the same time. Furthermore, speed was of the essence, and it was presumed that after the first rough draft, corrections would be made. However, on first reading the entire original transcript of the book, Warhol was delighted by the mistakes and decided to let them stand. Added to that was the necessity, he felt, to change the names of almost all the characters in the book and further confuse the issue by obscuring the text even more by randomly changing comments he liked or disliked. The job of making sure the final galleys were delivered to Grove in the form Warhol requested was given to the Factory's foreman, Billy Name. According to Name, the title *a* both refers to amphetamine and was used as an homage to e.e. cummings. Name also felt that the novel fell into the surrealist genre personified by Andre Breton's automatic writing, since it was automatic talking. He appeared to be the perfect man for the job.

Since the cast of *a* numbered over one hundred different characters, only those who play meaningful roles throughout the book have been identified in this glossary. Furthermore, since there is a great deal of confusing movement in the text, a separate section has been added explaining where each scene takes place. A third and final section of the glossary identifies the location of several key conversations or remarks that are the true heart of the book.

CAST OF CHARACTERS: A READER'S GUIDE

Page 120—MOXANNE is Genevieve Charbon, a French actress whom Edie had met in Paris earlier that year. Genevieve became her closest female companion, aka Lady in Waiting.

Page 196—ROTTEN RITA (Kenneth Rapp) made with Ondine and Billy Name the triumvirate of A-heads whose love for opera, amphetamine rapture, and a set of opinions that was diametrically opposed to the flower-power generation of the sixties had an enormous influence on the attitudes of the Factory in the mid-sixties. Rita was also known as the Mayor, just as Ondine was known as the Pope.

Pages 201–237—THE DUCHESS is Brigid Polk, aka Brigid Berlin. She was a major user of amphetamine and alcohol, yet, strangely, immensely fat. One of Warhol's favorites, like Edie Sedgwick she came from the upper crust of society. Her father ran the Hearst newspaper corporation. The dialogue with the Duchess conducted over the phone by Ondine, Rink, and Moxanne is one of the most hilarious sequences in *a*. Significantly, however, although Bridget would stay with Warhol for the rest of his life and he harbored a genuine affection for her, Drella did not take part in the conversation.

Page 257—BILLY NAME is Billy Linich, the manager and designer of the Factory, as well as the Factory photographer. Joining Warhol shortly after Malanga in 1963, he was responsible for shepherding *a* through publication. Once the entire twenty-four hours of tape were recorded (with, it should be noted, a few sides missing, and at least one side only two pages long because the mother of one of the high school girls had overheard what she was working on, confiscated it, and threw it in the trash!), Billy spent several days at Grove Press changing all the names, except Malanga's, putting runners at the top of each right-hand page, and, on Warhol's explicit instructions, making sure that all the errors in the transcriptions were preserved exactly as they had been typed. According to Name, his editor at Grove made no objections to his unusual manuscript, publishing it exactly as Warhol wanted with no questions asked.

THE FIRST NONSTOP TWELVE-HOUR TAPING SESSION ENDS ON PAGE 282.

Pages 282–283—DO DO (aka DO DO MAE DOOME) is Dorothy Dean. An extraordinarily intelligent woman who worked at *The New Yorker* in the mid-sixties, Dorothy was one of the very few women, along with Dorothy Podber and Oreon de Winter, who could keep up with, if not outdo, the jangling, vicious conversation of Ondine, Rotten Rita, and Billy Name. She was black, thin, attractive, and fast talking, and, like so many people of her nature, she had hidden beneath her armor a heart of gold. One of the major characters in the second half of the book, she is usually identified as Do Do.

Page 308—THE SUGAR PLUM FAIRY is Joe Campbell, who starred in *My Hustler* opposite Paul America. He was also in *Nude Restaurant*. Along with Rotten Rita and Billy Name, he was one of Ondine's best friends and a major member of the underground family.

Page 396—RON VIA is Ronnie Vial, another close friend of Ondine's and a member of Warhol's underground family.

Page 410—OXYDOL is OLYMPIO VASCONZALEZ, an actor in the John Vacarro school. He was in *Conquest of the Universe* along with Ondine and part of Ondine's circle.

Page 411—RUDINE is Orion, one of the black witches who hung around the edges of the Factory and was generally only accepted on her own terms by Ondine.

Pages 426–439—LOU or L. is Lou Reed of The Velvet Underground. Somewhat like the conversation between Ondine and Edie, this exchange between Reed and Ondine, largely about drugs and The Velvet Underground, represents the only time during this period that Reed ever appeared so openly in a public document. The whole scene takes place at Max's Kansas City in May 1967, two months after The Velvet Underground's first album, produced by Warhol, came out. They were playing a monthlong stint at The Gymnasium to promote it.

A GRAPH OF GEOGRAPHICAL LOCATIONS IN *a*.

Page 1—Ondine and Drella meet at Eighty-sixth Street and Fifth Avenue on a Friday afternoon in August 1965. They walk downtown to a coffee shop called Starks for breakfast.

Page 12—They take a cab from Starks to the Factory at 231 East Forty-seventh Street between Second and Third avenues. Then Ondine, Drella, Taxi, Moxanne, and Rink take a cab to Irving Du Ball's apartment at Fifty-ninth Street and First Avenue. They stay at Du Ball's until page 144.

Page 144—They take a cab from Fifty-ninth and First to Taxi's apartment on East Sixty-third Street.

Page 155—They say good-bye to Taxi.

Page 164—They take a cab from East Sixty-third to a restaurant in Greenwich Village.

Page 169—They arrive at the restaurant. By page 203 they have returned to the Factory.

Pages 203–237—There is a phone call from the Factory to the Duchess in the hospital.

Page 270—The group leaves the Factory for a club on Bleecker Street. Drella goes home and the first half of the book ends on page 282, after twelve hours of largely uninterrupted taping when Drella, at home, speaks to Ondine at the Bleecker Street club.

THE SECOND HALF OF THE BOOK.

Page 382—Ondine leaves Rotten Rita's apartment on Ninety-fourth Street in a
cab to Bickfords on Eighty-sixth Street. It is now July of 1966.

There is a strikingly different tone to the conversations in the second half of the
book. They are more frantic, less friendly, and much more fractured. This was
due to both the breakdown of the original Factory family (Taxi had left, Gerard
was on his way out) and the ravages from drugs that Ondine was taking in increas-
ingly large doses. Most of the 1966 tapes, made in three different sessions, take
place at Rotten Rita's apartment. By page 404, they have returned to the Factory.
It is now May of 1967. On page 424 they take a cab from the Factory to Max's
Kansas City, Warhol's favorite nighttime hangout on Park Avenue South between
Seventeenth and Eighteenth streets. They remain at Max's until page 445. The
final scene takes place back at the Factory.

KEY CONVERSATIONS

There are several key conversations in *a* that throw more light on Warhol than
anybody else:
  On page 38, Ondine defines Warhol as standing for All Woman and All Witch.
Ondine was greatly enamored of Warhol but equally aware that the Factory rep-
resented a certain vision of hell and that everyone, including himself, was being
manipulated by the greatest manipulator of the sixties, except perhaps Richard
Nixon.
  The most revealing conversation about Warhol takes place between Ondine
and Taxi (Edie Sedgwick) on pages 115–135.
  After dropping Edie off at East Sixty-third Street (page 164) Ondine warns
Warhol about how dangerously involved Edie is with drugs and that she could
easily kill herself by accident. Warhol plays dumb.
  Page 179 features the most revealing comment by Ondine about Warhol. The
first half of the book ends on page 282 with Ondine saying, "My last words are
Andy Warhol."

  The second half of the book is markedly more fractured and frantic than the
first half. Warhol's attention to The Velvet Underground from January to May
1966 took him away from Ondine et al. Later in the same year, the great critical
and commercial success of *Chelsea Girls* caused numerous schisms among the
unpaid superstars, particularly Ondine. While Ondine attacked Malanga on at
least three occasions at length, little remarks about Drella's Nazi tactics also creep
into the text.

Alternately, the second half of the book also contains some of the most interesting conversations with and about Warhol, in particular page 334, in which Ondine defines Warhol as the greatest humanist and its opposite!

The Sugar Plum Fairy's interview with Drella about his inability to be happy is on pages 344–345. It is the single most revealing statement Warhol ever made in public.

By page 346 Drella is literally pleading with Ondine to come back to the Factory and finish the taping.

Pages 368–381 feature the most harrowing conversation about drugs, in which Ondine admits he is so high that he is frightened. Some of this makes unpleasant reading for those to whom needles are not, in the words of Lou Reed, as necessary as toothbrushes.

Page 382 continues in this vein as the core A-heads—Ondine, Rotten, and Billy—listen to opera at ear-splitting volume while shooting amphetamine and generally teetering on the edge of sanity. It is a hard but accurate picture of their gone world. The book does not celebrate drug addiction, but is in fact a condemnation of it.

Toward the end of the book, The Velvet Underground is playing a monthlong stint at The Gymnasium to publicize their just-released album, the presence of Lou Reed and the beauty of their music appear to bring some calmness back to Ondine. This is particularly true in the scene at Max's (pages 425–445). Pages 426–427 on Lou Reed are particularly good.